The Last Hookers

By

Lieutenant Colonel Carle E. Dunn
United States Army, Retired

Book Cover Art by William Atkinson

"In Memory...."

ISBN: 0-75965-593-6

This book is printed on acid free paper.

1stBooks - rev. 09/29/01

Acknowledgements

Time

To everything there is a season, and a time to every purpose under the heaven: a time to be born and a time to die; a time to plant, and a time to pluck up that which is planted; a time to kill, and a time to heal; a time to break down, and a time to build up; a time to weep, and a time to laugh; a time to mourn and a time to dance; a time to cast away stones, and a time to gather stones together; a time to embrace, and a time to refrain from embracing; a time to get, and a time to lose; a time to keep, and a time to cast away; a time to rend, and a time to sew; a time to keep silence, and a time to speak; a time to love, and a time to hate; a time of war, and a time of peace.

Hebrew Bible. *Ecclesiastes 3:1–8.*

First, I must say thank you to Sammy. Sammy is First Lieutenant Samuel Harrell and he is the aviator who died in my seat. On 10 May 1972, Sammy climbed aboard a Chinook helicopter at Long Thanh North in the Republic of South Viet Nam to replace me. I left the ship to attend to a mundane chore that I cannot recall. Less than two hours later, Sammy died in the crash of that aircraft. Sometime I will learn why. For 30 years, I have yet to learn the reason and I know that I never will. I will have to wait until Sammy tells me.

On the same aircraft, others paid the supreme sacrifice for someone else. Unlike me, we do not know whom they saved. The persons could have been any crewmember in the 362nd Aviation Company. Those who made it home owe the following a deep gratitude for their sacrifice:

- Captain Barry Coley Tomlin
- Specialist Five Larry Steven Mustin
- Specialist Four Alvin Robert Elenburg
- Specialist Four Terry Duane Neiss

Aboard that same ship, a group of infantrymen were on their way for rest and relaxation in Vung Tau. For them, the war was over and soon they would leave for home. They did not go home, and again, there is no answer available to us as to why. However, an answer exists and, as with Sammy, one day we will know. Also, eventually, so will the rest of the 362nd Aviation Company. Sadly, some already do.

To CW4 Jay Wilhelm, another "Fly United" veteran, I say thanks for the inspiration to undertake the task of putting this book together. I had no idea at the time of what an immense task it would be. Jay, I hope I have accomplished what you expected.

To Jean, my wife, goes a major accolade for her tireless efforts. She kept me on the right path and gleaned page after page as my editor. Trust me; spelling and grammar checkers do not come close when it comes to editing manuscripts. She did. After 40 plus years together, she carried the load so I could put these words on paper.

To the United States Army Advisers, who carried the load at the Battle of An Loc, you did your profession proud. One in particular gets a special note of thanks. He was on the ground with these brave men until the enemy wounded him. He is Lieutenant Colonel James H. Willbanks, U.S. Army, Retired.

Colonel Willbanks is the author of *Thiet Giap! The Battle of An Loc*. This work, published by the Combat Studies Institute at the U. S. Army Command and General Staff College, Fort Leavenworth, Kansas, provided the soul of this book. Colonel Willbanks received the Silver Star for his action at the Battle of An Loc. Colonel Willbanks made available many of the charts and maps in this work. He now teaches at the Staff College.

Many thanks also go to the United States Army Military Academy at West Point. Their history department graciously made available details regarding battles in the Republic of South Viet Nam. They also provided maps depicting these historical events.

The Vietnam Helicopter Pilots Association gets credit for considerable historical information. Their interactive multimedia CDROM is a major source of aviation tactical detail about the helicopter's role in Viet Nam.

To all who served in the 362nd, I extend my heartfelt thanks for a job well done. You worked under trying conditions and at the worst of times. Month after month, I read the "MACV Safety Awards" as you set a new record each month for the safest flying hours in Viet Nam. This is no small achievement and it did not come easy. It required hard work and attention to detail. I applaud you.

To every Viet Nam veteran, please know this. You did not lose this war. You fought well and you fought hard. In every battle, you defeated the enemy. You risked your lives daily to carry out the orders of those appointed over you. That is the oath you took; and by God, you did it. Do not let the media or the politicians tell you different because they are the ones who failed you. I salute you.

Prologue

In May of 1975, the North Vietnamese Army entered Saigon, the capital city of the Republic of South Viet Nam. This ended a struggle that started in the early 20s of the last century. People in Southeast Asia fought a decades long battle against France, Japan, the United States, and finally, among themselves. The Communist north ultimately prevailed in their unification effort against the south.

One cannot understand what happened in Southeast Asia by solely examining the involvement of the United States. For the United States, Viet Nam is the site of its longest war. However, this involvement is a small portion of the overall picture. For many Americans, this is difficult to accept. The United States gave the lives of almost 60,000 in an attempt to provide freedom for others. These Americans died for a noble cause and they are true heroes everyone.

In these pages, you will find different perspectives. This takes place through the lives of fictional characters. These persons come from different countries and represent their societies. They are British, French, American, and Vietnamese. Two characters, in particular, give a parallel view of their lives. Dale Zane is the typical American teenager of his time. Nguyen Van Vinh is his Vietnamese counterpart. These two come from a common, agrarian background but their lives develop in stark contrast.

Nevertheless, the basic thread of the work is historical fact. Some people played such major roles in events that they are impossible to ignore. In these cases, they are not fictional. Some examples of these are presidents, secretaries of state, religious leaders, ambassadors, military leaders, politicians, and other key historical figures. Information about them comes from personal libraries, historical records, and the National Archives. Other details came from declassified National Security Agency and Central Intelligence Agency files.

Dates are important. Each chapter of this work starts with a date. To understand collateral events better, it is important to keep time in mind. The political arena, at a particular time, impacts heavily upon events in another part of the world. Hitler's fascist activities had a major impact in the Orient as well as Europe for example.

The rise of Communism in the Soviet Union spread to China and Southeast Asia. When we look at Communism today, we see a failed system. However, at an earlier time, it offered salvation to millions while threatening Western Civilization. Political figures, such as Ho Chi Minh, used the tenets of Communism to expand political power in Southeast Asia. Frequently, he did so at the cost of untold thousands of lives of those who opposed his ideology.

The appendix contains illustrations to help understand the major battles in this book. Maps 1 through 3 show General Giap's Spring Invasion of 1972. Map 4 depicts France's Operation Castor troop dispositions at Dien Bien Phu. North Viet Nam's leaders sacrificed millions to force their Communist system upon Southeast Asia. They did so at a time when they believed social and economic factors favored Communism. Today, they realize the grave fault of their reasoning. They can never justify their terrible disregard of humanity.

Chapter One

March 1954

"...All in the valley of Death,
Rode the six hundred."
Alfred, Lord Tennyson (1809-92)

The night's cold brought with it a bone piercing hurt that Vinh did not tolerate well. He crouched lower to avoid its raspy fierceness without success. He continued to shiver. He was wet, hungry and dawn was near. With sunrise, he would be able to see Muong Valley. Once it was his home, a place of personal joy and tranquility. Now, it was a killing zone. He could smell death from his observation post.

Vinh appeared malnourished, small and excessively thin. His light brown skin stretched taught, exposing his skeletal structure. His shoulder blades protruded, as did other bones of his body. His knees were bony protrusions falling away to legs deceptively weak in appearance.

His clothing was sparse. He wore a light khaki shirt with short, frayed sleeves. His trousers, the same color, ended above his knees. His foot protection was two rubber strips cut from a vehicle's tire. These were his sandal's soles. Thongs, made from rope, held them in place. Over his shoulders, two, olive drab straps descended to his waist. Suspended from them, a belt with ammunition pouches wrapped his middle. Hanging from his belt, on his right side, a bayonet lay protected in its sheath.

His most prized possession hung suspended inside a case around his neck, binoculars. This was an essential item for artillery forward observers. Other than his AK-47 assault rifle and ammunition, every military item he possessed came from the United States.

Morning sunlight began to appear over mountains behind him. With terrain blocking its warming rays, he continued to shiver. In his discomfort, he contemplated his enemy.

"What else could one expect?" He thought. "French Legionnaires are crazy. Another group parachuted into Dien Bien Phu last night. Many drifted and became prisoners. Others died in their harnesses before reaching ground. How insane they are."

"Yes, they are crazy," Vinh mused aloud. "They are cold and wet as I am. Yet, I will not die soon. They will."

Vinh wondered why French military leaders selected his valley for a fortress. It was not near anything significant. It was astride a highway between North Viet Nam and Laos. To the guerillas, this was of little importance. The French could monitor troop movements through this area. However, it was simple for General Giap's Viet Minh to use another route.

With the sun now higher, Vinh could see the valley's entire expanse. Its length was no more than 20 kilometers. At best, it was about five kilometers wide. One might say that it was a large gorge or a hole. A river, the Nam Youm, coursed through its middle.

The early morning sun felt good on his cold back. He had little sleep the night before and he was tired. With the warmth, he became drowsy and his eyelids began to close. He drifted and began dreaming.

"Hurry Vinh, bring some more shoots," Minh Thanh said in a delicate, singsong voice. "You are getting behind little brother."

Minh Thanh arose from her stooped position to await his return. She placed her hands on her lower back and stretched forward to gain relief from complaining back muscles.

Like her mother beside her, she wore black pants rolled up above her knees. This was necessary to avoid wetting them with rice paddy water. Her black blouse fell to slightly below her waist ending beside her black hair. She wore her hair tied back with a blue ribbon close behind her head.

Like the others planting rice, she wore a conical, straw hat to protect her from the sun. Beneath her chin, hat-retaining strings held it in place with a neat bow. She looked to her left at her family. They moved ahead at a steady pace placing rice seedlings in neat rows.

"Hurry Vinh," she encouraged her brother.

Vinh, nine years of age, splashed toward the rice paddy's corner as he ran. On a levee, near where they grew seedlings, small plants lay in bundled groups. One corner of each paddy was set aside to grow seedlings early in the year. When the season was right, they moved young plants to mature in the paddy's larger area.

Getting a bundle for Minh Thanh, Vinh also picked up additional ones for the others. He ran, creating an aquatic melee, to Minh Thanh and gave her some seedlings. Next, he moved behind his brother Anh and waited. Anh had the fewest sprouts remaining of the group. He would need more before the others.

Anh was his elder brother and his parents' first born. At 16, he did a man's work and his family treated him as such. Whenever Vinh needed help with a task, he went to Anh. He knew every thing in the world Vinh thought. Anh completed each course the local school had to offer. He knew mathematics and helped their parents plan how they would use money from cash crops. Whenever they took fish, geese eggs, or vegetables to market, Anh set the price and did any trading.

"Quit daydreaming Vinh," Anh said. "Give me a bundle."

Anh remained stooped with an outstretched hand behind him. Vinh immediately placed a bundle in it and moved right to stand behind his father. His bundle was diminishing rapidly as he moved forward gingerly putting each plant in place. Now, he would need replacements before the others.

His father's name was Nguyen Van Biep. He was the second eldest adult male living at their family home. His father still lived with them but was too old and weak to work in the fields. It was Biep's task to see to the fields and assure a living for his family. However, his father, lovingly called grandfather by all, had the final say regarding any major decisions.

Biep reached to his rear and Vinh promptly placed young plants in his open hand. He glanced at Vinh with a smile and winked.

His face said, "Good son," and Vinh swelled with pride.

Moving behind his mother, Xuan, Vinh waited to resupply her. She was known for her beauty throughout their valley. There was considerable gossip among other families when she became his father's wife. It was a favorite tale often told in the Nguyen household. After they had their evening meal, his father frequently told how she became his wife. Vinh had listened to the story many times. He never tired of hearing it.

"I first saw your mother at the market. She carried a water jug on her shoulder. She pretended that she didn't see me. I wasn't fooled because I could see her looking at me out of the corner of her eye," Biep bragged. "I started going to market more often."

"Other young men had their eyes on your mother and they came from wealthy families," he continued. "Their parents tried to arrange a marriage but they failed. While they had money, the Nguyens had land. Land is the greatest wealth there is. Grandfather taught me that."

Continuing, Biep told how his father's wisdom helped arrange their marriage.

"I told my father that I wanted to marry her and asked for his help. Your grandfather knew that your mother's parents lusted for land. In addition, he told me that I was going to market too much and that I should not let her family know how much I wanted to marry her."

Every time father told this part, mother would blush and hide her face. She would always deny that she watched him. She would also deny that she missed him at market when he stopped coming so often. Everyone would laugh when she said this.

Biep explained that his father would casually chat with Xuan's father after Mass.

"One night your grandfather mentioned that a grandson would one day likely inherit a large portion of his river bend property. Grandfather never mentioned this again to your mother's father. Finally, one night, your mother's father approached grandfather and mentioned that he had traded for land next to our river bend land. Your grandfather already knew this but he did not tell."

Your grandfather said, "Oh how nice. It is an honor to have your family as neighbors."

According to his father, their grandfather still avoided speaking of his intent to give river bend land to a grandson. He explained that, six months later, Xuan's father asked grandfather why his son avoided his daughter.

Grandfather answered him, "Oh, has Biep been rude. I will see to his manners. He should show respect."

Father explained farther, "I started speaking to her at market. It was only one month later that her father asked grandfather why I did not visit. Six months after that your mother's parents announced our impending marriage. No one in the valley understands how I obtained such a beautiful wife. I am very lucky. I have a wise father and you have a wonderful mother."

Explosions forced Vinh from his sleep. Projectiles passed overhead and ripped through morning's calm. Each high pitched whine was followed by a dull, echoing thump inside the French bastion. A low, growling noise sounded in Vinh's trench. The cold gone, he grabbed his field telephone. Answering hastily, he put the handset to his ear.

"Vinh," he answered.

"Are they on target?" He heard his brother ask.

Vinh strained to see through swirling fog, which obscured the valley. He tried focusing his binoculars but could only glimpse portions of the French positions. Swirling mist obscured his view.

Whispering, he responded, "I can't see for the fog Anh."

"Damn," Anh replied. There was a click, then quiet.

Slowly, sunlight evaporated the fog to reveal remnants of the besieged garrison. The sight was chaos. Vinh focused his binoculars. He first studied the northernmost devastation. The area was an airfield once. Now, it was burned aircraft, torn parachutes entwined with barbed wire and body parts. Artillery continued to pound, rip and tear amid giant earth eruptions thrown skyward.

A tank moved in the rubble. Vinh cranked his telephone's handle rapidly once, and then again.

"Fire mission," he yelled into the mouthpiece, not caring if the French heard.

"Tank! Tank," he screamed.

It was difficult for him to hear above an ever-increasing roar. Explosions from other artillery units pounded the target area. No answer came.

He cranked the handle while repeatedly yelling, "Fire mission."

Finally, a dejected Anh answered.

"We are out of ammunition. We cannot fire," he explained.

"Not again," he thought. "This is the third time since we began our attack."

He pounded the earth with clinched fists in frustration. He slumped lower in his hidden observation post. He could do little. He watched as other observers adjusted artillery onto the lucrative target.

He saw Legionaries crouching behind the steel vehicle, following close for cover. Their intent was obvious. A large container was to their front. It was undamaged. Dropped by parachute during the night, it likely held medical supplies, food, ammunition, or other desperately needed items. So needed that they were dying in an attempt to get it. An artillery shell struck the canister, spewing its mutilated contents into the air.

The armored vehicle stopped. Still firing its main gun, it reversed direction. Four wounded perished beneath its treads. Only two, of the original six behind it, retreated unharmed to a protective revetment.

French forces were growing less day by day while Viet Minh forces tightened their hold. This was not so when they made their first attacks. Initially, Viet Minh infantry attacked Dien Bien Phu directly. They crossed open ground from the forests to penetrate the base. Thousands would assault the perimeter only to die.

Anh had told him about two Chinese Peoples Liberation Army Generals, Wei Guo-ging and Li Cheng-hu. They were advisors sent to help. They convinced their commander, General Giap, to use human wave attacks. The Chinese used such attacks against United Nations' forces in Korea with success. Yet, the cost in lives was horrendous.

With time, casualties mounted from intense, defensive fires. In only three days, they lost 9,000 Viet Minh to the French guns. Of these, 2,000 were killed. They could not afford such losses.

According to his brother, General Giap did not approve of frontal assaults. He preferred patience. They would fight a protracted battle. Infantry units would dig trenches and tunnels. These would provide protection as they slowly approached strong points. This was to be a long siege. Giap knew the French were in a death trap.

Vinh removed a folded palm leaf tucked inside his shirt. Carefully, he opened it to expose a small rice clump. He ate directly from the leaf and licked it clean.

"Well, that's that," he thought. "I should get another ration before mid-day."

He turned to face the area to his rear. A cover, made from bamboo for his observation post, lay directly in front of him. He examined it and removed dead plant leaves used for camouflage. He crawled from his protective burrow to nearby plants. He removed fresh leaves and returned with them to his former position. He slipped into the hole and began putting new leaves on its cover. Satisfied, he pulled the arrangement forward so that it partially overlapped the opening to his underground refuge. Turning to face the valley, he lowered his body fully into the hole. Reaching up, he pulled the cover forward until it completely covered the opening. With a sigh, he relaxed knowing that his position was well hidden.

"Without ammunition, there is little that I can do," he thought. "Anh will let me know when I can start finding targets again."

Outside, explosions continued as other units bombarded French positions. The sun was full up causing the temperature to rise rapidly. Vinh leaned back to rest.

He thought about the French who were dying a short distance from his position. To avoid such thoughts he always liked to think about the days before the French. He liked to think about his family. He, Vinh, was a Nguyen.

"The Nguyen name was an honorable one that stemmed from the Nguyen dynasty from years long past. Unlike people from Western nations, Nguyens put their family name first. Ancestry was important and it was only reasonable that it should be first," he thought.

Vinh shifted his position in an attempt to obtain comfort but failed. He looked at the water standing in his observation post. Each day he dipped it out but, before morning, it returned. It seeped from the dirt walls. In desperation, he made a small mound on one side that provided a relative dry spot to rest. His thoughts turned to home, a few kilometers away along the Nam Youm.

He recalled his father returning one day from the market. He was angry and immediately went to see grandfather. They talked long into the night. He could hear them from where he slept with Minh Thanh and Anh.

"The damned French are demanding more taxes," Biep said. "Our land is not suitable for raising rubber trees so they are going to make us pay more taxes. They have already taken everything that grows rubber and now they want our land. If we do not pay the tax, they will sell our land to a plantation owner who will make us pay to live on it. Our only hope is Ho Chi Minh."

"That may be true," grandfather said. "However, he is in China. He and the others fled when the Japanese came. He cannot help us from China."

"We can help ourselves," Biep replied. "I will work with the Viet Minh."

"Look at my legs son. I cannot work the fields. All I can do is collect eggs and repair fish traps. Hell, I cannot even tend the traps. Anh does that now," the elder Nguyen said. "The French did this and you know it. The same will happen to you if they do not kill you."

Vinh crawled from the small mat upon which he slept. Anh and Minh Thanh tried to stop him.

"Get back here," Anh whispered. "They will catch you and you will be punished."

"No," Vinh replied. "I cannot hear everything."

Minh Thanh gripped his leg and said, "Listen to Anh. He is older than you are. He knows best."

Disregarding both, Vinh continued after removing Minh Thanh's hand. He arrived at the doorway to their small room. He rolled his body against the wall and crawled forward just enough to see into the next room. Biep and grandfather faced each other as they sat in a squat with a candle between them.

"You will be excommunicated," grandfather said. "If you start killing with the Viet Minh, our priest will remove you from the church. You will go to hell. The Viet Minh are Communists. They are a godless group."

"Are you going to hell?" Biep asked. "You killed the French. You killed Laotians working for the French. That's how you were wounded and almost bled to death. A priest came to this house and anointed you with oil. He gave you absolution after you confessed. I heard it."

"Ayah, show some respect," grandfather exclaimed greatly distressed. "Do you have no shame? Are you filled with so much disrespect that you listened to your father's confession?"

Biep lowered his head and reached for his father's arm. He gently touched it.

"I am sorry. I meant no disrespect. You are my father and I love you," he said in a hushed tone.

Biep retrieved a new candle from its storage box next to the candleholder. He removed the almost extinguished one and replaced it. He raised the old, short candle to light the new one. As he lifted it, Vinh saw a shiny reflection near his father's foot. It was a pistol. Vinh almost gasped aloud. He stared and dared not move. If they caught him, he would be punished for sure. This was something that he knew meant trouble. He remained motionless and listened.

Biep snuffed the old candle and said, "When the Japanese arrived, they let the French continue ruling. Now we have both with their boots on our necks. Uncle Ho promises that our land will always be ours. Everyone will be equal and there will be happiness for everyone. All we have to do is fight them. I believe him father."

"I cannot fault you my son," Biep's father said. "This house is now yours and the land is yours. My time is over and you must make your decisions. Whatever you decide, I will help."

Grandfather went to his mat and lay down. Biep took the candle and the pistol with him to their water buffalo's stall that adjoined their home. The large beast glared and watched as Biep lifted a large, grain storage jar. He placed the pistol beneath it and went to his room.

Vinh, still motionless, thought, "No one will find that. I won't go in the stall because that animal will gore most anyone except father."

Quietly, he returned to his mat and lay in a fetal position. He was afraid.

"Grandfather killed people? He would never do that. He is the kindest person in the world. Father must be mistaken," Vinh thought.

He felt a jolt in his side. Looking toward where he was struck, he saw Anh's foot. His older brother rolled next to him.

"If you do that again, I will tell," Anh said.

"No you won't," Vinh replied.

"Then I will kick your ass," Anh answered in a determined voice.

Vinh knew Anh meant what he said. He never listened again. He didn't have to because Anh did. He could always get Anh to talk.

From early as Vinh could remember, Anh went to parochial school. Teachers taught what local French landowner's wanted them to teach. Vietnamese children did not need an extensive education as far as they were concerned. It didn't take long for Anh to learn that history lessons were distorted. First, what they were told defied common sense. Second, Anh found history books that others kept hidden.

While history came easy to him, math was his true pleasure. It was pure and beyond distortion. With math, there was balance and form. To him, it was like abstract poetry that flowed in unison and the pieces had to fit. If not, flow failed and balance ceased.

Anh explained to Vinh about the Japanese and the French. He told him how the French took their country. They used force to make their nation a colony. They burdened them with taxes. They controlled every facet of their lives. They continued to do so even after the Japanese came.

Invading Japanese soldiers quickly subdued France's military at the beginning of World War II. The vile colonialists signed a treaty with Japan in 1941. The two governments mutually promised military cooperation for joint defense of French Indochina. They agreed not to arrange any thing with other governments that could adversely affect Japan. The Vichy French were happy to oblige.

Japanese were in his country for one reason. They wanted rubber. The same rubber France had stolen for almost a century. Now, since Hitler's Nazis Party controlled France, French officials worked with the Nazis. French colonialists did the same with Japan.

From documents distributed by the Viet Minh, Anh read to him how Henri Petain, a collaborator, ran France's government under Nazi control. Petain seemed to relish his authority when he established a new government at Vichy, France.

"Petain had fought the Germans in World War I, achieving a General's rank. How could he now pay homage to them?" Vinh wondered as Anh told him about it.

Vinh had watched Anh clean their father's pistol. It smelled of burned gunpowder when he returned just before daylight. Their father would leave shortly after sunset and return before daylight. He put his pistol beneath the grain jar and Anh would later clean it for him.

Vinh realize that his days were changing from joyous experiences to ones of worry. He would never forget a particularly tragic day in his life. Minh Thanh was teaching him how to get water from the Nam Youm and to their rice. He watched others doing it and it appeared easy.

"Show me how to do it," he pleaded. "I am big enough. Show me."

Minh Thanh relented and took him to a river levee adjoining their main field. She held one of two tethers that supported a basket between them. She told him to hold the other end. They stood atop the levee, which kept the river at bay.

"It's like dancing," she said.

"Follow what I do. Swing the basket over the river and let it fall. When it sinks slightly, help me lift it over the levee. This will throw water into the field," she explained.

"I know how to do that. You treat me like a child. Let's do it," I demanded.

She laughed when I spilled basket after basket. Her laughter was like wind chimes. It pealed with a bell like quality, pleasant to one's ears. It was a pure, happy sound sparkling with true, effervescent joy. She had joy in her heart.

No matter how clumsy my attempts, she continued helping until we moved the basket in unison. Each swing brought the Nam Youm to the rice. That's when we saw Anh running towards us on the levee.

He was crying and did not stop or speak to us. He slammed into Minh Thanh almost knocking her into the river. We followed him to the house. Inside, he and grandfather were locked in a vicious struggle. Anh had father's pistol from beneath the grain jar. Grandfather was trying to take it from him.

"I will kill them. I will kill them," Anh kept screaming.

Minh Thanh began helping grandfather. I tried but was knocked to the floor twice. Finally, grandfather had the gun and sat on Anh. It took all his strength but he held him.

"Tell me what happened," grandfather demanded.

Anh, now exhausted, turned his head aside and kept saying, "They took them both. They took them."

"Who took who?" Grandfather asked.

"The French police and the Japanese arrested father and mother. Our friends would not help. I begged them to help. They wouldn't. Let me go, I will kill them," he cried.

Grandfather's face turned pale and he began to tremble. Minh Thanh wet a cloth and put it on his head. He was sick and she had to get a basin for him. He was so sick that Anh stopped trying to get the gun. We thought he was going to die.

By late afternoon, he began to feel better. Still, he did not have enough strength to go to the market place. Grandfather agreed to let them go but the gun had to remain with him. He gave specific instructions to Anh.

"Go to your mother's father. He is a good man and he will be most disturbed by this. While he and I do not agree on some things, we both love Xuan. He knows the right people and has money to help. If anyone can get information or do anything, he can. Now go and come back as soon as you can," he directed.

The market was deserted. All stalls were empty and even the beggars were not in sight. The three made their way to their other grandfather's home. Grandmother saw them coming and rushed them inside.

"Hurry, they may come back. Get inside," she had urged.

Their mother's sisters were inside but not their husbands. Their aunts cried softly and their eyes were red and swollen. Across the outer room, grandfather was kneeling before a crucifix and was praying. They could hear his whispered Our Fathers and Hail Mary's as his hands moved across the beads of his rosary.

"Shush," grandmother said. "Your grandfather is expecting a priest at any moment."

"Where is our father and mother?" Anh asked in a low voice.

"The French police took them away in a truck with five others from the village," she whispered. "Follow me to a place where we won't disturb your grandfather."

Grandmother beckoned to her daughters to follow. They moved through another room and into a cleared area behind their house. A thatched roof covered an open area without walls. Corner posts, and the main structures, held it in place. Straw matting kept dirt from their bare feet. Hanging from the corner posts were strings of red and green peppers drying. There was a distinct odor of fish oil about the area. Two woven chairs with high backs were at the straw mat's edge. They faced east. Grandmother sat in one of them. She indicated for the group to sit in front of her chair.

"Now, I will tell you what we know. Biep and Xuan are under arrest by the French police. They said that Biep had been charged with sedition and sabotage. There will be a trial in Hanoi. Until the trial they will remain in prison," she explained.

Anh started to interrupt but grandmother raised her hand with her palm toward him, "Shush! Have you forgotten so soon."

Anh no longer cried. His jaw flexed as he ground his teeth. His neck seemed to pulse with each heartbeat. His eyes had a cold determination in them. Vinh had never seen his brother looking like he did.

"Grandmother, where are they?" Anh demanded.

"Calm yourself and watch your mouth. You do not speak to me in that fashion. You are a disgrace to you father," grandmother hissed.

Anh's shoulders slumped. He knew he must apologize for insulting her.

"Forgive me please. I am sorry and I did not mean to shame my family," Anh said with humility.

"Fine, now listen," grandmother continued. "Someone in our village told the French that your father worked with the Viet Minh. The police arrested your mother for helping him. They will have a trial in Hanoi. My husband will hire a French attorney to defend them. He is a good and honorable man who helps many of us. We will have to pay a high price to retain his services."

She placed a hand on Anh's head and said, "You are now responsible for your family. You must see to the land and your family young-man-no-more."

With her other hand on Minh Thanh's head, she continued, "Granddaughter, you are now the matriarch of the Nguyen house. Do what Anh says because he will have the wisdom of two grandfathers to guide him."

For a moment, she stopped to gaze at Minh Thanh's bowed head. A tear flowed from the corner of her eye and down across her cheek. Sadness washed across her face.

"You marriage must be delayed my Minh Thanh. I will explain to your betrothed's family. You must see to your grandfather because his death is near. You must mourn him according to our custom," she explained.

She arose from her chair and they all stood before her as she said, "Take Vinh and return home. I will see that you know everything that happens. Leave now for there is much to be done."

Vinh recalled that it was months before they received definite information about their father. His trial would be soon and his two grandfathers were to attend. However, Grandfather Nguyen could not stand the strain. Ever since his son's arrest, he grew worse.

His family already mourned his passing, although he lived. His death was imminent; thus, they grieved, as they should. Minh Thanh wore black and never wore her blue ribbon. She kept a note pad upon which she wrote everything grandfather said. She spoke to him in hushed tones.

This time was hard for her. Though details were in place, she could not marry because she was mourning. This special time usually lasted three years. However, these were strange circumstances. Nevertheless, she would grieve more than a year after his death to show respect. Her marriage would have to wait.

Anh tended three of grandfather's fish traps. He also worked and cared for their water buffalo. This horned beast pulled a crude plow to cultivate their rice field. It also pulled their vegetable cart to market. The mean tempered creature began to accept Anh as its master. No others in the family dared approach it.

Booming thunder rolled along Muong Valley and heavy rain began to fall. Vinh shifted his position, trying to remain above water in his dugout. He put on his pith helmet and pressed harder against the dripping soil. Unable to rest, he stood and slowly raised his post's camouflaged cover. He peered at his former home and the decimated French positions near it.

Raising his binoculars, he began looking for targets. He found none. With pouring rain partially obstructing his view, he looked again at the remnants of their home. Every levee was breached and river water flowed throughout the paddies. Small portions of their house's walls remained intact but the roof was completely gone.

Vinh stood with his elbows resting on the dugout's edge. He tried again to find targets but his binoculars' lenses were covered with condensation. His thoughts turned to the most terrible day in his life, the day of his father's execution.

"These six men are guilty of sedition," the French police officer read aloud. "By order of Hanoi's High Tribunal, they are to be executed by firing squad this date. May God have mercy on their souls."

His father, and five other men, stood bound to posts driven into their market's hard soil. A short distance in front of them, 12 French policemen faced them with rifles. Villagers, forced into the market by Japanese soldiers, watched.

He and Minh Thanh stood with Anh's arms around each of their necks. He held them close and listened to the words.

A policeman put a hood over each man's head and moved aside. On command, the riflemen fired in unison. He saw his father's body fall limp against ropes holding him to the post. He watched as a policeman stepped from body to body. He fired a bullet into the heads of his father and five other villagers.

Afterwards, he learned that their mother was in prison. She, like her husband, was found guilty but they spared her life. He learned from others that execution would have been a better sentence.

Anh, in his anger, began working with the Viet Minh at night just like his father. He and Minh Thanh did what they could to help. Still, it was a terrible time that became worse. He and Anh lost Minh Thanh.

Shortly after grandfather died, Minh Thanh went to Hanoi. She left a note. Anh was the family's elder and she should have asked permission to go. She explained that she was going to find their mother. An uncle lived near Hanoi and she would stay with his family. Minh Thanh knew Anh would not give permission so she went without it. Eight years had passed since she left the note. No matter how hard Anh searched, he never found her.

The rain stopped and sunlight began coming through breaks in the overcast. From the wood line to his rear, he saw Anh approaching.

"Anh's time with the Viet Minh has brought him rewards," Vinh thought while watching him approach. "The many nights, working in a Sapper unit, earned respect of senior officials. Now, he was a captain of Artillery, a most important position indeed."

Anh slipped into Vinh's camouflaged observation post.

"Anh, when will we have more ammunition?" Vinh asked.

"It will be at least two days before we will have enough to sustain a bombardment," he replied. "We have some now so stay alert. If you locate a good target, call."

Anh explained that French napalm attacks had almost been disastrous. Fortunately, monsoon rains had soaked the forested terrain. The flames died soon with little unit damage. Nevertheless, convoys now only moved at night. This was causing a major delay of every item they needed for their siege.

"General Giap issued orders to ration rice. Each person gets one ball a day and no more," Anh explained. "Wounded are getting less. Only able combatants receive one ball. Staff officers get one-half ration a day. I know that you are hungry but you must make do."

This was not good news to Vinh. He was already hungry. The portion reduction would make the situation much worse. At least he would get a full ration because his job was important. He was glad Anh arranged for his training as an artillery observer.

Chinese advisers arrived the previous year. They came to train Viet Minh how to use artillery weapons China supplied. The 105-mm howitzers came from Korea. Chinese forces captured them from retreating South Korean and United States' units. The Americans manufactured excellent equipment. He was surprised to see their markings on weapons supplied by China.

However, he had seen the same markings on equipment captured from the French. It seemed that most of their military equipment was American.

"Surely, they must be a rich country," Vinh thought. "They saved Europe; they fought in Korea; and, now they were supplying France. Yes, they had to be rich."

Vinh's thoughts turned to Minh Thanh.

"Tell me Anh, have you learned anything more about Minh Thanh?" He questioned.

Vinh watched Anh's shoulders slump as sadness filled his eyes. Turning, so as not to look directly at Vinh, he replied, "No. I've been to Hanoi twice. Where she used to be, is deserted. The French closed the building after the Japanese left. They don't use it for anything. I couldn't find the people who used to live at that address. I think they are dead."

Reaching for his brother, Vinh placed his arms around his shoulders. He could feel Anh shake as he stifled sobs. Pulling Anh to his chest, he held him close while Anh wept.

Maintaining his embrace, Vinh finally broke the awkward silence. Speaking softly, he reassured his brother.

"There was no way you could have known. The Japanese lied as did their French lackeys. They hid her, Anh. They hid her," Vinh said with compassion.

"Yes, the French will pay dearly," Vinh thought.

Next month he would be 17, old enough to go to advanced artillery training. He vowed to use his new skills to destroy the vile French.

Chapter Two

November 1953

"...And an end to the fight, is a tombstone white,
with a name of the late deceased,
And the epitaph drear, 'A fool lies here, who tried to hustle the East.'"
Rudyard Kipling (1865-1932)

Lieutenant Jean Danjou's first mission was to assure occupation of strong point Anne-Marie. His second was to place navigation beacons to guide aircraft with atomic weapons to their targets. If he survived long enough against the Viet Minh at Dien Bien Phu, he would accomplish both. He was a Legionnaire with a past and a good one it was.

Jean came from the family of a Legionnaire hero. His grandfather, Captain Jean Danjou, was one of the most famous Foreign Legionnaires in history. He died fighting in Mexico. The one-armed officer stood ground against a Mexican guerilla force. The Mexicans far outnumbered his 63 man, reconnaissance unit. Yet, he fought and died. The Battle of Camerone was certainly the stuff of legend. It was Jean's curse wherever he went. His peers did not recognize him for his performance. They compared him to his grandfather. He lost every time.

Anne-Marie was a strong point in General Navarre's plan to deny the Viet Minh access to Laos. In addition, Navarre hoped to draw General Giap into a fight he could not win. Jean had misgivings about how a battle at Dien Bien Phu would achieve either objective. Yet, he was on his way.

Jean felt the Dakota aircraft move and then stop. It was one of 65 in line at both of Hanoi's airports. They were to fly to Dien Bien Phu. Once over drop zone Natacha, his unit would parachute to begin Operation Castor.

"Did they select me to help plan this operation because of my name or my record?" He thought. "It was my performance at Na Son that drew their attention. We gave the Viet Minh a hard defeat, a year ago last October."

Navarre's adjutant had sent orders for him to report for duty not too long after the Na Son battle. Navarre had recently taken command of France's military in Indo China. He had a plan to stop the Viet Minh. He wanted the hero of Na Son on his team. Whatever Navarre wanted, he got.

"Congratulations on your promotion lieutenant," Captain Adjutant Andre Louis said.

"Welcome, we've been expecting you. General Navarre asked when you would be with us just this morning. The general is aware of your excellent job at Na Son," Louis continued.

"Thank you sir," Jean answered. "It is my pleasure to be with this headquarters," he lied.

"Navarre is making a big mistake with his plan," Jean thought.

Captain Louis grabbed one of Jean's bags and said, "Follow me to your quarters. You will live in the headquarters building. You might as well be here for you're not going to have time for much else. You're to brief the general day after tomorrow about Na Son."

They exited the adjutant's office and walked down a long corridor. The floors gleamed as if covered with glass. Along the walls were paintings and photographs of famous Legionnaires. At the quick step, there was no time to get a close look. He did see his grandfather among them.

Jean noted signs on doorways that identified offices for Operations, Logistics, and Personnel. On their right, they passed a large double door with guards. The guards came to attention at their approach and presented arms. Their heels clicking together echoed down the long walkway. A sign on the door stated, "Authorized Personnel Only."

After numerous turns, Captain Louis stopped at a door marked "4-A." He used a key to gain access and entered. The room was Spartan with one chair, a desk, a cot, and a small adjoining room with toilet facilities. It had two doors, which usually meant shared use.

Pitching the room key to Jean, Captain Louis said, "This is it. Shave, shower and get combat fatigues on and report to my office for a security pass. Questions?" He asked.

"None," Jean replied.

After Captain Louis's departure, Jean sat at the desk and examined his room.

"No comforts here," he mumbled.

Jean guessed the building to be 1800s vintage. Exposed electrical wiring was on the walls. Waterlines ran exposed along baseboards. The commode was an overhead, gravity feed box with a pull chain.

He undressed to shower, examining three scars on his right hip in the process. Red and tender to touch, he avoided them. He recalled receiving them while in a face-off with a Viet Minh guerilla.

He looked young and malnourished. His thin arms and legs didn't appear to be able to support his weight. In addition, he carried a Chinese SKS assault rifle along with an ammunition bandoleer. His eyes were white orbs in dark sockets. They grew wide with fear when he exhausted his ammunition. He just stood there pulling the trigger with no effect

Next came machine gun fire from Jean's right. He remembered that he fired as he was falling. His right leg gave way and he toppled to the ground. Blackness came but he felt no pain. He awoke in his unit's field hospital.

The battle was over and they withstood weeks of attacks by Viet Minh. They came in waves losing thousands to their guns.

"How can General Giap justify such losses? He slaughters his people as if they were nothing," Jean thought.

"I've had enough of that," he said aloud as he stepped into the shower.

He reported to Captain Louis. He felt refreshed and ready for whatever they were going to tell him to do.

"This is your security pass lieutenant. Wear it to gain access to our Operational Plans Room. We passed the guarded, doubled door earlier. You must return the pass to this office whenever you leave the room," he explained.

Captain Louis continued, "We require strict pass controls. They can only be at one of two places at any given time. It must be here in the vault or on your person. Don't ever forget to return it. I'm sure you would not like the consequences. Report to Major Bigeard. He is in the room now. Dismissed."

Jean rendered a crisp salute and did an about face. He departed to report to Major Bigeard, his new commander. The guards, again, rendered present arms. However, they stepped aside after examining his security pass. One opened the door for him.

Tables lined the room. Upon each was a topographic, terrain model. Above these, pins held maps to the walls. Various military symbols cluttered them. Large, overhead fans turned slowly, providing some heat relief. An officer approached while giving Jean's security badge a swift glance.

"Lieutenant Danjou, how glad we are to see you. We worried that your wounds might preclude your joining us in the upcoming operation," he said.

Jean knew this captain but exact details escaped him. For some reason, he had a bad feeling about him. He thought that perhaps he knew him in Algeria but was not certain.

"It will come to me," he thought as he accepted the captain's outstretched hand.

"My name is Pierre Prudhomme. My father and yours were at that Casablanca mess in 1908.

Those three German deserters were a sorry lot, not worth a bullet to shoot them," he commented.

"Now I remember," Jean thought. "This is that snot from Morocco. How in hell did he ever get in the Legion much less be a captain? His father must have done some heavy arm twisting to get him an officer's commission. This is a dangerous man."

Pointing to a nearby chair, Prudhomme said, "Have a seat lieutenant. I'll check and see if Major Bigeard can see you now. I'll be just a moment."

Jean watched as Prudhomme walked toward an office door. The door's window had closed Venetian blinds.

"He walks like a queer," he thought.

The Dakota's engines sputtered, withdrawing Jean from his reverie. They were taking off. Ahead, other planes flew toward their rendezvous. The flight from Hanoi would take almost two hours. He leaned forward to see other members of his unit.

"They are good men, well trained and hard. It is an honor to lead them," he thought.

Yet, he was concerned. He did not like many parts of Operation Castor. He had learned much at Na Son. He knew the Viet Minh to be determined fighters and not afraid of death. He also knew that General Giap was ready to sacrifice them without hesitation. He was sincere in his belief that planners had grossly underestimated the Viet Minh's capacity to make war. In addition, Prudhomme was a major player in that underestimation.

He remembered why he did not care for him. He was certainly his father's son. Major Prudhomme, Captain Prudhomme's father, played a major role in the Casablanca incident. If they knew the truth, he was a primary contributor to the problem. Jean recalled what his father said.

"Some Foreign Legion members deserted while stationed in Occupied Morocco in late 1908. Three deserters were German. In an attempt to leave the country, they made clandestine arrangements with personnel at the German Embassy. The consul had issued safe passage on a German ship. Additionally, the chancellor had extended his protection to the three," his father had said.

His father explained that through an informant, French officials learned of their plan. They became concerned what the reaction would be by Germany if they attempted to arrest the deserters. They contacted Major Prudhomme for an assessment.

Prudhomme was in charge of intelligence at Legion headquarters. He advised that the Germans would not contest a French arrest. He advised them to use a few Legion members to accompany police officials. He had information, from a reliable source that they should not worry.

During the arrest, German military attachě personnel fired on the Legionnaires. Two died and one received a severe wound. They arrested the German deserters but with a considerable loss of blood on both sides.

Prudhomme had made a serious mistake, according to his father. Prudhomme didn't know the difference between information and intelligence. Information only becomes intelligence when the information receives verification. He had not corroborated the informant's story.

"He is an arrogant bastard," his father told him. "He is a disgrace to the uniform."

Prudhomme's family was of aristocratic stock and quite wealthy. They had friends in high places who could bring political pressure to bear. Prudhomme never even received a reprimand.

Jean determined later that Major Prudhomme's son was worse. Major Prudhomme was now a lieutenant general. This fact Pierre used on many an occasion to his benefit.

"Yes," he thought. "He is a dangerous man."

Waiting patiently, Jean examined the room. There were three topographic models on separate tables. The center table was more than double the size of the other two. He could see models for bunkers, a large airfield, barbed wire, and trenches. Individuals working on the models were constantly making measurements on maps and comparing them to the models.

It was clear that they were preparing for a large operation. However, from where he sat, he did not recognize the terrain although it had a slightly familiar look.

"The major will see you now lieutenant," Prudhomme said.

Startled, Jean stood. Prudhomme pointed to the door he previously entered and immediately left for one of the tables. Jean walked to the door and knocked twice.

A voice said, "Come in, lieutenant."

Major Bigeard sat at his desk reading pages in an open file folder. He was dark from the sun and slightly gray at his temples. Rather small in stature, Jean noted that beneath his swarthy skin individual muscles were taught against it. Blood vessels stood stark where they crossed muscle. Jean judged him one of significant strength despite his size. He stepped smartly in front of Bigeard's desk and saluted.

"Lieutenant Danjou reporting as ordered, sir!" He said.

"At ease, lieutenant. Take a seat," Bigeard directed.

"Thank you, sir!" Jean replied

He sat in a chair beside the desk. Bigeard continued to examine the file while Jean waited.

Closing the folder, Bigeard said, "Tell me about what you did at Na Son lieutenant."

"Just my job, sir." He replied.

"Knock off the shit lieutenant and answer my question," Bigeard demanded.

"Well sir, this is what happened," he answered. "Me and my unit arrived at Na Son by chance. My platoon was a Special Operations Group. I divided them into five, nine-man teams. Each team made a night jump into Viet Minh territory in the Na Son region. Only certain persons knew their assigned areas. No one at Na Son was aware of our mission."

Continuing Jean said, "We were gathering information about guerillas. When we found supply depots, we destroyed them. Our instructions were to go to Na Son after 30 days for some rest and resupply."

"Just a moment, lieutenant," Major Bigeard interrupted.

Bigeard arose and walked to his office's door. He opened it and looked outside. He heard someone ask. "Can I help you sir?"

"Yes," Bigeard responded. "Bring us some coffee and the Special Actions folder."

"Yes sir," the voice responded.

Returning to his desk, Bigeard directed, "Continue."

"Sir, we arrived at Na Son while Viet Minh had it under attack. I decided it would be disastrous if we tried to infiltrate to gain access to the besieged garrison. Instead, I found a place where we could observe the Viet Minh by day undetected. At night, we attacked weak spots in their rear area."

"What kind of spots?" Bigeard asked.

"Well sir, for example, we took out heavy weapon positions. We used garrotes to kill the crews. We disappeared without alerting other guerillas. My teams did similar operations for two weeks," he answered.

Someone knocked on the door. "Come," Major Bigeard said.

A young man appeared with a tray holding a china coffeepot and cups. He handed a file folder to Bigeard.

"Thank you," Bigeard said.

The young soldier left, closing the door behind him. Major Bigeard opened the folder and said, "Help yourself to some coffee lieutenant."

While Jean poured, Bigeard leafed through the folder. He paused now and then to examine particular pages.

Bigeard said, "Proceed."

"Sir, that's about all I can tell. The rest is classified," Jean stated.

"That's fine lieutenant. Let me tell you," the Major answered.

Major Bigeard, reading from the folder, continued with details of Jean's mission. He revealed that many of Jean's teams disappeared without a trace. However, he related in detail what Jean told his superiors during his debriefing.

"According to this," he said. "You saw hundreds, if not thousands, of individuals delivering munitions to the Viet Minh by bicycle. Also, it says here, that you found a major delivery network of roads, trails and paths that appeared to come from China's direction. Additionally, you discovered truck parks with repair facilities, major fuel and munitions depots. In addition, you reported three hospitals treating Viet Minh wounded."

"Is that about right lieutenant?" He asked.

Dumfounded that Bigeard had access to such information, he answered, "Yes sir."

"You're not telling everything Jean. You left out a major part," Bigeard continued.

Jean noted that he used his first name rather than his rank. Still somewhat aghast that he knew so much, he answered with a question.

"Do you mean the sappers sir?" He asked.

"That's right," he replied. "It says in this report that you personally took out a sapper team. You found them placing charges. That is when you attacked. Is that how you received your wounds?"

"Yes sir," he answered.

Bigeard pushed his chair back and got up.

"Follow me," he said and started for the door. Jean followed.

Bigeard walked to the largest of three, model tables. He picked up a pointer and directed its tip to a town in the table's center.

"That's Dien Bien Phu. You are now the commanding officer of Red Team. It is attached to the Sixth Colonial Battalion for admin, quarters, and rations. However, you work directly for me, and the battalion commander knows. Try not to get his nose bent out of shape and do not interfere with his operations. You report only to me. The plan is Operation Castor. Learn it. Good luck with your briefing for General Navarre tomorrow. Report to me after you speak with the general. Questions?"

"No sir," Jean responded.

"Carry on then. We've work to do," Bigeard said as he turned and headed for his office.

Jean noted that Bigeard had a slight limp. In addition, he slapped the side of his leg with the file folder as he walked.

"He seems concerned about something." Jean thought. "It's not Operation Castor either. I wonder what it could be."

Jean went to the Adjutant's office to return his security pass. Captain Louis greeted him.

"Lieutenant, how did your visit go? He asked.

"Everything went fine," Jean answered as he handed his pass to the captain.

"Jean, are you free tonight? Louis asked.

"Well, that bare room isn't very thrilling. Why do you ask?" He questioned.

Captain Louis explained that he taught French classes at a local, Catholic school. The class that night ended at seven o'clock. After that, he would be free to enjoy Saigon's pleasures.

"Why not attend the class? We can leave from there as soon as I finish. This will save you from having to meet me. I'm leaving in 20 minutes. Transportation is arranged. What do you say?"

Jean figured he had nothing else to do. He would not see Navarre until 11:00 hours. There was plenty of time to prepare.

"See you out front in 20 minutes," Jean said.

"Fine," Captain Louis replied. "I must change clothes. We cannot wear uniforms outside the compound unless we are on official business."

Jean returned to his room to change to civilian clothes. He examined his room again.

"This is one hell of a place to spend the evening. Saigon is better. I'll enjoy getting away from things for a while," he thought as he unbuttoned his tunic.

Transportation was a three-wheeled Lambretta. Lambrettas were made in Italy and amounted to nothing more than motor scooters. Industrious Vietnamese added another wheel and a rear carriage. Passengers rode in a cramped, exhaust-filled box. It was ideal for travel on Saigon's filled, narrow streets. And, the fare was cheap.

They arrived at the Catholic school near the Chinese populated Cholon district. As with most buildings, it was surrounded by a high wall. Atop it, glass shards protruded skyward. This was to discourage thieves from trying to climb over it. He could see a cathedral's spire behind the wall. The wall's entrance was a solid steel door.

Captain Louis repeatedly pulled a cord hanging next to the entrance. From the sound, the cord connected to a bell. A small window in the door opened. An oriental woman's face appeared and immediately broke into a large grin.

"Ayah, Andre, Andre," she exclaimed in her singsong voice. "They are waiting for you."

This door opened into a small garden beside a cathedral. Next to it was another quite large building. It had wrought iron bars on every window and door. Various tropical plants surrounded a small pond filled with goldfish. A statue of the Virgin Mary stood with outstretched arms beneath an arbor covered with flowering plants. The area had a quiet serenity about it.

"Who is it Mey Ling?" A voice asked in perfect Chinese.

The words came from above them. Looking up, he saw a nun in traditional habit. She wore a long, black dress with a matching black hood lined with white. A rope-like sash crossed her midriff. From her clasped hands, a rosary could be seen.

"Andre, Mother Superior! It's Andre!" Mey Ling answered.

"Hello Andre," the nun said. "Please meet me after class. We will have some tea. Be sure to bring your friend."

Turning gracefully, she disappeared through drapes lining the balcony window.

Mey Ling said, "Follow me please," as she started down a stone path around the main building.

Attached to the main structure, a canopied walkway led to a smaller building. Mey Ling opened its door and stood aside to allow Captain Louis and Jean to enter. Jean followed Captain Louis into a well-lit room. Giggling filled the air. They stopped as Captain Louis proceeded down an aisle with school desks on each side. Jean remained at the room's rear.

Young girls dressed in white occupied each desk. They arose as Captain Louis reached a platform and stepped up and stood behind a rostrum. In unison, the girls bowed and said, "Good evening Monsieur Louis."

"Good evening Mademoiselles," he replied. "Please take your seats."

They sat and each opened a green textbook. The group looked toward Andre.

"This evening I have a special guest. His name is Monsieur Danjou. He recently arrived from Upper Tonkin," Andre said.

"Upper Tonkin," Jean thought. "The Viet Minh prisoner, taken at An Son, was correct. We were arrogant to rename his country. The North we called Tonkin. Farther south, it was Annam. And, in this locale, it was Cochin China."

The girls turned to see Jean. They covered their mouths as they giggled. Many blushed and excitedly whispered to girls on either side.

"Please give me your attention," Andre interrupted. "Turn to page 43 in your primers. We will begin with advanced grammar this evening."

Andre required French conversation. If there was a question, a student had to ask it in French. If could not articulate the problem, he would allow Vietnamese only to discuss the correct wording. This way the entire class benefited.

The lesson ended in one hour. Andre walked to the room's rear and the students stood while he departed the platform. Asians held educators in high regard. They received utmost respect.

Jean stood by the doorway as students spoke with Captain Louis as they exited. Jean glanced down the line and saw a girl who carried herself with exceptional grace. Her waist length hair seemed to glow. Obviously, she brushed it at length to achieve such sheen. She wore bangs slightly above her eye brows. A dark blue ribbon held her hair tight against the back of her neck. Her almond-shaped eyes sparkled. She laughed and chatted with her friends as the line worked its way past Captain Louis. She clutched her textbook to her breast with crossed arms.

"She is beautiful," Jean thought. "However, she does not look Vietnamese. She has features typical of Thais. I'll see if that is the case."

She spoke a few words with Captain Louis. As she approached Jean, he bowed with both hands together at this chin.

"Say-wa-dee crub," Jean said in perfect Thai.

Appearing somewhat surprised, she returned the gesture.

"Monsieur Danjou, do you speak Thai?" She asked.

"Very little mademoiselle, I learned some in Bien District at Muong Valley. Is your family Thai?" Jean asked.

"Only by heritage monsieur, my family moved into Muong Valley hundreds of years ago. We continue some Thai traditions. However, our true origin is from Tia tribes. They are the natives who live in the mountains," she answered.

Jean did not dare mention that he traveled lower reaches of Muong Valley during the Na Son battle. He did not want her to know he learned some of the language while interrogating prisoners. One of his Special Operations Group, commonly referred to as SOG, members spoke fluent Tia. He had taught him a few phrases.

"Excuse me, monsieur. I am blocking the door. We must attend Mass. Mother Superior will be upset if we are late," she continued.

She bowed and departed with Jean watching every step. He caught a slight wisp of lilacs from her. She appeared to glide above the walkway. Her long hair tied back highlighted her face. He felt a slight shiver seeing her face in the moon's light. She followed the walkway and entered the main building.

"God," Jean thought. "She's beautiful."

"Come along," Captain Louis said. "Mother Superior is waiting.

They entered the cathedral. Its interior was quite dark. Burning candles provided the only light. They had to wait until their eyes adjusted before they could proceed. They removed their shoes and placed them just inside the doorway.

To his left, Jean could see into a chapel. A Tabernacle was on a raised platform at the room's front. A Virgin Mary statue, to its left, flanked it. On the right, Joseph's statue held baby Jesus in its arms. Above the Tabernacle, a crucifix hung on the wall. Jean estimated it to be about 10 feet in height.

Girls from the class kneeled in the front pews. They were saying the Rosary. A nun, in black, led them through the "Hail Marys" and the "Our Fathers." Flickering candles gave the scene a ghostly appearance.

In the darkness, with their heads bowed in prayer, Jean could not see the blue ribbon. However, as his eyes adjusted, he saw the girl from Muong Valley.

"I must see her again. I wonder if they are allowed social visits." Jean thought.

Mother Superior entered the small foyer. She approached and said, "Andre, you and Jean follow me to the study."

Eyes now fully adjusted, they followed Mother Superior upstairs to a large room. Books filled shelves along one side. The carpet was soft and thick. Paneling covered the remaining walls that held various religious paintings. She took a seat next to a coffee table surrounded by chairs. She gestured for them to sit. A silver service was on the table along with fresh baked bread, cheese, and some fruit.

"Bon Appetite monsieurs," she said as she finished serving coffee.

They chatted about mutual acquaintances and local events. Jean could tell that she had other matters on her mind. Soon, she revealed her purpose.

"Andre, I am worried," she said. "The Pope recently sent disturbing information. I will discuss it only with your holy vow that it never leaves this room. I must have that from each of you."

Andre and Jean gave assurances that they would never reveal what she had to say. Jean felt reluctant. However, if Andre gave his word, he could do the same.

Mother Superior related how, in September 1945, the Marxist leader Ho Chi Minh declared independence for Viet Nam. He had used wording directly from America's Declaration of Independence. In addition, he was very tolerant of the Catholic Church. He showed this by nominating a Catholic as his economic minister. He is allowing Catholic Bishops and Vicars to continue holding services. She noted that about 40,000 Catholics demonstrated in Hanoi in support of Ho Chi Minh.

The Viet Minh leader, even though Marxist, tolerated various religious groups. He assured religious freedom to all. He had purposely selected the first Sunday in September as Viet Nam's Independence Day because it coincided with National Catholic Day. She knew of four Catholic bishops who had appealed to the Vatican. They wanted the Pope to recognize the new country with its new leaders.

Jean interrupted, "Pardon me, Mother Superior, I know from personal experience that Viet Minh hate Catholics. They do not hesitate to destroy their churches and schools. I know of priests executed in public squares. I don't see how you can maintain Ho Chi Minh promotes religious tolerance."

"My son, remember that the Japanese surrendered to British forces in the South. The British did not return control to the Vietnamese. They returned it to the French. Surely, you didn't expect the Viet Minh to tolerate their country's division into two parts. Ho Chi Minh declared freedom for the North and the South."

Jean persisted, "Mother Superior there is nothing secret about this. I follow orders from my superiors in France. They could not tolerate what the Viet Minh did to those who opposed them. They murdered entire villages."

Mother Superior poured more coffee for Andre and Jean. She leaned back in her chair and studied the two as she thought about what Jean said.

"Jean, who do you think the Viet Minh are?" She asked.

"They're a bunch of murdering terrorists," he replied.

"Oh Jean, this is so sad. The Viet Minh are Vietnamese. Their souls burn with an idea. You cannot destroy an idea," she emphasized.

Mother Superior's eyes pleaded with Jean to understand her position.

"You are right Jean," she said. "I've told no secrets. Please let me finish."

"I'm sorry. Please continue," Jean replied.

Leaning forward and lowering her voice, she said, "Think about this. Pope Pius XII will not recognize Ho Chi Minh's government despite pleas from his own bishops. He will do anything to destroy Communism. Why do you think he supported the nationalist movement in Germany? How could he align the Vatican with the Nazis? Why do you think he supported a dictator in the very home of the Vatican, Italy?"

Andre and Jean asked in unison, "Why?"

"Because he was on a divine mission to destroy Russia. He was reacting to a personal contact with the Virgin Mary. His mission was to assure the downfall of Communism in Russia. World War II ended with Russia the second most powerful nation in the world. Now, he must use other means to achieve their demise. France is part of his plan to destroy Communism be it in Russia or Viet Nam," she said.

Mother Superior explained that Pope Pius XII saw World War III as inevitable. It was the only way to rid the world of Communism. He was in contact with Cardinal Spellman in the United States. Spellman was working with Secretary of State John Foster Dulles on behalf of the Pope. He had convinced senior congressional members to support France in its battle in Viet Nam. President Truman had authorized equipment and money for France when the United States could be using it in Korea.

Jean saw truth in what she was saying. France's fleet of Dakota aircraft was American planes. They were Douglas C-47s. The Americans used them during World War II as a their main transport aircraft. Now, France had hundreds of them. Moreover, he knew that an abundance of weapons and ammunition was flowing into Viet Nam by the hundreds of tons. All of it went to Legion units.

"Yet, none of this was a secret," he pondered. "President Truman announced in 1950 that the U.S. would support France. He released to the press information regarding a $10,000,000 grant that same year. So, what was the big secret?"

"Mother Superior," Jean said. "There's nothing you've said that the world doesn't already know."

"Jean, have you ever heard of Operation Vulture?" She asked.

Jean looked at Andre. He shrugged his shoulders and gave Jean a "news-to-me" look. Both soldiers gave Mother Superior an inquisitive stare.

"Operation Vulture is a plan to use atomic weapons against the Vietnamese. Next, the U.S. will attack China. After that, the U.S. will bomb the Soviet Union. The initial attack will be by B-29 aircraft from Okinawa. The American Joint Chiefs of Staff have approved Operation Vulture. It could take place at any time," she said.

"My source in the Vatican is totally reliable," she continued.

Dumbfounded, the two officers stared at her in disbelief. The thought of what she said was so incomprehensible it had to be an outright lie.

"Mother Superior, with utmost respect, I cannot accept this information as truthful. Someone is misleading you in a horrendous manner," Andre said.

"I agree," Jean said immediately. "This is a cruel hoax. It is outrageous. You've said our Pope is supporting the death of millions. This I cannot accept."

Mother Superior gripped her Rosary and kissed its crucifix.

She said, "I swear to you upon my soul what I've said I believe to be true. Senior members of General Navarre's staff know of the plan. Andre, I thought sure you would know. My purpose tonight was confirmation. Now, it is suspect."

Andre replied, "I know how to expose this information as a hoax. My security clearance allows me access to files that would have to contain such information. I will let you know what I find if I can."

Relaxation swept through Jean. He had become extremely tense without realizing it.

"Yes," he thought. "Andre can learn if this is true or not. Prudhomme, as intelligence officer, would have to know. I would never breach the question with him. He's such an ass that he would lie if he did know it to be true."

Andre stood and Jean followed. Andre said, "Mother Superior, thank you for the coffee. We must go because of the curfew. We cannot be on the street in civilian clothes after curfew. I will contact you soon."

She saw them to the door. As they were leaving, Jean hesitated.

"Pardon me, Mother Superior" Jean said. "I have one more question."

"What is it my son?" She asked.

"One of the ladies in class tied her hair with a blue ribbon. I spoke with her briefly. She is a long way from home. Do you know her name?" Jean asked.

"Of course," she answered with a smile. "Her name is Minh Thanh. She is to be a bride of Christ."

Chapter Three

August 1953

"...On Blue Berry Hill."
Fats Domino (1928)

Falling to his knees, Dale Zane vomited. He broke his continuing fall with both hands.

"Jesus, I'm sick," he moaned.

Next, came dry heaves. They contracted his stomach muscles into knots. Nausea swept through his body bringing more contractions. He clenched his teeth, feeling the earth tilt. A distant voice penetrated his spinning world.

"Off your ass, Zane," Coach Ramsey yelled.

"You're supposed to be a hot shit player. At today's rate, you won't make the bench," he continued.

"It was enough to be new in town. But to fall out after two laps, he was going to die of embarrassment," Dale thought.

Slowly standing upright, he staggered after the others. However, he felt better when he saw a teammate in a four-point stance. He stopped to try and help him. Coach Ramsey was dead on his butt.

"Move it, Zane! You can't take care of yourself much less someone else. What a piece of crap, who said you could play football?" Ramsey screamed through Zane's face guard.

Dale stumbled at a sloppy gait as others passed. They leered over their shoulders. They had lapped him.

"Kiss my ass," he yelled in frustration.

Dale was not happy in Spartanburg. His dad moved his family to South Carolina's Piedmont because of a better job. It was a promotion for him.

"Good for dad," he thought. "Nonetheless, I prefer Florida. I would be a senior at Palatka High. I would be with friends and would be playing fullback on offense and linebacker on defense. This place sucks."

Coach Ramsey gave two long blasts on his whistle. "Everyone on the bus except Zane and Dybold," he yelled. "Zane, you and Dybold do another lap. Get to it."

"Hi, I'm Don," Zane's misery companion said between gasps. "The guys on the bus are going to be pissed. They may not be running but they're waiting. They're ready to hit the showers and we're a delay."

"I'm Dale," Zane replied. "I don't care. The problem is Ramsey. He's making them wait. We'll just take our time. He didn't say we had to run fast," Dale continued between gasps.

"Right," Don replied.

Slowing to a walk near the bus, the two removed their helmets. They boarded with their cleated shoes clanking on metal steps. Two seats remained at the back. They walked a gauntlet of catcalls and insults.

Collapsing onto the hard seat, Dale said, "I hope when Ramsey gets home his mother runs from under his house and bites his leg."

Dale, though a teenager, had a deep voice that resonated. His words carried the bus's length. Ramsey whirled to face a busload of laughing players. Some held their sides and tears streamed down their dirty faces. Clean streaks stretched to their jaw lines. Dale was the only one without a smile. He glared at Ramsey who returned his gaze forward without a word.

"Damn Dale, coach is going to have your butt for that," he said between chuckles.

"He won't get a cherry," Dale responded with a smile. "I just hope he respects me in the morning."

Don clasped his sides and roared with laughter.

"I like this new guy," Don thought.

"Where did you live before Spartanburg?" Don asked.

"Most anywhere you can imagine. This will be my 13th school since first grade," Dale answered.

"Is your ol' man in the Army?" Don questioned Dale.

"No, he's a company troubleshooter. Every time a branch organization starts having problems, they send my ol' man," Dale answered.

"The last place was in Florida. I hated to miss my senior year. I had a lot of friends," he continued.

Dale leaned back and closed his eyes. He thought about his dad. He shouldn't blame him for moving so much. Dad was one hell of a man. He was an Arkansas sharecropper when Dale was born in 1938. When World War II came along, he was too old to join. However, he did his part. Dad went to work at a local manufacturing plant. He started at the bottom and worked his way up to be top man in his field. His mechanical abilities made him a wizard with machinery. When he moved, he always got a promotion.

He worked hard to provide an excellent living for his family. He did it the hard way. His dad quit school in the sixth grade to work the family farm. They went under during the depression. Like many others, he became a hobo. He rode the rails to survive. He worked as a cook in logging camps when he could get work. Eventually, he returned to Arkansas. That's when he started tenant farming.

An elbow to Dale's side brought him from his daydream. Team members were getting off the bus.

Don said, "Come on man. You've been snoozing. Let's grab a shower."

Dale's muscles protested as he arose from his seat. They grew stiff during his brief rest.

"Man, I'm out of shape," he thought. "I'll be okay in a week though. It won't be long and I'll be able to perform up to my abilities."

The locker room smelled of sweat and dirty clothes. It was a sour stench. Dale sat on a bench and began untying his shoes. While undressing, he thought of Florida. He had started playing football in the ninth grade. Their team played differently from this one. This was a four-A school, much bigger than Palatka High was. Palatka did not have offensive and defensive teams. You played both teams or you did not play.

Furthermore, Palatka's team didn't use fancy plays. Their formations were straight-T with little passing. They ran drive plays. They used brute force. This was good for Dale because of his size. He weighed 185 pounds, which was big for a high school fullback. However, this paid dividends. He simply ran over anyone in his way.

Nevertheless, he had to change. Spartanburg played passing games. They did little over center, guard or tackle. Their ground game consisted of end sweeps. He did get a chance at the ball when the quarterback had to unload because a receiver wasn't open. He would lateral to him but this didn't happen often. Mostly, he was a blocker for halfbacks.

Additionally, he had another problem. Two fullbacks were returns and the coach knew them. They had played for two years at Spartanburg High. He had to overcome this and beat them for a position. This task was not going to be easy.

Grabbing a towel, Dale went to the shower. Placing his towel on a hook, he entered the steamy room. Joking and laughing, other players talked about their favorite subject, girls. Dale couldn't say anything because he had not met any.

He lathered his muscular body. His physique was perfect for football. His waist was 30 inches and his chest 56 inches. Dale's neck size was 18. Not tall at 5 feet 11 inches, some called him the fireplug. Dale let hot water soothe his aching muscles while rinsing the soap.

"Hey Zane," a player yelled. "Have you been to the mountains yet?"

Wiping soap from his eyes, he looked in the voice's direction. The starting quarterback was giving him an inquisitive look.

Dale answered, "Nope, sure haven't."

"See me outside," he replied.

"Okay," Dale agreed.

Leaving the building, Dale saw the quarterback talking with two other players. They motioned Dale to join them. The quarterback extended his hand and said, "Hi. My name is Jay Rode."

Pointing to the others, Jay said, "This is Barry Grant. He plays center. This guy is Jim Price. He's a quarterback"

Shaking hands with each in turn, Dale said, "I'm Dale Zane. You've got a good team going."

"Yeah we do and we should have a good year," Jay said.

"Yeah we will if we don't get caught cheating," Jim responded.

Dale, not having any idea what Jim meant asked, "What cheating?"

Jay explained, "Well, we're not supposed to be practicing as a team. State rules prohibit us from practice until August 15. We're two weeks early."

"Yeah," said Price. "We could get in big trouble. It would be Ramsey's ass."

"Ours too," Grant said.

Jay looked at Dale and said, "There's a group of us going to the mountains this weekend. It's only 20 miles to some cool places. Would you like to go with us?"

"Sure," Zane answered.

"I'll get details and let you know at tomorrow's practice," Jay added.

"Okay, I'll see you tomorrow. I've got to get home," Dale said, as he walked to the school's parking lot.

Dale came to his pride and joy, a 1939 DeSoto. A two-door, club coupe model, it was small. It was dark green and in perfect condition. It had the original mohair interior. The area behind the front seat was small. There was one fold-down seat on each side. When using these, passengers faced each other. This model had a rumple seat. Two could sit in it. However, rumple seat riders were at the mercy of the elements. Few vehicles had this feature. Dale thought it was sharp.

However, the good stuff lay hidden under the hood. The engine was a 1953 Dodge Ram 8. This eight-cylinder engine would really get up speed fast. The coupe, because of its lightweight, was a real mover.

He bought the car from a guy on his way to jail. Bootleggers made money bringing liquor from North Carolina to South Carolina. South Carolina liquor had high state taxes. North Carolina booze cost about half of what South Carolina charged. The car's owner had a load of bootleg booze when tax agents stopped him. He had to sell his car to post bail.

Nevertheless, the car caused problems. The previous owner had put oversized springs and shocks on the car's rear axle. This caused its rear to be abnormally high. The DeSoto looked normal when carrying a load. Alcohol Tax and Firearms agents were constantly stopping Dale. This was dumb because, if the rear was high, there wasn't any liquor. Still, they stopped him. Dale figured they had to be trying to hassle the previous owner. Maybe they would stop pulling him over when they learned Dale owned it and did not bootleg.

Dale got in and started the car. He raced the engine a few times to hear the mufflers. The noise from the dual exhaust and glass pack mufflers sounded tough. When idling, they had a low rumble. With acceleration, the rumble increased to a higher pitch. When he took his foot off the accelerator, the twin pipes would pop.

"Man, that sounds great," he thought as he left the parking area. "Now, if I can just find someone that will drag race, they would get a big surprise. The old looking DeSoto fooled them every time."

Dale returned from the mountain trip with mixed feelings. He had met Jay's friends. They were nice. Dale went in Jay's car. Four of his friends accompanied them. He felt out of place because of his clothes. He wore jeans, loafers and a tee shirt which were common in Florida. These guys wore wool slacks and quality shirts. The girls were sharp with their crinolines and knee high skirts. Definitely, he was a "country bumpkin."

Furthermore, other matters set him apart. They had prayers for everything. Saying grace was a common practice at home. However, this group prayed at rest stops. They prayed leaving and arriving at scenic spots. It seemed they spent more time praying than anything else.

Plus, as far as he could tell, none of them smoked. He was having a nicotine fit. This is how he met Buzz. Giving some lame excuse, Dale left the group and went behind a building to smoke. Upon turning a corner, there stood this guy with two cigarettes lit. He would puff one and then the other. He was really working up a smoke cloud. In addition, he was with their group. As soon as he saw Dale, he dumped both butts.

"Hey, man! Don't do that," Dale said.

However, it was too late. The guy squashed both cigarettes.

Glaring at Dale, he asked, "What business is it of yours if I smoke?"

"No, no, you don't understand. I wanted one," Dale explained.

"Oh shit, those were my last two. Your name is Dale. Right?" He asked.

"Right, what's yours?" Dale replied.

"My name's Eric Harrison. Most folks call me Buzz though," he said.

"Buzz, no sweat. I've got a pack," Dale responded.

The two lit their cigarettes. Frequently, one or the other would glance around the corner to see if anyone was approaching.

"What's with this bunch?" Dale asked. "They're always praying. And, there doesn't seem to be a smoker in the group. I bet they don't drink either."

"Right," Buzz answered. "They are a clique. I don't run around with them much. They only invited me because of my kid sister. She's trying to reform me. Frankly, I'm surprised they invited you. Trust me, they consider you lucky to be around them."

"Oh really," Zane said incredulously.

"Yeah, they're known as randy-bandies at school," Buzz commented.

"That's weird," Dale added.

"You said it. I didn't," Buzz said. "We better head back or they'll come looking for us," he continued.

Dale liked the Smokey Mountains. They were the first mountains bigger than the Ozarks he had seen. The view at Chimney Rock was particularly impressive. They ate lunch at picnic tables near the top. The Smokey Mountains spread for miles in the distance.

During the return trip, Dale learned about Thunder Road. This narrow road spiraled down into South Carolina. It was a prime bootleg route. Robert Mitchum starred in a movie about Thunder Road. Also, there was a hit song with the same title. He realized it was wise that he didn't bring his car. They would have stopped him every few miles. Later, some guy offered Dale $150 for every load delivered using this treacherous road.

Finally, registration for his senior year arrived. Dale took his Florida transcript. He learned that he had lost a grand opportunity. He could have skipped the twelfth grade and gone to college.

The lady in the office studied his records. Looking up, she said, "Mr. Zane. It appears Florida's graduation requirements are much higher than South Carolina's. You could have taken South Carolina History this summer and gone directly to college. The history course is mandatory for being graduated. However, you meet every other requirement."

"Mam, are you sure?" Dale asked.

"Quite sure. You've had every course we require and then some. Discounting the history course, we don't have any other courses that you haven't had. You can take fourth year Literature but you've had all the math and science courses we offer. The literature course is an elective," she said.

"Damn," Dale mumbled. "I could have saved an entire year. Now, I'm stuck with a bunch of do-nothing courses."

Registration was taking place in the gym. Walking through large double doors, Dale saw a typical gymnasium. Spectator seats lined each side of a basketball court. By folding them, they provided additional floor space. A large, electric scoreboard was above the far goal's basket.

Students were in line at various card tables to register for a class. He saw the South Carolina History line and joined other students waiting their turn. He noticed that the teacher appeared quite elderly. She was having difficulty holding registration cards. Finally, he reached the card table.

"Mam, I'm a new student," he explained.

"Have you been to administration yet young man?" She asked. "I think you must be in the wrong line. Only freshman students take this course."

"Yes Mam, I have," Dale answered. "Here's my clearance slip."

"My, my," she cackled. "You're a senior taking a beginner's class."

Dale failed to see humor in his situation. He watched as she wrote a time and room number on his registration card. She returned it and he started for another table.

Dale and Don saw each other simultaneously. Don waved and came in his direction.

"Hey man," Don said. "Didn't I see you in a freshman line?"

"Yeah," Dale answered, "I have to take South Carolina History. That's a freshman's course."

Don said, "Something stinks. Coach Ramsey had to know your courses and grades before you could come to practice. He has to check to be sure you have at least a C average."

"You think so?" Dale asked.

"I know so. For some reason, he didn't tell you. I bet he wanted to see what kind of player you were. If he had told you, you would never have come to practice," Don explained.

"From the way he carries on, I don't think he wants me on the team," Dale said.

"Don't sweat Ramsey. Head coach Goins decides who will play or not," Don replied.

Dale looked at his registration form. He could take Office Practice, Typing 2, Psychology and other mundane courses. "Well, this is going to be an easy year," he told Don.

"Yeah, it will be a breeze. See you at practice this afternoon," Don said as he left.

Like Don predicted, Coach Goins selected him to be a backup fullback. There was no way that he could overcome the returning senior. Nevertheless, he got as much playing as he wanted. The year went fast. The courses were easy. Also, there was an added benefit. He was the only guy in most of his classes.

The other class members were girls. Dale found that to his liking. He never wanted for female companionship.

He made friends. Don was his closest one. They lived near each other and shared rides to school. They double dated. Don knew most of the girls and steered him away from the dogs. There were dances, hanging out at the diner or the drug store soda fountain. It was a good time.

He danced to "Rock Around the Clock," "In the Still of the Night," and "You Ain't Nothing But a Hound Dog." He lived the birth of Rock and Roll and the phenomenon of Elvis Presley. His favorite song was "In Dreams" by Roy Orbison. It was a happy, carefree time.

Nevertheless, there was one major disappointment. After being graduated, he and Don would go to different colleges. Dale always planned to go to the University of Florida. Don was going to attend a private, local college.

After graduation, Dale got a job. He had to make enough money to pay college expenses. He had saved every summer, since he was in the ninth grade. Dale figured he would have enough by the time he was graduated. During early autumn, he drove to Gainesville, Florida. Filled with excitement, he registered. The heartbreak came when he went to the registrar's office.

"How will you be paying for this Mr. Zane?" He asked.

Dale answered, "By personal check if that's acceptable."

The registrar slid registration papers to Dale. He said for him to sign. The bottom copy would be for his records. As Dale produced his checkbook, he read the document. Suddenly, he felt alone. Everything around him ceased to exist. He read the document again with fear rising within him.

"Sir, what is this $1500.00 charge?" Dale asked nervously. He dreaded the answer.

"That is the out-of-state fee. You pay that every semester," he said.

"But sir, I lived at Palatka. I don't think I should have to pay this," he said, as his throat grew taught.

The registrar's words echoed with finality. Dale saw years of hard work wasted. He clenched his jaw teeth as the significance of his situation began to overwhelm him.

"Mr. Zane your address is in South Carolina. You are not a Florida resident. The fee is mandatory. Mr. Zane, are you ill?" The registrar asked.

Dale raced from the room bumping students waiting in line. One he knocked to the floor while another's books scattered across the room. He ran directly to his car.

He wanted to push the accelerator to the floor. However, he had presence of mind not to add to his troubles. Tears streamed down his face as he sobbed openly. When he reached the main highway, he could restrain himself no longer. He shoved the gearshift into second gear and pressed the accelerator to the floor. At 80 miles per hour, he downshifted into third. A puff of black smoke erupted beneath the DeSoto's rear tires as the car responded.

Dale turned on the radio and set the volume high. Yet, to Dale the music was distant, only slightly perceived. A disk jockey played "Long Tall Sally" by Little

Richard. He heard someone say, "Hello Mr. and Mrs. America, and all ships at sea."

The reporter kept talking about release of prisoners. They were French soldiers captured at Dien Bien Phu. Many of them had died on some death march.

Dale pressed the accelerator as far as it would go.

"Where in the shit is Dien Bien Phu," he mumbled as he changed to another station.

Chapter Four

August 1952

"Silence is the ultimate weapon of power."
General Charles deGaulle (1890-1970)

Lanny Briscoe did not like his job. Shuffling papers in Washington was boring. Although he was a key National Security Agency member, his NSA work didn't compare to being a field operative. As an Office of Strategic Services agent, he had made a difference. He could see direct results of his OSS work.

In the OSS, he used information decoded by an enigma machine. This encryption device's purpose was to protect Nazi transmissions of critical, combat information. He had used data from it to advise Eisenhower during WW II. Eisenhower listened and acted upon Lanny's advice.

In this job, politicians made major decisions. As president, Truman could not react directly to Lanny's recommendations. The president had to consult other politicians. Lanny despised politicians. Few politicians knew of the enigma. They wouldn't understand it if they did.

The Nazis, during WW II, used a coding device the Allies called the enigma machine. Considerable time went into its development by the Germans. Its origin was for business. Arthur Scherbius developed it to encode communications between corporations. Its purpose was to overcome business espionage. Scherbius displayed the machine at a few trade shows in 1923 and the German military took an interest. The device disappeared from the commercial market. German military security continued its manufacture and added improvements.

However, Poland's German Cipher Bureau was aware of the enigma. They knew Germany's intentions. Through dumb luck, the Poles got a gift. The Germans shipped a device to their Warsaw embassy by regular freight. Realizing their error, they made urgent inquiries about the package. This alerted Polish customs. Polish intelligence agents examined it for two days before forwarding it to Warsaw.

Nevertheless, having detailed knowledge of its construction was not enough. The device worked in such a way that it could change code daily. The operator did this by manipulation of various rotors and electrical contacts. Poland's best mathematicians worked hard to produce a means to accurately decipher enigma messages. They made progress but the Germans kept making changes. By December 1938, the Poles lacked resources to decode transmissions. They needed help.

The Poles met with British and French intelligence agents in January 1939. At the Paris gathering, the British offered services of their Government Code and Cipher School. At Bletchley Park, the British had a team of encryption specialists led by renowned mathematician Alan Turing. Considered by many to be a genius, Turing's group attacked the device and ultimately could decipher German communications. The Nazis never knew, throughout WW II, that their communications encryption effort was a failure. Lanny knew because he was the first American to see enigma information.

He was a military attache at the American Embassy in London in 1941. His job was to keep Washington advised of circumstances involving European operations. A major interest was shipping from the United States to Great Britain. German submarines were sinking British freighters at an alarming rate. American-made products were being lost. Yet, the British had an uncanny ability to predict where German U-boats operated in the North Atlantic. They simply did not have naval resources to cover every submarine. British situation reports first got his attention. How did they know where and when submarines would attack? He soon learned.

After Japan bombed Pearl Harbor, the United States declared war on their attackers. They did not take long before war with Germany began. President Roosevelt made Europe's war a priority. The Pacific Theater would have to wait. If the U.S. was going to fight in Europe, it was essential to assure reasonable safe passage for shipping. To do this meant dealing with the U-boat problem. The British had to share information to accomplish this. They told Briscoe about enigma.

Every senior commander, during WW II, had a special intelligence officer assigned. This individual passed enigma generated information for their use. Some ignored it while others based entire strategies on it. OSS officers knew, on a day-to-day basis, the status of every German unit. The Germans had distributed enigma code devices throughout their military. They thought it to be totally secure. Always meticulous, they made daily reports to Berlin. They accounted for every vehicle, ammunition available by type, petroleum products and troop status by unit.

General Patton had a field day. He wasn't a military genius. He knew every move the enemy was going to make before they did it. Only once did the Germans move without allied forces knowing it. The German attack, late in the war, known as the Battle of the Bulge never appeared on an enigma. Messengers delivered plans for this operation. This alone was cause for them to suspect compromise of their code device. Their arrogance caused them to overlook a major defect in their communication security.

Two weeks before D-day, 6 June 1944, Briscoe went ashore in southern France. He was there to help the resistance prepare for the invasion. While he could not tell them an exact date, he could help them prepare. His assignment involved extreme danger. The Vichy French actively sought OSS agents. They helped the Nazi Gestapo find and execute many operatives. French resistance fighters who helped him put themselves at maximum risk. One person in particular risked his life to save Briscoe from sure death. His name was Jean Danjou.

Eisenhower learned of Lanny's mission to France and was irate. Nobody told him that he was going. Europe's supreme commander went into a rage. The mere thought of his OSS adviser endangering enigma made him furious. Lanny knew too much and his capture could damage the entire war effort. Eisenhower asked General deGaulle for help.

DeGaulle was anti-Vichy and did not recognize Vichy France devised by Petain. He considered himself France's legitimate head of state. Also, he would go to any length to rid France of collaborators like Petain. He selected Danjou for the mission.

Danjou helped bring down the Vichy government in North Africa. He did this by assassinating important military leaders during the Allied Invasion. Additionally, he destroyed fuel depots critical to Germany's armored unit operations in North Africa's desert. He was the best man for this job.

Briscoe had been operating with the resistance for ten days when he received word to leave. A French agent would arrive by parachute and help him escape and evade to safety. The operative's code name was Baylou. In addition, he would rendezvous at Point Aspin near Calais.

There was much more to this mission than retrieving Lanny. Supreme Headquarters Allied Expeditionary Forces, better known as SHAFE, had a plan to mislead Nazi forces. This plan was to convince German military leaders that an invasion would be at Calais. So far, they were successful. Yet, with their imminent invasion, they wanted to assure their deception. Danjou was to give the appearance that a pathfinder team had parachuted in Calais' vicinity.

Pathfinder teams were first to arrive in advance of a major force. Their mission was to place radio beacons to guide aircraft. Moreover, they would place flares to show specific drop zones for airborne forces. Danjou was a trained pathfinder. However, pathfinder teams consisted of 10 men. Danjou was to place evidence to suggest that a 10-man team had entered the area. He must accomplish this before getting Briscoe to safety.

Two resistance fighters accompanied Briscoe to Aspin. They waited in darkness. Feeling secure in their hiding place, Briscoe felt a knife blade against his throat. A hand covered his mouth holding him tight without being able to move much less speak.

A voice whispered, "Baylou."

The hand across his face slightly reduced its grip. He could barely speak.

"Briscoe," he whispered.

The knife blade disappeared and the grip on his mouth disappeared. He started to speak.

"Remain quiet and listen," Danjou said.

Briscoe turned to see his attacker. The two resistance escorts lay dead, their throats cut. A shadow left the side of a nearby tree. It seemed to float without sound as if walking on air. It settled next to him. Lanny started to speak.

"Shut up and listen. They were double agents. It was their mission to kill us. I arrived last night, a day ahead of schedule. Remove your clothing and wear this. And, be damn quiet doing it," he ordered.

Examining the bundle thrust at him, Briscoe saw that it was a one-piece suit with a front zipper. Attached at its top was a hood. The material felt like silk and was black. He disrobed and donned the attire. It was a perfect fit.

"Be still," Danjou commanded. "You're going to need this."

A grease-covered hand touched his face. Soon, a fatty-like substance covered his face and hands. He noticed that he could hardly see his hands.

"Take this," Danjou told him. "It's a 9-mm Luger with a 20-round clip. A round is in the chamber and I've released the safety. It's ready to fire. Don't shoot unless I tell you. Follow me and don't make so much damned noise."

Briscoe held close to the specter-like figure before him. They came to a coiled, barbed wire barrier. He watched as Danjou pulled a loop aside and tied it to another barbed coil. The action was effortless and without noise. Occasionally, he would encounter a trip wire attached to a flare or explosive device. He quickly disarmed it. Danjou was making a tunnel through the wire just large enough for them to walk through in a squat. Soon the barrier was behind them and Danjou stopped at an iron grate in the ground. He removed it.

"Get on your back and enter feet first. It will be slippery so be careful. Do not move too fast. At the end, there will be some iron rods. When you arrive, move aside and let me pass," Danjou explained.

They arrived in England on D-Day. Briscoe recalled how Danjou had cut through the iron rods with a fine wire. They had passed beneath German defense positions through a storm drain. The drain emptied into the channel where a British submarine surfaced two miles from shore to recover them. He would have never made the swim without Danjou's encouragement and aid. He towed him the last mile.

Briscoe learned that Danjou placed low frequency beacons at Calais as a ruse. From a large canister, dropped with him, he was able to spread enough equipment to convince the Nazis that a pathfinder team was in the area. In addition, he placed explosives to destroy generators and transformers supplying power to Nazi gun turrets. The two partisans were Vichy spies and the Germans knew it. By leaving their bodies, it appeared that pathfinders killed them.

Danjou's efforts paid dividends. Hitler would not allow much needed armored units to move to Normandy. The Nazi leader would not admit that he was wrong. This cost them France and ultimately, the war.

Eisenhower wouldn't see Briscoe for over a week. He was too busy trying to get his forces organized. They stalled in hedgerow country. Nonetheless, when he did see him, he gave him a royal ass chewing. After that he stuck to his job and kept Eisenhower up to date with enigma reports. Also, he had to see that other OSS officers received daily updates. It was a long war.

After Japan's surrender, Briscoe began teaching theoretical mathematics at Princeton. In reality, he taught few classes. He left that chore to graduate students. His primary effort was research. Because of the enigma, he was fascinated with cryptography. After publication of his work in various journals, he received recognition as a theorist who could produce quality work. His research was fundamental to development of means to intercept encoded communications and decode them. Furthermore, he designed electronic devices to transmit sensitive information.

His developments drew the attention of a newly formed organization, the National Security Agency (NSA). In 1952, President Truman directed its establishment in order to monitor communications worldwide.

The Communist threat, perceived by Truman, required containment. He had affirmed his resoluteness by acting fast in Korea. Also, he had grave concerns regarding Southeast Asia.

Truman saw to it that France received support. The French were trying to maintain their prewar colonial regime in Asia. Although American units needed support in Korea, Truman diverted supplies to the French. Military equipment, stockpiled on Okinawa for use during an invasion of Japan, Truman shipped to Haiphong harbor. According to his sources, Ho Chi Minh took it for his use. He had declared independence for Viet Nam. France never got a single item of the shipment. The amount taken measured in the thousands of tons.

Truman acted in direct opposition to Roosevelt's intentions in Southeast Asia. Roosevelt's ultimate goal was to end colonialism. He saw that region free from France's determination to control it. Yet, Truman saw the French fighting Communism and containing it. Truman's desires became the Truman Doctrine or the Policy of Containment.

Briscoe found the offer to work for NSA a chance to carry out his research. Nonetheless, Truman was the ultimate politician. He feared Truman would use NSA as a political weapon. The monitoring of every communications means worldwide would give Truman the ability to intercept any political effort against him. Lanny did not trust the man.

Nonetheless, he accepted the offer. He felt he would be in a position whereby he could act if Truman started using assets for his own ends. In addition, he had a burning desire to implement his design for cryptographic devices. He had significantly improved techniques used by the enigma. Plus, he was aware of a research and development project to develop electronic computing systems. With the clearance he would have at NSA, he should be able to access that project. His cryptographic procedures saw human interfaces as error producers. Manual cryptography used in WW II was obsolete.

Lieutenant General Barron Lehouse welcomed him to the agency. He explained their mission and assigned him a desk. Lehouse told Briscoe to review files dealing with the status of cryptographic procedures. In addition, he was to examine current equipment and report any recommendations to General Lehouse. This is how he learned that Truman was definitely trigger-happy. Also, the Joint Chiefs agreed to a nuclear attack less than 10 months after the war ended. He went to Lehouse.

"Have a seat," Lehouse said gesturing to a nearby chair. "Are you through with your review already?"

"Not really sir, I do have concerns though," he answered.

"Spit them out," the general replied.

"For me to do my job, I need to know our threat priorities. According to what I have read, the Soviet Union and China must be at the top of our list," Briscoe stated.

"How did you come to that conclusion?" Lehouse asked, looking concerned.

"I knew we had an agreement with the Russians during WW II for the joint use of Iran. We had to do that in order to get war materials to them overland.

Plus, I knew we agreed to grant them oil concessions like we did with the British in the same area. Is that a fair assessment?" Briscoe asked.

"That's correct. So, what's the problem?" Lehouse asked.

"The documents I've seen state that the Russians moved armored units into Northern Iran after the war. In addition, they say that the Soviets demanded their oil concessions but we refused. Furthermore, I saw where President Truman told Soviet Ambassador Gromyko that they had 48 hours to get their military out or we would, 'Drop the bomb on you.' Is that true?" Briscoe asked incredulously.

"That's true and they got their asses out in 24 hours," Lehouse blurted with pride.

Briscoe, though apprehensive, continued, "Sir, if that was the end of it, I would not be concerned. However, there seems to be a determined effort to use atomic weapons. Our intelligence is not the best it could be. If we continue making threats without good intelligence, we could find ourselves in a nuclear war. We think we know what the Communist block has but we're not sure."

For the next 30 minutes, Briscoe reviewed specific incidents involving atomic weapons. He itemized them in chronological order.

The second major incident was an implied threat to Yugoslavia. The United States supported right wing Greek forces after WW II. When an American aircraft was shot down over Yugoslavia, the president authorized an over-flight of six B-29s. He clearly used the atomic capability to intimidate.

Lehouse interrupted. "They didn't shoot down any more planes," he said with a grin.

Continuing, Briscoe reviewed the third instance. It involved the Berlin Crisis and Operation Broiler.

The Soviets had blocked access to West Berlin. President Truman let it be known the he was prepared to use atomic force. Moreover, he had the support of Forestall (Secretary of Navy), George Marshall (Secretary of State) and Omar Bradley (Army Chief of Staff). Forestall asked Marshall to give authority to use the atomic bomb to commanders in the field. Consequently, the National Security Council gave Truman sole power to order an atomic attack.

The fourth atomic threat was now in effect. The Korean Conflict, coupled with the Soviet Union detonating an atomic weapon, has Truman's finger on the nuclear trigger.

Operation Shakedown had B-29 aircraft in position to deliver 20 atomic bombs on the Moscow-Gorki area. For this target, planes were on station in Maine. In Labrador, B-29s had 12 bombs for use against Leningrad. Plus, in the United Kingdom, there were 52 bombs destined for the Volga and Donets Basin in the Soviet Union. As if this was not enough, there were 15 atomic bombs in the Azores. Their target was in the Caucasus area. Plus, Vladivostok and the Irkutsk areas were targets for another 15 bombs.

Emotionally drained, Briscoe settled into his chair. With a bewildered look, he said to Lehouse, "Sir, President Truman can blast the world into the Stone Age."

"Listen Mr. Briscoe," Lehouse responded. "Your job is cryptology and not national policy. My recommendation is that you mind your business and leave such decisions to the appropriate persons. Is that clear?" He stated more as a directive than a question.

"Crystal," Briscoe answered.

"Anything else?" Lehouse asked.

"No sir," Briscoe answered.

"Good, I'm glad we cleared the air. Now, go secure our communications," Lehouse directed.

"Well," Briscoe thought, "At least I can get my hands on some equipment. I can get away from shuffling papers for awhile. Lehouse let me know that I would not be in the decision making process. At least I won't have to deal with politicians."

Lanny located the project officer's name for new equipment contracts. Their file showed that V. L. McNeese, of R. L. Meyers Systems, Inc., was in charge of research and development. R. L. Meyers Systems was a front organization for covert operations dealing with cryptography. They were preparing for testing the next generation of surveillance equipment. According to specifications provided them by NSA, the system would use the latest data processing technology. Lehouse made it clear that he had responsibility for security. He telephoned McNeese.

McNeese did not sound happy that Briscoe would have oversight of his projects. Nonetheless, he arranged an appointment for the next day. He gave Briscoe instructions on how to get to their office.

The offices of R. L. Meyers were on a new highway known as the beltway. It circled Washington; D.C. Defense contractors were opening offices along its length. These companies were called Beltway Bandits by those involved in government contract work.

Briscoe arrived on time. McNeese had left word for the receptionist to escort him to his office. They traveled through a cubicle maze to an unmarked door, down some stairs in the basement. His escort dialed a combination lock on the door and led him to an interior door marked Systems Group.

"Go on in Mr. Briscoe. He's expecting you," she said.

McNeese sat behind a kidney shaped desk. Various documents littered his desk. McNeese had a pot gut and jowls that shook when he spoke. He did not inspire confidence by his appearance.

"Hi Lanny, welcome to the NSA," McNeese said. "I'm glad to see you," he lied.

McNeese arose and extended his hand. Briscoe leaned forward and shook hands with him. In the process, he observed various documents on the desk marked Top Secret. They were open to any visitor's view.

"I see that you are working on the APPS project," Lanny said.

"Why yes I am," McNeese answered.

APPS was an acronym for Analytical Photogrametric Positioning System. It used aerial photographs to provide precise locations by geographical coordinates. These coordinates were used for targeting data on high priority attack missions. It had nothing to do with communications.

"I find that curious. NSA's mission is communications monitoring," Briscoe noted.

"Certainly, you are correct. I also work for a company interested in bidding on a contract for its development," McNeese answered.

"I see," Briscoe answered.

"You're a damn liar. APPS is a special project to which McNeese should not have access. Moreover, McNeese was supposed to be working solely for NSA. This is an obvious conflict of interest. He would have to do a background check on this guy," Briscoe thought.

"What can I do for you today?" McNeese asked.

"As you know, I'm new at NSA. My prime mission is to oversee development of devices to monitor communications. In particular, my expertise is cryptographic decoding devices. I understand you are a project officer on these devices?" Briscoe questioned.

"That's right. Most are ongoing at Massachusetts' Institute of Technology. I do have some preliminary reports. Would you like to see them?" He asked.

"No, I would much rather see the equipment. Who is handling the work at MIT?" Briscoe asked.

"That would be Dr. Jennings," McNeese replied.

"Bill Jennings?" Briscoe questioned.

"That's right. Do you know him?" McNeese asked with obvious concern.

"Yes, we've crossed paths a few times. I've read a number of papers he has written. He is more of an equipment man while I work theory. My best bet is to see him. It's essential that I learn hardware," Briscoe said.

"Want me to call him?" McNeese asked.

"No, that's okay. I can do that later. I must return to my office for an appointment," Briscoe answered as he arose to leave.

"Show you out?" McNeese asked, relieved that their meeting was at an end.

"Thanks but I know the way. I will be in touch from time to time. It's a pleasure meeting you," Briscoe said.

"Same here," McNeese answered.

The combination locked door opened from the inside by pressing a bar. He worked his way through the cubicles and to the reception office. The receptionist did not even look up as he exited the building.

"Jesus-H-Christ," he thought. "This place is a security risk from the front door to McNeese's office. No one asked for identification. He did not have to sign an entrance log. McNeese had top-secret documents open for anyone to see. Moreover, he wasn't even supposed to have them. He also let me loose to roam throughout the building."

Driving to NSA, Briscoe applied brakes at a major intersection. The pedal went to the floor with no effect. He never saw the delivery truck that struck his car on its passenger side. He hit his door with considerable force. Darkness gathered around him to the sound of shattering glass and torn metal.

Chapter Five

November 1952

"There are some who become spies for money,
or out of vanity and megalomania,
or out of ambition, or out of a desire for thrills.
But the malady of our time is of those who become spies out of idealism."
Max Lerner (1902)

The Arabian stretched its stride to maximum. The upcoming barrier would require a supreme effort. The rider leaned forward, low close to its mane. Her body pressed against the horse's withers. They became one, moving gracefully like an equestrian melody. Faster it went. Muscles flowed together in synchronization building power for that moment of release. Forward hooves rose skyward reaching for ground on the other side. The powerful steed became airborne with a push from its rear hooves. Sod flew upon impact and cries from the crowd drowned a whispered word of praise. Reins tightened to slow the stallion. Vanessa Earling dismounted as she entered the exit gate. The prize was hers and she knew it.

"My Lady, you've won again," Devon Elder said, as he grasped the halter. "It's another trophy for sure."

"Yes, you're correct. He has won," she responded. "I haven't seen another perform as well."

Lady Earling was used to winning. Her Arabian was a direct descendant of Lindentree, a stallion from Turkey. His Imperial Majesty Abdul Hamid II, a Sultan, presented two stallions to General Ulysses S. Grant in 1877. The two, Leopard and Lindentree, were sent to England. Later, Leopard was given to Randolf Huntinton who took the horse to America.

Lindentree remained in England to sire fine horses. These desert spawned Arabians came from once isolated Bedouin breeders. The Sheiks believed their horses to be spiritual as if bestowed by Allah. Her Arabian, Daytran, certainly had a majestic bloodline. Such ancestry made the Arabian intelligent, gentle and affectionate.

Vanessa stood with her left shoulder beneath Daytran's neck, as she reached around it with both arms. She caressed the horse from his mane to his shoulders. She used sweeping, gentle strokes to quiet him. She whispered the prancing animal into calmness. She knew exactly what to say.

"Devon," she said.

"Yes my Lady," he replied.

"Take Daytran and groom him until he shines," she directed.

"I want him to look his absolute best when they award that trophy. There are still 16 contestants remaining before the event closes," she continued.

Vanessa removed her gloves. She walked up a gentle incline to obtain a better view of the arena. Another rider was going through the course.

"What a beautiful creature," she thought. "Arabians have so much grace and confidence. They are truly remarkable sights. She loved them."

Nevertheless, there was a time when she could not afford to feed one. She was shanty Irish. Shanty Irish was different from lace Irish. Her father explained the difference.

"Listen little girl," he would say. "The difference between shanty Irish and lace Irish is simple. Lace Irish move the dishes out of the way before they piss in the sink."

She loved her father, Ian McBeal, to the depths of her soul. To her he was noble in every way except title. She cared for him in ways few could comprehend. She owed him so much for what he had made of her life.

He amassed a major fortune when prohibition ended in America. A few others had his insights. They also accumulated significant fortunes. Working through contacts abroad, he bought and stored fine liquors. He knew that prohibition would eventually end. When it did, he and his friends controlled the supply of the best scotch whiskies available. He invested profits wisely. He did not trust currency. Most of his fortune was in gold.

Nevertheless, there were those who considered him an opportunist. Before England declared war against the Nazis, her father had his family in Switzerland. Swiss bankers knew how to make money. They worked with her father to further increase his and their fortunes. It did not matter from what source or means.

Meanwhile, she attended the finest lady's school in Switzerland, the Geneva Academy of Arts and Science. She gained social graces. She met the "right" people. She received a superb education.

With nothing less than the finest wardrobe, she was beautiful to behold. She was taller than most women were. Her blazing red hair and green eyes struck many a suitor speechless.

Furthermore, she was not only intelligent but possessed her father's wile. She was fluent in French, Spanish, German and English. In addition, should the occasion arise, she could curse with the best of them in her native tongue, Irish Gaelic. She did not avoid hard courses in school. She had a particular liking for science and math. Her liking for these was quite different than her fellow students. They took the easy courses and spent their time looking for rich men to marry. As for her, she could have had her choice of many.

Her mother was her beauty's source. Molly O'Shea McBeal was of fairer skin. She was milk white sprinkled with light brown freckles. When angered, her eyes blazed and her tongue cut like a razor. She was the only person who could keep her father in check. In true Irish form, he would often linger too long at a pub. There would be hell to pay when he arrived home.

Molly's youth was spent in one of many, small houses in neat little rows. In winter, she carried coal for 2 miles each day to keep them warm. Her mother was often ill and her father seldom home. When he was not conspiring with the Irish Republican Army (IRA), he was usually with another woman. He was most certainly a lothario of the worst kind. A talker he was that man. For sure, he had kissed the Blarney Stone.

Molly grew up hard. When she married Ian, it was to escape. Yet, with time, she grew to love him. He was not in any way like her father. Oh, he loved to drink now and then but most often, he was doing business. For Molly, she was secure in the knowledge that Ian loved her. There had never been another.

Ten months after their marriage, Vanessa was born. Molly and Ian longed for more children. They never came. They knew not why so they considered it God's will. They followed their church's teachings and tried. Vanessa remained their only child.

Vanessa was a commoner. It did not matter that her education was the finest. Regardless of wealth, her station in life remained the same. At least it did until she met Sir Frederick Earling. It only took a few words and she became Lady Earling. Those words were "I do."

Now, Vanessa was a member of various organizations restricted only to nobility. She attended major social functions that appeared on the society pages. Yet, she felt that she was still an outsider. It was not anything someone specifically said or did, it was a feeling Frederick tried hard to dispel. Nonetheless, it remained. Most likely, it was a deep part of her unconscious that caused her problems. Nonetheless, it was of her own doing. Her secret was hers and a dangerous one it was. Frederick could cause it to fade at times.

Frederick gained her love through persistence. He was on leave from the Royal Air Force when they met. It was during Christmas 1938.

Her school closed for the holidays. She, and a classmate, Regina Phillips, went to the Alps to ski. Regina was an American whose family was Bostonian and old money. Her great grandfather made their family's fortune in the sea transportation business. There had always been a male Phillips heir to head the firm. Daughters went to the Academy and married well, always improving upon her family's fortune.

The snow was excellent. Each night brought a dry, fresh power that generated new slopes each day. After a full morning on the slopes, they ate lunch. The two lingered over superb hot chocolate to finish their meal.

Lunch at the Alpine Inn was an adventure for only those who could afford it. Its dining area had a cozy allure with its blazing fireplace, velvet drapes, and natural wood paneling. Its furnishings were solid, hand carved fine woods with their natural grains showing. A clock, on the fireplace's mantel, chimed portions of a Viennese waltz on each hour. Made in the seventeenth century, it represented the work of a skilled artisan's effort for an entire year.

The owner assured nothing but the best of chocolates prepared in a century's old method by hand. Mechanical processing never became part of their method. They did theirs the old way assuring the richest of flavor. Consequently, their Inn stayed crowded with the elite taking a break from the slopes.

Regina, sitting across from Vanessa in a luxurious booth, asked. "When do you think the terrible bombings will stop in Ireland?"

"When the Brits leave our country to determine its own future," she answered. "It could be next year or a 1,000 years but it will be."

"I just don't understand so much violence. What is that the British find so important about Ireland?" Regina asked.

"Being able to control it. They cannot adjust to the idea of another nation so close to their own. It is an islander complex," Vanessa responded.

Suddenly the Inn's ski slope entrance flew open amid a shouting of "Get out of the way."

A Ski Patrol member backed through the door clutching the handles of a stretcher. Standing customers stood aside as he passed. As the stretcher entered, a man on it came into view. He lay beneath a blanket and grimaced with each movement of the stretcher. He obviously was in considerable pain. Holding the stretcher's other end; another Ski Patrol member entered the crowded Inn.

After placing the stretcher on the floor, one Ski Patrolman rushed to a telephone and cranked its handle rapidly. The other one knelled beside the injured man and tried to console him.

"You will be fine sir. We will have you to the hospital straight away," he said softly. "Just remain still please."

The patrolman at the phone said quite loudly, "We know his leg has a fracture. We also think he may have a bad neck injury. Send an ambulance to the Alpine Inn."

Two other men entered and rushed to the stretcher. One remained standing while the other knelt beside the stretcher opposite the patrolman.

"I say Frederick ol' man. Had a bit of a fall did you now?" The one kneeling asked.

When Frederick did not answer, his apparent acquaintance asked the patrolman. "What happen?"

"We found him near a rockslide. We do not know how long he was there. He should not ski on a slope alone. In particular that slope, it is for advanced skiers," the patrolman answered.

The man on the stretcher began to move. The patrolman stopped him.

"Sir, please do not try to move. You could injure yourself quite badly," the patrolman ordered.

His friend placed a hand on his chest and said, "Frederick ol' boy, thankfully you fly a lot better than you can ski. As your wingman, it is thankful I am for that."

Looking across at the patrolman, he continued, "He's in the Royal Air Force here on leave. Aviators are a fearless lot. This one in particular thinks he's the best but he knows I am."

Soon an ambulance arrived. Medical personnel placed a splint on one leg. They braced the injured skier's neck. With the patrolmen helping, they took the injured flier out the Inn's front door to the ambulance.

Regina said, as she giggled, "Oh my Vanessa. You almost lost one of your oppressors."

That evening she and Regina went to a Christmas party at a private skiing lodge. Vanessa's parents were founding members. They decided not to attend. For the past month, Ian was away on business. They treasured their time together. With another trip impending, they remained at their chalet to enjoy their precious time together.

The private lodge, compared to the Alpine Inn, was the essence of opulence. One entire wall, in the great room, rose 30 feet. Constructed of local stone, it had a walk-in fireplace. Its hearth extended out six feet. Upholstered with genuine chamois, guests used it as a preferred seating place.

Six chandeliers descended from the roof's main beam. Hewn from natural wood, each had the shape of a Swiss Mountain cart's wheel. Each light was unique as its outer shell came from craftsmen who made them from blown glass. Walls, throughout the structure, were natural logs hewn by hand. Each one displayed axe cuts made by wood-crafters.

The lodge's Christmas party was the social pinnacle for the skiing season. Restricted to members only, and their guests, the huge facility still had a full house. Vanessa knew most attendees. They were regulars she had met over the years at other social events. They were the world's financial elite.

She was chatting with a small group when something from behind pushed her. She fell forward, spilling her drink and found herself pinned to the floor. As ladylike as possible, she tried to get up but found it was impossible.

Finally being able to roll onto her back, she looked Frederick in the face. He had a stupid grin, which just could not cover the blush of embarrassment on his face

"Pardon me miss," he said. "I haven't quite got the hang of these."

He was on his knees and elbows. In each hand, he held a crutch. His left leg was in a cast and he had a brace on his neck. Obviously quite flustered, he could not move. Not knowing whether to laugh or pitch an Irish fit, she said, "Sir, you are crushing me. Get up."

"I can't," he said with a thick English accent. "You will have to give me a hand now won't you."

Irate, she began cursing in Gaelic that would have made her mother proud. Finally, gaining her footing, she rolled Frederick onto his back and stood. With ire in her eyes, she stamped her foot causing her rumpled dress to fall into place. Watching the scene, some of Frederick's fellow pilots circled around him, roaring with laughter.

One reached for Frederick's arm, saying, "You're in a bit of a mess I would say mate."

Her ire vented, Vanessa also began to laugh. With one foot in a cast, the other caught in a crutch, and not being able to move with his head in the neck brace, he not only looked clumsy but helpless.

His embarrassment was so absolute his blush was the color of ripe cherries. With several sets of hands helping, he positioned his crutches and stumbled toward a sofa.

Vanessa thought, "Oh my, now I have hurt his feelings."

Throughout her life, Vanessa had a soft place in her heart for lost kittens and wandering dogs. Once, she almost caused a horrendous auto crash when she meandered through traffic pursuing a lost puppy. She had the same feeling looking at Frederick.

She noticed his spilled drink on the floor. It had been a martini with two onions. Picking up the empty glass she worked her way to the bar, ordering a replacement for him and a gin fizz for herself. Holding the glasses high, she made her way to the sofa.

Handing the martini toward Frederick, she said, "Sir, here's another. You now owe me a gin fizz."

Still blushing, he took it and tried to stand.

"Keep your seat," she giggled. "If you make me spill my drink again, I may just break your other leg!"

He promptly elbowed one of his friends sitting next to him.

"What the 'ell?" The man said.

"Get up and give the lady your seat," Frederick directed.

Seeing her, his friend promptly arose. With a big grin, he said, "Pardon me Miss. Our mate here did very poorly in ballet. He flies a plane the same way. He is accustomed to crashes."

Frederick swung a crutch at his tormentor, who easily evaded the blow.

Taking the offered seat, she asked? "Tell me sir, how are you at cricket?"

Somewhat composed, Frederick answered, "Much better than skiing I assure you. My name is Frederick Earling. What's yours?" He asked.

"Vanessa, Vanessa McBeal," she answered.

"I apologize for being a clumsy lout. This is my first visit to Switzerland. I tried skiing this morning for the first time. Somehow, I became separated from my friends. I finally saw them at the bottom of a rather steep hill. I decided to ski to them. I guess I did not do too well," Frederick explained.

Obviously smitten by Vanessa, he asked. "Do you come here often?"

"Only when I'm not at school. My parents have a place here that they like to visit. I try to come when they're on holiday so that we can spend some time together," she answered.

Vanessa lost track of time during their first meeting. She told this stranger things that she would not mention to other men. She was comfortable with Frederick. He had a likeable disposition that put her at ease. His maturity played a major role. In addition, he had a quick mind more than likely honed at Eaton.

Frederick explained that he was a captain in the Royal Air Force stationed in London. He told her that his accident would ground him for at least six weeks. If he could get convalescent leave, he would return to Switzerland to visit her.

While he was nice enough, she lied. She told him that she would be at school. School did not start for 10 more days. So, he would have been able to see her again. However, she did give him her mailing address. She had never done this with any man.

When she did return to the academy, there was a message for her. Frederick caught her in a lie. He had telephoned two days after their meeting at the lodge. He had called every day for a week. He left a number where she could contact him. She was too embarrassed to return his call. Over the following weeks, she frequently thought of him.

In early spring, Vanessa visited Germany with her father. His trip was business and she used the opportunity to complete a classroom assignment by one of her professors.

Shortly after visiting Germany with her father, Frederick surprised her. During April, she was in her dormitory when the housemistress rang her room. She told her that she had a gentleman caller. It was Sir Earling. She could meet him in the parlor. This was a complete surprise for two reasons. She felt sure that he would never try to contact her again. Also, she never suspected his title.

During following months, he courted her. She marveled at his persistence. Moreover, she grew to like him and looked forward to being with him. Finally, he met her parents at their villa in southern France. Her parents found him quite charming. He invited her to visit his parent's estate in England that summer. She agreed to let him know later. Frederick wanted marriage although he had not asked. This caused her deep concern. She had good reason. The secret in her life must remain hidden.

She dreaded this day. Often she wondered how she would handle marriage. She wanted it but there were consequences. In addition, she wanted children. As an only child, she desired a brother or sister. There seemed to be a void in her youth. Many times, she needed a confidant one could find in a sibling. Her vow was to see that this did not happen to her children. A decision was necessary and it had to be soon.

Devon Elder was the key. He would know what to do. This decision was not hers to make. Only Devon could resolve her dilemma.

Vanessa had met Devon her first year at the academy. He was a graduate student working to obtain a doctorate in international relations. He taught one of her required courses. His accent indicated he might be Bavarian. However, it never sounded quite correct. It was forced and he often stopped to think when he chose his words.

She wrote a paper on Mien Kamph. The other six girls in her class had the same assignment. Yet, he asked that she remain after class the day after she submitted her work.

"Miss McBeal, I am quite impressed with your paper," he said.

"Thank you sir," she answered.

"Don't thank me too soon. I did not say that it was a favorable impression," he stated. "Please have a seat while we discuss your submission."

Vanessa noticed that he had paper clips on numerous pages of her paper. He began to leaf through the pages stopping at the first clip.

"You state that the book is the work of a demented person. How can you justify that when the author has brought his nation from depression into a booming, economic power?" He asked.

Her response was swift and to the point. Hitler was a sick man. He was mentally unfit to rule anything. She explained that his socio-economic-darwinistic ideas were absurd. She explained that Hitler had used a sense of false nationalism to seduce his people.

He was the antithesis of President Roosevelt. Roosevelt used the American government to bring his country from the depression through public works for the benefit of his people. Hitler appealed to racism and his people's fear. He brought his people out of the depression through evil works. His effort was one of egotistical anarchy. Evidence of this was underway in Europe at this very time.

"Now, now," he exhorted. "There are a few million Germans who would disagree with you. They consider him another Alexander the Great or a Napoleon. What do you think of that?" he questioned.

"Sir, you are trying to provoke me. Why are you doing this?" Vanessa asked.

Devon smiled as he took a red ink pen and wrote something on the first page of her report. He handed the document to her. She read his note with disbelief.

It stated, "Temper, temper. Failed."

Vanessa tore the paper to shreds and left the room. She slammed his office door with evident rage. She cut his next three classes. She would never attend another.

She found a note from him in her mailbox. He asked her to meet him at a nearby coffee shop the next day at Noon. She never wanted to see him again. The only reason she went was curiosity. She wondered what kind of teacher would do such a thing.

She arrived on time. Devon sat at one of the coffee shop's outside tables. He seemed immersed in a book he was reading. He did not notice her approach.

"Hello professor. You wanted to see me?" She asked.

He immediately got up from his chair and turned to look at her. He was smiling. He moved behind a chair and pulled it away from the table.

"Please have a seat Miss McBeal," he said.

"Why should I?" She countered.

"Because it is of the utmost importance that you do. I apologize for my previous behavior. Please have a seat and you will learn why," he said.

Vanessa wanted to hear this. She moved to the chair and sat.

Devon sat immediately across the table from her. He had a determined expression on his face. His smile was gone.

He learned forward and said in a soft voice, "Do you love your country?" He asked.

Somewhat flustered, she had difficulty replying. She never expected this question.

After a moments reflection, she replied, "If you mean Ireland, the answer is most certainly yes."

"You do know that, if Hitler is successful, he will control Europe. When finished with that, he will direct his resources against Great Britain, Scotland and Ireland," he stated.

"He won't," she answered defiantly.

"If he continues his progress, he will," he replied.

Lowering his voice even farther, Devon leaned forward so that only Vanessa could hear.

"Would you like to assure that he fails?" He asked.

"Now, how would I be doing that?" She answered.

Devon began detailing her family's history for the past three generations. He even knew of her grandfather's work for the Irish Republican Army. He told about Molly and Ian McBeal. He knew of her father's wealth and its sources. He even named her father's contacts in the United States. She had never known who they were because her father never spoke of them.

"How does he know so much?" She wondered?

He ended his recitation with a question. "If you had an opportunity to help assure his failure, would you take it?"

"Of course," she replied promptly.

"Even if it meant your life?" He questioned.

She could see that he was serious. She saw a questioning determination in his eyes. She pondered his words.

"I might," she answered cautiously.

"Vanessa, you are in a position to do this. However, I am quite concerned about your temper. You would be in considerable danger should it control you," he commented.

Slowly, Vanessa began to realize the seriousness of Devon's proposal. She had heard stories from classmates about persons discovered as spies. Their fate was execution or they disappeared without explanation. A shiver overcame her at such thoughts. She was young with the promise of a full life. Why would she want to lose it? Doubt began to overcome her.

"Devon, I don't know about this," she said.

"Take a few days to think about it," he replied. "You can let me know when you come back to your studies."

"I have no intention of returning to any of your classes," she said firmly.

"Surely you're not upset about that paper. The paper is not important. Your reaction to the subject was important. The paper contained exactly what I was trying to determine. I had to have an indirect means of determining your feelings about the subject. You made that clear. However, your emotional response did create a problem that I have reconciled. See you in class?" He asked.

"Yes," she answered.

The next three days were agonizing. Her decision had to be solitary. In the past, she had strong concerns about evil spawned in Germany. She felt guilty because Spanish classmates had to leave school. She knew Hitler caused war in Spain and supported Franco. The Nazi runt used Spain as a testing ground for his war machine. In addition, Hitler supported the idiot Mussolini's taking of Ethiopia. Her conscience drove her to a decision. She would do it.

As soon as she heard the first condition, she wished she had said no to Devon.

"I will arrange a research course. Forget math and science. You will change your major to international relations next semester. You will begin traveling with your father. He moves freely between Germany and Switzerland. I know he wants you to travel with him. He even obtained a visa for you," Devon told her.

"In addition, you cannot tell your parents anything," he added.

"Why?" She cried.

"You are the only person to know. I have my instructions. You will have to trust me," he answered.

"Trust or not, you're not going to put my father's life in danger. I won't do anything if that happens," she said with resolution.

Lowering her voice to a whisper, she continued, "If my father gets hurt, you will pay a dire price."

A loud roar erupted from spectators in the arena. Vanessa ended her reflections. Looking up, she watched an exceptionally beautiful Arabian prancing toward the floor's exit. The young man riding him stood in his stirrups and waved his cap to the crowd.

"What a distasteful display of bravado," she thought with some envy.

Often she had wanted to do the same when riding Daytran. Yet, her social status forbade it. She moved forward a few feet to obtain a better view of the horse and its rider. She saw Devon watching her. He shrugged his shoulders and raised his hands with his palms upturned.

"Did I lose this event while standing here daydreaming," she thought.

She extended her right fist with her thumb pointing skyward. She had seen Frederick do this on many an occasion to indicate that everything was fine. She hoped it was now. Her thoughts returned to Devon and Switzerland.

What happened in Germany on her trip had to remain secret. She could tell no one. Only Devon knew and now she needed his help. He would have to provide guidance. While Devon understood her shame, others would not. Certainly, Frederick must never know. She could not put his life in danger nor hurt him in any way.

As arranged, she got word to Devon to meet her. He waited at the coffee shop. She approached and took a seat. She looked at Devon with a quiet desperation.

"Devon," she said. "I want to marry and I must make a decision. What am I to do?" She asked.

"Marry Frederick. You will move to England and remain there until further contact. Do not ask questions. Just do it," Devon directed.

Vanessa had not mentioned whom she wanted to marry. Devon knew. Surprise was unnecessary for Devon knew so much about her life.

"I'll see you in London," Devon said as he arose. He tucked his newspaper under his arm and calmly walked away. She would not see him again for a year.

Frederick was in London, as those on leave had to return. The situation in Europe was tense. She was safe in Switzerland but she wanted to be with Frederick. She left for England on 1 September 1939. Crossing the English Channel, she heard a radio broadcast. Germany invaded Poland because of a Polish attack on a radio station. War was inevitable.

"Your Ladyship! Your Ladyship, they're calling for you at the winner's circle," a distant voice called pleadingly.

Vanessa had lost sight of events in progress. While she actually saw them, her mind did not register them. Thoughts of her husband consumed her.

"Damn you Frederick," she thought. "You and your damned airplanes."

Increasing her stride, she wove through the crowd. Ahead she saw Daytran with Devon holding his reins. The Arabian's coat gleamed and his neck arched as he saw her approaching.

The announcer's voice echoed throughout the arena. Someone pushed flowers toward her. Another person put a horseshoe shaped wreath around Daytran's neck. She noticed little of it. Her thoughts were with Frederick and Laos.

"I don't care what he wants," she thought. "I am going."

Chapter Six

April 1954

Hence, that general is skilful in attack whose opponent does not know what to defend;
And he is skilful in defense whose opponent does not know what to attack.
Sun Tzu (5th –6th Centuries B.C.)

Vinh's replacement arrived. With a new forward observer in position, Vinh left for advanced artillery training. He was 16 and considered old enough for increased responsibilities. His trip to the training center was short. The Viet Minh used a tunnel complex, less than five kilometers from Dien Bien Phu, for training. Classrooms were deep underground, as were his living quarters. Academics included mathematics and ballistics. Eight other Viet Minh were in his class. He found the subjects easy to learn. His brother, Anh, taught him fundamentals before their Dien Bien Phu attack.

However, practical exercises with weapons were a major disappointment. There were no operational field artillery weapons available. They trained with heavily damaged howitzers to simulate firing. In addition, handling the 105-mm howitzers was exceptionally difficult. Nonetheless, they would have to do. Every operational weapon was in use against the French.

Vinh completed training in two weeks. Instructors recommended that he work in a fire direction center. He went to the 325th Division for which he had been a forward observer. Now he would work in the unit's nerve center. His fire direction team computed settings for the howitzers. They did this with information from forward observers. They determined how much to elevate the weapons. In addition, they selected the amount of powder necessary to cause a projectile to reach a target. Another important determination was which fuse to use. If they fired at personnel, they set fuses for an airburst. This caused shrapnel to rain down upon soft targets. It was particularly deadly against personnel without overhead protection. Delayed fuses allowed projectiles to penetrate bunkers and buildings before exploding. Vinh now understood why Anh insisted he give an accurate target description.

Vinh missed Anh. He was recently promoted to major. Their commander sent him to learn why ammunition was not readily available. They needed a continuous supply for they were constantly bombarding the fortress.

They had silenced French artillery early in the battle. The French deployed their weapons with little protection. It was as if they thought they could use them with impunity. They learned too late that the Viet Minh had a significant artillery capability. Obtaining this capability did not come easily.

The Viet Minh moved an entire artillery division into the battle area. The French discounted any such ability. The terrain was too mountainous and roads did not exist upon which to move the heavy weapons. Undaunted, the Viet Minh disassembled each weapon to its smallest component. They carried these parts through the roughest terrain in Tonkin. It took thousands of personnel to achieve this feat. Parts came by bicycle, carts pulled by oxen and on soldiers' backs. Volunteer laborers carried a single projectile for thousands of kilometers. Next, they gave it to other volunteers in the transportation chain. They continued the journey until reaching mountains surrounding Dien Bien Phu. At their destination, artillery crews assembled the weapons into their original configurations.

There were many reports about the Viet Minh leader, General Giap. They told of his riding a horse along the muddy trails. He would stop and help pull a weapon's barrel up a particularly difficult slope. He shouted encouragement to the soldiers. He was one of them and that made their chore easier. Indeed, what they accomplished seemed an impossible task. Yet, they did it. The French were now paying for their underestimation.

Vinh worked a 12-hour shift. He ate his small rice ration and then collapsed. In the tunnel's wall, he dug an area just big enough to hold his small body. While drifting into a fitful sleep, he often recalled Anh's story of his quest to find Minh Thanh. His reflections were heart wrenching. He took a personal oath to have vengeance upon those who took her from him. He remembered Anh's words all too well.

Anh arrived at a small village outside of Hanoi to find their uncle's house deserted. He knew this village from many visits by his family. It used to have a market filled with vendors. Now, only a few stalls sold items. Many of the other village homes stood silent. Residents denied any knowledge of his uncle. He knew this to be untrue for he had played with their children as a youngster. For some unknown reason, they did not even want to talk to him. Totally confused, he made his way into Hanoi's industrial district.

He stopped at a large building he knew about from previous visits. One summer Anh had worked for a friend of his uncle. His family lived in this large warehouse. They had living quarters inside to discourage thieves. The place looked deserted but he went around the building. In the rear, railroad tracks passed a loading dock. He saw children's toys on the platform. Also, there was a pen with chickens. Someone still lived in the building.

After knocking on the heavy wooden doors, he heard noises inside. His former employer opened the door a slight amount. He recognized Anh and opened the huge doors enough for him to enter.

"Come in quickly," Bhan Van Duc said in a frightened tone. "Hurry before you are seen."

Anh could barely see in the darkened building. In one corner, he saw flickering light from a candle. Bhan held his arm and rushed him toward the light.

"Move quickly," Bhan stated. "We must hurry. I hope no one saw you coming to this building."

Unable to see well, he stumbled along with his former employer. He could not understand his obvious fear.

"What's the matter? Where is everyone?" Anh asked.

They entered a small room made from packing material. Much of it was cardboard. If it were outside, it would not last through a heavy rain. Inside, it was protected. Through an open doorway, Anh saw Bhan's wife and three children huddled around a small table.

Bhan moved a packing crate for Anh to use as a chair. He closed the door to the next room and joined him on the crate.

"Have you been to your uncle's house," Bhan asked.

"Yes," Anh answered. "It was deserted. Actually, there were few people in the village. What happened to them?" He asked.

Bhan explained to Anh the situation in Hanoi. Bhan had been a member of the Viet Nam Quoc Dan Dang revolutionary party.

Bhan said, "People knew us the VNQDD, it was a secret party established Christmas 1927. Your uncle and I joined two years later. Our objective was an armed uprising aimed at destroying French colonialism throughout Viet Nam. We intended to gain independence, institute democratic reforms and gain happiness for our people."

"When we joined, the VNQDD was well organized and armed. We planned a revolt against the French to take place in early 1930. Your uncle was an important leader in his village. We attacked on 10 February 1930."

Anh watched Bhan swell with pride. Anh already knew that his uncle was an important person to his neighbors. This fact he could not reconcile with the reception he received from his former neighbors.

Continuing, Bhan said, "We caught he French by surprise. They suspected nothing. We caused significant damage for a few days. However, French forces struck brutally against our uprising and soon defeated our group. They arrested known leaders and sentenced them to death. They guillotined 13 of our leaders on 17 June 1930. The French thought this would cause fear. It did not. All it did was make us hate them more. Your Uncle Diem, once a Tia tribesman in the mountains, hated them more than anyone."

Anh knew that his father was once a Tia tribesman but he never thought of Uncle Diem as one. Many times his father told them of his life with the Tia. They were great hunters and lived as part of the forest.

"I wonder why Uncle Diem never mentioned them," Anh thought.

"The Communist Party staged a protest later that same year. Their protest had little impact. However, it received praise from Communist groups. The people still preferred our group and had little use for the Communists. The Communists always tried to take credit for what we did," Bhan explained.

"What happened after that?" Anh asked.

"The brutality of the French only served to drive the VNQDD farther underground. We took our time building a stronger and more powerful organization. We were Nationalists and had major support throughout our country. Nevertheless, we had to retreat to Southern China," Bhan answered.

"Uncle Diem never spoke of these things to me," Anh said. "He only talked about his life as a Tia tribesman. What did you do in China?"

Bhan responded, "While in China, we consolidated our leadership. In addition, we formed an alliance with other disenfranchised Vietnamese. We formed a new organization with the VNQDD as its major organization. We called our new alliance the Vietnamese Revolutionary Allied League, known as the VNCMDMH. We allowed the Vietnamese Communist Party to join. Your Uncle Diem did not like this. He did not trust them. Anytime that we did something worthwhile, they took credit for it."

Thinking about what Bhan said, Anh commented, "This explains many of my early memories. My father left at night to fight with the Viet Minh against the French. I kept his pistol clean. He never told any of us exactly what he did those nights but I know he hated the French."

"Yes he did," Bhan said. "However, Japan took control before we could overcome the French. The Japanese did nothing more than use the French for their chores. The Vichy French fell when Japan removed them from power in 1945. This did not help the Japanese or us. Japan surrendered later that year. They surrendered to the British. Shortly thereafter, the British returned Viet Nam to French colonialists. We could not take any more French control. It was time for us to attack again."

"In Hanoi, we started a major protest. By most estimates, over 10,000 people protested the return to French control. The leader of the Communist Party, Ho Chi Minh, took advantage of the situation. He claimed leadership of our group. This was a major violation of a previous agreement with us. Ho Chi Minh did exactly what your father and Uncle suspected. He took credit for what our people did."

Bhan explained that the Communists began killing League members as they returned from China. Ho Chi Minh was determined that he and his party would rule. A reign of bloody terrorism began.

"Wait," Anh said. "Are you telling me that Ho Chi Minh was having Vietnamese killed. I cannot accept that," Anh said with determination.

"It's true," Bhan replied. "And matters became much worse," he continued.

Anh sat quietly wringing his hands as Bhan continued his horrendous story. Bahn explained that it was Ho Chi Minh who signed an agreement with France in early 1946.

"Anh, you cannot imagine the killing that Ho Chi Minh had done. It was carnage at its worst. He had subordinates killing members of non-communist parties. It was one of Ho Chi Minh's main followers that attacked your uncle's village. They killed tens of thousands throughout this region in 1948. It was an unbelievable bloodletting of the worst sort," Bhan exclaimed.

Anh felt fear rising within and he dreaded to ask the question. Nevertheless, he had to know.

"Was Minh Thanh at my uncle's house?" He asked.

Bhan lowered his head and looked away. Anh asked louder, almost screaming.

"Was Minh Thanh there during the killing?" Anh said with anguish.

Bhan nodded his head. His eyes brimmed with tears. They finally overflowed, coursing down his face.

"Yes," he whispered. "Yes she was."

Anh arose and gripped his face in his hands. His jaws trembled as he ground his teeth. A stifled sob burst in echoes across the empty warehouse. He whirled to face Bhan. His eyes blazed with determination.

"I will kill the son of a bitch. I will kill him as sure as the Nam Youm flows," he screamed.

"No," Bhan said. "She is not dead. Ahyaahh! She might as well be," he exclaimed.

Anh grabbed him by his shoulders, shaking him mercilessly. He glared at Bhan.

With a subdued voice, he asked, "What do you mean?"

"The French took her," he blurted. "The French took her," he said as his voice trailed away to almost nothing.

"Where?" Anh yelled.

"I don't know," Bhan replied totally dejected.

Anh pushed Bhan and he fell backwards across the crate. "Did she find our mother?" Anh continued. "Is she alive?"

Before Bhan could answer, they heard a loud, repeated pounding on the entrance door.

"Who is in there?" Someone yelled in French. The pounding continued.

Bhan, with urgency in his voice, whispered, "Go! It is the police. Go!"

Anh ran from the cardboard shelter. The entrance door was moving back and forth as someone tried to force it open. He saw light beaming through a ventilator cover at the far end of the warehouse. He ran for it.

Climbing junk crates, he kicked the metal cover. It split and he pushed with his shoulder. A splinter embedded in his cheek from a bullet hitting the ventilator's frame. As if in slow motion, he jumped to the roof. Other shots echoed behind him.

He continued across the flat roof to its edge. Without hesitation, he leaped into an alley filled with cardboard boxes. Unhurt, he wriggled through them. A high fence closed the alley on one end. He scaled it and ran between abandoned railcars. He ran until shouting behind him ceased. Out of breath, he leaned forward placing his hands upon his knees. He gasped for air.

"In here," a voice whispered.

He felt a tug on his arm pulling him through a doorway into total darkness.

"Be still," the voice said.

For what seemed hours, he waited. The only sound was his heart pounding and his raspy gulps for air. Finally, someone touched his arm.

"You can go now," came the whisper. "Keep going and don't return. It is dark and you can go where you belong. You are not safe in Hanoi."

Anh arrived at his uncle's village before sunrise. He hid in the house he knew so well from his youth. At dusk, he began his journey to Muong Valley. The trip was over 300 miles. It took two weeks traveling only at night.

Vinh could never reconcile Anh's actions in support of Ho Chi Minh. He was responsible for their uncle's death. At least indirectly, Ho Chi Minh caused the loss of Minh Thanh. Yet, Anh embraced the Communist Party. He fought hard for the Viet Minh. Perhaps his hate for the French outweighed his sister's loss.

Regardless, Anh was a rising star in Viet Minh ranks. He was a major and in a position of high responsibility. He loved his brother and was proud of his achievements.

Awakened by the roar of aircraft, Vinh crawled from his dirt cubicle. He could hear antiaircraft weapons firing. Wriggling his way outside, he looked skyward. He did not see the aircraft. They were on the other side of the mountains separating him from Muong Valley. It had to be another supply attempt. Each night C-119 aircraft tried to make low-level, aerial supply drops to the fortress. Their failures dotted the valley's floor with blackened aircraft remains. Few supplies made it into French hands. Of the many drops made, Viet Minh infantry got most of the bounty. Nam Youm Rats got the remainder.

The Rats were a group of deserters from the French forces. When the Viet Minh began their attack, many conscripted soldiers deserted their posts. They could not escape the valley so they gathered in an area near the river. They were no threat to the Viet Minh so they ignored them. The French had neither the time nor the resources to capture them. They remained between the warring factions and built crude huts for shelter. They lived on what they could steal. They often risked death by gunfire in order to get one of the air dropped containers.

Vinh had watched the supply drops from his observation post. Aircraft had only two directions to fly. They had to travel from north to south or the reverse. Each course took the planes in front of him. He could hear them first and then they would appear from the mists. Green tracers streaked at them as they flew the valley's length. Sometimes Vinh fired at them but he couldn't see that he did any damage. Once, he saw a captured aircrew.

While training on the 105-mm howitzers, Vinh saw three prisoners led down a road. Two of them were Caucasians and the other Asian. Each had his arms tied behind his back and a rope around his neck. The neck rope extended from the front prisoner to the last. This forced them to walk single file at a given distance apart. They were not in French, military uniforms. They wore white shirts with epaulets showing gold stripes. One, the Asian, wore a flight suit. He thought this to be most unusual.

Rumors spread fast. Gossip was that crews on aircraft supplying the French were mostly Americans. This created considerable concern among Viet Minh leaders. They were afraid that the United States would come to rescue the French. If so, they would have to withdraw. They would not be able to withstand a major bombing assault.

Later, in the fire control center, Vinh learned details of the capture. Their intelligence officer gave a briefing so that they would be alert for any possible American targets. The intelligence officer said that a patrol captured three crewmembers near their downed aircraft. They took them to division headquarters for questioning. After two days, the Asian told interrogators everything they wanted to know. He said that he was a pusher. His job was to push supplies from their aircraft over drop zones. The two pilots were one crew among many now flying from bases in Laos. They worked for an organization called Air America. They had a large headquarters in Lao's capitol. Logbooks, found in the crashed aircraft, verified the Laotian's story. Additional information caused concern.

The Laotian said that Air American was supplying weapons to the Laotian military. If they should receive enough, they would be a dangerous threat. They knew the valley well and were determined fighters. They could attack in the Viet Minh's rear and disrupt their supply system. If this happened, they would have to withdraw from their attack on the French. The intelligence officer said that General Giap had left for Hanoi to consult with Ho Chi Minh. The hope was that they could convince the Chinese to intervene since Americans were now helping the French. Their hopes were high because they provided troops to help North Korea.

Vinh returned to the tunnel complex. He mixed his rice ration with some noodles and water. He placed this over a small cooking fire to heat. Other members of his fire direction team began to arrive. It was almost time for their shift to begin. When that happened, there would be little time for eating.

One of the men stated aloud, "I understand that another strong point fell yesterday. Giap's attack method is working well for us. There are those in the intelligence section who say the French will soon surrender."

"I don't think so," another answered. "The French are stubborn devils. They may fight until they are all dead."

Excited by the thought of a French surrender, Vinh asked. "Does this person in intelligence have an important job?"

"Yes," came the reply. "He is a courier. When he delivers a message to a commander, he waits to see if he wants him to take a reply. He listens to them discuss the battle. Just yesterday one said that the French had retreated to their final strong point."

Stirring his food, Vinh said, "My home is on the other side of the mountains. If the French surrender, my trip home would be short. May will be here soon and it is a good time to plant. I hope this person knows what he is talking about."

While he ate, Vinh thought of him and Anh working together in the fields. It would not be the same without Minh Thanh. If only they could find her.

"I know she is alive," he thought. "We will find her and we will be together again."

Chapter Seven

November 1953

*"The Angel of Death has been abroad throughout the land;
you may almost hear the beating of his wings."*
John Bright (1811–89)

"That meeting seems light years in the past," Jean thought. "Mother Superior's suspicions proved correct. What's worse is my helping. If we must use Operation Vulture, France will inherit a wasteland."

The two-hour flight from Hanoi passed quickly. Muong Valley's early morning fog dissipated, leaving their intended drop zone clear. Dien Bien Phu was visible, as was Jean's objective area north of town. In full view from the cockpit, the pilot activated a jump light switch.

Jean saw a red jump light illuminate. Cold, damp air rushed through the aircraft as engine noise became louder. Their jumpmaster had opened the door.

"Stand up," he yelled to assure they heard him above the noise.

Airborne soldiers stood in unison. Each began checking harness on the man in front of him.

"Hook up," came the next command.

Jean gripped a metal snap that tied a lanyard strap to his parachute's ripcord. Like others, he hooked it to a metal, overhead cable running the craft's length. Upon exiting, this strap would automatically open his parachute. If this failed, he could use a reserve on his stomach. His main parachute had always opened. Still, he clasped his reserve with both arms.

A green light illuminated and the jumpmaster yelled, "GO!"

Each person exited at two-second intervals. Jean moved forward and jumped. His parachute's opening pulled him upright with a hard jolt. Wind whistled through his parachute's rigging. He heard gunfire below him.

He saw individuals firing from various locations. They were not organized and he returned fire. His attackers ran into the forest for cover. Nearing ground, he placed his legs tightly together to absorb his impact.

Jean's parachute landing fall was perfect. He bent his knees slightly as his feet touched ground. He rolled to one side causing his body to land smoothly. Immediately he stood and collapsed his canopy. Next, he began pulling his parachute. Soon he had a tight bundle and set the silk mass aside, as he looked for landmarks.

He was near a north-south highway that bisected the valley. He could see Dien Bien Phu to his south. He was not in strong point Anne-Marie. It was north about 400 meters. Gathering his equipment, he ran along the road and then turned northwest.

Once in place, he raised one arm and yelled, "Red team, form on me."

Jean watched as some Legionnaires floated to earth while others gathered parachutes. He saw familiar faces coming toward him. He counted as they approached and determined that one man was missing.

Jean did not hesitate. He ordered his group to take defensive positions. They used the road's ditch for protection. Jean knew that defenders had an advantage during the initial phase of an airborne attack. He had to get his unit organized should the Viet Minh attack.

"Where's Leopold," he yelled as he ran parallel to the ditch, checking each man's position as he went. No one answered.

Small arms fire erupted from trees across the road. Impacting bullets kicked up dirt immediately behind Jean, as he dove for the ditch. An automatic weapon began firing from the same area.

"Twelve O'clock at 300 meters, engage," Jean yelled.

Jean's team began firing at the trees. Green tracers continued streaking from the forest at their position.

Jean yelled, "Radio!"

A soldier rose to a squat and ran toward him. He stopped at Jean's position and handed him a handset. Jean contacted fire support. Soon, mortars began firing. Explosions began appearing in the trees to their front. The green tracers stopped.

While his team defended their sector, other Legionaries secured the airfield. It was essential to their success. Soon other planes would arrive. They carried much needed supplies. Without a secure airfield, they would return to Hanoi. Mission success depended on aircraft delivery. Re-supply overland was not an option.

Operation Castor was going as planned. Still, Jean feared that General Navarre's operation had major flaws. He looked in every direction. Their position was at the valley's lowest level. Mountains surrounded them. He had voiced this problem in Saigon. Yet, Navarre would not change anything. Jean recalled briefing him.

General Navarre listened without comment. Jean explained his earlier mission and how he had come upon Na Son under attack. He ended his briefing and asked for questions.

"Tell me, lieutenant. Have you studied Operation Castor?" Navarre asked.

"Yes sir," Jean replied.

"Do you see any similarities with what happened at Na Son?" The general asked.

"No sir, I do not," Jean answered. "The situation at Dien Bien Phu is different in many ways."

General Navarre leaned forward and asked. "What's that, lieutenant?"

"Sir, Na Son was a single strong point. It was easy to defend. Operation Castor has too many strong points widely dispersed. The enemy can penetrate areas between and isolate them. Next, they will be able to defeat each at their will. In addition, the number of units is too small to defend such a large area. I believe we would need almost triple what has been allocated," Jean explained.

General Navarre turned to a general sitting next to him and said, "Tell me Charles. Do you think you might need more artillery? You could provide better coverage between strong points. Perhaps, the lieutenant is correct."

Seated next to Navarre, an one-armed brigadier general cleared his throat. He was Charles Pieroth, France's foremost artilleryman.

"I have the artillery we need," he said. "There's six batteries of 105-mm howitzers, a battery of 155-mm guns and three heavy mortar companies. I can assure strong defensive fires anywhere in the valley. Besides, I thought this was an offensive operation. What's all this talk about defense?"

"Of course you're right Charles. I'll explain to the lieutenant," Navarre said.

"Lieutenant, someone at this headquarters has not done his job. You obviously don't understand Operation Castor," Navarre said. "I'll explain."

Jean listened as Navarre explained that Operation Castor was an offensive plan. It would include 10 tanks for that purpose. He expected infantry to take the battle to the Viet Minh. They were not to sit idly by in a defensive posture. However, Navarre stated that he would not mind if Viet Minh should mass forces and attack. They would receive a resounding defeat.

Navarre arose from his seat, causing all in the room to rise and come to attention.

"Thank you, lieutenant," he said. "I'll see that you are properly briefed."

Navarre stalked from the room as Brigadier Pieroth followed.

Jean was perplexed. The two senior officers ignored his observations at Na Son. He had reported how the Viet Minh could move soldiers and munitions rapidly to a battle. Although their means were crude, they were effective.

Andre opened the door and looked around the room. He obviously was looking to see if others were present. Satisfied that they were alone, he looked at Jean.

"Jean, what in the hell did you say to Navarre?" He asked.

"For some reason, he thinks I don't understand Operation Castor," Jean replied.

"Come to my office and get your security pass. Major Bigeard said to report to him immediately. He didn't sound happy," Andre said.

Jean showed his pass to the guards. They opened the door and he entered the planning room. He saw Major Bigeard at the center table talking to Captain Prudhomme. They seemed to be having a heated discussion about something. He kept a respectful distance until Major Bigeard saw him. Bigeard pointed to his office and Jean immediately went and entered. In about 10 minutes, Major Bigeard arrived.

"Sit," he ordered.

Jean sat and looked inquisitively at Bigeard. The major leaned forward and whispered to Jean.

"You are a dumb ass," he said. "You don't piss on Navarre's plan. What were you thinking? Or, were you thinking?"

"Sir, I simply gave my briefing. The general was the one who asked my opinion. So, I gave it," he answered.

"Tell me what you told him," Bigeard directed.

Jean explained about the road network he saw near Na Son. He detailed how the Viet Minh could mass forces and supply them. He also gave his opinion about Operation Castor. He detailed his concerns about using Dien Bien Phu.

To his surprise, Bigeard responded, "I agree."

Furthermore, Bigeard explained that he thought Captain Prudhomme's intelligence was grossly inaccurate.

"I don't believe we have a true picture of what awaits us at Dien Bien Phu. The Viet Minh are determined fighters. We will be isolated over 300 miles from our support base. This will be what General Navarre calls 'an airhead.' Frankly, I think we are going to have a big problem. Nevertheless, we will have to make do as best we can. If we find ourselves in trouble, everything depends on you," Bigeard stated.

Jean took this as a supreme compliment since it came from Bigeard. Major Bigeard never intended to be a professional soldier

Jean learned, during his OSS mission in France, that Bigeard was a deadly saboteur. The Gestapo knew of Maurice "Bruno" Bigeard. There was a $500,000 reward for his capture. Other resistance fighters, in France during World War II, told of his heroic exploits. Bigeard received a direct commission because of his competence and leadership. Now, he had the respect of the Legion.

"Sir, we need to talk in private. Can we use the back channel room?" Jean asked.

"Certainly," Bigeard answered. "You have a Special Intelligence-Crypto clearance. We can use it now."

They left his office and entered the hall. Bigeard led the way to the operations office. Inside, they crossed it to where an armed guard sat at a closed door. The guard examined their security passes. Next, he checked a book containing names of individuals with special intelligence clearances. The guard opened the door for them.

They descended stairs to arrive at a long hallway. At its end, another guard sat. A single steel door was next to the guard's desk. He repeated the procedure used by the first guard. However, this time, they had to empty their pockets. The guard signed a receipt for their personal items and gave each a copy.

"Gentlemen," the guard said. "You can make notes while in the security vault. Pens and papers are available inside. However, you cannot bring any documents with you when you leave. This includes any notes you may make. Do you have any questions?"

"No," was their mutual response.

The guard pulled the 6-inch thick, steel door to open it. He closed it behind them as they entered. A large table, and six chairs, dominated the interior. Another door had a sign on it which stated, "Communications Personnel Only."

Senior officers, and intelligence officials, used the back channel room for special communications. Messages from this room did not go through official channels. In addition, technicians used electronic devices to screen the room three times a day to detect listening devices.

Bigeard took a seat and asked, "What's so secret?"

"Sir, Operation Vulture is not secure," Jean Answered.

"How so?" Bigeard responded.

"I was told about the operation by a civilian source. I did not believe it until you assigned me to help put the plan into effect," Jean explained.

"Does Prudhomme know this?" Bigeard asked.

"I don't think so," Jean answered.

"Don't tell him," Bigeard directed.

"Who told you this?" He continued.

"Sir, with utmost respect, I am not at liberty to say," Jean answered.

"How would you like to spend the rest of you life on an island near South America lieutenant?" Bigeard asked with determination.

Jean noticed Bigeard addressing him by rank. He had changed from personal to official. Nevertheless, he gave his solemn word to a holy woman. Yet, he had a responsibility to his fellow Legionnaires. In particular, he had a trust with Bigeard that only a soldier would understand. This man was his commander. He had a duty. He had to answer Bigeard's question.

"Sir, it was Mother Superior at the Cholon District Nunnery," Jean answered.

"How the hell did she know anything about this?" Bigeard said, as he slammed the table with his fist.

Bigeard remained deep in thought while he rubbed the back of his neck. Next, he paced the room muttering words that Jean could not hear.

"Okay, nothing has changed for you. Be prepared to put directional beacons in place as planned. They will arrive packed as communications equipment, after the airfield is secure. Do not go near that nunnery. Do not speak of this to anyone. If the situation gets bad, I will tell you where to put the beacons. Do not tell men in your red team anything other than the beacons are for our aircraft to use in bad weather. Do not mention this to Prudhomme. Do you understand?" Bigeard asked.

"Yes sir," Jean answered. "What about Mother Superior?"

"Let me take care of that. You do your job. Once again, stay away from that nunnery, Jean." Bigeard directed.

Bigeard's words still echoed in Jean's mind as he lay in the ditch. He watched airborne forces and equipment being delivered. Continuing flights dropped steel plate by the hundreds of tons. An important supply item was a bulldozer. Delivered the first flight, it broke apart upon impact. Nevertheless, an aircraft returned with another. It survived. It was essential that the old airfield be rebuilt. This construction project had first priority.

General Gilles jumped with the first group despite ill health. He commanded the airborne force. He had a persistent heart condition. Some considered him too old for airborne duty. Nevertheless, at 49, time began to exact its toll. Over 4000 airborne soldiers arrived with the first flight. Gilles was the oldest.

Men placed barbed wire to form perimeters. Sharp barbs tore at their gloved hands. Jean saw troops bent low and running north toward where strong point Gabrielle would .be. Gabrielle was the northernmost position in Navarre's scheme.

Across the road, to the east, men were digging in to form a small perimeter named Beatrice. They found Corporal Leopold. He died during the jump. He was a victim of ground fire.

There had been others killed with the first flight. A major loss was a unit surgeon. He, like Leopold, died from ground fire. They could ill afford this loss. Medical personnel were hard to find.

Jean signaled his team to start preparing their position. He did not speak. A simple nod sent his men scurrying for barbed wire. They would see their part done with elan. Their team was the best and they knew it. This feeling came from numerous missions with Jean. They had complete confidence that he knew best. He did not have to demand their respect. He earned it.

General Navarre's Operation Castor had Dien Bien Phu at the center of numerous strong points. Each had a woman's name. Circling the town, in a clockwise direction, Dominique was on the immediate northeast. Next, on the southeast, was Eliane. Claudine was to the southwest. To the northwest was Huguette. Each strong point sat astride a road leading into, or out of, the village.

Two roads went north from Dien Bien Phu. One went northwest and the other northeast. Jean's team was digging in slightly northwest of Huguette at Anne-Marie. This was the largest of the strong points. Yet, further northwest a small strong point, Gabrielle, would engage any force moving into the valley. On the northeast road, another strong point, Beatrice, was much like Gabrielle. It would detect any force coming into the valley from their direction well before it could get to Dominique.

A single road entered Muong Valley from the south. Slightly into the valley, strong point Isabelle was at the juncture of the main road and a smaller trail that went north into Claudine. However, Isabelle was approximately six kilometers south of the strong points surrounding Dien Bien Phu. It sat alone isolated from the others.

Jean, with the Na Son experience behind him, firmly believed the plan would not work. The Viet Minh could isolate individual strong points and defeat them. As each fell, center areas around Dien Bien Phu became vulnerable. Nonetheless, the only thing he could do was to try to make it work. In addition, he instilled this in his men. He surely hoped that other leaders would do the same.

"Quiet, it's too damn quiet," Jean thought.

Viet Minh leaders were not idle. They had started moving equipment and supplies to surround the valley. The first major engagement was a harbinger of things to come. The first battle would come soon. The Legion would suffer major losses. Yet, it would not come close to the blood bath a few, short months away.

Chapter Eight

September 1954

"It takes twenty years or more of peace to make a man;
it takes only twenty seconds of war to destroy him."
Baudouin I, King of Belgium (1930-1933)

After returning from Florida, Zane visited Wofford College in Spartanburg. Wofford was a private, liberal arts college with a reputation for excellence. The student body was small with 300 students. In addition, it was male only. However, it was co-ed during summer months. Students received considerable, individual attention. Moreover, since it was private, it was more expensive than state schools.

His Florida and Wofford visits had exposed Zane to hard truths. First, to attend college was expensive. Second, he did not have enough money to complete degree requirements.

Giving up his prized car was hard. However, if he wanted a college degree, he had to sell it. The savings in insurance costs would pay for one semester. His original savings, plus cash from the car sale, could handle the rest of his first year. Still, he would need more to get a degree. His Dad provided a workable solution.

"Son, I cannot afford to pay for college. However, I will do this. You live here and I will provide a place to live, eat and study. In addition, I can get you work every summer. I will do this as long as I am convinced you are trying. You make passing grades and I will help. Nonetheless, if I think you are not trying, the arrangement ends," he said.

Zane agreed instantly. He did not mind being a day student. He might miss what some people called, "the whole college experience." Nevertheless, he preferred his home over a dormitory. Moreover, he would not have to eat cafeteria food. His mom's cooking had to be better.

Furthermore, he remembered an event at Spartanburg High School's Career Day. Potential employers met with seniors. He remembered what one army captain said.

"For you young men, I suspect that you have never heard of Universal Military Training (UMT). UMT is a law that requires each of you to serve your country for six years," he said.

Zane remembered punching Don and asking; "Did you know that shit? I want to go to school not the army."

Continuing, the captain said, "For those of you planning to attend a local college, there is a way to meet that obligation and go to school. In addition, you can earn a few dollars. You can join a local nation guard unit. The guard meets once a week and you go to a summer camp for two weeks. You will receive pay and dispose of two years of that UMT requirement. If you will drop by my table, I will explain in more detail."

Zane made a point of seeing the captain. This UMT thing could screw up his plans.

"Have seat son," he said. "I am Captain Graham. I've with the local recruiting office. Would you like to go into the service when you finish high school?"

Zane took the offered seat and answered, "Sir, my name is Dale Zane. I definitely do not want to join. I plan on going to the University of Florida for college. I do not want to enter the service."

Graham said, "Sooner or later you will have to meet the UMT requirement. You join the local guard unit in Gainesville, Florida. That way you will meet two years."

"Why can't I stay in the guard for four years?" Zane asked.

Graham answered, "You can Dale. However, there is a better deal. Take R.O.T.C. while you are in college. After the first two years in the guard, you can take Advanced R.O.T.C. You will accumulate another two years toward meeting UMT requirements. When you are graduated, you will be a second lieutenant in the army rather than a private. Do two years of active duty and you will meet full UMT requirements. In addition, during those two years, you will draw maximum pay while on active duty because your time spent in the guard and R.O.T.C. counts for pay."

Zane went to the local National Guard Headquarters and enlisted. He raised his right hand and took an oath of enlistment administered by a warrant officer.

"Welcome aboard son. I am Chief Warrant Officer Begoins. You unit of assignment is the 51st Division Artillery Headquarters. With your background in math, I'm assigning you to the survey section," Begoins said.

"What's a survey section?" Zane asked.

"Private, you know about surveying property don't you?" Begoins asked.

"Yes, sir," Zane answered.

"A survey crew in the artillery does surveys to determine accurate locations on the ground. We have to know where we are before we can shoot," he explained.

"Uh, sure thing," Zane answered, not understanding a thing Begoins said.

Begoins added, "Be here Monday night at 19:00 hours. Wear the boots and fatigues that supply gave you."

"Sir, what time is nineteen hundred hours?" Zane asked.

Begoins grinned and said, "It's the military's way of telling time. It is a 24-hour system. For example, 7 A.M. is 07:00 hours. Nine A.M. is 09:00 hours. Six P.M. is 18:00 hours and midnight is 24:00 hours. Got it?"

Thinking for a moment, Zane said, "Then I'm supposed to be here at 7 P.M."

"That's it private. See you Monday night," Begoins answered.

While his income would be better, Zane still needed more for books, supplies, and other expenses. Zane figured he would try to get a football scholarship. Colleges had not recruited him. This meant he would have to be a "walk-on." As such, he would have to excel enough to gain a spot on the team.

He went to Wofford's head coach and told him his desire. The coach told him to report for practice.

College football was different than high school. Each player was serious. The training was difficult and designed to determine who would go or stay. Zane had it tough. This year's team was the best Wofford had produced in 25 years. The quarterback, Charley Bradshaw, and his best receiver, Jerry Richardson, were returning stars. At their grueling pace, Zane wondered how he could possibly get a good education and play ball. However, Bradshaw and Richardson, had high grade point averages. If they could do it, he could also.

"To the locker room," the coach said. "There will be a skull session after lunch."

A skull session was classroom work on how to run various plays. It was necessary to attend these between morning and afternoon field practices. Zane was doing his best and hoping it was enough.

On the way to the skull session, he saw Coach Ramsey. His former high school coach was standing near the classroom entrance.

"Zane, what in the hell are you doing here?" He asked.

"Trying to make the team," Zane answered.

Ramsey took Zane by his shoulder and turned him toward an adjacent room. Once inside, he looked at Zane with an amazed stare.

"Zane, I cannot believe you are doing this. With your grades, you have no business out here getting your head beat to a pulp," he exclaimed.

"Coach, I need the money. This place is expensive and I have to pay my way," Zane stated.

Ramsey thought for a moment and said, "You attend tomorrow morning's practice. Meet me at Dean Lambert's office at 11 O'clock. What you are doing is senseless. You be on time."

Zane wondered what Ramsey intended to accomplish at Lambert's office. He arrived 15 minutes early. Coach Ramsey had a manila folder tucked beneath his arm. He led the way into the dean's reception area. His secretary looked up as the two entered.

"Good morning Coach Ramsey. Dean Lambert is expecting you. Give a knock and enter," she said.

The dean greeted Ramsey like a long, lost friend. They made some small talk and Ramsey introduced Zane. Lambert directed Zane and Ramsey to a sofa. Dean Lambert sat in an easy chair in front of them. An antique coffee table separated them. Ramsey handed the folder to Dean Lambert. He browsed through it and then looked at Zane.

"Tell me son, are you registered yet?" He asked.

"No sir," Zane answered. "I will be doing that tomorrow."

"Coach Ramsey tells me that you will be living at home. Do you plan on staying with Wofford until you get a degree?" The dean asked.

"Yes sir," Zane replied.

The dean stood and said, "Pardon me for a moment."

He walked to his desk and opened a large, ledger-like book. He scanned a few pages and returned. He sat and looked at Zane.

"Mr. Zane," he said. "Wofford is a small school. What we lack in size we like to think we make up for in quality. I see potential for you. Your high school grades are excellent. We can award small academic scholarships from time to time. With Coach Ramsey's recommendation, we can do that for you," he explained.

Stunned, Zane stammered, "Thank you sir."

"That's not all," the dean continued. "Has anyone ever told you that you have a quality voice? By this I mean, you could be a radio announcer with proper training," he explained.

Zane watched as the dean removed a small notebook from his coat pocket. He flipped the spiral bound pages until he had an empty one. He wrote a few lines and removed the page from its binder. He handed it to Zane.

"Call WSPA radio and ask for the manager. His name is Ralph Deerborne. He will be expecting to hear from you. Give him the note. You need not report for ball practice this afternoon. I will tell the coach. We're glad to have you with us Mr. Zane," he said with a wide smile.

"Anything else Coach?" He asked.

"No Jim, thanks for the help. I'm sure you won't be disappointed," he answered.

After shaking hands, Zane and Coach Ramsey left the Dean's office. Ramsey said farewell to the receptionist. They stopped on the main stairs leading to the building.

"Zane, don't disappoint me. I hope things work out for you. Give a call now and then to let me know how you and Wofford are doing," he stated, as he turned to leave.

"Wait coach," Zane said. "What happened in there just now?"

"Dean Lambert, Ralph Deerborne and I were Wofford classmates. I played ball for the school. My grades suffered because of it. You're a good kid. I did not want you to suffer the same results. Just keep your nose clean and get an education," Ramsey directed.

Totally, at a loss for words, Zane watched Ramsey skip down the stairs. He turned a corner and was gone. Zane, with hands shaking, removed the dean's note from his shirt pocket. It stated, "Ralph give Zane a try for 'Wofford Now.' I think he is exactly what you need. Stay in touch."

Zane sat on the steps and read the note again. He wondered what "Wofford Now" was. Evidently, it was a radio program of some sort. While pondering the note, he felt a slight nudge to his shoulder. He stood up to face a slightly balding, older guy with a wide grin.

"Hi, my name is Howard. What's yours?" He asked.

"Uh, Dale, Dale Zane," he answered.

Howard asked, "You a student here?"

"I will be come tomorrow," Zane replied.

"Are you going to wear one of those stupid hats?" Howard asked.

"What hats?" Zane questioned.

"You haven't registered yet have you?" Howard asked.

"No, I'm supposed to do that tomorrow," Zane replied.

"Oh, you're a jock," Howard stated with a smirk.

"Well, not anymore, I guess. How did you know?" Zane responded.

Howard explained that tomorrow's registration was for athletes. The regular students were registering already. He added that today was the registration deadline for other students. In addition, Howard already had his class schedule. He also explained about the black hats.

Freshmen had to wear small, black caps. They could not walk on sidewalks and upper classmen called them "Rats." If an upper classman asked for a favor, you did it. They also required that freshmen sing Wofford's Alma Mater on command. Howard removed a card from his pocket.

"This is my class schedule. It is for the first semester. You will get one when you register," Howard explained.

Continuing, Howard said, "There's not a whole lot of choices. First year students have few electives. Actually, they have none unless some special arrangement exists. I know some guys that transferred. They brought credits from another school."

"You have to take religion and R.O.T.C. for two years," Howard told Zane.

Zane thought about this for a moment and then asked. "Tell me Howard. Don't you find those two requirements at odds with each other? One is for love and peace while the other trains people to kill. In addition, if a student takes the four-year ROTC course, they become officers. They train others to kill. You don't have a problem with that?" Zane asked.

Without hesitation, Howard answered, "Never thought about it. I just pulled a hitch in the service and the idea never entered my head."

Explaining farther, Howard said, "I am attending school as a G.I. Bill student. The government sends me a check each month. I couldn't afford Wofford when I left high school. I went in the Army so that I could attend college when my enlistment ended."

Howard was older than Zane. However, they had a common interest to get an education.

"Listen Dale," Howard said. "Don't worry about things you can't do anything about. If you want a degree from this school, you will take the courses. Save you questions for the professors. They receive pay for that shit. You better get your butt to registration today. I will go with you. Since I've been through it, I can save you all kinds of time."

After registering and paying the registrar, Zane did not have much money left in his checking account. He still needed to buy textbooks and supplies. He was not going to have enough money. He told Howard.

"Don't sweat it," Howard said.

"You can buy used books. Actually, they are better than new. The old ones have notes made by the previous owner in them. They give a good indication of what to expect on an exam," he explained.

Howard was correct. Zane got his books and had money remaining in his account. It was getting late in the day.

"At least I'm not on the practice field getting beaten to a pulp. Things are going to be fine," he thought.

He and Howard went to the student post office. The registrar had given them combinations for their mailboxes. They wanted to assure they were correct.

Walking across the campus, Howard asked, "Let's go get a beer. What do you say?"

Zane had to decline. He didn't have the money and it was a long walk home. He explained this to Howard.

"No sweat, the beer is on me and I've got wheels," he said.

Their mail box combinations worked fine. A short time later they went to what was to be a favorite haunt, The Trade Winds Bar. Howard seemed to know everyone in the place. He constantly fed nickels to the jukebox and ordered beer. To the tunes of Patsy Cline and Jim Reeves, they reveled away the remainder of the afternoon. It was drink beer and flirt with the waitresses. Over years to come, Howard Timbers and Zane cemented what was to be a life-long friendship. Many adventures awaited the two.

Zane enjoyed National Guard drills. Each Monday night he went to the armory for training. He was a private, the lowest rank a person could be. This did not bother him. He learned how to use a slide rule and conduct surveys for artillery units. Much of the equipment was obsolete but it was functional. They taught him marksmanship with an M-1 Carbine. The first year went fast.

Wofford was his most enlightening experience. His freshman classes seemed like high school. Most of the courses he had already studied. With two years of high school Spanish, the Wofford course helped him master the language. His grades kept him on the Dean's list with a solid 3.7 grade point average. In high school terms, that was a high B plus.

Zane went to mandatory ROTC classes. In addition, he attended ROTC drill on Monday afternoons. Most of it was basic stuff. Upperclassmen taught close order marching and the manual of arms. They conducted inspections to assure their uniforms were in order. There was a disciplinary procedure consisting of merits and demerits. If a person did something wrong, they received demerits. This required menial chores doled out by upperclassmen.

Furthermore, Zane liked order and discipline. There was an honor code. Lying, cheating and stealing were serious offenses and not tolerated. The military code called for honor, integrity, and trust.

"Son, whenever you do something, do it well. Never do anything that you are not willing to sign your name to," his father told him in earlier years. Following his father's advice enhanced his military experience. He did well.

The military history classes extolled the price paid by others to assure his country's freedom. Zane took the lessons to heart and gained a newly found respect for those serving their country.

The National Guard summer training meant two weeks at Fort McClellan, Alabama. The summer of 1955 was his recruit training. He had already mastered recruit-training requirements in ROTC. Senior officers observed Zane during training. They noticed that he knew the basics better than most of their instructors. They assigned him instructor duties. He wore a white band around his cap, indicating that he was an instructor not a recruit. Many resented this.

They felt that, since they went through recruit training, he must do the same. Zane ignored them.

Nevertheless, he had recruit duty requirements. There seemed to be a duty roster for everything. He did KP in the mess hall. KP was an abbreviation for Kitchen Police. The dirty jobs came his way. Cleaning pots and pans was the worst. He dug six-foot deep sump holes and latrine trenches. One event burned indelibly into his brain. He had to prepare and maintain the commanding general's tent in the field. On a Sunday morning, he arrived to find vomit covering the tent's floor. Numerous liquor bottles lay strewn across the tent's interior. As he cleaned the foul regurgitation, he vowed to never impose such foul duty on another.

Furthermore, there came the inevitable manhood challenge. The unit bully caught Zane between tents one night.

"I understand you want a piece of my ass," he said.

Zane said not a word. Their fight took place in the dark between tents. The bully made a mistake challenging Zane. He lost miserably and had the marks to prove it. Zane never mentioned the incident to anyone. The bully did not either. Nonetheless, the others knew and Zane received no more challenges.

After completing summer camp, Zane returned to continue attending weekly drills. These did not interfere with his class schedule or his work scholarship. Zane realized that he owed much of his ability to attend Wofford to Coach Ramsey.

Coach Ramsey's assistance paid dividends. Zane went to WSPA with the note from Dean Lambert. Mr. Deerborne asked him to read a short manuscript aloud.

"Mr. Zane, you have an excellent voice. However, the southern accent has to go," he said. "I have just the way to do that."

The station manager left the room. Soon, he returned with a piece of cork. It came from someone's Thermos bottle. He cut the stopper into four even pieces.

"Mr. Zane, place two of these in your mouth. Put one between your rear molars on each side and bite. Now, read the manuscript," he instructed.

Zane's natural inclination was to release pressure on the cork. Deerborne would have none of it. He insisted that Zane read while biting hard on the cork pieces. This forced him to pronounce words using his lips and tongue. The words were crisp, clear and without accent.

"Son, you're going to do fine. The corks stay in place until you can speak like that without them," he stated.

Deerborne explained the work scholarship. "Wofford Now" was a radio program twice a week. It aired on Tuesday and Thursday nights for 15 minutes. It consisted of one night's music of original Jazz and the other contemporary. There would be Wofford announcements and interviews. Zane would host the program. The first series would last for 13 weeks. For each completed series, WSPA credited Zane's tuition $50.00. It was easy money as far as he was concerned.

Furthermore, there was the academic scholarship. At second semester registration, he had $100 credit to his account. This, combined with the radio program, the National Guard pay and his savings, provided enough to get through his first year. His grade point average kept his dad, not just happy but proud.

Howard had wheels for dating and helped with the costs. The freshman year was indeed good. Unfortunately, his second held some distasteful experiences. One would be a strong integrity test.

Zane looked forward to his second year. He was tired of his monotonous, summer job. Yet, he needed the money so he had to live with it. He liked simply walking on campus. The trees were losing their leaves and the early morning air had a chill to it. He had made many friends. In addition, Don Dybold and he were good friends after a year together in high school and one at college. Don became his study mate. He and Howard still hit the Trade Winds on weekends. Howard seldom studied. He was too busy partying.

Being a sophomore had advantages. He could select some elective courses. Hazing the "Rats" was a pleasure after what upperclassmen put him through his first year. He knew his way around campus and adjusted to its routine. He had little time for a social life but he liked what he was doing and why.

Some of his classmates joined fraternities. They seemed to like being a member.

During his freshman year, a few fraternities invited Zane to parties. This they called "rush week." Zane's lack of interest must have showed. He did not receive an invitation to join. Most of them preferred on campus students. Day students seldom received invitations for memberships. Zane did not care because he could not afford dues.

Nevertheless, one invited Howard and he became a member. The fraternity houses had living space for two. Howard not only lived in one of the houses; the members elected him president. The gossip was that Howard, because of his age, could easily buy liquor.

Howard invited Zane to visit. As soon as he met them, he knew why Howard was president. These members were party people. They liked their booze and Howard was a party king. Zane knew many of the members. One in particular put his integrity to a test.

Zane took Spanish 201 his sophomore year. The course was a "gimme" for an A. He arrived home, after staying late for a Biology Lab class. His mom met him at the door. She told Zane that Tim Bush was in his room. Tim told her that Zane said it was okay. He needed to get some study material.

Flustered, Zane wondered why Tim was in his room. They were casual acquaintances from high school and college. Friendship was not a mutual trait. Upon entering his room, Zane saw that Tim was copying his homework.

"Tim, what the hell are you doing?" Zane asked heatedly.

"I didn't make a couple of Spanish classes. You are always making As. I figured you wouldn't mind my catching up with your notes," he sheepishly explained.

"The hell you say. You cut those classes and that is just tough. I worked on that translation until three O'clock this morning. You do your own damn homework. Get the shit out of my room," Zane said, seething with rage.

Tim hurriedly gathered his books. He inched toward the door mumbling as he moved. Tim exuded fear. It swirled around him permeating his physical presence. He wanted out and fast.

Once clear of Zane and the door, he said, "What a prick. Screw you Zane."

In his haste to depart, Tim left his notebook on Zane's desk. It had a partially copied translation in it. Zane ripped pages from it and tore them into shreds. These he threw into a trash can by his desk.

"Son of a bitch," Zane thought. "I can't stand a liar and a cheat. I should have whipped his ass."

Nonetheless, Zane knew better than create a scene with his Mom present. His Dad would most definitely have been upset. It would not be because of whipping Tim's ass but because he did it in the house. This was still his Dad's home.

Two weeks later Howard asked Zane to go to the Trade Winds with him. They met after class and Howard drove his beat-up, 1951 Ford. On their way, Howard seemed uneasy.

"Dale, would you like to be in my fraternity?" He asked.

"Man, I sure would. However, you know I cannot afford the dues," Zane explained.

"Would you join if there were no dues?" Howard continued.

Zane knew Howard rather well. Something was amiss because dues were mandatory in fraternities.

"What's up?" Zane asked.

Howard related events from his fraternity's last membership meeting. Howard nominated Zane for membership. After a secret vote, there was a black ball in the voting cup. Someone did not want Zane to be a member. This person "blackballed" him, which meant he could not join. According to Howard, members present could not believe the vote. They looked at each other in amazement with one exception, Tim Bush. Another member made a motion for a show-of-hands vote. There was a second and another vote taken. Tim Bush voted against Zane's membership.

"What's with you and Bush?" Howard asked.

Zane told Howard of the Spanish homework incident. Howard did not seem shocked.

"That's Bush alright," he said.

Howard continued, "By our constitution you cannot be a member. I'm sorry. However, those present at the meeting, granted you honorary guest status. You, if you want, can participate in every function except voting. Feel free to come by the fraternity house anytime. We have hot coffee and doughnuts every morning. You have a non-dues status so don't worry about money."

"What about Bush?" Zane asked.

"He'll keep his mouth shut. If he causes a problem, we will vote his ass out," Howard answered.

Beer at the Trade Winds tasted particularly good that afternoon. Zane knew that he had a true friend in Howard. Howard must have told them that they could get another president. On the other hand, Zane had more friends than he realized. Though they met often at the Frat house, Bush never voiced a complaint about Zane's presence.

Zane continued his National Guard training. While doing so, he gained an embarrassing nickname, "Sweets." The headquarters staff had to go to a weekend staff test at Fort Gordon, Georgia. The unit exam was a simulation of staff procedures during combat. The various staff elements operated from a large tent. Simulated tactical situations came to the headquarters by telephone. The staff had to process this information and make tactical decisions. Zane, because of his advanced training, went with the headquarters.

His assignment was to receive incoming messages. He distributed these to various headquarters' elements. These elements would update operational maps and issue directives to simulated units. These orders went to a test group who evaluated the tactical decisions. The test was an around-the-clock exercise.

Zane operated a telephone for 24 hours with few breaks. He was tired and craving sleep. An unusual message arrived. It stated that civilians were pouring sugar into vehicle gas tanks. The sugar destroyed engines. Zane, in an exhausted fog, rushed the message to the operations officer. Zane took the message to be real. He asked the operations officer's permission to check vehicles for damage. He wanted to catch someone putting sugar in his Dad's fuel tank.

The staff had a big laugh over his reaction. Upon returning to Spartanburg, his unit commander told Wofford's Professor of Military Science. Word spread throughout the military community. For almost two years, Zane was the brunt of many jokes. Finally, the joke wore thin and his nickname disappeared. It was none too soon to suit him. Yet, people knowing him throughout the military community, had an advantage to it. Later, it would pay dividends.

Classmates began making choices as to their major studies. Zane found his interest in biology and chemistry. He wanted to practice medicine. Although Wofford was a liberal arts college, its science department was excellent. He talked with various professors about becoming a doctor. One in particular, Dr. Dewitt, advised Zane to drop his desires to be a medical doctor.

"Mr. Zane, doctors are nothing more than glorified body mechanics. You should do research. If you really want to make a difference in this world, do research. I'm sure you would do well," Dr. Dewitt advised.

Others recommended that he take a Pre-Medical Course. He would have a major in biology and a minor in chemistry. In addition, he should join the Pre-Med. Society. This was a student group who participated in extra-curricular, medically oriented activities. They received night lectures from visiting physicians. They watched movies of numerous surgical procedures.

Furthermore, Zane was dating regularly. He found dates, with ladies attending college, not to his liking. Their perspective was either marrying someone rich or their careers. On one date, he spent the evening in a parlor listening to his date play classical piano music. He preferred dating local girls. A mistaken identity, involving one of them, changed his life forever.

Chapter Nine

April 1948

"Blunders are an inescapable feature of war,
because choice in military affairs lies generally between the bad and the worse."
Allan Massie (b. 1938), British author. Marshal Pétain, *in* A Question of Loyalties,
pt. 3, ch. 11 (1989)

Minh Thanh's mother was free. Minh Thanh's Uncle Diem, who lived near Hanoi, wrote of Xuan's release. When she did not arrive home in a month, Minh Thanh's anxiety increased.

"Surely," she thought. "She will at least write."

She never did. A year passed and Minh Thanh knew what she must do. She would go to Hanoi.

Traveling was dangerous. Nevertheless, Minh Thanh knew she must go because something was seriously wrong.

Minh Thanh regretted leaving her brothers. Yet, she did not mind leaving her hamlet. She suffered scorn from its people. She mourned too long after her grandfather's death. Her betrothed, and his family, became angry when she would not marry. His family was important. They brought shame upon her. She had no friends and the isolation tore at her soul.

Minh Thanh put her home in order before she left. She wrote a letter for her brothers. She explained why she had to go. They suffered grief like Minh Thanh. However, they had to work the fields. She knew they needed her to help. Yet, they could handle matters until her return. They would understand. Hopefully, she would bring their mother home. Although concerned, she tried to be optimistic. Her uncle's letter sounded certain as to her release.

She traveled south from the valley. Her bicycle was sturdy and in good condition. Traveling only during daylight, she rested at Catholic churches after dark. A priest warned her that she was in danger. Communist party members were following instructions from Ho Chi Minh. They were trying to eliminate Catholics. This was confusing because Ho Chi Minh had embraced Catholics in his declaration of independence in 1946. She did not understand politics. Her desires were the same as her neighbors. They wanted to live their lives in peace.

Minh Thanh stopped in a village about half way. Its church was small but the sisters were quite friendly. She ate with them and they allowed her to have a room for the night.

During the evening meal of rice and vegetables, a sister mentioned that their priest, Father Cicero, would be going to Hanoi the next day.

"Father Cicero travels to Hanoi each month for supplies. While there, he always visits various missions throughout the city. He does this for the bishop. He is ill an unable to visit," she said.

"Dearest sister, do you think Father Cicero would allow me ride with him?" Minh Thanh asked.

Responding immediately, she answered, "Of course my dear. In the morning, put your bicycle in the truck's rear. He has a lot of room going to Hanoi. It is his return trip when the truck is full."

Minh Thanh explained, "My uncle lives almost in Hanoi. He lives in a small village this side of the city. Traveling by truck will save me four days. Bless you for your kindness."

Before sunrise, Minh Thanh put her bicycle into the truck's open bed. She climbed into its cab and waited.

"Good morning, you must be Minh Thanh," a priest said as he approached the truck. "I am pleased to have your company. I am Father Cicero."

By dawn, the two began their trip. The road was not a good one and this required that Father Cicero drive slowly.

At noon, Father Cicero stopped and parked near a church. He opened his door to exit. Minh Thanh did not move.

"Come along little one. We can have lunch with these nice people. You are welcome," Father Cicero said.

"Thank you father," she said. "I accept."

Minh Thanh ate with the sisters in the kitchen while Father Cicero dined with the local priest in another room.

Minh Thanh enjoyed the food immensely. She did not realize how hungry she was. The rice had pork in it for flavor. By her standards, it was excellent.

Suddenly, they heard noises outside. Part of the sound was loud voices. Dogs began barking and guard geese sounded their alert cries. One of the sisters grabbed Minh Thanh by her elbow.

"Come child," she said urgently. "You must take refuge. Follow me."

Holding Minh Thanh's hand, she rushed from the kitchen into a small chapel. She pulled a candle stand aside and parted a wall tapestry behind it. She opened a miniature door that revealed stairs.

"Go inside and remain quiet. I will return for you when it is safe," she said.

Darkness enveloped her as the sister closed the door. From her hidden chamber, she listened as the local priest answered questions.

"Whose truck is this? It does not belong to anyone in our village. Tell us who it belongs to," a man demanded to know.

"It is mine sir," she heard Father Cicero say. "I am on my way to Hanoi for supplies. I stopped for lunch."

Another man asked. "Who owns that bicycle?"

"It is mine. My truck is old and often fails to operate. I use the bicycle to ride for help," Father Cicero explained.

Minh Thanh, hearing this, thought, "Oh my father. You must go to confession as soon as possible. I do not think such lies are venial sins."

During questioning, she heard footsteps moving from room to room above her. Someone entered the chapel but did not move the candle stand. Minh Thanh trembled with fear as footfalls echoed through her sanctuary. Soon the interrogators departed.

Hours passed while Minh Thanh remained hidden. She leaned against a wall that she could not see. In the darkness, she slept.

Someone opened the door to her hiding place. She awoke confused. For a moment, she almost panicked. Awakening to total darkness caused her disorientation. A bright light momentarily blinded her.

"You can come out," a nun said. "Hurry, you must move quickly."

Ushered out a side entrance, she saw that it was night. The old truck's engine rattled in the darkness.

"May God be with you," a nun said as she helped Minh Thanh into the truck's bed. Covered with a piece of canvas, she felt her bicycle placed on top of her.

From beneath her covering, he heard Father Cicero say, "Do not move. We are leaving this village. I pretended to work on the truck until darkness fell. The local Communists think that I am alone. There are reports of young girls becoming prisoners of such groups. They are never seen again."

The truck had not gone far when Minh Thanh heard its brakes screech. She slid slightly forward as the truck stopped. They were at a checkpoint outside the village. She recognized a voice from the previous day.

"I see you have this piece of junk working," he said.

"Yes," replied Father Cicero. "I wasn't sure I was going to be able to fix it."

"You're probably going to need that bicycle before long," another person commented with a loud laugh.

"On your way," the first voice said

Gears growled in protest and the vintage vehicle lurched. The road was little more than a dirt trail. The bicycle pounded Minh Thanh beneath her cover. Every bump bounced it upward and it crashed back onto her. One of its pedals dug into her rib cage causing extreme pain. Try as best she could, she could not move to a position that kept it from gouging her. She was coming from beneath her covering when the vehicle slowed to a stop. She remained motionless gripped by fear.

"You're safe here," she heard Father Cicero say. "We're away from prying eyes."

Moving caused her cramped body to scream with pain. Moving slowly, she pushed from beneath her cover. With lights off, the truck was on the roadside. The father helped her dismount. She left with considerable relief.

Darkness prevailed beneath a cloudy sky as frogs disturbed an otherwise silent night. There were no visible signs of human presence.

"Excuse me Minh Thanh. I must answer a call of nature," Father Cicero said as he disappeared.

Minh Thanh moved in the opposite direction for the same purpose. She returned to find her escort had already arrived. She entered the truck's cab as Father Cicero started onto the road. Slightly before dawn, she could see a lighted sky on the horizon. Hanoi's lights reflected from low hanging clouds. She could not imagine a city so large that it lit the night's sky. Fumbling in her bag, she withdrew a worn letter from her uncle. In it, she had a crude map. It showed where he lived. She trembled with anticipation. After so many years, she would soon see her mother.

They drove into the village's market area. It was quite busy as vendors were setting up for the day's business. Vegetable stands had an array of products for purchase. The aroma of Nuc Baum, a spicy condiment made from fish, filled the tiny square. Villagers crowded around their vehicle as they moved slowly through the market. Women wore traditional garb consisting of conical straw hats and flowing, loose, one-piece robe-like garments. The men wore two pieces, a black shirt, and trousers. Footwear was the same for all, thong sandals. It was a busy place.

Using her map, the pair found her uncle's house with ease. Her father's brother, Nguyen Van Diem, rushed to meet her. He recognized her immediately. Other family members, her aunt and cousins, retrieved her bicycle and small bag. They pleaded with Father Cicero to stay and eat. He explained that he should be at the bishop's cathedral in a short time. He gave them his thanks and blessed the group. Soon he was lost in traffic swirling through nearby streets.

"Ahhyahh, my little Minh Thanh, you have grown into a beautiful lady" Diem said excitedly. "Come in! Come in! It is time to eat. We have so much to tell since we last saw you."

They entered a small, courtyard that fronted on the main street. Mats, woven from rice straw, covered most of its space. They held various green, red and yellow peppers drying in the sun. These would add flavor to their rice and vegetables. Everyone removed their sandals upon entering a small foyer. The home was typical of those found in most suburban hamlets. The foyer and main living areas had wood floors. The kitchen floor was dirt. The room had various crock pots strewn about it.

After much genuflecting and greetings, Diem asked for tea. Diem's family gathered and sat upon the floor at a small table. Diem's wife, and her daughters, brought tea in their best china pot. Tiny cups filled a serving tray. It had some rice cakes stacked upon it. The atmosphere was gleeful with a lot of giggles and chattering.

Minh Thanh looked for her mother, Xuan. Every time someone entered the room, she looked hoping to see her. Everyone noticed her concerned looks. However, the group ignored her, preferring pleasure of the moment. Nonetheless, the reason for Minh Thanh's visit required satisfaction. The task fell to Diem. He cleared his throat to quiet the group.

Diem blessed their meal and said a prayer. Each person crossed themselves in typical catholic fashion.

Looking into Minh Thanh's eyes he said, "My dearest brother's daughter, you honor us with your presence. It is my privilege to tell you of your mother. She is free and lives near us."

Minh Thanh's bewilderment showed. She sensed their discomfort.

"Why isn't she here?" She thought.

Anticipating the obvious, Diem continued, "She is not with us because she could not come. However, you will see her tonight. Do you remember the gentleman for whom your elder brother worked during summers with us?"

Minh Thanh nodded that she remembered and answered, "Yes."

She could feel everyone looking at her with anticipation. There was a hint of concern in their eyes. They saw in her a natural grace. She sat with her hands in her lap. Her fingers interlocked with her palms upturned. Her waist length black hair reflected shimmering light from a nearby window. With her back straight, she peered downward at her hands. She waited for her uncle to continue.

"Bhan Van Duc is an honorable and considerate person. I am one of his employees as is your mother," he explained.

Minh Thanh slowly raised her head. Her eyes began to fill with tears. Those in the room saw her take a deep breath as she looked into Diem's eyes with a questioning gaze.

"Why didn't she come home? Why did she not write?" Minh Thanh questioned softly.

"She will answer those questions for you," Diem replied as he positioned himself close beside Minh Thanh. He reached around her delicate shoulders and gently pulled her near.

"Xuan asked that I prepare you for what will come," Diem continued. "Your mother escaped from prison. She was able to get here to recover from her ordeal. Minh Thanh they hurt her. I did not recognize her at first sight," Diem explained.

Diem felt her shoulders begin to tremble. Yet, she maintained her outward composure.

Softly her words came, "What have they done to her?"

Diem noticed Minh Thanh's beauty and gracefulness. Even under such stress, she seemed to radiate peace. However, Diem knew it was a deception. It was obvious that she was in great emotional pain.

"Her love must be profound," Diem thought.

Continuing, he said, "After your father's execution, the Vichy French brought Xuan to Hanoi. I tried to visit her. The prison officials said they knew nothing of her. After months, I lost heart and thought she must be dead. They killed so many in that terrible place."

Overcome with emotion, Diem began to lose control. He gazed out a window so that they would not see his tears. Minh Thanh dared not look at him for fear of embarrassment. The room remained silent. In the distance dogs barked and a peacock wailed its lonesome cry.

"Our tea is cold. Heat some more," Diem ordered, without looking at anyone.

Onlookers left the room. They knew not to return until Diem called for them.

He swallowed hard and held Minh Thanh even closer. He leaned his head next to hers.

"My dear Minh Thanh, there is no easy way to do this," he whispered. "You will not recognize Xuan. Her hair is white and her face disfigured. The French gave her to the Japanese for their pleasure. Out of shame, she took poison. She did not die but it did terrible damage to her. A doctor at the prison said she had leprosy. Some lepers helped her escape."

Minh Thanh placed her hands over her face as her shoulders slumped. Between words, she gasped for air.

"Why didn't mother come home?" She asked. "We love her so much."

Diem explained that she was afraid for them. She did not want her tormentors to believe other family members might side with the Viet Minh. She feared her fate would befall Minh Thanh and her brothers.

"She came to us at night. We hardly recognized her. She was like a ghost. We helped her gain strength but her mind never recovered. She cannot overcome her terror. Her sleep brings nightmares," Diem told Minh Thanh.

Diem's wife appeared with a lighted candle. She told Diem that it was time to go.

"We will go to your mother now. She lives near where I work as night watchman. She could not stay with us. Communist neighbors were getting suspicious. We will take food to her tonight," Diem said.

They went to the foyer and donned their shoes. Some trucks and small cars traveled the streets but bicycles were the main transportation means. As they traveled, Diem explained that the warehouse where he worked was prosperous. Bhan Van Duc managed it.

After the Japanese left, British soldiers fixed the railroad. It suffered significant bomb damage from air raids. Most warehouses near railroads suffered total destruction. However, the one where Diem worked had little damage. When the French arrived, they needed storage space for their plantation equipment. They immediately made use of the facility. The warehouse's owner hired Van Duc. With so much valuable equipment stored, he needed a watchman. Diem worked for Van Duc before the war, so he was Van Duc's first choice.

Soon they arrived in the industrial district. Road traffic began to increase. Vendors' roadside stands lined the street. When they approached a railroad crossing, Diem told Minh Thanh to stop. He explained that they would have to push their bicycles.

"This is the short way to the warehouse," he said. "It is too difficult to ride because of the railroad ties. Also, this route will take us directly to your mother's home. She does not work at the warehouse. Her place is on an alley near the building. She braids twine that we use to package materials. It is excellent for her because she does not like being around too many people," he explained.

Diem led the way. After a short distance, he left the tracks. He followed a narrow path through high weeds to an alley. It ended at a high chain link fence with a locked gate.

"That gate is the entrance to the warehouse area. I have a key. If you want me, ring the bell on the gate. I can hear it from anywhere in the building. I will come and let you in," he explained.

Confused, Minh Thanh asked. "Where does she live?"

"Directly in front of you," he answered. "Tap lightly on the door. She will know it's you."

Minh Thanh stood transfixed as she watched Diem ride his bicycle toward the gate. She turned and saw a dim light piercing darkness from beneath a small door. Leaning her bicycle against the building, she tapped on the door. She saw a shadow cross the light as someone approached.

"Minh Thanh, is that you?" An unrecognizable whisper asked from behind the door.

"Yes mother, let me in please," she cried.

The worn door opened slowly to reveal a hideous person. She was far beyond anything that Minh Thanh expected.

"This is not my mother," Minh Thanh thought as her heart broke at the sight.

"Who are you?" She asked.

"You mother Minh Thanh. Come in before you are seen," she said.

Minh Thanh was certain this was not her mother.

Chapter Ten

February 1953

Force, and fraud, are in war the two cardinal virtues.
Thomas Hobbes (1588–1679), English philosopher. *Leviathan,*
pt. 1, ch. 13 (1651)

Briscoe had major problems using crutches. Nevertheless, if he wanted to walk, he had to use them. Six weeks in a body cast did not overjoy him either. He struggled through his recovery. Various ladies offered to make therapy more pleasant. He declined. His body cast would have frustrated both.

He heard a taxi's horn blaring. He made his way to his apartment's door. Clumsily he exited into a hall. Turning to lock his door, he fell.

"Damn, that's four times today," he grumbled, climbing upright.

The horn continued to blare as he exited his apartment building. The weather was cold with a mixture of snow and rain. He grasped a railing that helped him navigate steps to the sidewalk. It was a difficult task hopping on one foot while balancing with a crutch. Once on level ground, he moved rather well. Still, caution was necessary to avoid slipping.

He grasped a rear door handle. As he swung it open, his driver looked straight ahead ignoring his plight. Briscoe found it necessary to enter rear end first. Next, he moved both legs into the cab. He placed the crutches on his lap and closed the door.

"Where to?" The driver asked sounding bored.

"The White House," Briscoe answered.

The taxi driver gave Briscoe a sideward glance, "Yeah, right," he said.

"Damn straight," Briscoe answered. "You could have got off your dead ass and given me a hand," he added.

Without a word, the driver pushed down the meter's flag. Simultaneously, he accelerated causing tires to spin and his cab's rear to fishtail. Frozen slush sprayed from beneath its tires.

Thrown sideways, Briscoe grabbed his seat with one hand. With the other, he held onto the front passenger's seat. After his crash, he felt ill at ease traveling in any car. This driver definitely caused anxiety.

"Take it easy," he said with obvious anger. "One wreck is enough for awhile."

He could see the driver looking at him using his rear view mirror. With a smirk, he reduced speed. Briscoe relaxed as best he could and began to recall events.

His hospital stay lasted three weeks. The main problem was a collapsed lung. In addition, he was in a coma for six days. To add to these, he suffered a broken leg, a fractured skull and collar bone. His doctor told him that he almost died from internal bleeding.

It was three months before he learned what caused his crash. He, and his attorney, went to the police impoundment yard to examine his car. Police, investigating the accident, charged him with failure to yield and reckless driving. When he was able to speak, he explained that his brakes failed. He also maintained that his auto was in good working condition. Their response was, "Tell it to the judge."

A thorough examination revealed a partially severed brake line. Someone used a hacksaw to make a cut close to the wheel. This caused leaking fluid to accumulate in the tire's metal rim. This cutting method did not allow fluid to go where it would be readily seen.

"It had to be a professional," Briscoe thought. "Now, I must learn why. I haven't been in Washington long enough to piss anyone off that much."

Briscoe's cab made little progress through snarled traffic. Snow fell as large flakes blurring visibility to almost nothing. Disgruntled drivers tried to weave through traffic with excessive speed. Most of them either crashed into a vehicle or became stranded sideways on a curb. Briscoe's driver had one redeeming trait; he could drive through snow. Soon they were on Pennsylvania Avenue. Next, they were at a White House entrance gate. Briscoe waited for the guard to come to his taxi. He was not about to try to go to the guardhouse. He rolled his window down as a guard approached.

"Good morning, I need to see your identification please," the guard stated.

Briscoe handed him his National Security Agency (NSA) identification. The guard went to his small shelter. Briscoe could see him check a clipboard and then make a telephone call. He returned taking care to avoid ice patches. He opened Briscoe's door.

"Come with me Mr. Briscoe. It is warm in the guardhouse. Someone is coming to take you inside," he explained.

Briscoe paid his driver who, again, did not attempt to help. However, the guard noticed Briscoe's condition and assisted.

"Be careful sir. The ice is bad in spots," he explained as he guided Briscoe to shelter.

"How about some coffee sir?" The guard asked.

"It will be awhile before someone arrives," he added.

"Sounds great. I like mine black," Briscoe replied.

While sipping his steaming brew, Briscoe gazed at the White House grounds. It was picturesque with snow covering trees, shrubs, and lawn. A black, iron fence stood in stark contrast to the snow. Over years, security needs changed, sometimes because of a president's desires or enhanced security. At one time, there had been a solid wall on one side. Now, it was iron fencing so that citizens could have a clear view of their White House.

During World War II, President Roosevelt used the White House's East Wing for military staff. Truman also had his particulars about use of the president's home. After Puerto Ricans attempted to kill him a few years before, Congress approved additional security for Blair House and the White House. The days of people wandering in from the street ended.

He watched a black staff car approaching. Upon stopping, the driver came to the guardhouse.

"Good morning, Mr. Briscoe. My name is Neil Burnum. I am an assistant to the Chief of Security Affairs. Let me give you a hand. I apologize for keeping you waiting. President Eisenhower is keeping us rather busy getting settled," Burnum said.

Briscoe shook hands with Burnum. He explained that he could navigate well with crutches but snow and ice did not help.

Burnum helped Briscoe keep his balance as they went to the sedan. The drive only took a few moments Soon they were entering the White House through a side door that led to the West Wing.

Inside, activities ran at a chaotic pace. Various persons rushed from place to place while typewriters' clatter bombarded them from every direction. Burnum led Briscoe to an office, which opened onto a long hallway.

"Have a seat," Burnum said. "Can I get you some refreshment?" He asked.

"I'm fine, thanks," Briscoe answered.

Burnum pressed an intercom button and spoke into its microphone, "Katherine, get me the Briscoe file please."

"I see you've had a hard time. We missed you at the various social functions after inauguration," Burnum commented.

"I'm rather lucky," Briscoe replied. "My doctor said that it was touch and go for awhile. However, I'm in good shape now except for the crutches."

There was a knock on the door and a young woman entered. She held a thick, manila folder. In bold, red type, the words "TOP SECRET" covered its front. She handed it to Burnum.

"Thank you, Katherine," Burnum said as she handed him the folder.

She smiled, gave Briscoe a quick glance, and left the room. Briscoe could not help but notice that she was quite attractive. In particular, she had done away with the hairstyle popular during World War II. Hers fell in golden strands to her shoulders. He noted her clear blue eyes that seemed to dance with an inner light. She was lovely indeed.

"Lanny, is it okay to call you Lanny?" Burnum asked.

"Certainly, is Neil okay with you? Briscoe questioned.

"Sure is Lanny. This folder is for you to study. Take what time you need. I have a meeting with the chief of staff and must leave for awhile. Please remain in my office. If you need anything, simply press the intercom button and Katherine will get it for you. I hope that I can get you in to see the president this afternoon. Any questions before I leave?" Burnum asked.

"None that I can think of just now," Briscoe replied.

Burnum left, closing the door as he went. Briscoe looked around Burnum's office. It was in considerable disarray. Cardboard boxes lined walls with their tops opened. Markings adorned their sides. Some were campaign, funding, contacts, and budget. It was obvious that Burnum had not occupied his office for long.

Briscoe examined the folder. A string, wrapped around a button, held it shut. He quickly opened it and removed a binder. The binder had a heavy plastic cover. It's front had a stamped notice which stated, "Top Secret." Beneath the bold heading, another stamped statement listed the agency classifying it, the date classified and the authority for classification. Also, a declassification date stated "February 2003."

His curiosity rising rapidly, Briscoe opened the binder. Each page had a plastic cover. The cover had a stamped seal across its top. It was necessary to break this seal to remove a page. Pages had sequential numbers to make it easy to determine that a page was missing. He read the first page's title and he felt a strange rigor pass through his body.

ATOMIC WEAPON UTILIZATION
SOUTHEAST ASIA

BACKGROUND:

1. Communist Movement — The Vietnamese Communist movement began in Paris in 1920, when Ho Chi Minh, using the pseudonym Nguyen Ai Quoc, became a charter member of the French Communist Party. Two years later, Ho went to Moscow to study Marxist doctrine and then proceeded to Canton as a Comintern representative. While in China, he formed the Vietnamese Revolutionary Youth League, setting the stage for the formation of the Indochinese Communist Party (ICP) in 1930

2. French repression of nationalists and Communists forced insurgents underground, and others escaped to China. Other dissidents went to prison, some emerging later to play important roles in the anti-colonial movement. Ho Chi Minh was abroad at that time but later imprisoned in Hong Kong by the British. Ho's release took place in 1933, and in 1936, a new French government released his compatriots who, at the outset of World War II, fled to China. While in China, Ho organized the Viet Minh. Purportedly, a coalition of all anti- French Vietnamese groups joined them.

3. Official Vietnamese publications reveal founding of the Viet Minh by the ICP. Because a Vichy French administration in Viet Nam during World War II cooperated with occupying Japanese forces, the Viet Minh's anti-French activity was also directed against the Japanese, and, for a short period, there was cooperation between the Viet Minh and Allied forces.

4. When the Japanese ousted the French in March 1945, the Viet Minh began to move into the countryside from their base areas in the mountains of northern Viet Nam. By the time Allied troops—Chinese in the north and British in the south—arrived to take the surrender of Japanese troops, the Viet Minh leaders had already announced the formation of a Democratic Republic of Viet Nam (DRV) and on September 2, 1945, proclaimed Viet Nam's independence.

5. Deep divisions between Vietnamese Communist and non-communist nationalists soon began to surface. However, especially in the south, the DRV began negotiations with the French on their future relationship. The difficult negotiations broke down in December 1946, and fighting began with a Viet Minh attack on the French in Hanoi. Hostilities continued in Cambodia, Laos and Viet Nam.

6. Two previous administrations (Roosevelt and Truman) provided significant resources to support France in Indochina.

7. Support for France is ongoing. The United States (US) pays 80 percent of France's costs to continue operations in Southeast Asia. Most of these costs are for support in Viet Nam. France intends to expand military operations in Northern Viet Nam this fall. US costs will increase.

FACTORS BEARING ON THE PROBLEM:

1. Communist China continues its effort to disseminate Communist doctrine in Asia. The Chinese intervention, during the Korean police action, resulted in North Korea coming under Communist control.

2. Communist China continues its effort to overcome the Peoples' Republic of China (PRC) on Taiwan. Continuing battles, involving the islands of Matsu and Quemoy, keep the region volatile without hope of stability in the near future.

3. Nationalist forces in Cambodia and Laos are under continuing attack by Communist supported forces to overthrow their legitimate governments.

4. The United Soviet Socialist Republic (USSR) provides extensive resources to support Communist China's continuing spread of Communism in the region.

5. The USSR is in a position to provide a rudimentary, atomic capability to China.

6. China is doing extensive atomic research. It is the consensus of intelligence agencies that China will soon possess an atomic capability.

CONCLUSIONS:

1. China, if left unchecked, will continue extending its doctrine and territorial control throughout Southeast Asia.

2. It is necessary for the Eisenhower administration to continue support to France, the PRC, Cambodia and Laos.

3. Communist China will expand its efforts to include Indonesia.

RECOMMENDATIONS:

1. It is necessary for the US to take decisive action in the near future. If not, the US will face an atomic threat on two major fronts, Europe, and Southeast Asia.

2. Implement Operation Vulture (See Joint Chiefs' File BC-RL006) with atomic support for France. Preposition atomic assets for immediate use if needed.

3. Prepare to expand atomic operations to Communist China and the USSR.

4. Immediately dispatch covert operatives to the PRC. They will prepare PRC military resources for invasion of Communist China.

5. Acquire controlling interest in CAT Airlines (Taiwan) for Cambodian and Laotian operations. Establish covert operation from Thailand with aerial support assets designated Air America.

Briscoe's hands trembled as he read a concurrence / non-concurrence card attached inside the folder. This card showed who had read the document and whether they agreed or not. A list contained names of essential governmental leaders. Beside their names, they initialed as to their position on a particular matter. This card showed that the document had concurrence of the Secretary of State, Secretary of Defense, chiefs of each armed service, the Senate and House Armed Service Committees' Chairmen. Each did so without comment.

"Shit," Briscoe thought. "This is serious. Surely to God, this is not going to happen. How am I involved?"

Closing the binder, he went to Burnum's desk. He pressed the intercom's button. Katherine answered with her name.

"Katherine, do you have the international coordination pages for this binder?" He asked, hoping his anxiety did not show in his voice.

"Yes, sir. Give me a moment to get it from the vault. Do you need anything else? I will be going by the break room. Coffee, maybe?" She asked.

"That would be great. Black please," he answered.

Returning to the sofa, Briscoe sat and put the binder on a coffee table. Leaning back, he looked at the ceiling while removing a cigar case from his inside, coat pocket. He liked his cigars as long as they were Partega number eight. While breaking its tube, he immersed himself into what he had just read.

"People like me do not get to read these things," he pondered. "That is unless there is a need to know. Who in this place thinks I need to know?"

Wringing this question through his mind, finally an answer came. It rang like the entire percussion section of the Philharmonic Orchestra, "Eisenhower."

He heard a light knock and Katherine entered. Under her arm, she carried another manila folder. She held a small, silver tray. On it was a glistening, coffee urn. A coffee cup, adorned with the president's seal, bounced lightly as she crossed the room.

"She is one gorgeous woman," Briscoe thought. "Her feet don't appear to touch the floor. What grace?"

She leaned forward to place the tray on the coffee table. Doing so, she revealed cleavage that hinted at hidden treasure. Next, she unwrapped the folder and withdrew a page.

"Sir, if you do not mind, I need you to sign for this," she said with a heart stopping smile.

"Certainly," he replied and took the document.

"It is a standard, controlled document ledger. Kindly print your name and sign beneath it," Katherine explained as she poured coffee.

Briscoe saw that she signed to get the binder. He completed its receipt section and returned it to her.

"Thank you sir. Just buzz when you are ready to return it. Anything else?" She asked.

"Nothing I can think of," he replied.

She turned and walked to the door. Briscoe noted how she dressed. Her clothes fit the way they should and they were in good taste.

"If she looks back as she goes out the door, I have a chance," he thought.

It was momentary but a glance nonetheless. Her smile leaped across the room as she departed.

"Okay Katherine, I understand," he thought as he lifted his cup.

A classification glared from the binder's cover, "Special Intelligence – Crypto." Briscoe puffed his cigar twice and lifted the binder's cover. This file had the same security arrangement as the other. However, its contents dealt with foreign affairs and the proponent was the Secretary of State. The first page was a non-concurrence by Great Britain followed by another from Japan. There was no surprise about Japan but the British, totally unexpected. Briscoe read their position with care.

Britain had strong interests in India. Also, they felt that Australia could suffer severely if the US initiated atomic warfare in Southeast Asia. In addition, they could see the European continent plunged into an atomic bloodbath because of subsequent attacks on the USSR and Communist China. Britain had major problems in the Middle East. The Suez Canal was of major concern. They considered the US proposal outlandish war mongering. They wanted no part of it.

However, France concurred without comment. Briscoe felt sure there were secret agreements between France and the US.

Burnum entered saying, "Well, I see you are into this at the international level."

"When can I see Ike," Briscoe said. "This is the dumbest crap I've ever read."

Burnum stared in disbelief.

Chapter Eleven

March 1939

First, one hopes to win; then one expects the enemy to lose; then, one is satisfied that he too is suffering; in the end, one is surprised that everyone has lost.
Karl Kraus (1874–1936), Austrian satirist. *Die Fackel,* no. 462/71

Vanessa felt comfortable on her father's arm. They ascended steps covered with bright red carpet. Soldiers, in black uniforms, stood rigid lining their route. The entrance stairway spread wide in concave arcs on either side. Although massive searchlights lighted their way, flaming torches blazed from tall, black stands. From inside, she heard a Viennese waltz.

Glancing over her shoulder, Vanessa saw limousines lining a curved drive. To gain access to the driveway required traveling through a large, barricaded gate. Men, in civilian clothing and wearing overcoats, checked each vehicle's occupants. When satisfied, they signaled drivers to proceed. Vehicles moved slowly to the stair's base. Here, passengers left their limousines assisted by tall, blond soldiers. They wore Nazi SS uniforms. Drivers took their cars to designated parking areas.

Outside the tall, iron fence, reporters took photographs and camera crews recorded film footage. Behind the media, a crowd strained to see those arriving. The group was enormous with lights reflecting white faces that disappeared into darkness far from the fence. They were Germans waving Nazi flags. They pushed and shoved hoping to obtain a glimpse of their savior, Adolph Hitler.

Germany's Führer brought their nation from depression to economic stability. Employment was high. The indignities of the Versailles' Treaty no longer brought shame. Hitler ignored it and he was their hero. Across Germany, his picture hung with honor in homes.

Sometimes Hitler would appear on a second story balcony for similar events. For now, the crowd had to watch celebrities. These privileged few had invitations. They arrived in elegant splendor.

Her father looked grand indeed. His long coat trailed split tails. He held a high, top hat cradled atop his left forearm. A wide cummerbund wrapped his waist and a large, diamond stickpin adorned his cravat. Ian looked ambassadorial.

They arrived at a large doorway 30 feet high. From their position, they could see into a great ballroom. Red banners, adorned with black swastikas, hanged from the ceiling. Sparkling chandeliers reflected light beams throughout the room. Before them a staircase descended into the great hall.

Vanessa gently lifted her Parisian gown ever so slightly. With her head up, never once looking down, she and Ian descended toward a reception line. The music stopped. She heard their names echo as a doorman announced their arrival. She felt eyes from the gathering sweep across her. Around her neck, she wore a diamond necklace studded with green emeralds that matched her eyes. It nestled an exceptionally large diamond at the top of enticing cleavage. The necklace was vulgar she had told Ian. He did not care. He wanted his daughter to look her finest. Whispers skipped across the room like tiny zephyrs across a pond. The music started.

An aide, wearing a formal mess jacket, caught her eye at the reception line's head. Beside him, she saw Hitler in a black, dress uniform of the German Army's elite guards, the SS. The aide whispered into Hitler's ear at their approach. A little smile grew beneath the Führer's square mustache. Gently, Ian placed his hand in the small of her back and moved behind her. The aide introduced Vanessa as she extended her hand. Hitler leaned forward and kissed it. She felt nausea engulf her. Yet, outwardly, she appeared delighted. She managed a petite curtsey.

"Welcome fraulien," Hitler said. "We are honored by your beauty. Your father understated your elegance. Please enjoy yourself."

Vanessa answered, using impeccable German, that it was her honor to join the celebration. Not a trace of Irish brogue tainted her response.

Next, to receive her was President of the Reichstag, and Commander and Chief of the Luftwaffe, Herman Göring. Devon was correct. The man was an oversized oaf. Yet, he was founder of the dreaded Gestapo and a man to fear. While he appeared a lummox, he was Hitler's named successor.

Down the reception line they went. It was as if she and Ian were traveling along a rogue's gallery. Next in line was Heinrich Himmler, Reichsführer-SS, chief of the German Police. She recalled what Devon told her that Himmler had once said.

"I know there are many people in Germany who feel sick at the very sight of this black (SS) uniform. We understand this and we do not expect to be loved. All those who have Germany at heart will and should respect us. All those who, in some way or at some time have a bad conscience in respect to the Führer and the nation, should fear us."

Finally she faced her nemesis, Reinhard Heydrich. Known as the "blond beast" among Nazis party members, he was her special danger. He founded the Nazis' intelligence arm as a young officer. If she was to accomplish her mission, this man had to be overcome. His spies were everywhere.

He considered himself a grand lover. She must use this to her purpose. She prayed he could not sense the fear in her.

Thankfully, Ian led her to the dance floor. He was an excellent dancer. The orchestra continued playing Viennese waltzes. There was a reason for this. Hitler, and his Nazis, was celebrating the first anniversary of their annexation of Austria. Austria was now part of Germany.

Last year, at this time, signs appeared throughout Austria banning Jews from restaurants, theaters, and other public gathering places. There were an estimated 200,000 Jews in the country. Devon told her of German plans to eliminate them. The Nazi's final solution was gaining momentum.

Ian danced in graceful arcs. When they passed a table of young SS officers, they would rise and bow. She felt their lust. She did not mind. Her intent was to make fools of them with it.

Onlookers became a blur as she recalled her last meeting with Devon. They never met at the same place twice. Always, the places were public and outside. Yet, some students noticed them. Those who knew them assumed they were lovers. This assumption was wrong.

"You must make certain your visit to Germany appears as a simple father-daughter venture. You are his guest and he is on business. If asked, say that you are majoring in international relations. Convince them you want to see how they achieved their depression recovery. Flatter them but do not overdo it. Do you understand?" He asked emphatically.

"Of course," she answered.

"Use the letter of introduction. It will get you a meeting with Joseph Goebbels. He is their Minister of Propaganda. Meeting with him will add legitimacy to your visit. He will be glad to make governmental changes appear to be the people's will. He will see your visit as a grand opportunity. Take advantage of it," he directed.

Continuing, Devon explained that she would meet a covert operative. Devon did not know where this person would make contact but he explained that she would know when it happened. The individual would recommend that she visit the Buergerbraeukeller in Munich. This large hall served excellent food and beer. It was one of Hitler's favorite haunts.

"This person needs photos of your father's order forms. It is essential that you make them available. From these, we can determine items that Germany must import. Do not worry about your father. He is not part of the Nazi movement. He is not aware of Germany's intentions. Nonetheless, he is naïve to think that their intentions are worthy," Devon said.

"Just one minute," Vanessa exclaimed. "Don't you even imply that my father is a fool. He is a businessman. He represents knowledgeable, Swiss clients. If they thought for one moment that he supported the Nazi regime, they would not hire him. So, you watch what you say or get someone else. Do you understand me?" She stated as her Irish blood heated.

"Calm down, Vanessa. I did not mean to imply that your father was a dupe. Do not worry about that one second. Get order forms available and get out in one piece," Devon explained.

"Remember this," Devon continued. "There are individuals in Switzerland whose only concern is making money. Whatever the source, they could care less. If the money comes at the cost of lives, so be it. I will do everything I can to see that your father does not fall prey to them. If I have to tell him, I will. You must leave that decision for me to make. You keep out of it," he stated.

Vanessa listened intently as Devon explained reasons for obtaining photos of her father's order forms. Germany lacked vital minerals. Foremost among these were copper and tin. Copying the orders would provide the source and quantity of these items.

Copper and tin were needed to make brass. Every artillery projectile required brass for it to function properly. These projectiles had a brass band around them. When fired, this metal strip formed a seal between the projectile and the weapon's barrel. Without it, gases from ignited powder could escape past the projectile reducing its range. Furthermore, copper was a primary component of ammunition for small arms and automatic weapons. Its need was immense for wiring, electronic devices and other assorted electrical needs. Germany had few copper and tin resources within its borders; thus, they must import it.

The special parts were for a specific purpose. They were for oil processing equipment. Germany probably produced the best precision, machined parts in the world. Yet, they had few used for petroleum refinement. Their energy base consisted mostly of coal of which they had ample supplies. Still, this was not enough to support their mechanized war machine. They needed petroleum and, eventually, they would have to take it. In the meantime, they would use imported parts as templates to produce their own refinery equipment. They would need this equipment in the near future.

"Vanessa, don't believe the Nazi's cooperation with the USSR. It will not last. Hitler will attack the Soviets. He will do it for two reasons. First, he wants control of oil from southern Russia. He will take oil fields at Baku in the Caucasus. Second, he hates Communists. He will invade. Count on it," he said with determination.

She felt fear at Devon's words. It was certain that she had crossed the line between curiosity and deadly serious. Her feelings were almost surreal.

"How did I let this happen," she thought. "She had a grand life and a certain future. Now, she was risking it all as a spy."

The music stopped again. Ian led her to the table where he had left his top hat before taking the dance floor. The hat was not there but three officers were. One of them was Reinhard Heydrich.

"Oh my God," she thought. "He will see through my ruse. I hope what Devon told me about him is true. If so, his ego will shield my purpose. His racial activities will blind him."

Heydrich hated Jews. During his youth, children taunted him by saying he had Jewish ancestors. He did not participate in group activities because of this. Instead, he concentrated on his studies. As he grew, he excelled at academics. Also, he displayed natural athletic talent. He became an award-wining fencer.

His father founded the Halle Conservatory of Music and was a Wagnerian opera singer, while his mother was an accomplished pianist. Young Heydrich trained seriously as a violinist, developing expert skill, and a lifelong passion for the violin.

His family enjoyed high social status and wealth. Their life style was well above that of most Germans. Heydrich took advantage of this. Nonetheless, rumors persisted about his ancestry. Yet, his physical characteristics were a perfect example of what Hitler considered a pureblooded German. He had a high forehead sweeping back to blond hair. His eyes were pale blue.

Too young to fight in World War I, he joined a group of racist war veterans. They relished degrading Jews at every opportunity. He participated to dispel rumors about him. Only 16, he roamed the streets attacking known Communist Party members and Jews.

Germany's defeat in World War I destroyed his family's social status and wealth. Their life became one of chaos. Heydrich found this hard to bear. He had to have an education. He turned to the military.

Treaty terms allowed practically no military development. Yet, there remained a small, elite naval force. With no money for an education, Heydrich obtained an appointment to Germany's naval academy. He did well and soon became a lieutenant in the navy's intelligence branch. A personal weakness would cost him his career.

Heydrich was a womanizer. His sexual exploits became notorious throughout the navy. Unfortunately, he impregnated a young lady whose family had influence. According to rumor, her father was a senior director at a major shipyard. A close friend of his was Admiral Erich Raeder. When Heydrich refused to marry the girl, Raeder withdrew Heydrich's commission for conduct unbecoming an officer and a gentleman. It was 1931.

What had brought his downfall with the Navy was his salvation with the Nazi Party. He met and became engaged to an active member of the party. She spoke to the "right people" and arranged his membership in Hitler's personal guard, the Schutzstaffe, or "SS."

This group of young soldiers had to have the correct physical characteristics. Heydrich was perfect. Moreover, he had formal, military training regarding intelligence matters. Himmler assigned him the duty to develop an intelligence branch within the SS. He excelled. Heydrich proceeded to create the intelligence gathering organization known as the SD (Sicherheitsdienst), or SS Security Service.

His ruthless ambition and racist beliefs brought quick rank. He became a brigadier general before age 30. He commanded the SD. His informer network was international in scope. He received special commendation for causing Stalin to slaughter most of his senior generals. By having his operatives spread rumors of an overthrow, Stalin had the officers killed. Heydrich was dangerous.

As Ian and Vanessa approached their table, Heydrich arose, as did the others. In one fluid motion, the notorious SS Intelligence leader clicked his heels, bowed and pulled a chair aside for Vanessa. He motioned her to have a seat next to him. Fear almost consumed her as she felt Ian's hand leave hers.

"Thank you general," she said. "You are most kind."

Heydrich introduced her to the other officers. One was an aide and the other a colonel on his staff. She nodded to each. While introducing Ian, she studied Heydrich.

"He is impressive. His manners are impeccable. His tailored, black uniform fits him well and his decorations add a special touch to his appearance. He is attractive," she thought. "I can see how he obtained his reputation."

"How long will you be with us fraulien," he asked.

Vanessa recognized this as a first test. As chief of intelligence, she felt sure he had a dossier on her and Ian. He knew their departure date and their itinerary.

"Unfortunately, we must leave in three days. I have to return to my classes. While father handles his affairs, I will be gathering information for my international relations assignment," she replied with a demure smile.

"Where do you attend school?" He asked.

"Another test?" Vanessa wondered.

"The Geneva Academy for Arts and Science," she replied.

"An excellent institution, my dear. You are fortunate. Only a few are able to meet their entrance requirements. What aspect of our county is of interest?" He questioned again.

Before she could answer, a wine steward appeared. He showed an unopened bottle to Heydrich by resting it label up in his palm. A simple nod caused the steward to remove its cork. He passed it to Heydrich. Leaning back slightly, Heydrich closed his eyes and sampled its aroma. Vanessa saw his jaw muscles bulge as he frowned. An eyebrow arced upward and he whispered to the steward. She watched the steward grimace, visibly shaken. He left in a rush.

Turning quickly, he glared into Vanessa eyes, he asked, "What aspect?"

"Economic recovery," she replied.

A miniature smile appeared on his face. Visibly relaxing, he shifted his position in his chair.

More comfortable, he said, "My dear, I seldom attend public events like this. They are crowded and a bore. My preference is to remain at my living quarters outside Berlin. It is quiet there and I can think. I do, however, like companionship. Perhaps you can visit during your stay?"

"That's possible," she answered with a widening smile.

"Did you have a particular date and time in mind?" She asked.

The wine steward appeared with another bottle. He showed it to Heydrich who nodded approval.

Attempting to remove the cork, the steward's hands trembled causing him considerable difficulty. With dread in his eyes, he handed it to Heydrich.

Heydrich glared at the obviously frightened waiter. Vanessa saw liquid accumulate beside the man's shoes. His trousers were wet and his knees trembled.

Without even an attempt to test the cork, Heydrich returned it. He shifted his gaze to Vanessa and smiled broadly.

"Pour the wine," he ordered.

As if in a stupor, the steward did not move. Evidently, he realized he could not pour the wine without spilling it. Fear consumed him for what Heydrich might do if he did. Finally, Heydrich's aide took the bottle and dismissed the brunt of Heydrich's play.

"This dance fraulien?" He asked.

"Certainly," Vanessa answered but remained seated.

Heydrich arose and removed her chair. He took her hand and led her a few steps to join other dancers. Vanessa noticed couples moving away and providing additional room. He was an excellent dancer but could not approach Ian's expertise.

She watched her father engaged in animated conversation. Ian was surely making contacts that would prove valuable for future business. His talent was a gift and it had made them wealthy. He did not have to work but it was his joy. He would not be Ian without it.

"Day after tomorrow?" Heydrich asked.

"Pardon?" Vanessa replied.

"We can meet day after tomorrow. I will have my driver come get you. What time is best?" Heydrich continued.

"It is too early to tell. My research must come first. Tell me how to contact you and I will let you know," Vanessa explained.

"That is good. However, I will contact you tomorrow evening. Perhaps you will know by then," Heydrich replied.

On their circuit around the floor, Vanessa caught sight of Hitler and Himmler engrossed in conversation. Hitler did not drink any alcoholic beverages of any kind. She thought this peculiar for a pure German. On his table, he had a seltzer bottle and some ice. Himmler drank coffee. The occasional glances from the two caused her to think they were talking about her and Heydrich. It was a sixth sense that she had. She knew it had to be.

Vanessa left the party disappointed. No one, other than Ian and Heydrich, danced with her. She thought surely, one of the two at the table with them, would ask. They never did. Additionally, none of the other officers approached their table.

The problem had to be Heydrich. Everyone seemed to fear him. She could not understand why. To her, his high pitched voice almost made him somewhat effeminate. Nevertheless, she knew she danced with evil that evening. If the choice remained hers, she would never see him again. Unfortunately, it was not.

The next morning Vanessa entered Joseph Goebbels office building. Construction workers scrambled about doing a complete renovation of the facility. It was appropriate for the Reich Minister for Public Enlightenment and Propaganda to have a building worthy of his status. He created Hitler as a savior and redeemer and Hitler knew it. Goebbels position in the Nazi party was firm. Hitler saw to that in 1933 when he appointed Goebbels to his position. He had total control of media throughout Germany. He held a tight grip on radio, the press, publishing, movies, and the other arts.

Vanessa made her way through a maze of scaffolds, drop cloths, extension cords, and other construction equipment. Goebbels office was at the end of a long, marble hallway. Lining its sides, busts of great men sat atop pedestals. She arrived at a receptionist's desk. The woman seated behind it met Vanessa's smile with a smile.

"Good morning," she said. "Can I help you?"

"Yes, I hope so. I have an appointment. My name is Vanessa McBeal," she explained.

The receptionist opened an appoint book and moved her index finger down a column of names. She found Vanessa's.

"Please go in and have a seat in the anteroom. He will be with you in a moment," she explained.

Reaching beneath her desk, the receptionist activated some electrical device. Vanessa heard a sharp clicking sound come from the door. It opened partially.

Picking up her briefcase, she moved the door aside and entered. The anteroom was luxurious. Grand portraits decorated its walls. The largest was one of Hitler. It dwarfed the others. An SS lieutenant occupied a large desk covered with telephones by another door. He arose to attention and genuflected, clicking his heels in the process. He greeted her and asked for her papers. Vanessa opened her briefcase and removed her passport and letter of introduction. She gave them to the lieutenant.

"Are these sufficient?" She asked.

The lieutenant examined her documents. He read her letter of introduction in its entirety.

"Have a seat," he said and entered the main office.

Vanessa sat on a sofa from which she could watch the office door.

"When will I make contact?" She wondered. "I have no idea whether the operative is male or female. I'm getting nervous carrying this case."

She examined its rectangular shape on her lap. Its genuine alligator exterior was most elegant. Her initials were embossed in gold leaf. Plus, it was lightweight and convenient. Nevertheless, as she moved her hand across it, she became apprehensive.

"If they only knew its purpose," she thought. "I would likely disappear."

Devon explained its structure before her trip.

"This case's basic material is plastic explosive. This is a recent development from a research firm in America. A reinforcing matrix, composed of magnesium fibers, gives it strength. It's totally harmless without a detonator," he said.

"However, with a detonator, it will explode with tremendous force. Additionally, it would burn with ferocious heat," he said.

Devon explained that her contact would have a similar case. When "invited to Munich," she was to place her case on the floor for an exchange. The new case would contain identical documents.

"Fraulien, come with me please," the lieutenant said. She had not seen him open the door.

"Stupid, how stupid. I'm daydreaming when it could cost me my life," she thought.

Goebbels appeared larger than expected. However, she noticed that his desk was on a raised platform. From his position, he looked down at everyone. When he came from behind his desk, she saw his disfigured foot.

Off the platform, face to face with her, she was taller by six inches. Yet, he had a powerful voice that belied his runt stature.

"Runt is a correct description," she thought. "He's the type to have a Napoleonic complex."

There were no surprises from the man. He extolled the virtues of Hitler as if he was a deity. He moved aside a portion of one wall to reveal a movie projector. Goebbels showed films of Germany's youth movement. She watched displays of the "Nordic" types Hitler explained in his book.

"The same damn book that got me into this," she thought.

She stayed for lunch in Goebbels private dining room. He sat at the head of a large table 12 chairs from her. They were the only persons in the room. Goebbels exercised his resonating voice in order for her to hear. He provided details of how Hitler moved Germany from depression to a world, economic power. The Nazi party was the salvation with Hitler as its leader. Without Hitler, they would still be a depressed nation with the Versailles Treaty boot on their neck.

"In 1936, the world witnessed Germany's greatness in Berlin at the Olympic games," he said.

"Yes, and you got your asses kicked," she thought.

After lunch, the meeting ended. She entered the long hall with workers busy around her.

From behind, she heard a man's voice say, "While in Germany you must visit the Buergerbraeukeller in Munich."

Turning slowly, she sat her briefcase by her right foot. Another was already by her left. She watched as a nondescript man, by his dress obviously a carpenter, slide her case beneath a drop cloth. She took the new case and left the building. The entire event took seconds.

Ian was not at their hotel when she arrived. Vanessa did what she could to relax. She examined the replacement case. It was an exact duplicate down to the finest of details.

"Oh, I'm so glad to be rid of the other one," she thought. "It was damning evidence if caught with it. There would be no way to explain it. It would have meant the end for me and father."

She undressed for her bath. She removed her toilet articles and placed them on a large, marble stand in the bathroom. Full-length mirrors flanked the stand on both sides. She could not resist admiring her lithesome body. Her athletic activities kept her in excellent condition. While slim, she was not overly so. Her firm, upturned breasts fell away to a flat stomach. Her long legs ended above small ankles. Removing pins from her hair, she shook her head. She watched waves of red flow across her alabaster shoulders. Here and there, freckles sprinkled across her skin. Yes, she was pleased.

Remaining chaste had been difficult. Twice she almost succumbed but realized doing so would have been an affront to her mother's teachings and her faith. She would wait and take comfort that she did.

Frederick was her strongest temptation. She knew she loved him. Yet, they had only met the previous Christmas. She hoped to see him in the spring.

Nonetheless, the situation between England and Germany seemed to get worse each day. Hopefully, Chamberlain had matters under control. If not, Frederick would not be allowed to visit her. He had warned that getting leave was becoming more difficult.

She prepared her bath. She swirled scented oils into the sunken tube's warm water. A mild soap, with an aroma of roses, mixed freely with the oil and water mix. She entered the bubbly liquid using four steps on the tub's end. Relaxing, she spread her arms across the tub's rim. Her hair remained dry, held in place by a turban formed from a towel. She floated while she dozed.

"Vanessa, you in there my girl?" Ian asked.

Partially awake, Vanessa answered, "Yes, father."

"My dear, I will be missing supper for a meeting. I will likely be late. Either call room service or the dinning room here has excellent fare. I will meet you for breakfast. Please don't wait up for me," Ian said from outside her bathroom door.

"Oh, I am sorry Father. Won't it wait?" She asked.

"I'm afraid not. It's an important order or I wouldn't miss supper with my darling," he answered.

"Well, all right then but it will be breakfast at nine," she said disappointedly.

"I'll lock your door on my way out. Love you darling," Ian explained.

She heard the door close and Ian's key turn in the lock. She realized she had slept soundly for she never heard him enter.

Vanessa walked slowly up the tub's steps, drying herself as she did so. The oversized bath towel felt soft and warm. She pulled it together in front. The large towel overlapped so she pushed a portion down between her breasts. The towel remained in place as she sat before a large vanity mirror. She brushed her hair with long, gentle strokes. Each wave in it glistened with a vibrant sheen. She heard a knock from her entrance door.

"Fraulein McBeal?" A familiar voice asked from outside her suite's door.

"Yes," she answered hesitantly.

"Room service," came the reply.

"There must be a mistake. I did not order," she explained.

"This is a special order," the voice advised.

"Father has been here many times," she thought. "It would be like him to order something special for me. One moment, please," she answered.

Vanessa donned an elegant bathrobe. Her intent was to have the waiter leave it in her room but decided against it.

"Leave it, please," she directed.

"Yes Fraulein," the voice said.

Waiting a few moments, she opened her door. A room service cart was in front of her. It held shining silver dishes with large covers. A vase held roses. It was lovely.

"Good evening, Fraulein. The dinner for two is this hotel's renowned specialty. You will like it," Reinhard Heydrich said as he stepped from his unseen position beside her doorway.

Vanessa's initial reaction was total freight. She gasped at Heydrich's unexpected entrance from nowhere. She grabbed one side of the door's facing with one hand and clutched her throat with the other. She was speechless.

Heydrich looked on with an amused grin. He stood legs apart, as if posturing for a photo. He held a riding crop behind his knees with one hand on each end. He laughed once and stepped forward to support Vanessa, who appeared about to faint. He helped her to a nearby divan in the apartment's foyer. She leaned against one of its pillows catching her breath.

Heydrich pulled the cart into the room and shut the door. Vanessa, recovering quickly, realized her situation.

Angrily, in perfect German, she yelled, "Get out of here you Nazi pig."

In one fluid movement, Heydrich responded. Vanessa never saw the blow coming. Darkness consumed her consciousness.

Satin pressed against her face as an all-consuming pain spread from her abdomen. It was so powerful that nausea caused her to choke. She pulled her knees to her chest and moved into a fetal position. Rolling onto her side, she saw Heydrich standing in front of one of her bathroom mirrors. He was adjusting his tie.

Noticing her reflection, Heydrich spoke without turning.

"Ahh, Fraulein, you have a sharp tongue. Our evening could have been most pleasant but you had to spoil it for yourself," he said as he turned sideways to examine the tuck of his shirt. He turned to check the other side.

Vanessa emitted a low, moan filled with pain. Her nausea became worse.

"Cover yourself, my dear. You are most tempting," Heydrich said as he pulled on his jacket. He turned to face her as he buttoned it.

Only now did she realize she was nude. Heydrich's silhouette went out of focus as she tried to find her gown. She was too weak and her sickness too strong. She retched and the pain continued. Heydrich's voice echoed as if from inside a deep canyon

"My dear, we shoot spies. As long as Ian McBeal provides what we need, he will not come to harm. This very moment he is arranging to provide us copper. We do not care who knows. The machined parts are another matter. It would be a terrible shame for him to face a firing squad. You would not want that now would you?" Heydrich asked with sarcasm wrapping each word.

Heydrich gripped his jacket's bottom on each side and pulled. Watching his mirror image, he turned slowly to be sure it fit neatly beneath his belt. Gripping his side arm's holster, he pushed it into a satisfactory position. He removed his hat from a nearby stand and walked to the bed's side. He reached and lifted Vanessa's chin.

"Have a safe journey tomorrow. Give Herr McBeal my regards. Be sure that your papers are in order before you approach the border. They will be checked. I look forward to your next visit."

Vanessa heard a door close in the distance. Blackness and peace returned.

Chapter Twelve

May 1948

Love is a great beautifier.
Louisa May Alcott *(*1832–88*), U.S.* author. *Little Women,*
pt. *2,* ch. 1 *(*1869*)*

With her hood removed, Xuan's white hair cascaded onto her stooped shoulders. Like ivory, it framed a face reflecting insufferable agonies. It showed ravages and shame beyond concept. A morass of grief and fear existed where once beauty lived. Minh Thanh was incapable of grasping what Xuan had become.

Placing her hands on her shoulders, Minh Thanh wept as she turned her mother's face to the flickering candlelight. From within her heart, profound pain spread.

"Oh, what have they done to you?" She asked between gasping sobs.

Pulling away, Xaun shuffled toward a chair, breathing heavily as she went.

"Come, sit with me," she said with a raspy voice. "There is much I have to tell so that you will not become a victim of this evil place."

Minh Thanh heard dread in Xaun's voice. Where once there had been joy, it was now grief. It permeated Xaun's presence. This could not be the mother she once knew. This person was a stranger.

Xaun's gnarled hands gripped her chair's arms as she slowly settled into it. She groaned.

Swiftly, Minh Thanh went to her. Falling to her knees, she placed her head in Xaun's lap. She reached around her, pulling close. She felt little flesh. Her mother was taught skin over bone, nothing more than a shell.

Minh Thanh felt Xuan's fingers stroking her hair. She remembered how, many times, she brought peace to her this way. This time was different. Her fingers were bent and twisted, hard knots where once joints had been. Peace did not come.

"Dear one I perished when your father died. The murderers took my body to their prison. My heart remained with him," she said.

"French police took me to Hoa Lu. They built a prison where our ancient emperors used to live," Xuan explained. "They respect nothing."

"Our resistance was a major problem for the Japanese and French. They wanted to know whom, in Muong Valley, was attacking them. They found an informer in our village. This treacherous person told them about your father. That's when they arrested and killed him," she continued.

Minh Thanh could not believe that anyone, in their hamlet, would inform on her father. He had respect and people knew him to be honorable.

"Who did such a despicable thing?" Minh Thanh pleaded.

"It was your fiancée. You did not marry did you?" Xaun asked.

"No," Minh Thanh answered sadly. "They became angry when I would not stop mourning grandfather. They spread lies and brought great dishonor to me."

"They did that to hide their shame. They could not face you after what their son did," Xuan explained. "When the truck came for me, our neighbors gathered to protest. When I did not see your fiancée's family among them, I knew. The truck took me to Hanoi."

Continuing, Xuan spoke with evident sadness, "We left our valley with one truck. When we came to other villages, more people joined us. They either put them on our truck or another full truck joined the convoy. Along the way, Japanese soldiers had checkpoints. French truck drivers stopped for the night at these places. At one of them, a Japanese officer ordered us out of our truck. He took two women from another village into a nearby building. We heard them screaming. We waited for two hours after the screams stopped. The officer came from the shack and ordered us onto the truck. A father of one of the two women asked when they would return. A soldier with the officer killed him with a bayonet. The officer laughed."

Xaun, obviously shaken, stopped and sighed as her hands trembled. She was weak.

"You must rest. Stay here I have something for you," Minh Thanh said.

She arose and went outside where her bicycle lay. Behind its seat, there was a small bundle. Minh Thanh removed it and returned to her mother.

"Please stay still. I will make some broth. I also have some rice cakes," Minh Thanh said.

Earlier, when she first entered, she noticed a glow at one end of the room. It was charcoal in a makeshift stove. A clay pipe, from outside, entered a small, iron cylinder. Another pipe extended up through the ceiling. Next to the stove, charcoal lay in a storage bin. She removed two pieces and placed them on the embers. As they heated, they created an updraft that pulled in fresh air from outside the shack. She opened her bundle and removed a piece of chicken with fat on it. She also had four rice cakes, each about the size of a saucer.

She needed water. Outside, near her bicycle, there was a barrel for rain collection. Minh Thanh took a small bowl and went to it. She returned with rainwater and rushed to the fire. Mixing chicken and water, she placed the container above glowing coals. Soon, she had a hearty broth.

Again, she exited. This time to get her bicycle. She moved it inside a small foyer, where she left her shoes earlier. Now, she could attend to Xuan.

"I don't have much but it will give you strength. One of my cousins gave me food. It will be ready soon. Please rest," she implored.

Xuan did not respond or move and remained slouched in her chair, her face toward her lap.

Frightened, Minh Thanh felt one of her wrists and detected a weak pulse. She returned to the small fire.

Minh Thanh said a prayer repeatedly, while stirring the slowly heating broth, "Hail Mary, full of grace, the Lord is with thee. Blessed art thou among women.

Blessed is the fruit of thy womb Jesus. Holy Mary, mother of God, pray for us sinners now and at the hour of our death."

Getting a tiny cup from a nearby shelf, she filled it with steaming liquid and moved to her mother. Gently, she raised her head by tilting her chin. Using both hands, she placed the cup near her lips.

"Sip some. Please," she pleaded as she touched her mother's lower lip with the cup.

Xuan's eyes moved almost imperceptibly as she sipped some broth. She took more.

Next, Minh Thanh broke a small rice cake and slipped a piece between Xuan's lips. She began to chew. She swallowed more broth. This loving dance continued until the cup was empty and rice consumed. Xuan slept.

Minh Thanh dozed on the floor by her mother, her rosary entwined among her fingers. She slept an innocent's sleep.

Diem entered without waking them. It was almost dawn. He placed a large bag near the fire and left. There was a note attached to the container.

A beam of morning's light penetrated dingy curtains and, filled with smoke and dust, fell upon Xuan. Without moving, she saw Minh Thanh asleep at her side.

"Oh, sweet one," she thought. "So many times I've held you to my breast. I have protected you. Your father, and his father, died to give you peace. The fight is now for your brothers."

Sighing softly, she closed her eyes as a tear slowly found its way down her cheek. She leaned backward in the chair.

"These are terrible times," she thought. "When the British came, the Japanese surrendered. For awhile, we were free. Ho Chi Minh's independence declaration did not last. The French returned and now the fighting is worse than at any other time. Why can't they leave us alone?"

Xuan recalled her prison time when Japan ruled. She did not think that there could have been a worse fate. The trip to prison cost many lives and they were the lucky ones.

"The Japanese occupation made servants of the French," she recalled. "These 'Vichy' French were scum. They killed my husband and put thousands of us in prison. It was not that long ago when they arrested me. I will never forget."

Xuan remembered her trip. As the trucks traveled to Hanoi, more prisoners were loaded onto them. They did not allow them to tend to their needs. They slipped in their excrement and retched at the stench. Foul air engulfed them. Death found the elderly first. Their bodies remained aboard, as heat permeated their midst and flies swarmed.

Finally, they reached Hanoi. The arrival was a welcomed relief but it did not last.

They saw little light as drivers backed their trucks to open doors. Room existed for tailgates to fall. As they tumbled from the filth, a glimmer of sun struck them. For most, it would be the last they would ever see.

Inside, ancient corridor floors were wet from stifling humidity. From somewhere ahead, screams echoed along dank, tunnel-like halls. Herded through a maze, they arrived at a large room. Dim light came from one bulb surrounded by a metal cage. Finally, there was space to move.

Suddenly, they were on the floor, knocked there by powerful water streams. Attempts to stand were futile. Everyone writhed, pounded by strong, stinging water from fire hoses. Men in French police uniforms held hoses. Two men on each leaned forward to offset strong water pressure. Prisoner's rotten clothing flew from their bodies leaving most naked.

The water stopped as guards stepped among them. They used their batons to prod them to their feet. Those who did not move fast enough were struck repeatedly. Those on their feet, staggered through an exit to another room.

A powdery cloud descended upon them. Above, on walkways, guards emptied drums of an eye burning insecticide over their balcony's edge. They gasped for air while more guards, wearing masks, rushed them to another door.

Forced into a single line, Vietnamese behind a counter threw two pieces of clothing at each prisoner. At the counter's end, each received a wooden bowl. They moved continuously. Those who slowed, or stopped, received baton strikes.

Xuan's nightmarish trek ended in total darkness. An iron door slammed shut behind her. Her companion was silence for two months as madness tore at her mind.

"Surely, this is hell," she thought.

Once a day, someone opened a small slot in the iron door. This opening was at floor level. They took her empty bowl and gave her a replacement. It contained gruel made from rice, water and grease.

Stumbling in the dark, she found a narrow trough at her cell's rear. She used it to relieve herself. Every few days, she could not remember how many, a guard sprayed water into the indentation from an overhead opening. There was barely enough light to see a grate. Some of the mixture went into this outlet and disappeared. If the purpose was to remove body wastes, it failed. The water scattered most of it. This became a terrible problem when diarrhea struck.

Attempts at sleep were constantly interrupted. Flies crawled over her body as they tried to enter her nose and mouth. They were incessant, causing a constant buzzing, background noise. She felt her sanity going.

Two guards pushed the cell's iron door open wide. Light filled her dismal pit and she could not see. Each guard grabbed her emaciated body under her armpits. They dragged her to another room. Her feet and legs failed to function. She could not walk so they pulled her. They left her on the floor. Whimpering she curled into a fetal position. How long she stayed like this she had no way of knowing.

Later, she felt a boot pushing her. She opened her eyes enough to see another guard.

"Get up," he ordered. "Clean yourself and get dressed. Everything you need is on the stool."

When the guard left, she half rolled to a position to see the room. A large, three-legged stool sat in a corner. Stacked on it were clean clothes, towels, soap, and sandals. Arching her body, she got to her knees and sat upright. The room appeared to spin. She put one hand on the cool, tile floor for balance.

From her new position, she saw a showerhead on one wall. Except for the stool, the room had no other furnishings. She crawled to a spot immediately below the shower outlet. Gradually, she was able to remove her clothes and climb to her feet.

Turning a valve brought a steady stream of cold water. She stood still, head down, and let it wash through her hair and over her. Next, she quenched her thirst. While doing so, she examined her body. She saw that her pelvic bones protruded causing two peaks beneath her skin. Areas, between her toes, appeared red and raw. Slime oozed from between them. Her teeth were loose and her gums bled. She had to get clean.

Xuan took soap from atop towels and clothing on the stool. She washed and scrubbed. Although clean, a smell remained. It was the odor of her cell.

Exhausted, she stumbled toward the stool. Removing items on it, she sat to rest. Moments later she placed her feet upon braces supporting the stool's legs. She dried each foot removing dried blood from between her toes. Her skin, once smooth, had a leather-like texture. Her gums continued to bleed.

As she dressed, she noticed that the cloth was silk. She had never owned silk garments. These felt good to her skin. While putting on the sandals, a Frenchman entered. He was not a guard.

Dressed in white, he wore the uniform of a French officer. She did not know his rank. He stood, with legs spread, and a fist on each hip. In one hand, he carried a swagger stick. His trousers had fine pleats. His boots shined as if they were patent leather. On each shoulder, a braided cord encircled the juncture of his arm to his torso. One cord was gold and the other blue.

He had a thin, narrow mustache and wore wire-rimmed glasses. His glasses were pinch-nose and appeared ready to fall at any moment.

"I must apologize for your treatment. As soon as I learned that you were in solitary; I ordered your release. I believe your name is Xuan?" He asked.

She did not answer.

"Oh well, good enough. Follow me," he instructed, as he stepped from the room.

Slowly, she tried to stand. Her legs trembled and she felt dizzy. She kept one hand on the stool to avoid falling. The French officer returned.

"I'm sorry," he said. "I should have known. Please have a seat. I will return in a moment."

Xuan sat. Her trembling stopped and she felt much better.

"What is this?" She wondered. "This is most unusual. Frenchmen, particularly military, do not treat her people with such kindness. They never apologize."

Again, the same Frenchman entered. This time he had a long, cigarette holder that he held between his left index finger and thumb. His swagger stick remained in his right hand. Again, he posed with his spread legs stance.

"In here," he barked. "Come along now, in here."

Two guards entered. They wore uniforms same as other guards. In addition, they wore pith helmets. They stared at Xuan with obvious disdain.

"About your business now. Help the lady. Follow me," he ordered.

With an incredulous look, the two approached her. Each grabbed an arm and pulled her from her perch.

"Easy now men, easy," came the command.

Xaun hardly felt her feet as they followed the white peacock. The two guards dug their fingers hard into her arms. She winced as they grinned with pleasure. This continued until they came to an exit into a courtyard. She squinted at bright light blazing through the door. They continued across but she saw little because she had to close her eyes to avoid bright light. Her eyes could not bear it.

Across the courtyard and down another hall, they stopped at a door. The peacock pushed it open and she felt cool air flow over her. They entered.

"Thank you men," the peacock said. "Return to your duties."

Looking around the room, Xaun saw other women dressed like her. They seemed bewildered and fearful. Some sat in easy chairs while others stood, lining the walls.

Overhead, large fans turned circulating air. Coolness came from these. There were sofas, easy chairs, tables with lamps and carpet covered the floor. Varnished mahogany walls seemed covered with glass plate. Xuan never saw such luxury.

"Take a seat my dear. I will return shortly," the peacock instructed. "I will arrange transportation. Meanwhile you must rest."

He went to those standing and walked them to comfortable chairs. He never remained quiet. His chattering continued as he helped others to seats. Once each had a seat, he walked to the door. He stopped and placed remains of his cigarette in a trash can. Carefully, he opened his tunic and placed his cigarette holder in a hidden pocket.

Turning to face them, he said, "Ladies, please rest. I am arranging transport. However, I will have light refreshments delivered before you leave."

He closed the door and they were alone. Each looked at the others with wide-eyed fear. They expected the worst and it would come.

Minh Thanh moved in Xuan's lap. Xuan had her hand in her daughter's hair. She started stroking it as she did so many times in the past.

Slowly awakening, Minh Thanh remembered where she was. Swiftly, she looked at Xuan who smiled.

"How long have you been awake?" Minh Thanh asked?

"I have been dozing. I feel much better Thanks to you," she answered.

Minh Thanh noticed the large bag near the charcoal stove. She saw the note and got up. She walked toward it with suspicion.

"Don't fear," Xaun said. "It has to be from Diem. He leaves something every week. I owe him so much. He is a loving brother-in-law. He makes my life bearable at considerable risk to himself."

Minh Thanh removed the note and read it. Smiling she gave it to her mother. While she read, Minh Thanh opened the bag. Inside she found fruit, dried and fresh, plus cans of fish, beef, and other assorted items. One cardboard container held chocolate bars. Also, writing on the containers was in English. Each can and bag had a quarter moon emblem on it. In large type, the words "Property of the United States Government" appeared.

Pointing to the phrase, Minh Thanh asked, "Mother, what does this mean?"

"My darling, the United States helps France. They provide food, medical supplies, weapons, and many other valuable items to them. Diem takes it from the warehouse where he works," Xuan explained. "If he gets caught, he will be in serious trouble. Few Vietnamese have important jobs like him. He would lose it and likely be executed as a spy. He knows how to alter documents so that missing items appear to go to French military units," Xaun answered.

Minh Thanh put charcoal in the makeshift stove. Soon she had hot tea ready. She served Xaun and then prepared some that she tasted.

"This tea is not good," she said. "Our tea tastes much better."

"My feelings were the same when I first tasted it. Nevertheless, I learned to like it. On the black market, one container like that costs $150 American," she explained.

Smiling broadly, Minh Thanh replied, "It tastes better already."

Happiness filled Minh Thanh's heart. Her mother looked refreshed compared to the previous evening. Nevertheless, she was not the mother she remembered. Walking to her, Minh Thanh embraced Xaun.

"Mother, I love you," she said, her voiced filled with obvious joy.

"My darling, you are the sun in my sky. My greatest hope is that you will still love me when I explain my long absence," she whispered, her voice filled with emotion.

"I will always love you. Nothing will ever destroy that. You do not have to tell me anything," Minh Thanh said as she pulled Xuan even closer.

"We will have to see," Xuan replied as dread engulfed her.

Xuan told of her truck trip, solitary confinement, and the peacock incident.

"When the peacock left, we talked. Most prisoners had treatment similar to mine. A few were not in solitary and related events, of which we were unaware," she told Minh Thanh.

"Where were you for so many years?" Minh Thanh asked.

"I was in prison," she answered. "I did not have to be. The circumstances causing me to not return are of my own doing. I hope you understand."

Her mother explained that the prison's commanding officer was a French colonel. The peacock was his aide. The guards were French.

"A Japanese officer inspected every two weeks. I never saw him because I was in solitary confinement. The women who had regular cells saw him. According to them, he seemed concerned for their welfare. He asked many questions. They were not interrogations. He wanted to know if we had enough food. He also asked if we received good medical care. They all agreed that he seemed like a good man. Eventually, I met him and he was not a good person. He was more evil than the French. He was the cause of my long absence," Xuan explained.

Continuing, Minh Thanh's mother told of the peacock's return with transportation. The vehicles were confiscated French sedans. The drivers were Japanese. It took 15 cars to move them as a group.

The trip was not long. They arrived at a group of buildings inside a high fence. Japanese soldiers manned guard towers around the buildings. There was a smaller fence inside the outside fence. The distance between the two was about two meters. Guard dogs roamed free between the two.

A barrier blocked the main gate. Japanese guards manned this entrance. When the sedan convoy arrived, the guards stood aside and waved them through into the compound. The guards leered as they passed. Many laughed and waved.

"They seemed happy to see us," Xuan said. "I knew this was not going to be a good trip when I saw their stares."

Xuan told how their vehicles passed between outer buildings and into an area with privacy fences. It was impossible to see behind them. The convoy stopped at an outer fence that blocked an entrance. The prisoners left their sedans. The peacock led them around this fence and into an opening in the main fence. The outer fence kept anyone from seeing through the entrance.

Once inside, the prisoners were amazed. Thick green grass grew everywhere and palm trees lined walkways. Adjacent to one building was a large swimming pool. Around it, nude Japanese soldiers basked in the sun. Some saw them and waved. Japanese music came from speakers located around the pool area.

The peacock promptly moved them into a large building. They entered a room much nicer than the one they waited in at the prison. In the center, a long table held foods of every description. The centerpiece was a large, roasted pig surrounded by fresh fruits. The variety seemed endless.

Along the wall, stood Vietnamese waiters holding silver trays. They smiled and bowed as the prisoners entered. The peacock told them to take seats, which they promptly did. However, most could not take their eyes from the table. The aroma was overpowering.

Xuan stopped her description as her newfound strength waned swiftly. She needed rest.

Minh Thanh prepared a meal while her mother slept. While doing so, she heard someone talking outside near the door. She went to investigate. Two young Vietnamese boys were unloading rolls of hemp strips. They stopped at Minh Thanh's approach.

"We're here to get the twine," one said.

From Minh Thanh's expression, they knew she did not understand. The older of the two explained that they delivered hemp that Xuan braided into twine. He knew where she usually put the twine and would get it. He walked behind the rain collection barrel to a large storage bin. From it, he removed balls of twine and placed them on their cart.

"We will be back the day after tomorrow with more materials," the older one said.

They pushed their cart toward the warehouse, leaving Minh Thanh staring at a large stack of hemp. She placed it in the bin. She returned to her meal preparation. Xuan still slept.

"What is Spam?" She wondered. "The picture on the container looks strange."

She quickly determined how to open the can. Taking the key from beneath, she used it to twist the metal strip. Soon it was open and she tasted the contents.

"This is delicious," she said aloud to herself. "I will chop this and put it with noodles."

"You will tire of it soon enough," Xaun said. "I've been eating it for almost two years."

"Mother, I didn't mean to wake you," Minh Thanh said apologetically. "You need more rest. I will wake you when this is ready," she said.

"Did they bring the hemp?" Her mother asked.

"Yes, and they took twine from the outside bin," Minh Thanh answered.

"After our meal, I must work," her mother commented. "I braid hemp into twine for use at the warehouse. The work pays for this place. It's not much but my needs are few," Xuan explained.

"We will eat and then you can show me how. I will help" Minh Thanh replied.

Sitting on the floor, the two picked through their noodles and canned meat. They held their bowls close to their mouths and used chopsticks to eat. They deftly transferred morsels with ease as they chatted. Joy was in Minh Thanh's heart. Xuan hoped that her revelations would not destroy their love. It could happen.

Chapter Thirteen

September 1958

Here dead lie we because we did not choose
To live and shame the land from which we sprung.
Life, to be sure, is nothing much to lose;
But young men think it is, and we were young.
A. E. Housman (1859–1936)

Dale Zane saw an opportunity and took it. By increasing his classes, he could graduate early. His medical preparation program was difficult but he realized he could do more.

"That's a big load for any student," his counselor said. "Twenty-four hours a semester is double the normal class schedule. Moreover, the courses you are taking are difficult. You will have a laboratory class four days a week. If you weren't doing so well, I would not agree with your proposal."

"Sir, I can handle it," Zane said almost pleading. "Let me give it a shot for one semester. If it doesn't work, I'll drop some courses."

Next, with his counselor's approval in hand, he went to the Professor of Military Science and Tactics, Colonel Mulholland. Anxiously, he waited in his outer office.

"Shit! This will work. I know it will," he thought. "I missed my chance to save a year in high school. I'm not going to make that mistake again."

Upon entering Mulholland's office, he stepped in front of his desk and rendered a crisp salute. Mulholland returned it. Standing rigidly at attention, Zane said, "Sir, I have a special request."

"At ease, Zane. Pull up a chair and relax. What can I do for you?" Mulholland asked.

Zane explained that he could be graduated a semester early. To do this would require that he take one semester of junior and senior ROTC the same year. He would have sufficient hours for graduation by the end of the first semester of his senior year. He gave a detailed listing of every course and his proposed schedule.

"Has your counselor seen this?" Mulholland questioned.

Reaching into his pocket, Zane retrieved his counselor's permission sheet. He handed it to the colonel. The sheet did not state that it was only good for one semester. And, Zane was not about to tell the colonel.

"Zane, I see a real problem. Department of the Army (DA) will have to authorize your commissioning as a second lieutenant. The rest of your class will get their commissions in June. That is when they will have the paper work done. There are no provisions for this. I don't see us being able to get DA permission for an early commissioning," Mulholland explained.

Zane, anticipating this, said, "Sir, if they don't want to commission me, the National Guard will. They said when I had my diploma to come see them. They would pin my bars on that day."

Mulholland sat quietly. Zane could see that he was mentally working his way through regulations. If regulations did not provide for it, Mulholland did not do it. Zane knew Mulholland to be a good man and was always willing to help any student when he could.

"Sir, how about this? If I get a letter from the registrar stating that I will graduate early, you can include it with a request for an early commission. Will that help, sir?" Zane asked.

"All right Zane, go see the registrar. While you are doing that, I will make some telephone calls. Don't be disappointed if we can't get this approved," Mulholland said.

"Yes, sir! Right away, sir," Zane said as he came to attention. "Permission to leave, sir?" Zane requested.

"Get out of here Zane," Mulholland directed.

Saluting, Zane responded, "Sir, yes sir," and rushed from Mulholland's office.

Lester Shultz peered above his wire rimmed glasses at Zane, "You want what?" Shultz asked.

Lester Shultz had been at Wofford forever, or so it seemed, as registrar. Wofford professors, some with tenure, remembered Lester Shultz from their days at the Spartanburg College. No one ever graduated from the school unless Lester Shultz said so. He was the keeper of the keys, the guardian of the sheepskins, and numerous other titles bestowed by students. Now, Zane was trying the man's patience with what Shultz considered a "hair-brained scheme" to circumvent, time honored procedures.

"Mr. Shultz, I can do it," Zane exclaimed. "It's there on the proposed class schedule. Just look at it. It will work," Zane continued.

"Mr. Zane, sit down," Shultz ordered as he took the proposal from him.

Zane sat. While doing so, he watched the hawk-nosed registrar slide a ruler down each page. Line by line he looked for errors. Finding one, he grinned with satisfaction.

"Thought so," he mumbled as he continued his examination. After thoroughly inspecting each class and its hours, he looked up at Zane.

"Mr. Zane," he said while beckoning Zane to his desk. "There's a problem with this. You added the hours wrong. You are actually over by one hour. Now, tell me again what it is that you want?"

Jubilant, Zane grinned with pleasure. Now, he had to get the needed letter.

"Sir, Colonel Mulholland needs a letter from you stating that I can graduate early with this schedule," Zane explained.

"And, why does he need that?" Shultz asked.

Zane explained in detail the nature of the letter. Mulholland would send it with a request for an early commission. The army would not arrange for one unless he had documentation to show he would get his diploma early. Satisfied, Shultz said he would have the letter the following week.

Exploding from the registrar's office, Zane ran to call Janice, his fiancée. This accelerated graduation would have a major impact upon her plans. Wedding plans were Janice's forte.

Zane's first date with Janice Bolling was blind and an accident. She had a twin sister, Joyce. He called for a date with Joyce but Janice answered. Getting the two confused, he arranged to date Janice the coming weekend. Later, this would prove to be most disconcerting because they lived less than a block from his home.

Carla, who lived next door to Zane, was an old flame. When they were courting, he drove her to Spartanburg High School each day on his way to Wofford. Carla knew Janice and Joyce Bolling. She had Zane give them a ride along their way. Zane paid no attention to the pair. It was only later that he realized he had been giving them rides for almost a year. Now he was going to marry one of them.

Janice was a hit with Zane. They began dating regularly. They had many things in common. She loved the outdoors, which Zane found appealing. Their first date was a fishing trip with her parents. Her father was most intimidating because he was a sheriff's detective. Furthermore, he was a big man and quick to let a person know his mind. Zane avoided him.

Marriage was not a priority. Having to work, and his heavy class load, kept Zane from making any commitments. He would not agree to marriage until he could provide for a family. Now, he could see a future with the army. With an income secure, he could agree on a date to marry.

"Oh, this is great," Janice said, bubbling with excitement. "When can we get married?"

"The first semester ends in January. They should have my commission ready by then. What do you think about 14 February, Valentine's Day?" Zane asked.

"Yes, oh yes! I cannot wait to tell Joyce. When will you ask Dad?" She asked with a doubtful tone.

"Do I really have to?" Zane replied.

"Sure you do. I cannot get married unless Dad says it is okay. When are you going to ask?" Janice questioned again.

"How about I wait until he's in a good mood. This weekend, maybe," Zane said with some dread in his voice.

"Robbie, had to ask Dad. You will too," Janice said.

Joyce, Janice's twin, married Robbie earlier in the year. Janice had suffered through her sister's bragging about leaving home. Also, Janice had arranged various social functions for her sister. Now it was her turn. Janice

looked forward to the showers, making plans and other rituals associated with marriage. "Oh, this is going to be so much fun," she squealed. "I must get to the jewelry store and select my silver service and china."

While Janice prepared for her wedding, Zane spent the following months-attending classes. Classes were more difficult than anticipated. Zane spent an average of three nights per week as all-nighters. His goal was to qualify for medical school.

He arranged with the military to hold his orders, if he went to medical school. The army agreed. They needed doctors and they would gladly defer him. One thing that could not have a deferment was marriage. Things were going to get a lot harder if he went to medical school and tried to support a family. Fate would have it that Zane's future was going to have some major changes. Lester Shultz would see to that.

"One hour, you are short one hour," Shultz said. "You cannot graduate in January."

Zane felt numb. Thoughts raced through his mind and went no where. Speechless, he glared at the registrar. The nausea came. Small perspiration beads formed on his forehead. In ten weeks, he had to graduate, marry, and be on his way to Fort Sill, Oklahoma. Unable to raise enough money for medical school, he was to go on active duty as a second lieutenant. Department of the Army sent orders for his assignment to the field artillery. The basic officers' course was his first assignment. Now, none of it was going to happen.

"But, you wrote a letter certifying that I would have enough hours. That letter went to DA and they have approved my commission. I am getting married three weeks after the semester ends. You changed the hours from what I provided. It's your mistake. Why in the hell should I pay for your screw-up?" Zane asked, his voice a chilling whisper.

Shultz leaned back in his chair as Zane leaned across his desk. He could see Zane's jaw muscles growing taught as he ground his molars. Obviously, he was trying to maintain self-control. Zane's face was now no more than a few inches from his. Zane lowered his voice to an almost inaudible hiss.

"This is wrong. You make it right. I will return in the morning and you will make it right," Zane said.

He whirled and left Shultz's office, gently closing the door. Now, he had to face Colonel Mulholland. The receptionist met him at the entrance to the R.O.T.C. building.

"Mr. Zane, the registrar just called the colonel. He will not see you. I highly recommend that you leave. You do not want to see him. Believe me, you do not want to see him," she said with sympathy in her voice.

Howard went with Zane to the Trade Winds. The night ended with Zane hugging his commode at 3 A.M. Unable to attend class; he remained in his room the entire day. His mother took numerous telephone calls for him. And, he was not about to tell Janice. He figured there must be a way out of his predicament. There was not.

The following day Zane had a note from Dean Lambert in his student mailbox. It stated for him to come to his office.

"Well, I guess cutting class is now going to bite me in the butt," Zane thought.

"Go on in Mr. Zane, he is expecting you," the receptionist said.

Reluctantly, Zane knocked twice and entered. Lambert was at a window looking across the campus grounds. He stood with legs spread and his hands clasped behind his back. He was rocking forward and backward slightly by bending his knees. He was humming a tune that Zane did not recognize.

"Have a seat Dale," he said.

"First names, what gives?" Zane wondered.

Taking a seat on the leather sofa, Zane watched Lambert's back. He continued his gentle, rhythmic rocking while humming. Zane waited for what seemed an hour but was only seconds.

"Why didn't you tell Mr. Schultz about the research course?" Lambert asked, still gazing out the window.

Time slowed for Zane. Typing noise from the outer office stopped. All was silent.

"Sir?" Zane asked.

"Dr. DeWitt just left. He told me about your registering for the one hour, biology research course. He explained that he forgot to turn in the registration slip. Why didn't you tell Schultz?" Lambert asked again.

Zane's mind whirled. He could hear the clock above his head click as its second hand snapped the seconds.

"He's testing me," Zane thought. "I never signed up for any research course. This is my way out of this mess. Yet, if I lie, I am in big trouble if this is a test. Also, if DeWitt did tell him that I was in a research course and I tell the truth, DeWitt could lose his job. He doesn't have tenure."

The clock became louder, resounding seconds like a bass drum.

"Sir, I never registered for a research course," Zane said with a grimace.

"Thank you Dale. You may go," he said without turning.

Dazed, Zane left. He went directly to Dr. DeWitt's office. His door was open and he saw Zane approaching. He smiled with a wide grin and said, "Come on in Mr. Zane. I looked for all day yesterday. You have never cut a class of mine. I really did need to talk to you. I called your home twice. Your mother said you had the flu. Your counselor came to see me yesterday morning about the one-hour mess. Do not worry about that. I have taken care of everything. However, you do have to get to work. You must do a semester's work in a few weeks. I know you can do it without any problem."

"Oh my God," Zane thought. "He did it. He lied to Dean Lambert. Now, DeWitt will be on the street. Lambert will fire him for sure."

Overwhelmed by the irony of the situation, Zane leaned against the door's frame. He pulled his texts to his chest and gazed at the ceiling.

After a long sigh, he half cried and laughed as he replied. "Sir, I've really dropped my dick in the dirt on this one."

With an intense look of concern, DeWitt asked, "What do you mean?"

Zane told him details. He expressed his fear about DeWitt lying for him. He did everything he could to impress upon DeWitt his sincere grief for exposing him. DeWitt's expression never changed throughout Zane's explanation.

"Don't worry son," he said. "Dean Lambert is my godfather. His father and mine have been life-long friends. They fought in World War I together. I am sure he will not fire me. He will likely suspend tenure for a year or two but I can live with that. But know this, you now occupy a special place in relation to the dean. You showed exceptional integrity and Lambert will not forget it."

Zane entered DeWitt's office and took a seat. The reality of his situation became clear. He would register for a one-hour course the second semester of his senior year. He would not attend classes. Moreover, he would have to pay for the one hour. His scholarship now belonged to another student, since he was to leave in January. The earliest he could graduate was June.

Furthermore, he had his marriage taking place in February. He could not cancel it. Janice had the church reserved. She already had her wedding dress. The invitations were in the hands of those to attend.

He had to find them a place to live. They could not live with their parents. This would be a significant expense increase. They had to have more income. Janice could continue working which would help. Nevertheless, he had to have a full-time job.

"What a damn mess," he thought.

DeWitt explained his research assignment. Zane had to gather insects found in the Piedmont section of South Carolina. His task was to preserve and classify each one. DeWitt set a minimum of 1500 insects to complete the project.

"There's not 1500 insects in the world," he thought.

Janice took the bad news in stride. The marriage would still take place. They cancelled plans for a honeymoon. Zane would be bug hunting.

Furthermore, Zane solved his employment problem. He had been selling aluminum cookware at night. The job required that he sell to single women. He had sold enough cookware sets to pay a large portion of his college expenses. His sales manager assigned him exclusive rights to a nearby region. He and Janice selected an apartment close to the area to help with travel expenses. Two days before the wedding, another disaster struck. Janice's maternal grandmother died.

Her grandmother was the granddame of her mother's family. Her demise cast a dark cloud throughout her relatives. It was unthinkable to have a large wedding one day and her funeral the next. After much serious consideration, Zane and Janice agreed to a small, private wedding after the funeral. Only their closest friends would attend. Immediately after the ceremony, they would leave for their apartment in a nearby town. Janice would continue her job and Zane would continue his studies. The situation was bittersweet, indeed.

During Zane's final semester, a previous mentor contacted him. It was Coach Ramsey. He called Zane at home.

"Hi Dale, you been doing okay," Ramsey said.

"Well, sort of I guess," Zane replied.

"I received a call from Dean Lambert about your situation," Ramsey said. "He explained about the one-hour screw-up. He also told me you would not be going to medical school. Why?"

"I cannot afford it coach," Zane answered.

"Can you get free about 1 O'clock tomorrow?" Ramsey asked.

"I hate to tear myself away from the bugs. Sure, I can arrange that. What do you have in mind?" Zane responded.

"Meet me at First Federal Savings Bank," Ramsey said.

Zane agreed to meet Ramsey as he requested. He arrived 15 minutes early but Ramsey was already in the bank talking to one of its officers. Ramsey spotted him and beckoned him to join them.

"Mr. Littlejohn, this is Dale Zane. He is the Wofford student I was telling you about. Dale, this is Albert Littlejohn. He is a senior vice president," Ramsey explained.

Littlejohn extended his hand and said, "Hi Dale. I've heard some good things about you."

Zane shook hands and replied, "I hope coach didn't go into some of the bad things."

Littlejohn smiled and told Ramsey and Zane to follow him to his office. Once inside, Littlejohn took a seat behind a large, kidney-shaped desk. The interior reeked of importance. Its shining, paneled walls held various plaques, photographs and framed awards. Of particular interest to Zane was a diploma from the prestigious Wharton Business School.

"Mr. Zane, I've talked with Dean Lambert and Coach Ramsey at length about your situation. They tell me that you cannot attend medical school. They say you cannot afford it. Are they correct?" Littlejohn asked.

"Yes sir, that's correct. Vanderbilt approved my application because Doctors Waldron and Bemayer sponsored me. They wrote Vanderbilt on my behalf. They provided the endorsements I needed. However, I cannot afford the microscope required for the first year much less the tuition," Zane explained.

Lambert opened his desk and removed a loose-leaf binder. He glanced through its vinyl-covered pages. Looking at Zane, he said, "Your transcripts are most impressive. To maintain a 3.8 grade point average in a Pre-Med Program is no easy task. I'm impressed."

"Thank you, sir," Zane answered.

"Dale, if the decision was mine alone, I would advance the cost of your schooling. However, I presented your situation to our directors. They agree that your success is likely a sure thing. Nonetheless, they must answer to depositors. If you attend one year, and maintain your current grades, the bank will loan you enough to complete medical school," Littlejohn explained.

"Sir, at the best I will have to work for one year to raise enough money to attend the first year. Will your offer be good for two years from now?" Zane asked

"Unless there is a depression, it will be available," Littlejohn answered.

Ramsey and Zane excused themselves. They stopped outside to discuss the situation. Zane expressed his deep gratitude for Ramsey's assistance.

"Coach, this is the second time you have helped me. I appreciate it and I want you to know I will do my best," Zane told Ramsey.

"I know you will," Ramsey answered. "Stay in touch. If you need help, contact me," Ramsey said while shaking Zane's hand.

With his research course and graduation behind him, Zane sought other employment. He would continue selling cookware but he needed a consistent income source. He applied to numerous companies throughout the Piedmont. Many personal interviews took place but no offers were forthcoming. Zane could not understand why he did not receive any employment offers. A personnel manager at one organization told him why. He still had an impending military obligation.

"Mr. Zane, others won't tell you but I feel we have an obligation to be up front with you," the manager said. "If we hire and train you for a career, you will leave us. You have a two-year, active duty obligation. Until you complete it, your chances for a permanent position are almost non-existent. I'm sorry but that is the truth."

Zane did not tell him that his intention was only to work one year. However, it was obvious that he would not be able to save enough for medical school. He discussed the situation with Janice.

"Hon, that's the situation. I think I should contact the Army and ask for active duty. What do you think?" Zane asked.

"I agree," she said. "Do what you have to. I will support you decision."

The army told him to report for duty in ten months. This was unacceptable. Zane contacted Senator Mendel Rivers of South Carolina. He was chairman of the Senate Armed Services Committee. Five days later, he had orders to report to Fort Sill, Oklahoma in two weeks. Dale and Janice left South Carolina in September 1960. They in no way realized the adventure upon which they were embarking. They conceived their first child across Oklahoma's border in Sallisaw. Later the same evening, they watched Senators Richard Nixon and John F. Kennedy debate in their campaign for the United States Presidency. Both candidates would have a direct impact upon their lives.

Chapter Fourteen

February 1953

The ability to get to the verge without getting into the war is the necessary art ...
If you try to run away from it, if you are scared to go to the brink, you are lost.
John Foster Dulles (1888–1959)

"Eisenhower looked strange in civilian clothes," Briscoe thought. "After their years together in Great Britain, he knew Eisenhower to be a warrior. And, modern warriors wore uniforms. However, Ike was now a politician. So, it was only logical that he wore a politician's uniform. Still, he seemed out of place in it."

"Lanny, what a pleasure to see you again," Eisenhower said, while pumping Briscoe's arm. "I need your special talents again."

Briscoe noted that the president did not look well. He had lost weight and his eyes sat in darkened sockets. However, he still had his wide, winning smile.

"Being President is a killer job," Briscoe thought. "Why would anyone fight to be one?"

"Same old Ike, huh Mr. President?" Briscoe replied. "No time for chit chat, let's get to the point."

Eisenhower laughed aloud. "I save chit chat for the golf course," he answered.

"How can I be of service Mr. President?" Briscoe asked.

"Lanny, do you remember Claire Chennault?" Eisenhower asked.

"Yes sir. I remember that he formed the Flying Tigers and flew against Japanese forces in China. If I remember correctly, he was a maverick to some people. He conducted combat operations before the United States declared war," Briscoe replied.

"That's right Lanny. He was a fine general officer when I was a major. His men named him 'old leather face,'" Eisenhower explained. "The man was a true visionary. In matters concerning aviation, he had insight when the rest of us were blind. After the war, he remained in China and supported the Nationalists. He formed an airline called China Air Transport or CAT for short. General Chiang Kai-shek lost his war with the Communists and moved his forces to Taiwan. Chennault went with him and took CAT," Eisenhower continued.

Turning away, Eisenhower activated a small, desk switch. He spoke into his intercom, "Hold all calls."

"Yes, Mr. President," someone replied.

Eisenhower left his desk. Without Briscoe hardly noticing, Eisenhower maneuvered him to a nearby sofa. Eisenhower began pacing the room.

While Briscoe watched, Eisenhower continued, "We've bought CAT Lanny. Including the two of us, no more than ten people know this. We call it Air America and the airline continues to conduct commercial operations. However, Chennault had money problems and we saw a grand opportunity in Southeast Asia. We saved his airline but now it also conducts covert operations for the United States. Our operatives have their fingers on the pulse of the region. Lanny it is going to the Communists. While France fights the Viet Minh in northern Viet Nam, Ho Chi Minh has troops taking Laos."

Eisenhower stopped pacing. He turned and faced Briscoe.

He said, "We're organizing and equipping the Laotian military. Our government must help them. Also, my guys tell me that the French are going to lose in Viet Nam. We have lost North Korea. Laos is catching hell. Soon the Viet Minh will control Viet Nam. We must stop the Communists Lanny. We must," Eisenhower said.

Placing his fists on each hip, he looked at Lanny with a nervous mix of anxiety and fear.

"Lanny, you have to help. Can I count on you?" Eisenhower asked, almost pleading.

Briscoe's planned protest about atomic weapons melted before Eisenhower's winning ways. Answering quickly, Briscoe said, "Mr. President, you know you can. Tell me what you want."

"I cannot do that," Eisenhower answered. "You will receive word very soon. Just stay loose. Thanks Lanny. I appreciate this very much. You are helping stop a world menace."

An intercom chimed. Eisenhower answered, "Yes, Nell?"

"Senator Barclay is here Mr. President," a soft voice said.

"Thanks Nell. Give me one minute," Eisenhower replied.

Before he realized it, Briscoe was with Neil Burnum and on his way to his office. Briscoe turned over one trash can with his crutches and stumbled into a number of desks. He knew that onlookers thought he was spastic. Before long, he saw Katherine who greeted him with a warm smile.

"Have a nice visit with the president Mr. Briscoe?" She asked.

"I sure did. He is quite a guy. Does anyone ever tell him no?" Briscoe answered.

"I've not heard of anyone. However, he has only been in office a short time," she said.

Briscoe was vaguely aware of Burnum trying to say something. Now, his effort was of little interest. Katherine had his complete attention.

"Sir, you need to go with Mr. Burnum. Please be careful until you shed the medical garments," Katherine advised.

"You bet," Briscoe replied.

Once in Burnum's office, he explained to Briscoe his contact information. Burnum did not provide mission details. He claimed not to know anything about them. He did tell Briscoe that an operative would make contact soon. Briscoe would know the person as "Turk."

Burnum asked Katherine to have a driver come for Briscoe. She stopped Briscoe when he left Burnum's office. She helped him with his topcoat.

"Please leave your pass at the gate," she explained. "A driver is waiting for you at the door where you entered earlier. Do you need me to show you the way," she said as her hand left Briscoe's coat pocket.

"No that's not necessary," Briscoe answered. "I know the way. Thanks for the help."

Upon reaching the hallway leading to his exit, Briscoe stopped and looked across the room. Katherine was still standing and gave him a demure smile.

"All right," Briscoe thought excitedly.

A taxi awaited him at the guardhouse. Once in the cab, Briscoe checked his topcoat pocket. He retrieved a small piece of paper. There was a telephone number, a date, time, and a large question mark on it. A large K appeared at the bottom. Briscoe understood.

Later, at his apartment, he had time to reflect on the day's events. He could not believe the United States would use atomic weapons in Asia. Moreover, they intended to do so without any effort through the United Nations. Surely, the Secretary of State would exhaust other approaches before using atomic weaponry.

Briscoe chastised himself. He did not use his opportunity to protest such a plan to Eisenhower. Briscoe tried his best to visualize what national interest was at stake in Southeast Asia. While he was not knowledgeable of circumstances surrounding Viet Nam, he did know a great deal about China.

He attended classes at the Army's War College. This was necessary to gauge the caliber of instruction given to students. The college asked him to function in a visiting fellow capacity. He would present lectures on cryptography and assess intelligence capabilities of various nations. China was one of them. His research gave him a broad perspective about the Asian leviathan. Their threat was Communism.

Mao Tse-tung used its teachings to gain power. He espoused Communism throughout his country as a way to liberate his people. After World War II, he left his stronghold and drove nationalist leader, Chiang Kai-shek from the continent.

However, Briscoe saw no future for Communism. As a way of life, he felt sure it would fail. In undeveloped countries, with a population of "have-nots," it had appeal. Yet, in the long term, it destroyed initiative. He felt that, one-day, its beliefs would implode with disastrous results for the country involved. However, the philosophy represented a direct threat to United States' interests. Communism would likely spread throughout Southeast Asia. He had to fight it and Eisenhower knew this.

Furthermore, he had to accept Eisenhower the politician. As a military leader, he gave instructions without fear of reprisal. As a politician, he could not give Briscoe mission instructions. If someone caught Briscoe in a covert operation, Eisenhower had protection. He had plausible deniability. When Briscoe did similar missions for Eisenhower in Europe, his orders came directly from Ike. Now, the situation was quite different.

That night, Briscoe telephoned Katherine. His anticipation ran high as he listened to the rings. She answered.

"Hi, this is Lanny," he said.

"Well, hello," she replied.

He explained that he knew of a family-style, Italian restaurant with excellent food. The meal was eight courses and required at least four hours to consume. He asked if she would like to go with him on the date and time of the note. Feigning surprise that he selected a time when she was free, she accepted. It would be two days before he would meet her. He was most pleased at the prospect.

Meanwhile, he had to determine who sabotaged his car. He felt sure that McNeese played a major part in that. Also, he had to correct the poor security at McNeese's office. He figured his best bet was to have another agency do an unannounced inspection. He had friends at the Army Security Agency (ASA). He would contact them. They would rip McNeese a new one. However, there was a problem with McNeese's involvement. To Briscoe's knowledge, McNeese had never heard of him until he telephoned.

"The man did not have time to do anything," he thought. "Perhaps it was someone else. Nevertheless, he is the only lead I have. While ASA wrings him out, I will do a background check. Delaney can handle this with ease."

Bryan Delaney worked at the Central Intelligence Agency, better known as the CIA. Delaney was a former OSS operative during World War II. Briscoe worked with him on a dangerous operation involving Army General Mark Clark.

Clark traveled with a group brought to Southern France by submarine. The Allies needed to know if the Vichy French would help the Nazi's repel an allied invasion. In particular, their concern was the allied invasion of North Africa. Briscoe went ashore in France to arrange a meeting between General Clark and a senior, French general. Delaney was an undercover OSS officer on Vichy France's General Staff. He was Briscoe's contact to arrange the clandestine gathering.

The meeting took place at a small beach house. General Clark, and some troops, came ashore by rubber boat. While France did not agree to allow the Allies to come ashore unopposed, General Clark did obtain valuable information. He learned details of Vichy France's naval forces and troop dispositions in North Africa.

The operation almost failed when stormy weather kept General Clark's group from returning to their submarine. The rubber boats were no match for the boiling surf. They hid on the beach for days, waiting for the weather to abate. They did not know if the submarine would be in place to retrieve them or not. Finally, the group was able to leave for the sub.

They still had to launch their boats by pushing them through the surf. General Clark undressed to do this. Clark forgot to take his clothes with him. Delaney found Clark's trousers on the beach after their departure. They were marked with the general's name. Delaney destroyed them. If a German patrol had found them, their subsequent investigation might have exposed Delaney and the French general.

After the Allies invaded Normandy, Delaney fought with the famous, French saboteur Bigeard. Delaney had the respect of French resistance fighters. France recognized Delaney's efforts by decorating him with their highest award after the war.

Delaney met Briscoe at Arlington National Cemetery. It was normal for Briscoe to visit Arlington. He visited at least once a month. He walked among the fallen heroes to visit lost friends. The weather was clear and sunny as if a harbinger of spring. He almost did not recognize Delaney.

"Good Lord Bryan, look at you," he said in amazement. "How much weight have you lost?"

"About 60 pounds Lanny. You are looking well considering your recent accident. What can I do for you?" He asked.

"You know about the accident do you?" Briscoe answered.

"You know D.C. Lanny. Word gets around," he said smiling.

They walked among the tombstones, talking as they went. It was quiet, with only flags snapping in the breeze. Briscoe's pace was erratic because of his cast and crutches.

"Bryan, I need your help," Briscoe said. "I need a background on a guy named McNeese. You should have a file. He is a contractor representative on the beltway. He is handling some projects for which I have oversight. He's sloppy Bryan. Moreover, I'm certain he's dirty," Briscoe stated.

"Glad to help Lanny, but shouldn't the FBI handle this?" He asked.

"No," Briscoe answered. "You are the right people, if this guy is doing what I think he is."

"Well, if he is a defense contractor, we have a file. I'll let you know what I find," Delaney said.

"My brakes failed because someone cut one of the lines. I know McNeese did not do it. However, I think he knows who did. I need to know his close associates. There's something rotten going on and we need to stop it," Briscoe explained.

"You've got it my friend," Delaney said.

"Oh, by the way, you still married?" Delaney asked.

"Not for six years. We separated for two and the divorce was final four years ago," Briscoe replied.

"Sad to hear it. You and Rosalind made a fine couple. How's the kids taking it?" Delaney asked.

"Not too bad. Their step-dad is a jerk-off. He's an accountant in San Francisco. He and Rosalind have a place in Oakland. Next year my son starts college. Jesus, I'm getting old Bryan," Briscoe said.

"Tell me about it. The younger guys at the company do not seem dedicated. They want to start at the top. Seems like they feel they don't have to pay their dues," Delaney commented.

"Bryan," Briscoe replied. "I have to eat the charges against me resulting from the wreck. We cannot afford to let the locals know what happened. If I do not survive another accident, odds are that someone took me out. Let the right people know," Briscoe continued.

"For sure my good friend. I will be in touch about McNeese. Meanwhile, you stay alert. Are you carrying?" Delaney asked.

"No, I'm not but I will after tomorrow. They are removing this damned cast," Briscoe explained.

The two arrived at a walkway leading to the main exit. Delaney departed while Briscoe remained. He wanted to check the burial site of a close friend. While walking the manicured grounds, he noticed a momentary light flash from a row of trees outside the grounds. Not able to determine its source, he stepped behind a statue. This placed the statue between him and the observed light glimmer. He waited.

"Hell, I cannot stay behind this thing forever," he thought.

Lingering for a few more minutes, he stepped from behind his cover. Nothing happened.

"Guess they figured I made them and left," he wondered.

Nevertheless, he moved from obstacle to obstacle as best he could to maintain cover. Finally, he reached his vehicle. Walking around the auto, he checked fine hairs placed on each door. They were undisturbed. If one was misplaced the slightest, he would know that the car was likely rigged to explode. A detailed look underneath revealed nothing.

"I am getting tired of this fast," he mused.

Briscoe drove to his safe house. This was a small apartment on Washington's West Side. He kept it for those times when he wanted to disappear. It was his haven and no one at NSA knew about it. He closed the main garage doors from the inside and secured them with a steel bar. Another exit gave access to the apartment's kitchen. He reached inside and turned on the lights. He stood a moment in the darkened garage. Everything appeared in order. He entered.

He crossed the living room and entered his bedroom. Adjoining it, there was a full bath. The building was quite old, constructed before there was indoors plumbing. It was necessary to raise the bathroom's floor to install plumbing. This left a small step up to enter. Briscoe knelt on one knee. He pressed on the right end of the panel covering the six-inch rise in the floor. The panel opened.

Briscoe removed a steel container three feet long and two feet wide. He took it to a kitchen counter and opened it. Inside were two handguns and a rifle. One handgun a .357-Magnum, five shot revolver and the other a .45-cal., semi-automatic. The rifle had four subgroup assemblies.

He removed the semi-automatic and two ammunition clips. Taking a towel from the counter top, he spread it on a small, kitchen table. He placed the pistol on the towel. Next, he removed a container from the steel case and sat. Opening the container, he did a quick inventory of cleaning supplies.

First, he removed the weapon's ammunition clip. He then pulled the pistol's barrel assembly rearward in one quick motion. A bullet sprang from its chamber and landed on the towel. Lifting the pistol, he applied pressure to its barrel and swiftly removed it from its slide. Soon the disassembled weapon spread across the table.

Holding the weapon's barrel toward a light fixture, he examined its interior. It shined without a mark to mar its surface.

"Ah old girl, we have spent some time together haven't we," he said aloud. "I risked a lot for you because you've always been true," he continued with a small chuckle.

After the war, the Army asked for the pistol's return. They were not happy when he told them it was lost. He signed a statement of charges and the Army deducted the pistol's cost from his pay. It was worth the price. While in England, a Jewish refugee from Germany customized it for him. Its outward appearance was that of Army standard issue. However, in use, there was no similarity. It fit him as though it was an appendage. A once powerful recoil no longer existed. At 40 yards, he could put six rounds inside a six-inch circle. The Jewish gunsmith worked miracles. Briscoe was not about to return it.

Briscoe quickly assembled the pistol after cleaning each part. He pushed a clip into its handle and quickly chambered a round. He placed the weapon in a shoulder holster, leaving both on the table. He placed the other items in their storage site while coffee percolated on the stove.

Filling a cup, he returned to the table. Many evenings he went through this same ritual, daydreaming about Rosalind.

"I had it coming," he thought. "When the war ended, she wanted a home and children. She deserved them because she waited for me. Others were not so lucky; their wives dumped them while they fought the war. They came home to nothing."

Staring into his cup, he recalled when problems started. "All was well until I started doing research. I was home every evening and she liked that. Our weekends were ours to do with as we saw fit. I am the one who started staying at the laboratory late in the evenings and on weekends. She was right to leave," Briscoe determined as usual. He went to bed.

The telephone on his nightstand dragged Briscoe from his slumber. He looked at his beside clock. It was 3 A.M.

"Who in the hell could be calling me here? Few know about this place. And, of those only two have the phone number," he thought as he grappled for the shrieking telephone.

"What?" He answered.

"Check the partegas. Turk needs some," an unknown voice said.

There was a click and then a dial tone. Briscoe replaced the handset on its stand. He felt for his pistol. It was where he could reach it quickly. He drifted to sleep trying to determine the message's meaning. He had his answer early that morning.

Briscoe removed the steel bar from his garage doors and opened it. Moving to his car, he checked the fine, black hair stretched between the driver's side doorpost and door. Reaching low, he removed it. Before entering, he glanced at similar devices on the other doors. They were inside and intact. He checked his other tampering indicators. They were undisturbed. He opened his door with reassurance.

Opening the glove compartment, he placed two ammunition clips inside. He saw a partega cigar as he did so. He removed it and examined its protective cylinder. It was okay. He opened it. He saw a small message written on the seal's underside.

"Mount Vernon – 03/14/ 1600 hours," it read.

"That's today," Briscoe thought.

Again, he examined the other three hairs. There was no indication of removal.

"Hell, how did he get in?" He asked aloud in amazement.

"Better yet, how did he get out? The garage door had an interior locking bar. Other apartment doors had deadbolts. This guy is good," he commented, as he backed from the garage.

He drove to Bethesda Navy Hospital northwest of Washington. An intern removed his cast. As he left, they advised him to not put much weight on his injured limb for a number of days. He promised he would not.

Briscoe drove southeast to Mount Vernon. Only 15 miles from Washington, the drive was short. He parked and walked up the hill toward President George Washington's former home. It was now a national monument. It was a major tourist attraction even during the cold and wet days of February. Tourist groups moved with their guides in various parts of the site. Others examined pamphlets deciding which portion to visit next. Many posed for photographs.

Briscoe sat on a vacant bench alongside one of the many walkways. He noted the time. It was 3:50 P.M., or 1550 hours, as military people preferred. After watching visitors for a few moments, he removed the Partega from his inside coat pocket. Lighting it, he leaned back with both arms stretched across the bench's backrest. He puffed the fine cigar with pleasure. Partegas were a favorite.

Darkness was near when Briscoe noticed a groundskeeper. He was a short, elderly man. Dressed in denim, he moved across the lawn impaling pieces of paper trash on a stick. As he neared, Briscoe unbuttoned his topcoat pushing it aside. Also, he opened his inner suit jacket to provide easy access to his sidearm.

"Evenin'," he said. "Is that cigar a blend smoked by Turks?"

"I don't think so," Briscoe responded.

The grizzled caretaker slowed. Briscoe noted his stooped stature and gnarled hands. Appearing to continue retrieving litter, the old man spoke again.

"Try something else. The hairs do not work," he said.

"Pan Am tickets and instructions will be at Washington National," he continued. "Be there on the 20th for an extended leave of absence. A contact will meet you on the plane. Good luck," he instructed, moving away from the bench.

Briscoe watching his contact leave. He continued removing litter that he put in a bag slung around his neck. His bag captured Briscoe's attention. He felt sure he could see a weapon's outline.

"That guy is dangerous," Briscoe thought. "I bet he would take a person down and not blink."

Next morning Briscoe found a note on his desk. It was from General Lehouse. He asked Briscoe to see him when he arrived. He waited an hour to see the general.

"Hell Briscoe, you just got here," Lehouse exclaimed. "What is this leave of absence business?" He asked.

Surprised, Briscoe did not respond immediately.

Bewildered, he thought, "How did he find out so fast?"

Gaining his composure, Briscoe answered, "Sir, you need to talk to George Burnum."

"Who is George Burnum?" Lehouse asked.

"He works in the White House," Briscoe answered.

"White House my ass! I run this operation not some ass kissing, aide to the President," Lehouse exclaimed.

"Get out of here," the general ordered.

Briscoe left. He never saw Lehouse again before his departure. However, he did get an "eyes only" memo. It said, "Forget going to court. The charges have been dropped." Briscoe sighed with relief.

The restaurant looked like a middle-income, frame home. Inside there were only a few tables. All tables had diners except for one. It sat in a corner with a candle for illumination. The headwaiter led Briscoe and Katherine to it. Briscoe intercepted the maitre de's attempt to seat Katherine.

"Why, thank you sir," she said.

Briscoe sat across from her and asked for the wine steward.

"Right away sir," the maitre de replied.

"This is so nice," Katherine commented.

"I think so," Briscoe answered. "Prepare yourself for a treat. We may be here four hours to enjoy all the courses. The food is absolutely great."

"I like good Italian. There are many Italian restaurants in Washington. A lot of them do not prepare food the way they do in Italy. They try to adjust it to American tastes," she noted.

"Not here. This is the real thing. I do hope you enjoy it," Briscoe explained.

Briscoe was not disappointed. From the anti pasta through a succulent desert, the wines were superb. He knew Katherine enjoyed their excellent repast. Their four-hour meal took six. Later, they danced until 3 A.M.

His GSA leased vehicle was poor transportation for a princess. However, he knew she understood. He took her to a small brownstone in Georgetown. She invited him in and they had homemade cappuccino. It was excellent. For the first time in many years, he was at ease with someone. Katherine had the unique quality of being a good listener. Also, she was quite articulate.

"But what the hell," Briscoe thought. "She didn't get to be an executive secretary at the White House being a dummy. I like her. She is a true lady."

During the evening, he told her about Rosalind and the two children. Katherine explained that she was a widow. She lost her husband during World War II. They had no children. They planned for some after his return that never happened. She reverted to using her maiden name, Ingersoll.

Briscoe detected a deep sadness within her. She had lovers in the past. One was married with children. Her mistakes lingered and her trust did not come easy. While they talked she played music from her pre-war record collection. One or two songs made her eyes misty. Briscoe understood and she knew it.

He told her he would be on an extended leave of absence. She agreed to see him before he left. Often her hours at the White House ran late. She would call him.

Dawn approached as he drove to his apartment. He could smell her perfume in the car. As he entered, he whistled one of the songs she played. There was an extra bounce in his step. Unfortunately, he had no idea how long he would be gone or even where he was going.

Unfortunately, the last time he saw her was from his airplane. It was taxing for takeoff. She stood behind a barrier fence waving a scarf. He returned her wave but never knew if she saw it. Formosa, now Taiwan, was his destination and he could not tell her.

"Soon Katherine. As soon as possible," he thought.

Chapter Fifteen

November 1939

It's easy to forget what intelligence consists of: luck and speculation.
Here and there a windfall, here and there a scoop.
John Le Carré (1931)

In Munich, Johann George Elser ate his dinner. A waitress saw to his needs as she had during past weeks. The Buergerbraeukeller served superb food and drink. Elser had his usual after dinner beer. At 10:30 P.M., 30 minutes before closing, he picked up his carpenters' toolbox and went to the front counter. He paid his bill.

However, instead of leaving, he went to a rear staircase. Shrouded in darkness, it led to a balcony overlooking the main gallery. He climbed them unobserved. Construction material covered the area. He moved behind it and took refuge in a work closet. He waited. In Elser's mind, it was Hitler's time to die.

By 11:30 P.M., the cigar lady fed some cats. Next, she made sure tables were ready for business the following day. She locked the building not knowing of Elser's presence. Elser listened for 30 minutes. Hearing nothing, he left his hiding place with his tool chest. It was in this container that he brought explosives into the building. He also used it to remove waste from his work. No one ever suspected.

Moving aside some boards, Elser revealed a cavity within a large column that provided support for the gallery. He put the final portion of his explosive device in place. He examined the new plastic explosive with its magnesium matrix. He placed it over conventional explosives taken from a munitions factory. He set the timing mechanism to activate during the evening of 8 November. Elser knew Hitler would be in the building that evening. German's leader always kept his Buergerbraeukeller meetings. He had for many years.

Hitler had a deep, sentimental attachment to the Buergerbraeukeller. It was during his years with the Brown Shirts that he used it for meetings. He held rallies to organize the Nazi party in his beloved beer hall. Now that he was Führer, he made regular visits.

Furthermore, the visits were always the same. Crowds began gathering by 06:00 P.M. Thousands of avid supporters filled the building. Many remained outside to listen to the public address system. They knew Hitler's speech was near when the band played the Badenweiler march. Nazi troops carried their blood flag high through the milling crowd. Inside, at 10:30 P.M., Hitler would arise and speak. He continued until 11:00 P.M. when he would leave for the airfield and his flight to Berlin.

Elser set the timer for 09:20 P.M. He knew that Hitler would be with his senior staff at the drinking tables. Hitler did not drink alcoholic beverages, not even beer. However, Himmler, Goebbels, Ribbontrop and Sepp Dietrich drank their share. Hitler did not mind and he reveled in tales of previous exploits with them. They helped him establish the Nazi party. They deserved to enjoy themselves.

Finished with his work, Elser returned to his hiding place. He waited for morning. It was quiet and he had time to think. He recalled how and why he was going to kill the Führer.

Most Germans considered Hitler their savior. Elser did not. He was a union member. He was a skilled carpenter. Yes, there was more work now but so what. Since Hitler's rise to power, he worked more but for less. He couldn't remember a single pay raise during Hitler's time as their leader. Others had the same problem but would not admit it. They seemed to want another World War. Hitler was giving it to them with his invasion of Poland. Elser knew about war.

Elser was too young for World War I. At 15, he began training to be an iron turner to support the war effort. When Germany lost, he had to leave his job. He was destitute and without work. He needed a skill and carpentry was a good one. It paid well and there was always a need.

He became an apprentice. His specialty was construction and furniture. With time, he drew recognition for his attention to detail. Because of this, he went to work in a Konstanzer clock factory. He did this for seven years and became well known for his expertise. To build excellent clocks was a proud, Germanic skill.

Furthermore, his developed talent allowed him to open his own business. He left the clock factory and moved to Koenigsbroon to open a small carpentry shop. Unfortunately, the world depression eventually caused him to lose everything. He had to seek work elsewhere.

He found employment in an armature factory in 1936. He hated it. As a master carpenter, he found the dull, conveyor line work boring. However, it paid much more than he could earn as a carpenter. Hitler didn't need furniture. He needed war machines.

Hitler's rise to power was complete when Elser began planning to kill him. He could see that the Führer was leading Germany into another war. He saw what happened during World War I and he had to assure it didn't happen again.

Next door to the armature factory, a new company started producing explosives to support Hitler's growing military. Working with an employee of the ordnance plant, he collected small amounts of high explosives daily. These he hid in a one-room apartment he rented in Munich. It was in Munich that he learned of the resistance.

Everyone was not pleased with Hitler. There were those who found his treatment of the Jews abhorrent. Plus, many had ancestral ties with Jews. They lived in fear that the Nazis would send them to a prison or use them as slave laborers.

There were others besides Jews who were discontent. There were a number of reasons. Transferring to a better job was almost impossible. Hitler youth were destroying their families. Catholics were targets of the Gestapo. Religious freedom was fading fast. There was even a prohibition against sparkling wines. Personal liberties withered from the Nazi onslaught. Some people complained openly. Elser met three of them in a beer hall. They scared him. They considered themselves members of a resistance movement.

The trio talked too much. One, an elderly woman, made her views known openly and loud. She attracted attention so Elser stayed away from her. Soon, the Nazis arrested her and disappeared. He preferred the other two. One, a brick mason, he knew from the armature factory. Like Elser, he worked there because it paid more. Yet, he would rather work construction. The other member, a man, worked at the explosive factory. He was the one who helped Elser get needed explosives. He also gave Elser the name of a resistance member in Berlin.

Nonetheless, Elser did not care for their public voicing of their disdain for Hitler. He knew that they too would suffer the old woman's fate. He decided to become a loner and moved to Berlin.

He made contact with the person identified as anti-Nazi. He went to see him for one reason, work. Seeing him had nothing to do with his political views. The man was a construction foreman overseeing renovation of Joseph Goebbels' Ministry of Propaganda building. Elser's guild papers got him immediate work.

Elser grew to like this man. He was smart, quiet, and determined. Each day, after work, they drank together. Once his foreman learned of Elser's combination of clock and carpentry skills, he devised a plan to kill Hitler. It was a year before he mentioned anything of it to him. Elser had gained his trust.

It was while Elser worked at the Propaganda Ministry that he received delivery of explosives from a foreign operative. She had red hair and left him a briefcase molded from magnesium and plastic explosives. This was the final item needed to construct his bomb. A bomb so powerful that it would bring down a large building. That building was in Munich. And, Hitler would be in it.

Fortunately, Elser did not have a family. He never married and was able to save his earnings. He used most of it to pay for his Munich apartment. After leaving Berlin, he used it as a base. He left every afternoon at the same time and returned early the next day. He always carried his toolbox. Neighbors thought of him as a quiet, hard working man. One who obviously worked a night shift.

He put his experience to good use. His clock and armature training served him well. His most difficult problem was to assure the timer did not activate in the morning rather than the evening. He created a simple electrical circuit around the morning settings. Once set, the device would ignore A.M. times. By setting the device on 7 November, he would be across the Swiss border before the explosion took place on the eighth.

While dozing slightly, Elser heard a loud noise. Instantly awakened, he listened. He heard men talking and laughing. Their voices came from beneath and to his rear. Moving slowly, he looked through a small space between two storage containers. Below, in the main hall, he saw four German soldiers. The cigar lady was with them. Terrified, he watched.

The soldiers seated themselves at a long table. From their conversation, Elser determined they were with an air defense unit. As he watched, he recognized two of them. They had waved at him when he left the building each morning. They manned weapons on the roof.

After Hitler invaded Poland, he stationed antiaircraft units in every major city. Usually these were powerful, 88-mm, antiaircraft guns. However, the crew atop the Buergerbraeukeller used smaller weapons. Evidently, the roof was not strong enough to support 88s.

The cigar lady brought steaming mugs of chocolate to the soldiers. She chatted as she wiped her hands on her apron. She seemed nervous. Never, during Elser's month placing his bomb, did anyone arrive with her. She went to the kitchen and returned with pastries. She talked awhile longer and excused herself. She went about her normal, morning chores.

Elser could not leave the building. If the soldiers lingered, he would not be able to leave undetected. Previously, while the cigar lady was in the kitchen, he simply walked out the front door. Soon, customers would start arriving. He had to leave or risk explaining his presence. He could not explain his presence in the building if confronted. He had to go and it had to be now.

Elser crawled to the staircase's juncture with the balcony. Slowly, he arose. He turned and leaned against the wall and sidestepped down the stairs. With palms flat against the wall, he pressed himself as flat as possible to remain in shadows. The smell of fresh baked strudel became intense. They were so close. He put one foot on the floor and then the other. Quietly, he turned right and moved beneath the stairs. In this location, anyone in the hall could not see him. However, to use the back door, he would have to move across a small open area. Suddenly, he realized he had made a major mistake.

"Damn," he thought. "My toolbox is upstairs."

He almost panicked. The longer he remained his chance of exposure increased.

"It is more important that I get to the Swiss border. At least I will be safe. There is no way they can learn whose tool box that is. The explosion would destroy it.

"I must leave," he convinced himself.

Elser moved swiftly to the back door. He slowly turned its knob and eased through without fully opening the door. November's cold air hit him full force. Yet, he perspired. He closed the door and starting walking down the alley. A loud voice called to him. He stopped. Expecting the worst, he trembled and turned.

"Have you seen our friends?" A soldier on the roof asked.

Engulfed with fear, he answered, "Yes. They are having chocolate and strudel."

Three soldiers stared at him from their antiaircraft position. Two stamped their feet and rubbed their arms to ward off the cold. The one who called to him muttered something to the others. They made gestures toward a ladder that provided roof access. Seemingly frustrated, the caller moved to the ladder and stopped.

"Thank you," he said. "Their break time is over and it is our turn. They simply don't give a shit."

"You are welcome," Elser responded and continued walking from the area.

Elser had one goal in mind. He must get to his apartment and gather his papers. He had documentation as an importer. His passport showed many trips to and from Switzerland. However, Hitler's Polish invasion complicated matters. He had not planned for such a situation. Security was intense. Yet, with his papers, he did not foresee any problem. He had a good suit, proper papers, and money. His identification appeared authentic. He was sure he would get into Switzerland. For now, he had to get to his apartment.

A different person left Elser's apartment. Wearing a nice suit and overcoat, he carried an expensive suitcase. His departure did not go unnoticed. Two neighbors were curious about Elser's changes. They dismissed their misgivings thinking that he was likely taking a holiday. It was early morning 7 November 1939.

By that afternoon, Gestapo agents arrested George Elser. He was 30 meters from the Swiss border. While he was an excellent carpenter, he knew little about passports. With many Jews trying to leave, Gestapo agents manned every border crossing. They identified his passport as a fraud with one glance.

Elser was in a holding cell when his bomb exploded with devastating effect. His device destroyed the building, killing many inside of it. Newspaper headlines the next day gained considerable sympathy for Hitler. They explained that Hitler kept his scheduled visit. However, he departed 13 minutes before the explosion. Thick fog canceled his Berlin flight. He had to leave early to travel home by train.

The following day, the Gestapo found a picture postcard of the Buergerbraeukeller in Elser's suitcase. With it were notes about ammunition production made while he was collecting explosives. Employee survivors of the explosion quickly identified Elser. Ultimately, he confessed.

Hitler and Himmler concluded that Elser was part of an anti-Nazi underground. They had no doubts that he did not almost kill Hitler while working alone. After intense interrogation, the Nazis sent Elser to Dachau. He underwent the worst kinds of questioning without revealing any confederates. On 9 April 1945, camp guards killed Elser on orders from Berlin. Soon the Allies would liberate the Dachau death camp.

After the war, Allies learned of 16 attempts to kill the Führer. All failed.

Chapter Sixteen

May 1954

Living by chance, loving by choice, killing by profession.
Régiment étranger parachutiste Legionnaires

General Pieroth pulled a grenade's pin; placed the armed weapon against his chest; and died in the blast. His military career ended in failure and death. His assurances to General Navarre became lethal errors. Pieroth was France's foremost artilleryman. He selected and organized artillery units for Operation Castor. His fellow Legionnaires paid dearly for his mistakes. Viet Minh artillery destroyed Pieroth's units with ease. He never expected the devastation brought to bear against his artillery batteries. The Viet Minh outgunned the Legion from the beginning.

Lieutenant Jean Danjou watched the carnage. Tears made clear trails down his blackened face. From his hidden position, he watched Dien Bien Phu in its death throes. His fellow soldiers fought desperately but overwhelming numbers of Viet Minh swept across their defensive positions.

Where he was, with his remaining men, was bittersweet for Jean. They accomplished their mission. Yet, the price was high. Only six men remained of his red team. These men were special. Each was a member of Groupement Mixte d'Intervention, better known as the GMI. They, like Jean, were field intelligence gatherers. They parachuted anywhere and sought the enemy. Their mission was not to kill but find and report. This they did with great skill.

They surrounded Jean's observation post atop a ridge. Their perimeter extended only 10 meters in thick jungle. Nearby, a Viet Minh antiaircraft weapon fired repeatedly. Its firing heralded another heroic effort at aerial resupply; most failed. The enemy was close. Yet, his men remained still, quiet. Their ability to remain calm resulted from extensive training. In addition, they also trained others.

They organized and trained native tribesmen to fight for France's colonial government. French success at Na Son rested heavily with the GMI. They organized and trained over 3,000 Meo tribesmen to fight. The Meo played a major role in this significant victory. It was at Na Son that Jean saw what Viet Minh could do. He reported it. Few listened.

Unfortunately, some senior officers did not heed information from the GMI. Their arrogance was such that they placed their own beliefs above information from the field. Captain Prudhomme was an excellent example. General Navarre was another.

If Jean survived, he would settle with Prudhomme. What Prudhomme did was out of ambition. He purposely made reports to curry favor with superiors. He knew the disdain with which generals like Navarre held for Viet Minh forces.

Instead of providing a true picture, he told them what they wanted to hear. Prudhomme was the ultimate sycophant. His desire for favor cost the lives of thousands.

General Navarre was arrogant and aloof. He gave no credit to the Viet Minh. His sin was misplaced pride. Once he set into motion Operation Castor, he would not change it. He did so with the knowledge of his plan's dangerous aspects.

"Hell," Jean thought. "Our job is always dangerous. But what Navarre did was stupid, fatal dangerous."

Jean's goal now was to save his men. After the way they fought the past three weeks, they deserved to live. They fought with skill and achieved their mission's goal. The navigational beacons were in place. His men put them there but that was only a small portion. They had been with him throughout the battle. They parachuted into the deadly gorge and fought like true Legionnaires.

Jean recalled the Viet Minh's falling upon Dien Bien Phu like a mad horde. General Giap's first attacks were human wave assaults. They charged across open ground into withering French fire. While they inflicted French losses, their casualties were much higher. Giap finally disregarded recommendations of his Chinese advisors. He changed tactics and began using trench warfare.

From every direction, they dug toward strong points. Incessantly, night and day, they moved closer. Whenever Legionnaires fired, trenches protected their attackers. The process was slow but effective.

As the end neared, General de Castries isolated himself. He would not talk to his staff or make command decisions. Outposts furthermost from the airfield began to fall. Viet Minh actually tunneled into some positions and sprang upon the defenders. It was havoc.

Major Bigeard knew it was time for Operation Vulture. He sent for Jean. He listened in disbelief. While he had trained for the mission, he never imagined it would take place.

"Jean, it is time," Bigeard said. "Move the transmitters to their positions."

Jean noted Bigeard's haggard appearance. He had not shaved in days and his eyes peered from inside dark caverns. His voice was shaky and sounded unsure. Yet, Jean knew that he was deadly serious.

"Yes sir," Jean replied. "We leave as soon as it is dark. I do not need the full team. Twenty of them can remain here to help."

"No Jean," Bigeard ordered. "Follow the plan. We have not had any communications for over a week. I do not know if the mission has approval. Still, you must go and you must follow the plan. Get the transmitters in position. After that, get as far away as you can. Do not return to this place. Do you understand?" Bigeard asked wearily.

"Yes, but," Jean said before Bigeard interrupted.

"Damn it Jean. Do what you are supposed to do and do it now," Bigeard said sharply.

Continuing, Bigeard asked. "Do you have your piece with you?"

"Yes sir, I do. You have my solemn word that I will get it home," Jean answered.

Bigeard arose from his seat behind a meager field table. He walked around it and stood in front of Jean. Amid artillery explosions, the dugout shook and dirt sprinkled onto them. Bigeard straightened his shoulders. Solemnly, he placed his hands on Jean's shoulders and embraced him. Stepping back, he extended his hand. Jean took it.

"It is a brave thing you are about to do. I could not live with it. Now, get the hell out of here Jean. Do not look back," he ordered. That was the last time he saw Major Bigeard.

Bolting outside, Jean ran low along a trench to another dugout. Moving inside, he opened his shirt. He removed a piece of cloth. Torn, dirty and rumpled it was a portion of their unit's flag. Rather than allow the Viet Minh to capture it, they tore it apart. There were nine pieces. Jean, and eight others, took a piece vowing to return their portion to France. One day their flag would be complete again.

"I will get this to France," he said aloud.

He began gathering his equipment. It wasn't much. He made sure he had extra ammunition clips, his knife, and some black grease paint. In the corner, he removed a small box from beneath a canvas cover. He took a key hanging from a chain around his neck. He swiftly unlocked the box. Opening it, he removed three cylinders no larger than lipstick tubes. Raising his trouser leg, he taped them behind his right knee. To assure they were secure, he flexed his knee a few times. Taking a final look around the dugout, he pushing aside the door's canvas covers. Artillery shells were impacting in every direction. Shrapnel whistled above his head. During a brief, firing lull, he ran to where his men waited in an underground bunker.

Jean gathered them and explained their mission. He had trained them to place, and put into operation, radio transmitters. Originally, he said they were for French aircraft navigation. Actually, they were for United States' B-29s. These bombers carried atomic weapons from Okinawa.

They were supposed to place three transmitters. Nonetheless, the B-29s could reach their targets with as few as two transmitters operating. The B-29 crews had receivers set to intercept low frequency transmissions carrying identification codes. They would plot any two of four specified signals to determine a course to their targets. Where two of the radials intersected, indicated an initial point (IP). From that there, they would fly known directions and distances to release points (RP). At their RPs, they would drop their bombs from 30,000 feet. Parachutes would slow their descents. This allowed aircraft time to be far as possible from the detonations.

In addition, Jean did not know when, or if, B-29s would arrive. Transmitter batteries were good for four days. If the B-29s did not arrive during that time, their attack would not take place. For all he knew, they had already arrived and gone.

Jean told his men to activate their transmitters and not return to Dien Bien Phu. He stressed that they avoid enemy contact and make their way to Laos. He told them that they must move swiftly to avoid being in a detonation area. He removed two of the three tubes from behind his knee. He taped the remaining one back into a snug position. He gave a tube to each team leader.

"These are the encoding controllers for the transmitters. Do not lose them. The transmitters are useless without them," he explained. "You've been trained where to put them. Do just like you did in the rehearsals."

Continuing, he said, "I will take one transmitter with me and Sergeant LeMarc's team. We will move from here to our departure bunker. Follow at staggered intervals. Let's go."

It was at least four hours until sunset. Jean moved his team along a trench leading north. They stopped at an abandoned dugout near the northeast perimeter. It was a tight fit but he had everyone move inside. He slipped his small backpack from his shoulders and opened it. He removed a sealed, wooden box.

"Okay, let's relax for awhile," Jean said as he opened the box.

Visibly, tension flowed through the group and they began muttering to one another. They watched Jean.

"Here you are," Jean said with a smile. "There's a couple here for each of you."

Jean began passing slim cigars among the men. They began removing their coverings and pulling them beneath their noses.

"Ah, rum," someone said.

"My favorite flavor," said another.

There was nervous laughter. Some tried joking remarks while others lit cigars.

"Sergeant LeMarc, pull the sand bags out," Jean said.

"Thought you would never get to it sir," came LeMarc's reply.

"Out of the way," LeMarc said.

He pushed through the group to the far wall. He examined it and removed two sandbags. He reached into a small hole and retrieved two, full Cognac bottles.

"Pass them around," Jean directed.

The cramped space filled with bluish smoke. Monsoon rains made the air humid, the floor mud, and the stench almost unbearable. Yet, they laughed. There was no more than a swallow for each man. Some took it and smiled. Others took it and choked. Each drank. In this moment, they were one. This instant became an inedible imprint on their souls. They would never forget it, no matter how far or old. They were Legionnaires and soon they expected to die.

"It's time," Jean said. "LaSalle, take your team first. LeMarc, we will leave last. Any questions?" Jean asked.

After a momentary lull, Jean said, "Let's do it."

Jean moved to the small doorway and pulled aside the canvas. He touched each man on his shoulder as he went through. There were no words but this simple gesture said so much.

Soon LeMarc stood by Jean's side. Bending down, Jean removed the last cylinder. He gave it to his trusted sergeant.

"Take this. You have one concern. Get this in the transmitter no matter what happens," Jean told him.

LeMarc nodded and followed Jean's example by taping the tube behind his knee. Once finished, he stood upright and looked at Jean. They exchanged knowing glances. Jean went through the door and into darkness. The others followed.

They traveled northwest. Bloated corpses lined their small trench. Death's odor permeated everything. Sadly, they grew used to it. They gave it little thought. Soon they arrived where barbed wire crossed their path. They were at the northeastern edge of strong point Anne Marie.

For defensive purposes, Anne Marie was no longer a threat to their attackers. They could occupy it whenever they desired. Most forces left it the day before and moved into Huguette. Evidently, the Viet Minh intended to remain in their ever-increasing trenches until inside the perimeter. When they arrived, they would find it deserted.

They listened. Outside the wire, they heard digging. They were close. Silently, each man unsheathed his knife and slipped over the trench's edge. Knowing every mine's position, every tripwire, they slithered through mud thrown skyward in a thunderous downpour. Occasionally, Jean would see someone's eyes when lightning flashed. Otherwise, they were invisible. Eight Viet Minh died in their protective trench without a sound.

From there, they crossed the main road. Following its edge, they traveled toward Gabrielle. This was the first French position to fall into Viet Minh hands. Its defenders served their purpose. They alerted the others to their enemy's nearness. They died over six weeks ago.

After Gabrielle, their destination was atop a mountain to its east. Once in position, they would assemble their transmitter and activate it. The Laotian border would be near. It was an easy day's travel to relative safety.

Soon Viet Minh soldiers moved openly around them. The enemy had nothing to fear. French artillery was silent and their tanks destroyed. Jean's force attacked no more. They must get past Gabrielle and into the jungle. It would be a horrendous climb through slippery mud to their final position.

They arrived undetected. Dawn was soon. Quickly they assembled the transmitter and activated it. LeMarc installed the encoding cylinder. It would be necessary to remain at their position until night. It appeared that the only Viet Minh in their vicinity were antiaircraft crews. However, there was constant movement by ammunition bearers supplying the fast-firing weapons. Supply aircraft made repeated attempts to deliver much needed medicine, ammunition, and other tools of war.

Directly to their front, Jean and his men saw a C-119, "Flying Box Car," take direct hits. The nearby antiaircraft gun fired round after round of 37-mm into the aircraft. Trailing smoke, the severely damaged plane plummeted toward the jungle. A large fireball and smoke erupted from beneath thick canopy. No one could have survived.

As noon approached, they sweltered in the heat and humidity. Cicada's high-pitched drone filled the jungle air. Their sound rose in volume and then faded, only to rise again. Insects chewed at their flesh but they dared not move. Still and silent, they awaited night. In a short while, the Viet Minh discovered them.

An ammunition bearer walked into their midst to relieve herself. She met a deadly fate. But, not before she screamed an alarm. A one-half second's hesitation to kill a woman brought death to four of Jean's men. Six remained after the short firefight and their disappearance into the jungle. Fortunately, as best he could tell, the Viet Minh did not find the transmitter.

At night's approach, Jean decided not to leave for Laos. He did not tell the others until darkness was upon them. He had to assure the transmitter remained secure. When he did tell them, LeMarc objected to Jean's decision.

"So what," he said. "There is not a damned thing you can do if it has. Forget it."

The others mumbled in agreement.

"I have to know. The B-29s may come. If they do, I want to be there to see the Viet Minh die," Jean explained.

Jean knew that the French would die with them. If necessary, so would he.

"I'm staying," Jean said with finality. "You men head for Laos. See if you can make it to Vientiane. It's a long haul but we have friends among the native tribes. They will help you. Beware of the Pathet Lao. They are as bad as the Viet Minh."

The others refused to leave. They would not go unless Jean did. He led them to the vicinity of the antiaircraft position. The transmitter was in place and operating. They moved farther up the mountain. A ridge extended toward the northwest. From it, they could see most of the final, French controlled strong point.

The next morning they watched as Viet Minh overran the position. He saw his comrades herded into groups with their hands atop their heads. Six Viet Minh soldiers waved their flag from atop a large command bunker.

"They didn't get ours," he thought.

He felt the small scrap of cloth lumped inside his tattered shirt. As if to provide better protection, he moved it to a position underneath his left arm. He handed his binoculars to Sergeant LeMarc.

"Everyone take a short look. We're leaving for Laos," Jean said.

Each Legionnaire watched for a moment and passed the binoculars to the man next to him. They watched as tens of thousands staggered through mud as Viet Minh prodded them with bayonets. If a man fell, the captors killed him. Despite best efforts at being stoic, each observer wept.

Jean retrieved his binoculars and said, "Okay, let's get out of this hell-hole."

Before they could leave, they heard intense small arms' firing. Viet Minh walked through the Nam Youm Rat's encampment destroying it. They killed anyone they saw. Women, children, and deserters from the French forces, succumbed to death execution style. The soldiers collected supplies dropped for the Legionnaires.

Jean moved slowly as waning light filtered through openings in the jungle's canopy. The Viet Minh, engrossed with joy, never noticed six shadows fade as night drew nigh. Laos, and relative safety, were only a few miles north. It was the night of 7 May 1954. The B-29s never came. They remained at their base in Okinawa. Other nation's objections to the planned attack resulted in cancellation.

Later, Jean learned their that two Americans were flying the C-119 he saw shot down on 6 May 1954. They were James B. ("Earthquake Magoon") McGovern and Wallace Bufford. They were the first Americans to die fighting Ho Chi Minh's Communist inspired forces. He never imagined that thousands of Americans would later die in this nondescript part of Southeast Asia.

It was a long way to Vientiane through rough, mountainous terrain. Jean and his group still had to escape and evade their way across Laos. Even after crossing the border, their lives were in jeopardy. It was essential that they locate a native tribe to rest and recover. They were exhausted after months fighting at Dien Bien Phu. Three of his men had severe jungle rot. Their feet would soon fail and they could walk no more. He decided to hide them while he and LeMarc sought safety and rest with a native tribe.

The Viet Minh presence in Laos was strong. Jean and LeMarc were not safe. Viet Minh military and covert agents roamed freely in this northernmost province. They would have to avoid the Pathet Lao. They were the Laotian equivalent of the Viet Minh. Though France was loosening its hold on Laos, there was a violent effort to evict them.

Terrain was exceedingly rugged. Laos had mountains as high as 9,000 feet. Large limestone cliffs dropped away to deep valleys. Jean led the way to a major stream. It would take them near a village atop a mountain ridge. He had lived with this group for six months on another mission. He would have little problem convincing them to retrieve his men.

Nevertheless, Communist forces traveled the same valley. It was a major route from North Viet Nam into Laos. Again, they would travel at night and hide during the day. One luxury they afforded themselves was a bath. Each stood guard while the other cleaned filth from their bodies. While the water was cold, it brought new life to each of them. Clean, and with leeches removed, they rested. LeMarc killed a large snake that they ate raw. They could not dare a fire.

On the fourth day, they located a small trail. It came from above and ended at water's edge. While no boats were present, it was obvious that it was a major launching site. They climbed, not on the trail, but beside it in the heavy foliage. Soon they heard children's laughter. Remaining hidden, they peered through dense brush at a native village.

This was the land of the Hmong. They migrated into the region from China. Over the years, factions arose with some supporting the Viet Minh. However, one person named Touby organized settlements to direct anti-Viet Minh warfare. He strengthened village militia units in an attempt to contain military attacks by the Viet Minh. This was one of his settlements. These people were committed to an anti-Pathet Lao stance. Here, Jean knew they would receive help.

Suddenly, a loud roar descended upon them. Overhead, an airplane swooped low over the village. Men, women, and children ran between thatch-covered huts. They disappeared from view on the village's other side, away from Jean and LeMarc. They heard the sound of an engine sputtering typical of a taxing aircraft.

Jean nodded toward the nearest building. He and LeMarc, staying low, ran to it. They flattened themselves against the bamboo wall. Jean, in the lead, slowly looked around the hut's corner. In the distance, dust boiled skyward behind an airplane making a take-off run. It was rapidly airborne leaving swirling dust on the short, dirt runway.

From behind the pair, a loud voice said, "Danjou, what the shit are you doing here?"

Startled the pair turned rapidly, ready to fire. A Caucasian man stood in the middle of the trail they had just left. He walked rapidly toward them with outstretched arms.

"Lanny Briscoe, your sorry son-of –a –bitch. I figured you had drowned somewhere by now," Jean said with a loud laugh. The two embraced.

Chapter Seventeen

May 1954

Communism is the opiate of the intellectuals [with]
no cure except as a guillotine might become a cure for dandruff.
Clare Boothe Luce (1903–87), U.S. diplomat, writer.
Newsweek (New York, 24 Jan. 1955)

Fire missions stopped and, for the first time in months, they did not have targets. Vinh found the silence strange, foreboding. Their sergeant told them to rest. He watched as he spoke with their forward observer by telephone. Suddenly, he put the telephone down and smiled as he turned to the group.

"It's over," he said. "It's over, the French have surrendered."

The sergeant began circling the room, sometimes dancing and sometimes singing, "It's over, we're free. We're free."

Vinh, and his team members, looked incredulously at each other. They watched their formerly stoic leader acting like a child.

"Is this true?" Vinh wondered. "Can this possibly be true."

Loud voices began echoing throughout the underground passageways. From outside, a captain entered their fire direction center. His eyes gleamed and he walked with a confident swagger. He went to the room's center and stepped up upon a chair. He looked about and ordered quiet.

In anxious silence, they waited for him to speak. Slowly, he looked about him at gaunt, upturned faces and then, smiled.

"Today, 7 May, the French commander was captured. Our flag now flies atop his bunker. The battle is finished. You are to await further orders," he announced.

Vinh leaned against a dirt wall, stunned. He saw the captain on the chair. He watched as fellow soldiers hugged and danced about him. It was pandemonium. Radios along the opposite wall began to crackle and hiss with message traffic. Lights blinked off and then on again. He heard singing.

"I'm going home," he thought. "I'm really going home."

He saw his brother enter and look about the room. Vinh rushed toward Anh with outstretched arms. Just slightly before grabbing him, Anh recognized Vinh and laughed aloud.

In a tight embrace, the two pounded each other's backs. Finally, Anh said something but Vinh could not hear above the noise. He beckoned Vinh to follow him outside. Vinh began looking for his sergeant to get permission when Anh pulled him toward the nearest exit.

Outside there was intense weapons fire. Tracers climbed skyward as antiaircraft crews fired with wild abandon. Individual soldiers emptied clip after clip, firing their weapons. Joy flowed like an opiate rush throughout the Viet Minh. Anh and Vinh embraced again.

Stepping back, Anh held his brother at arm's length and said, "Little brother, this is a grand day. This means the end of French oppression. Our country can now grow without the French sucking our nation's lifeblood. We have beaten them. They will never fight us again after this."

Vinh felt his heart racing. Euphoria engulfed him as his brother spoke. "Now, we will all be equal. The French plantations will be no more. We will be free from the French tax collectors."

Almost sobbing with joy, Vinh asked. "When can we go home Anh?"

"Not right away," Anh answered. "There is still much to do. The weapons and ammunition are valuable. We must move it to storage. There are thousands of prisoners to move. You need not worry about them. Other units will see to that. However, the situation in Laos continues and the Pathet Lao need our help. We're not going home soon."

Vinh's elation faded. His original fear that the situation was not true returned. Sadly, he looked at Anh.

"How long will this take," he asked.

"I'm not sure," Anh answered

Anh could see that his brother was deeply distraught. It was time to tell him.

"Tell me little brother. How would you like to go to the Soviet Union?" Anh asked.

Puzzled, Vinh answered with a question. "Why would I want to go to Russia?"

"One reason would be to keep me company," Anh replied. "However, there are two more reasons."

"Why are you going?" Vinh responded immediately.

Anh saw his chance to perplex his brother with a cryptic answer. He replied, "To keep you out of trouble."

"Quit it, Anh. Tell me the truth," he demanded.

"Okay, okay," Anh said as he led Vinh to a nearby boulder. "Take a seat to hear this."

The two sat close. Around them soldiers continued firing their weapons in jubilation. They had fought long and hard. Many feared they would never see their families again. Pent-up emotions burst forth causing them to cry, sing, or fire their weapons. Anh almost had to yell as he explained future events to his brother.

"You are going to attend an officer's training course for a year. If you are graduated, you will be a second lieutenant of field artillery. How does that sound?" Anh asked proudly.

Vinh had no desire to remain in the military. He wanted to return home to live in peace. He thought that Anh wanted the same. He had difficulty understanding why he would want him to leave. He could never farm their home alone.

In as stern a demeanor as he could exhibit, he told Anh, "That does not sound good. I want us to go home. Our home is why our grandfather and father fought. It is why you and I fought. Now that the French are defeated, you want to send me away. Never!"

"I am not sending you away. We will go together," Anh explained. "While you are attending school, I will also be in training near you."

Vinh did not like this. He respected his elder brother, as he should. Nevertheless, he did not understand why they should leave their home for military training. Ho Chi Minh made it clear that they fought to remove the French. If they were defeated, they could go home.

Quietly, with the most respectful demeanor possible, Vinh asked once more. "If the French are defeated, why can't we go home?"

Anh loved Vinh. He must explain or Vinh would not go. He was not ambitious. He wanted one thing, to stay on the ancestral lands and live in peace.

"Vinh, we have won a battle but not the war. The French remain in Laos and are still in the southern provinces. However, Uncle Ho does not believe that our country will be one country. The political factions in the south intend to divide us. A need will remain for a strong military. We must prepare to make sure the western capitalists do not prevail. Part of that preparation is our going to the Soviets for training. This is a great honor for you and me," Anh explained.

Vinh listened while gazing at his torn feet in the mud. He knew what Anh said was true but he still did not like it. Nonetheless, if Vinh thought they should go to Russia, he would do so. Yet, he still yearned for home and Minh Thanh.

Vinh asked. "Will we not get to go home at all?"

"Yes," Anh answered. "We will have a few months before we leave. We can go home and we can try to find Minh Thanh. With the French defeated, perhaps they will return her. My last information was that they took her. If what Uncle Ho believes is true, we must go and try to help him. Meanwhile, we will do our best to find Minh Thanh."

The two sat quietly. They watched others celebrate their great victory. In their hearts, they knew there would be many more battles with more killing. Somehow, the two seemed alone on that rock near Dien Bien Phu. Moving closer, they took comfort in each other's nearness.

Vinh knew what was to come but he dared not tell Anh and break his heart. Ho Chi Minh was going to build a great Army with the help of the Soviets and the Chinese. He was going to bring equality and peace to their strife torn nation. They would embrace Communism as the Soviets and Chinese had. The western powers and their corrupted governments sought only to exploit workers for the rich. Their country would be different. Uncle Ho had said so.

Vinh listened to the gunfire. His brother's words echoed in his mind as truth. Yet, in his heart, he wanted the life of his youth on the Nam Youm. Just across the mountains, their home waited. He wanted to toss water across the levee again with Minh Thanh. He wanted to smell the morning air as it glided across young rice fields that he had planted. His needs were few, a water buffalo, some chickens, ducks and soil to till. This was his peace. If he had to go to Russia to gain it, he would. He would do it because Anh said he should.

Anh broke the silence, "I must go. Report to your sergeant and await orders. I will bring them. We will have time to find Minh Than and we can do some work in our fields."

The two stood, awkward in their departing, "Hurry," Vinh said. "The sooner we go, the sooner we can be home."

Vinh watched as his brother followed the main trail into the forest. Two soldiers met him and saluted. One gave Anh a map and pointed to something on it. There was an agitated conversation. Anh folded the map and put it in his small backpack. The three disappeared into the jungle at a rapid pace. Vinh wondered why.

Since Anh's visit, Vinh's sergeant treated him differently. Once he was boisterous and overbearing. Now, he seemed eager to please. He assigned four men to Vinh and sent them to Dien Bien Phu to search for artillery equipment. They found little of worth. Every weapon was useless. Most of it fell to their guns early in the battle. The French destroyed the rest before surrendering. They did obtain some fire direction equipment, radios, and code books.

Viet Minh infantry guarded large groups of French Legionnaires. They lived in an open sea of mud. They had no protection from the elements. Wounded soldiers suffered without medical care. Many were dying or already dead. In addition, many more would die on their trek to prison camps. He noticed that their eyes held no light. They were void of life as in death but they lived.

One severely wounded soldier lay in a fetal position; a gaping wound festering in his leg. His head rested in the crossed legs of a comrade who stared at Vinh. His eyes seemed to follow his every move. No matter where he went or what he did, he felt him staring. He turned quickly to check. The soldier gazed blankly into space with a stream of spittle draining down his stubbled chin. Yet, when he turned away, the sensation returned. He checked again. The man lay dead in driving rain and mud. He had fallen forward covering his wounded friend.

Vinh did not sleep. He felt the eyes. From his dirt, sleeping place, he saw two piercing lights gleaming in quiet darkness. No weapons fired. Firing charts lay unattended beneath a single lantern surrounded by flying insects. Radios belched some occasional static but no voices. Bolting upright, he pushed aside his mosquito netting and leaped to the floor. The eyes disappeared.

Dripping with perspiration, he ran outside to cool, night air. His hands trembled. Night insects made no sounds. It was strange, this quiet.

"Is this peace?" He thought.

He felt the eyes. Turning slowly, he peered into the jungle's darkness where two eyes leered. And, then blinked. With total abandon, he ran toward them. They moved deeper into the jungle. He followed with barbed vines clawing at his bare legs. Earth dropped from beneath him. He plunged downward into agonizing pain. Finally, the eyes were gone.

"Is this peace?" His mind asked as darkness and pain consumed him.

"Sir, this is where we found it," the antiaircraft gunner explained to Anh.

Other Viet Minh watched as Anh walked toward an olive drab cylinder. It had tripod legs and rose above the ground about two feet. Squatting, Anh moved his hands around the object's surface. He felt a small indentation and pressed. A small, spring-loaded door opened with a snap. Others, standing nearby, jumped backward from fright. When nothing happened, they looked at each other laughing nervously. Anh never flinched.

Looking inside, he saw a circular indentation. It appeared to be the top of an insert.

"Perhaps, a timing mechanism," he thought.

He placed his bayonet into a groove across it. Pressing gently, he turned it counter-clockwise. It moved.

"Stand back," he said as he arose. Walking around the device, he examined it from various directions.

"This is not an explosive device," he concluded. "It's too obvious and there are no attachments to cause it to explode, no trip-wires, nothing."

Gesturing for a nearby man with a radio to join him, he continued studying the device. Anh removed the radio's handset, pressed its transmit button and spoke into it. He explained what he had found and listened. He put the handset on the radio. He knelled again.

Reaching inside the opening, he twisted the loose device with his fingers. It made a slight squeaking sound but moved outward. He continued turning it. Soon the screw-like threads gave way to smooth metal. He removed a small cylinder. He set it aside to further examine the main body. He did not find any markings. Turning it over, he looked closely at its underneath, nothing.

"Strange," he thought.

He retrieved the small cylinder. By rotating it, he could see a small inscription. Raising it to obtain a better view, he read the markings, "Mil-Spec-00378-01A."

"American," he thought.

Speaking to the group, he said, "Do not touch it. Specialists will arrive soon. They will take it with them."

Anh knew that two other devices, like this one, were in their battle area. They did not yet know their function. He felt certain their electronics experts would find what their use was. Other than what its purpose might be, he had no concern that the removable cylinder was America. They had great quantities of American equipment. Most of their artillery weapons were American.

"Sir, you have an urgent message," his radio operator said.

Anh took the handset and listened. He asked that the message to be repeated.

While returning the handset to its cradle, he said, "Let's go and be quick. We're returning to Division's main fire direction center."

The two soldiers found it difficult to keep pace with Anh. He moved at a slow run made difficult by heavy undergrowth. He was not following the trail but making a direct course for where they met him earlier.

"Vinh's no deserter," he worried. "This must be a mistake."

Semi-conscious and suffering intense pain, Vinh could see jungle canopy. The upper growth lay inside a dim circle above him. He fainted. Later, he awakened again. The pain was much worse and seemed to come from his right leg. Struggling, he moved his upper body to an almost upright position. He leaned on his left elbow and looked toward the pain's source. A sharpened, bamboo stake protruded from his leg's calf. Blood seeped from where it exited his flesh. Each time he tried to change position, other sharp stakes prevented it. He was in a punji pit.

Vinh knew punji pits well. He helped build hundreds while with the Viet Minh. Their primary purpose was a passive, defense measure. They dug holes and placed sharpened stakes at the bottom. Frequently, they urinated or defecated on them to make them more dangerous. They hid them with matting covered with debris taken from the jungle's floor. If someone stepped on one, they fell into a deadly trap. If the initial fall did not kill them, they died later from deadly infections. Now, he was a victim.

He lay in muddy water accumulated from monsoon rain. His impaled calf barely remained above water. Again, he tried to move but could not. Most of his body was wedged between a stake row. Whoever made this pit was neat. Normally, they placed stake randomly about the bottom. Someone put these in neat rows. Their tidiness saved him because most of his body fell between a row. Unfortunately, his right leg landed directly upon a contaminated stake.

Moreover, he was fortunate not to have drowned. Water was almost a foot deep. His contorted position rested his head upon his shoulder. This held his head above algae covered, slime floating above the brownish sludge. However, starving leeches attached themselves over most of his torso. He could not remove them as they swelled with his blood.

Furthermore, yelling did not bring aid. By this time, he didn't care who heard him, French or Viet Minh. The chance of Legionnaires coming was small. However, he didn't care for he was dying. Nausea returned and he began to retch and convulse. Foliage over his pit blurred and disappeared into darkness.

"I don't care what your damned report says. My brother is no deserter," Anh yelled at the bespectacled personnel officer. "We were going on leave to our home. He would not leave. He was waiting for me."

Quite intimidated by Anh's verbal attack, the personnel officer pointed to a line on the paper he held and said, "I have to go by what his sergeant reported. Your brother left during the night and did not return. Search parties did not locate him. I have to report him as a deserter, sir."

Hearing the loud exchange, the administrative unit's commander left his field table and went to the noise's source. He pulled aside a beaded curtain and saw an irate captain standing at his personnel officer's desk.

"What is the problem?" The colonel asked.

Anh answered immediately; "My brother is being reported as a deserter. It's not true. He is not a deserter."

"Give me the report lieutenant," the colonel told his staff officer.

Examining the papers, the colonel asked. "What is your brother's name, captain?"

"Nguyen Van Vinh, sir. He's a corporal," Anh answered immediately.

Turning toward a dim overhead lantern to better see the report, the colonel moved his finger slowly down a list. Speaking aloud, he said, "I know that name. I saw it somewhere recently. Oh yes, I remember."

Turning to Anh, he asked. "Was your brother on orders to the Soviet Union?"

"Yes, sir. I have his orders. I have not given them to him yet. However, I told him. He knew that we were going together. He had no reason to desert," Anh explained.

"I see," the colonel replied as he turned to his personnel officer. He walked to his desk and placed the papers before him.

Pointing to a place on the form, he said, "Mark this as missing in action. There has not been enough time to determine that he is a deserter."

"But sir," the lieutenant said, before his colonel interrupted.

"Do it," the colonel ordered.

Looking at Anh, the sympathetic colonel said, "Find your brother captain. Report it when you do. You're dismissed."

Calmer now, Anh answered crisply, "Yes sir. Thank you sir."

He saluted and left the thatched hut. Once outside, he thought, "Do not worry little brother. I will find you."

Vinh smelled smoke. Its aroma was that of burning wood and meat cooking. As if from a deep cavern, he heard children giggling. Their high pitched voices echoed with a vibrating quality. A stabbing pained ripped him into consciousness.

A face materialized close to his. Long, stringy black hair fell around it. In places, it appeared matted with grease. A wide grin slashed across it, showing pointed teeth colored red. Around the mouth, red stain spilled onto its chin below and up to its nose. The face left and a blissful feeling raced through Vinh. He felt it surge throughout his body. The throbbing leg pain was gone.

"I can stay here forever," he thought.

Again, the aroma came but stronger. Opening his eyes, he saw a leathery hand holding a bamboo sliver with cooked meat on it. Suddenly, he was extraordinarily hungry. He grabbed the offered morsel with his teeth. He allowed it to melt in his mouth as his stomach cried for more. He tried to rise but could not. Once more, another piece appeared but larger this time. He grabbed the gnarled fingers holding it, while gulping another delicious piece. This was better than the first. Still gripping the hand, he pulled upwards with renewed strength. A throbbing fire burned his leg and he collapsed.

Euphoria engulfed him while he dreamed of what he saw. The hand was that of an old, bare breasted woman. Slightly stooped, she was of small stature and horribly ugly. Her breasts were flat and hanged from her body. Her clothing was a mere animal's skin over her pelvic region. From her neck, many strings of beads dangled. Behind her, he could see glaring daylight. In it, shadowy figures moved like dark ghosts.

In his dream state, mountain tribesmen moved about a fire skinning a monkey. Children passed where he lay in a hammock, often stopping to stare. The old woman frequently came and went, always giving him something to drink. Sometimes, she gave him morsels of tender, cooked flesh that he relished. He slept often. His pain was less frequent.

"Up, you must get up," a voice kept repeating.

It started from a distance, coming closer with each exhortation. He felt his body shaking and the commanding voice well upon him. Opening his eyes, he repeatedly blinked against the bright light.

"Ayah, welcome to the world of the living. It is time for you to get out of your comfortable bed my friend," the person stated. "With what they've been giving you, I can understand why you want to remain."

"Who are you and where am I?" Vinh asked as he arose.

Vinh pushed his legs over the hammock's side. He winced as a sharp pain sprang from his leg. He became dizzy and felt weak. Grasping the hammock, he steadied himself while looking at his tormentor. Before him, a Vietnamese man stood. Around his waist, he wore a military belt with pouches containing ammunition clips. A large machete-type knife was protruding from a sash around his waist. Knee length trousers, with frayed leg openings, covered his lower body. His chest was bare. Around his neck, he wore a red and white, checkered kerchief. It hung loosely with a long end below his chin. On his feet, he wore sandals made from automobile tires and leather strands. They were the kind that he wore.

"Take it easy. You've not walked for some time now. Let me look at that leg," he said.

Kneeling, he began removing green leaves from his still painful leg. Clear fluid oozed from beneath each leaf as he neared the wound.

Examining the swollen gash he mumbled, "Lucky. Yes, lucky. Another day and you would have been dead."

Vinh guessed him to be middle-aged. He had wisps of gray at his temples. Looking down his back to where his sash crossed, he saw a pistol inserted. It was a 9-mm, Luger-type weapon. Also, leaning against a post behind him, there was an AK-47 assault rifle. It appeared well maintained.

Arising, the man said, "You may call me Diem. That is all that I am going to tell you so don't ask. What do you like to be called young warrior?"

"My name is Nguyen Van Vinh," Vinh answered.

"That is a fine name. Your family is a great one. If I could pick any name I wanted, that would be my choice," Diem said with unusual sincerity in his voice.

"Where am I and how long have I been here?" Vinh asked.

"By whose calendar do you want to know?" Diem questioned.

Puzzled by this strange man, Vinh did not know how to reply.

"By my country's," Vinh answered.

"And what country might that be?" Diem asked, smiling broadly.

"The Democratic Republic of Viet Nam," Vinh answered indignantly.

"Oh, that country. I've heard of it but I do not think it exists. In the rest of the world, it is June," Diem replied laughing.

Incredulous, Vinh cried aloud, "June, I've been here a month?"

"That's what I'm told. It has been a hard month for you also. You have these tribes-people to thank for your life young warrior. You were delirious for two weeks. You did considerable praying to the Virgin Mary. I guessed that you are Catholic." Diem said.

"That's true Vinh," answered. "Does it make a difference?"

"Yes, it does," Diem answered. "If you had been a godless Communist, we would have returned you to the jungle to rot."

Diem pulled a wicker basket to him and removed its cover. He reached inside and removed a handful of bright green leaves and plant stems. Each stem had a round bulb on one end. Separating a bulb from the group, he held it toward Vinh.

"Here, take this. Chew it. If you don't you will be very sick soon," Diem stated.

Hesitant, Vinh took the plant. He knew what it was. It was a bulb from which tribes people extracted a powerful drug for pain. Many also used it for pleasure. From the plant's flower-base, they collected a white, creamy liquid that they made into a powder. It was definitely a strong, painkiller. He remembered his dreams and his blissful feeling. He realized the old woman gave it to him for pain. Too much of it for too long and a person's body became addicted. He chewed the bulb. A bitter taste filled his mouth.

Vinh watched Diem. He had an infectious smile. His dark eyes sparkled with life. He did not walk. He flowed. Walking was not an apt description for his movements. Sinewy muscle writhed beneath his tight skin indicating strength. He retrieved his assault rifle and deftly placed its strap across his chest. He turned to face Vinh.

"You are in a rare place," Diem said. "This is the largest village of Tia tribesmen in our county's mountains. There are others scattered throughout the area. They are my friends and they have my protection. Your people have treated them badly. They are moving farther south. I am going ahead with two of their best men to scout for Pathet Lao. I will return in one week. You should be able to travel by then. I will help you on your way young warrior."

Although Diem was standing in Vinh's clear view, he did not see him leave. One moment he was speaking to him and the next, he was gone.

Pain from Vinh's leg eased. Feeling drowsy, he reclined into his hammock. He was not asleep but dwelled in a place between sleep and consciousness. It was familiar. Most often, he was here in the mornings before arising. Answers to troubling questions frequently came to him when in this world. If ever he needed answers, it was now.

In two days, Vinh could hobble to a cook-fire to eat. Using a makeshift crutch under his arm, he could move to privacy to relieve himself. After four days, he could see that his wound was healing. It was still red but the swelling went down considerably. Soon, he would be able to remove the neat rows of stitches along its length. He often wondered who among the Tia had such skill.

Late one evening he sat by the cook-fire eating rice when a voice from across the fire said, "Hello Vinh, I see you are much better. Are you ready for me to remove those stitches?"

Vinh did not hear or see anyone approach. The flames kept him from seeing who it was across the fire. However, he recognized the voice.

"Hello Diem. How was your trip?" He asked.

Moving from behind the flames, Diem answered, "It went well young warrior. We will move in three days."

Vinh watched Diem move closer and remove a knife from a sheath strapped to his leg. As he sat beside him, he placed the knife's blade into hot coals in the fire. He rested its handle on a stone.

Turning to Vinh, he asked? "What are your plans?"

"I guess I will return to Muong Valley and the Viet Minh," he answered.

"Most of them are gone. There are a few remaining to salvage what they can. There's not much left," Diem explained.

Continuing, Diem said, "Once I asked you what country you were from. You said the DRV. It appears there may be such a place in the near future. Talks are underway in Geneva, Switzerland to settle details. The French will soon be leaving."

Vinh jumped to his feet and said, his voice ringing with jubilation, "Finally, peace. Now there will be peace."

Diem reached forward and rotated his knife's blade while pushing it farther into the coals. He watched Vinh's exultation as he did a mini-dance around the fire.

Finally, Vinh's leg gave way and he hobbled to collapse beside Diem. He looked at Diem and noticed his grim appearance. He stared directly into the fire.

"Aren't you glad the French are leaving and there will be peace?" He asked.

Still staring into the flames, Diem stated, "There will be no peace. Ho and his Communist party will not be happy until they dominate Viet Nam, Laos, and Cambodia. He is a treacherous man filled with Communist zeal. He sees a salvation for the world in Communism. He makes sure that anyone who does not agree dies. No, there will be no peace."

"You don't know that," Vinh said incredulously.

"Oh but I do," Diem answered quickly. "And so does Xuan."

"What," Vinh exclaimed. "What Xuan do you mean?"

"Your mother of course," Diem replied without changing his demeanor.

Vinh quickly grasped Diem's shoulder and pulled. This caused him to face Vinh. He looked directly into Diem's eyes.

"What do you know about my mother?" Vinh asked almost as a challenge to Diem's truthfulness.

Diem did not blink. He met Vinh's glare with a look that only comes from confidence born of truth.

"My name is Nguyen Van Diem. I am your uncle from Hanoi," he said. "I knew your brother. He visited with my family when he worked for my friend. You and I never met. During your fever, you kept calling for your father and mother by name. I saw the resemblance. I knew who you were then."

Speechless, Vinh stared in total disbelief.

"Why would he lie?" He wondered.

"Why didn't you tell me this before you left?" Vinh asked seething with doubt.

"Because you were weak, sick and needed rest. If I had told you, you would have done something stupid," he answered.

"If you are my Uncle, then tell me about our family. I can tell if you lie," Vinh demanded.

Diem turned the knife again. He began stoking hot coals with it. Almost casually, he detailed the birth date and place of every family member for two generations. Vinh felt disbelief slipping away and acceptance taking hold.

Interrupting Diem's recitation, Vinh demanded. "Where is my mother? How is she? Do you know anything about Minh Thanh?"

Diem related details about Xaun's arrival and then Minh Thanh's. He explained everything to include Xuan's physical condition.

"When word spread in Hanoi of your victory at Dien Bien Phu, Ho Chi Minh started a purge of his enemies. He had his followers roving in gangs killing people because of their religious or political beliefs. It was a nightmare. I was on my way to where they lived when a terrible storm struck. They were not at their place near the warehouse. Someone tore their door from its hinges. While there, a group saw me and knew I worked at the warehouse. They knew I was a catholic. They ran after me through the streets. I was able to lose them and return to my home. My house was in flames. I tried to go in but couldn't, the fire was too hot. Rain helped put the fire out and I examined the remains. My entire family was dead. I went into my chicken coop and armed myself from a stash I had. I made my way here," Diem said without taking a breath.

As he related events, tears streamed down his checks. Vinh could see them change from despondent to anger tears. By the time he finished, his eyes flashed vengeance.

"Vietnamese were killing Vietnamese because they were Catholics. That is your damned Uncle Ho, the Communist bastard and you want to join him. As your father lies in his grave, I will kill you before I will let you dishonor him by being a Communist," Diem blurted.

Fear rolled over Vinh for Diem still held the knife's handle. He knew that Diem meant what he said. He expected to die any moment.

Vinh lowered his head and said in a hushed tone, "Uncle, I will never dishonor you, father or mother. I hate the French. I killed them for what they did to my parents. I thought once the French left, we would live in peace, and the killing would stop. I believe you."

Diem released his grip on the knife. A deep sadness moved into his once fiery eyes.

Pulling Vinh to him, and holding him close, he said, "Tia are a freedom loving people. They are leaving here and moving south. They want nothing to do with the Communists. All they want is to live in peace. Their blood is your blood young warrior. Come with us," Diem pleaded.

"I will go with you to the south. Teach me the ways of the Tia. I too love freedom," Vinh said.

"Lay on your stomach," Diem directed.

Vinh watched as Diem removed the white-hot knife from the fire. He turned and did as Diem directed. He looked over his shoulder as Diem slowly moved the glowing blade toward his wound. He watched as each stitch snapped apart without the blade touching his skin.

"You will be able to travel in three days. I hope we find freedom. If not, we may have to fight for it. I will be proud for you to be at my side," Diem said.

Vinh could only wonder what life with the Tia would be like.

Chapter Eighteen

January 1962

There are no signposts in the sky to show a man has passed that way before
There are no channels marked. The flier breaks each second into new uncharted seas.
Anne Morrow Lindbergh (b. 1906), U.S. author.
North to the Orient, ch. 1 (1935).

Orange, gnat-like helicopters flitted above desolate Texas desert. Over scorpions, tarantulas and rattlesnakes, they dived and dipped as if taunting the scorched wilderness. Dale Zane watched with intense interest as he neared Mineral Wells, the Army's primary flight training school. Soon, he would board one of the small craft. By aerodynamic standards, they could not fly. Yet, the Army expected him to learn to fly them and do it well.

Janice slept with her head on a pillow against the right door's window. In the back seat, Susan slept a fitful sleep in spite of desert heat. She was their first born and controller of Dale's heart. If a "daddy's little girl" ever existed, she was one. The three were leaving one adventure for another. Their short time at Fort Sill had been an initiation into the military. They learned it was a way of life and not a job. Military members lived it every day, seven days a week.

Eighteen months earlier they arrived at Lawton, Oklahoma, for Dale's active duty tour. Janice wept in abject sorrow as they drove through Lawton's darkened streets. The dismal scene was heartbreaking after South Carolina's green hills. The only hills seen here were dirt mounds that separated traffic lanes on narrow, litter-strewn streets. In what appeared to be Lawton's municipal center, intersecting side streets were dirt. Green plants and trees were practically non-existent. The only vegetation was mesquite and cactus. It seemed only seconds and they were through the city, northbound.

"Was that it?" Janice asked.

"I guess so. I'll find a place to turn around and see if we missed a sign to Fort Sill," Dale replied with disappointment.

Tired from their long drive, they needed a place to rest. They saw a motel sign hanging from a broken frame. It swung back and forth emitting an irritating squeak as hot prairie wind pummeled it. Small, wood-frame cottages, weather beaten and worn, were the only overnight accommodations found.

"Oh hon, let's not stay here," Janice cried.

"I'm afraid this is it. Have you seen any others?" He asked empathizing with her apparent distress.

"No, but this is so bad," she answered with sincere consternation.

Their room was more disappointment. A musty odor permeated its shabby furnishings. In an effort to remove the smell, Dale crossed the room to what appeared to be an air conditioner. Starting it caused moist air to flow. It wasn't cold, not even cool but damp. Listening, Dale could hear water circulating inside the device. It was not an air conditioner. It was an evaporative cooler designed to moisturize air giving an impression of cooling.

Quite surprised, Janice said, "It does feel cooler. Perhaps we can sleep."

Dale, an early riser, slipped away the next morning. He left a note that hc would locate a place for breakfast. Janice greeted him upon his return.

"Let's get out of here. At least the car's air conditioner really cools," she pleaded.

"You bet," Dale said. "I've got a surprise."

They entered a different world. Manicured lawns and large oaks came into view as they entered Fort Sill's main gate. They had passed near it the previous night. Well-paved streets meandered through beige, stucco-like buildings with red tiled roofs. They followed signs to the installation's guesthouses. They obtained a neat, clean cottage as a temporary residence until they had permanent housing. They had breakfast at the Officer's club. Compared to what they had seen, this was magnificent.

It was Saturday morning and most student facilities did not open until Monday. With little else to do, the two lingered over coffee.

"Hon, let's drive around Fort Sill and see what its like," Janice suggested. "I have a brochure in my purse that was in our room at the guest house. It sounded interesting."

"Okay, let's do it," Dale replied.

They followed signs leading to South Boundary Road. They traveled west and immediately became awed by the immense prairie. Short grass, already tinged brown by cold weather, spread to the horizon. Here and there, a thorny mesquite bush dotted the terrain but other wise the vista remained unbroken. As they traveled farther west, the tops of what appeared to be mountains came into view.

"Those must be the Wichita Mountains," Dale said.

"That's wonderful," Janice exclaimed. "Let's visit them. I miss the Smokies so much. This flat dry terrain is depressing. It will be great to be in mountains again," Janice said.

"Don't get your hopes too high," Dale answered. "These aren't mountains like the Smokies. From what I remember from military history classes, they are an old group of hills worn smooth over the centuries. Nevertheless they dominate surrounding terrain."

"Look out," Janice screamed as four deer dashed across the road.

"Damn," Dale said applying brakes with considerable force.

The deer stopped a few yards from them and turned to watch Dale and Janice with curiosity. They began grazing while moving away at a leisurely pace.

"They're beautiful," Janice said watching them with intense interest. "They're not afraid of us at all. They act like pets."

"Well," Dale said. "They almost got killed with that stunt. We'll have to be more careful. Help me watch for them," Dale requested, still nervous from their near miss.

Soon the road they traveled became dirt. Dust billowed in great clouds behind their car. Coming to a slight rise in the terrain, Dale stopped. Nearby, a small knoll rose from the prairie. Its top was mesa-like with a deeply rutted trail to its top.

"Let's climb that hill for a better view," Dale said. "Those mountains don't seem to be getting any closer."

As soon as they exited their vehicle, dry desert heat engulfed them. They did not perspire climbing the knoll. Hot dry air adsorbed moisture like a sponge from exposed parts of their bodies. The climb was steep and the trail rutted by vehicles with large tires.

From their vantagepoint, the grandeur of the plains had a strong impact. They marveled at the vastness before them.

"It's so big," Janice commented.

"Yeah," Dale said. "Can you imagine what it was like living in this place 100 years ago?"

Continuing, Dale explained how Fort Sill came into being "After the Civil War, the Army sent Major General Sheridan out here to stop Indians raids on settlers living along the Kansas and Texas borders. This place teamed with Apaches and Commanches. He had his hands full. He had help from 'Buffalo Bill' Cody and 'Wild Bill' Hickock. They served as scouts in one hell of a winter campaign. Where Sheridan settled his post, the Indians called it 'the Soldier House at Medicine Bluffs.' Later, Sheridan named it after a classmate of his from West Point. He was Brigadier General Joshua W. Sill. The first Indian agent was Colonel Albert Gallatin Boone, grandson of Daniel Boone."

"Gosh," Janice exclaimed, "This place had a lot of famous people."

"Yeah, now they have us," Dale quipped.

"Dale, you are absolutely terrible," Janice commented.

"Would you believe Geronimo and his Apaches could have been standing where we are now?" Dale asked.

"Really," Janice answered.

"That's right," Dale continued. "He lived and died here. I'm told if you come out here during a full moon at midnight, you can hear them singing while they do war dances."

"Stop it. You're making that up. You cannot do such a thing," Janice answered.

Laughing, Dale asked, "Why would I lie?"

As the pair continued, they saw a large, brown mass moving across the prairie in the distance.

Janice asked. "What in the world is that?"

"I can't tell. They are too far away," Dale answered.

"My goodness, they are buffalo," Janice exclaimed.

"Bison," Dale said.

"What?" Janice asked.

"They are bison. They are not buffalo," Dale explained.

"Okay smart ass, I guess you're going to change your story," Janice said with a malicious grin.

"What story?" Dale questioned.

"The one you told about 'Bison Bill Cody,'" Janice retorted.

"Okay, I surrender. You got me," Dale replied with a large grin.

Shortly, the base of the mountains came into view. They were treeless, rolling hills covered with brown grass. Rising among them, a plateau-like mountain was much taller than the rest.

"Hey, there's cars driving up the side of that big one," Dale said. "Check that brochure about the mountains. See if they mention anything about that."

Looking at the brochure, Janice said, "That has to be Mount Scott."

"Let's drive up. Okay?" Dale asked.

"Okay," Janice agreed.

They drove to the top of Mount Scott on a narrow, curved road. They could see for what seemed 100 miles in any direction. It was the highest peak in the region. Below, a prairie dog city held thousands of the creatures whose burrows extending across the prairie.

Near sunset they listened to coyotes, wail a sad song calling one to the other.

"There's your Apaches and it's not even dark yet," Dale said with a chuckle.

"You are terrible. You gave up." Janice replied.

Dale laughed and said, "I couldn't resist."

Later, Janice tried to coax a badger to her by calling, "Here doggie. Here doggie."

It spread its body and threatened to charge until Dale intervened. He explained that the best approach to badgers was one of retreat. Their disposition wasn't that of the "cute prairie dogs" that Janice saw.

After dinner at the officers club, they collapsed in each other's arms in their cozy cottage. They were two alone having fun but far from home and feeling small in a big world. That night they slept the sleep that only lovers can.

Second Lieutenant Dale Zane was not the first junior officer to attend the Field Artillery Officer's Basic Course. The school had procedures in place to take young men from college and make them into "officers and gentlemen." Signs gave directions to arriving students as to where they should report. Dale went to the student battery headquarters. With his four years experience, he felt at home. He knew that other Army unit's used the term, "company," to designate their basic, organization unit. The field artillery used battery.

Nevertheless, most of those reporting knew little of artillery units and procedures. The purpose of the school was to take near-civilians and teach them the ways of "The King of Battle."

The first week was administrative time devoted to getting students organized. The army expected each officer to have specific uniforms. Each student officer purchased his clothing. Part of their processing was to assure that they did. Not only did they have to have the proper clothing; they had to demonstrate how to wear it. Their first test was to report for an early morning formation in fatigues, the Army's field uniform.

The night before Dale and Janice were preparing for Dale's first day on active duty as an officer. In a three-room apartment they rented, Janice was pressing hard with an iron on their kitchen table.

"Hon, I cannot put any more starch in these trousers," Janice said. "They are so stiff that they stand by themselves."

Dale, lying on the sofa reading, responded with a grunt. He held "The Officer's Guide."

"Hey Janice," he called.

"What?" She replied.

"It says in this guide that we have to make a social call on my commanding officer. You must wear a hat and long gloves. Get this; I have to leave a calling card. I don't have any calling cards," Dale said.

Janice replied, "You can get some printed. I think that is neat. I need a new hat and gloves."

"We're going to need some money from somewhere. I have to buy a dress blue uniform. They are expensive," Dale explained. "Hey, here's something else. Would you believe I have to pay for my meals when I eat in a unit's mess hall?"

"That doesn't seem right," Janice commented. "If you are in a war, you have to pay for your meals?"

"That's what it says in this book," Dale answered.

Janice laid her iron aside and lifted a pair of fatigues that stood rigid as if made from plastic.

She asked. "Are these stiff enough?"

Dale put down his book and looked toward Janice. She was standing by the kitchen table. The trousers stood upright leaning against the table without Janice touching them.

"I would say that's enough starch," Dale commented.

Janice walked across the room and sat on the sofa's edge. Leaning forward, she kissed Dale. Next, she lay down and pushed Dale against the sofa's back holding him in place.

"Now, I've got you," she said as she put her head on Dale's shoulder. "Hon, this is so different being in the military. Is this what you really want?"

"That's what the next two years are about I guess. I don't have a choice and what I want doesn't matter. It's something that my country thinks I should do and I will. As a private, I liked the National Guard. I think this is going to be fine," Dale answered.

Snuggling closer Janice looked Dale in the eyes and asked with a grin. "You ready for bed?"

"You bet," Dale answered.

Cold wind, a harbinger of Sill's harsh winters, blew across the student battery parking lot. It was early morning, slightly before sunrise. The new officers gathered in a parking lot. Mostly strangers, they milled about introducing themselves. Each wore heavily starched trousers tucked into their boot's tops. Their boots gleamed with a shiny sheen. Most of the neophyte artillerymen walked like stiff-legged puppets. They avoided bending their knees to keep from breaking their trousers' sharp crease.

Dale noticed that one officer's boots and trousers appeared strange. Only the lower portion of his boots shined. The tucked trousers looked peculiar near his boots. Yet, before he could get a closer look, a colonel approached their group.

"Attention," someone yelled.

It was likely that the colonel was a veteran of World War II and Korea. He had row upon row of award ribbons on his tunic. He had eight overseas bars on one sleeve. He had a look about him that screamed, "hard-bitten and tough as nails."

The colonel pointed to a nearby lieutenant and ordered, "Form the class."

Raising an arm, the lieutenant screamed in an adolescent like voice, "Everyone form on me."

Not totally without training, the group began forming rows with the designated officer as a start point. By placing one hand on the shoulder of an adjacent officer, the group began to look like an organized unit with neat, equally distant rows. Once accomplished, the designated officer stepped forward, saluted in front of the colonel, and reported, "Sir, the class is formed."

This group had almost 400 new lieutenants. The formation was large. Dale, in the last row, noticed the officer with the strange boots standing in front of him. He wore low-quarters, standard shoes for the dress uniform. He had his trousers tucked into black socks. By stretching his socks, the combination gave the appearance of high-top boots. Dale suppressed a laugh and then realized this was a serious situation.

This man had put an important formation at risk. During processing, a briefing officer explained about their first formation. The Staff and Faculty Commandant, Colonel Ludlow, would inspect their class. If they did not pass, the entire group would have to have formation every morning for a week. There was no possibility of passing with this officer's sophomoric attempt at subterfuge.

Dale punched the officer next to him in the ribs. It was a painful blow, causing the struck officer to turn his head and glare at him. Remaining at attention, Dale began exaggerated nods at the weirdly dressed officer to his front. By directing his glances downward, the situation became immediately apparent. With open mouth, the struck lieutenant stared in disbelief. He also realized they were doomed to early formations for the next week.

Colonel Ludlow, still inspecting the first rank, stopped in front of each officer. He gave him a close examination from his hat to his shoes. He would make a crisp left face and move to the next soldier. He was completely engrossed in his inspection.

Dale reached forward and grabbed the offending officer's belt. In one quick movement, he pulled him from his position and stepped into it. Totally surprised and off balance the guilty man started to speak.

Before he could say anything, Dale hissed a firm whisper, "Get the hell out of here, now."

The punched officer grabbed the surprised lieutenant's shoulders and gave a twist. This caused the offending soldier to face away from the formation. Next, he received a hard shove. He staggered forward and saw that there was a deserted building in front of him. Quickly understanding, he ran around it and out of sight.

The entire event did not take more than a few seconds. Colonel Ludlow, engrossed with his task at hand, never noticed.

After passing inspection, Dale and his classmate went looking for the lieutenant with the weird boot deception. He was standing behind the building with a guilty look about him.

"Hi, my name is Dale Zane. I'm sorry about handling you like I did. What is the deal with the shoes instead of boots?" Dale asked.

"No sweat," he said. "I appreciate your quick thinking. I had a money crunch. My brother mailed me a pair of new boots but they didn't make it on time. I didn't have the money the get another pair. By the way, I'm Neil Burnsides," he answered.

As they were talking, the other officer who pushed Burnsides approached them.

"My name is Scott. I couldn't help but hear what you said about your brother's boots. I hope you don't mind me pushing you like I did."

"No big deal," Burnsides said. "I didn't know that they were not going to call the roll. If I had known that I would not have showed."

"We can't have you walking around post like that," Scott said. "I have a pair of boots in my car's trunk. They should get you through the day."

"Thanks a million. I really appreciate the loan," Burnsides commented.

This incident forged a bond for life between Second Lieutenant Dale Zane and Second Lieutenant Daryl Scott, Dale's fellow conspirator. Only three knew how close it came to failure. None of them ever spoke of the matter. After getting boots on Burnsides, they went to their first class.

"My name is Peter Blake, Sergeant Major, United States Army Retired. I will be your instructor for the next three days. During this time, you will learn everything you ever wanted to know about artillery projectiles. You will leave this phase of instruction at least knowing which end of a projectile leaves an artillery piece first. Now, on with the show," their eloquent instructor said.

Sergeant Major Blake walked with a limp. He had a patch covering his left eye. In his right hand, he held a long, white pointer with a tip painted red. Limping across the classroom's stage, he pointed to an artillery shell standing on end.

"Gentlemen, this is an artillery projectile. It weighs 200 pounds and contains high explosive. Its purpose is to kill the enemy and not you. Therefore, you will take this hellish piece of steel apart and learn every component," Blake said as his voice faded from Dale's mental attention.

Dale knew this subject. This was basic information that he learned in the South Carolina National Guard. It was the upcoming gunnery instruction that caused him concern. Gunnery training lasted six weeks. It was the hardest part of the course. If he passed gunnery, he would graduate. If he didn't, he would lose his commission.

He was a reserve officer. Unlike regular army officers, his initial duty tour was two years. The officers, who graduated from West Point, and other military academies, were regular officers. Their duty tour was indefinite. However, most had to serve at least four years.

If a reserve officer did not pass, he received a discharge and was no longer a service member. His commission ceased to exist. A regular officer became a "graduate student pending." This was an army term meaning that the officer must take the course by correspondence. If he did not pass it the second time, he would possibly lose his commission.

The reservists referred to West Point graduates as "ring-knockers." This moniker came from a reported habit of academy graduates knocking their rings on a table to let people know they were "West-Pointers." A distinct rift existed between reservists and regulars. Much of it was unspoken. There was a feeling that regulars received better assignments and special consideration. However, this was to be expected. Regulars made a 30-year service commitment.

The utmost desire of any officer is command duty. Command positions did not exist for second lieutenants in the artillery. However, this school would teach him the basics needed to command. His first chance would come upon promotion to captain. Captains commanded artillery batteries.

The ultimate test of an artillery battery commander was reconnaissance, selection, and occupation of position, known by artillerymen as a RSOP. In artillery lingo, they called it an R-SOP. The most difficult RSOP took place while traveling. A forward observer would locate a target and contact the moving artillery battery. The commander had to make an immediate occupation of a position. Lacking a readily available off-road site, the commander placed his six weapons on the road.

Fire direction personnel were solving the firing problem while this activity was underway. Within three minutes, the unit had to be in place and have projectiles on their way to the target. Putting fire on a target had first priority and the success of doing so rested with the battery commander. His class would learn these techniques. Their gunnery instructor would do that.

A gunnery instructor's challenge was to assure his class knew every facet of artillery battery operations. The forward observer portion was popular because the observer saw the fruits of his efforts. He could watch targets destroyed. Firing big artillery weapons had its moments but paled against fire direction center procedures. The FDC coordinated everything. They were the conductors of a deadly symphony. Their maestro was their gunnery instructor.

To new artillery lieutenants, gunnery instructors were god-like. Each class section had the same one for six weeks. They were seasoned artillerymen with vast knowledge of the artillery process. They solved complex mathematical equations while talking and writing on the blackboard. A gunnery instructor was a walking, talking epitome of what every second lieutenant wanted to be. Graduating students showered them with lavish parties and gifts. The gunnery instructor sent them into battle armed with knowledgeable control of vast firepower resources.

Yet, there was a major drawback about being a forward observer. During the Korean War, the enemy made forward observers a primary target. They knew if they could kill forward observers, the infantry lost their best firepower sources. The average life span in combat, for forward observers, was 20 minutes.

"Wake up Zane," Daryl said. "It's break time."

Dale felt his seat toppling sideways. Quickly, he righted the upended desk and looked to his right. Daryl Scott gave him an elfish-like look and a laugh.

"You're damned lucky I didn't kick you over during instruction," Daryl advised. "You were into some heavy daydreaming."

Classmates gathered in small groups consuming snacks and sodas. Dale and Daryl went outside to smoke. It was early November. Stinging blue-northers had already begun ripping into Fort Sill from the northwest. Blue-northers were fast moving cold fronts that approached with low hanging, bluish black clouds. They brought dust storms, followed by heavy lightning and hail. As if that was not enough, tornadoes also skipped across the plains destroying entire cities. Next, temperatures plunged to below zero chill factors because of strong winds.

"We should get orders soon," Daryl said shivering slightly. "A guy in personnel said they usually have them by our fifth week. Do you have any preferences as where to go?"

"Not really as long as it's not here. Janice hates this place," Dale answered.

"Yeah, my wife's sick of it. I'm not exactly fond of the place. It's a crock having to check my boots for scorpions each morning," Daryl commented.

"Janice has to jam newspapers beneath outside doors to keep dirt out of the house. It still gets in somehow," Dale replied.

"Time for another?" Daryl asked, offering Dale a cigarette.

"I don't think so. That crusty, old sergeant major has a fit if we are not in our seats when he starts," Dale answered.

With introductory classes finished, their class met their gunnery instructor. He was a Marine Corps Captain. They considered this unusual until he explained that the Marine Corps did not have an artillery school. Fort Sill trained Marine Corps students. Later Dale learned that the Marine Corps selected their best officers for instructor duty at Fort Sill. Their section was lucky to have him.

Soon afterwards, class members received assignments. Dale received orders to Korea. Dale did not look forward to this assignment. It was an unaccompanied tour. He and Janice would have to part for 13 months. This was tough to take for newly weds.

Duty would be with a unit near Korea's Demilitarized Zone. DMZ duty was the hardest in Korea. Installation facilities were primitive at best and the hours long. North of their unit, untold thousands of elite North Korean forces continually probed defense facilities for weak spots. Frequently, covert Special Forces crossed into South Korea. They conducted terrorist activities and sabotaged critical facilities. Those who interfered, civilian or military, usually did not live to tell about it.

Dale and Janice agreed she should return to Spartanburg. Under no circumstances did she want to stay in Lawton. Second lieutenants did not qualify for on-base housing. They had rented a small house near Fort Sill's main entrance. It wasn't much. They could not afford anything better because of his low pay.

To make matters worse, Janice was pregnant. She would have their first child while Dale was in Korea. Janice was developing an aversion to military life. She wanted Dale present when she gave birth.

Daryl received orders to attend advance training. His assignment was to an Honest John missile battery. The Honest John was a ground to ground missile capable of delivering nuclear warheads. Daryl could not tell Dale where he was going for training. Much to his chagrin, his assignment after advanced training was to Fort Sill.

Two weeks before being graduated, Dale received a memo to report to the Commandant of the Staff and Faculty Battery.

"How have I screwed up?" He wondered.

The commandant was the colonel who inspected their class in October. His reputation was that of a bad-ass. Rumors were that he had zero tolerance for screwed-up students. Their class had already lost many students for dumb mistakes. Dale could not think of any attributed to him. Nevertheless, he approached the meeting with considerable anxiety.

"Tell me lieutenant. How would you like to be a gunnery instructor?" Colonel Ludlow asked.

The significance of Ludlow's question staggered Dale. He found the question so unbelievable that he failed to respond.

"Come on lieutenant, I do not have all day. Do you or don't you?" Ludlow asked again.

"Absolutely sir but I have orders to Korea," Dale finally answered.

"Forget them son. They no longer exist," Ludlow replied. "After graduation, report to the personnel officer in Headquarters. They will be expecting you. Now, get out of here."

Dale saluted; did an about face; and left Ludlow's office without his feet touching the floor.

"What?" Janice exclaimed. "We're staying in this terrible place. Honey, I do not believe I can stand this place for two years. While I hated that you were going to Korea, I looked forward to going home. The only good thing I see is your being with me with our child arrives. That's wonderful."

She began to cry. Dale took her into his arms to console her. Holding her close, he tried to explain. She mumbled something about laundry and ran from the room. Dale knew better than to follow. Lately, morning sickness had not been only in the mornings.

Dale sat on their lumpy sofa and interlocked his fingers behind his head. Leaning back, he stared at the ceiling.

"There are no lieutenant gunnery instructors," he thought. "Hell, there's damn few captains. Most are experienced majors who have commanded artillery batteries. Many of them did so in combat. This must be a mistake. I will call Daryl."

Daryl was sure Dale was setting him up for a practical joke.

"Yeah, right. They are going to let some shave-tail teach gunnery. That's about as likely as the Pope joining the First Baptist Church. Zane, what the hell are you up to this time?" Daryl asked.

Two weeks later Daryl left for missile training. Dale reported to Headquarters. Janice cried every time he mentioned his new assignment.

Major Bennett was Dale's new commander. He commanded an instruction group in the Gunnery Department. Each group taught students in Officers Candidate School and the Officers Basic Course. A few senior officers taught classes in the Artillery Officers Career Course, the last artillery courses for individuals selected for position of high responsibility. Dale met one of those instructors. He was his new boss.

"Here's the deal," Bennett said. "You will attend a three week methods of instruction course. They will teach you how to be an effective instructor. After that, report to Sergeant Major Blake. He will spend two weeks helping you with lesson plan preparation and presentation. When Blake says you are ready, report to me. Any questions lieutenant?"

"Yes sir," Dale responded. "Why me? I didn't have the best grades in gunnery. It's an honor to be here but I find the situation quite unusual. Don't you sir?"

"You bet your ass I do. You will be the first second lieutenant to teach gunnery. Honestly, nothing personal, I don't like the idea. Nevertheless, the commandant saw that you have enlisted experience in an artillery unit. He thinks you will be able to better relate to officer candidates and lieutenants than senior officers. We will see about that in good time," Bennett answered with considerable doubt in his voice.

Dale had watched Bennett as he spoke. He was slightly bald and developing a paunch. He held the ends of a pencil in each hand. He rolled it back and forth with his thumbs and forefingers. The more he talked, the faster he rolled the pencil.

For a major, he appeared older than most. Wrinkles spread from the corners of each eye and ended in thinning hair above his ears. With his lower body behind his desk, it was difficult to judge his height. Dales guessed he was short, perhaps five feet, nine inches.

Bennett confirmed Dale's guess as he arose and said, "Let's take a break lieutenant."

Dale followed Bennett. The diminutive major retrieved his blouse from a nearby coat rack. As he was putting it on, Dale saw an impressive array of awards and decorations. Among them was a Distinguished Service Cross ribbon with an oak leaf cluster. This indicated he had received the nation's second highest award twice. The next highest award was the Medal of Honor.

Bennett led the way down a hall to a small, break room. A counter on one side held a coffee machine with two coffeepots on it. There was sugar and some plastic spoons. Next to these containers, a cardboard box held a variety of doughnuts. Bennett poured a cup for Dale and one for himself.

"Sugar lieutenant?" Bennett asked.

"No sir," Dale answered as he watched Bennett go to a small table in a corner.

Dale joined Bennett and sat directly across from him. He noticed that Bennett had a puzzled look.

"How old are you lieutenant?" He asked.

"I'm 23 sir," Dale answered.

Stirring his coffee, Bennett said, "Here's some advice. Do with it what you will."

Dale nodded and waited for Bennett to speak. Bennett blew softly on the steaming liquid in his cup and sipped some. He took a larger swallow.

Clearing his throat, he said, "You stick to Sergeant Major Blake like glue, son. Listen to him and learn. He has more experience leading men than you do years. Doesn't be an ass kisser or he will drop you quick. If Blake believes you sincerely want to learn, he will teach you everything he knows."

Bennett removed a pack of Camel cigarettes from his shirt pocket. He tapped it upon the tabletop until its tobacco packed tight. He took a silver, Zippo lighter from the same pocket. It had a large, military unit crest on it. The insignia was a yellow patch with a black line diagonally across it. A black horse's head appeared behind the line. Bennett lit his cigarette, took another sip of coffee, and continued.

"Furthermore, if you ever get in a combat unit, listen to your non-commissioned officers. They can make or break you. Treat them with respect and they will bust their asses for you. Screw with them and you're doomed."

Suddenly, Bennett arose swiftly saying, "Let's go."

Dale was sure he saw Bennett's eyes go slightly misty before he abruptly stood. They headed toward Bennett's office but he stopped at the door.

"Go see Blake lieutenant," Bennett ordered and left Dale in the hall.

Dale stood for a moment staring at the doorway. He turned slowly and went to the break room. Opening his wallet, he took a dollar and put it in a jar next to the coffeepots. He looked and Bennett's cigarette still smoldered in an ashtray. He twisted it into the tray.

Dale knew something extremely important just happened. It was imperative he remember every word. In addition, he noted Major Bennett's nervous use of his hands. They trembled when lighting his cigarette. Dale left to see Blake.

Sergeant Major Blake worked in an office complex next to where he taught classes. Dale entered and looked around the large room. He estimated there were at least 30 people seated at desks. Each desk had a nameplate bearing each person's name. There were another 10 desks without nameplates or persons seated at them. He searched the room for Blake. He finally saw his desk but Blake was not at it. Wondering what to do next, Dale saw an NCO leave his desk and walk toward him.

"Can I help you L-T?" The staff sergeant asked casually.

Dale found the sergeant's manner strange. He had expected him to salute and report. Instead, he called him "L-T." Some senior officers called lieutenants L-T but not enlisted.

"Yes, sergeant," Dale answered. "I'm assigned to work with Sergeant Major Blake. Do you know where he is?" Dale asked.

"Well, hell L-T. I heard we were getting a shave-tail but I didn't believe it. I'm Staff Sergeant Malloy," the sergeant said extending his hand.

Dale reluctantly took the offered greeting. Remembering what Major Bennett told him, he held a firm grip and shook the sergeant's hand.

Dale asked again. "Sergeant, do you know where Blake is?"

"Right here L-T," a voice said from behind him.

He turned to find Sergeant Major Blake smiling at him with outstretched hand. Dale took it and shook Blake's hand.

"Sir, Major Bennett told me to report to you," Dale explained.

"Don't sir me L-T. I work for a living," Blake replied with a grin as Sergeant Malloy laughed.

"It is going to be interesting here," Dale thought.

Dale followed Major Bennett's advice. He and Blake developed a close working relationship. Blake was an "old school" artilleryman. He liked to say he was from the "brown shoe army." He lied about his age and joined the Army when he was 16. He fought with Roosevelt at San Juan Hill during the Spanish American War. He fought in World Wars I and II. He received a medical discharge after a serious wound in 1945. Every assignment was in an artillery unit providing direct support for infantry troops in battle.

Regarding Korea he said, "Hell, if they won't let me fight the commie bastards. I will train others how. I applied for this job when the war started. I've been here ever since. They will have to roll me out of this place on a caisson."

His relationship with Sergeant Malloy was different. He, and his wife Nell, were almost surrogate parents for Dale and Janice. Nell helped Janice with her pregnancy. She already had six grandchildren and considered Janice's to be her seventh.

At work, Malloy was all business. On weekends, he and Dale hunted quail on Oklahoma's prairie. Malloy had three bird dogs of championship quality. When the mother dog went on point, the younger two honored her by holding. With one front leg poised, they stood rigid while scenting the covey. On occasion, the older dog would move if the birds ran. However, it was slow and deliberate.

Malloy would say in a low voice, "Whoa girl, whoa. Good girl, bird, bird."

He most often motioned Dale forward for a first shot that he usually missed. Malloy always brought down Dale's missed birds.

"What's the matter L-T? Those little birds scare you?" he asked when Dale over-reacted to a flushed covey.

Each hunt ended with a session of bourbon and water. He always had a pint in his pickup. Malloy never drank during a hunt. Whether they had birds or not, he always honored the hunt. Malloy had bourbon under control now but it was his downfall in earlier years.

"You know L-T, if I had been Nell, I would have thrown my butt out years ago. She's a fine woman who always picked me up when I fell and I fell a lot," Malloy told Dale.

He explained how he had lost two stripes because of drinking, "With a few drinks L-T, I was the toughest thing going. I would fight a telephone pole if it were in my way. I should be a first sergeant but drinking too much cost me the honor. I was too stupid to realize that I was a runt looking for a fight. I lost every time. Not only did I get my butt kicked, I lost my stripes."

Malloy explained how Blake had intervened to save him, "He gave me the job as coach of the post boxing team. Can you believe that?" He said with a laugh.

"Hell, I know how to fight but not when I'm drunk. Blake knew that L-T. It took a while but the guys I coached always ended up in the finals. I never go to bars any more. Instead, I go to the gym. During hunting season, I always have a pint at day's end. Now, I share it with you. You're going to do okay L-T," Mallow said as he petted one of his dogs.

Months passed rapidly while becoming a gunnery instructor. When Blake told Barnett that he was ready, he assigned Dale to another instructor. For six weeks, he followed the seasoned instructor's every move. He prepared lesson plans, firing charts and gathered tools needed in class. At the end of six weeks, Major Barnett sent for him.

"Zane, I'm starting you with an OCS class. They are enlisted personnel undergoing rigorous training to become officers. As artillery professionals, they must master gunnery. You are the one held responsible to see that they do," he said.

Dale watched as Barnett either chain-smoked or grappled with pencils. He couldn't keep his hands still.

Barnett continued, "You will teach for six weeks and be off for six. I expect you to use those six weeks off to get ready for your next class. If you can get ready at home mowing the yard, fine. I will monitor your classes on a random basis. If I find that you're not ready, you're out of here cause I did not want you doing this."

"Is there anything you do not understand about what I just said?" Barnett asked.

"No sir," Dale replied.

"Good, you're dismissed," Barnett directed.

Colonel Ludlow was correct. Dale had a natural rapport with young students. Major Bennett finally conceded to Dale's expertise. This brought comfort for Dale because Barnett decreased his visits to his classes. To Dale, this meant trust and Barnett's trust was important to him.

Master Sergeant Blake explained Barnett's nervousness, "L-T, the major has had a rough go of it. He was with Task Force Smith in Korea. They were the first combat unit to try to blunt North Korea's invasion. They made first contact near Pyontaek, South Korea. This is near the bigger town of Osan south of Seoul. He was an artillery battery commander. His battery of 105-mm howitzers was no match against tanks. The North Korean infantry would simply flank his position on both sides and attack from his rear. Meanwhile, tanks pounded his front. They forced him to continually fall back to a new position. Eventually, they destroyed or captured every weapon he had. He and his men were captured."

"Damn, Sergeant Major, I had no idea," Dale said. "No wonder he's nervous."

"He finally escaped L-T. He made his way south and eventually found his old unit, the 1st Cavalry Division. You've seen that lighter he uses haven't you?" Blake asked.

"Sure, many times," Dale answered.

"His men gave him that immediately after the cease fire. He treasurers it more than the two Distinctive Service Crosses he received. You don't know how lucky you are to have him as your boss," Blake continued.

"Hell Sergeant Major, I didn't know any of this about Korea. However, I sure respect him for what he did for me not too long ago," Dale said.

"What's that?" Blake asked.

"I was 20 miles out on the West Range teaching an observed fire class. I received a message to report to Colonel Bigalow as soon as I returned. You know Bigalow. He runs the Tactics Division in the Department of Instruction," Dale related.

"Sure I know him. What's he got to do with you?" Blake asked becoming concerned.

Dale continued, "I had to cut my class short in order to return before he went home. He was just leaving his office when I reported. He took me inside and chewed my butt big time. His wife is one of the organizers in the Officers Wives Clubs. She had a luncheon and Janice didn't go. She called her husband who sent word for me to report to him. Hell, Sergeant Major, she was in the hospital having Susan. She couldn't go."

"Jesus H. Christ L-T, you don't have to put up with that crap," Blake exclaimed.

"Well, I told Major Barnett the next morning," Dale continued. "He called Colonel Bigalow and chewed his butt royally. He told the colonel that he had better never go around him to one of his men. They do not work for him and if he has something to say, say it to him. He made Bigalow apologize to me. I didn't believe it."

"I'm not the least surprised," Blake said. "He is good people."

Dale and Janice were soon at a decision point. In six months, Dale's active duty tour would end. The two discussed what to do when Dale left the service. Despite the low pay and long hours, they liked military life. Their friend Daryl helped them with their decision. Daryl was applying for flight school. He wanted Dale to do the same.

Dale liked the idea. There were advantages. Aviators received flight pay. The amount received depended upon rank and years in the service. Dale would soon have six years. He would draw maximum pay for his rank. This would help with finances.

He liked the idea of learning to fly. He had flown in an airplane one time. A high school friend was in the Civil Air Patrol. He took him for a night flight over Spartanburg when he was in college. At the time, he liked it but had forgotten about it. Now, he had a chance to become an aviator. He and Janice agreed he should apply.

Selection for flight school was difficult. There were extensive tests to pass. One psychological evaluation required an entire day. After the written portion, he met with a psychiatrist for a mental evaluation. Dale thought questions that he asked were outlandish.

"Tell me lieutenant. What do you think the phrase, 'People who live in glass houses gather no moss,' means?" He asked.

Initially befuddled by this question, Dale answered, "It is meaningless. It is a mix of two views about human behavior. The first part is from the phrase, 'People who live in glass house should not throw stones.' The second part is from the phrase, 'A rolling stone gathers no moss.'"

"Thank you lieutenant," the evaluator said. "That's it."

The most difficult part of being qualified for flight school was the physical. It was exacting with no room for physical problems. Visual testing was the most extensive part. However, one portion caused Dale a major problem. He could not weight more than 176 pounds. He had never weighed less than 176 since he was 13.

His football coach referred to him as the "fire-plug." He was five feet and 11 inches tall with an 18-inch neck. His chest was 56 and his waist was 31-inches. What served him well in football was now a major difficulty.

Dale passed the physical except for weight. He weighed 191-lbs. The flight surgeon informed Dale of the problem. He prescribed a diuretic, gave him a diet to follow, and told him to come back in two weeks. Totally dejected Dale returned to his office.

"What's the matter L-T?" Sergeant Malloy asked. "You look like you just found out the IRS was going to audit you. What's up?"

"You know I applied for flight school. Well, I flunked the physical for being overweight," Dale answered.

"Overweight! You are not overweight. There's not an ounce of fat on you L-T," Malloy exclaimed.

"How much?" Malloy asked.

"I weigh 191-lbs. and I cannot weight over 176-lbs.," Dale answered.

"L-T, you wait here. I thought you had a problem. You don't have a problem. I will take care of this," Malloy said with confidence.

Malloy returned with a large bag filled with lemons. He went to Dale's desk and sat across from him. He removed a lemon and placed it in front of Dale. He began to roll the lemon back and forth while pressing with his palm.

"L-T, this will make the lemon juicy. Don't you already feel your mouth watering while I roll this thing?" Malloy asked.

Dale agreed as he felt his mouth begin to accumulate liquid. It watered even more when Malloy sliced the yellow fruit in half.

"Fighters use this method to meet weight limits in boxing matches," Malloy explained. "This will work for you but you must do exactly as I say. From this moment forward, you cannot consume liquids of any sort. I mean none. You suck these lemons and spit out the fluid. Do this all night and continue to take the diuretic. You are not going to believe the weight loss. You going to do what I said L-T?" Malloy asked.

"Yeah, I will try it," Dale said unbelievingly.

"Don't try L-T. Do it," Malloy emphasized.

Dale weighed at the flight surgeon's office the next morning at 175 pounds. Once the doctor signed the qualification form, Dale ran to a nearby water cooler.

Dale and Daryl had orders to flight school within a month. They were to report to Camp Wolters at Mineral Wells, Texas, for primary training. After primary, they had to report to Fort Rucker, Alabama, for advance training.

Major Bennett's words stayed with Dale. He never forgot them. The NCOs made him a successful gunnery instructor. The NCOs got him in flight school. He knew NCOs could make or break an officer. Without them, he was nothing.

A well-known odor came from their old car's back seat. Susan began crying. She was awake and, from the aroma, in need of a diaper change. Janice took her head from her pillow and sat upright.

Stretching, with a big yawn, she asked. "Are we there yet?"

Dale watched Janice reach for a large diaper bag and answered, "Almost, the last sign said Mineral Wells 10 miles. I'm watching for a Camp Wolters' sign."

Deftly moving Susan to the front, Janice laid her on the seat. She removed the soiled diaper while holding two safety pins in her clenched teeth.

Mumbling, Janice commented, "I hope it's better than Lawton."

In the distance, Dale saw a large hotel. It seemed exceptionally large for such an isolated area. Later he learned that people used to come to bath in its spring fed pools. Many people believed the springs had medicinal qualities. The town got its name from the well's presence.

Slowly, mesquite covered ranch land gave way to suburban homes. A road sign noted that there was an exit to Camp Wolters ahead one-mile. Dale reduced speed and followed signs. Turning left at an intersection, he drove two miles to a large sign that arched over an entrance gate.

"Welcome to Camp Wolters," appeared on the arches upper part. Directly beneath, "Above the Best," appeared with a set of aviator's wings. He read the sign aloud for Janice since she had her hands full.

"Catchy," he thought.

Chapter Nineteen

May 1954

Immature love says: "I love you because I need you."
Mature love says: "I need you because I love you."
Erich Fromm (1900–1980), U.S. psychologist. *The Art of Loving,* ch. 2 (1956).

Minh Thanh pulled her bed covering tight. She did so, not because of mother superior's desires, but it seemed the natural order of things. Besides, it was no great burden since little else in her small chamber required much care. After genuflecting and crossing herself, she removed a crucifix from the wall at the head of her bed. It was the only object adorning the room's walls. She cleaned and replaced it with care.

Knelling to pray she kissed a prized, hand-carved rosary that had belonged to her mother. Her prayers finished, she crossed herself and arose. With tenderness and care, she returned the rosary to her only worldly possession, a small, black lacquered box. Inlaid mother of pearl dragons adorned its surface. Sighing, she dusted it to a high sheen.

She poured water from a pitcher into a small porcelain bowl and washed. Afterwards, she sat at her desk-like table. She reached behind her head and parted her long, black hair. She pulled half of it over her right shoulder, holding it with her left hand. She opened the table's drawer and removed a crude brush. She began applying long strokes to remove tangles. She repeated this procedure on her left side. After putting away the brush, she used both hands to pull her ebony tresses together directly behind her head. Placing her hands, fingertips to fingertips beneath it, she shook her head. Her hair tumbled to her waist. Without a mirror, she could not see that it was in order. The thought that she wanted a mirror caused concern. Such a desire was worldly and possibly a sin of vanity.

From a wooden peg on her door, she removed a single-piece; beige gown made from homespun cloth. She placed both hands into its bottom opening and raised it above her head. She let it fall. It stopped its descent immediately above the floor. From the same peg, she took a rope-like sash and placed it around her diminutive waist, tying it in an overhand loop. She slipped her feet into sandals and made a quick look around her room. Everything was in its proper place.

She opened her room's door to allow light to enter from the hallway. Next, she returned to her table and extinguished her lone candle. It was five A. M. and time for morning prayers.

Afterward, she went to the cathedral for confession. She pulled the confessional's curtain closed as she entered. Turning, she went to a small seat but did not sit. Reaching forward, she moved a sliding cover that revealed a grid carved as tiny flowers growing on twisting vines. The decorations made it impossible to see the priest on the other side.

Facing the open portal, she genuflected and made the sign of the holy trinity and said, "Forgive me Father for I have sinned. It has been two days since my last confession."

A male voice answered, "Be seated my child and we shall pray."

Clasping her rosary to her breast, she sat. Bowing her head, she recited the Lord's prayer with her confessor. When finished, the two said Amen in unison.

A momentary silence ensued before she said, "Father, I want to become a bride of Christ. My love for him is so powerful that I feel I should devote my life to him. Yet, my heart must not be pure because I have disturbing dreams. They come in the night and I pray that it is not Satan. I pray every morning after the dreams but they still return. During the day when we have meditation, my mind wanders from Christ. I dream of another. He is a man I met only once but cannot forget. I try Father. I try so hard but I cannot stop it."

Minh Thanh began to weep. Her shoulders heaved for the hurt within was strong, powerful. Despite every effort she could not stop. The booth was silent and the priest did not speak. Finally, exhausted, Minh Thanh breathed deeply while moving her rosary through her fingers.

"My child, the time is near. You will soon have to decide. Do not despair because what you feel is not Satan. It is love and it is natural. God, through love, gave his only son for us. Christ is our redeemer and is not one to condemn you because of love for another. Do you have anything else to confess my child?" The priest asked.

"No Father," she answered.

Minh Thanh leaned forward and kissed her rosary.

She tucked it beneath her chin and said, "Oh my God, I am heartily sorry for having offended thee. I despise all my sins because I fear the loss of heaven and the fires of hell. But, most of all, because I have offended thee, my God, who is all good and deserving of all my love. I firmly resolve, with the help of thy grace, to do penance and amend my life."

"An act of contrition was not necessary. Neither is absolution or penance young one for you have not sinned. Go to the Chapel and pray for guidance. Christ will show you the way. Have faith and trust in him. He will let you know in your heart what you must do," the priest advised.

Next, he blessed her and closed his side of the grid. Minh Thanh closed hers with trembling hands. She arose and pushed the curtains aside as she left for the chapel. Quickly and quietly, she moved through the cathedral like an apparition. She seemed to glide across the inlaid, tile floor. Her only stop was to genuflect before the tabernacle.

Great arcs and spires rose about her. Columns climbed to a high ceiling with paintings of Christ and his apostles. Day's first light scattered varied colored beams throughout pews as it entered through massive, stained glass windows. Each window's light stood stark against waning darkness as it penetrated Saigon's largest cathedral. It was South Viet Nam's major refuge for many seeking to become nuns.

At the cathedral's rear, Minh Thanh stopped to lightly touch holy water by the exit. Again she faced the tabernacle, genuflected and completed the sign of the holy trinity with her moistened fingers.

A short distance down the hall, towards an exit door, the chapel was on her right. It was in this chapel that she became aware of Jean's eyes upon her. It was just outside that her heart raced when they spoke as she left her French class. She never forgot. Once in the chapel, she started to pray.

She began, "Almighty God and Father, we give you thanks. We praise you for your glory."

Her throat became constricted and she had difficulty breathing. In her chest, a great ache grew. It was almost as if someone had a large strap around her and was tightening it.

"I do not understand this," she thought. "I only saw him for a moment. We said a few words. What kind of madness is this?" She asked herself.

In her ensuing prayer, she begged for Jean's life and safety. She knew that many Legionnaires went north last fall. She plagued Captain Louis, her French instructor, for details but received none.

"If he was here and safe, he would tell me," she reasoned. "They have gone to fight the Communists. They will kill those considered Satan's disciples. I cannot believe that God's commandments apply to Satan's allies."

With a massive mental effort to overcome her distressing emotions, her thoughts turned to her mother, Xuan.

"Oh, if you were only here. You would know what to do," her mind wailed in a long, distressing cry.

The few years they had together in Hanoi were assuredly a blessing. After nursing her back to health, the two made twine for the factory. They spent every waking moment together. After Xuan's ordeals, her being alive had to be miracle.

The French almost killed her in prison. Her solitary confinement was inhuman. They treated her as if she was less than an animal. Vichy French treated their pigs with more kindness. Starved, she could not resist the Japanese. Their abundance of food overwhelmed her.

Xuan told her everything. She explained that she slept with Japanese officers to live. As she regained her strength, her natural beauty returned. This lessened her exposure to the attentions of the group because their commander made her his concubine. The others dared not make an overture. Still, she found no peace with what she was doing.

She had only been with her husband before the Japanese. Although he was dead, she considered what she did a breaking of the holy sacrament of marriage. Finally, not able to bear her disgrace, she committed a mortal sin. She tried to kill herself. She reasoned that Purgatory had to be a better place. She would stand before her God and leave her soul to his judgment.

Her attempt failed only because the officers feared their commander. He was away when she drank poison. His subordinates thought he might find them at fault so they made sure she received excellent medical care. Xuan's heart broke because she lived.

Nonetheless, the mercury-based poison caused her to become ill. She could not eat and, despite intravenous feeding, her health continued to deteriorate. While ill, her hair changed from ebony to white. Malnutrition caused her to start losing her teeth. Her lover rapidly lost interest and found another. Her medical care stopped and they returned her to prison.

A French doctor diagnosed her condition the result of leprosy. Xuan knew he lied out of compassion. He could not bear to see what his fellow countrymen were doing to her and others. He knew they would move her to a leper colony where she might survive. In their prison, death was certain.

Minh Thanh remembered Xuan telling of the leper colony. It was much better than prison. Guards never entered their compound. They feared contracting the disease. Prisoners were not in dark cells but had access to fresh air and sunshine. They lived in bamboo huts with thatched roofs. Each was on a raised platform to remain away from the mud and water.

They aided each other. They had few medical supplies but did have better food than the prison. They shared and made sure that the severely sick received priority for medicine and food.

The lepers knew immediately that Xuan did not have leprosy. In addition, she was not the first to arrive without the dreaded ailment. The prison doctor had sent five others.

One of the afflicted was once a nurse in Hanoi's largest hospital. She examined Xuan and found her crippled from swollen joints. Her open sores resulted from filth in prison. Grief, despair, and residual effects of the toxin caused her weight loss. She told Xuan that she could not remain at the colony. She must leave as the others had. She explained that each month a medical team visited. They would expose Xuan and the doctor who sent her.

The lepers revealed their escape method. The others, who did not have leprosy, had used it and gained their freedom. It was imperative that Xuan do the same.

The leper's escape plan was simple. Each day a truck came to remove the dead. French drivers would not touch bodies or enter their compound. They backed their truck through the gates for lepers to do the loading. They took bodies, wrapped in burlap, to a pit on the outskirts of Hanoi and dumped. Heavy equipment operators pushed dirt over them.

Xuan's opportunity would come when a truck arrived late. This was a frequent occurrence. The drivers, as usual, delivered their ghoulish load to the pit. However, they arrived after sunset. They tilted their truck's bed, causing bodies to fall into the pit where they remained uncovered until the next day.

Heavy equipment operators never remained in the area after dark. Their superstition kept them away. They feared that, in darkness, a leper's soul could take their body. They would then become lepers. Xuan waited anxiously for her opportunity. It came soon.

When it became obvious that the truck was late, they prepared her. They gathered some shelled coconut and fruit from their hidden stash. They wrapped it in a palm leaf for her to eat later. They gave her a hooded shroud to wear and put her in one of their body bags. Everything almost went as planned. One failure almost cost Xuan her life. When they dumped her into the pit, she lost consciousness from the fall.

Slightly before dawn, Xuan awoke and freed herself. It was necessary to push through other bodies but she did so with great difficulty. She climbed the pit's side to reach its top just at sunrise. Three equipment operators, arriving on their bicycles, saw her silhouetted against the morning's sunrise. She wore her hooded shroud and made a horrific figure to the arriving workers. They crashed in a tangled heap of arms, legs, and spinning bicycle wheels. They ran away screaming. Xuan always drew great pleasure relating this event to Minh Thanh.

Xuan met no resistance traveling to her brother-in-law's home in Hanoi's suburban area. A distinct odor from the leper's bodies traveled with her. She made no pretense of hiding. Crowds parted to let her pass.

In a market place, she saw two policemen watching her. They appeared suspicious and one ordered her to stop.

"You there, in the black robe, stop," one said firmly.

They started toward her on their bicycles. The one in front wore a sergeant's uniform. Xuan removed her hood as they approached. The lead rider stopped suddenly almost causing the other policeman to crash into him. They stood astride their bicycles, as their fear became obvious.

"On your way old woman," the sergeant said in a most disrespectful manner. He felt the crowd watching him.

"Keep going and do not return here," he ordered.

Xuan covered her head and started toward an exit street. She moved without haste or any evidence of concern. The police remained in place and watched, glad to see her leave their area.

She arrived at Nguyen Van Diem's home at midday. Her husband's brother ordered her away until she revealed who she was. Even then, he reluctantly admitted her. Only after she told what had happened did they relax.

She lived with Diem and his family for two weeks. He approached her one morning after work. He had just returned from his night shift as a warehouse guard. He seemed excited.

Diem said, "You cannot stay here for it is not safe. Our neighbors are already suspicious and the Communists among them will report you."

"Where can I go? How can I provide for my needs?" Xuan asked.

"Do you remember Anh working for a warehouse owner?" Diem questioned.

"Yes," she answered.

"He is a good man. I work for him and we are friends. I told him about you. He made an offer I think you should take," Diem revealed.

Interested, Xuan asked. "What is the offer?"

Diem replied, "The warehouse needs a lot of twine that is in short supply. You can braid twine to earn an income. In addition, he will provide a place for you to live. He will not require rent. You can live there for free."

"He must be a good man," Xuan answered. "What is his name?"

"His name is Bhan Van Duc. He is a kind man and a good Catholic. He hates the Communists. He helps many people and puts his family in great danger," Diem explained.

"I accept," Xuan said. "When can I go?"

Diem sat beside Xuan. He reached around her shoulders pulling her close. He gazed at her white hair with wonder. Her face bore many scars where once sores festered.

"My dearest sister, I will take you tonight. We will leave early so that I can help you at your new home. It is not much but I will be close every night to help you. I will see that you receive food. Much comes through the warehouse. The small amount you need will not be missed," Diem explained.

Diem took Xuan's right hand and examined it. Its knuckles were swollen and reddish. Her fingers were twisted and scarred.

Gently stroking her hand Diem said, "I am lucky that you married my brother. Your family is a great one with a rich heritage. Their name remains a legend in Thailand and Laos. Few know that my ancestors are of the Tia mountain tribes. My great grandfather took the Nguyen name and left the mountains many years ago. He was able to pass among the Vietnamese who hate our tribe. The Catholic missionaries taught him enough so that he was able to appear a true Vietnamese. We owe much to the leaders of our faith."

Diem continued, "I have six children. Two daughters are my first and second born. My eldest son is only nine. I make sure that he maintains his Catholic faith. Your sons, Anh and Vinh, are of great concern to me. If they do not leave the Viet Minh, they will become godless Communists. I teach my children the ways of our faith. Your husband did the same with your family. We must hope that his teachings allow Anh and Vinh to see the Communists for what they are."

Xuan thought for a moment and replied, "Anh has a fiery hate for the French and the Japanese. He holds them responsible for killing his father. He puts his faith and Communism secondary to obtaining revenge. Minh Thanh is young yet and does not understand many things. Vinh is younger still. I do not know what will happen to them. I cannot return to our home. If I do, her betrothed will alert the police."

"You must go with me tonight then," Diem said.

"Will you get word to my children that I am no longer in prison?" Xuan asked.

"Yes, I certainly will. Also, I will warn them of what is to come," Diem answered.

"What do you mean?" Xuan asked.

"Our nationalist leaders are in China. They have formed a league so that various factions are united. However, I do not trust the Communists. I am afraid that they will try to destroy Catholics so that they can impose their beliefs upon our country. I foresee a great internal struggle coming. Our families are in great danger," Diem answered.

"Remember this," he continued. "If you are ever in trouble and cannot find me, go to the South-side Cathedral. Tell the sisters who you are. They will protect and care for you."

Minh Thanh recalled that she owed a great debt to the sisters at Hanoi's convent. When Ho Chi Minh began slaughtering Catholics, she and her mother made their way to Diem's home. They found his family burned in their home. While searching for Diem, a marauding Communist group saw them.

It seemed only yesterday that she saw them surround her mother. Unable to run anymore, Xuan insisted that she continue without her. She did not want to leave her and tried to get Xuan to her feet. She was too weak and the screaming mob would soon be upon them.

"Run to the mission," her mother urged. "Run now, please."

With great reluctance, she ran. Stopping once to look back, she saw them leading Xuan away. It was a scene burned indelibly into her memory.

"Kill the Communists Jean. Kill them all," she thought.

Now, she knew what she had to do. She left the chapel to see mother superior.

"I understand completely, my child," mother superior said, as she put her teacup on its cart. "Do not be ashamed of being human. I want you to stay with us although you will not become a nun. You are important to us and we love you."

Minh Thanh's chin trembled and she bit her lower lip. She knew her heart and she could never become Christ's bride. Mother superior's kindness was overwhelming. Being able to remain and continue her studies was a gift she had not expected.

"Thank you mother superior," she said. "I am so grateful. I feel as if I have failed you and the church. I owe you so much and have returned so little."

"My dear, we do not keep score. You have no debt. You will learn with time that love does not have a price upon it. It is free to give to anyone and to expect nothing in return. True devotion is that which is free, otherwise love would be nothing more than a commodity. It would be like a fish at the market or a loaf of bread for sale," mother superior replied.

"What price do you place on your love for Jean?" Mother superior asked. "What must he pay for it."

"Why nothing of course. He already has it and doesn't even know it," Minh Thanh answered.

"You see, I'm right," Mother superior told her.

Mother superior reached for a silver teapot on the nearby teacart. Lifting it, she filled Minh Thanh's cup and then hers. Next, she raised her saucer and cup and stirred in one teaspoon of sugar. Sitting the spoon down, she quietly sipped her tea and appeared to be in deep thought.

Minh Thanh, concluding her visit ended, asked. "Mother superior may I be excused?"

"Not just yet my dear," she answered.

"I have a proposal for you. You complete your French class with Captain Louis in two weeks. You have done well and are fluent in the language. We have a new student group consisting of mostly refugees from Laos. Would you like to teach them French?" Mother superior asked.

"Oh yes, I would enjoy teaching French," Minh Thanh responded. "How many are in the group?"

"Now, there are 17 but we expect a few more. There are still some on their way. They are coming the same way that you did, through the safe house system. Two arrived last night," she answered.

Minh Thanh knew the system well. It consisted of Catholic families' homes, convents, and churches. It extended from the Laotian border through Hanoi and south to Hue and, finally, to Saigon. Some refugees elected to remain in Hue while others continued. A few men traveled the route but mostly its travelers were young girls. Traveling distance seldom exceeded one day's travel by foot.

Viet Minh attacks were not the only dangers faced. Along the way were unscrupulous men and women who abducted girls to sell for prostitution. Some went willingly, succumbing to promises of fast wealth and comfort. Youth did not seem to be a factor. Early adolescents, as young as 12, found themselves in brothels. It was common to find many addicted to heroin. They sold their bodies to obtain drugs.

A significant increase in the number of refugees was taking place. During the last three months, thousands began moving south. These were entire families traveling in groups. They arrived with what they could carry. It was necessary for them to leave most of their belongings.

Young girls, traveling alone, benefited most from the safe houses. Many found their way to Saigon where mother superior and the bishop gave them sanctuary.

Minh Thanh, always seeking news from the north, quickly asked. "Did the two have any information about the battle that we have been hearing about?"

Mother superior, keenly aware of what might happen to the Viet Minh, was also sensitive to information from northern areas. She already knew details about Dien Bien Phu but never revealed it to any person at their convent. She never even spoke of it to the bishop. Operation Vulture remained very much on her mind after her meeting with Captain Louis and his friend Jean.

"They are in the infirmary. I have not yet spoken to them," she answered.

"May I speak with them?" Minh Thanh asked with considerable anxiety.

"Not yet. They are exhausted and need medical care. One has a serious leg wound from a Viet Minh attack. You may speak with them when they've had time to mend. We need to discuss the French classes," mother superior said firmly.

From her tone, Minh Thanh understood she must stay away from them. Yet, her desire for information was compelling. She looked at mother superior in desperation. Her eyes pleaded with her for a different reply. It never came.

Obviously avoiding Minh Thanh's pleading gesture, Mother superior said, "You will teach fundamentals. These students, for the most part, have little education. You must keep your classes at the most basic level. Your teaching will be a prelude to Captain Louis's class. Please present your instruction outline to me in two weeks. You have my permission to tell Captain Louis about your upcoming class. I am sure he will have sound advice for you."

Minh Thanh knew she should leave. While departing, she did not reveal her excitement about teaching.

"I will be able to see a direct result of my efforts. My students, she liked the sound of the phrase, will be the best students ever," she thought. "I wonder how many 18-years-old, French teachers there are? Not many, I suspect. Mother would be proud."

Across town, General Navarre's headquarters was in chaos. Operation Castor was a total failure. With French forces at Dien Bien Phu killed or captured, France's Department of State was in an uproar. The operation that was to reestablish French colonialism throughout Viet Nam now meant that a military solution was no longer an option. French leadership now saw that they must come to terms with the Viet Minh at a conference table and not on a battlefield.

"I do not give a shit what Colonel Bittare wants," Captain Louis screamed into a telephone. "He will keep his forces in barracks until given written orders to do otherwise."

As soon as his telephone was back on its cradle, it rang. Every telephone in his office was ringing, adding to an already inflamed bedlam. Clerks and junior officers could not answer them fast enough. Courier's, in line six deep, waited to take messages. Louis would write a memo in haste and then tear it from its pad. He threw most in a nearby trash can to burn later. When he did complete one to his satisfaction, he handed it to a courier with instructions as to where and whom to deliver it.

His orders were clear. There would be no operational orders delivered by telephone. He had to write each one and encode it. Once complete, couriers delivered the messages.

Captain Andre Louis had not slept for 72 hours. He was near exhaustion as was the rest of his staff. The situation in operations was worse. For a month, they had tried to coordinate support for Dien Bien Phu through a combat command headquarters in Hanoi. They were tired, hungry, and frustrated.

A general's aide rushed to Louis's desk, and said, "Sir, you're needed in operations immediately."

"They will have to wait lieutenant. I cannot be in two places at once," Louis replied angrily.

"Sir, this is not a request. You will report to operations now," the lieutenant ordered firmly.

Louis slammed his desk with his fist and said, "All right, don't stumble or I will run over your ass."

Operations was quiet where minutes before it had been almost impossible to speak without yelling. Captain Louis stood just inside its entrance, staring in disbelief.

"What the hell?" He thought. "What's going on?" Louis asked the general's aide standing beside him.

"Sir, I do not know. It was like this when I came to get you. Something is going on but I cannot say," he answered.

Across the room, Captain Prudhomme sat in a metal chair. He was leaning forward at the waist and staring at his boots. In a rhythmic motion, he would lean farther forward and raise his heels so that only his toes remained on the floor. Next, he would lean rearward and look at the ceiling. He held the end of a pointer in each hand that stretched across his knees. He applied pressure to bend it almost to its breaking point and then released the pressure. He seemed in a trance and oblivious to his surroundings.

Other personnel sat quietly. They avoided eye contact with anyone. Some would doodle on pads or play with paper clips. None of them spoke. It was eerie to watch.

Louis heard the door opening behind him. He moved to his left without looking to allow the person to pass. The lieutenant next to him announced, "Gentlemen, the chief of staff."

Everyone in the room moved at once. They stopped whatever they were doing and immediately came to attention. From the corner of his eye, Louis saw Major General LeClare enter the room. General LeClare walked to the room's center and stopped.

"At ease gentlemen," he said. "As of 12:00 hours today, a cease fire exists. Combat units will remain in place throughout Tonkin, Annam and Cochin China. No units will fire unless fired upon. Troops in barracks will remain in barracks. This cease-fire is in effect until further notice. That is all, thank you."

Everyone came to attention as LeClare walked quickly from the room. When the door closed, random mumbling flowed throughout those present. One major sat with his face in his hands obviously weeping. Turning to speak to the lieutenant, he noticed that he was no longer present. Louis concluded that he left with the chief of staff.

Louis returned to his office. The telephones were quiet and personnel were putting scattered documents in order. As he entered the room, everyone stopped what they were doing and looked at him inquisitively.

Louis said to them, "It's obvious that you are aware of the cease fire. This does not mean we stop working. There are casualty reports to make; notices to next-of-kin to prepare; and normal administrative actions to complete. We will continue our 24-hour manning schedule. However, each of you will have an opportunity to get some rest and food. Sergeant Major prepare a new duty roster and post it on the bulletin board."

At his desk, Louis tried to organize papers scattered upon it without success. His hands began to shake and his legs to tremble. He sat and pulled his chair tight against his desk. Crossing his arms, he laid his head upon them.

"Jesus God in heaven, there were over 10,000 of them," he mumbled as exhaustion engulfed him.

News of Dien Bien Phu's fall raced through Saigon like a fire through a dry forest. Church bells sounded throughout the city. Their chimes came at a pace that one would expect during a funeral dirge. Their sounds caused Minh Thanh to drop the bread dough that she was kneading. Untying her apron, she wiped her hands and walked to a nearby window. She opened it and saw that street traffic was at a standstill. People gathered in groups to read newspapers. Across the traffic circle, frightened onlookers read posters placed on storefronts. Even from her faraway location, she could see the headlines.

"Mother in heaven, are we next?" She thought.

Like a coiled spring wound too tight and then released, people in the streets burst into motion. Some ran while others raced away on sputtering Lambretas.

"Where are they going?" Sister Margaret asked.

Turning, Minh Thanh looked into Sister Margaret's wide eyes. She was attempting to wipe a small amount of perspiration from her eyebrow with the back of her flour-covered hand. She was a buxom woman and one of only three American nuns in their convent. She was responsible for food preparation and this was Minh Thanh's week to work with her. Sister Margaret was a nun in Europe during World War II. She had worked in the Vatican and had actually talked with the Pope. Because of this, she enjoyed a special status among the nuns. A few sisters seemed distressed by some of Sister Margaret's worldly mannerisms.

On occasion, she drank too much wine and used inappropriate language. She liked to listen to American music that some considered risqué. Twice she began dancing to fast-paced tunes. Nevertheless Minh Thanh knew her to be kind and totally devoted to serving Christ.

"What do you mean?" Minh Thanh answered.

Lifting her apron, Sister Margaret wiped her hands while watching the outside commotion. Minh Thanh could not help but marvel at her size. Her breasts strained her habit and she had three chins. When she walked, she shook from head to toe.

"Well, look at that couple with a mattress," she said pointing to the street. An elderly man and woman were struggling to mount a rolled mattress onto a bicycle's rear.

"Where are they going and what are they running away from?" She asked.

"They are afraid Sister Margaret. With so many Legionnaires out of the city, they are afraid the Viet Minh will attack Saigon. This would be a good time to try to seize control of our government. I suspect they may be trying to leave the city. All I can do is guess Sister Margaret," Minh Thanh answered still somewhat puzzled by the question.

"Surely, she understands the dangers surrounding us," Minh Thanh thought.

"Well, bless them," Sister Margaret said. "Come Minh Thanh, we have bread to bake."

"Sister Margaret there is an important matter that I need to do. Will you excuse me for awhile?" Minh Thanh asked.

"Of course dear but do hurry back because we must prepare tonight's meal," Sister Margaret answered.

Restraining herself, Minh Thanh walked slowly to the kitchen's exit. Once through the door, and out of Sister Margaret's view, she ran through the hallway to stairs leading to the ground floor. She had to find Captain Louis and demand to know Jean's fate. Bounding down the stairs two at a time, she ran into mother superior. She had a firm grip on the banister and remained upright.

"Oh mother superior please forgive me. I am so sorry. Are you okay?" Minh Thanh asked, totally embarrassed.

"I am fine child," she said trying to regain her composure. "Where are you going in such a hurray?"

Minh Thanh held mother superior's free arm in an attempt to help her. She lowered her head and answered, "I was going to find Captain Louis."

"There is no need," mother superior answered quickly. "I have the answer to what you seek. Lieutenant Danjou's fate, like many others, is not known."

"Did Captain Louis tell you this?" Minh Thanh asked.

"No, but my source is much more reliable than Captain Louis. We will not be likely to know for months. Everything depends upon the outcome of a meeting scheduled to take place in Switzerland. You may return to the kitchen," mother superior responded with obvious sympathy.

"But Mother," Minh Thanh started to speak before mother superior interrupted.

"Trust me and pray for the lieutenant. We know that most of the Legionnaires are now captives of the Viet Minh. I hope that they will release them soon. We must wait," mother superior said as she embraced Minh Thanh.

"Oh mother superior, I love him so much," Minh Thanh said between sobs.

"Yes, I know," she replied

Chapter Twenty

March 1953

It is only the enlightened ruler and the wise general who will use the highest intelligence of the army for the purposes of spying, and thereby they achieve great results.
Sun Tzu (6th–5th century BC), Chinese general. *The Art of War*, ch. 13, axiom 27 (c. 490 BC)

"The Straits of Taiwan are a festering sore between the Communist mainland and China. It reeks with the blood of many that have tried to gain control of it. Fortunately, Mao Te Sung has not forced the issue. If he does, the only course will be to bring them down with atomic firepower. I hope matters do not come to that," Lieutenant General Gary Masterson said.

Lanny Briscoe listened intently as the Chief of Operations for Far Eastern Affairs briefed the Commander In Chief Pacific (CINCPAC) Admiral Homer R. Eastland. Briscoe had to use every ounce of his concentration to remain focused on the briefing. The last 72 hours dulled his perception ability.

He arrived in Hawaii suffering from time distortion after crossing multiple time zones. His flight from Washington took him to Seattle, Washington, where he immediately boarded a flight to Anchorage, Alaska. He tried to sleep but failed. Upon arrival in Anchorage, a stewardess advised him that a gentleman was waiting to see him in the airport's lounge. With only a 15-minute stay to refuel, his flight would soon leave for Hawaii. He hurried toward the lounge but was intercepted by Lieutenant Commander Bereland, United States Navy, who escorted him to Pan Am's VIP lounge.

Bereland kept a constant stream of instructions flowing as he escorted Briscoe.

"Sir, what happens here you will never mention to anyone unless they have the proper clearance and a need to know. Once inside you will show your credentials to the gentleman who asks for them. You need not ask questions as those present will not, or cannot, answer them. I apologize for the haste but events driving this equation are beyond our control."

Lanny listened while nodding his head affirmatively. Once inside, two Air Force policemen took position outside the door. Another one locked it and stepped in front of the other two. The three stood at a rigid "At Ease" position with legs spread and backs straight, looking directly ahead. They held batons in a port arms position. Their right hands gripped the baton's handle with its leather thong around their wrists. Their left hands held the other end at chest level.

Inside, a well-dressed man stepped from behind a bar and asked for Briscoe's credentials. He wore a tailored suit with an opened coat revealing a vest. He had a bulge beneath his left arm indicating that he wore a sidearm. He was well groomed and wore his hair short. Briscoe guessed him to be a senior government official or an operative with one of the intelligence branches.

Briscoe gave his identification documents to him. While examining them, the stranger pointed to a chair and asked Briscoe to take a seat. He sat in one of two easy chairs facing a coffee table. The individual examining his documents looked at Briscoe and then back to the documents. He did this numerous times. Satisfied, he walked to the other chair and sat.

He returned Briscoe's papers and said, "I once knew a Turk who liked cigars. Have you met him?

"Yes," Briscoe answered. "He preferred Partegas."

The stranger handed him a folder while Bereland brought him a double-bourbon on the rocks.

"Briscoe, you are to read the contents of this folder," the stranger said. "Remember what you see because you must return it to me. In addition, you will sign for a diplomatic pouch that I will handcuff to you. Bereland will issue you a sidearm that you must sign for after you receive the pouch."

Events were taking place too fast to suit Briscoe. He sat back and took a long swallow of the bourbon. Almost immediately, he felt its effect begin to relax him. He opened the folder.

Inside was a sealed envelope marked "Del-Ray" in bold letters. Following that there was a standard "Special Intelligence Crypto" stamped impression signed by an individual from the National Security Agency. He did not recognize the name. Adjacent to the signature an "Eyes-Only Mr. L. Briscoe" stamped seal held the envelope closed.

The envelope opened on one end. Briscoe tilted it to remove its contents. Three aerial photographs fell into his hand. His initial exam revealed that they were terrain photographs. Individually, the three seemed to be of the same area. However, closer examination showed that these were special pictures. Each had a cross mark on opposite corners. By placing the marks one above the other, a single, stereo-optic image resulted.

"Damn," Briscoe thought and immediately looked closer.

Thinly marked, across the bottom of each photo, was the notation, "Jennings-MIT." Briscoe held the superimposed photos toward an overhead light. The terrain was mostly mountainous and heavily forested or possibly jungle. He saw an airfield in a narrow valley. High mountains were on every side. Someone, using drafting equipment, had inscribed lines connecting three dots. Each dot had geographic coordinates beside it.

"This has to be an APPS product," he thought. "Dr. Jennings produced this at MIT. What the hell are the dots for?" He asked himself.

Someone pulled Briscoe's left arm with a downward motion. He looked to see Bereland attaching a courier's pouch to his left wrist with a handcuff.

"Just a minute, damn it," Briscoe complained as he almost dropped the photos.

"I'm sorry sir but it's almost time to go," Bereland replied. "Please sign here."

Bereland held a clipboard with documents on it. At the bottom of the top document, Briscoe saw his signature block and date typed. With his left hand now free, Briscoe transferred the photos and took a pen offered by Bereland. He glanced at the paper and saw that it was a form to sign for a standard issue, 38-cal., revolver and shoulder holster. He signed the document and Bereland pulled Briscoe to his feet.

"Let me help you sir," he said. "We need to get this on you."

Fortunately, the shoulder holster strap had a snap that went beneath his left arm. Otherwise, they would have had to remove the pouch and his coat to fit the holster.

"Here's two quick change units sir," Bereland said as he handed him two cylinders with six cartridges in each. "The weapon is loaded."

Briscoe placed the quick-change units in his right coat pocket and thought, "How in the hell am I supposed to reload with this damn pouch on my left wrist?"

The stranger reached for the photos and envelope. Briscoe pulled them away.

"Just a minute I'm not through," Briscoe said in desperation.

"Commander, go to OPS and tell them to hold the flight," the stranger said.

"Yes sir," Bereland replied.

"Take your time Briscoe. Whoever rushed these here, I do not know but it was obviously important. Pan Am can wait," he said after the commander left.

Briscoe sat and returned his attention to the aerial photographs. They were of an unusual clarity and resolution. The added advantage of being in three dimensions made examination even better. By the notation, there was a date and time expressed in Zulu units. If accurate, the photos were less than 48 hours old. He looked up from the photos in astonishment.

"Don't ask," the stranger said.

"This is Bill Jennings' work and he does not have a thing to do with communications. Why is it necessary that I see these?" Briscoe thought. "The coordinates on these photos are of Southeast Asia near the Laotian border. Shit! Operation Vulture, that's what these are for."

Getting to his feet, he placed the photos in the envelope. He opened the folder, put the envelope inside, and closed it.

Handing the folder to the stranger, he said, "I've seen enough. I'm ready to go."

During the flight to Hawaii, Briscoe tried to answer the question as to why APPS kept rearing its head. The Analytical Photogrametric Positioning System was in its infancy. It was a research and development prototype at best. Nonetheless, the photo quality exceeded anything that he had seen. He could only conclude that his requested background check on McNeese revealed something. Whatever it was, the CIA could not reveal it directly so they sent the photographs. Yet, this did not explain the NSA seal. If his CIA contact sent the photos, the NSA seal would not have been on the envelope.

"There has to be a link between R. L. Meyers Systems and APPS. R. L. Meyers, while a front organization, still has overall responsibility for overseeing research and development dealing with cryptographic devices. Also, the guy McNeese, had documents relating to further APPS development when he should not have," Briscoe thought.

Two bourbons and he slept. He never felt his craft's touchdown in Hawaii.

As he walked down the ramp, he saw a jeep with a sergeant standing by it. He met Briscoe as he left the off-loading ramp.

"Sir, I'm Corporal Michaels. I have your baggage," the young airman said. "We'll get you disconnected from that pouch first and then I'll take you to the Bachelor Officer's Quarters. You will have time to freshen up. I'll wait for you," he said.

Briscoe looked at the jeep and saw his two bags already loaded and asked. "Got coffee hidden anywhere?"

"You bet sir. There's a thermos in the jeep," he answered.

"Well hell, let's go," Briscoe said.

Corporal Michaels drove to a United States Customs building where a customs officer inspected his baggage. After the baggage check, Michaels showed him to a room marked United States Department of Defense, CINCPAC. An official unlocked his handcuff and signed for the diplomatic pouch.

"Sir, I have instructions for you to keep the sidearm," the official said.

Michaels drove him to the BOQ. He showered and changed clothes. Michaels took him to an unmarked, but obviously a military building. It seemed that the military always got the worst buildings to use for offices.

Now, here he was with the Pacific's top brass. He still wasn't sure why but hoped he would soon learn. Otherwise, someone spent a lot of money to get him here for nothing. Thankfully, Michaels' coffee was strong and black. He was able to stay semi-alert to hear what General Masterson had to say.

"Sir, thanks to the efforts of Mr. Lanny Briscoe, I have been able to prepare a comprehensive overview regarding events in Southeast Asia. In particular, sir, I will provide background information from the Pentagon regarding activities that play a part leading to the current situation in the Taiwan Straits. Sir, Mr. Briscoe is seated to your rear," General Masterson said.

Admiral Eastland turned to face Briscoe and said, "Welcome aboard Lanny. We're glad to have you.

He extended his hand over his chair's back to Briscoe. He took it and returned Eastland's firm handshake.

"How was your trip?" Eastland asked.

"Fast sir," Briscoe replied.

Eastland gave Briscoe a knowing grin and turned to face the briefing officer.

"Go ahead Gary," he said.

"Sir, France contributed directly to the current situation. To understand, it helps to review the situation existing in Southeast Asia at war's end; what subsequent events took place, and how they brought about the current problem."

"Military considerations governed United States policy in Indochina. President Truman replied to General de Gaulle's repeated requests for aid in Indochina with statements to the effect that it was his policy to leave such matters to his military commanders. At the Potsdam Conference, the Combined Chiefs of Staff decided that Indochina south of latitude 16' North was to be included in the Southeast Asia Command under Admiral Mountbatten."

"Based on this decision, instructions were issued that Japanese forces located north of that line would surrender to Generalissimo Chiang Kai-shek, now on Taiwan. Forces to the south of that line would surrender to Admiral Lord Mountbatten."

"Pursuant to these instructions, Chinese forces entered Tonkin, also known as North Viet Nam, in September, 1945, while a small British task force landed at Saigon, in South Viet Nam. Political difficulties materialized almost immediately sir. For while the Chinese were prepared to accept the Vietnamese government they found in power in Hanoi, the British refused to do likewise in Saigon, and deferred to the French there from the outset."

"According to authoritative documents, there is no evidence that serious concern developed in Washington at the swiftly unfolding events in Indochina, sir. In mid-August, Vietnamese resistance forces of the Viet Minh, under Ho Chi Minh, had seized power in Hanoi and shortly thereafter demanded and received the abdication of the Japanese puppet, Emperor Bao Dai."

"On V-J Day, September 2nd, Ho Chi Minh had proclaimed in Hanoi the establishment of the Democratic Republic of Vietnam (DRV). The DRV ruled as the only civil government in all of Viet Nam for a period of about 20 days."

"On 23 September 1945, with the knowledge of the British Commander in Saigon, French forces overthrew the local DRV government, and declared French authority restored in Cochinchina, or what we refer to as South Viet Nam. Guerrilla war began around Saigon. Although American OSS representatives were present in both Hanoi and Saigon and ostensibly supported the Viet Minh, the United States took no official position regarding either the DRV, or the French and British actions in South Vietnam."

"Pardon me Gary," Admiral Eastland interrupted. "I have a question for Lanny."

Once again, the admiral turned in his chair and said, "Lanny, come sit up here with me. I'm liable to wrench my neck if I have more questions."

Briscoe moved forward and sat next to Admiral Eastland. He asked. "How can I help sir?"

"Didn't you serve in the OSS?" Eastland questioned.

"Yes sir. However, I never became involved in Pacific operations," Briscoe answered.

Admiral Eastland hesitated a moment and then asked. "I know but your primary field was cryptography wasn't it?"

"That's correct." Briscoe answered.

"Fine Lanny, let's meet after this briefing. We need to talk," Eastland said.

"Sorry Gary, please continue," Eastland directed.

General Masterson nodded toward an Army captain standing next to an easel. The officer removed a red cloth to reveal large display charts. The first, in large letters, stated:

"In October, 1945, the United States stated its policy in the following terms:"

"The United States has no thought of opposing the reestablishment of French control in Indochina and no official statement by the United States government has questioned, even by implication, French sovereignty over Indochina."

"However, it is not the policy of this government to assist the French to reestablish their control over Indochina by force. The willingness of the United States to see French control reestablished assumes that French claims to have the support of Indochina's population is borne out by future events."

General Masterson gave ample time for the admiral to read the chart. When it appeared Eastland was finished, he gave the Admiral an inquisitive look.

When Eastland did not ask any questions, he said, "Sir, French statements to the United States looked for an early end to the hostilities, and spoke reassuringly of reforms and liberality. In November, Jean Chauvel, Secretary-General to the French Minister for Foreign Affairs, told the U.S. Ambassador information indicated on the next chart."

The captain removed the previous chart, revealing a new one. It read:

"When the trouble with the Annamites (Northern Vietnamese) broke out, de Gaulle was urged by the French Mission in India to make some sort of policy statement. The expectation was his announcement of France's intention to adopt a far-reaching progressive policy. The policy's design was to give the native population much greater authority, responsibility and representation in government."

"According to our information, De Gaulle considered the idea but rejected it. He did so because, in the state of disorder prevailing in Indochina, he believed that they could not implement such a policy. He felt such a statement, without restoration of French authority, everyone would consider just more fine words. Furthermore de Gaulle and the Foreign Minister believed that the situation was still so confused, and they had so little information really reliable on the overall Indochina picture, that such plans and thoughts as they held heretofore may have to be very thoroughly revised in the light of recent developments."

After reading the chart, Admiral Eastland struck his chair's arm and said loudly, "What an egotistical ass-hole. He knows exactly what he is doing."

After a short pause, Eastland said, "I'm sorry. Go ahead Gary."

"Sir," Masterson said, "the following charts are direct quotes from documents brought by Mr. Briscoe. Their origin is the Pentagon. However, we know with certainty their proponent is the State Department with President Truman's concurrence. Next, chart please."

Eastland and Briscoe read the displayed chart.

"Despite the fact that the French do not feel that they can as yet make any general statements outlining specific future plans for Indochina, Chauvel says that they hope 'very soon' to put into operation, in certain areas programs, including local elections which will by design grant much greater authority and greater voice in affairs to the natives. This he said would be a much better indication of the sincerity of French intentions than any policy statement... The French hope soon to negotiate an agreement with [the King of Cambodia], which will result in the granting of much greater responsibility and authority to the Cambodians. He mentioned specifically that they would integrate many more natives integrated into the local administrative services. They hope to hold local elections soon. The French (Chauvel) intend to follow the same procedure in Laos when the situation permits and eventually also in Annam and Tonkin. When order is restored throughout Indochina and agreements have been reached with the individual states Chauvel said the French intend to embody the results of these separate agreements into a general program for all of Indochina."

General Masterson again watched Admiral Eastland for any indication of questions or comments. With no indication given, he asked. "Homer, how about we take a break. There's coffee and refreshments in the adjoining room. How about you Mr. Briscoe?"

"Whatever Admiral Eastland wants is fine with me," Briscoe answered.

"Gary, it's about time we take a break. I have to piss so bad my back teeth are floating," Eastland said with a chuckle. "Join me Briscoe?"

"You bet Admiral. Lead the way," Briscoe responded.

Briscoe followed the admiral down a hall and into a latrine. General Masterson's office building was a barracks converted for office use. The latrine had 12, exposed toilet seats and a urinal trough.

While the two urinated side by side into the trough, Eastland said, "I guess I should have followed my doctor's advice."

"How's that?" Briscoe asked.

Still urinating, Eastland looked at Briscoe with a wide grin and said, "Because of my bad back, doc said for me to always sit to take a whiz. He doesn't want me to lift anything heavy."

Both men laughed and went to the sinks to wash. Eastland, now serious, began wiping his hands with a paper towel.

Eastland, while looking at his hands, lowered his voice and asked. "Briscoe, do you ever buy cigars from a Turk?"

Briscoe turned off the sink's spigot and answered, "Only when I can buy Partegas."

Eastland walked to a window and gazed at the Pacific crashing on a nearby beach. Briscoe stepped beside him. Both men remained quiet for a moment before Eastland asked. "Did you see the photos?"

Briscoe replied, "Yes, if you mean the APPS shots."

"It is imperative that you and I talk before you leave for Taiwan. Don't forget to remain after the briefing," Eastland ordered.

"If you know anything about those photos, there is no way I'm going to leave without talking to you sir," Briscoe responded.

Both went to the room adjoining where the briefing was taking place. A long table had a large, two-gallon, stainless steel coffee thermos on one end. Along its length, there were a variety of fresh baked rolls, croissants, and doughnuts. Grabbing two croissants on a napkin and a cup of coffee, Eastland returned to the briefing area. Briscoe, preferring cinnamon rolls, followed with steam wafting from a large, full coffee cup.

General Masterson saw them enter and left his seat. He stepped behind the podium and asked. "You ready Homer?"

"Sure thing Gary. Could you have a pot of that coffee brought in here?" Admiral Eastland asked.

Masterson nodded toward the captain who promptly left the room. He returned shortly with two coffee urns. He placed one next to the Admiral and one by Briscoe. He returned to his former position by the easel.

Masterson said, "From the autumn of 1945 through the autumn of 1946, the United States received a series of communications from Ho Chi Minh. He depicted calamitous conditions in Viet Nam, invoking the principles proclaimed in the Atlantic Charter and in the Charter of the United Nations. He pleaded for United State's recognition of the independence of the DRV, or, as a last resort, trusteeship for Vietnam under the United Nations."

"While the United States did not act on Ho's requests, it was also unwilling to aid the French. On January 15, 1946, the Secretary of War was advised by the Department of State that it was contrary to United States' policy to employ American flag vessels, or aircraft, to transport troops of any nationality to or from the Netherlands' East Indies or French Indochina. The same applied to use of such craft to carry arms, ammunition, or military equipment to these areas."

"However, the British arranged for the transport of additional French troops to Indochina. They also bilaterally agreed with the French for the latter to assume British occupation responsibilities. The British signed a pact on 9 October 1945, giving full recognition to French rights in Indochina."

"French troops began arriving in Saigon that month. Subsequently, the British turned over to them some 800 United States Lend-Lease jeeps and trucks. President Truman approved the latter transaction on the grounds that removing the equipment would be impracticable."

"The fighting between French and the Vietnamese that began in South Vietnam with the 23 September 1945, French coup d'etat, spread from Saigon throughout Cochinchina, and to southern Annam. By the end of January, 1946, it was wholly a French affair, for by that time the British withdrawal was complete; on 4 March, 1946, Admiral Lord Mountbatten deactivated Indochina as territory under the Allied Southeast Asia Command, thereby transferring all control to French authorities."

"From French headquarters, via Radio Saigon, came announcements that a military 'mopping-up' campaign was in progress; pacification was virtually complete; these reports of success were typically interspersed with such items as those on the chart. Next chart please."

"20 March 1946:

Rebel bands are still (wreaking destruction) in the areas south of Saigon. These bands are quite large, some numbering as many as 1,000 men. Concentrations of these bands are in the villages. Some have turned north in an attempt to disrupt (communications) in the Camau Peninsula, northeast of Batri and in the general area south of (Nha Trang). In the area south of Cholon and in the north of the Plaine des Jenes region, several bands have taken refuge.

21 March 1946:

The High Commissioner for Indochina issued the following communiqué this morning: Rebel activities have increased in the Bien Hoa area, on both banks of the river Dong Nai. A French convoy has been attacked on the road between Bien Hoa and Tan Uyen where the rebels had laid a land mine.

"In the (Baclo) area, northwest of Saigon, a number of pirates have been captured in the course of a clean-up raid. Among the captured men are five Japanese deserters. The dead bodies of three Japanese, including an officer, have been found at the point where the operation was carried out.

"A French detachment was ambushed at (San Jay), south Annam. The detachment, nevertheless, succeeded in carrying out its mission. Several aggressions by rebel parties are reported along the coastal road."

Continuing Masterson said, "Violence abated in South Viet Nam somewhat as Franco-DRV negotiations proceeded in spring, 1946, but in the meantime, French forces moved into further confrontation with Vietnamese rebels in Tonkin. In February 1946, a French task force prepared to force landings at Haiphong, but became forestalled by diplomatic maneuver. A Franco-Chinese agreement of 28 February 1946 provided that the Chinese would turn over their responsibilities in northern Indochina to the French on 31 March 1946."

"Next chart please," Masterson said.

"On March 6, 1946, a French-DRV accord was reached in the following terms:

1. The French Government recognizes the Vietnamese Republic as a Free State having its own Government, its own Parliament, its own Army and its own Finances, forming part of the Indochinese Federation and of the French Union. In that which concerns the reuniting of the three "Annamite Regions" [Cochinchina, Annam, Tonkin] the French Government pledges itself to ratify the decisions taken by the populations consulted by referendum.

2. The Vietnamese Government declares itself ready to welcome amicably the French Army when, conforming to international agreements, it relieves the Chinese Troops. A Supplementary Accord, attached to the present Preliminary Agreement, will establish the means by which relief operations will take place.

3. The stipulations formulated above will immediately enter into force. Immediately after the exchange of signatures, each of the High Contracting Parties will take all measures necessary to stop hostilities in the field, to maintain the troops in their respective positions, and to create the favorable atmosphere necessary to the immediate opening of friendly and sincere negotiations. These negotiations will deal particularly with:

a. diplomatic relations of Viet Nam with Foreign States
b. the future law of Indochina
c. French interests, economic and cultural, in Viet Nam.

Hanoi, Saigon, or Paris may be chosen as the seat of the conference.

DONE AT HANOI, the 6th of March 1946

Signed: Sainteny
Signed: Ho Chi Minh and Vu Hong Khanh

"Sir, French forces quickly exercised their prerogative, occupying Hanoi on 18 March 1946, and negotiations opened in Dafat in April.

"Hence, as of April 10, 1946, allied occupation in Indochina officially ended. French forces took position in all of Viet Nam's major cities. The problems of United States policy toward Viet Nam then shifted from the context of wartime strategy to the arena of the United States relationship with France."

Masterson paused for a drink of water from a class he kept at the podium.

Next, he looked at the admiral and said, "Homer, if you will excuse me, I need to use the latrine."

"Good grief," .Eastland replied. "When are you going to learn that's a head and not a latrine?"

"When this worn out building gets christened and set afloat," General Masterson said as he exited the room.

Admiral Eastland poured coffee from his urn while speaking to the captain still on the platform, "Captain, why don't you hit the head too."

The captain said, before being interrupted, "Sir, I really don't...."

"Hit the head captain," Eastland ordered as he turned to Briscoe.

With the captain gone, Eastland said to Briscoe, "What do you make of those coordinates in the photos?"

"They're navigation points sir," Briscoe responded.

Incredulous Eastlake asked. "What kind of navigation points? Who the hell needs navigation points in the middle of a jungle?"

"Admiral, are you familiar with Operation Vulture?" Briscoe asked.

"Not at all," he answered while munching on a croissant.

Briscoe explained, "Vulture is a contingency plan. It provides for the use of atomic weapons to support French operations in North Viet Nam. The plan also mentions follow-on attacks against main land China and the Soviet Union."

Eastland immediately choked on a half-swallowed portion of his croissant. Quickly gaining his breath, Eastland gulped a few swallows of coffee.

"Briscoe, you're nuts," Eastland exclaimed. "If any such plan existed I would know about it. Not only would I know about it, I would have to approve its implementation. Where did you get such a wild idea?"

"Sir, I cannot tell you that but believe me its true. I'm certain the French are going to establish a major force in North Viet Nam. As a contingency, if they get in trouble, we're going to launch B-29s with atomic weapons. They will use those coordinates to navigate to their release points. The B-29s will start their missions on Okinawa," Briscoe explained.

"Ready Homer," Masterson said as he entered the room.

"Sure thing Gary," he answered.

Eastland, using a low whisper, said, "Briscoe, you will damn sure stay after this."

Gesturing to the captain who had returned with him, Masterson said, "Next chart please."

"Just a moment," Eastland said. "Gary I'm sure your staff busted their buns putting this presentation together and I appreciate that. However, it looks like you have another dozen charts over there. Tell you what, just tell me as quickly as you can, how we got into supporting France in Indochina."

Masterson dismissed the captain and placed both hands firmly on the podium. He thought for a moment and looked directly at Eastland.

He said, "Homer I know you've heard of Bao Dai, the last Emperor of Viet Nam. Well, when the Japanese surrendered to the British, he tried to regain his previous position as leader of the Vietnamese people. Ho Chi Minh, and his Communist thugs, threw his ass out and created the Democratic Republic of Viet Nam better known as the DRV. Ho even had the balls to use a portion of the United States Declaration of Independence when he wrote a governing document to unify Viet Nam. They let Bao Dai live and he fled south to Saigon."

"France cut a deal to put Bao Dai into power again. Everyone wants to think the French did that hoping he would gain support from the populace. That wasn't it at all. The French did it to get our support and it worked. Bear with me on this Homer. I want to read what Secretary of State Acheson said in a statement he released in Paris on 8 May 1950. President Truman had to approve this of course, and I quote:

'The French Foreign Minister and I have just had an exchange of views on the situation in Indochina and are in general agreement both as to the urgency of the situation in that area and as to the necessity for remedial action. We have noted the fact that the problem of meeting the threat to the security of Viet Nam, Cambodia, and Laos, which now enjoy independence within the French Union, is primarily the responsibility of France and the Governments and peoples of Indochina. The United States recognizes that the solution of the. Indochina problem depends both upon the restoration of security and upon the development of genuine nationalism and that United States assistance can and should contribute to these major objectives.

The United States Government, convinced that neither national independence nor democratic evolution exist in any area dominated by Soviet imperialism, considers the situation to be such as to warrant its according economic aid and military equipment to the Associated States of Indochina and to France in order to assist them in restoring stability and permitting these states to pursue their peaceful and democratic development.'"

Masterson looked up from the statement he read and said, "You know what happened next. North Korea invaded South Korea the following month. They figured we would be so mired down with the Indochina mess we couldn't help South Korea. We've been paying the bill for France to the tune of 80 percent of their entire costs in Indochina."

"Homer, we did this while our guys were doing without in Korea. In addition, if that wasn't bad enough, MacArthur made public a proposal to invade main land China with Generalissimo Chiang Kai-shek's forces on Taiwan. He openly advocated using atomic bombs. That's why the Straits are so damn hot right now. The Chinese are looking for any excuse to invade Taiwan and I'm afraid they have one now."

"The Chinese are playing us Homer. They indicate that they want to resume peace talks this month in Korea. Yet, they're concentrating forces across the strait. It's blackmail. In addition, they know we're pouring resources into Viet Nam. Our resources are too thin and they're using that against us. My worry is that we may have to use atomic weapons to make up the difference."

A long silence engulfed the room as General Masterson concluded his presentation. Briscoe wasn't aware of any of this information. Admiral Eastland appeared to be in deep thought.

Rising from his seat suddenly, Eastland stomped his feet as if to bring them back to life and asked. "Gary, you and Madeline are going to be at Diamondhead tonight aren't you?"

Appearing somewhat befuddled, Masterson answered, "Sure Homer, we'll be there. And you?"

"Yeah, me and the little lady will join you. Thanks Gary. Great job and thank your guys for me. They do good work," Eastland answered.

Sensing his dismissal, Masterson excused himself and the captain. They left the room. Eastland turned to Briscoe.

"Let's see if there are any more of those goodies in the next room," he said to Briscoe.

Eastland made sure no one was in the break room. He also checked the outside hallway for possible listeners. He took a now stale roll from the table and walked to the same window as earlier. Briscoe went with him.

"Briscoe, if you're right about those photos showing navigation points, I need you to do something for me. You're a civilian and this is something that is out of your chain of command. I guess I could send some of my guys to do this but I would prefer a civilian handle it. If you don't want to, I will understand," Eastland said.

"What's that Admiral?" Briscoe asked.

"I want you to piss in someone else's sandbox. It pisses me off to know that something like Operation Vulture planning took place and no one consulted me. If those are navigational beacon sites, there is only one device in our inventory that can handle such a task. Someone will have to deliver these special beacons to the French. Each beacon has a coding device that provides identification data to an aircraft tracking on it. Without this device, an aircraft probably couldn't even receive it, much less identify it. I want you to replace the beacon coding devices with dummies," Eastland said.

"Sir, if you do that it will screw-up follow up mission in China and the Soviet Union," Briscoe said. "If the French are counting on the atomic strikes, and they don't get them, they will likely get creamed."

"Are you familiar with details of Operation Castor?" Eastland asked Briscoe?

"No sir," Briscoe answered. "All I know is that it's a scheme by some French general to try and get the Viet Minh drawn into a battle to destroy them. I also know that Operation Vulture is in support of that plan."

"You know enough," Eastland said. "Here's what I want you to do. First, intercept the navigation beacons before the French get their hands on them.

Second, remove the code cylinders and replace them with dummies. If you cannot intercept and replace, go to their sites and replace the cylinders."

"How am I going to get to those three sites in the middle of a mountainous jungle?" Briscoe asked unbelievingly.

"Air America will get you there," Eastland replied. "From here you will go to Taiwan. In Taiwan, you will meet an operative who will get you to Thailand and then to Laos if you cannot intercept the devices. At a staging area in Laos, Air America will fly you to within a few kilometers of the site. Go in from there and change the cylinders. I don't think you will have to do this but we cannot take any chances. My hope is that you will intercept the beacons before they get to the French."

"What if the beacons are protected by French troops?" Briscoe asked sounding considerably concerned.

"You will have to terminate them," Eastland answered unflinchingly.

Two days later Corporal Michaels drove Briscoe to Hawaii's Naval Air Station. There he boarded a Douglas C-46 for a turbulent ride to Taiwan. It was a grueling affair with many fuel stops at desolate islands. Along the way he chatted with the flight crew who were an amiable group but obviously professionals. They wore uniforms typical of many airline pilots. However, they seemed different. He couldn't decide if it was their friendly attitude or the way they conducted themselves. He came to one certain conclusion. They were not typical pilots found on most civilian airlines. Hell, those people seldom spoke to a passenger unless it was over an intercom.

Looking unkempt, and definitely almost exhausted, Briscoe arrived in Taiwan. The airport near Tainan was crude with few services available. He stood beside his baggage watching for someone to meet him. A government surplus sedan arrived for the flight crew.

"Hey, Briscoe," the craft's captain called from the olive drab car. "You want a lift to Ops?"

"Sure do," he replied.

"Wait there, we'll come over and get your gear," the pilot said.

The vintage vehicle coughed and started towards Briscoe. He noticed a heavy, bluish smoke pouring from its rear.

"Well hell, it beats walking," he thought.

It was a crowded ride across the tarmac. The three crewmembers' gear took most of the luggage space. Briscoe's two bags bounced precariously atop the weary auto. Inside, crammed together in the rear seat, the ship's captain introduced himself and his crew.

"I'm Jerry Meyers and this is my first officer, Reggie Green. That's Barry Wilson, our flight engineer, up front," Meyers said. "Where're you headed?"

"I'm not sure Briscoe," said. "Someone from CAT Airlines was supposed to meet me."

"Somebody in Ops will know. Welcome to Tainan," Green said and extended his hand.

Briscoe shook it and replied, "I'm Lanny Briscoe and thanks, this is my first time in Tainan."

"Hell, we'll be gentle," Wilson said with a chuckle. "I would shake your hand but this clunker might run away."

"Pleased to meet yah," Green said with a hint of Irish accent.

Wilson stopped in front of a Quonset hut with peeling, lime colored paint. Large portions were missing causing OD green patches to show. Wilson jumped from the front seat and opened a rear door from the outside. There were no handles inside, only corroded stubs.

"All ashore that's going ashore," Wilson said. "I'm going back to help with the post-flight. You ladies have fun."

With barely enough time to grab his bags, Briscoe watched the wretched vehicle lay a smoke screen across the ramp. Parked in neat rows, he saw C-46s, C-47s and C-119 aircraft. Located in various locations, he could see a few shiny C-54s. He estimated at least 50 aircraft of varying models parked on the tarmac. He saw above a screen door on the Quonset's side a sign that read, "CAT Airlines Operations."

"So, this is what's left of the Flying Tigers," he thought.

Lifting his bags, Briscoe entered while Green held the screen door open. It slammed with a bang once he entered. Overhead, a large four-bladed fan turned at a slow pace. Along one wall, there was a bulletin board with various notices and messages stuck to it. A few chairs lined the wall. A long counter ran completely across the building's end. About midway, there was a lift up door in the counter's top that allowed access to the area behind it. On the wall behind the counter, there were numerous maps and charts with pins stuck in various parts. Red lines connected one pin to another evidently indicating flight routes. On the northwest portion of the map indicating the Taiwan Strait, large red lines crisscrossed. Bold, red letters stated, "No Fly Zone."

Midway of the wall behind the counter, a sign above a door read, "Authorized Personnel Only." On the door's face, in small letters, the title "CAT Airlines, Inc." appeared. Electrical wiring ran exposed throughout the area. This way typical of Quonset buildings used by the military. While their half-moon shape did not lend itself to ample interior space, it did allow swift construction and maintenance.

Captain Meyers raised the counter top door and walked through lowering it behind him.

He knocked on the door and said, "Meyers here."

A muffled voice from inside replied, "Come on in Jerry."

Meyers entered while Green removed a clipboard from the wall. He sat in a nearby chair and crossed one leg over the other. Placing the clipboard on one knee, he began to write. From outside, the sound of the sedan grew louder and stopped immediately outside the entrance door. Wilson entered and removed a towel hanging from the wall. He began removing grease from his hands.

"How about something cold to drink Lanny?" He asked.

"Sure thing," Briscoe replied.

"We've got hard stuff, mild stuff and kid stuff. Name your poison." Wilson said as he moved behind the counter.

"Right now hard stuff sounds great to me," Briscoe stated.

"Coming up," Wilson said as he set two large tumbler-style glasses on the counter.

Wilson reached beneath the counter and opened a container that Briscoe could not see. However, he recognized the scooping sound of cracked ice. Wilson opened his raised fist above each glass allowing ice to fall.

"Green doesn't drink," he said as he lifted a bottle of Ancient Age bourbon.

He filled each glass and pushed one in Briscoe's direction.

"Come and get it before I do," Wilson said looking at Briscoe with a smile.

Briscoe moved to the counter and gripped the cold glass already covered with condensation. He sipped slowly because he had not had any thing to eat for almost 18 hours. He didn't want his knees to crash just yet.

Meyers opened the wall's door and stuck his head around its edge in order to see Briscoe.

After a quick glance around the room he said, "Come on back Lanny and bring your drink. Where's mine Wilson?" He asked.

"Coming right up," Wilson replied as he lifted the counter top's door for Briscoe to pass.

Briscoe stepped into a small anteroom where a lavish Oriental rug spread across parquet tiles. Each wall's lower half was a pale green. From this point up to a false ceiling, woven palm strips formed a delicate beige pattern. Soft indirect lighting reflecting from overhead mirrors almost caused Briscoe to experience vertigo. He kept his eyes on Meyers who appeared in a rectangle straight ahead.

"It's disconcerting isn't it," Meyers said. "Persons coming through that entrance always have the same reaction unless they're drunk. To them everything appears normal."

After a few steps, the foyer opened upon a mahogany walled room. Beneath heavy varnish, the wood's natural reddish brown color acquired depth and richness. Overhead an opened parachute's silk spread outward to form the room's ceiling. Rugged looking furniture filled the room. Chairs and tables appeared to be hand carved in a Polynesian motif. Low table lamps provided illumination. Directly across from the foyer's entrance sat a gaunt man with high, cheekbones and a sullen expression. He did not look up when Briscoe entered.

Meyers gestured for Briscoe to join him beside the desk. As Briscoe crossed, he could not feel the floor. Its carpet gave a distinct impression of nothing beneath his feet. After the foyer experience, Briscoe was better prepared and soon adjusted. Meyers grinned as Briscoe moved toward him. Once beside Meyers and the desk, he could see that the seated man had extensive scar tissue on the right side of his face. The thickened skin disappeared beneath his shirt's collar. As if feeling Briscoe's stare, he lifted and turned his head to look at him.

"So, you're Briscoe. What's so damn special about you?" He asked brusquely.

"Depends upon who says it. My dog thinks I'm great," Briscoe responded.

With a loud laugh, he stood and faced Briscoe. Extending his hand, he said, "Homer said you were okay."

Briscoe immediately saw severe damage to his hand. Two fingers were missing and the remainders were nubs. Taking it, he noticed a lack of strength.

"Make your skin crawl Briscoe?" He asked.

"Yeah, at first. Why?" Briscoe quickly replied.

"It's an attention getter. You would be amazed what I can tell about a person from their initial reaction. You're a stoic Briscoe. Have a seat," he said.

Meyers crossed the room and stood beside the foyer entrance. Briscoe sat in an easy chair. His initial impression was correct. The furniture was solid wood and hand carved.

"Briscoe, for now call me Redford. Later, if things gel, we'll see," Redford said.

Continuing, he explained, "My job is to get you to Naha Naval Port on Okinawa. In addition, I'm to supply you with documents authorizing you to inspect outbound cargo going to Saigon. One of my guys will accompany you dockside and into the warehouse. He'll cover your back until you do whatever it is you're supposed to do. After that, he will get you back to Taiwan. You can leave your sidearm with us. You will not need it and we don't want to be stopped because you're wearing one."

"Reggie will see that you get some rest. He will also provide your new papers and clothing. In addition, there's a package for you that I have stored in a vault. You can pick it up the day you leave. That's it on my end. Is there anything else I should know?"

"I cannot think of anything. It seems the admiral has been busy," Briscoe replied.

"For some reason, I have a bad feeling about this," Redford commented. "Homer has a tendency to over extend himself at times. This one may bite him in the butt."

"If that's it," Briscoe said. "I could handle some rest. Reggie mixes a tough drink and this one is definitely telling me its bedtime."

"Jerry, have Reggie see to Briscoe, will you?" Redford asked.

"Yes, sir," Meyers responded. "Come with me Briscoe."

Redford returned to his work without comment. Briscoe followed Meyers through the hallucination foyer and outside to Ops. Reggie Green sat in one of the chairs reading the "Saturday Evening Post."

"Reggie see to Briscoe please," Meyers ordered.

"Sure thing. Follow me Briscoe," Green said.

Meyers, without a word to Briscoe, closed the door while remaining in the foyer. Green raised the counter door and motioned Briscoe through. The two exited the Quonset.

"Let's take the Green Hornet," Green said while pointing to the sedan. "They call it Green because I have to maintain it. You would think Wilson would do that considering he's a mechanic. He claims he doesn't know a thing about automotive engines."

Once inside Green started the beast and steered toward a double gate with a guardhouse. A Chinese guard stepped from the building and indicated for them to halt. He glanced throughout the automobile and gave Briscoe a long look.

Focusing his attention on Green, he asked. "He number one Leggie?"

"He's fine. Open the gate," Green answered.

Green drove to small, stucco building on a beachfront road. Oyster shells served as paving through the sandy soil. The place was what one would expect for an aviator living alone. It was a mess. The walls held numerous nude photos of women in various enticing poses. A trashcan, near the kitchen sink, was full of empty, Blatz beer cans. Some lay on the floor around it. Numerous squashed Lucky Strike cigarette packages also circled the filled container. In one corner, There was a double bunk bed in one corner. A mosquito net covered it.

"Ah, home away from home," Green said as he opened a small refrigerator. "Blatz beer is all I have. The guys say I don't drink because I leave the hard stuff alone. They do not keep beer at Ops. Want one?"

"No thanks," Briscoe answered but I would like a piece of that bunk.

"Help yourself mate. The bottom is mine," Green answered.

"He's either Irish or Australian," Briscoe thought. "It hard to tell."

Briscoe stripped to his shorts and climbed to the top bunk. He lifted the netting to see that there were no sheets or a pillowcase. He didn't care. Immediately he was asleep to the sounds of the Taiwan Strait's surf.

Briscoe awakened with a demanding urge to urinate. The room was totally dark and he was momentarily lost. It took awhile to remember where he was. He raised the mosquito net and felt for the ladder with one foot. He couldn't find it. He tried his other foot without success. Nature's urge demanded he proceed. He placed his knees on the bunk's edge and pushed away. The netting caught his head and shoulders and brought the top mattress crashing on top of him as fell to the floor.

"Be Jesus mate," Green cried. "You trying to kill us?"

"I have to piss damn it. Where's the john?" Briscoe asked.

"Through the porch door and on the beach. If it is serious work you might want to be doing, the shitter is around the porch's corner," Green answered. "It's a two-holer; nothing but class for us."

While relieving himself, Briscoe could hear the surf to his front. The beach could only be a few yards ahead. He walked forward and up a sand dune. He could see foam from crashing waves leaving a line extending left and right. It was nearly dawn and the light from behind him illuminated two islands in the distance. He reveled in the scene's beauty. For a moment, there was no war only peace; people were not trying to kill each other; it was a blissful feeling that he did not want to lose. Nevertheless, the sun's heat on his bare neck and back pulled him into reality. Much relieved he made his way through the sand to the outhouse. Inside he found an ample supply of "Wings" comic books. He glanced through them amused at their simplicity.

"We will never stop killing as long as we glorify this stuff," he thought.

It was full daylight as Briscoe made his way from the outhouse onto the small building's porch. He could hear Green's snores from outside. He felt famished and doubted if Green had anything other than Blatz beer in his refrigerator. He decided to look anyway.

He walked quietly across the room. Green was asleep in a fetal position with his back to him. His snoring continued. Opening the refrigerator's door, he examined its contents. Amid the beer, he saw four papayas. They appeared ripe so he removed two. He took a butcher's knife from the kitchen counter near the sink and sliced both into halves. He sat and consumed both quickly. He remained hungry.

He picked up a squashed beer can and threw it at Green. It struck the netting and fell to the floor with a loud, clanking noise. Green did not stir. Briscoe threw another with the same result.

"Hey Reggie. Where can a man get some steak and eggs?" Briscoe yelled.

"In heaven you dumb shit which means you get nothing," Green mumbled.

Eventually, Green left his bed with a big yawn and headed for the beach. Shortly he returned and went to the sink and washed.

Briscoe had already showered. He put on clothes laid out for him near his bunk. He asked again. "Is there any hope of steak and eggs?"

"No steaks around here but we can get some Spam and eggs at the airfield," Green finally answered. "You should be damned well hungry. You slept through two nights and a day."

"No way," Briscoe answered doubtfully.

Green, drying his head with a towel, said, "You must have been one tired fellow. We figured you needed the rest so we left you alone. Let's go eat."

Compressed pork, or whatever Spam was, never tasted so good to Briscoe. He and Green ate in a mess hall near Ops. On the way to the airfield, Green gave him identification documents. They showed that he was an official with the United States Department of State. He also had a false passport indicating the same. The best item of all was his diplomatic immunity card. It indicated his immunity anywhere in Japan and its islands.

"Lanny, I'm going to preflight. Meyers is filing our flight plan to Naha Port. He said for you to come by Ops and get a package. He said you would know what he means. See you at the plane mate," Green said.

Enroute to Naha, Briscoe examined the three cylinders. They were identical copies of encoding devices for a navigational beacon. The particular beacon was low frequency and anyone could receive its signal. However, if their receiver did not have a decoder, the signal was essentially useless. His task was to remove the real ones at the Naha warehouse and replace them with the dummies. He wasn't looking forward to the task.

Green looked sharp in his Army uniform. In every respect, he looked like a United States Quartermaster Captain. He stood aside as the Naha Port Authority official unlocked the main gate to the storage yard. Briscoe, in Army fatigues, carried a clipboard with a three-inch thick manifest attached. He wore the rank of staff sergeant. Green entered first and Briscoe followed. The official locked the gate behind them.

"Push the buzzer by the gate when you finish captain," he said. "I will unlock it for you."

"Thanks," Green replied.

In every direction vast stores of vehicles stood in neat rows. There were large crates and CONEX containers. They surrounded a large open sided warehouse. Beneath its roof, olive drab tarpaulins covered items hiding them from view. Green and Briscoe marched, in step, directly for it.

"Hell, this is a breeze mate," Green said.

"Shut up," Briscoe said with a hiss. "There are others in this yard. They might hear your damned accent."

Supplies beneath the roof were in stacks of various sizes. Briscoe estimated that the stacks covered an area of about two acres.

"Damn, we will never find such a small crate in this place," he thought.

Briscoe handed the clipboard to Green while he lifted one tarpaulin. Green watched, looking very official, while he compared markings on each crate with the manifest. After two hours, they had not found the specific container they needed.

Briscoe, now sweating profusely, said, "We could be at this for days."

The two heard a vehicle's engine approaching them. From around a corner of one row, they saw a forklift turn in their direction. As it got closer, they could see that the driver was Oriental. He stopped and dismounted next to them.

Neither Green nor Briscoe could understand what he was saying. They knew it was Japanese but knew nothing else. Finally, the Oriental bowed deeply and reached for the manifest. Green started to pull it away when Briscoe took it from him. He handed it to the Oriental who began gesturing with one finger at the description line on each page.

Briscoe stepped beside him and turned to the manifest's fifth page. He pointed to a description that read, "Mil-Spec-00378-01A. The small man began bowing profusely with a wide grin. He mounted the forklift and indicated for Green to join him. He ignored Briscoe.

"He's not stupid," Briscoe thought. "He knows whose ass to kiss."

The Japanese driver took them directly to the desired container and left. First, Briscoe opened the large metal container. This required him to break a lead seal. Inside, protected by packing material, he found a small box. The container was about one foot square. With the Oriental gone, Briscoe opened the small box. He removed three cylinders and replaced them with others that appeared identical. He closed it and put it into the larger, metal container. He pushed four spring-loaded snaps into place. He ran a wire through a tiny aperture and crimped its lead seal. He put the original cylinders into his pocket.

Briscoe repeated this process on two more beacons. He crimped the final lead seal.

Rolling the heavy tarpaulin over the large stack, he said, "Let's get the hell out of here."

Chapter Twenty One

June 1962

A puff of wind, a puff faint and tepid and laden with strange odours of blossoms, of aromatic wood, comes out the still night—the first sigh of the East on my face. That I can never forget. It was impalpable and enslaving, like a charm, like a whispered promise of mysterious delight. ...The mysterious East faced me, perfumed like a flower, silent like death, dark like a grave.
Joseph Conrad (1857–1924), Polish-born English novelist.

Vanessa Earling did not miss her title in the least. In England, it was expected but she never felt comfortable with it. In Laos, it was meaningless and she was happy without it. Her world interlocked with others like hers. They watched their men leave never knowing where they went and if they would ever return. Every month had emotional highs and lows. She held Frederick close before he left and after each return. She cried alone and never complained. Such was her life and she savored moments as they came. She relished the fullness of each moment for its presence and prayed for the next for it might never exist.

From her balcony, Vanessa could see across Vientiane, Laos, to the northeast. The largest urban center in Laos, it suffered from urban sprawl. It grew in random fashion without any evidence of control. Poverty resided next to wealth with blooming flora between both. From her vantage-point, she watched Mercedes mixed with pushcarts swirl through narrow streets conducting life's business. There existed those businesses open to public view. She knew there were others whose existence remained hidden. Some were clear and bright while others were dark and sinister.

Many tried to place Air America in a category but failed. She did not know because she was not supposed to know. What she did know was that Frederick flew for them. They were good to her and wives of other pilots. That was enough.

Air America made it possible for her to join Frederick in Laos. They knew she would anyway, so they made it easier. Vientiane was a name she never heard until she decided to join Frederick. Getting to Laos was an adventure unto itself. Its isolation went without question as soon as she tried to locate it on a map. Again, Devon came to her aid.

She had put Daytran out to stud after his latest win in 1954. He sired many great stallions. One of which was Daytran IV that she now had at stud. Her Arabians consumed massive amounts of her time before she decided to join Frederick. Her graceful stallions held every honor available and she saw no need to fill more display cases with trophies. She could count on Devon to see to them.

She was at their estate adjacent to Chatsworth, home of the Duke and Duchess of Devonshire when Devon brought her the map.

"My lady are you sure you want to travel to such a place?" He asked while unfolding a map.

"Devon, you found it," she said excitedly.

"Yes, I have. I will finish grooming Daytran while you examine it," he answered. "I have marked a recommended travel route for you."

Devon took Daytran's reins with one hand while holding the much sought after map with the other. Daytran, recognizing Devon, greeted him with a slight neigh.

Vanessa removed the grooming brushes from each hand and took the map. She thanked Devon and began walking slowly between horse stalls on each side. There were 24 of them. This building was one of three and the largest. The other two did have stalls but their primary purpose was for storage. One held farm implements to maintain the large fields required for grazing. The other contained fertilizer and feed for their 15 horses. In addition, this building held a birthing room to bring colts into the world.

She exited and turned left. Packed sawdust crunched beneath her feet. A white-boarded fence, on her right, enclosed a breeding area. Other fences extended across bright green grazing fields. Some Arabians grazed lazily raising their heads occasionally to gaze at her. One stallion raced toward the fence. A mottled gray, his head stood high upon an arching neck. His mane was streaming in the wind. His tail had a sharp upturn near his body while the rest flailed the air with each hoof's beat. He stopped at the fence and called to Vanessa while curling his upper lip. His large teeth gleamed white.

"What am I going to do with you Galag?" Vanessa asked walking toward him.

Shaking his head, the stallion neighed and pawed the ground. Near the fence, Vanessa reached into her sweater pocket and removed two lumps of sugar. Seeing her movement, the stallion reared high as if with pleasant anticipation.

"Here you are you phony," Vanessa said as she extended her open palm holding the sugar. With her other hand, she put the map in her riding pant's pocket.

Gently, Galag removed the sugar cubes while Vanessa caressed his large jaw. The sugar gone, she reached with both hands to rub above his muzzle. The giant stallion stood still as if to say, "Thank you."

"I'm going to miss you Galag," she said.

"You are going to have a big job living up to your father's reputation. I've retired the Daytran name so it's up to you now to establish your own. I won't be here to help," she said with a tightening throat.

Vanessa turned and walked to the building's north corner. She opened the door to where they either made or repaired harness. She went to a worktable and completely unfolded the map. Reaching to her left, she turned on an overhead light. With her finger, she traced Devon's red markings to Vientiane.

"Oh my," she thought. "This looks near where Frederick served with Admiral Lord Mountbatten. I had never noticed exactly where it was."

Turning the map over, she examined a larger depiction showing Southeast Asia's peninsula. First, she located Saigon in Viet Nam. Moving her gaze westward she found Laos on Viet Nam's western border. There, in the middle of the peninsula was Laos.

"No wonder I didn't notice it," she said aloud. "It's landlocked. Everywhere Frederick went there was a port. There has been mention of it on the Tele of late but not that much."

Looking closely, she saw that China was to Laos' north and Burma to the northwest. Thailand was to the west and Cambodia to the south. She looked forward to the trip. She found it easy to adjust to new places. Her trip from Switzerland to England proved that.

Recollecting, she looked through a window toward Chatsworth. She remembered the first time she ever saw Chatsworth on the way to her new home, Haugton House, in England.

In 1939, she arrived to a nation plunged into war. Hitler's drive into Poland was a call to arms for England. The Nazi leader crossed a line into a situation from which he could no longer extricate himself with talk. He laid his grand design for a master race at the world's door and they rebuffed it. He had allies but they were never part of his grand design. They were convenient and nothing more.

With war spreading, it became apparent that all of Europe was in jeopardy. Many began to flee France and other countries. Her parents remained in Switzerland but Ian insisted that Vanessa leave. He had not recovered from his last encounter with Nazi Germany.

She and Ian were returning to Switzerland from Berlin when Gestapo agents removed them from their train. They focused their attention on Vanessa for reasons Ian did not know and they would not say. They seemed wary of Ian.

Nevertheless, they continued to question her with Ian not present which infuriated him. He demanded use of a telephone that they promptly provided. They searched her luggage relentlessly and seemed frustrated when they did not find anything. Next, two female agents appeared for a body search. This was the ultimate insult. Ian tongue lashed them until Vanessa could see fear in their eyes. This was not normal for the Gestapo. They knew Ian had important German friends.

She felt certain she knew the reason for their treatment. Heydrich had sent them thinking that his position was powerful enough to cause their arrest. Fortunately, he underestimated Ian's influence. It was necessary for him to use the full extent of it to get her safely across the border. Vanessa suspected that their clearance came directly from Hitler but Ian never said.

When safely across, Ian asked. "Is there anything that you have not told me? Do you know why the Gestapo treated you that way?"

"No," she lied.

She dared not tell him about Heydrich's attack in her hotel room. Ian would return and demand justice. He could very well have Reinhard Heydrich court martialled. Heydrich's background would make his defense difficult. Once before the German military removed him from their ranks. It was for the way he treated a young woman. There still existed rumors about him having a Jewish heritage.

However, an ensuing investigation might reveal her activities during their visit. Ian knew nothing about what she did. She would never expose him to a spying charge because he didn't. In fact, she failed an important part of her mission. To her knowledge, no one ever got copies of orders made by the Germans with Ian. If they did, they did so without her knowledge. It was best to leave matters alone.

The day she arrived at England's coastal city of Skegness Frederick did not meet her. His family's butler, Neville, was there to greet her. A stately man with graying temples, he had been with the Earling family for 28 years. He apologized for the family. Her arrival was on short notice and Frederick's father and mother had other commitments. Neville assured her that they would greet her at dinner. Frederick could not obtain a leave from his duties with the Air Minister's Office in London. He would speak with her by telephone as soon as they arrived at Haugton House. Haugton House was their country estate in Derbyshire near Bakewell.

Neville rode in front with the driver who he introduced as Welford Jamesway. He explained that Welford was available to drive her when she desired.

"Miss, the staff is looking forward to meeting you. Duke and Duchess Earling are quite pleased that you are joining us. They expressed deep concern about your trip. Hitler seems to be making European travel a hazardous affair. We are available at any time. Simply let me know your need," Neville explained.

"Thank you Neville. I am glad to have made the journey without difficulty. I appreciate your kindness," Vanessa answered.

Vanessa knew about Haugton House and Chatsworth House. Chatsworth was one of many estates belonging to the Cavendish family. Their heritage sprang from William Cavendish in the mid-1500s. There had been many William Cavendish heirs over the centuries. In the late 1700s, there had been a land dispute between the Cavendish and Earling families. It was not until the 1800s that the conflict ended amicably. Now, they were close friends and often traveled together to various equestrian competitions.

What brought the two families together to settle the dispute was a mutual love of Arabian horses. It was in the 1870s that one of President Grant's stallions made its way to England. From this lone stallion, many Arabians became the property of Cavendish and Earling families. Frederick had told her about their horses and she was anxious to see them. She had always had a fascination with them but never had one of her own. At the academy, she rode regularly. The various steeds seemed to sense a fondness from her.

"Pardon me Miss, we are here," she heard Neville say.

She had drifted to sleep during their long ride from the coast. Haughton House was about 160 miles north of London and inland amid rolling hills in Derbyshire.

"Thank you Neville," she replied. "I must have dozed."

"That is quite all right Miss. Please follow me. Welford will attend to your luggage," Neville explained.

She had bathed and changed clothes when Frederick's call came. He sounded genuinely exhilarated that she arrived safely. He explained that he would join her by tea-time the following Friday. He could not be away from his duties until then.

Their marriage was a major social event of 1942. She recalled how the calves of her legs ached from so many curtseys. They never let the seemingly incessant German bombing interfere. Frederick no longer served on the Air Ministry's staff. Being fighter qualified, he spent his days responding to alerts. His commander allowed him a 48-hour holiday for their honeymoon.

Ian gave her away. He looked so dashing in his formal attire. Her mother cried throughout the entire ceremony. Ian drank too much at the reception and spilled whiskey on an exquisite dress belonging to a Baron's wife. By the time he finished with his characteristic blarney, the lady thought he had done her a favor. It was all so wonderful and fantasy like. A fairy tale could not have been better. It ended too soon with Frederick returning to his airfield as bombing raids continued.

Vanessa joined Britain's Air Defence Force. She helped track incoming raids detected by radar. During her shift at an operational control center, she helped show locations of friendly and enemy forces on a large table that almost filled an entire room. Senior staff members watched from their overhead positions and assigned missions to Royal Air Force Air Defence interceptor squadrons. She often displayed Frederick's squadron responding to alerts. She watched with intense anxiety as reports came in regarding aircraft losses. She feared the worst every time Frederick flew a mission.

Twice he cheated death. He had to parachute into the English Channel on one occasion because of severe damage to his aircraft. His recovery was swift. The second time he returned to the airfield with critical damage to his aircraft. He had to land immediately because of low fuel. It was the practice for interceptors to launch with low fuel. This increased their speed and maneuverability. At the field, he could only extend one landing gear. He made one landing approach and struck the field hard with one gear in an attempt to cause the other to descend. This attempt failed. He made his landing with one tire extended. He walked away from his wrecked fighter with minor cuts and bruises.

Frederick rose in rank rapidly and commanded a Royal Air Force Squadron. Subsequently, he joined England's prestigious Central Air Defence Command as Aviation Advisor to the Admiralty. Vanessa and Frederick grabbed brief moments together after his posting to London. However, this soon ended when Lord Mountbatten, Chief of Aviation, Southeast Asia Attack Group, selected Frederick for his staff.

Prime Minister Churchill appointed Lord Mountbatten Supreme Allied Commander South East Asia. Mountbatten had free rein to select those he wanted on his staff. Frederick was his first choice to coordinate aviation activities. Mountbatten told Frederick to accompany an advance group. They were to proceed to establish a headquarters in Delhi, India. It was September 1943.

Before his departure, they had a week to holiday on the coast.

"Oh what bittersweet days those were," she thought. "Each second was precious and succulent. We loved and hurt at the same time."

Light beamed into the room as the door opened, "Pardon me," Devon said. "What do you think of the travel route?"

Looking back to the map, Vanessa realized that she had not looked at Devon's recommendation.

"I'm sorry, Devon," she answered. "I've been sitting here thinking of old times. I've found Laos but didn't examine your routing suggestion."

"That's fine, mam," he replied. "I need to talk to you about another matter."

"What's that?" She asked.

"I wanted to let you know that I will be leaving Haughton House shortly after you go to join Frederick. I thought it important that I tell you in person," Devon answered.

"Why Devon?" She asked deeply concerned. "Who will see to Galag and Daytran? They have never known another trainer that cared so much. Plus, you are practically family."

"Unfortunately, I cannot explain. You know how that is," Devon replied.

"Devon, you're not doing that again are you?" Vanessa asked.

"Mam, you know I cannot even answer that," he said.

"Devon, you promised. After what happened the last time, you promised," Vanessa exclaimed.

She arose from her seat and walked to Devon. She took his hand and led him to a window seat. She sat on one end and indicated for him to sit on the other which he did. She took his hand and placed it between both of hers.

After a few moments gazing at their hands in her lap, she said, "Devon I owe you my life and that of my father. In addition, were it not for you, England could have suffered significant damage during the war."

Stopping for a moment, she continued, "The wounds you suffered will never heal. You are in no physical condition to go back to that life. You promised Devon. How can you break that promise?"

Without hesitation, Devon promptly replied, "Sometimes events are so important that they exceed any other consideration. In this case, I must break my promise. Someday, I might be able to explain and then you will understand."

Pulling Devon to her, they embraced. With her head next to Devon's, her eyes filled with tears. With her arms around him, she could feel the indentations in his back where flesh had once been. Now, hard scars lined multiple concave spots across his shoulder blades.

Gently Devon removed her arms. Taking each shoulder in his hands, he pushed Vanessa to arm's length.

He looked into her misty eyes and said, "I will let Neville know. In addition, I contacted a superior trainer. He will see that Galag realizes his full capabilities. I have work to do and must go. I will accompany you to the airport when you leave," he said with a wistful smile.

He arose and went to the door. He opened it half way and placed one foot over the threshold.

Looking at Vanessa, he said, "All will be well. Please do not worry. I will remain in contact whenever it is possible."

Devon closed the door. Vanessa remained in her seat staring at her hands. She recalled the time that Devon advised her to marry Frederick. He said then that he would see her again and he did. She prayed that was true this time. Again, she gazed at the white fences flowing over rolling green hills. She noticed that leaves on the oak trees were beginning to change color. It was this time of year when Devon saved her and Ian. It was also the time that he almost died. There was no way she could ever repay him. It was all so clear now.

Devon saw her one year after she arrived in England. She was leaving church on Sunday morning in Bakewell. As she reached the bottom step, she looked ahead and saw him across the street. She recognized him immediately and almost yelled his name and started to run to him. His negative gaze stopped her. It took every ounce of her being to appear that she did not see. She knew enough to continue her routine. After chatting with some of the local ladies, she drove to Haughton House. She waited to hear from him. It was another week before he contacted her.

She was in the local library to find a book on Arabians. As she searched the stacks, a voice came from behind.

"Meet me at the reference table," Devon said.

She turned but he was not behind her.

"He must have spoken from the other row," she concluded as she looked for the reference desk. "Why is he being so cautious? We're safe here."

She visually searched the library's main reading area while appearing to examine a book. Devon sat at a table looking through London newspapers. She went to the magazine rack next to the reference table. She selected a magazine and began looking through it. Putting it back she selected another and glanced in Devon's direction. He indicated with his eyes for her to take a seat across from him.

Vanessa returned the second magazine and went to the newspaper table. She looked through them and selected one. She casually thumbed through it. Again, she glanced at Devon. Once more, he indicated with his eyes for her to sit across from him. She went to the chair and sat. She opened the newspaper and pretended to read.

"Do not look up. Continue what you are doing and listen," Devon directed. "We missed him by ten damn minutes. You did great but the bastard is simply lucky," he whispered with a hiss indicating disgust.

After a moment, Devon said, "The photos of your father's orders were perfect. That was a complete success."

"No one took photos," Vanessa replied whispering.

"They did and you just don't know it. While your father was on the telephone at the border, our agent got the photos. What did you think all that searching was about?" Devon asked.

Vanessa considered what Devon said.

"It made sense," she thought. "That Nazi animal wasn't behind the search. Devon was."

"Why didn't you tell me when I got back to Switzerland?" Vanessa asked.

"Because you did not need to know," he answered. "Listen carefully and do not panic. You must promise to stay calm," Devon stated firmly.

Vanessa hesitated for a moment and thought, "What is wrong? It must be about someone close. Ian!"

She glanced around the area to see if anyone was watching them. It appeared that no one was interested.

"What's wrong Devon?" She asked.

"Tell me now," she ordered, rising slightly from her chair.

"Sit and read the paper," he answered nonchalantly.

Vanessa knew Devon. While he might sound casual, there was an icy tone in his voice that meant he was serious.

"I need your help one more time," he said. "If there was anyone else, I would not bother you. Only you can do what is necessary. It's about your father."

"I knew it," she thought. "Oh God, let him be okay. If he's hurt because of me, I will never be able to forgive myself for using him."

"What is it?" She asked with her teeth tightly closed and her words breathed through them.

"Drive five kilometers south on the main road to London. There is a historical marker and a maze. Meet me at the marker in one hour," Devon said as he arose from his seat.

He placed the London newspaper in the correct stack. He casually walked past the librarian's desk and spoke to her. Vanessa could not hear what he said. She watched him leave as her stomach began to churn. She could taste bile. She remained in her seat and appeared to read the entire paper.

After 45 minutes, she arose and went to the librarian's desk and asked. "Miss Wallace will you request a book from London for me?"

"Certainly, Vanessa. What can I get for you?" She questioned.

"Sir Riley's 'Equestrian Etiquette, Fourth Edition'," Vanessa replied.

"It will be here next week. If there's a problem, I will give you a ring dear," she advised.

"Thank you," Vanessa responded.

Outside, she looked for Devon. He was nowhere in sight. She tried not to run to her car. Her hands trembled as she fumbled for her keys. In her haste, she dropped them in the gutter.

"Damn," she thought. "Calm down."

As she arrived at the historical marker, she saw Devon standing next to it. He saw her enter the parking area. He turned and went into the maze.

Hurriedly, she parked and went directly to the maze. Devon was waiting around the first turn. He had a dour look about him. She became even more concerned.

"Devon please, what is it?" She asked with desperation permeating every word.

"Walk with me," he replied.

On both sides, heavy foliage rose ten feet. The walkway was cobblestone with ground lights along the way at regular intervals. It was fall and the air had a tinge of impending winter in it. Consequently, they were the only persons visiting the popular tourist attraction. Few visitors came to the site this time of year. She walked beside Devon and listened intently.

"Your father is still making trips into Germany. He is attracting attention and is becoming suspect by our people. He is putting his life in danger and you must stop him," he said.

"I can get word to him right away," Vanessa answered.

"No, you must go to Switzerland and tell him in person. He is on a personal crusade against the Nazis and it is going to get him killed," Devon said sternly. "I hope he will listen to you. He has been warned twice but he ignores us."

"What crusade? What are you talking about? And, who's us?" Vanessa asked.

"You know that your father never put faith in currency. He considered gold the best exchange medium. Well, he strayed and accepted British pound notes instead of gold. The payment came from Germany. He didn't like the look of the money. He took some of it to three Swiss banks. Senior officials told him that it was fine. After depositing the total, the same bankers now say it was counterfeit," Devon explained.

Vanessa stopped walking and turned to Devon and said, "I don't doubt that he's upset. A stunt like that would make anyone enraged. With his temper, I imagine he demanded the bankers make it good."

"They did," Devon answered.

"So, what's the problem? Who is 'us' and what crusade?" Vanessa demanded.

"You know I cannot reveal anything about the organization I work with," Devon continued. "Through whatever sources your father has, he learned who made the plates for the phony money. The Gestapo did not have the technical expertise to create quality, printing plates to produce genuine looking currency. They learned that they had Jewish engravers in their concentration camps. These engravers were some of the best in the world. Threatened with death, they made the plates. The result was pound notes identical to the real thing. As a test, they took some of it to Switzerland. They showed it to the same bankers your father saw about it. Supposedly, they told the Nazis they would take all they could get. There is some question as to whether the bankers knew it was fake. Your father doesn't care and he's set into play events that are going to get him killed. In addition, he will probably cause the engravers' deaths. He must be stopped."

"Are you saying that you would kill my father?" Vanessa asked incredulously.

Without hesitation, Devon answered, "Yes."

Blind rage engulfed her. She began pounding Devon's chest with every ounce of Irish fury she could muster. Tears streaked her face and she began to curse him. Realizing her strikes were not effective, she slapped his face repeatedly. Finally, Devon grabbed her wrists and she collapsed against his chest racked with anguished sobs.

"Oh Devon," she finally cried, "What can I do? Tell me, please."

Devon placed one arm around Vanessa heaving shoulders. Gently, he led her back along the walkway to their last turn into the maze. From this position, he could see anyone entering the popular attraction. He was certain that they were alone but he wanted to make sure.

He gave Vanessa his handkerchief and said, "Ian has hired mercenaries to form an attack team. He has them at a camp high in the mountains along Switzerland's northern border. He plans to attack a train moving the engravers to their original concentration camp. He thinks he can rescue them and escape. We cannot allow the attack for two reasons. First, we don't want the Nazis to learn their counterfeit scheme did not work. Second, there is a Nazi spy among the mercenaries. He will be able to reveal how Ian learned of the Jewish group and expose many of our agents. He will listen to you."

Vanessa, now composed, asked. "What do you want me to do?"

"That's my girl," Devon said. "Here's the plan. We're going to take out that camp. Your job is to lure your father away before we attack."

"Father is no fool," Vanessa responded. "He will be suspicious as soon as he sees me."

"You're right. He's no one's dummy. We're going to have to trick him. That's why it's so important that you come with us," Devon said.

"Devon, I hate this. I've only deceived him once. That's the time we went to Berlin and I've not forgiven myself for that," Vanessa explained.

"If we can save him by lying, we have to do it. To help reduce suspicion, a man he trusts will take you to his camp. Ian recruited most of his men from the Irish Republican Army," Devon said before Vanessa interrupted.

"He did not do the recruiting himself. He used a go-between that he trusts. He's a second cousin of yours from Northern Ireland. He works for us. The IRA thinks he's a deserter from the Royal Air Force. He will take you to Ian's camp. Tell Ian that you learned of his plans from me. He knows I was your teacher at the Academy. He also knows I gave you the writing assignment for your Berlin trip. He doesn't know the true nature of our relationship unless you've told him," Devon said.

"I've never told him or Frederick about that trip Devon," Vanessa answered.

"Fine. Get Ian away from the main building. Use any excuse immediately after you arrive. Our man will take care of himself. You take care of Ian and we will take care of the others. Vanessa, you need a good excuse for the Earlings. I have to have you on your way day after tomorrow," Devon explained.

"Devon, at this point, more lying is not going to matter. They know father doesn't want me in Switzerland. How are you going to get me out of England?" Vanessa asked.

"You will have to go to Ireland first. The Ireland trip is a cover. Otherwise, we would start at Land's End. We will bring you back to Land's End, England. You will board an aircraft with Spanish markings. We will follow a route through Spain to San Sabastian and then Gerona."

"From Gerona, we will make our run to Switzerland through Monaco. Our destination from Monaco is Frauenfeld, Switzerland. You're in for a long trip with many fuel stops. Get as much rest as you can on the flight. You will need all your strength after Frauenfeld because we will travel overland to Ian's camp. Expect heavy snow along the route. We've got everything you will need on the plane."

"Once we have Ian, we will return directly to England. We will be flying low-level and fast to avoid Nazi aircraft. Any questions?" Devon asked.

Vanessa shook her head indicating that she did not. At this point, events overwhelmed her.

"You will receive a cable from Ireland. It will say that your father is there and seriously ill. Just get to Ireland and we will handle the rest. Be ready to go day after tomorrow," Devon instructed.

"Devon, I'm afraid," Vanessa revealed.

"We all are. Just be ready, okay?" Devon said.

"Okay," she replied meekly.

Vanessa could not believe her fear. This was different than her Berlin trip. Most of those events she had direct control. In this situation, she was at the mercy of many others. If it were anyone but Devon, she would devise her own plan. Somehow, on her own, she would get to Ian. Still, she realized that she did not have Devon's resources. Her profound anxiety stemmed from being at the mercy of strangers.

"Let's get out of here before someone comes along. That's all we need right now is for some busybody to think you are having an affair shortly before your wedding," Devon told her.

Neville drove her to London for her flight to Dublin. The Earlings were very concerned, as was Frederick. She was able to get word to him about her having to go.

Vanessa left her remembrances and returned to her map. She traced the route drawn by Devon to Laos. She knew that he had checked every detail. That was his way for he never left anything to chance. He made up his mind to do something and he did it with no second-guessing or excuses. Had it not been for Frederick, she felt she could have loved him. Yet, she never felt for Devon what she felt for Frederick.

"How strange," she thought. "Devon had done for her more personally than Frederick ever had. Still, she gave her life to Frederick after Devon saved it for her."

Looking at the red lines on the map reminded her of the map Devon showed her on the plane to Spain. The difference was that the lines he showed her were blue. She understood now that they had to be blue to see them with the red night lighting aboard the plane. How simple she had thought at the time. However, the selection was critical. Those were the kind of things Devon was good at, details.

The 16 men with them looked like ghosts. Everything was white, their weapons, faces, clothing, everything. They could disappear in snow. She, and her escort into Ian's hideaway, dressed the same. All of it was so dangerous but Devon had put her fears to rest.

She remembered how dumbfounded Ian looked when he realized who she was. With the white clothing and facemask, he didn't recognize her. He immediately started chastising the man who brought her without his permission. Others in the room were cleaning weapons and preparing explosives for their train raid. They too became concerned. When she spoke Ian became confused.

He couldn't attach her voice with what he saw. There was no logic to it. She couldn't be there in his mind.

On the long flight, she had studied over and over how to get him out of the building. It was so simple. Whenever she really wanted something from him as a young girl, she always called him daddy instead of Da. It worked then and it worked that cold, wintry night. He came like a lamb.

"Daddy, please," she implored him. "I must talk to you in private, daddy. Please daddy," she whined and stamped her feet.

The others in the room laughed. Here was the little rich girl, begging daddy for something foolish. Ian, quite embarrassed, put on his winter clothing. He followed her into the howling, snowstorm. They took refuge beside an outbuilding.

Events after that were a blur of explosions, weapons firing, and flashing lights. An acrid odor of burned explosives permeated the air. Ian grabbed her and took her behind the nearby building for safety. Devon confronted him; they argued; and Devon struck Ian unconscious. Four others unfolded a portable sled and strapped Ian to it.

"Stay here with Ian and do not move," he told her forcefully.

Devon took one man with him and sent the other three around the building's other side. They took firing positions at alternate corners of the building. From there, they attacked the main building with their automatic weapons. The noise was horrendous.

She had never let what happened next enter her mind before their arrival. Her focus and been on Ian. She never thought through why Devon had 16 men with him. They were killing everyone in the main building. They were not having an easy time of it. Their opponents were well armed and experienced fighters. Many escaped into the surrounding forest. One by one, they were hunting and killing them.

Finally, there was quiet. Devon returned with his men. Three had severe wounds and one was missing. Her escort into the building was the missing man. As the building blazed, they figured he died during the initial attack. Two more were killed later.

Three men donned a harness connected to the sled and began pulling it from the area. Devon told her to follow. As they left the outbuilding's cover, an automatic weapon began firing at them from a stand of trees. Devon threw himself upon her. He caused her to fall on Ian strapped to the sled. Devon made a small groan and went limp atop her and Ian. She felt warm blood on her face.

Meanwhile, the others attacked the lone gunman. He was in a ravine and well protected. Finally, while others kept heavy fire on his position, one team member circled behind and killed their attacker with a grenade.

Ian, now conscious, demanded they release him. Some were skeptical but finally they removed his restraints. They needed the sled for Devon.

Ian helped Vanessa attend to Devon. They cut his parka apart to reveal five, gaping wounds. While Vanessa continued removing Devon's heavy coat, Ian gathered five compress bandages from the others. Two men held Devon's torso up so that she and Ian could apply the compresses. With Devon secured, they began their return to Frauenfeld.

At Frauenfeld, they attended to Devon's wounds. It was essential that they stop his bleeding. In addition, he was in shock. After applying fresh compresses, they wrapped him in a warm blanket and put him aboard their aircraft. The pilot had little visibility and expressed concern about trying their flight in such adverse weather. After some discussion, he agreed to try. With a strong crosswind, their flight crew got them airborne and on the return leg to Land's End.

Devon received continual care while they made their perilous, low level flight. Vanessa and Ian's attention was on Devon. Had they been in the cockpit they surely would have known an even greater fear. With blinding snow and severe turbulence, it took every ounce of the pilot's skill to navigate across mountains and down narrow valleys. They finally were able to relax as conditions improved over the channel. They radioed for an ambulance in violation of Devon's previous orders of strict, radio silence.

At Land's End, Vanessa insisted she accompany Devon to the hospital. Team members and Ian had to restrain her. Once refueled, they departed Land's End for Ireland. Along the way, Vanessa explained to Ian their reason for abducting him. At first, he was irate. After Vanessa's continued persistence that the mission was necessary, Ian relented. Vanessa finally slept in Ian's arms until landing at their origin.

At the memory, Vanessa began crying. Her tears fell upon the map causing its red lines to smear as tears struck. Their impact caused the ink to form wet circles similar to wounds on Ian's back. She tried to stop but couldn't. Finally, she rushed outside to find Devon. He was gone.

For whatever reason, Devon did not go with her to the airport. She kept watching the boarding area for him. He never appeared. Frederick's parents walked her to the loading gate. She could only hear some of their parting comments. She promised them that she would make Frederick write more often.

As her plane climbed over England, she could see the coast where she came ashore in 1939. Again, she was joining Frederick in a war torn land. However, this time his missions were peaceful ones for a commercial airline.

He grew to love Southeast Asia during the war. He had returned to England afterwards but was restless. He loved his flying and he was good at it. He flew with British Overseas Airlines for 15 years but grew to dislike it immensely. At first, she thought it might be a mid-life crisis. Perhaps he missed the adventure but that wasn't it. He said that he felt like a truck driver. He wanted to feel the airplane and be a part of it. She understood and agreed to his desire. Eventually, he returned to Southeast Asia to fly for Air America.

Vanessa recalled her arrival in Thailand. Frederick was there to meet her. They finally had their honeymoon for two weeks. He loved his work and it was what he wanted. He was again the man she married.

They next flew to Vientiane on an Air America flight. The captain had them ride in the cockpit with him. These were the first of many others she would meet. If being in Laos was happiness for Frederick, it was for her also.

Chapter Twenty Two

February 1960

There can be no reconciliation where there is no open warfare. There must be a battle, a brave boisterous battle, with pennants waving and cannon roaring, before there can be peaceful treaties and enthusiastic shaking of hands.
Mary Elizabeth Braddon (1837-1915), English Writer

Colonel Nguyen Van Anh looked through the documents on his desk. Setting one file folder aside, he looked through another and rejected it. He selected three more and did the same.

"Where is the damn thing," he thought. "Our effort in the south is a total failure. It is not going to work. As long as that treaty exists, we're in trouble. We simply do not have the resources."

With one sweep of his arm, he sent documents, paperweights and file folders crashing across the room. Everything previously on his desk now lay scattered about his office floor. He pushed his chair straight to the rear, crossed his arms in disgust, and stared at the ceiling.

A series of rapid knocks sounded outside his officer door.

"What?" He yelled, with a voice indicative of his deep frustration.

A meek, female voice from outside asked. "Colonel, are you okay?"

"I'm fine. Leave me alone damn it," he answered.

The same voice, but now trembling, responded, "Yes sir."

After a few minutes, Anh arose and began collecting items from the floor. He began placing them on his desk with sighs of resignation. With the last folder in hand, he returned to his seat. As he turned to face his desk, he threw the folder onto it causing another folder to slide from within it.

"There you are," he mumbled.

He immediately sat and grasped both chair arms while pulling himself close to the desk. He glanced at the file's title. It stated, "Unification, Geneva Accords – 1959, National Liberation Front (NFL) and Beyond." Opening it, he read the title of the file's first page, "SEATO Analysis, Party Impact-Capability Vs. Threat."

Anh turned to the next page and directed his attention to its "Table of Contents." He quickly scanned down the page to a title, "Overview July 1954 – July 1959." He opened the manuscript to the referenced page and began reading.

The party's intent for the Geneva Accords, signed on July 20 and 21, 1954, were overridden by pressures from the Soviet Union (USSR) and the Peoples Republic of China (PRC). The USSR and the PRC did not want another confrontation with the United States and/or France so soon after the conflict in Korea. While the objective of removing France from the Democratic Republic of

Viet Nam (DRV) was achieved, the division of Viet Nam at the 17th parallel gave nationalist causes in the south an opportunity to garner support from the West. In addition, the election of Diem and his followers further complicated any effort to expand control to the south with hope of reunification.

The National Liberation Front (NLF), established to expand the cause of reunification was a failure from the outset. This should have been clear when the United States Secretary of State John Foster Dulles and then President Dwight D. Eisenhower stated their position regarding the accords. Their position stated:

1. It (DRV) will refrain from the threat or the use of force to disturb them, in accordance with Article 2(4) of the Charter of the United Nations dealing with the obligation of members to refrain in their international relations from the threat or use of force.
2. It (US) would view any renewal of the aggression in violation of the aforesaid agreements (The Accords) with grave concern and as seriously threatening international peace and security.

While the United States' thinly veiled their threat in the disguise of the United Nations, they subsequently began unilateral negotiations with multiple nations in Southeast Asia. The consummation of these negotiations resulted in the formation of the Southeast Asia Treaty Organization (SEATO). This capitalistic arrangement was nothing more than a ruse to expand imperialistic tools into the region for monetary and political gain.

Ngo Dinh Diem's election in 1956 was a major step toward the failure of our political process to bring about the reunification of our country. Diem's repeated solicitation for capitalistic support in the form of military support to include materiel, training, and advisory support were successful. Of particular importance was the recent implementation of numerous acts to impose military law in the south. Most recently, Law 10/59, enacted May 6, 1959, gives him essentially dictatorial powers over the southern portion of our nation.

The new president of the United States, John F. Kennedy, must be convinced that continued support of Diem is not in the best interests of the United States. It is our recommendation that previous plans for this contingency become effective immediately.

Furthermore, an increased effort to use influence from religious organizations in the south is imperative. In particular, Buddhism will be effective due to their dissatisfaction with western influence on the tenets of their faith. Growth of Catholicism is a particularly sensitive issue with the Buddhists."

"There's no reason to read farther," he thought. "I've read the details a dozen times and they have not changed."

Anh considering the implications of the committee's report.

"This will require us to make major changes to the current, and the upcoming, five year plan. The increase will be beyond what we can afford. The Soviets, for some reason, are being very careful with Kennedy. They have something very costly underway. I know it," he thought. "The PRC can help us the most. The supply lines are short and there are many supply routes into the south without having to ship by marine vessels."

Leaving his seat, Anh went to a wall map showing Asia. He examined the borders of Cambodia, Laos, South, and North Viet Nam.

Moving his gaze to Muong Valley, he thought, "That was so long ago. I wonder where he is. Official records show him as killed in action. If they find him, they will execute him as a deserter. My only hope is that you are safe and happy little brother. I do not for a second believe your are dead. You must never use our name again."

Anh glanced at a clock above the map. Surprised at the time, he looked at his watch.

"Another meeting! I am sick and tired of meetings. I have been behind a desk long enough. Perhaps today I can get that changed," he thought as he reached for his hat.

He opened his office door to an outer office with a secretary seated at her desk. She heard his door open and turned from her typewriter to look at him.

"Do you want me to have your driver meet you out front?" She asked.

"No thank you," he replied. "I will walk. I need the exercise. That desk is turning me into an old man."

Placing her hand over her mouth, she giggled and answered, "Oh no colonel, you have many years before you are an old man. Are you going to the minister's weekly meeting?" She questioned.

"Yes," he replied. "After that I will visit my mother. I won't return today. I will be here at the usual time tomorrow. You have a nice evening."

As she turned to her typewriter, she said, "You too colonel. I hope your mother is better."

Anh left his office through a side exit to the street. Heavy traffic flowed in both directions with a mixture of automobiles, Lambrettas, pull carts, and mostly bicycles. The air was alive with incessant ringing from bicycle bells as thousands fought for position in the churning mass of humanity. He made his way through a myriad of vendors trying to make a living.

"If the minister has his way, there will be no vendors on the street Monday," he thought. "He is not going to tolerate capitalists on Hanoi's streets. They will either be in a reeducation camp or working a state farm."

Soon, he neared the old prison across from the lake. The same prison almost brought about the death of his mother. He recalled his first attempt to find her. The police almost shot him. He could still hear her voice in that darkened room. They were together and he never suspected. It was later, when she told him about it, that he scolded her for not letting him stay. She didn't want her son to see her in such a devastated condition.

"Oh, how she cried," he remembered. "What kind of son was I to scold my mother after her ordeal? I will never forgive myself for that."

Along the way, Anh returned salute after salute. Military personnel were in abundance in Hanoi. Many were on leave for Hanoi's Tet celebration that ended two days before. Soon they would return to their inadequately equipped units.

"There's one advantage having a driver," he thought. "It saves wear and tear on my arm."

While chuckling to himself, he saw his destination ahead to his left. The entrance to the offices of The People's Minister for Finance and Military Planning was an innocuous archway over a doublewide brick drive. Immediately inside and to the left, a small room opened onto a courtyard. It was necessary to pass through the room to gain access to the building. Otherwise, the drive led directly to an open quadrangle. However, no entrances existed from the courtyard into the building. Bricks filled bottom floor entrances and windows to preclude passage. Upper floors opened onto the courtyard via balconies.

Everyday at 5 P.M., guards closed the drive's entrance with two, steel reinforced wooden doors. Once shut and bolted, access was through a normal sized door cut into the main door. The entrance had guards 24 hours a day, seven days a week. Formerly the headquarters for the French Secret Police, the minister found it excellent for his needs. He laid claim to it as the French left under terms of the Geneva Accords.

Inside the guard's checkpoint, three DRV soldiers came to attention when Anh entered. The sergeant in charge saluted.

"Good afternoon colonel, the minister will meet you at the usual place," he said as Anh returned the salute.

"Thank you," Anh replied without breaking his stride.

The guard post opened into a long corridor. At the far end, a large mural of Ho Chi Minh, superimposed over a DRV flag, dominated the view. Along the corridor's sides, chest high pedestals held memorabilia from Dien Bien Phu. Engraved brass plates described each item. Above the pedestals, various photos of Ho Chi Minh with world leaders appeared.

Reaching the corridor's end, Anh stopped to glance left and right. Immediately to his left, another mural showed Mao Te Jung's head in a celestial pose looking down at workers building a dam. To his right, another corridor ran the building's length. At its end, a right turn formed another side of the building's quadrangle design. On its wall, a floor to ceiling picture showed Lenin reading from a book to a group of people. They looked up at him with adoration on their faces.

On the right, where once doors and windows existed, ornate inlaid terrazzo depicted pastoral scenes. On the left, doorways led to offices. Each, with one exception, had a sign above it. The lone door had a guard on either side. Before he entered, the senior guard examined his identification at length. Satisfied, he opened the door and Anh entered an empty foyer where he removed his boots. Proceeding, he opened a door to his immediate front and entered a gymnasium.

Various martial arts paraphernalia dominated the room's furnishings. Around the sides, a single bench provided seating. Two doors allowed access to a steam bath and a tiled hot tub. On Anh's right, in a far corner, one man sat on a bench reading from a book. He was Minister Le Phuong Bien.

He was old with gray hair and a short beard. His complexion was quite pale and his appearance gave an aura of being fragile. He wore a solid white robe tied at his waist with a black belt.

"Few people even know of that man," Anh thought. "Outwardly, he appears to be someone's kind uncle or grandfather. Yet, he is the architect of more mass killings than anyone in our government."

Anh recalled their first meeting.

"I, like many others, fell prey to an initial impression. He was the personnel colonel who allowed me to list Vinh as MIA while I looked for him. With that gesture, I thought him to be a kind and considerate person. It was later that I learned the depths of his depravity," he thought.

Anh remembered spending two days trying to find Vinh's trail. By questioning members of his unit, he learned of Vinh's running into the forest. A fellow soldier, from the FDC, was relieving himself when he saw Vinh come from their tunnel complex.

"Sir, he seemed upset. He kept staring into the heavy foliage in that direction. Then, suddenly, he started to run. That's the last I saw of him. He never returned to our unit."

He had thanked Vinh's fellow soldier and entered the jungle where he indicated last seeing him. After two hours, he found a collapsed punji pit. There was a considerable amount of blood in its bottom. Overhead, someone had placed two strong vines on a tree limb. It appeared that they used the vines as a lift to remove whomever was in the pit. By examining the pit's edge, he knew that four or five people were at the pit. Their trail led into the jungle and disappeared. Whoever it was made a conscious effort to hide their trail.

Later, back at his unit, he received word from electronics specialists about the three cylinders. They were not functional. Their report indicated that they were encoding devices of some sort. Someone rendered them useless by removing essential, internal components. Why the French did this still puzzled him.

It was after this incident that he again met Le Phuong Bien. He was attending a commander briefing by General Giap. Giap made Colonel Bien responsible for moving captured French soldier to their internment camps. So many Frenchmen died during their march that it was a major problem at Geneva. His instructions to his troops resulted in more prisoners dying than during the infamous death march from Bataan during World War II. His methods were particularly vicious and cruel. Yet, he received praise and recognition for efficiency. The Central Committee approved his nomination for promotion to brigadier general.

His rise was swift. He gained a reputation for being prompt, efficient, and reliable. He began working directly for Ho Chi Minh during Ho's purges of his political enemies. He led the campaign to eradicate Catholics. Tens of thousands died as a direct result of his efforts. Indeed, he was a ruthless man. His position as The People's Minister for Finance and Military Planning gave him tremendous power.

As Anh approached, Bien laid his book on the bench atop some file folders and stood. Anh stopped, bowed, and said, "Good afternoon Minister Bien. I see you are staying fit."

Also bowing, the minister replied, "Everyday I spend here reminds me that I am no longer a young man. Anh, please have a seat."

Pointing to a red bordered folder on the bench beneath his book, Bien said, "Anh, read through this while I bathe. Let me know your thoughts when I return."

Without waiting for comment, he went to the door leading to the hot bath. Anh watched him enter and close the door.

"What is he up to this time," Anh thought as he retrieved the folder.

Opening it, Anh began to read.

The Path of Revolution in the South, 1956.

"The situation forces bellicose states such as the U.S. and Britain to recognize that if they adventurously start a world war, they themselves will be the first to be destroyed, and thus the movement to demand peace in those imperialist countries is also developing strongly.

Recently, in the U.S Presidential election, the present Republican administration, in order to buy the people's esteem, put forward the slogan "Peace and Prosperity," this showed that even the people of an imperialist warlike country like the U.S. want peace.

The general situation shows us that the forces of peace and democracy in the world have tipped the balance toward the camp of peace and democracy. Therefore, we can conclude that the world at present can maintain long-term peace.

On the other hand, however, we can also conclude that as long as the capitalist economy survives, it will always scheme to provoke war, and there will remain the danger of war.

Based on the above world situation, the Twentieth Congress of the Communist Party of the Soviet Union produced two important judgments:

1. All conflicts in the world at present can be resolved by means of peaceful negotiations.

2. The revolutionary movement in many countries at present can develop peacefully. Naturally in the countries in which the ruling class has a powerful military-police apparatus and is using fascist policies to repress the movement, the revolutionary parties in those countries must look clearly at their concrete situation to have the appropriate methods of struggle.

Based on the general situation and that judgment, we conclude that, if peaceful negotiations resolve conflicts, peace is achievable.

Because the interest and aspiration of peaceful reunification of our country are the common interest and aspiration of all the people of the Northern and Southern zones the people of the two zones did not have any reason to provoke war, nor to prolong the division of the country. On the contrary, the people of the two zones are increasingly determined to oppose the U.S.-Diem scheme of division and war provocation in order to create favorable conditions for negotiations between the two zones for peaceful unification of the country.

The present situation of division exists solely because of the arbitrary U.S.-Diem regime, so the fundamental problem is how to smash the U.S.-Diem scheme of division and war-provocation.

As observed above, if they want to oppose the U.S-Diem regime, there is no other path for the people of the South but the path of revolution. What, then, is the line and struggle method of the revolutionary movement in the South? If the world situation can maintain peace due to a change in the relationship of forces in the world in favor of the camp of peace and democracy, the revolutionary movement can develop following a peaceful line, and the revolutionary movement in the South can also develop following a peaceful line.

First, we must determine what it means for a revolutionary movement to struggle according to a peaceful line. A revolutionary movement, struggling according to a peaceful line, takes the political forces of the people as the base rather than using people's armed forces to struggle with the existing government to achieve their revolutionary objective. A revolutionary movement struggling according to a peaceful line is also different from a reformist movement in that a reformist movement relies fundamentally on the law and constitution to struggle, while a revolutionary movement relies on the revolutionary political forces of the masses as the base. In addition, another difference is that a revolutionary movement struggles for revolutionary objectives, while a reformist movement struggles for reformist goals.

With an imperialist, feudalist, dictatorial, fascist government like the U.S.-Diem, is it possible for a peaceful political struggle line to achieve its objectives?

We must recognize that all accomplishments in every country are due to the people. That is a definite law: it cannot be otherwise. Therefore, the line of the revolutionary movement must be in accord with the inclinations and aspirations of the people. Only in that way can a revolutionary movement be mobilized and succeed.

The ardent aspiration of the Southern people is to maintain peace and achieve national unification. We must clearly recognize this longing for peace: the revolutionary movement in the South can mobilize and advance to success on the basis of grasping the flag of peace, in harmony with popular feelings. On the contrary, U.S.-Diem is using fascist violence to provoke war, contrary to the will of the people and therefore must certainly be defeated.

Can the U.S.-Diem regime, by using a clumsy policy of fascist violence, create a strong force to oppose and destroy the revolutionary movement? Definitely not, because the U.S.-Diem regime has no political strength in the country worth mentioning to rely on. On the contrary, nearly all strata of the people oppose them. Therefore, the U.S.-Diem government is not a strong government it is only a vile and brutal government. Its vile and brutal character means that it not only has no mass base in the country but is on the way to being isolated internationally. Its cruelty definitely cannot shake the revolutionary movement, and it cannot survive for long.

The proof is that in the past two years, everywhere in the countryside, the sound of the gunfire of U.S.-Diem repression never ceased; not a day went by when they did not kill patriots, but the revolutionary spirit is still firm, and the revolutionary base of the people still has not been shaken. Once the entire people have become determined to protect the revolution, there is no cruel force that can shake it. However, why has the revolutionary movement not yet developed strongly? This is also due to certain objective and subjective factors. Objectively, we see that, after nine years of waging strong armed struggle, the people's movement generally speaking now has a temporarily peaceful character that is a factor in the change of the movement for violent forms of struggle to peaceful forms. It has the correct character of rebuilding to advance later.

With the cruel repression and exploitation of the U.S.-Diem, the people's revolutionary movement definitely will rise. The people of the South have known the blood and fire of nine years of resistance war, but the cruelty of the U.S.-Diem cannot extinguish the struggle spirit of the people.

On the other hand, subjectively, we must admit that a large number of cadres, those have responsibility for guiding the revolutionary movement, because of the change in the method of struggle and the work situation from public to secret, have not yet firmly grasped the political line of the party, have not yet firmly grasped the method of political struggle, and have not yet followed correctly the mass line, and therefore have greatly reduced the movement's possibilities for development.

At present, therefore, the political struggle movement has not yet developed equally among the people, and a primary reason is that a number of cadres and masses are not yet aware that the strength of political forces of the people can defeat the cruelty, oppression and exploitation of the U.S.-Diem, and therefore they have a half-way attitude and don't believe in the strength of their political forces.

We must admit that any revolutionary movement has times when it falls and times when it rises; any revolutionary movement has times that are favorable for development and times that are unfavorable. The basic thing is that the cadres must see clearly the character of the movement's development to lead the mass struggle to the correct degree, and find a way for the vast determined masses to participate in the movement. If they are determined to struggle from the bottom to the top, no force can resist the determination of the great masses.

In the past two years, the political struggle movement in the countryside and in the cities, either by one form or another, has shown that the masses have much capacity for political struggle with the U.S.-Diem. In those struggles, if we grasp more firmly the struggle line and method, the movement can develop further, to the advantage of the revolution. The cruel policy of U.S.-Diem clearly cannot break the movement, or the people's will to struggle.

There are those who think that the U.S.-Diem's use of violence is now aimed fundamentally at killing the leaders of the revolutionary movement to destroy the Communist Party, and that if the Communist Party is worn away to the point that it doesn't have the capacity to lead the revolution, the political struggle movement of the masses cannot develop.

This judgment is incorrect. Those who lead the revolutionary movement are determined to mingle with the masses, to protect and serve the interest of the masses and to pursue correctly the mass line. Between the masses and Communists, there is no distinction any more. So how can the U.S.-Diem destroy the leaders of the revolutionary movement, since they cannot destroy the masses? Therefore, they cannot annihilate the cadres leading the mass movement.

In fact, more than 20 years ago, the French imperialists were determined to destroy the Communists to destroy the revolutionary movement for national liberation, but the movement triumphed. It wasn't the Communist but the French imperialist themselves and their feudal lackeys who were destroyed on our soil.

Now, 20 years later, the U.S. and-Diem are determined to destroy the Communists in the South, but the movement is still firm, and Communists are sill determined to fulfill their duty. Moreover, the revolutionary movement will definitely advance and destroy the imperialist, feudalist government. U.S.-Diem will be destroyed, just as the French imperialists and their feudal lackeys were destroyed

We believe that: the peaceful line is appropriate not only to the general situation in the world but also to the situation within the country, both nation-wide and in the South. We believe that the will for peace and the peace forces of the people throughout the country have smashed the U.S.-Diem schemes of war provocation and division.

We believe that the will for peace and Southern people's democratic and peace forces will defeat the cruel, dictatorial and fascist policy of U.S.-Diem and will advance to smash the imperialist, feudalist U.S.-Diem government. Using love and righteousness to triumph over force is a tradition of the Vietnamese nation. The aspiration for peace is an aspiration of the world's people in general and in our own country, including the people of the South, so there will not be a separation between our struggle and peaceful line.

Only the peaceful struggle line can create strong political forces to defeat the scheme of war provocation and the cruel policy of U.S.-Diem. We are determined to carry out our line correctly, and later the development of the situation will permit us to do so. Imperialism and feudalism are on the road to disappearance. The victory belongs to our people's glorious task of unification and independence, to our glorious Communism we must pledge our lives. We shall win."

Anh closed the folder and set it aside. He gazed toward the bath's door and thought, "This didn't work four years ago and what makes him think it will now," Anh thought. "I know he has reasons but without essential supplies we cannot sustain our effort much longer. In addition, people in the Southern Zone are not carrying the revolution with the force for peace, as they should. We must convince them that the Communist party is the answer they seek."

After a half-hour, Bien exited the bath and walked slowly toward Anh.

As he approached, he asked. "Well, what do you think?"

"It's a failed effort," Anh replied. "It will continue to fail unless there is a major change."

"Exactly," Bien said. "We now have the change we need."

"And what's that?" Anh questioned.

"A new president of the United States," Bien's answered promptly with a smile.

Continuing, Bien explained, "Eisenhower tolerated Diem and his corrupt regime. Kennedy views things in an idealistic fashion. It is not within Kennedy to tolerate Diem's dictatorship tactics. He will insist that Diem have another election for him to demonstrate that he represents the people. While he is occupied with that, a new force will come at him from another direction."

Stopping to take a deep breath, Bien continued, "He is in for a rude awakening in the near future. That will be the time to bring Diem down. We can do it if we embarrass him before the world. We will start with the Buddhists."

"Pardon me minister," Anh interjected and asked. "What threat at home?"

Bien placed one hand on the bench and leaned forward. He had a look about him that Anh had seen before with Bien. His expression was that of someone who knew a secret that you did not know.

Lowering his voice almost to a whisper, he said, "The American's place great store by their Monroe Doctrine. They think they can isolate themselves in their hemisphere from any political ideology other than their own. Kennedy will have to show the world that he will not tolerate anyone threatening that policy. While he is distracted, we will topple Diem."

Anh knew better than to ask what Bien knew to give him such confidence. His reasoning seemed confused. The Buddhist could help but how. Bien liked his achievements to come unexpected. His pleasure was to leave others staring wide eyed in amazement.

"No, he has told me all that he will," Anh thought.

"How can I help?" Anh asked.

Bien began stroking his small, gray, beard. A tiny smiled formed at the corners of his mouth.

"You will soon receive orders. You are to be our special liaison to the Pathet Lao. You are to assure adequate supply routes from China though Pathet Lao controlled territory. Give priority to routes that enter our country from the northwest. Use the road network through Muong Valley if you think that's best. When you're satisfied with that, scout southern routes. We need to improve roads through Cambodia. I want to assure supplies to Can Tho and districts to coastal waters. I'm particularly concerned with routes to Long Bien Province. We must be able to resupply if our main harbors become unusable. You will receive a detailed briefing in a week," Bien said.

Rising to his feet was Bien's signal that their meeting was to end. He tucked his book and folders beneath his arm and looked at Anh with determination.

"We will win," he said as he turned and walked away.

Anh watched Minister Bien until he exited the gymnasium. He could not help but marvel at his optimism.

"Out of the office I wanted and out of the office I got," he mused. "This assignment will require at least a year. I must make arrangements for mother's care."

It was almost dark when Anh arrived at his small villa. As usual, he scrambled through his pockets for his gate key. Finding it, he lifted the chain held in place by a small lock. Pushing aside one side of the double gate, he entered a small courtyard typical of most apartments in this area of Hanoi. He re-locked the gate and continued to an entrance door on the ground floor of his two-story residence. Once inside, he removed his shoes and placed them on a rack next to the entrance. On the wall directly above, an autographed photograph of Ho Chi Minh hung for all to see. He turned and pushed a sliding door to his right. He stepped up to enter his main living area.

"Something smells good cooking," he thought after sensing the aroma of food being prepared. "I've told her that she should not be going to market and cooking. She has been today because she knows I usually forget to stop and purchase something."

Anh moved across the small room to another sliding door. He gently moved it aside without making a sound. Inside, was a step down into a kitchen. Directly ahead, he saw his mother standing at a cutting board. She was totally unaware of his presence as she chopped vegetables. She was humming a favorite song.

"Oh mother," he thought. "You have been through so much and hurt so badly. How can you possibly be happy? What ever happened to you to turn your hair white?"

Anh moved forward until he was inches from Xuan.

Moving quickly, he reached over her stooped shoulders and covered eyes and asked, "Who is it young lady?"

"Ayah," she cried, "it must be a thief to steal my son's dinner. You are in trouble because you have scared his mother. He is a colonel and respects me. Now leave before he comes home."

Releasing Xuan, he spun her around and embraced her saying, "I am not afraid of your son. I shall kidnap you for a great ransom. If he cares so much, he will pay a vast fortune for you."

The two, still embraced, laughed aloud.

Anh finally released her and said, "Come with me. I have an offer to make."

The two moved into the living area and sat at a table used for serving tea. Xuan reached across and held Anh's hands, while gazing at him with a wistful smile.

"If only I could have my three children together. I would die happy," she said.

"Mother don't dwell on that. It makes you feel bad and we have to take you to the doctor," Anh commented. "I know you do not care for that."

Anh took his mother's hands into his and asked. "Would you like to visit Muong Valley?"

Continuing before she could answer, Anh recommended, "You could stay with your sister. You can visit with your mother and have a grand time."

"What do you think about that?" Anh asked with a broad smile.

"Can I take my crucifix and rosary," Xuan asked.

"It would not be wise mother. Your mother has one I'm sure. It is best not to travel with them in your baggage. Someone may stop us and check," Anh answered.

"Oh Anh, are you going?" Xaun asked cheerfully.

"Yes I am. I have business in that area. I can take time to visit with your family if you want," he told Xuan.

"Oh, that is wonderful. We will get to see our friends. When will we leave?" Xaun asked.

"We should be able to leave in a week. I will stay a few days in the valley and then go on an assignment for a few months. I will come back and visit again. After that I can leave you there or bring you here. Whatever you want mother," Anh explained.

Anh watched her eyes begin to sparkle. He had not seen that since she first left the valley for her terrible nightmare in prison.

"That was a long time ago," he thought. "That was when the Japanese occupied their country and held power over the Vichy French. What a long time that has been."

Still excited, Xuan arose and said, "I am not getting dinner ready for my son while I sit. He will be here any minute. You best leave now inept kidnapper."

On her way to the kitchen, she began humming in earnest. She had not prepared the vegetables and she must fix the fish. Taking the fish she purchased earlier that day, she lay it upon a cutting board. Inserting a carving knife's blade near its anal fin, she pushed toward its head. Reaching inside the cut, she began removing entrails. As they fell upon the cutting board, Xaun stopped and stared.

"They look almost like that man's the night Minh Thanh escaped," she thought.

Continuing, she removed the remainder. Again, she stared. She could see Minh Thanh safely escaping into the night. The crowd around her grew. Two men grabbed her arms to lead her away.

She remembered the crowd's words, "Catholic witch! Catholic witch! They screamed."

The man on her right released her arm and grabbed her shroud. He pulled it from her head. She remembered that the crowd became quiet and stared at her horrid appearance. This moment gave her time to remove her large carving knife from beneath her clothing. She struck swift and hard at the stranger bent upon killing her. He stood staring at her with his mouth agape. She looked directly into his eyes and saw understanding coming.

He looked down at his stomach and saw the blood. His shirt stood open and his intestines fell forward. He grabbed at them trying to put them inside his large wound. As he tried, others watched, giving her time to strike again. She pulled free from the man holding her left arm. Her next thrust went deep into his side. As hard as she tried, she could not move the blade in any direction. It was wedged between his ribs. She jerked it from his body and ran. The crowd watched as she stopped before turning a corner.

At that moment, there was a bright flash of lightning followed by thunder. They saw her outline with a knife dripping blood in her hand. It started to rain. The crowd was not moving but just staring, too full of fear to follow.

Xuan's weak condition precluded her running far. She was drenched with pouring rain. Exhausted, she stumbled through an open gate to rest. Between lightning flashes, she saw a weathered sign. She could barely read the words, "St. Joseph's Mission." There was no glass in the building's windows. She stepped under the porch to escape the rain. Glass crunched beneath her feet.

Remaining still she continued to examine the building between lightning flashes. It was deserted.

Slowly she stepped into the building through a large, broken window. Once inside, she placed her hands on her knees and gasped for air. The moisture-laden air made it difficult for her to breathe. Her right side ached from her exertion running. Suddenly, a bright light blinded her. Xuan raised her knife to defend herself although she could not see.

A calm voice spoke from the darkness, "Do not fear. I will do you no harm. My name is Father Cicero and perhaps I can help."

Still gripped by fear, Xuan backed toward the window. She kept her knife pointed toward the light. Raising one foot to step over the low windowsill, she caught her foot on a downed curtain. She began falling backward when someone grabbed her wrist and waist. The grip was firm but did not hurt.

"I will take the knife. I will not hurt you," the voice said again.

She felt the room spin and she collapsed into quiet darkness.

Xuan remembered how she awoke later. Outside, a storm still raged and rains continued. A moist cloth was on her forehead. She learned that her benefactor was a priest, Father Cicero. He too was hiding in the building. Earlier a Communist group attacked the mission where he was visiting. The mob threw rocks and broke all the windows. He and the volunteer workers remained out of sight. The roving crowd had tried to burn it but torrential rains quickly drenched the flames. He and the workers dared not leave for fear of their lives. Two parishioners, young girls, were hiding with him. They were waiting for the girl's parents when Xuan arrived.

She remained with catholic families for over two years. When word came that French forces lost their battle at Dien Bien Phu, a great fear spread among Catholics. They began fleeing south. The new Democratic Republic of Viet Nam claimed religious tolerance but did not adhere to it.

Anh did not recognize her with a refugee group as they traveled south. He stood tall and handsome beside the roadway watching. His unit was responsible for the area through which they were traveling. He was raised as a Catholic and had sympathy for refugees. He kept locals from harming them.

Xuan had stopped and stared at Anh. He looked directly at her and did not know. Finally, she moved in front of him and called his name. A puzzled look washed across his face as he looked at her.

"Anh," she said. "It's me."

First, disbelief filled his eyes followed shortly by recognition.

"Mother," he said excitedly. "Mother," he yelled and ran to her. Holding her in his arms, they both wept.

It gave Xaun pleasure to recall how she found her eldest son. Now, it was time to prepare his dinner. Xuan placed the fish amid a vegetable bed. She pushed their dinner into a charcoal oven. Xuan hummed her favorite song as she cleaned the cutting board.

Chapter Twenty Three

January 1961

The conventional army loses if it does not win.
The guerrilla wins if he does not lose.
Henry Kissinger (b. 1923), U.S. Republican politician, secretary of state

"We left our home in North Viet Nam and moved to Laos to be free of the North Vietnamese. They followed us and trained Laotians to be Communists. They called themselves Pathet Lao. We moved into these mountains in South Viet Nam to avoid them and remain free. The time for moving is finished. Our home is now these mountains in South Viet Nam. We cannot move again. There is no other place to go," Diem said.

Vinh watched from the building's doorway. Above him, a convex, thatched roof provided protection from the elements. At the roof's apex, an opening allowed wisps of smoke to escape from the elder's meeting place. Inside, men sat in a circle around a smoldering fire. Diem paced in front of them to explain a recent visit by an officer of the South Vietnamese Army.

"We know that we must change how we fight the Communists from the north. Our weapons are old and we do not have adequate equipment. The officer came from Kontum. He wants us to go there and he will give us modern weapons and equipment. We will learn together as Tia and we will fight together as Tia. We will learn the modern ways to fight effectively as a group with modern equipment. To go to Kontum and do this is our only hope. The North Vietnamese will soon move their soldiers into Laos and claim it as their own. They are just across the border in Cambodia building roads. We have seen this coming and we all know that I speak the truth. I leave now for you to decide," Diem said as he walked through an opening in the circle and toward Vinh.

As Diem passed, he said in a hushed tone, "Come with me. I have important information."

Vinh followed Diem to a hillside. It overlooked a valley a short distance from their meeting house. From this location, they could see east toward Kontum and Pleiku. In the opposite direction, was Cambodia's border. Slightly north-northwest was Laos.

Diem squatted and said, "You have learned the ways of the Tia. Now, it is time for our brothers to learn the modern way. You can help for you have experience and understand how the Viet Minh fight."

Vinh squatted next to Diem and looked toward Kontum.

He replied, "I have no experience fighting as a guerilla with the Viet Minh. I was with the artillery and my experience was conventional warfare."

"I know that but you have organized military experience and can provide leadership. It will be important that the Tia learn. It will be difficult for the South

Vietnamese to train them. You know our language and can make it easier for them," Diem stated.

"You know I will do what I can. You have taught me the Tia way for seven years. They are fierce fighters and are better at guerilla warfare than the Viet Minh," Vinh answered.

"The Tia way is freedom and peace. They want to live their lives their way. You and I know that the South and North Vietnamese look down upon mountain tribes as inferior. They come to us only because they need us. Maybe, just maybe, if we stop the Communists, the south will provide a safe home for us," Diem said.

Diem and Vinh heard a noise behind them and turned. It was Lai, one of the elders.

"Come, we have an answer," Lai said.

Diem and Vinh followed at a respectful distance as Lai returned to the circle of elders. He squatted with his forearms across his knees. The elders stared ahead and stillness filled the room. They were about to make a serious announcement.

The oldest member, Biale, arose. No one knew his age for he had lived longer than any one in their tribe. His skin lay in wrinkles over his body and made stiff by time. Across his back, he wore an old, breech-loading rifle. Some said it was older than Biale. Others said that he slept with it. Nevertheless, over the years, he showed that he could kill at great distances. Others, with more modern weapons, took many shots to strike a target when Biale did so with one.

He stepped to the circle's middle, turned slowly looking at each elder, and said, "Diem has lived in the city and knows the North Vietnamese way. He brought Vinh to us and he knows the army's way. Both agree that we should go to Kontum and learn to fight with modern weapons. I, as you have, agree with them. The modern way is not the way of all our people. So, as agreed, those who want to leave for Kontum can do so with our blessing."

Biale raised his right arm and pointed at Diem and said, "You may go among our people and ask for volunteers. Anyone who wants to leave may do so. We will see to their families while they are gone. They are welcome to come back to us at any time. The task is yours Diem."

The old tribesman returned to his position in the circle. Other members nodded their heads in agreement. Diem and Vinh left to gather volunteers.

In January 1961, 900 Tia tribesmen gathered near Dak To, South Viet Nam. Diem and Vinh led the unorganized group to Kontum. Along their way, South Vietnamese villagers watched in wonder at so many mountain tribesmen traveling together. It was rare to see more than a few at any time. They were recluse and avoided cities and crowds. Following instructions given by the officer, who visited them, they arrived at their destination. For the first time, they saw an American.

"He must be French," Vinh said to Diem. "You told me that the French had to leave all of Viet Nam not just the north."

"I assure you that he is not French," Diem answered. "I will ask who he is and what is he doing here."

With Vinh and Diem's help, South Vietnamese military instructors started processing the Tia volunteers. It took a week to issue them clothing and weapons. During this time, Diem asked Captain Dam Van Kinh, the officer who recruited them, about the American.

"He is from the United States. Their government sent him to us as an adviser. He is from an elite Army organization called Special Forces. He is Sergeant Major McKenzie. They have special training to fight and live as guerrillas. He is here to help us organize the Tia into a division consisting only of your people," Kinh explained.

"Everyone thinks he is French because he wears a beret. Elite French units wore berets," Diem commented.

"The American government is concerned about North Vietnamese troops invading parts of Laos. The North Vietnamese say that the areas they take have always been theirs. The true reason is that they are getting ready to improve their supply routes into South Viet Nam. They are providing supplies to the Communist insurgents throughout South Viet Nam. The Americans call the southern Communists Viet Cong or VC," Kinh told Diem.

After two and one-half months training, the Tia began to function as an organized unit. Both Diem and Vinh received commissions as second lieutenants because of their obvious leadership abilities. At a graduation ceremony for the Tia, an Army of the Republic of South Viet Nam (ARVN) General, presented their unit their official designation as the 22nd Infantry Division.

The ARVN tried to convince Vinh to transfer to an artillery unit.

"Lieutenant Vinh, I would think you would rather be in the artillery. You would be a forward observer," Captain Kinh suggested.

Vinh, somewhat dismayed at the prospect, answered, "I have already been a forward observer. Besides, there is nothing for a lieutenant to command in the artillery. Here I can command a platoon of my people."

"You did say that Tia would stay together as a unit, didn't you?" Vinh asked.

"Yes, I did and you may do that. I thought you might want to return to the artillery," Kinh responded.

"No, thank you sir. I will remain with the Tia," Vinh said.

"That's fine. Return to your platoon. Get them ready to move to the combat confidence course this afternoon. I would like to see how they are doing. You're dismissed," Kinh directed.

While returning to his unit, Vinh mentally reviewed the last few months. He was proud of his men's progress. To be mountain tribesmen almost six months ago, they had come a long way. They marched like soldiers; worked as a team; and had mastered their weapons' training. One thought nagged him.

"When they fought as Tia, they were not fettered with so much heavy equipment. They moved silently through the jungle without being seen or making so much noise," he reflected. "They made it almost impossible for their enemies to locate them. They would strike swiftly and then disappear to fight again somewhere else."

Vinh moved his 20 men to the combat course as directed. The course was a series of obstacles that they had to overcome both as individuals and as a team.

The final portion was moving through a defensive position with barbed wire obstacles and simulators exploding. While moving through the barbed wire, machine guns used live ammunition. The weapons were set to fire no lower than 18 inches. He had taught his men to move through it on their backs to avoid snags on the wire.

"I do not see this," he thought. "The VC fight like the Viet Minh fought against the French. They are not going to sit in a defensive position and let us attack them. They ambush and then leave. We need to be teaching the Tia to do this. We need to teach them how to fight at night."

"Lieutenant, this is an infantry company. You will train your men to fight as a team," his company commander said.

"Perhaps, if he had been at some of the battles against the French, he would understand," Vinh thought. "However, he had been to the United States for training. He also had an American advisor so he should know."

As Vinh moved beneath the last barbed wire obstacle, he saw Diem standing over him. Covered in mud and with his trousers torn in three places, he climbed to his feet. He greeted Diem while watching his men's progress.

"Hello uncle, would you have believed that six months ago our tribe could do this?" He asked.

"They can do a lot more with proper training. This is not the way we should train to fight," Diem answered.

"I agree but how do we convince our trainers?" Vinh questioned.

"I have not been able to get them to listen," Diem said. "However, I came to talk to you about something else."

"What?" Vinh asked.

"There are units who fight as we believe. They are here looking for volunteers," Diem said.

"Tell me more," Vinh replied with interest.

"I am told that they are special units that use helicopters and parachutes for mobility. They use small forces to go into enemy territory to gather information or sabotage enemy bridges, facilities, and such. I am interested. Are you?" Diem asked.

"Yes I am," Vinh replied anxiously. "How do we join?"

"Meet me at battalion headquarters when you finish this afternoon," Diem said.

"I will," Vinh replied as Diem walked away.

He returned his attention to his men. The last one was completing the course. He had his sergeant form his platoon and they ran in formation to their company area to bathe and change clothes. After evening formation, they would be free to conduct personal business.

Vinh went to battalion headquarters and saw Diem waiting for him. There were other Tia in a group with him. He knew most of them from his years with the Tia. Each man had a reputation in their villages for their hunting skills and ability to avoid detection by North Vietnamese patrols moving through their mountains. They would return to their villages with reports about North Vietnamese movements. They were valued members of their tribes.

He approached Diem and asked. "Are these Tia here to volunteer?"

"Yes, there is a major inside from Saigon. He is interviewing volunteers. We must get in line," Diem urged.

A line extended from the headquarters tent for about 30 yards. Other Tia tribesmen were converging on their location. It was obvious that considerable interest existed for the new unit. Diem entered the door first. Above his head, a sign indicated for officers to proceed to a table on their right. An ARVN major sat at the table looking bored.

Diem stepped in front of the table, saluted and said, "Lieutenant Nguyen Van Diem reporting for interview sir."

"Can you read and write?" the Major asked.

"Yes sir," Diem answered.

The major did not appear particularly impressed. He took a clipboard from the table and thrust it at Diem.

"Have a seat over there and complete the form. There is a pen attached to the clipboard. Next," he said.

Vinh repeated Diem's reporting and received his clipboard. He walked to where Diem sat on a folding chair and sat. He began reading the form. The first questions dealt with personal background information. Information that he had to furnish before he received his commission. There were many questions about religion.

Diem was still completing his form when Vinh returned his to the major. Vinh saw boredom disappear and interest arrive as he read Vinh's form. The major sat up straighter and looked at Vinh twice as he continued reading.

The senior officer looked at Vinh and asked, "Lieutenant, you fought at Dien Bien Phu?"

"Yes sir," Vinh answered sharply.

Pointing to a chair beside his table, the Major directed, "Have a seat lieutenant."

While Vinh took the offered chair, the major continued, "I am Major Huan, lieutenant. If this information is correct, you may be changing units. If you were at Dien Bien Phu, you must have seen many men parachute into that fortress. What do you think about them?"

"I considered them crazy sir," Vinh responded quickly.

"Why is that?" Huan asked.

"They were jumping to their deaths. They had to be crazy to go into that trap," Vinh answered with a wry smile.

"I take it you don't think much of soldiers jumping out of airplanes," Huan continued.

"It's not that sir. It is the place they jumped into that I think is crazy. I don't have anything against soldiers jumping out of airplanes," Vinh replied.

"Have you ever heard of Airborne Rangers?" Huan asked while pointing to patches on his uniform.

Next Huan reached under his table and retrieved a beret that he placed in front of Vinh.

"That's the hat that airborne rangers wear. It is for special people that do special work for their country. I think you would make a fine one," Huan commented.

"Will those selected be able to stay together as Tia?" Vinh asked.

"Yes lieutenant, they will," Huan promised.

"Okay, I volunteer. What do I have to do?" Vinh asked.

"Lieutenant, you be here in the morning at 07:00 hours. Bring all your gear. You will be going to some special schools. You are dismissed for now," Huan directed.

"Yes sir," Vinh replied as he stood to leave.

Vinh moved through the entrance line and waited outside for Diem. Diem came from the tent with a wide smile on his face. He waved and moved quickly to join Vinh.

"They thought I was too old. I had to arm wrestle Major Huan to show him different. He said I would quit the first week of training. They are in for a surprise," Diem said while laughing.

"Let's go get some beer to celebrate," Vinh suggested.

"I'm for it," Diem answered gleefully.

At times during the next three months, Diem wished he had not volunteered. Vinh's encouragement kept him going. They went through Ranger and Airborne training at a base north of Saigon. Vinh sincerely believed, if he had not lived with the Tia, he would not have completed the harsh training.

However, this was his kind of unit. They trained to operate as independent, small teams. They had to be self sufficient and lethal. While they learned how to use practically ever nation's weapons, they learned to kill with their hands. They moved fast and quiet. They trained to parachute into areas at night; something he thought that he would never do. He could stay in an enemy's area and report on their activities. Vinh loved it.

Vinh and Diem graduated from Airborne and Ranger school at Thu Duc, slightly north of Saigon. They received their berets with pride. They knew they were special. Two hundred Tia tribesmen completed school. They became an elite, special unit, the 1st Airborne Ranger Company.

After having endured three months confinement to their base, the company received passes to visit Saigon. Vinh looked forward to it because he had never seen a city. The only cinemas he had seen were training films. His total, metropolitan experience was the village at Dien Bien Phu.

"Hey Vinh," Diem yelled. "I guess I showed them that I'm not too old. A truck leaves in 20 minutes for Saigon. Let me show you a big city."

Excited, Vinh knew that Diem lived in Hanoi. He knew about big cities. From stories told by others, Saigon was a wonderful place of exotic smells and beautiful girls. There were grand restaurants, movie theaters, and oriental operas to see.

"Guide! I cannot be your guide. I've never been to Saigon. We will get lost together," Diem said playfully.

As they waited for transportation, a sergeant approached them and saluted. He explained that their new commanding officer had arrived. He said for his officers to report to his headquarters immediately.

"Ayah," Diem cried. "Wouldn't you know it. It never fails. Anytime we're going to do something we look forward to there is work."

Crestfallen, the once jubilant duo began walking to the company's headquarters tent. As they approached it, two other lieutenants joined them. They knew each other from their village. One of them, Lieutenant Bien, he had hunted with in their mountains. They had killed a large Sambur deer that feed their group for two days. The other one, Lieutenant Bhan, he did not know well. He was quiet and did not speak much.

Vinh asked, "Do you know who the new commanding officer is?"

"No," Bien answered while the other lieutenant shook his head indicating agreement.

Lieutenant Bien said, "We've heard that he is an experienced fighter. He fought with the French Airborne at Dien Bien Phu."

Vinh stopped dumbfounded.

"You're sure?" He asked.

Diem immediately saw the irony. Vinh's army defeated their new commanding officer's forces. Now, the victor and the vanquished would join to fight Vinh's former army.

"He's Tia like us," Bhan commented.

Diem said, "I know most of the Tia. I do not know one who became an officer and fought with the French. Some Tia, who fought with them, brought shame upon our tribe by deserting. They called them Nam Youm Rats. I was told that the Viet Minh executed them."

"You're correct," Vinh said. "I saw them along the river. They almost had a small city. Someone told me that they had a brothel that serviced soldiers from both sides."

The other three looked at Vinh and laughed. The four entered their headquarters tent continuing their good-natured bantering.

"What the hell is so damned funny?" A stranger's voice demanded.

The four stopped suddenly and looked toward the tent's right rear. Standing in an opening leading to the commander's office, an ARVN captain glared at them. He was in Class A uniform with spit shined jump boots and wearing an Airborne Ranger's beret. His left chest had five rows of award ribbons. His blouse had airborne wings and a ranger's tab. Around his right shoulder, he wore a blue and gold citation cord. This meant that he had served on President Diem's personal staff. The name on his blouse was Captain Voong Van Hoi.

"Which one of you is Nguyen Van Minh?" Captain Hoi asked.

"I am sir," Vinh answered while coming to attention and rendering a crisp salute.

"Come into my office. The rest of you wait until I ask for you," Hoi directed.

"Sit," Hoi said.

Vinh sat in a folding, metal chair directly in front of Hoi's desk. Hoi sat across from him and stared inquisitively. He continued this, making Vinh uncomfortable with the continuing gaze.

"You are not Tia and you are not from Dien Bien Phu," Hoi stated.

Vinh started to speak but Hoi interrupted him, "Don't until I say so lieutenant," Hoi ordered.

Hoi removed Vinh's photograph from a file folder and studied it. He would alternate between looking at the photograph and at Vinh.

Finally, laying the photograph aside, Hoi said, "Explain please."

"Sir, you see my name in the file. It is a well-known name and is common. I have heard my grand parents say that our origin was Thailand but I'm not sure. My father's brother told me that I was Tai. I lived with them for the past seven years before joining the 22nd Infantry Division," Vinh explained.

"Who is your uncle?" Hoi asked?

"He is Lieutenant Diem and he awaits outside your office," Vinh answered.

Vinh watched as Hoi visibly relaxed. He could see tension released from his body's posture.

"I wonder why he is so nervous," Vinh thought. "He appears satisfied about me but there is something still bothering him."

Hoi opened the lower right drawer of his desk. He removed a bottle of Johnny Walker scotch and two glasses. He filled the glasses and set one in front of Vinh.

"Drink lieutenant," He said. "I will drink with you twice. The first is when we meet. The second is when we depart. I hope that you will be alive at that time. The rest of the time everything is business. I will not develop a personal relationship with you. When I give an order, do it. Too many lives are at stake."

Each man set his empty glass on the desk.

"Lieutenant Vinh, I will see you Monday morning at formation. Have your men mission ready. Be sure you sanitize them and yourself. See the supply sergeant for details. Send Diem in as you leave. That's all," Hoi instructed.

As Vinh left Hoi's office, he said with a whisper, "Hard core, go on in."

The four 1st Airborne Ranger Company lieutenants shared a taxi into Saigon. They went to the Cholon District as recommended by some of the cadre. As they entered Saigon's suburbs, traffic became a seething mass. Diesel smoke filled the air mixed with numerous aromas of food, spices, and unknowns. Their driver stopped in front of a cinema. Diem and Vinh got out and the other two remained.

"We're going to find some girls," Lieutenant Bien said, while Bhan nodded in agreement with a large smile.

Vinh watched in amazement as "The Day The Earth Stood Still" unfolded on the cinema's large screen. It was about a space traveler who came to Earth to meet people. Instead, people attacked him. Vinh wanted to see it again but Diem insisted they leave.

"First, we have to get a safe house," Diem said.

"A safe house?" Vinh asked.

"Yes, a safe house. We pay for a nice hotel room in advance. We put enough piasters in their safe to pay for transportation back to the base. After that, we can enjoy ourselves. If we spend our money, we have a place to sleep and can get to the base," Diem explained.

Continuing, Diem said, "Now, we get a full dinner at a fine restaurant."

"I'm not hungry," Vinh stated.

"I don't care," Diem replied. "We are not going into a bar with an empty stomach. The girls will drink Saigon tea while we get drunk. We'll get robbed within an hour."

"Saigon tea?" Vinh questioned.

"Yes, Saigon tea. It's colored water that the girls drink. There is no alcohol in it. They will gulp it and quickly order again. On an empty stomach, you cannot stay sober long. When you're drunk enough, they ask you to go to their room. Instead, they hit you in the head and rob you. You must be careful," Diem cautioned.

"Damn, I'm glad I'm with Diem," Vinh thought.

After a grand dinner, they began walking deeper into the Cholon District. In the distance, Vinh saw a cathedral's spire.

Vinh asked. "Should we go to Mass?"

"Absolutely not, we can go tomorrow when we will have plenty to confess," Diem said with a laugh.

As they stumbled through crowded sidewalks, Vinh kept noticing Caucasians wearing shirts with wild, flowery designs on them. They were always in pairs.

Vinh asked. "Do you think those are Americans?"

"I suspect they are," Diem answered as he placed an arm around Vinh's shoulder.

With a hard tug, he turned Vinh to face an open doorway. Diem led him into a bar. Inside he saw a smoke filled room with blinking neon lighting. Tables filled most of the room. A long bar ran the length of one side. On the other, there were booths to seat four. At the far end, a dancing area had a rotating, glass ball above it. Light, reflecting from it, gave a surreal appearance to the dimly lit interior. Immediately on the other side of the dance floor, a five-piece band played a rock song.

Oriental girls were throughout the interior. Some sat at tables while others danced with military men. Many, by themselves, sat on barstools lining the bar. They wore heavy makeup with bright red lips and rouge on their cheeks. Their skirts were bright satin with long splits up their sides, exposing hips and thighs. All of them smoked, or rapidly chewed gum. As Diem worked his way through the heavy crowd toward an empty table, girls clawed at them.

"Airborne Ranger, you come with me. We have good time. Buy me a drink," they said.

As soon as they sat, two girls were at their table. They put their arms around their necks and sat on their laps. A waiter appeared and took their drink order. He promptly returned with four drinks. As Diem said, the girls promptly downed theirs and coaxed them to do the same. Vinh noted that his scotch tasted strange. He had heard stories about bars putting formaldehyde in their liquor. He had scoffed at the notion until he tasted this particular drink.

Church bells rang in unison with Vinh's throbbing head. His tongue felt swollen and his mouth was dry. In the distance, he could hear someone being sick. He gingerly opened his eyes to tiny slits and still daylight hurt them. He closed them and moved his right leg that fell to the floor with a thud. Nausea began welling from his stomach up to his throat. Trying to open his eyes again, he felt his bed spin. Retching sounds became louder and he heard Diem moan.

"We can go to confession after a while," he groaned. "First, I have to remember what I did so that I can confess it.

Diem returned to his retching while Vinh held tight to his bed.

"Maybe," Vinh thought. "Just maybe, if I stay still, the spinning will stop."

Suddenly, Vinh realized he did not feel his wallet in his trousers. He grabbed for his hip and he opened his eyes. Immediately, he closed them again. After one hour, he found his wallet on a table. It was empty. Slowly, he unlaced his right boot and removed it. Reaching inside he removed a tightly packed square of piasters.

"While Diem may be sophisticated, I'm not stupid," Vinh thought. "I guess a safe boot works."

Vinh put the money in his wallet and went to the bathroom door. Diem lay curled around the commode. He held it tight with both arms. He appeared at ease on the cool tiles.

Vinh looked at his watch and said, "It's only 11 P.M. We can make it to Mass. The cathedral I saw cannot be too far from here."

Diem groaned in response.

"I need to use the toilet so come out of there," Vinh insisted.

Forty-five minutes later, the pair entered the cathedral's large, front doors. They rolled their berets and tucked them beneath epaulets on their shirts. Beside inside arches, they used holy water to make the sign of the holy trinity as they faced the tabernacle. Walking down one of the long aisles, they stopped at a pew and kneeled on one knee, making the sign again. Side by side, in the pew, they lowered the prayer bench and began to pray. Both realized it had been over seven years since they had been inside a church. They also realized that they could not take communion until they went to confession. After the homily, they remained seated as parishioners took communion. After the service, Vinh stopped to talk with the priest standing at the door.

"Father, I have a special request," Diem said.

"What is that my son?" The priest asked.

Diem explained their situation. He also told him that they did not know when they would be able to attend mass again.

"Father, we are leaving tomorrow. We need to confess and take communion. Will you help us?" Diem asked.

"Certainly," he answered. "Return and pray. I need to remain here for awhile. Watch for me to enter the confessional. I will give communion afterward."

They thanked the priest and returned to pray. Diem entered the confessional first. When he returned for penance, Vinh entered.

Vinh detailed his life from the time he joined the Viet Minh. He told about losing his mother and father. He begged absolution for his mortal and venial sins.

He told of losing Minh Thanh and his brother Anh. Vinh told of every burden on his soul.

After absolution, the priest told him what he had to do for penance. He explained that afterwards he would give communion to him and Diem at the same time.

Vinh returned to his pew and began saying his prayers beside Diem. Later, as promised, they received communion. Once finished, they prayed again before leaving the church.

Outside on the steps, they removed their berets and were putting them on when they heard a soft, female voice.

"Vinh," he heard in an unforgettable, melodic tone.

Vinh felt numb and whirled to the sound. From behind a pillar, a beautiful woman dressed in beige stepped from the shadows. A blue ribbon held her long hair behind her head.

"Oh, Mother of God," he cried. "Minh Thanh! Oh Jesus, my Minh Thanh."

Throwing his beret aside, he ran hard into her waiting arms. Joy filled his being and happiness descended on them both. Amid tears and tender embraces, they held each other.

"Oh Minh Thanh, it is you. I thought you were dead. Oh my God, I thought you were dead," he wailed.

Stepping arm's length away from her, he leaped into the air. Looking skyward, he threw both arms toward the heavens and screamed, "Thank you God! Oh, thank you!"

Vinh reached beneath her arms and lifted her. He began spinning Minh Thanh in a wide circle.

"Diem, it's Minh Than! It's Minh Than," Vinh yelled in jubilation his heart awhirl with joy.

Diem watched in stunned wonder. It was Minh Thanh without a doubt. She was older but still a picture of angelic beauty. He ran and grabbed them both in a bear hug and squeezed.

"Uncle, stop! You are breaking my ribs," Minh Thanh said with a squeal.

She kissed them both on each cheek and forehead.

"Come inside, come inside. It has been so long," she said with tears streaking both cheeks.

Minh Thanh took them to a small, sitting room near the main entrance. Waiting to meet them was the priest who gave them communion.

"Vinh, Diem, this is Father LeTruc. He came and told me you were in the church. I could not believe it. Oh this is so wonderful," she said.

Vinh and Diem thanked Father LeTruc, not for giving communion but for bringing them Minh Thanh.

"I wasn't sure," Father LeTruc said. "I could only hope. I went and found Minh Thanh immediately after Vinh's confession. I will leave you three alone."

Minh Thanh sat on a satin covered sofa with an arm around Vinh and Diem. She looked at each in turn and pumped her feet up and down squealing with joy.

"I have prayed and God has answered my prayers," she said.

The trio talked until late afternoon. When it became apparent that evening services were near, Minh Thanh suggested they go to the classroom building. She did not want to interfere with services. Father LeTruc gave permission and told her that mother superior wanted to visit after services. She would bring a light dinner.

Into the night they continued. Minh Thanh told them that she was teaching Latin at the church's school. She explained that she once taught French but that changed in 1955. She studied English and knew it well. Soon she would begin teaching it.

Mother superior left early explaining that Vinh and Diem could stay in their guest quarters. A driver would take them to Thu Duc early the next morning.

One cloud darkened their reunion, Anh. As far as Vinh knew, he was in North Viet Nam in the military. He told of their last meeting. He explained that they were to go to Moscow. Vinh could only guess that Anh went.

"Minh Than, Anh is a respected officer. He was a major when I last saw him. They were sending him to the best schools. He must be a high ranking officer by now," Vinh surmised.

"God brought you to me. If we both pray, maybe he will unite the three of us. Oh, how I hope for that," Minh Thanh responded.

After midnight Vinh and Diem went to the guest quarters. Minh Thanh returned to the same room she lived in for years. She kneeled beside her bed and prayed.

"Thank you God for bringing me Vinh and Diem. Please guard them and keep them from harm. In addition, I beg thee to protect Anh. I know in my heart that he is not a Communist. Care for Jean wherever he may be. In the name of the Father, the Son and the Holy Ghost. Amen," she prayed.

Before dawn, mother superior joined them in the kitchen for sweet rolls and tea. She seemed disappointed when Vinh and Diem could not say where they were going.

"We have no idea mother superior," Vinh said. "They have not told us. All we know is that we are going somewhere today."

Vinh stared through the rear window of the car taking them to their base. Minh Thanh stood at the cathedral's gates waving and smiling. She appeared to grow smaller and finally vanished as their vehicle turned a corner.

"Uncle," he said, "This has been the most wonderful day of my life. I know that she is safe and in a place where she will remain safe. If only I could know the same for Anh. I worry about him.

"So do I," Diem said. "I sincerely hope that he does not become an ardent Communist. They have brought so much harm to our family. I find it difficult to believe that Anh would forget that."

After arriving on base, Vinh and Diem went to their company supply sergeant. They had to prepare for their mission.

"Good morning," the supply sergeant said as he rendered a salute. "Your unit's clothing is in those boxes. None of it has insignia. There is nothing to indicate what country or unit the person wearing it represents. You are to use Swedish K submachine guns. Get your basic load of ammunition at the arms room. Also, there are white phosphorous grenades and a variety of smoke grenades. Here are your signal instructions for the smoke's use. You must commit that to memory and return it to me. Bring your teams to the supply room's side door for equipment issue. Your radios have new batteries in them. Since you will be gone for an extended period, there are spares. Our new company commander left instructors for you to go to battalion for a map briefing. If you have any special needs, please let me know today. Tomorrow will be too late."

The two thanked the supply NCO and left for battalion headquarters. The other two lieutenants joined them in their company, Bien, and Bhan. Intelligence specialists told them that there was major North Vietnamese activity near Tchepone, in Laos. They could expect significant patrol activity. In addition, there were company sized, infantry units providing security for an airfield. After close study of intel reports, they left to take charge of their men.

Captain Van Hoi formed four, 15-man teams for their mission. Each lieutenant would command a team. A team consisted of three, four-man sub-units. A medic, with advanced medical training, was available for problems the sub-units could not treat. Each lieutenant had a communications specialist that stayed with him.

Each sub-unit could operate independent of the other three. However, if necessary, they could fight working together. Two units would provide covering fire while the third unit maneuvered.

As they approached where their men were gathered, Lieutenant Bien said, "Now, I know why we rehearsed so much using team tactics. Looks like Hoi knew what he wanted before we ever came to training."

Diem replied, "I like this better than trying to handle platoons. Tia like to move fast and silent. With large groups it is to hard to control them and they make too much noise. Hoi is definitely Tia."

"Yes," Vinh interjected, "this also explains why they reduced our company from 200 to 160."

After the lieutenants prepared their teams, they reported to Captain Hoi for final instructions. They met him outside his headquarters tent.

"Hello gentlemen," Hoi said. "Gather around so that you can see."

Hoi spread a map on the ground and kneeled by it. Two lieutenants moved to either side of Hoi and kneeled.

"This is Tchepone, Laos," Hoi said as he pointed to his map. "It is where North Vietnamese forces are staging their operations from. They occupied it with an infantry battalion almost a month ago. I believe that three infantry companies are at the locations that I have marked. Somewhere, there is a heavy weapons company that we cannot locate. I believe they have assigned a platoon to support each of the companies. You can expect heavy mortar fire if you are detected so move like hell if you make contact. Any questions so far?"

"Yes sir," Diem answered. "Where do you want us to go if we do make contact?"

"Good question, Diem," Hoi replied. "Let me explain something so that I can answer your question. We are going in on foot gentlemen. There will be no airborne or helicopter insertion. We're to fly to Khe Sanh by C-46. The C-46 is an

Air America bird. Khe Sanh will be our staging area. We will move to Lao Bao inside Laos here. Three teams will proceed from Lao Bao and one will remain behind to assist anyone who gets into trouble."

Each team leader watched Hoi's indications on his map. They updated their maps to indicate the route in by foot. They had expected an airborne jump and had not planned on the overland insertion.

Hoi continued, "Diem, you take you team to point xray southwest of Tchepone. Vinh, you move you men due south of Techepone to point yankee. Bien, you take up position to the southeast at point zulu. Bhan, your team will remain at Lao Bao with me as a reserve if one of the teams cannot break contact. You will provide supporting fire to cover any of the other teams as they return to Lao Bao if they need it. How are we doing so far? Any questions?"

"Yes sir," Vinh replied. "What are they trying to accomplish by taking Tchepone?"

Looking at Vinh, Hoi said, "My information is that they are using Tchepone as a forward support area to improve their road network. That is the heart of our mission. You are there to observe. We need to know what they are doing at Tchepone's airfield. Are they bringing in road working equipment? Watch for engineer units. If you see any, report how many? What is their strength? What exactly are they doing? Do not wait to give reports. Radio the information when you see the activity. Be damn sure you use your shackle codes. Change them daily. Any more questions?"

When no one responded to his question, Hoi said, "Fine gentlemen, return to your teams and get your briefings completed. Have your men at battalion headquarters no later than 15:00 hours. We will load trucks to go to Tan Son Nhut airfield. When we get to Khe Sanh, it will be getting dark. Form your teams on the tarmac north of the runway. We'll move from there to Lao Bao. You're dismissed."

Vinh watched the weather worsen the closer they got to Khe Sanh. From his window seat, he could see their aircraft wings disappear frequently the farther north they flew.

"This could be a big problem," he thought. "We're going in with three day's rations. If we do not receive airborne re-supply, because of the weather, we'll leave earlier than planned. We're supposed to be in there for two weeks."

Vinh removed his map from inside his shirt and began studying it. Khe Sanh was in the northwest corner of South Viet Nam near the demilitarized zone. It sat astride an excellent route into the south for North Viet Nam forces. Drawing upon his experiences with the Viet Minh, he recognized Khe Sanh as a vital tactical objective.

The C-46's engines roared making talk impossible without yelling. Vinh elbowed Diem sitting next to him. He gestured for him to lean closer.

Yelling, Vinh said, "They are going to be watching us the entire time we're at Khe Sanh. They will see us head for Lao Bao. They will alert the Tchepone forces to expect us."

Diem nodded in agreement and said, "When we leave Lao Bao let's leap frog our teams. We can cover each other as we move."

Vinh raised his right hand with his thumb extended upward and nodded agreement. Diem leaned against his seat's nylon webbing. He pushed his hat over his eyes and went to sleep.

Watching his uncle, Vinh grinned and thought, "You are one cool customer."

Realizing that his team was watching, Vinh did the same. He squinted with one eye slightly open and saw his men relax. He understood what Diem was up to from the start.

In Laos, at Tchepone, Colonel Nguyen Van Anh sat in the command post of the North Vietnamese Army's (NVA) 53rd Engineer Battalion. Across from him, Lieutenant Colonel Huen, the unit's commanding officer, poured rice wine into Anh's glass. Next, he filled one in front of him.

"If we keep making progress like today, we will be able to move tanks through here," Huen said.

"I couldn't agree with you more. This is going well. Hanoi will be pleased colonel," Anh replied.

Anh lifted his glass and drank half of its contents in one swallow. He placed his glass on his forehead and slowly rolled it back and forth.

As he gazed across the room at a map, he said, "In the morning, I will go south to take a look at the truck repair area. We're going to need good camouflage to reduce detection. I'm going to get some sleep now."

Chapter Twenty Four

February 1962

Of all the inventions that have helped to unify China
perhaps the airplane is the most outstanding.
Its ability to annihilate distance has been in direct
proportion to its achievements in assisting
to annihilate suspicion and misunderstanding
among provincial officials far removed
from one another or from the
officials at the seat of government.
Madame Chiang Kai-Shek (b. 1898), Chinese educator, reformer.

"Zane, park this damn thing over there," Harold Oates yelled in the most disgusting manner he could muster. "Now, Zane now," he continued while pointing to a clear area on the tarmac.

Dale Zane had a seemingly death grip on the controls of the H-23 helicopter. Every time he changed one control, he had to change three others. His hands and feet were constantly making changes to maintain a hovering position. It was difficult enough to do without Flight Instructor Oates screaming at him.

While rocking fore and aft and swaying from side to side, Zane made slow headway. Eventually, he arrived at the designated location.

"Put it down, Zane," Oates yelled. "Do you expect me to get out three feet in the air?"

"Get out! What does he mean get out?" Zane thought as he reduced power.

As the helicopter struck hard, Oates removed his shoulder harness and connecting seat belt. He stepped from the plastic bubble directly onto the pavement. It was hot and they had removed the ship's doors. Oates removed his flight helmet and leaned inside.

"Okay, go kill yourself Zane. That's what we need is a big crash and burn show. See if you can make it around the pattern twice without crashing," Oates ordered.

"Jesus," Zane thought, "He's going to let me solo."

Oates turned and walked toward the stage field training building. He held his helmet by its chinstrap, swinging it back and forth. Inside, other instructors, and their students watched. Oates had a large grin on his face that Zane could not see.

Slowly adding power, Zane brought the Hiller to a three-foot hover. He moved forward until reaching a runway-like training lane running from left to right.

"Brazos Tower, this is Army 547 request permission to taxi lane 4, over," Zane said using his radio.

"Roger Army 547, you are cleared for lane four, over," an air traffic controller replied.

"Army 547, roger," Zane answered, indicating he understood.

After receiving clearance, he entered the lane and turned right. Hovering forward, he continued until reaching a white square painted on the lane.

"Brazos Tower, this is Army 547 lane four, request permission for takeoff, over," Zane requested from the tower.

"Army 547, this is Brazos Tower, you are cleared for takeoff, over" the controller answered.

"Army 547, roger," Zane answered.

Zane felt a nervous sensation pass over him. He looked left and right to make sure no one was approaching. He gradually added power while adding a small amount of left pedal to overcome engine torque. By adding power, the aircraft turned right around its crankshaft. To overcome this, required left pedal to cause the ship's anti-torque tail rotor to push in the opposite direction. This kept the craft's nose straight.

Gradually, the plastic canopied helicopter began to accelerate. Its nose dipped causing it to shudder slightly. Zane watched his airspeed increasing while checking his altimeter. At 45 knots, he adjusted power for a 500 feet per minute rate of climb. As he approached 500 feet, he looked left and right to assure his intended flight path was clear. With no one in sight, he turned right onto the traffic pattern's cross wind leg. He continued climbing toward 1,000 feet. As he approached his desired altitude, it was time to begin his next turn 90 degrees to the right. Again, he looked for other craft. Seeing none, he turned right and was level at 1,000 feet. He was now on the pattern's downwind leg with an increased airspeed of 60 knots.

"Glory, glory, hallelujah. Glory, glory hallelujah," he sang aloud. "Damn, I am actually flying this mother on my own," he yelled.

With only 18 flying hours, he had 182 to go before he could get his wings. Others soloed earlier and there were those that had yet to do so. In any case, he was glad to still be in the program. From day to day, none of them knew when they might "wash-out." He had discussed that possibility with Lieutenant Scott, his stick-mate that morning.

"Dale, how many pink slips you got?" Scott asked.

"A bunch," Zane answered.

The two had the same flight instructor, Harold Oates. Candidates, with the same instructor, were stick-mates. Oates was a retired navy commander with thousands of hours flying. He flew fighters in Korea. Zane and Scott surmised that Oates must find flying the Hiller trainer degrading.

Continuing his anxious inquisition, Scott asked. "Do you know what the wash-out rate was for the class ahead of us?"

Before Zane could speak, Scott answered, "Sixty percent! Sixty damn percent! That's how many. They started with 100 and 40 graduated. Shit! That's tough."

The two stick-mates were having coffee at Zane's house before going to academics. Each training day was divided into two parts, academic and flight.

Each week the courses alternated between mornings and afternoons. This week they had academics in the morning. This was Scott's week to drive, so he came in for a quick coffee before continuing to class. They sat at Zane's kitchen table. Janice and Susan were asleep so they kept their voices low.

Zane lit a cigarette and gave one to Scott. With the day to day tension, Zane and Scott both chain-smoked.

"Oates gives me a pink slip on Thursdays and Fridays to make me sweat the weekends. He knows damn well it's three pink slips and you are out of here," Zane stated. "I am a nervous wreck by Monday. When I climb in that thing, I am so nervous I could barf. Oates is constantly screaming which does not help."

"It's part of the training," Scott commented. "They want to see if you lose control under pressure."

"Yeah, I know but it doesn't make it any easier," Zane replied. "We better get moving. We don't want to be late. They'll use any excuse to run us off."

Zane relished the ground school part of the program. In particular, he liked the weather portion. It was a major part of their training. It was necessary that they be able to understand weather in detail. Many pilots had crashed because they flew into bad weather when it could have been avoided.

Other courses dealt with aerodynamics, mechanics, and flight safety. They attended four hours of ground school a day. They would do this for almost six months.

Zane quit singing when he approached the point where he would turn and begin his descent. At every turn, it was necessary to look left and right.

After assuring his route was clear, Zane contacted the tower, "Brazos Tower, this is Army 547. Turning baseleg for landing, over."

"Roger, Army 547," the controller replied.

Reducing power, Zane began a slow right turn while his craft descended. He reduced speed to 45 knots and adjusted his rate of descent to 500 feet per minute.

"Here comes the moment of truth," he thought. "As some of the guys say, a landing is nothing more than a controlled crash. I can handle the crash part."

At 500 feet, Zane contacted the tower, "Brazos Tower, this Army 547 turning final for landing over," he said.

"Roger, Army 547, you are cleared to land. Altimeter is two niner point niner two," the air controller advised.

"Army 547, roger, two niner point niner two," Zane confirmed.

It was necessary to assure that his turn to final was to the same lane from which he took off. With students, it wasn't unusual to overshoot and try to land on an adjacent lane. This meant a major problem because other students were making approaches to the other three parallel lanes.

Zane aligned his helicopter with his landing lane. Down its middle white squares indicated landing points. Each square was three feet on each side. The object was to stop forward airspeed and be at a hover above one of the squares.

He could hear Oates, "When you get the correct sight picture, hold it. Adjust your power and airspeed to maintain that sight picture. Follow it all the way to your landing point while gradually adding power."

In Zane's mind, he was not alone. He could feel Oats' presence in the cockpit.

"Hell, he might as well be in here," he thought.

Zane brought the H-23 to a shaky hover above the square. He taxied down the lane at the speed of a brisk walk. He had to do the same pattern again. With this one out of the way, his confidence soared.

Later, Zane, Oates, and Scott returned to Camp Wolters main heliport. Zane sat in a daze through Oates' debriefing. Once completed, they were dismissed to catch buses to return to where their cars were parked. In the parking lot, Scott and four other students wrestled Zane to the ground. While they held him, another student cut the tail from Zane's shirt. In his happiness about making his solo flight, he forgot this tradition.

"Okay, you turd," Zane said to Scott. "Tomorrow your ass is mine. Oates is going to put you up for solo. If you live, I'll have yours."

Both friends laughed as they arose. After brushing off gravel, they made their way to Scott's car. Neither one spoke during the ride to Zane's house. There was a quiet understanding that this day, this moment together was special. It was something that had never happened before and never would again. They were in their twenties. Life was good and they were friends. They had a special bond that only others like would understand.

Ensuing months saw memorable moments pass. Not only did they learn to fly, they had experiences with comrades that would remain always.

Zane climbed aboard the bus to go to the flight line. As he walked the aisle to an empty seat, he heard students making statements that he did not understand.

As he sat, one in front of him said, "I've got six."

Another farther forward stated, "Nine is mine."

This continued until one cried, "I'm the winner!"

At the stage field, Zane asked Scott. "What's that business on the bus?"

"What business?" Scott asked.

"You know. The guys picking numbers," Zane explained.

"Oh that, you mean you don't know?" Scott asked incredulously. "Haven't you been watching Waldrop? When he gets on the bus, he makes sure he has a window seat. Next, he starts picking his nose. He gets a bugger and rolls it into a ball while staring out the window. Whenever he gets it the way he wants, he flicks it away. The guys are betting on how many seconds, between the time he starts rolling it, before he flicks it."

"You are kidding," Zane answered.

"No, I'm not. You just watch," Scott challenged.

It was as Scott said. The betting lasted until Waldrop got his third pink slip. He failed his check ride, which meant he flunked the course. He left without wings.

Nervous tension ran high and had strange effects. With time, it got worse. Janice usually fixed a soup and sandwich for lunch. She never gave Zane a spoon. It was impossible for him to keep soup in his spoon. His hands shook so much that he would spill it before getting it to his mouth. He picked the cup up and drank it like coffee. Sometimes he used both hands.

Another afternoon, two weeks before the course would end another event took place. An instructor, who Zane spoke with often, invited Zane to the Hut after class for a beer. The Hut was a small bar in Mineral Wells most often used by instructors. There was an unwritten rule that it was off limits to students.

"Yes, thanks. I would like that," Zane answered.

"Well come on let's go," he said.

Being invited to the Hut was an honor. Zane accepted the invite and was thrilled at the prospect of drinking with instructors. Later, still excited, he explained what happened to Janice over dinner.

"Honey, I learned so much just listening to those guys talk. They ought to schedule classes that way. It was great," Zane exclaimed.

After dinner, Zane watched the evening news. Janice was at the sink washing dishes.

Looking out the kitchen window, she asked Zane. "Hon, where's the car?"

Zane seemed to shrivel in his chair and said, "Oh shit, I left it at the parking lot. I wonder how Scott got home?" He said deeply embarrassed.

"I will never hear the end of this. I have to call Scott and see how he got home. In addition, I have to ask him to drive me to the parking area to get the car. He will never let me live this down."

The prospect of drinking at the Hut completely removed Zane from reality. Scott made sure he never forgot.

Both Zane and Scott received orders promoting them to first lieutenants on the same day. Since this promotion was routine, there was no official ceremony. However, the two started a practice that became a tradition between the pair. Scott brought his wife Georgia to Zane and Janice's quarters. Each removed his second lieutenant's gold bar. They placed their new silver bars in water glasses filled with bourbon. Before either one could pin on his new rank insignia, it was necessary to drink his bourbon non-stop. Then, and only then, could that person pin on his new, silver bar. The two vowed to make this ceremony a rite of passage at every promotion. Their mutual bond gained strength.

On a return flight from the stage field in June, Zane, Scott, and Oates were aboard. Oates took the flight controls.

"Well gentlemen, I have taught you everything I know. Tomorrow, I am putting you up for your final check rides. Don't worry. You will pass easily. It has been an honor flying with you," Oates said. "It's time for you to go to Fort Rucker for advanced training.

The only sound was the roar of the aircraft's engine and its rotor blades. There was deep satisfaction to know they were going to complete the course. They were two of 40, out of 100, to do so.

The instructors and students went to the Hut as fellow aviators after receiving their wings. A considerable amount of liquor went down that night. While rattling around in that old bar, Zane went to Oates and thanked him for his excellent instruction. As he turned to join the others, he saw tears in Oates' eyes. His time was over and he knew it. Zane immediately choked and went back and hugged the big man.

Fort Rucker sits nestled in Alabama's southeast corner. Outside its gates on the south is the small town of Daleville. To the southeast, Dothan is the locale's largest city. Two towns are on Rucker's north, Enterprise and Ozark. Among Army Aviators, the installation will always be Mother Rucker.

Zane and Janice arrived in July 1962, for Zane's advanced training. Forty others from their class arrived with them. It was a bittersweet time. Zane and Scott had orders for Korea for their first flying assignments. Ironically, as at Fort Sill, Janice was pregnant. What they escaped in Oklahoma caught them in Alabama. As before, they planned for Janice to remain in Spartanburg while Zane completed his 13-month, Korean tour. In the mean time, Zane had to master flying the Army's H-19 cargo helicopter.

"Can you believe the beautiful trees. It's so long since seeing trees that I had almost forgotten what they look like. They are gorgeous," Janice exclaimed.

"I will admit that I missed them," Zane answered. "The humidity here in July is horrendous with temperatures in the high nineties everyday. We're not lucky enough to find a place with cool temperatures, no humidity and glorious forests."

The three rented an apartment in Daleville near Scott and Georgia. They had places scattered throughout towns encircling Rucker. In addition, they had to learn to fly different aircraft.

Part of the class received assignments to fly the CH-34. This was a large, single rotor helicopter with a reciprocating engine. It had a reputation for power and versatility. It was relatively new in the Army's inventory.

Others, like Zane and Scott, reported for training in the CH-19. The H-19 made history saving lives in Korea. Many wounded owed their life to pilots flying this aircraft. These craft were old and worn and without much power.

The remainder of their class was envied. They were learning to fly the new, turbine powered UH-1. The UH-1 was the Army's new utility helicopter. It sat low and sleek. Hearing its turbine whine on startup was music compared to the cough and bang of the other craft. The UH-1 was nicknamed "Huey." There was no mistaking its distinctive rotor sound as it passed overhead with a "whop, whop, whop."

Rucker's program of instruction was similar to Camp Wolters except that the instruction was much more detailed. The CH-19 was a larger craft than their Hiller trainer and immensely more complex.

Their academic classes included a realistic field exercise on escape and evasion. The instruction was at night and simulated a situation where the students made a forced landing into enemy territory. Each student had basic survival equipment. It was necessary to cross a jungle-like swamp with enemy forces in pursuit. To check that students knew how to navigate with compasses, they had to navigate to specific points. To determine whether a student accomplished this, each point had information on it to get to the next one. Without information from each point, it was not possible to reach a partisan who would help them escape.

If captured, a student went to a realist prisoner of war (POW) camp. There he received intense interrogation, psychological manipulation and mild, mental torture. Attempts to escape were encouraged. It was a difficult test of a person's ability to survive in a wilderness and evade the enemy.

Students ate rattlesnakes, grubs, grasshoppers, and ants. They prepared snares for trapping wildlife and had to clean and cook it. Instructions on how to identify wild plants for consumption composed a large portion of the program.

Zane and Scott met their flight instructor their first day at Rucker. He was Chief Warrant Officer Gary Purdom. His training approach was completely different than that received at Wolters. This was one aviator to another training. It was comfortable and without undue harassment. This approach paid big dividends when it came time to fly the H-19.

"Good morning lieutenants, I'm Chief Warrant Officer Gary Purdom and together we are going to learn to fly the sickest cargo helicopter in the Army," he said. "You will have to fly this aircraft because, if you don't, it will not leave the ground."

During their first pre-flight inspection, Purdom noted the aircraft's struts and said, "See these, if you do not land this bird correctly, it will literally shake itself to pieces with you in it. You will either learn to do this or it will happen to you. The process is ground resonance. Touch down on one wheel first and that strut will bounce. That will rock you onto the other strut that will return the favor. This rocking intensifies rapidly until the aircraft beats itself to pieces. Remember this when you get ready to touch down. Any questions on ground resonance?"

Neither Zane nor Scott replied so Purdom said, "Let's get aboard."

A crew chief and one pilot rode in the cargo compartment. The instructor pilot and student rode in the cockpit above the cargo area. With this load, the H-19 could not hover. July's heat, combined with high humidity, reduced the craft's ability to lift. It simply did not have the power. Purdom was correct, you had to fly this aircraft.

For two months, they trained. Purdom showed them that, with a gentle touch, the H-19 was a performer. A pilot might not be able to hover but he could make a rolling take off in a few feet. In addition, skillful use of the wind helped immensely. Purdom's instruction heightened a pilot's feel for his aircraft. Learning to fly the H-19 served Zane and Scott immensely when they transitioned to more powerful aircraft.

Scuttlebutt was aviator's rumors. Scuttlebutt focused on one thing, Viet Nam. There were wild tales about the place and most had never heard of it. Zane learned of it soon after arriving at Rucker at happy hour.

"Hey Zane," Scott said, "Have you heard the latest?"

It was Friday afternoon after work. The officers' club sold drinks for half price. They had cold cuts free. Aviators swarmed the place. Janice and Georgia always met them for happy hour. They arrived early to get a table before a mob arrived. They already had two drinks for them when they arrived.

Zane gave Scott an exasperated look and asked. "What is it now?"

"Our orders are going to be changed. We're going to Viet Nam," he said excited.

"Where's Viet Nam?" Zane asked.

"It's in Southeast Asia. Haven't you heard of Dien Bien Phu?" Scott asked.

"Yeah," he answered. "I heard about that place on the news. The French got their butts kicked. Right?"

"That's the place," Scott responded as he leaned across the table and lowered his voice. "The word is that a guy in personnel said that we're being diverted to go there instead of Korea. No shit, this is on the level."

"Didn't President Kennedy give a speech about that place?" Janice asked.

"He sure did," Georgia answered. "It was on the news. He was at a joint session of congress. He said that assassins in Viet Nam had killed over 4,000 civil officers in 12 months."

"I don't remember that," Zane commented.

"Hon," Janice said. "We were at Fort Sill. You were on a night exercise. Georgia came over and we saw it together. I'm sure."

"Who is doing the killing?" Zane asked.

"The guerillas are," Scott answered.

"Janice, don't you remember that Sunday morning news program we watched about it at our place?" Georgia asked.

"I'm not sure," Janice replied.

"It's the one that had some republican senator complaining about the money Kennedy wanted. It was in the summer of 1961. We had gone to brunch that morning and went to our place for the guys to watch baseball on our new color TV," Georgia explained.

"Hey, I remember that," Zane interjected. "We had your birthday party at the club the night before and got shitfaced."

"That's it," Georgia exclaimed. "Kennedy wanted over two billion dollars to use in Viet Nam and other places like that. The senator was complaining about how we didn't have the money."

"Dale, that's how we got the new UH-1s. Kennedy got additional money to buy them. He also is increasing our Special Forces," Scott said.

Zane looked at his watch and said, "Happy hour is about over gang. Let's get another round before they shut us down. Your turn Janice."

"Okay, I will be right back. I hate fighting through those guys to get to the bar," Janice said.

Zane looked at Scott and asked. "Didn't that guy at the escape and evasion course say something about Special Forces?"

"Yep, he sure did. He said that's where he received training to get the course going," Scott replied. "I'm telling you this guy in personnel knows some crap. He said Special Forces guys were already in Viet Nam training people. The country has a lot of jungle and they are going to need helicopters to move troops."

"Korea is looking better by the minute," Zane said as he finished his drink. "Where's Janice?"

"Damn, Dale don't you want to go where the action is?" Scott asked.

"I'm not looking to get my butt shot off if that's what you mean," Zane replied. "Here's Janice now. Let's have a toast."

The four raised and touched their glasses as Zane said, "Here's to having only one hole in our butts."

After completing advanced training, Zane and Janice returned to South Carolina on leave for a month. Scott and Georgia went to Tennessee for leave. The two new aviators agreed to meet in Oakland, California, to board ship for movement to Korea.

During October of 1962, Zane and Scott were on board ship in mid-Pacific traveling to Korea. Onboard, there were seven officers and 400 soldiers. Also on board were some civilian wives and children going to join husbands in Japan. The trip's duration was 23 days.

The ship's captain formed a voyage staff from the Army officers on board. They were responsible for activities involving troops. The staff's commander was Lieutenant Colonel James R. Grinder. He appointed Zane provost marshal for the trip. Zane's duties were to enforce military discipline. The trip was a pleasant voyage until Colonel Grinder called a special staff meeting.

"Gentlemen, we are now at Defcon 2. This is the next highest readiness condition before actual war. I have special orders received an hour ago from Washington. I suggest you have seats," Grinder said.

Grinder remained at his desk as the officers found seats in his office. Each wore a deep expression of concern. They knew what Defcon 2 was and they were helpless in the middle of an ocean.

Once everyone took seats Grinder continued, "Our orders are to prepare for redirection to another port at any time. I have no idea which port. When we arrive, we will be prepared to engage in combat activities against hostile forces. I do not know which forces. Any questions so far?"

"Yes sir," Zane said. "Why?"

Grinder answered, "The United States is under imminent danger of nuclear attack. The Soviet Union has nuclear capable missiles in Cuba. United States armed forces are moving to positions to invade Cuba."

Subdue whispers of "Oh my God," "Damn," and "Shit," rippled around the room.

Immediately Zane thought of Janice, "Oh my God, she's there alone with Susan and a kid on the way. She must be scared to death. It wouldn't matter if I were in the U.S. because I definitely wouldn't be at home. They would have me going to Cuba."

Grinder continued, "It may be small satisfaction to know that you are probably in the safest place to be in an atomic attack. There's not a damned thing in any direction for 1,000 miles. We are remaining on course for Japan. We will remain overnight and depart for Korea early the next day barring any changes. I will be announcing this information over the ship's public address system to the troops. Some of them may not take this too well. Zane, get your military police together and brief them. Be prepared for any undisciplined response to my announcement."

"Yes sir," Zane affirmed.

"Unless you have something else. That is it for now. I ask each of you to pray to your God that this does not happen. There will be world chaos. Thank you. You are dismissed."

Zane gathered his seven school trained military police corps soldiers who were on their way to Korea. He explained the situation and they had an expected reaction. They had loved ones for whom they cared in harm's way. However, they realized there was nothing they could do. Each donned his MP armband and drew a baton from supply.

"Sergeant Willard, I am assigning you three men. Take them to the forward hold and wait for the colonel's announcement. You have authorization to use force only to protect yourself and your men. If someone creates a major problem, you can only use enough force to take them into custody. Take them to the mid-ship brig. The colonel will decide what disciplinary action to take. If everything is in order 30 minutes after the announcement, report to me in the aft hold. Any questions? Zane asked.

"No sir," Willard answered.

Continuing, Zane said, "Specialist Bingham, you are in charge of Billings and Holt. You are with me in the aft hold. Do you understand the use of force as I explained it to Sergeant Willard?"

"Yes sir," Bingham answered.

"We have 30 minutes. Let's go," Zane directed.

As Zane moved aft with his MPs, the ship's captain announced over the public address system for Army personnel to move to their bunk areas fore and aft. He posted Bingham and Holt at one exit from the aft hold. He and Billings took position at the other.

He watched soldiers streaming into their sleeping areas. Many passed directly through his post on their way. Their chatter sounded like bees buzzing as they wondered why they had to return to their areas.

"Now hear this. Now hear this," a speaker blared above Zane's head. "The voyage staff commander has an announce."

The aft hold's soldiers became totally silent. There was no horseplay or talking. Everyone listened intently. As the nature of Grinder's announcement became evident, they glanced at each other. Then mummers spread throughout the group. There were quick glances towards the exit doors where Zane and Sergeant Willard stood.

The nature of the group changed. Where once there were 200 individuals, groups of four and five men each began forming as friends found each other. Zane observed exaggerated hand movements as men argued among themselves.

Finally, one of the men walked toward Zane and stopped a few feet away. He wore a tee shirt so Zane could not determine his rank. After quick glances around the area, he spoke.

"Lieutenant, what's with the MPs?" He asked.

Zane learned from his NCOs to never lie to troops. They can tell when they are getting bullshit.

Zane answered, "We're hear in case someone overreacts to the disturbing news you just heard."

The man looked over his shoulders at the others as if saying, "Watch me get this shavetail."

Stepping closer, he said in an insolent tone, "We want to go back to the states. Tell Grinder to turn this ship around."

Zane noticed that some men, who had been sitting on bunks, got to their feet and looked toward him. A few of the small groups moved towards him and stopped.

"This can get out of control quick," Zane realized. "I have to do the right thing quick."

Zane stepped forward, gave the soldier a friendly look, and said, "So do I. Get your shirt and we will go ask him."

Behind the soldier, Zane saw men passing a shirt forward. Others seemed to relax and began whispering to each other. A man stepped forward and tapped Zane's challenger on his shoulder. He gave him his shirt. Anxiously looking around while he put his shirt on, he saw other soldiers avoid his look. He quickly realized he was alone.

"I'm ready sir," he said while tucking his shirt into his trousers.

Zane looked across at Specialist Bingham and indicated with a head movement for him to follow. He felt sure that the possibility for an ugly incident passed without any difficulty.

Colonel Grinder spent ten minutes with the young man. After he left Grinder's office, he spoke to Zane.

"Thanks L-T, I will tell the guys," he said.

"You are welcome. If anything else comes up let me know. Okay?" Zane requested.

"You bet L-T," he answered.

Their ship made port at Yokohama, Japan without incident. Civilians disembarked to meet family members on the dock. Colonel Grinder decided, against Zane's recommendation, to grant overnight liberty to the soldiers.

"Sir, these men have been locked away for almost three weeks. We sail at 08:00 hours tomorrow morning. A lot of them will end up drunk and miss ship," Zane said to Grinder.

"Lieutenant," Grinder said, "I will bet you a beer at Inchon, Korea, that they all make it."

The next morning 30 minutes before getting underway, Zane stood at the gangplank's top watching soldiers return. Five were yet to arrive. After checking his watch, he started to give the signal to raise the walkway when he heard tires squeal. Looking toward the dock, he saw a taxi stop and five men jump from it. They started running toward the ship. Close behind them, their Japanese driver was in hot pursuit, screaming as he ran. The five soldiers raced past Zane as he reached the dock to intercept the cab driver. Not able to speak Japanese, Zane held $20.00 in American currency in the irate man's face. He grabbed it immediately and walked away slowly, humming to himself as he went. Zane owed Grinder a beer.

Once aboard, Zane signaled to move the gangplank. They began moving on their way to Inchon, the land of the morning calm.

During the trip, Scott was supply officer. He had a nice, air-conditioned office from which he seldom ventured. Zane went to see him shortly after getting underway.

"Aren't you something," Zane said as he entered Scott's office. "You've been cooped up in here for three weeks. How did you stand it?" Zane asked.

"Easy, my friend," Scott said as he held up a book. "I've been studying this."

In his hand, he held a book titled, "The Soldiers Guide To Korea."

"Do you know what banjo means in Korean?" Scott asked.

"No, what?" Zane asked amused.

"The latrine," Scott said. "You never know when you need to know a word like that.

"Get off your ass," Zane said. "We are sitting at the captain's table tonight for dinner."

"No shit," Scott responded. "I've heard that the captain lays on a special meal for voyage staff members. Let's go."

Later, after dinner, the two stood on the foredeck. They watched dolphins leaping at their ship's bow. They watched as the water changed from deep blue to muddy brown. They could see Korea's mainland behind many small islands.

The pair rested their forearms on the ship's railing. They had been quiet watching the sunset. It was a beautiful scene.

"Daryl, did your book tell you about what happened here a few short years ago? Did it explain how so many American soldiers died so that the south could remain a democracy?" Zane asked.

"No it didn't," Scott answered.

"Over 50,000 died just beyond those islands. I am certain they did not want to die. Yet, they did. There were many more thousands maimed for life to keep South Korea free. First, the North Koreans invaded followed by the Chinese Communists. Our guys stood their ground to keep this small piece of Far Eastern territory non-communist," Zane explained.

"They weren't only Americans," Scott commented.

"Yeah, I know," Zane responded. "They were United Nation's troops but the United States bore the brunt of most of it. I can see the same thing happening in Viet Nam. Jesus, when are we going to stop trying to be the world's policemen?" Zane asked.

Scott answered, "We're still at Defcon 2. I will bet you that the DMZ here is hot. If there's going to be a shootout between the USSR and the US, the North Koreans are going to storm across the DMZ to take the south. They will figure we cannot handle the world."

"We better hit the sack," Zane stated. "We'll be at Inchon in the morning. We'll find out if this is really the land of the morning calm."

Zane lay in his bunk with his hands clasped behind his head. He stared at the bunk above his where Scott slept.

"Dear God, let them be safe. Don't let us destroy a great home you've built for us. Take care of Janice and Susan for me. Amen," he said.

Waiting ashore were teams issuing steel helmets, gas masks, and M-14 semi-automatic rifles to everyone leaving the ship. They boarded trucks to go to the replacement depot near Seoul, Korea's capital. Although, the Korean War was over for almost ten years, its damage was still evident along their travel route. Gutted buildings, destroyed temples and refugee beggars lined their way. They yelled at the passing trucks begging for anything they could get. Abject poverty existed everywhere Zane looked.

At the replacement depot, Zane and Scott received their assignments. Scott had orders to report to an infantry division manning the DMZ. He would be flying Bell H-13s, which was a light observation helicopter. His unit was a cavalry, recon company.

Zane learned that he was going to the 38th Air Defense Brigade (ADA). They were responsible for the air defense of South Korea. Their headquarters was at Osan Air Force Base south of Seoul. Zane would fly with their aviation detachment farther south at Camp Humphries, at Pyongtaek. A sergeant was waiting for him with a three-quarter ton truck. He would drive Zane to Osan where the commanding officer of the aviation detachment would fly him to Camp Humphries. This was the same place that his commander at Fort Sill fought the North Koreans with Task Force Smith. Somehow, this seemed ironic but did not know why.

"Dale, if you are ever up north, look me up," Scott said at their parting.

"You do the same sport," Zane said as he took Scott's hand. He did not shake it but gave a tight squeeze with both hands. Scott looked at Zane with sad eyes. There was pain in their parting.

Zane slung his rifle over his shoulder and picked up his heavy duffel bag. He walked away toward the waiting NCO and truck. His eyes became misty and his throat grew tight.

"Shit," he mumbled with his head down.

The NCO came to attention at Zane's approach, saluted and said, "Good morning sir. I'm Staff Sergeant Dearon. Let me help you with your gear," he said.

Zane placed his duffel bag on the ground while grasping his rifle's shoulder strap with his left hand. He returned Dearon's salute.

"Good morning sergeant, I'm new meat for the 38th ADA," he replied.

Sergeant Dearon laughed and picked up Zane's duffel bag. He placed it in the truck's rear.

"Sir, here's your basic load of ammo. There are 120 rounds in clips. There may be insurgents along our route. Ready to go?" Dearon asked.

"Let's do it," Zane answered.

Their road south soon changed from asphalt to dirt. Houses along their way had mud walls and rice straw roofs. The terrain was rugged hills blasted barren during the war. Beside the road, someone recently planted small saplings. As they passed, children waved. They seemed to be everywhere he looked. He noted that toddlers had no crotch in their britches. Their genitals and rears were bare. Older children carried small ones on their backs like papooses in old western movies.

"Sir, get ready for this," Dearon said. "It is a stinker."

Ahead they approached a cart with a large, soiled cylinder on it. Its wheels were solid with no spokes. A water buffalo pulled it with a wooden yoke around its neck. As they passed the odor struck and Zane gagged.

"Sir, I warned you," Dearon said. "They are everywhere with those honey-wagons. They fertilize with human feces. That was a collection of it we passed."

"You won't have to tell me again sergeant. I will be on the lookout," Zane answered.

Sergeant Dearon stopped their vehicle as the road disappeared into a river and explained, "If you ever drive this way watch this place. There's a cement ford beneath the water about a foot. There are no markers for the edges. Never try to pass a vehicle on it even if it is coming from the other direction. The only safe way to cross is to watch where the road exits the river. Align you vehicle with its center and enter. This thing is narrow and dangerous."

Zane leaned out a window as they crossed. He saw large swirls around their tires.

"I wouldn't want to cross this place in a jeep," Zane commented.

"No sweat sir, you can do it. Just take your time," Dearon replied.

Air police, at Osan Air Force Base, threatened to arrest Zane because he didn't have a pass. He presented a copy of his orders and his identification card. They reluctantly let him enter.

"What gives sergeant? Why the hard time?" Zane asked.

"Nukes sir," he answered. "This base is loaded with them. The brigade has Nike-Hercules missile batteries on most mountaintops in this area. Their mission is air defense. However, they have a ground to ground capability. The Air Force moves the warheads through Osan. The brigade takes them to the missile batteries. Right now with Defcon 2, they are ready to nuke North Korea if they so much as fart."

Zane thought about what Dearon said and then asked. "If the Nike units are on ground targets, who provides air defense?"

"Hawk batteries sir. They have Hawk and Nike batteries integrated. You will go to every one of them very soon. They are also on mountaintops. Driving there is a bitch. So, the brass goes by helicopter," he answered.

Zane looked at huge mountains in the distance and swallowed hard. At Rucker, they landed on miniscule hilltops not mountains. He could see problems ahead.

His commanding officer, Captain Marvin Hinson, met Zane at Osan AFB Operations. The first impression Zane had was Hinson's size. He couldn't be over five feet, ten inches tall.

"I bet he doesn't weigh over 150 pounds. Here we go with the overweight crap from a runt," Zane thought.

Zane and the sergeant saluted as they approached him.

Zane said, "Sir, Lieutenant Zane reporting for duty."

Hinson returned his salute as he dismissed the sergeant.

Putting out his hand, he said, "Zane welcome aboard. Are we glad to see you. Well, I take that back. There is one who will be disappointed."

"Sir, why is that?" Zane asked.

"Second Lieutenant Harrellson won't like your arrival. He's tired of all the shit details because he's the junior officer of our bunch. He hoped for someone he outranked. He will get over it. Harrellson is good people. Let me take that duffel bag. Jesus, the only thing you don't have is grenades," Hinson answered. "Follow me, our flight plan is filed and we can go."

Hinson took a route through a large maintenance hanger and outside to an aircraft parking area. Zane followed and noted that Hinson could hardly handle his duffel bag.

"That's her on the end," Hinson said. "We have two of them."

Looking down the row of huge cargo aircraft, he saw an L-19 Birddog. Zane was expecting an H-19 or H-34. Never did he expect this tiny aircraft. The L-19 was primarily a reconnaissance aircraft. The Army did use it for aerial artillery observation and adjustment. Its single engine was extremely powerful for such a small airplane. There was no civilian equivalent because it couldn't meet Federal Aviation Administration (FAA) requirements. It was overpowered enough to damage wings if not careful. It had seating for two persons in tandem with a small cargo space behind the rear seat.

"Damn, with the two of us, and this extra gear, it may not be able to get airborne," Zane wondered.

Hinson seemed cheerful about something. He opened a frail looking door and removed a parachute from the backseat. Next, he playfully tossed his duffel bag into the rear seat with a groan.

Holding the parachute in front of him, Hinson said, "Put this on."

"Ahh, sir I don't know how," Zane responded.

"What? You went through flight school and never wore a parachute?" Hinson asked in disbelief.

"That's correct sir. I'm only helicopter rated and we never received instruction about parachutes. As I'm sure you know there are no parachutes in helicopters," answered.

"Okay, I will show you how," Hinson stated.

Zane removed his gas mask container from his hip. In addition, he took off his ammunition belt and helmet. Hinson began adjusted straps so that it would fit. After three attempts, he had it on Zane.

"You are a big one Zane," Hinson said with a chuckle. "I hope we can get off the runway, ha!"

"Now, take it off," Hinson directed.

"Sir?" Zane responded.

"Take it off. We don't wear the thing. We have it ready if we need it," Hinson explained.

With gear stowed and Zane aboard, Hinson taxied to the run-up area and did his preflight checks. When cleared, he taxied onto the runway and added full power while holding the brakes. The tiny ship trembled from end to end. He released the brakes and they lurched ahead.

Finally, they were airborne. Zane looked at the runway remaining ahead. It disappeared in the distance. They had not used one tenth of its length. Later he learned that the runway was 10,000 feet long, far more than an L-19 would ever need. Hinson flew south. To the right, Zane could see the Yellow Sea. Looking left, large mountains were silhouettes for a setting sun. From the air, it was a beautiful scene. Dark was near.

Hinson landed without so much as protest from the craft's tires. He taxied to a lone hanger far from other buildings on the airfield. He moved to a parking spot next to a line of observation helicopters. Zane counted four H-23s and two H-13s. Also in the line was another fixed wing, the Army's L-20 Beaver made by Canada's DeHavilland. A favorite of bush pilots this single engine, high winged craft was almost impossible to stall and had amazing short landing and takeoff capabilities. Once stopped, a jeep raced from the lone building and parked beside them.

"Hey captain, what kind of new meat have you got on board?" Someone in the jeep bellowed.

"He's a heartbreaker for you Harrellson," Hinson roared with laughter.

The distance between the front seat's back and the doorframe on an L-19 is small. Zane had to squeeze through the space with his back to the outside and could not see.

As his feet touched the ground, he turned to hear Hinson say, "Second Lieutenant Harrellson meet First Lieutenant Zane, ha!"

With only the jeep's headlights for visibility, Zane could make out the outline of a medium build officer. He was about six feet tall with a small pompadour in his hair. Through the middle of the pompadour, there was one silver streak about one inch wide.

"That's strange for a young man," he thought.

He noticed that he was unarmed and wearing heavy wool, winter olive drab (OD) shirt, and trousers. He had his trousers tucked in his boots. Underneath his chin, he wore a white scarf puffed up with a unit insignia of some sort on it.

He promptly saluted Zane and said, "Welcome to Camp Humphries and the 38th Air Defense Brigade Aviation Section sir. I hate to say that I am sorry to see you sir."

Zane returned his salute and held it by not lowering his arm. Until he did so, Lieutenant Harrellson had to remain in place. Finally Zane began to laugh as did Hinson and Harrellson. Zane dropped his arm to his side.

"I wished I could say that I'm glad to be here but it would be a damned lie," Zane said with a chuckle.

"Sir, I'll get that duffel bag. On the way to our hooch, we'll stop by the arms room and relieve you of your armaments. The Russians blinked by damn," Harrellson said.

"No shit," Zane said.

"That's right. We're at Defcon 4, which is normal for here. How about that," Harrellson replied.

After signing for Zane's weapon and ammunition, Harrellson locked the arms room. They drove up a dirt road to a group of Quonset huts in neat rows.

Stopping at the last one in one of the rows, Harrellson said, "We're home. This is the famous hooch of the 38th ADA Aviation section. Let's have a drink."

"I'm for that," Zane replied.

Midway along the side of the Quonset, an entrance allowed access to a central living area. In the middle was an oil burning, potbellied heater. On two sides, general issue, Army sofas sat. Two easy chairs completed the seating. Directly opposite the entrance along the far wall, a waist high counter ran parallel to the wall. Harrellson stepped behind it and removed three mugs from a shelf. Each mug had the name of each officer in the aviation section imprinted upon it. Directly above the name, a red shield with a clenched fist inside held three lightening bolts.

Reaching beneath the counter, Harrellson retrieved another mug. It was blank.

Looking at Zane he said, "This drink is on us. If you want, this blank is your mug and I will get it embossed. Eighth Army restricts booze to four-fifths a month. If you don't drink, we would appreciate the donation of your ration to our bar. Name your poison."

"Bourbon and water's fine," Zane answered. "By the way, I assume a hooch is where we live."

"Captain, we have a winner. You're quick there Zane," Harrellson said laughing aloud.

"I might as well keep a winning streak going. Who is Laughton?" Zane asked.

"Watch it folks. Zane's bucking for the CO's job," Harrellson chuckled.

Continuing, Harrellson said, "Laughton is one each, Chief Warrant Officer Three Frank W. Laughton. He will join us shortly as he is out actively protecting our asses. Tonight he is Officer of the Guard and is checking our perimeter. He is due any minute," Harrellson answered.

As the mugs passed to individuals, Zane noticed that Hinson's had a gold star on it.

"I guess the gold star is for the CO?" Zane asked.

"Nope that's for the man with less than 30 days to go before leaving?" Harrellson replied. "Our Captain Hinson is short. He will soon leave the land of the morning calm for the land of the big PX (Post Exchange)."

Looking up from his copy of "Playboy," Hinson said, "Eat your hearts out."

The entrance door flew open and a giant of a man entered with arms outstretched, he said, "Your protecting angel is in your midst. Rise and be recognized or I will shoot."

Throwing his fatigue hat across the room, he reached for his sidearm saying, "Who is first?"

Laughing, he crossed the room and slapped Zane on his back and extended a hand, "I am CW3 F. W. Laughton. The man whose dad almost named him Long John Silver so he could call him Long for short!"

Catching his breath from the hard blow, Zane took his ham-sized hand and returned his welcoming shake. The man's blue eyes sparkled beneath brush-like eyebrows. He was totally bald with a glistening head. At least six feet four inches tall, he was lean and decidedly strong. His hand engulfed his large mug and it disappeared within.

Raising his mug, Laughton said, "Here's to new meat."

The others raised their mugs and shouted in unison, "Right on."

Hinson laid his magazine aside and said, "Have a seat Zane. I'll bring you up to date on our outfit."

Everyone became quiet. It was clear that the time for horseplay was finished.

"Zane, we're a small operation. At most, we have five officers in the unit and ten enlisted. Located on the base with us is the Sixth Transportation Helicopter Company. They are a CH-21 outfit. You know the ship that looks like a banana with big rotors on each end. That's Sixth Trans and they are our mother unit. Eighth Army attached us to them for meals, quarters, and direct support maintenance. You will meet all of them soon enough. The uniform during fall and winter is OD wool. During daylight, we wear a red neck scarf. After 17:30 hours, we change to white. We seldom wear flight suits but that is your choice. Go by Sixth Trans supply tomorrow and they'll get you what you need. Frank, you fill him in on operations," Hinson said.

Laughton sat on the sofa next to Zane and said, "I will arrange qualification flights for you in the H-23 and H-13, you will be flying both. In addition, before you fly anywhere, you must have a DMZ orientation ride. A qualified IP will take you into the tactical zone. He will show you how to identify the DMZ from the air. Fly across it and the North Koreans will shoot your ass down quick. In fact, they often shoot if you're close so pay attention. Any questions?"

"None," Zane answered.

"Fine," Laughton continued, "Forget everything Rucker taught you about flying into high, confined areas. If you try their technique here, you will not last a day. Your IP will demonstrate that for you. Captain Hinson appointed you maintenance officer. Ours left a month ago so we need you big time. Every night you tell me how many helicopters are available for the next day. I schedule the missions with 38th ADA operations. Have the tail numbers to me not later than 17:00 hours each day. Okay?"

Harrellson added, "I've got all the good jobs. You name it; I have it. First, hooch maids, they are $5.00 a month. They do your laundry, shine your boots, and clean your room and other minor chores. You will meet her tomorrow. Her name is Mama-San. Of course, that's not her real name but that's what she expects so address her that way. Another chore of mine is the slush fund. Each month you pay another $5.00. This fund is illegal but every unit has one. It pays for your mug, bar supplies, a going-home plaque, and your black hat. You will learn about the hat later. Are you broke yet?" Harrellson asked while the others laughed.

"Not yet but you're getting there," Zane replied.

"There's another five for the officer's club each month. You won't find a better deal anywhere for the price. Mixed drinks are five cents as is beer. Various bar snack items are free. We have a hail and farewell each month. The $5.00 goes to expenses for that. I collect money on the third of each month. No welching allowed," he continued.

Hinson arose and looked at his watch and said, "That's enough for the first day. It's late. I am going to bed. See you in the morning."

Zane watched Hinson walk to one corner of the living area. He opened a door with "Hinson" displayed on it and entered. He closed his door and a light came on simultaneously. The light showed over the top of a wooden divider running perpendicular to the Quonset's length.

Harrellson said, "Come on Zane, I'll get you setup. This will be home for the next 12 months."

Zane noted earlier that there were five doors to the living area. One was their initial entry and the others were inside the hooch. Three, including Hinson, had names on them. One did not. Harrellson walked toward the unmarked door and opened it. He and Zane stepped inside.

Furnishings were sparse but adequate. In one corner, a three-quarter-size bed dominated the area. A small desk and chair was on one wall. Immediately inside the doorway on the right, a small chest of drawers sat. Next to it, in a corner, was a freestanding closet with curtains for a door. Pushing it aside, Zane found ample hangers. He guessed the room to be about eight feet wide and 20 feet long. The walls had numerous staples in them where once pictures or posters were on display.

"If walls could talk," Zane mumbled.

"Sir?" Harrellson asked.

"Nothing, just thinking aloud," Zane responded.

"Your bedding is in the bottom drawer of that chest. If you need more, ask Mamma-San. The banjo, excuse me, the john is the small door behind the bar. Shower in the evenings, the water is hot then. Do not wait until morning. You will freeze your but off. Captain Hinson runs every morning and showers at his office. That helps with only three using the one here. See you in the morning," Harrellson explained.

As the door closed, Zane thought, "Twelve months. Why does that sound like a jail sentence?"

Chapter Twenty Five

April 1962

Love does not consist in gazing at each other but in looking together in the same direction.
Antoine de Saint-Exupéry (1900–1944), French aviator, author.

"Sir, it has been one damned coup after another. Every time the military gets their nose out of joint, they take over the government. If someone has to be military and in charge, Sarit Thanarat is the best we could hope for," Pontier Gevereaux said. "Sarit used to command the Bangkok garrison and is hard core anticommunist."

Colonel Jean Danjou listened intently as his assistant military attaché provided insights about Thailand's government. Jean knew that Major Gevereaux was an administrator. His field experience was nonexistent. Yet, he thoroughly understood the inner workings of Thailand's politics.

"Tell me about Phao and Phibun," Jean directed.

"Those two have been stirring the pot in Thailand since they participated in a coup in 1932. Phibun's full name is Luang Plaek Phibunsongkhram. Since everyone refers to him as Phibun, I will continue doing so," Gevereaux said.

"That's fine with me," Jean replied.

Continuing Gevereaux explained, "Phibun was an ambitious army officer. He was also politically active, which, by our standards, was a dangerous game. Eventually, he became Field Marshall Phibun. Most agree this was because of his political connections. He helped overthrow Thailand's government in 1932. Phibun considered Thailand a backward nation and thought they should be more involved with the West. After the coup, he sat on a three man commission that ran the government."

"Where does Phao fit in?" Jean questioned.

"Phraya Phahonphonphayuhasena, better known as Phao, was the senior member of the group behind the coup. He represented old-line military officers dissatisfied with cuts in appropriations for the armed forces. Without his support, the overthrow would have been a dud," Gevereaux explained.

One of three telephones on Jean's desk began ringing. He raised his hand indicating that Gevereaux stop speaking.

Lifting it from its cradle Jean said, "Danjou."

"Good afternoon colonel. This is Belton. I'm calling to remind you of our four o'clock," a voice with a long, southern United States drawl said.

"Thanks Jim," Jean answered. "I may be delayed but it will not be more than 15 minutes. Is that a problem?"

"Not at all colonel. I will explain to the others. See you then," Belton said as he broke their connection.

"I'm sorry Ponteir. Please continue," Jean said.

"These two worked with a guy named Pridi. He was the real kingpin. However, he only lasted until about 1938 when Philbun took over through political maneuvering. He became Prime Minister. Philbun threw Pridi a bone by keeping him as Finance Minister. As Prime Minister, he was a nationalist and strongly anti-French. He even collaborated with the Japanese during World War II. That's why the heavy reparations at war's end," Gevereaux continued.

Interrupting, Jean leaned back in his executive's chair. He asked. "What about Sarit?"

"Shit, it's the same old story in Thailand. General Sarit Thanarat was commander of the Bangkok garrison. As time passed, Phibun's stock within the military declined as a result of plots against him. Phao and Sarit grew more powerful than Phibun. However, Philbun did stay Prime Minister for awhile. This happened in 1951. By 1959, after other coups and some assassinations, Sarit began ruling the country," Gevereaux said, somewhat out of breath.

Jean reached on his desk and picked up an OD green cylinder. He began moving it from hand to hand while thinking. He pushed his chair back and opened his desk's lower left drawer. From it, he removed a cylinder identical to the one in his other hand. He closed the drawer and looked at Gevereaux.

"I will be away for a few months doing some field work," Jean said as he held the two cylinders in front of him.

Leaning across his desk, Jean extended a hand with one cylinder in it and said, "Take this and keep it. If anyone brings you another identical to it, take action on whatever message they might give you."

Gevereaux took the device and examined it curiously. On its side, he noted the inscription "Mil-Spec-00378-01A."

"Yes sir," Gevereaux answered. "By the way, what's this good for?"

"Nothing, absolutely nothing," Jean answered cryptically.

"One more thing before I have to leave," Jean said. "Is it true that Sarit put in force a defense treaty with the United States."

"Yes sir, he did but it was more of an understanding between Foreign Minister Thanat Khoman and Dean Rusk, United States Secretary of State. The agreement was that the U.S. would come to Thailand's aide in time of trouble from any aggressor nation. Two months later, President Kennedy started pouring armed forces into Thailand. You cannot believe the construction. They are building major air bases. It is unbelievable the amount of money they are spending. Thailand's government is not officially recognizing the U.S. effort but they are not protesting either," Gevereaux answered.

"Thanks major. I will see you in a few months. You're dismissed," Jean said.

Jean watched his assistant leave his office while examining the cylinder given to him. As soon as Gevereaux left the room, he picked up a telephone handset. He pressed a button on the telephone's base.

"Yes Colonel," a female voice answered.

"Get me Benton on a secure line please," Jean directed.

"Right away, Colonel," she said.

Jean listened for one long tone and two short ones. This indicated that the line was secure without taps or anyone listening on another handset.

"Benton," a man said.

"Danjou," Jean replied. "Tell the others I will be late no longer than 30 minutes."

"Yes sir," Benton said.

Jean listened for the same tones after Benton broke their connection. He heard them indicating that his call was secure.

Jean left France's embassy in civilian clothes. He found his way through a raging sea of people to a clock shop. Upon entering, a bell above the door chimed. An oriental man came from the shop's rear area.

Jean stood straight and placed his palms together with his fingers pointed up. He bowed his head while bringing his chin to the apex of his fingers. He made sure that he bowed first, and quite low, to show respect for the older gentleman.

"Sawasdee Ka," Jean said.

Taking the same posture, the oriental man replied, "Sawasdee Ka, colonel. Follow me please."

Jean followed him to the store's rear and up one flight of stairs. Along his way, many types of clocks filled the room with a barrage of ticking sounds. The oriental opened a door and they entered a room filled with workbenches. Many clocks, in various states of repair lay upon them. The pair arrived at a wall filled with shelves containing clock parts. The oriental leaned his full weight against the shelves. At the same time, he removed a paint can that activated a counterweight causing a portion of the shelved wall to move aside. He entered with Jean close behind him. The door closed causing a light to automatically illuminate.

Inside the small room, Jean asked. "Preecha are they ready?"

"You only had to ask colonel. Have I ever been late," Preecha asked in return.

"No you have not. Let's have a look," Jean said.

Preecha removed a vinyl case about the size of a cigar box from a nearby shelf. He placed it on a table and turned on the table's lamp. Opening the case, Preecha removed an ordinary looking ballpoint pen.

"Shall I demonstrate colonel?" Preecha asked.

"Certainly," Jean answered.

Preecha twisted the pen at its midpoint causing it to come apart in two pieces. He removed its ink tube and replaced it with an identical one from the case. He reassembled the pen. He pressed a small silver colored knob at the pen's top causing the pen's point to extend. As far as Jean could determine, it worked exactly like any ballpoint pen.

"Colonel this functions as any ball point pen when used in this fashion," Preecha said as he wrote on a piece of paper.

He pressed the pen's top and the point retracted as he said, "Colonel press the pen against someone and push its top and hold it. This causes a membrane to burst allowing a deadly toxin to flow. A minute needle extends from the toxin chamber and through the writing point. It functions as a hypodermic needle injecting the toxin. Death is almost instantaneous."

"Excellent Preecha. What about the other item?" Jean asked.

Preecha placed the pen in its case and removed a gold pocket watch. He pressed its stem causing one side to open. Inside the opened portion, there was a picture of a young woman holding a baby. He showed the picture to Jean.

"Lovely," Jean commented.

Preecha closed the watch and pressed it stem twice in succession. The watch's other side opened revealing a watch face with a minute and hour hand. The indicated time was incorrect by two hours. Inside the cover, there was an inscription. He held it for Jean to examine it.

"To Jean with love, Monica," it stated.

"Colonel, to activate the device pull its stem out to set the correct time. This activates a miniature powder train. It will burn for ten seconds to a detonator. The detonator causes highly explosive nitrogen compounds to detonate. The explosion will remove a person's hand. If it is in a pocket, it will destroy a hip. The time will always be exactly two hours in error," Preecha explained.

"Clever," Jean said. "If someone takes it and tries to set the time, they are in for a big surprise. How am I going to keep the thing operating?"

"Not to worry colonel. It does not require winding. A lithium battery powers it. The battery also activates a crystal mechanism that is accurate to one second in five years. The battery will last that long," Preecha responded.

"How much do I owe you?" Jean asked.

"Colonel, you dishonor me. After what you did for my family, I can never repay. The items are a gift, sir," Preecha said with grateful emotion in his voice.

"You are kind Preecha," Jean said. "I must leave. I am already late for an important meeting. Thank you."

Jean connected the watch to a belt loop by its gold chain and put the explosive device in his trousers' pocket. Next, he removed the pen from its case and placed it in his left shirt pocket.

Jean bowed, according to custom, and left the hidden room. He went down the stairs two steps at a time. Walking briskly, he departed the shop and hailed a taxi.

"International Airport please," Jean told the driver.

Autos, bicycles, carts and motor scooters seemed to battle for position in the horrendous traffic. As they passed the Erawan Shrine in central Bangkok, his driver took both hands from the steering wheel to wai the image of Brahma housed in the shrine. His driver placed his palms together as Jean had earlier at the clock shop. The driver showed respect as their custom dictated.

Jean never became used to this practice. He did not understand why major accidents did not take place. Perhaps their paying homage protected them. Jean's first lesson about Thai respect he learned from Preecha. Jean recalled the event in June 1954.

"We'll arrive at Ubon in about 15 minutes captain," the flight engineer yelled in the cargo compartment of Air America's C-46.

Without a headset, the engine noise from the aircraft was overwhelming. The flight engineer had to yell to make himself understood as wind whipped through their compartment. Because of a malfunction, the FE removed the cargo compartment's main door. This was the source of the wind.

Ubon, Thailand had a small airfield used by Air America. His flight originated at Vientiane, Laos with a short stop at Korat. The Korat stop was necessary to replenish the C-46's oil supply and repair the door. They were now inbound to Ubon for an overnight stay for maintenance. They would depart the next day for Bangkok.

Upon landing, the pilot taxied to a dimly lit hanger. From inside, a man exited with a lighted flashlight in each hand. He began giving taxi instructions via hand signals. He directed the pilot to a specified parking area and gave him the engines off signal.

As Jean exited the aircraft, the flight engineer, Bryan Keefland said, "Sir, our people will get your baggage. Go with the pilots to operations while I get to work on the magnetos."

"Sure thing," Jean replied and waited for the others.

From where he stood, Jean could see the pilot and copilot completing their after landing checks. They made some notations in the aircraft's logbook and exited the C-46.

As the pair approached Jean, the pilot, Billy Denfield, said, "Come along with us Jean. We'll get you some chow and a place for tonight."

With Denfield, the craft's copilot Sam Galfine took position on Jean's left and said, "It won't be the Hilton. Count on that captain."

He met both men after Lanny Briscoe arranged transport for him to Thailand. When the crew picked him up, they commented about their mission. The pilot told him that he must have friends in high places because they received a mission change to get him. They were flying Operation COGNAC, the evacuation of civilians from North Vietnam to South Vietnam following the signing of the Geneva Agreement. They were short aircraft and were really surprised when told to get Danjou.

"Meeting Briscoe in that Indian village had been one hell of surprise," Jean thought. "I wonder what he was really doing in that place."

Jean and the two pilots ate something that he had not been able to identify. It was quite spicy and tasted excellent. It was a stew-like combination poured over rice. Later, they left him at what appeared to be an Inn of some sort. He had a straw mat for a bed and a cushioned brick for a pillow. It wasn't too uncomfortable after the accommodations he shared in Laos with Briscoe. Still, he was restless and indigestion kept him awake. That's when he heard a commotion outside his room.

His quarters had a window for sake of calling it anything else. It was nothing more than a woven panel covering a rectangular hole in the building's side. By pushing out, he could raise it. A wooden pole, about five feet long, held it upright.

As he raised the cover, he saw an elderly man and woman hugging some bundles. They were on their knees screaming something in a Thai dialect that he did not recognize. Circling them were two young men laughing. One had a knife and kept making thrusts with its blade toward the woman. She gripped a black, lacquered box to her breast.

"You there, stop it," he yelled.

The pair of thugs looked in his direction. One grabbed his crotch with his had and made humping gestures with his hips toward Jean. The other one gave him the finger.

The elderly couple stared at him with pleading eyes. The punks continued their harassing motions. The one with the knife grabbed the lady's box but she held it tightly. He raised his knife as if to strike and screamed at her.

Jean put one hand on the window's edge and vaulted outside. He took the window cover's supporting pole with him. In one fluid motion, he was upon them. Putting his right foot forward, he took a wide stance. In an instant, he brought the pole back over his left shoulder and slammed it forward into the knife wielding attacker's temple. He began collapsing in place. Before he was on the ground, Jean placed his arms forward allowing the formidable pole to slide through his hands as he whirled. He stopped the pole's slide at its fullest length slightly before it struck the other man. Standing transfixed watching his comrade's downfall, he took the blow's full impact across his throat. He fell to his knees gripping his throat while gasping for air. The first attacker died instantly. The other gagged for a moment and then fell prostrate. He was dead within four minutes.

Jean turned to the old couple. He saw a gaping wound on the man's forearm. Blood gushed profusely over his cloths and onto the ground. His wife immediately dropped the box and tied a scarf tight around her companion's wound. Jean kneeled and forced him onto his back.

"You must remain still sir," Jean said.

"I know," the bleeding man answered.

Jean amazed at his reply, asked. "Do you speak French?"

"Fluently," he answered.

Turning to the woman, Jean heard her say, "So do I."

"Good, keep pressure on that wound while I get help," Jean directed.

Jean, barefoot, ran to the Inn's entrance and pounded on its entrance door. He saw light come on inside and he waited impatiently until a man opened the door. Jean grabbed his arm and pulled him around the corner. He pointed to the couple in the street. Recognizing the pair, the innkeeper ran to them. Satisfied they were okay, he ran into the Inn. The police arrive shortly afterwards. They arrested Jean and took him to a filthy cell where he remained overnight.

"You are one bad ass captain," Denfield said from outside Jean's cell.

Jean awoke to see the C-46 pilot standing with a policeman who was unlocking his cell. His jailer smiled and motioned that Jean leave his cell. He did so without hesitation.

"You will be needing these," Denfield said as he handed Jean his boots.

"Thanks," Jean said as he began donning them.

"In case you are interested, you are on your way to provincial court for this region. Killing a couple of folks is bad enough but a Frenchman without a passport, that spells trouble," Denfield commented.

Jean felt ridiculous in the courtroom. He wore the same fatigues he wore at Dien Bien Phu. He was unshaven and generally unkempt. A judge entered the room and everyone stood at the announcement of his entrance. He appeared solemn and serious as he sat behind his high rostrum. He lifted documents in front of him and began reading. Everyone in the courtroom sat.

At what Jean considered the defendant's table, he sat with a stranger. Numerous times, he tried to speak to him in English and French. He just shook his head that he did not understand.

After a few moments, the judge looked at Jean and said in flawless French, "You sir are most fortunate. The gentleman attacked is a revered person in our province. He is Praphat Kittikachorn whose brother is Prime Minister Thanom."

As soon as the judge made this announcement, the man at the table with him patted Jean's knee. Jean turned to him and received a wide grin and a whispered chuckle.

Continuing, the judge said, "The two persons attacking him were known Communist party thugs. Our national police have been trying to apprehend them for years without success. You sir, accomplished in a few moments that which I have wanted done for a considerable time. You have my appreciation. In light of these events, I rule as follows. You are released into the custody of Mr. Praphat Kittikachorn who will personally escort you to the French Embassy in Bangkok. You are to leave our country promptly, never to return without proper authorization. Does the prosecution have anything to add?"

From a table next to Jean's a man stood and said, "We concur your honor. Also, we recommend that all charges be dismissed and stricken from the record."

The judge quickly said, "So be it," and struck a blow with his gavel. He promptly stood and left the room.

Jean's attorney, who never said a word during the proceedings, hugged Jean and commenced putting papers in his brief case. Mr. Kittikachorn and his wife approached Jean's table.

He greeted Jean with a deep and prolonged bow of his head, which Jean promptly returned. Kittikachorn gave Jean's attorney a knowing look and both smiled.

"Come with me captain," Kittikachorn said. "I have transportation waiting. Your pilot friends had to leave because of pressing matters they could not ignore. They returned to Viet Nam after making repairs."

What few belongings Jean had were already loaded aboard the small sedan. He and Kittikachorn road in its back seat while his wife followed in another car. In front of the two sedans, a provincial police vehicle provided escort. As they crossed into the next region, another police car took the lead. This procedure took place all the way to Bangkok's airport. While traveling the long distance to Bangkok, Jean and Kittikachorn came to know one another.

"Captain, I have a familiar name by which you may address me. Kindly refer to me as Preecha," he told Jean.

Jean responded, "You can drop the rank and speak to me as Jean."

Preecha explained that he could never do that. It would be a gross insult to do so.

"Captain, my wife handles most of my family's financial matters. The box those two were trying to take contained rare gems belonging to my customers in that province. They were settings for watches that I was going to make for them," Preecha explained.

Continuing Preecha explained that Jean saved him from a vast dishonor. In addition, he saved his business. The cost to him of replacing the stolen gems would require that he borrow money from his family. He would lose considerable face by having to borrow. He would forever be in Jean's debt. If, in the future, he ever returned to Bangkok Jean was to contact him in advance. He could assure his not having difficulties with customs. In addition, he would be able to honor him as he should now but could not because of the judge's instructions.

At the airport, a first class reservation to Paris awaited Jean. He boarded never expecting to see Preecha again.

"Here I am back in Bangkok and legal," Jean mused while watching traffic stream past. "The American's are trying to accomplish what we couldn't. They have my hope for success."

Jean's taxi driver began maneuvering toward the baggage boys in front of the airport. Cars were triple parked resulting in a traffic jam. One narrow line was open on the left side.

Jean leaned forward and told his driver, "Do not stop here. Go around and continue to the far end of the outside lane. I will get out at the double gates."

His driver jerked his steering wheel hard to the left causing a car horn crescendo behind them. He cut into the outside lane and stayed close to the vehicle in front of them. He continually blew his horn. Breaking free of the bottleneck, he went to the far inside lane on their right. He stopped directly in front of the double gates. Jean paid his fare and gave a handsome tip. The driver smiled broadly and gave repeated nods of his head indicating his thanks. Jean watched him speed to the long line waiting for pickups of inbound passengers.

Lifting his one handbag, Jean went to the double gates. He pressed a button that summoned an airline official by ringing a bell inside an aircraft hanger. Within a few seconds, a door opened in the hanger's side from which an armed guard exited. He carried a clipboard and walked toward Jean.

Reaching inside his bag, Jean removed a wallet sized, credential holder. He held it open for the guard to inspect through openings in the chain-link fence. Neither of the two spoke while the guard inspected Jean's documentation against a list on his clipboard. Satisfied, the guard removed a key ring from his waist and unlocked the gate.

Jean entered and began a brisk walk toward the door that the guard had exited. Opening it, he stepped inside. Four Douglas C-47 aircraft were in various stages of assembly. Mechanics were busily working on them. The sounds of their tools echoed throughout the high ceiling supported by open steel beams. Fluorescent lights ran in long rows along overhead beams. To Jean's right, high sliding doors provided hanger access for large aircraft. To his left, windows and doors indicated two floors. Steel stairs provided access to doors on the second floor. Above the first door on the ground floor, a sign read "Air Asia."

Jean went to the Air Asia door and entered. Two rows of desks, four deep filled one side of the room. At each desk, Thai women were typing briskly and paying no heed to his entrance. Continuing forward, he stopped at a steel door with a small window. He looked through the window to see rows of steel lockers. Reaching to his left, he pressed a buzzer. From between the lockers, he saw Jim Belton approaching.

Belton, seeing Jean through the glass, increased his pace to the door. He unlocked and opened it for Jean to enter.

Once inside, Jean removed his pocket watch and opened it. It showed the time to be 18:30 hours. He was on time.

"Hi colonel, everyone's hear. I'll lockup while you join the guys," Belton said.

Jean was always amused to hear Belton talk. It seemed to take him forever to say anything. When he did, he exhibited a dialect peculiar to his home at Enterprise, Alabama. The group had a nickname for him. They referred to him as "peanut." Jean understood this to be a reference to an agricultural product in abundance where Belton lived.

Moving along a narrow path between benches dividing the lockers, Jean made his way to the room's rear. He arrived at another steel door that he promptly opened and went inside.

Six men turned to face him as soon as he was inside. They wore coverall, flight suits. There were no identifying markings on the garments. Usually, flight suits had leather patches on their fronts. The patches would contain a person's name, and often, their rank or title. These men's suits had a slight discoloration where patches once were. Everyone got to their feet when he entered.

"Be seated," Jean said as he went to a rostrum at the room's far end. "I apologize about the 30 minutes but it could not be helped."

"Briscoe here?" Jean asked.

One of the men answered, "Yes, he is. He went to calibrate a piece of equipment. Belton is going to get him."

"Good," Jean replied. "We have time. We'll wait for him before we get started.

Jean turned to a blackboard that ran across the wall behind him. At its top middle, a tube ran for four feet. From it, a cord with a metal ring attached, protruded. Jean grasped the ring and pulled it toward the blackboard's bottom rail. Attached to the ring was a topographic map showing the junctures of North Viet Nam, Laos and South Viet Nam. Southwest of these, the map showed Laos, Cambodia, and Thailand.

Reaching into his handbag, Jean removed a roll of plastic. He began unrolling it. As he did so, he attached two corners of the transparent plastic to grid line intersections on the map. Once completely unrolled, he attached two bottom corners. The plastic had no markings on it.

While Jean was smoothing the plastic sheet, the room's door opened. Jim Belton entered first, followed closely by Lanny Briscoe. Belton took a seat with the other six men while Briscoe continued walking toward Jean. He carried an OD metal case with silver latches with one hand. With the other, he held a handbag similar to Jean's. As the two met, Briscoe set his equipment on the floor. Briscoe took Jean's offered hand. While shaking hands, the two pulled close and rendered hearty slaps on each other's back.

"Damn glad you're with us on this," Briscoe said as he pulled away from Jean.

"Me too," Jean replied. "Why don't you get started."

"Right," Briscoe replied as he retrieved his handbag.

Briscoe opened the bag and removed a rolled, plastic sheet similar to the one Jean attached to the map. As Briscoe unrolled it, markings came into view.

Simultaneously, Jean began marking his map covering with a grease pencil. He made seven small Xs and three triangles. As he finished, he stepped aside as Briscoe approached.

Briscoe aligned his plastic sheet so that the markings on it overlaid Jean's grease penciled items.

Looking at Jean, Briscoe said, "I will hold this in place while you attach the corners. There are some thumb tacks in my bag."

After Jean pinned Briscoe's sheet to his, he took a seat with the others. Briscoe stepped behind the rostrum.

Looking at Belton, Briscoe asked. "Belton, you swept this place?"

"Yes sir," Belton answered. "There hasn't been another person in here but us since."

"Great," Briscoe replied as he looked at each person in the room. "You have been training for this for two years. It's time. Direct you attention to the chart please."

Briscoe positioned himself beside the altered map where everyone could see. He remained in easy reach of the chart. He picked up a pointer leaning against the blackboard. He pointed to the three triangles and explained, "First, observe the triangles. Any transmission of any sort passing thorough the indicated zones will be detectable. I don't care what frequency it is we can received it," Briscoe explained.

Continuing he said, "As you know from your training, if we can receive it we can decipher it. Today, in Geneva, representatives are meeting to try to work out a diplomatic solution to problems in Laos. Each day, the North Vietnamese contact Hanoi to coordinate their proposals with those of the USSR and the PRC. We must intercept, decipher, and report the contents to our people."

Briscoe set the pointer aside and returned to the rostrum. He retrieved the OD case he had when he entered. He released the silver latches and removed its cover.

Tilting the case so that all could see its instrumentation, he continued, "We must assure that our representatives in Geneva know the USSR, PRC and North Vietnamese daily position at the Geneva talks. We must assure that our representatives know before the USSR, PRC, and North Vietnamese representatives do. Our people will not be surprised about anything. That is our sole mission and we're going to accomplish it with this."

Briscoe held the device above his head to give the group a better view. He held it high momentarily and then placed it on the rostrum.

Looking at Belton, Briscoe said, "Jim get each man a set please."

Belton went to the room's rear where a six-foot long container sat. He opened it and removed a device identical to the one Briscoe held.

"Okay guys, I'm not a delivery service. Come get one," Belton directed.

Each person in flight suits filed by Belton; took a device from him; and, returned to their seats. Belton took one for him and went to his seat.

Briscoe continued, "The unit you hold is functional. They are not mockups like you used for training. These are integrated ARC 102 high frequency radios and Mark 55A6 decoder/encoder cryptographic units. Direct your attention to the yellow and black switch cover. Beneath the spring-loaded cover is a thermite activation switch. Set the switch to on and the entire device will melt in 15 seconds. Do not hold the unit while activating the switch. Ignition is instantaneous. If, for any reason, there is a possibility someone might capture the device, activate the switch. Any questions?"

One of the six men raised his hand. He was Barry Homesfeld from Indiana.

"Yes, Barry. What's your question?" Briscoe asked.

"Sir, I understand this team will be on station for three months. We're not commandos. Who will cover our butts while we're on station?" Homesfeld asked.

"Good question Barry. Let me cover one more item and Danjou will answer that for you," Briscoe advised.

Briscoe returned to the map and used the pointer to indicate the seven Xs and said, "These are dirt airstrips. They are under Hmong control. Air America will provide air support from these strips. They will use Dornier DO-28 short takeoff and land (STOL) aircraft. Once daily either Jean or I will board a Dornier and climb to 10,000 feet. Our Mark 55A6 units will interface with yours and retransmit collected data directly to Geneva via encoded Ultra High Frequency (UHF) radio. We will use one of the seven strips on a random basis. You will never know which one. That completes my part. Jean will you cover tactical please?"

Jean had watched Briscoe throughout his presentation. He marveled at the man he first met during World War II.

"Hell," he thought, "I still know so very little about him. The few days together at the Indian village after Dien Bien Phu didn't reveal a thing about him. What in the world could he have been doing in that wilderness? He definitely knows his way around Air America that I am sure connects him to the CIA or NSA. If I had to guess, I would think the NSA. They are the Crypto people and he sure knows that. I wonder what he did there after he got me out?"

"He most certainly is not a military man. However, he has a mind like a steel trap. He is one smart man. He got me hooked up with the Air America people and on my way to France. Otherwise, I could have been stuck in that jungle for ages. As it was, the Legion figured I was among the captured or dead after that battle."

"What's remarkable is how he got me on this assignment in the first place. He has a connection that's for sure. I guess the intelligence people in Paris figured I could learn what the Americans are up to but I don't feel like a spy. Guess I am though."

Jean stepped behind the rostrum as Briscoe took a seat. He made eye contact with each of the six men before speaking.

"You men may not be commandos but you are not choir boys either. The six months we spent together, you learned a lot. I would gladly have any one of you covering my back on any operation. With that said, I realize your mission is not as a combatant. Each man will have a Police Aerial Reinforcement Unit (PARU) assigned to you. These are elite teams. They were originally used to reinforce widely dispersed military units that found themselves in trouble. They are tough and will protect you while on station," Jean explained.

Continuing Jean said, "Each of you will go to one of the airstrips by Dornier aircraft. You will arrive during daylight. A platoon of Vang Pao's Hmong will secure your gear near the strip. Vang Pao is the leader of the Hmong resistance in Laos. He gave me his personal assurance that your mission is a priority so don't hesitate using his people."

"That night the PARU teams will jump into your area. They will travel with you to your designated monitoring zone. While you are on station, they will patrol to intercept any Pathet Lao forces. Remember this, when they say go, go. They will leave without you so trust these guys. They are good. If you have no questions, your gear is in your lockers. Get it on and assemble here in two hours. Our first leg out of Bangkok will be by C-46 to Ubon. After that, it will be Doniers. Anything else Lanny?"

"Yes," Briscoe answered. "Leave your coding units in the case at the room's rear. We will redistribute them at Ubon. That's all."

"Okay, you are dismissed," Danjou said.

With only Danjou and Briscoe remaining in the room, Danjou asked Briscoe. "What were you at that village for in 1954?"

"Jean, I'm sorry. I cannot say. I am sure you understand," Briscoe answered.

"Just curious," Jean responded as he fondled the cylinder in his pocket. "We better get our gear. You go ahead. I will guard the units until you send Belton to relieve me. I'll go change then."

Jean watched Briscoe leave. He recalled Briscoe waving to him from that dirt strip in the Laotian Mountains. Because of Briscoe, he arrived in France without a scratch. He was able to continue his career and didn't spend time in a POW camp or suffer that deadly march from Dien Bien Phu.

However, Jean recalled his being on leave when he, again, had to fight a war. He received a telephone call that would propel him into another bloodbath. It was November 1, 1954, All Saints' Day that he received word. He had been in France for one month after his escape from Southeast Asia.

"Jean darling, it is for you. I think he said he was Major Prudhomme. He insists that it is urgent," Monique said.

Jean, nude in bed, slipped into a light robe. He could detect the aroma of Monique's culinary expertise at work in the kitchen. He sat on the bed's edge and lifted the telephone's handset, he said, "Danjou."

"Jean, this is Prudhomme. You must report to headquarters immediately. The Front de Liberation Nationale (FLN) guerrillas have launched attacks throughout

Algeria. You must report for duty now," Prudhomme squeaked in his adolescent voice.

"I am on my first leave in three years damn it. I am sure our forces can handle this without me for two weeks," Jean answered, his voice reeking of venom.

Prudhomme replied excitedly, "This is not a local skirmish. The maquisards (guerillas) have hit military installations, police posts, warehouses, communications facilities and public utilities. They are making continued broadcasts from Cairo. They're making a proclamation for Muslims in Algeria to join in a national struggle for restoration of the Algerian State. They are inciting revolt within the framework of the principles of Islam."

While listing to Prudhomme's ranting, Monique sat a steaming demitasse filled with rich, black coffee on the nightstand. With it, she provided fresh baked croissants and orange marmalade. She sat close beside Jean and began applying marmalade to a croissant. It was difficult for Jean to concentrate on Prudhomme's whining.

With what attention he could muster, he said to Prudhomme, "Look, I am staying here until I hear something official. Calm down. I will call day after tomorrow. I have to go."

Jean placed the handset in its cradle and turned to Monique. He slipped one hand inside her transparent gown and the other on her back as he pulled her to him. They descended to the bed and the telephone rang again.

"Don't answer it," Monique said, her voice husky with passion.

She moaned as Jean lifted the handset and said with impatience, "Day after tomorrow, Prudhomme, day after tomorrow."

"No Major Danjou, now. This is Colonel Broussard. I expect you in no less than two hours. Understand?" Colonel Broussard stated emphatically.

"I am sorry sir. I thought you were someone else. I am on my way," Jean answered.

Jean saw parallels between Algeria and Viet Nam. France invaded Algeria in 1830 and took control of the country. Over the years, colonists moved to the country and seized prized land. Civil servants established a bureaucracy that held in check any hope of freedom for the Muslims. Colonists, known as Colons held considerable political and financial power.

Jean deployed to Algiers in late 1954 and served a three-year tour. While there, he enforced his country's laws. Thousands died at the military's hands. He took no pride in it. While there, his skills became evident to senior officers and they recommended him for France's prestigious War College. Few Majors ever attend this stepping stone to higher rank. While in attendance, in 1958, they promoted him to colonel. If he continued performing as he had, many said he would receive an early promotion to general. His one fault was failing to court the politicians needed to gain favor.

His next assignment was perfect to enhance a possible promotion to general. Jean graduated first in his class at the War College. France's Defense Minister personally selected him for his staff. It was the type of assignment that Jean avoided. However, he could not get out of this one. It was during this assignment that Colonel Prudhomme made a major mistake.

Prudhomme used his political shrewdness to gain promotion to colonel. Always a sneaky one, he was not to be trusted. His ego was his downfall. Jean saw it coming during November 1961 when Prudhomme contacted him.

"Jean join us," Prudhomme said. "France needs to rid itself of de Gaulle. We can see that he goes. France despises his regime. There are forces afoot in Algeria that will bring him down by force."

Jean had heard rumors of an Organisation de l'Armee Secrete (OAS). It was a secret organization in league with elements of the French Foreign Legion in Algeria. He had no idea that Prudhomme was an essential player.

"Be damned glad this is a secure line Prudhomme. One whiff of this and you are a dead man. You are in for a big fall. I recommend you detach yourself from the OAS as soon as possible," Jean told him.

Prudhomme realized he had made a major judgment error by letting Jean know about the OAS. He never contacted Jean again. However, Jean did not forget the mutinous talk. He immediately alerted the intelligence arm of the minister's office that got word to de Gaulle. He received word to report to de Gaulle.

"Sir, I know there is going to be a major insurrection. I simply do not know when. Intel knows about it and I suggest they get an operative into Algeria's Legion headquarters," Jean recommended.

"Danjou, you are going to be that operative," de Gaulle said.

"Sir, that will not work. Prudhomme knows where I stand on this. He will make sure I never get close to anything to do with the OAS."

"Sadly, I must concur. You form a team to infiltrate. They will report to you as their controller. Pick your best men for this. Our nation is at stake. There are those who believe they would invade France," de Gaulle stated.

Jean sent his men and they worked as moles throughout Algerian Legion units. In late March of 1961, Jean received a report that an insurrection would take place in April. Jean went to de Gaulle and received permission to eliminate Prudhomme along with nine other conspirators.

As reported, an insurrection took place in April. Panic swept through Paris because of a report of an impending invasion. Known as "The General's Putsch," the insurrection fell after four days. Early warning allowed de Gaulle to garner support from the air force and regular army units.

"It's done sir," Jean reported to de Gaulle.

"All of them?" de Gaulle asked.

"No sir but the main ones. Prudhomme went first. It appeared because of fighting in the street. No one knows that my operative eliminated him. Three others died the same way. We have evidence to court martial the remainder," Jean explained.

"I am sending you on a special mission. You do not need to be in one of the Legion units for a couple of years. Intel thinks that they could learn that you were in charge of this operation. Report to intelligence. They have details on this mission. You will be returning to Southeast Asia," de Gaulle directed.

Jean reported to France's embassy in Bangkok, Thailand, as Chief Military Attaché. Everyone knew he was a spy.

After settling into his new job, he contacted Preecha. It had been seven years since they parted. Now, he was here officially with proper papers. He did not have to contact Preecha in advance because he did not need special treatment at customs. Nonetheless, Thailand officials knew who he was. The presiding judge at his trial placed his record on file with customs. As soon as he arrived, they took three hours verifying his credentials.

"We know what you are doing here and we do not care," Preecha told him. "You are anticommunist and that's what counts. Our little country has few secrets of value to France. However, it is important that you be here to help stave off the Communists. If you ever need my skills, they are at your disposal."

Soon Briscoe contacted him. He was on record as being an accountant for CAT. CAT still flew commercial missions throughout Southeast Asia. Their Air America arm handled the covert stuff. Being an accountant fit Briscoe perfectly. He looked the part. Few would suspect that he was a United States operative.

Briscoe had him flown to a base in southern Thailand to train crews for their current mission. Jean eliminated 90 percent of attendees to his training course. For one reason or another, nine out of ten did not complete the course. The six going with them on this mission were excellent graduates.

"You get bored sitting here?" Briscoe asked as he entered the room. "Go get ready. Have two men come by here to get this equipment container. One man cannot carry that thing."

Briscoe simply did not look military in his tiger striped fatigues. His appearance was exactly what he was, a civilian dressed like a person in the military.

"Sure will. It won't take me long. I will come back with them," Jean said as he departed.

At Ubon, they drew weapons and ammunition. Each man departed for his assigned sector on Doniers. Danjou and Briscoe flew to the southernmost of the seven airstrips. The nearby Hmong villagers were staunch followers of Vang Pao. The other six dirt airstrips followed a line 25 miles south of the Plain of Jars. According to intelligence reports, over 10,000 North Vietnamese and Pathet Lao forces occupied the Plain.

Sitting on the edge of a hammock, Briscoe asked. "These surroundings look familiar Jean?"

"I would say so. North Viet Nam is only a few clicks (kilometers) northeast. If the word gets out that we are here, we are in big trouble," Jean replied.

Briscoe got up and walked to the hut's opening to the outside. He glanced around the area. There were a few armed Hmong around a small fire; the remainder was women and children. He returned to where Jean sat at a folding table.

Briscoe sat across from him and said, "I figure you know by now we are not here to intercept Geneva information. Aren't you interested to know why?"

"I know why," Jean answered. "This entire thing is a cover to monitor radio traffic on North Vietnamese units inside Laos. In addition, you will gladly take note of what is going on with supply efforts towards South Viet Nam."

"That's correct," Briscoe answered. "Our people doing the scans don't know that just as our decoders don't know the difference. They accept any transmissions and retransmit them to listening stations. That's where the actual decoding takes place. Our president will know in detail, around the clock, what's happening."

Continuing Briscoe explained, "Last year in June, President Kennedy met in Vienna with Nikita Khrushechev. There was a major confrontation underway between Laos and the North Vietnamese. Kennedy was behind the power curve because Khrushechev knew details and he didn't. He swore that would never happen again."

Jean reached into his pocket and removed an OD cylinder about the size of a lipstick tube. He rolled it across the table toward Jean.

As Briscoe grabbed it to keep it from rolling off their table, Jean asked. "Does that look familiar to you?"

"Not really," Briscoe replied. "What is it?"

"What a poker face," Jean thought. "He didn't even blink. I know damned well he had them at that village in 1954."

Watching Briscoe for any sign of recognition, Jean answered, "It's supposed to be a coding device for American navigational beacons. That one is a dummy," Jean explained.

Briscoe held the device toward Jean and said, "Here, I have no use for it. Why are you carrying it?"

"Hold onto it for me. If we separate and you make it to Bangkok, give it to my assistant at the embassy. I told him that if he ever received it to follow any instructions the carrier might have," Jean explained.

Briscoe flipped the device in the air and caught it during its descent. He placed it in his pocket.

"Glad to help. What do you want me to say?" He asked.

"Until I say otherwise, just let them know where I am," Jean answered.

"He is a cold fish. I saw three fall from his pack in 1954. He has to miss them and wonder where they went. Now he knows. I wonder how long he's going to play this game," Jean contemplated.

An hour after sundown, Briscoe received reports that PARU teams were in place with their individual operatives. They reported considerable radio traffic. Briscoe went to where Jean was napping in a hammock. Briscoe's intent was to shake Jean's foot to awaken him.

As he reached for Jean's boot, Jean said, "Not needed. I am awake. What's up?"

"Our Doniers landed slightly before sunset. They are waiting for us," Briscoe said.

"Waiting for us, Doniers? Why do we need more than one?" Jean asked.

"There is a change in plans. Both of us will simultaneously receive and retransmit data. You take the area above strip six. I will remain above this one. If for any reason one of us should go down, the other should get through. In addition, the Dornier pilots won't attempt landings here after dark. These strips are too bad and there's no feasible lighting. We'll both return to Ubon tonight," Briscoe explained.

While Briscoe was explaining the situation, Jean strapped a survival knife to his right thigh. He slipped into his survival vest and checked his emergency radio. He gave a close look at his nine-millimeter Luger and made sure a round was in its chamber. Next, he retrieved his sawed-off, 12-gauge shotgun. He checked its ten round magazine to assure it was full. He looked in his ammo belt for 11 more shells.

Satisfied, Jean said, "Let's do it."

The takeoff for Briscoe was nightmarish because of inexperience. Their takeoff run was downhill into total darkness. He felt his rear leave his seat slightly as his pilot stopped ascending at 10,000 feet. He plugged his headset into the Mark55 device and immediately started receiving signals that sounded like static. He turned up the gain while watching an indicator light change from red to green. He next pressed the retransmit toggle switch to its on position and pressed a retransmit button, a red light began glowing. Adjusting a gain control knob, he watched it glow green.

Briscoe thought, "Somewhere in the South China Sea, a nondescript trawler is plowing through swell after swell. Inside, an operator is monitoring two green lights and two signal strength gauges. Each represents a transmission from Jean and him. Beyond the trawler, over the Pacific, a Boeing 707 crammed with electronics flew a race track pattern. This will be a lot easier when their satellite becomes operational. That could be any day now."

Slightly before dawn, Briscoe watched Jean's Dornier taxi to a halt at Ubon. Jean exited first followed closely by his pilot. The two walked to where Briscoe waited.

Jean said, "I want you to meet my pilot. He knows where we can get some hot breakfast. Lanny Briscoe this is Frederick Earling. Fred, Lanny."

Briscoe extended his hand and said, "The pilot I flew with went to the john. He will be with us in a minute. Pleasure to meet you Fred."

"The pleasures all mine mate," Frederick said.

Chapter Twenty Six

December 1962

For what is love itself, for the one we love best?
—an enfolding of immeasurable cares which yet are
better than any joys outside our love.
George Eliot (1819–80), English novelist, editor. Daniel Deronda,
bk. 8, ch. 69 (1876).

"I'm so sorry dear. It is a terrible lot I have given you in life. This constant moving from place to place must be a horrendous burden," Frederick said.

"It's not so bad," Vanessa replied. "I like Thailand much better than being in Laos. There seems to be an inability to decide who is in charge in Laos. It was a fearful situation in Vientiane. Our landlady told me about Kong Le taking over Vientiane before I arrived. He's Communist. Right?"

Frederick walked from their hotel room's picture window to where Vanessa sat on a sofa. His black tie hung loosely below his unbuttoned shirt collar. He still wore his CAT pilot's uniform with its white, short-sleeved shirt and dark blue trousers. His epaulettes showed his rank of captain with gold stripes. Sitting beside Vanessa, he propped his stocking feet on their coffee table while putting his right arm around her shoulders. Gently, he pulled her to him so that she rested her head on his right shoulder.

Staring at the window, he answered, "Kong Le claims to be neutral. Yet, he and his forces are on the Plain of Jars, in Northeastern Laos, receiving aerial resupply by the Soviet Union. With him, he has an estimated 10,000 Pathet Lao and North Vietnamese forces. He continues to fight Laos' government although a neutrality agreement is in place. I cannot accept his neutrality claims. If he's neutral then Hitler was a pacifist."

Lowering her left shoulder, Vanessa pushed it farther under Frederick's right arm to get closer. She wore a dainty chemise that she allowed to creep farther above her knees.

She turned her head and looked up at Frederick and said, "I have difficulties following the names. I hear about Souvanna Phouma one day and next day, Phoumi. I get lost."

Leaning his head down, Frederick placed his nose in Vanessa's hair and inhaled. He always liked her faint aroma of jasmine.

He responded, "Souvanna Phouma is the main reason we are in Udon Thani. The world is giving the Laotian politicians an opportunity to abide by their neutrality agreement they signed in Geneva this past June. That's the main reason we had to come to Thailand."

"I know that but you're still flying missions in Laos," Vanessa noted.

"Of course, the Laotian government contracted with CAT for commercial services. There's nothing to keep them from hiring us," Frederick explained. "The first neutrality agreement cost a lot of good pilots their jobs for awhile. CAT and Air America had to lay off a lot of crews."

"Well, they kept you because you are their best pilot," Vanessa answered with a giggle as she kissed Frederick's neck.

Vanessa's gesture did not go unnoticed. Frederick turned more to his right to face Vanessa. He kissed her full on her lips with a passion that never wavered.

Later, they lay in bed snuggled close basking in each other's nearness and contentment. Vanessa curled Frederick's chest hairs with her index finger.

With her gaze fixed on her efforts, she casually asked. "Hon, what were those two men doing in Laos last June?"

Frederick leaned his head back with a knowing smile on his lips and commented, "Still trying to weasel information aren't you ol' girl?"

"Don't ol' girl me. You're no wee bit of a lad yourself," Vanessa replied while extending her lower lip in a feigned pout.

Frederick laughed loudly and asked. "How can you say that after the last hour?"

With a wide smile, she responded, "They called you Fred."

"Oh, you mean the two chaps, Lanny and Jean?" He replied. "You know Yanks. They will brutalize the King's English to appear non-colonial."

"That's blarney. A good friend of mine, Regina Phillips was from Boston. Don't you remember her the first time we met? Americans do that for people they know well. Regina used to refer to me as Van. Besides, the Frenchman also called you Fred," Vanessa argued mildly.

"Darling, we spent some time together on the job and that's all I'm telling you," Frederick stated firmly.

"Well, I saw the American at the market yesterday," Vanessa stated as if revealing a major secret.

"What did he have to say?" Frederick asked as he rolled onto his side.

"Got your attention didn't I. We didn't speak. I don't think he saw me," Vanessa answered.

Continuing, Vanessa explained seeing many Caucasian men at the market, she said, "There are too many of them to be tourists. Most do not have wives with them. They are not CAT people. I know all the CAT wives. I am a thinking that they are doing dirty business."

"Dear, think what you like but I am not going to succumb to your interrogation," Frederick stated.

Vanessa leaped upon Frederick straddling his waist. She placed a hand on each shoulder and pushed him against the bed. Putting her face close to his, her red hair fell brushing his cheeks.

"Interrogation is it? I will show you interrogation. What is it you will be wanting for Christmas?" Vanessa asked while moving her nose back and forth across Frederick's.

"You are right. It is only one week from today. Hum, I wonder what Saint Nicolas might bring you? As for me, I have you." He stated with a sly smile.

Vanessa grabbed Frederick's ribs with both hands and began tickling him. He rolled from side to side laughing.

Breathless, she fell forward, placing her full weight upon him and said, "You are a devil of a man Frederick Earling. And, it is my failing that I love the likes of you."

Placing his arms beneath hers, Frederick spread his hands on her shoulder blades. He placed his lips next to her right ear.

Whispering, he told her, "You, my bonnie Irish lass, stole my heart when I was weak and injured. You should be ashamed Mrs. Frederick McBeal Earling for taking advantage of a cripple."

After their loving, they lay entwined atop their sheets as an overhead fan made slow sweeps stirring Thailand's humid air.

Frederick left before dawn as usual. Vanessa awoke famished and searched for something from the previous day. Her search failed. A quick look at the clock revealed she could still get breakfast in their hotel's dining room. She didn't particularly care for eating there but there was little choice, at least for now.

After a quick shower, she dressed and was at the dining room's entrance in time for breakfast. She waited for someone to seat her. Finally, she gave up and selected a table with an outside view.

Eventually a waiter appeared with a menu. She did not need it for she knew their fare by heart.

"I will have the fruit delight platter. Two slices of dry toast and coffee now please," she said.

Her waiter bowed from his waist and backed away while mumbling something she did not understand. He returned shortly with what they considered coffee. Its consistency was much like that of molasses. She finished filling the coffee cup with water. It was the only way she could drink it. While stirring the mix, she saw the hotel manager enter the dining area. He stood still looking around the deserted room until seeing her. He gave a broad smile of recognition and walked toward her.

"Good morning, Mrs. Earling. I hope everything is satisfactory," he said.

"Everything is just fine. Thank you," Vanessa replied.

He reached inside his jacket and removed an envelope and said, "This came for Captain Earling early this morning. The front desk did not see him leave so I held it for you."

He handed her the letter and excused himself. She saw that Frederick's name appeared as addressee. Its postmark was from The Royal Academy of Medicine, Bristol, England.

"What could it be?" She wondered, while placing it in her purse.

Her fruit platter arrived with her side order of dry toast. She asked for more coffee. She could not stop staring at the envelope.

"Oh, he won't mind if I open it. At least, I do not think he will," Vanessa thought with misgivings.

Still staring anxiously at the envelope protruding from her purse, she thought, "He will be home before dark today. I will give it to him then."

Once she tasted a fresh mango, she realized how hungry she really was. She consumed everything on her plate and began eating her dry toast. She did so in a way that Frederick never approved. She dipped it in her coffer before eating it. She always told him that it was the shanty Irish in her.

When finished, she left a tip for the waiter. She passed the cashier without stopping. Frederick had their meals charged to their room. Air America was paying for their food and lodging until they found adequate housing.

Inside their room, Vanessa went to one of their few possessions. It was Frederick's Akai, reel to reel, crossfield-head, tape player. For amplification, Frederick bought a Pioneer stereo receiver. He also bought and installed four speakers, two for the living room and two for the bedroom. With a large tape reel, recorded at slow speed, they had eight hours of continuous music on each side. When a tape reached its end, the reel automatically reversed. This stereo system was one of Frederick's favorite toys.

It seemed that each pilot tried to outdo the others with their electronic gadgets. They stalked camera shops and audio stores trying to find an "ultimate system." No one ever did because new models with enhancements were always arriving in the stores. In any case, she liked the music when she was home alone. She turned the amplifier on and set the volume. Next, she pushed down on the toggle switch on the tape player. The twin gain indicators immediately began moving as one of their favorite songs began playing. "Sentimental Journey" always brought happy memories of their stolen moments during the Battle of Britain.

She closed the door to their bedroom. An unmade bed always irritated her and she did not want to look at it.

"Maid service will change the linen soon," she thought.

Removing her shoes, she sat by their window to watch the street leading to the market. Like Laos, the street was a teaming sea of humanity. She enjoyed watching streets filled with people and vehicles.

"Where are they going in such a hurry," she reflected. "Surely, nothing is so important to cause them to push and shove like they do. These are a graceful, gentle people until they get in traffic."

In the distance, almost on the horizon, she saw a black speck in the sky. It grew larger rapidly and soon there were two black objects.

"What can they be?" She wondered, as they became larger still. "They are moving so fast."

In a few seconds, she discerned that they were airplanes, fast ones. They passed directly overhead and she had time to see that they bore camouflaged paint and America markings.

"Oh my God," she said aloud as two engine blasts struck milliseconds apart.

Windows shook and dishes fell from shelves. She cringed, thinking that the ceiling might fall.

"Mother of God, what are they doing here?" She thought as she saw two more specks approaching.

This pair made a steep climb slightly before reaching the hotel. She could see moisture curling from their wing tips as they began their ascent. When the craft engaged their afterburners, their rate of ascent increased rapidly. Again, the building shook from the roar.

Vanessa pressed her hands over her ears. She held them in place until she could not feel any vibrations. Taking them away, she heard the final chorus of "Sentimental Journey."

She went to the sofa and sat on the end next to a table lamp. She removed the handset from a telephone sitting on the table. She dialed the number of her close friend Grendel Faverson.

"Yah," Grendel answered.

"Grendel, this is Vanessa. Did you see those planes?" She asked.

"Yah, they were so close to the ground. Were they American?" Grendel asked, her Dutch accent very strong.

"They had American markings so I guess they were American. I thought they were going to hit our hotel. Has Ludwig mentioned anything about American fighters coming here?" Vanessa inquired.

"Never," she replied. "Oh, by the way, are you going to market today? If so, I will meet you at the melon cart," Grendel explained.

"Yes, I will meet you in 15 minutes. Bye now," Vanessa responded.

"Bye," Grendel said just before Vanessa put the handset onto its cradle.

Rushing into the bathroom, she began brushing her hair. She reached for her purse to get lipstick and Frederick's letter was in the way.

"I don't have time for this now," she muttered as she put it on the coffee table and returned to the bathroom.

Vanessa applied her lipstick in four easy strokes and pressed her lips while curling them inward. Smiling in the mirror, she was pleased with the result. She closed the bathroom door and looked at her image in a full-length mirror on it. She turned to see her back while looking over her right shoulder. She did the same over her left shoulder. Her dress was unwrinkled.

Satisfied she reached for her purse when there was a knock at the door.

"Linen service," a voice said.

"Wouldn't you know it. I get ready to go somewhere and they show up," she grumbled.

"Just a minute," she answered as she went to turn off the tape player.

As she was reaching for the toggle switch, she heard a key enter her door and its knob rattle.

"Damn," she thought as she turned off the player. "At least they could wait until I get there."

She turned to go to the door when she heard a soft popping sound. Immediately, she felt as if someone had hit her in the chest with a brick. She began sinking to her knees despite her every effort. While on her knees, she saw a person standing in her doorway. The individual wore a ski mask and she could see oriental eyes. She could not tell if the person was a man or a woman. There was another popping sound and she fell sideways into darkness.

Frederick applied 20 degrees of flaps and reduced power. With a slight touch of left pedal, he turned his steering to his left and watched the black ball on his aircraft's instrument panel remain centered. On baseleg of his landing pattern, he felt his descent begin. He rolled his wings level when 90 degrees left of his downwind leg. He repeated his turn procedure to align his craft with the runway. Sensing that he was slightly short of his intended landing point, he gently nudged his throttles for more power. His plane responded perfectly.

"CAT 459, you are cleared for a full stop runway 32 right," Udon Thani's tower operator said.

"CAT 459, roger," Frederick acknowledged.

He watched the runways over-run pass beneath him. Ahead, he saw white stripes rapidly approaching. His sight picture and airspeed were excellent. Upon crossing the over-run's juncture with 32 right's runway, he reduced power and raised his aircraft's nose ever so slightly. He felt his forward gear touch following by his tail wheel. He heard a minute squeak as they touched the runway. He reduced power for taxi speed and touched his toe brakes.

"CAT 459, turn right next intersection. You are cleared to CAT parking," the tower operator advised.

"CAT 459, roger," he answered.

Frederick looked toward the CAT parking area and saw Ray Wilouby holding signal flags straight above his head. Ray was one of CAT's crew chiefs. He had a certification for engines and airframes. Most of his experience he got in the military but he did an excellent job for CAT. Frederick followed yellow taxi markers toward Ray. Ray guided him into position and gave him the signal to cut his engine. Next, Ray grabbed some wooden blocks and placed them on both sides of each landing gear.

After completing entries in the logbook, he left the aircraft and went directly to CAT operations. Inside he saw Roger Wilcox at their radar screen.

"Hey Roger do you see any fast movers?" Frederick asked.

"Not now but I did about an hour ago. Why?" Roger asked while still looking at the radar screen.

"I need to file a near miss report," Frederick responded.

Roger slowly stood upright and turned to face Frederick and said, "You know there's no such thing in Thailand."

Roger had been with CAT for six years and knew Frederick well. Something was decidedly wrong. He could tell by Frederick's voice and body language.

"You can bet the United States Air Force does," Frederick exclaimed. "I want the butts off four of their people."

Roger became quite concerned because Frederick kept a cool head. Seldom did he complain unless something was strongly amiss. He walked to the counter separating them and took a clipboard off the wall.

Roger handed it toward Frederick and said, "Put down the details and I will see if I can find where they came from to get in our control zone. Be sure to include their tail numbers," Roger explained.

"You got it," Frederick replied.

While his attention was on details of his near miss, he did not see Ludwig Faverson enter operations. Ludwig approach from Frederick's rear and stood beside him at the counter. He put his arm around Frederick's shoulders.

Frederick looked up and turned to face him.

With a wide smile, he asked. "My friend, when are we going to get some more of Grendel's pot roast?"

"Anytime you want," Faverson answered rather solemnly.

Frederick, with one look, sensed dread in Faverson's eyes.

"What?" Frederick asked anxiously.

"It's best that we speak outside," Faverson suggested.

Hesitantly, Frederick said, "Roger, be sure and let me know about those fast movers."

Faverson lead the way outside with Frederick close behind. When he figured they were out of hearing distance of anyone, he stopped.

Frederick immediately saw his friend's eyes begin to mist and his chin knot and trembled, as he spoke, "I have bad news. Vanessa is severely injured. She's on her way to Bangkok as we speak. I am so sorry. Grendel is with her."

"How? When? Was it a traffic accident?" Frederick asked with a deepening concern.

Faverson had to take time to regain his composure. His throat seemed locked and his words were difficult to muster.

"Someone shot her. Grendel found her at your hotel. She has lost a lot of blood. You barely missed her departure for Bangkok. She has two nurses and a doctor with her. Oh Frederick, I am so awfully sorry," Faverson explained as his voice trembled at his words.

"Shot, who in God's name would shoot Vanessa?" Frederick cried. "God's blood she never harmed anyone. Perhaps a damned thief?"

Not being able to answer Frederick's questions caused Faverson to experience a deep sympathy. He clutched Frederick to him.

"Let's go," he said. "There's a C-130 on run-up now. We need to get to Bangkok," Faverson said gently as he pulled at Frederick to follow.

Frederick stumbled along with Faverson pulling his sleeve. He was in a dazed like state unable to comprehend. As soon as the two walked up the C-130's ramp, the aircraft began to taxi. The ship's loadmaster helped strap Frederick into his nylon-webbed seat. Next, he gave Faverson a headset that he plugged into an audio jack. He would be able to communicate with the crew.

"This will be a short flight. We should be at Bangkok in 20 minutes. There's a car waiting on the ramp. The latest word about Vanessa is that she is in surgery. The doctors have not announced a prognosis. She's listed as critical," the ship's first officer explained.

"Thanks," Faverson answered.

Looking at Frederick, Faverson thought, "I've never seen him like this. We have flown into some bad shit and he was always the cool one. He's really taking this hard. Hell, so would I if it was Grendel."

Leaning close to Frederick, Faverson cupped a hand around Frederick's left ear. The C-130's four engines created a roar and this was necessary for Frederick to hear. He relayed the first officer's message. Frederick only blinked. His facial expression never changed. He continued to stare straight ahead.

There was a slight buffeting as the aircraft's flaps extended. This was the first indication of their nearing Bangkok. Another mild jolt occurred as its landing gear went into a down position. It was as if someone slapped Frederick's face. He immediately became animated. One moment he stared out a window and the next he gave Faverson a pleading look. As soon as the wheels touched, he began unbuckling his seat belt. While taxiing, the pilot let the ramp down to its half-opened position. When stopped he lowered it to the ramp and a company sedan stopped near it. Frederick ran to the vehicle and began yelling at the driver as he entered.

"Get this damned thing moving," he yelled.

As soon as Faverson's door closed, the sedan driver pressed the accelerator to the floor. A pale, bluish smoke appeared at its rear tires and an ear-piercing squeal erupted. With emergency lights flashing, they exited the airport's gate and raced to Bangkok's Royal Medical Center.

Subduing Frederick was no easy chore. His agitated state was so high that he was almost unmanageable. His first frustration was trying to make medical staff members understand what he wanted. They would shake their heads indicating they did not speak English. Finally, he found the operating room doors. He started through them when Faverson brought him under control from behind.

Faverson put his right arm around Frederick's neck. With his left hand, he grabbed his right one. He placed his right knee behind Frederick's and pulled Frederick's torso rearward. He went to the floor quickly where Faverson sat on his chest.

"No, no, no," Faverson yelled. "You are staying here. You cannot go in and disturb her surgeons. You could endanger her so stop it."

Frederick visibly relaxed. Finally, he asked to stand. He insisted that he was fine and would remain in the waiting area.

Faverson arose from Frederick's chest. He extended his hand to help Frederick get to his feet. Frederick's push combined with Faverson's pull brought him up quickly.

"I say there Faverson, that's a fine chap. I'm sorry for my behavior. I do sincerely hope you understand," Frederick said with sincerity.

To Frederick's chagrin, he often lapsed into his home's accent when disturbed. Faverson had seen this in the past and didn't mind how he talked. While they spoke, swinging doors to the operating room opened. An oriental man, wearing a pale green surgical gown emerged.

He loosened his surgical mask and asked. "Are either of you gentlemen Frederick?"

"I am," Frederick answered hurriedly.

"I am Doctor Sarrandnak. We need to speak," he said gesturing for Faverson to leave.

Sarrandnak led Frederick to the OR waiting area. He asked him to have a seat, which he promptly did. Sarrandnak sat beside him with no show of emotion.

"Sir, your wife is still in critical condition. She is in recovery. I removed two bullets, one from her abdomen and the other from her left shoulder. The shoulder wound was not a problem like the other one. The bullet did considerable damage to her liver and spleen. I removed her spleen and repaired her liver. We will know within 24 hours what the outcome will be," Sarrandnak explained.

"When can I see her?" Frederick begged more than asked.

Sarrandnak appeared to give this question considerable thought and answered, "In a few hours, if there are no complications."

As they talked, two Asian men entered the waiting area. They remained at a discreet distance until the two finished speaking and Dr. Sarrandnak appeared to be leaving. They stopped the doctor, spoke with him a few moments, and then approached Frederick.

Bowing their heads deeply, they greeting him and he returned the gesture. The older of the two completed an introduction and showed his credentials. He was from the Royal Thai Police. He was the lead investigator.

"Sir, I assure you that we will bring to justice the person or persons who did this terrible thing. It is extremely important that we speak with your wife as soon as possible. We will wait until you see her but then we must visit with her. We hope you understand the need," he explained.

"Sure I understand," Frederick replied. "However, you must wait until the doctor says it is alright."

Excusing themselves, the two detectives left Frederick alone with his grief. He looked about for Ludwig but he could not find him. Finally, at a nurse's station, he was able to communicate his desire for a chapel. One of them showed him the entrance to a small room. Ludwig was inside praying.

"This is a catholic chapel," he thought. "I don't care I need help."

A single praying bench sat before a crucifix on the wall. On each side, and lower, two statues stood on pedestals. One was Mary and the other Joseph. To the right, a bank of candles stood. Some were burning while most were not. He was of a strong Protestant belief but that did not matter now. He knew enough to light a candle and join Ludwig in prayer.

Vanessa existed in a world of sounds, changing lights, and darkness. People came and went. She could hear them speak but soon their voices faded. She experienced pure bliss while, at other times, it was absolute agony. Ian talked to her at length, as did Frederick. Then a bright light came and she was content to bask in its warmth and comfort. She remained for what seemed years. The only way that it could be better was if Frederick was there to share. Devon came and she was joyful. She bemoaned his departure. She galloped aboard Daytran and fed him sugar cubes while listening to his delightful neighs. She skied down snow covered slopes with Frederick at her side. Another time she tended Devon's wounds while their aircraft swept across Europe in darkness.

More pain came and it was intense. Nerves in her left arm burned with enormous suffering.

"Be still. Help me with this Vanessa," a woman said to her. "I must get this in."

Flickering light partially blinded her as she began seeing fuzzy images moving about her. They started taking form. At her left arm, a nurse was trying to tape a shunt into place. Beside her a persistent beeping sound continued. Moving her eyes slowly, she saw Frederick's head resting upon his arms across the foot of her bed. He appeared to be asleep. Light began to fade but she wanted to stay with Frederick. She cried out to him and he answered.

"Vanessa, you are fine darling. Thank God, you are fine. Rest now, you will be up and around in no time," he said.

She walked across an Irish hillside as the ocean crashed upon boulders below. Stacks of rocks formed fences marking the land into a world of squares and rectangles. Atop a hill, a cottage stood with a thatched roof and rock sides. Smoke drifted lazily from its chimney. She heard children laughing at play near the quaint structure. She moved closer to see over a rock barrier. On its back steps sat Molly O'Shea, her eyes aglow and red tresses hanging below her shoulders. She watched her brothers and sisters at play.

The door opened behind her and Grandfather O'Shea leaned against the doorframe and smiled. This was a happy time for the O'Shea's before they had to move to the city.

Grandfather O'Shea saw her watching. He stepped around Molly and walked to the rock barrier.

"'Tis a good time for children to be a-playing I'm a-thinking," he said, his voice in full Irish brogue. "I'll help ye over the fence wee bonnie lass. Ye can join them."

Her desire to play joyously with them swept through her. She raised her arms for the burly Irishman to lift her over when a loud noise sounded behind her. Lowering her hands, she turned to see Daytran leaping fence after fence. After each jump, he pranced in circles with his head and tail held high.

Suddenly, he stopped and looked at her. Shaking his head from side to side, he reared skyward pawing the air with his front hooves. Next, he pranced toward her but stopped a few meters away. He shook his head again and his glorious mane flew back and forth. Daytran began clawing the earth with one hoof while raising and lowering his mighty head. He whirled and ran a few meters and did the same.

"He wants me to follow," she thought, while the children's voices grew in volume. She looked over her shoulder and Grandfather O'Shea waited with outstretched arms and a wide smile.

"Come a-long lass or you'll be a-missing all the fun," he said.

Daytran's neighs filled the air and she looked at him again. He continued pawing. She made one short glance at Grandfather O'Shea and ran toward Daytran laughing. A short distance before reaching the massive stallion, he whirled and ran a few meters and stopped. He looked back at her as if to say, "What are you waiting for?"

She began chasing him as hard as she could run until she could almost touch his tail. During her desperate run to reach him, he began fading from view. Then, he was gone. Pain returned to her arm.

"That's a girl. I told you that you would make it. God promised," she heard Frederick say.

Chapter Twenty Seven

December 1962

Asia is rich in people, rich in culture, and rich in resources.
It is also rich in trouble.
Hubert H. Humphrey (1911–78)
U.S. Democratic politician, vice president. Speech, 23 April 1966

Lanny Briscoe fumed with frustration. He sat in a room with paint peeling from its ceiling and cobwebs in every corner. On three sides, a partition enclosed his work area. Three trays on his desk, sat stacked one upon the other. From top to bottom, a hand painted notice appeared on each, "Out," "Hold," and "In." The three were empty.

Outside, above the building's entrance, a sign stated in faded red color, "Collins and Belbow, Imports and Exports." What was once a glass window, in front of a display area, had warped boards covering it. A narrow, dirt street provided vehicle access but not for autos. Builders never intended it for anything more than bicycles.

His frustration grew as he contemplated his situation. He was the only NSA operative sharing a poorly disguised, CIA regional headquarters. He felt like a bastard at a family reunion. No one talked to him and he returned the favor. He was in the worst of situations, a man without a mission.

"We should have been monitoring Geneva's radio traffic," he thought. "If we had, we would have seen it coming. We weren't on station more than six weeks when Laos signed a neutrality agreement. Some CIA jerk blew this one he knew it. Damn they ordered us out of Laos on 23 June after Souvanna Phouma took office in the second coalition government in Lao's history. Hell, we arrived on station in April. What a screwup."

He looked at the survival knife on his desk. He remembered how Jean used one like a surgical instrument while for him it was nothing more than a paperweight. He recalled their last night together.

"Go without me," Jean said. "We're too close to Viet Nam's border for me to leave. There are some things I have to do."

"What things?" Briscoe asked.

"The things I was going to do when this mission ended," he answered.

"There's no need to swamp me with facts and figures. When were you going to do these things had our mission not been canceled early?" Briscoe asked, somewhat upset with Jean's evasive answer.

"When we finished the mission we had, I was going to stay anyway. The only thing that's changed is that I am going to start my mission a little earlier than planned. I do need you to do something for me," Jean said.

"I will do what I can," Briscoe agreed.

"Remember the cylinder I gave you?" Jean asked.

"Yeah, sure. I have it in my backpack," Briscoe answered.

"When you get to Bangkok, go to the French Embassy. See the assistant military attaché Major Pontier Gevereaux. Tell him that Joan of Arc is in the tobacco fields. He will know what to do. Do not give this message to anyone else," Jean told Briscoe.

"I will be glad to do that providing I make it to Bangkok. We're not out of this place yet. There's still considerable danger until the remaining teams get to their pickup points," Briscoe said.

Continuing, he reviewed how one man did not heed the PARU's warning.

"You know I thought that Peanut was the best of the bunch. The PARU told him that an NVA patrol was approaching. He didn't listen. I thought sure that the PARU would leave him but they didn't. They gave him just enough time to activate the thermite switch. Evidently, the NVA saw his silhouette in the bright light from the burning unit. The PARU brought him out of there. Jim Belton was a big guy for those small Thais to carry," Briscoe explained.

"Damn," Briscoe thought. "How does he do it? I was talking to him one moment and the next, vanished. I hope he makes it."

Briscoe delivered Jean's message as requested. Jean's assistant could not hide his distress when he received it.

When Briscoe contacted his controller, he ordered him to Udon Thani, Thailand. His instructions were to "standby" for further orders. He took up residence with a group of CIA operatives supporting Vang Pao's forces in Northeastern, Laos. Because of the neutrality treaty, they were not supposed to be in Laos. So here he was cooling his heels.

The rightmost partition of his cubicle shook from a resounding blow causing Briscoe to leap from his chair.

"What the hell," he cried.

"Jesus Briscoe, you sure are jumpy," Greg Hampton said as he looked at Briscoe across the partition's top.

Although he would not admit it, Briscoe knew that Hampton was the region's Station Chief. He also knew that Hampton was their money man. Once a month, he left with a large suitcase that was sealed and locked. He always had someone help him carry it. However, when he returned, he could carry it easily alone. The suitcase had to contain money to pay General Vang Pao's Hmong forces. Briscoe often wondered what would happen if someone tried to force the suitcase open. He sincerely believed the result could only be instant death.

"That's a good way to get your throat cut," Briscoe replied, pointing to the knife on his desk.

"You Briscoe, not a chance. You coneheads aren't into the blood and guts business," Hampton said with a chuckle.

Coneheads was a term the CIA used for electronics people. It did not matter if it was Crypto, computers, or whatever, if it took brains, you were a conehead.

Hampton gestured with his head toward the room's rear area and said, "Come with me. You will find this interesting I think."

Briscoe knew what Hampton wanted. He intended them to go to their safe room. This was a 12-foot by 12 foot; copper mesh lined room swept daily for surveillance devices. Its construction was such that electromagnetic energy could not leave nor enter it. Furthermore, they could discuss sensitive subjects without fear of long range detection equipment monitoring them.

Hampton led the way down an aisle between cubicles. He carried a brief case in his left hand with a chain attached to his wrist. He opened the safe room by inputting the correct combination. He gestured for Briscoe to enter.

The safe room's furniture was Spartan to say the least, one OD folding table and three folding chairs. There were no electrical outlets, lights or anything posted on its walls. Hampton nodded toward a box of candles on the table indicating that Briscoe light one. If he didn't, the room would be totally dark. With a candle lit, Hampton closed and locked the door behind him. Moving to the table, he placed the briefcase on it and dialed in a combination. Briscoe heard the lock retract.

"Take a seat," Hampton said as he proceeded to sit in one of the chairs.

"Sure thing," Briscoe said as he selected a chair across from Hampton.

"Lanny, can I call you Lanny?" Hampton asked.

"Sure," Briscoe answered.

"Lanny, when you moved in here I had a background check run on you. The results did not show anything other than you taught mathematics as a college professor. I don't mind telling you I had a hard time establishing your need to know status. It finally came from the White House. That's enough for me," Hampton explained.

Hampton removed an opaque, vinyl document case. Holding it closed was a twisted wire passing through a lead seal. He cut the wire with a fingernail clipper and began removing glossy photographs. He placed them upside down on the table so that the image side was not visible. Each had a number on its back, progressing from one through 11.

"I had to get a clearance to show these to you. It was not a clearance for you but for me. I didn't know anything about this capability until three days ago. My instructions are to explain where they came from and show you something about them. After you see them, you have to let me know whether you need to return to the states. If so, I will arrange transportation," Hampton related.

Hampton turned photo number one to reveal its image. Briscoe picked it up and held it closer to the candle to see it better.

"You may have seen that photo before," Hampton said. "It came from a satellite launched by Discoverer 14 on 19 August 1960. A Corona Keyhole 1 camera (KH-1) took the photo. The area covered is in the Soviet Union. Note that it is fuzzier than U-2 photos but it comes from a region the U-2 cannot cover," Hampton explained.

Briscoe replied, "You are correct. I have seen this photograph. What else have you got?"

Hampton turned over photographs numbered two through eight. Briscoe picked up photograph number two. He immediately thrust it toward the candle.

"Light some more candles," Briscoe said excitedly.

Lacking candleholders, Hampton lit a second candle from the first. He then dripped wax on the table and set a candle upright in it. He did the same for another one.

"Jesus," Briscoe exclaimed. "These are great. I never saw so much detail. Do you know anything about their origins?"

"Yes I do," Hampton answered. "A KH-2 camera put up by Discoverer 18, on 10 December 1960, shot those."

Briscoe examined every photograph intensely. He kept putting one down and looking at another. He was totally enthralled with them.

"Don't tell me you have more?" Briscoe asked exuding anticipation.

"Yes," Hampton answered. "Before I show these, you need to know that they are the ones you use to determine whether you remain or leave. Okay?"

"Sure," Briscoe blurted as he grabbed the three remaining photographs. He began examining number nine first.

Hampton said, "That photo was taken by a KH-3 camera on 30 August 1961. Note that the detail is twice that of photos numbered two through eight. I was told for you to note the minute punctures on each photos' corners."

"Well, I'll be damned. I'll be damned," Briscoe repeated as he examined the pinhole punctures.

Throwing the photo aside, he clutched at photo number ten. He held it away from his body placing it between him and the candles' light. On each corner, he saw pinholes.

"That photo, and number 11, came from an even more advanced KH-4 camera. It went into orbit on Discoverer 38 on 27 February of this year. I am certain that more exist but I could only get a clearance for these 11," Hampton told him.

Briscoe retrieved photograph number 11 and held it and number ten between him and the candle's light. He looked closely from one to the other. Next, he placed the two where he could examine the image.

"Shit, shit, shit," Briscoe said loudly as he raised the two photographs above his head. "Get me on a plane to the states. They told you where, right?"

"They sure did. Are you through examining the photographs?" Hampton asked.

"Not yet, give me more time," Briscoe demanded.

"You don't have much time Lanny," Hampton said. "I was told you would want to leave. There's a C-130 waiting to take you to Tan Son Nhut airfield in Saigon. From there, you will board a flight on Cathy Pacific to Hong Kong. There will be a short layover and you will board a Pan Am 707 for San Francisco. From there, you will have a five-hour flight to Washington's National Airport. You will be met and escorted to another destination in D.C."

"Let's get on the road," Briscoe said impatiently.

"Not until you witness my burning these," Hampton said as he gathered the photographs.

Outside the safe room, Hampton crumpled some typing paper, lit it, and dropped it into a trashcan. He lit the corner of each photograph while Briscoe watched it burn in the trashcan. Briscoe stirred the ashes into a fine powder.

"Sign here," Hampton said.

Briscoe signed the witness document and asked. "Can we get out of here now?"

"On our way," Hampton answered.

Briscoe had known fears before but the landing approach to Hong Kong's airport never failed to top most of them. It simply did not seem safe to be looking into people's homes while landing. Cathy Pacific's Boeing 707 turned erratically as it twisted between skyscrapers to its landing point. Takeoffs at Hong Kong were fine. They exited over open waters. Landings, however, twisted between buildings while making a rapid descent. It was just scary as hell.

What was it that Hampton said? "A short layover at Hong Kong."

His flight did not leave for two hours. Meanwhile, he could not leave the airports duty free area. To make sure no one tried, armed guards manned all exits but one. The one unmanned was the boarding area's loading ramp. To try to leave that way meant serious injury unless an aircraft was in place. Otherwise, it was a 20-foot fall to cement.

Flights came and went while Briscoe waited. Passengers would unload for a few minutes and then board a plane to another destination. Hong Kong was a major hub for air travel in Asia. The standard joke was that a person could not go anywhere in the Orient without passing through Hong Kong's duty free area.

"They must really be making big payoffs to arrange that deal," Briscoe thought.

A voice over the public address system announced a flight from Seoul, Korea. Passengers spilled onto the waiting area. Korean tourists almost ran to the duty free shops. Other passengers examined flight schedules posted on television displays. Invariably, they checked their watches and muttered some obscene phrase. What Briscoe thought amusing was their checking the time with their watches.

"Good grief, a clock three feet in diameter was immediately above the flight display. Guess they figure their watches are better," he thought with a chuckle.

Briscoe felt the presence of someone near him. He looked to his right and saw an U.S. Army first lieutenant leaning against the wall about three feet from him. He wore a rumpled khaki uniform with aviator wings on his shirt. Tucked under his left arm, he held an unopened box of Partega cigars. As if detecting Briscoe's gaze, he looked directly at him; gave a brief smile; and nodded his head.

Caught totally by surprise, Briscoe gradually worked his way toward the flier. At his approach, the soldier looked again but with a puzzled expression.

Briscoe asked, "Did you get those cigars from a Turk?"

The aviator glanced to his left and right. Next, he returned his gaze to Briscoe.

"Beats the hell out of me. He sure looked Chinese," he answered.

Realizing he had made a mistake, Briscoe quickly asked. "Where you headed?"

"Saigon, Republic of South Viet Nam," he answered with a note of anxiety in his voice.

"Just left," Briscoe said.

"Beg your pardon?" Zane asked.

"Just left there a few hours ago," Briscoe explained.

"Really. What unit were you with?" Zane asked with interest.

"None. I was flying Space Available (Space-A) on a C-130 and Saigon was a stopover," Briscoe responded.

With his interest aroused, Dale moved closer and asked. "What was it like?"

"Never got out of the terminal. It is jammed with people trying to get home for Christmas. They're sleeping on the floors, benches, and air mattresses. When a ticket agent does appear, they mob him trying to get a boarding pass. The person who puts the most money on the counter gets a seat. I had to fight for a seat that was already reserved in my name," Briscoe told Zane.

"One thing's for sure. There's no one here fighting to get there," Zane commented with a note of sarcasum.

An attractive woman in uniform walked to the boarding area entrance. She had a badge identifying her as an employee of Cathy Pacific Airlines. Removing a velvet rope across the entrance, she walked to a rostrum and picked up a hand microphone.

Pressing its talk button, she announced, "Those passengers for Saigon please come to the boarding desk with your passes please. Cathy Pacific Flight 451 for Saigon departs in 15 minutes.

"That's me. Guess I had better get aboard. Nice chatting with you," Zane said.

"Me too," Briscoe answered.

On his way to the boarding desk, Dale felt a hand on his shoulder. He turned to find Briscoe with his hand extended. Dale turned and accepted Briscoe's handshake.

Looking Dale in the eyes, Briscoe said, "Take care of yourself. There are some of us who care."

"Thanks. I appreciate that," Dale said, caught by surprise.

Zane found his window seat. Once seated, he put on his safety belt and stared through the window into darkness. He could see some blue taxi lights but nothing else.

"That was a nice guy in the waiting area," he thought as he put his cigars beneath his seat.

Briscoe arrived to a totally changed Washington, D. C. There was a new administration in the White House, and General LeHouse at NSA had retired. He knew that there had to be a case officer assigned to contact him. He went to National's Airport coffee shop to wait. He waited less than five minutes.

A man slipped into the seat next to his at the counter. He ordered coffee. After his waitress delivered it, he kept looking straight ahead.

"You're Briscoe?" He asked.

"That's right. Do you smoke Partegas made by a Turk?" Briscoe asked.

"Nope and I cannot reply to your ID code. I do not have any earthly idea what the response is," he answered.

"Let's do it the old fashioned way. I will show you mine if you will show me yours," Briscoe quipped.

"Gorge Wilson, Agent, National Security Agency," Briscoe read aloud. "You must already know everything about me?"

"Pretty much Lanny, you've been in the field for almost nine years. What I know I learned from your file. They do not always give a complete picture," Gorge mentioned.

"Pictures, that's why I'm here. Let's talk pictures," Briscoe stated.

"Can't do that here. Ride to Fort Meade with me and we can," Gorge suggested.

"I'm sorry Mr. Wilson but Mr. Briscoe cannot enter until he gets cleared at personnel," the burley gate guard said. "A vehicle is on its way. You can wait with me Mr. Briscoe. You go ahead Mr. Wilson."

Briscoe's feet were not on the ground yet when a black suburban arrived. Wilson waved to it as he drove away.

One man opened the front passenger's door and gestured for Briscoe to enter. He held a rear door open until Briscoe took a seat. As it closed, Briscoe heard door locks snap to their locked positions. Separating Briscoe from the men in front was a one-way glass pane. He could not see who was in front. He knew they could see him.

"It's probably bullet proof," he thought.

From hidden speakers, a voice asked. "Mr. Briscoe, what was the name of Neil Burnum's secretary?"

Somewhat surprised, Briscoe had to think a moment, he answered, "Katherine Ingersoll."

"We've been holding your mail. You have quite a stack waiting. Most of it is from Katherine Ingersoll. We had a dickens of a time finding out who she was," the voice explained.

Memories flooded Briscoe's mind. He remembered her delivering coffee with a silver tea service set. They had a grand Italian dinner. She waved goodbye at the airport.

"So long ago," Briscoe thought. "This is a rotten life. There was really no way that I could have stayed in touch. Moreover, there was nothing I could do if I had. She couldn't be with me where I've been going."

Personnel quickly verified Briscoe for new credentials. One identification method was new to him, retinal scans. He knew the method was under study when he departed. Now, it was standard procedure. The next six days he spent in debriefings and filing reports. While he continually demanded to meet his new supervisor, they ignored him.

His retreat on Washington's West Side was in order as he left it. Filled with dust and spider's webs he considered it livable. His evenings he spent reading and rereading Katherine's letters. After working at the White House, she went home to Iowa to work in the state's Republican Party Headquarters. Her letters stopped for three years. She married a state senator but that marriage failed. Now, she was working as a legal secretary for a Supreme Court judge in Washington, D.C. Her last letter, mailed six months ago, indicated a new love in her life. Somehow, this caused hurt in Briscoe's heart although he knew he had no claims on her life.

Foremost in his mind were those photographs. He never mentioned his suspicions to his NSA debriefers for good reason. They would consider what he knew to be a matter for the Army Security Agency (ASA) or the CIA. This was too important to pass on through normal channels. This problem required a careful approach. If Ike were still in office, he would have gone to him. However, it was the Democrat's ball and he did not know their interest or priorities. After the Cuban crisis, he felt they would have considerable interest but he did not know whom to approach.

"I busted my butt to return in record time only to spend a week dealing with red tape," he thought. "I must make the correct contact about those Keyhole photos."

"General this is Lanny Briscoe. He is in from a nine-year stint in the field. I think you have his file sir," Lieutenant Colonel DeLaney said as he introduced Briscoe to NSA's Director.

Lieutenant General Robert A. O'Conner extended his hand across his desk to Briscoe and said, "Welcome back Briscoe. Glad to have you in from the cold as our CIA counterparts like to say."

"Thank you, sir," Briscoe replied.

"General, unless you have something else, I will leave you two alone," Colonel DeLaney said.

"That's fine Bill. Have Melanie hold my calls for an hour please," General O'Conner responded.

"Yes sir," DeLaney said as he departed.

"Sit down Briscoe. I see we've had you away from your primary duty for a long time. However, whatever the president wants he gets. You and Ike were tight I guess. I hope we can let you apply your considerable talent to cryptographic equipment for awhile," O'Conner said.

"Sir, I did get considerable hands-on time with the UHF crypto units. They are fine devices," Briscoe replied.

"Yes, I saw that from your debriefing reports. I hated to see that we lost Peanut," O'Conner commented.

Briscoe could not help but notice O'Conner's palatial office. He guessed the room to be at least 1,500 square feet. Mahogany paneling covered every wall from three feet to the ceiling. Directly behind the General, there was a 32-inch photograph of President Johnson. Smaller photographs of the Chairman of the Joint Chiefs and the Secretary of Defense flanked it. To the right, and behind the general, was an American flag. He did not recognize the flag on his left because of its folding. One wall was a bookcase filled with various reference books.

"I guess a lieutenant general earned it," Briscoe thought.

"Briscoe, I don't see why you can't start where LeHouse had you assigned. You will serve as a Special Assistant to the Director unless things change. I see in you file that you express an immediate need to speak with your supervisor. That's me," O'Conner said.

Briscoe leaned forward in his chair and asked. "Is this room cleared sir?"

"Yes, it is. Proceed," he answered.

"Sir, someone sent me photographs in Thailand. That someone knew my background and what I was doing to help President Eisenhower. I have no idea who contacted me so I am not sure to whom I should speak," Briscoe told O'Conner.

"You will speak to me Briscoe. If I think it goes to anyone else, I will advise you of that. Now, please continue," O'Conner commented with some irritation showing in his voice.

"General, the photographs I saw came from the Corona Keyhole camera series. The most recent ones had what appeared to be a resolution of six inches. My understanding is that there are newer cameras going into orbit soon. The latest photos that I saw were most significant," Briscoe said.

"Briscoe, you have not mentioned anything that falls within your realm of cryptography. We monitor communications and try to decode transmissions. That's why you are here. We need to move this to another agency," General O'Conner said firmly.

"Sir, I do not think so," Briscoe disagreed.

"And why not?" O'Conner asked gruffly.

"Sir, someone used APPS on those photos," Briscoe stated fully expecting an astonished reaction from O'Conner.

Instead, he asked. "What the shit is APPS?"

Briscoe explained that APPS used aerial photographs to provide precise coordinates for targeting. If the photographs were accurate and high resolution, precise coordinates for a target could be within one meter or even less. He also told that he believed that the front organization, R. L. Meyers Systems, responsible for Cryptographic Devices using data processing, had compromised the APPS project. He detailed his contact with McNeese and the subsequent attempts on his life.

"Sir, Bryan Delaney at the CIA was doing a background on McNeese when I left. If I can get that report, it may well answer a lot of questions," Briscoe continued.

"Wait a minute. Was that the Bryan Delaney that saved Mark Clark's operation in France?" O'Conner asked, now showing intense interest.

"Yes sir," Briscoe answered.

"That was his son who brought you to my office. I knew his dad well. I went to his funeral at Arlington in 1955. He committed suicide," O'Conner exclaimed.

"No way," Briscoe promptly said. "Delaney would never commit suicide. I knew him too well. This stinks sir."

"That's what his son says. Okay Briscoe, I am listening. Continue," O'Conner directed.

"If my suspicions become known within the ranks of those associated with APPS development and use, they will go to ground. We will never know who they are," Briscoe stated with obvious concern.

General O'Conner leaned back in his executive chair and began rubbing his chin while deep in thought. After a few moments, he rocked forward and firmly placed his elbows on his desk. He propped his chin on his extended thumbs still thinking.

A short time later, he told Briscoe, "See Colonel DeLaney. He will provide you an office down the hall. Review every R & D document published regarding APPS that you can get with your clearance and need to know status. It may not be much. However, you have clearance for everything dealing with the Air Force's continued satellite deployment. They've slapped a tight security status on that project so you may get some resistance. If you do, tell Colonel DeLaney. I need to do some things. I will get back to you in one week. You're onto something Briscoe."

After his office space in Thailand, Briscoe felt he could get lost in his new office. He even had his own executive secretary, outer office, and private restroom. DeLaney explained that he would have a secretary from the office pool assigned for a few days until he could get someone permanent. He also got limited access to APPS development documents and full access to GPS. He began researching with relish. He also began looking for Katherine.

Briscoe found Katherine's telephone listed as K. Ingersoll. This gave his heart some hope since she still used her maiden name.

"She could be living with her new love," he thought with rising anguish. "There was one way to know. Ask."

"Hello," she said and Briscoe recognized her voice immediately.

"Hi Katherine, this is Lanny Briscoe. It has been a long time. I am in D.C. and thought I would check to see how you are doing," Briscoe said nervously.

After a prolonged silence, she said, "Hi, it has been awhile hasn't it. Did you get my letters?"

"Yes, I received them all about a week ago. That was the first time I had seen them," he explained.

"I kept hoping I would hear from you but after a couple of years I quit trying for awhile. I remarried," she explained with an obvious melancholic tone growing in her voice.

"I'm so sorry it did not work out for you. Any children?" Briscoe asked.

"Yes, a girl. She's in kindergarten and the joy of my life," Katherine answered.

"Any chance of seeing the two of you?" Briscoe asked with apprehension gnawing at him.

"No Lanny. I think I wrote about that," she responded. "I was very lonely Lanny. When I never even received an acknowledgement of my letters, I figured that you didn't care."

"That wasn't it Katherine. I did not know that your letters existed. While I could have contacted you, there was a potential risk to you. I hope you understand my work," Briscoe continued, trying to justify his inaction.

"I understand you have obligations Lanny. They are important I am sure. That's likely why our situation worked out the best for both of us. It would be best if we avoided further contact. They would only serve to kindle dreams best kept as fond memories. Thanks for calling. Bye now," Katherine said as she ended Briscoe's call.

Briscoe held the handset to his ear and listened to the lifeless dial tone, he thought, "She is right. She evidently has a new life and love. She has always impressed me with her intelligence. While it hurts, her valuation of our situation is the best for the both of us."

On Monday morning, he found a memo to get an appointment to see General O'Conner. Its marking indicated that he was to expedite. He immediate called Colonel DeLaney.

"Thanks for calling Lanny," DeLaney said. "Let me talk to the General and I will get back with you right away."

After an anxious two hours, DeLaney contacted Briscoe by telephone, "Lanny, be at the high security room in an hour. Be prepared to discuss in depth your observations as expressed to the director."

Present at the meeting was a representative for the Special Assistant for National Security Affairs, Grahm Williams, Senior Executive Assistant to the Director of the CIA, Kevin Greenbriar, and General O'Connor. O'Conner introduced Briscoe.

"Gentlemen, with us today is Lanny Briscoe, my special assistant. He will brief you on matters that I seriously consider of major importance," O'Conner said.

The room was small with one table. There was barely room for them to sit. Briscoe could easily shake hands with everyone without rising from his seat.

After doing so, Benjamin Phillips, Williams' representative, immediately asked. "Mr. Briscoe didn't you do research and teach at MIT?"

"That's correct. I hold a Ph.D. and taught advanced mathematics to graduate students. However, most of my effort was devoted to research. I produced some algorithms that were of use to the APPS project. My primary focus was the mechanics of cryptography," Briscoe answered.

Phillips stated, "You must know Dr. Jenkins."

"Yes, but not personally. I am intimately familiar with some of his work. Why do you ask?" Briscoe questioned.

"Just curious," Phillips replied.

Kevin Greenbriar, sitting next to Briscoe, opened his briefcase while Phillips was asking questions. When it appeared that Phillips was through, Phillips opened a file folder and placed it in front of Briscoe.

He said, "Mr. Briscoe that's a synopsis of information we have regarding the late Bryan Delaney. He was a senior operative with us and highly respected for his diligence on any task that he attempted. We found his apparent suicide inconsistent with his personality, duty performance, and psychological profile. In addition, we could never find a motive for his termination. Perhaps you can shed some light on the matter."

Briscoe glanced through the file. He found no reference for the background investigation on McNeese. This didn't surprise him because it was on a personal basis and out of command channels. Delaney would never have documented it.

"I think I can," Briscoe began. "There is nothing here to have caused you to look at what I suspect may be happening. I will get that underway now."

Briscoe presented in detail events beginning with his acceptance of a NSA assignment to oversee security relating to equipment used for cryptography. He also told of his work for Eisenhower. He explained the Analytical Photogrametric Positioning System (APPS). Those present listened intently and made notes. Phillips, in particular, voiced exclamations at some parts of Briscoe's presentation.

In summation, he concluded, "Gentlemen, first, when I showed the slightest interest in R. L. Meyers Systems and their man McNeese, repeated attempts were made on my life. I am certain I was close to something of dire importance.

Second, a senior naval official, CINCPAC, had me intervene in an executive decision to cause it to fail. Frankly, I do not believe that intervention was what it appeared. It was nothing more than an effort to get me off course. I have since learned that Operation Vulture was never a viable mission. Our allies killed it.

Third, someone with intimate knowledge of our operations sent me to intercept the wrong radio traffic. I firmly believe I was there to intercept communications to Geneva.

Fourth, my assignment sent me to the middle of nowhere in Thailand when the Cuban Missile Crisis took place. Had I been on station during that crisis, I could have decoded their radio traffic with ease. I've examined files here that show there was no effective interception of Soviet Communications during that crisis.

Fifth, I would have been able to provide precise coordinates of every missile launcher in Cuba. There was no need whatever for U-2 flights. Instead, I was flying traffic patterns in Laos. Any of NSA's crypto specialists could have handled that job.

Sixth, someone in our government was using APPS to provide targeting data to the Soviets. I have seen photos viewed and analyzed using APPS. Those photos were of Washington, D. C., Miami, Atlanta, Pensacola Naval Air Station, New Orleans, Mayport Naval Transportation Center near Jacksonville and numerous communications centers, air traffic control facilities and power generation plants.

Everyone stared at Briscoe as if frozen in time. Their minds were trying to grasp the magnitude of what his speculations meant for the United States. Had the Soviets not blinked, there would have been consequences far beyond those originally determined.

Briscoe continued, "There is one friend on our side. Someone with access had aerial photos sent to me by courier. Those photos were the actual ones used on APPS. I saw them destroyed. However, identical photos exist and I have seen them. An APPS processing of those photos never took place. They lack the punctures caused when photos are fixed into the feed tray that moves them through the stereoscopic viewer."

Phillips hurled a pen onto the table and began cursing, "This is absolutely outrageous. How in the hell could someone get in so damned deep. The president is going to shit little green apples when he learns of this. We better have some damned good answers when he asks what we've done about it."

Greenbriar said, "I guarantee you that Bryan Delaney had those photos sent to Briscoe. Knowing Delaney, if something happened to him, he arranged for Briscoe to get those photos. He knew in 1955 that there was a deep penetration. He arranged, seven years in advance, for this contingency. He knew that he could trust Briscoe and he would recognize what was happening."

Briscoe turned to Greenbriar and stated, "I agree. That's Delaney at work."

General O'Connor interjected, "This is way outside my ballgame. If you need surveillance, interception and decode services, you have it. There's one big question remaining. What are we going to do about this mess?"

Everyone at the table looked at Briscoe.

Chapter Twenty Eight

December 1962

The gates of Hell are open night and day;
Smooth the descent, and easy is the way:
But, to return, and view the cheerful skies;
In this, the task and mighty labour lies.
Virgil (70–19 BC), Roman poet.

At Kimpo Air Base, near Seoul, Korea, Dale Zane was trying to stay warm. He wore summer a khaki shirt and trousers. He had his boarding pass and was killing time waiting for his flight to Viet Nam. He had a short stop in Japan and then Pan Am to Hong Kong. After that, he would travel via Cathy Pacific Airlines to Saigon.

Three months before, he knew little about the small, Southeast Asia country. When 6th Transportation Company had his first "Hail and Farewell," he obtained some insight. He was new meat and had to earn his black hat. The old timers were going home. Some others had returned to Korea from Viet Nam. They had been there on temporary duty.

To lose the title of new meat meant earning a black hat. The hats were nothing more than black baseball caps with a unit crests on them. Once a month the 6th Trans CO told the guys who were short goodbye. After that, they welcomed the new guys. Their right of passage was an insidious scheme. Each new aviator had two persons assigned to provide special attention. Their purpose was to assure that new meat pilots never had a hand empty of an alcoholic drink. This continued for an hour before their ceremony. Simply, they make sure the new guy was falling down drunk before the ceremony.

The club's dining tables became one, large horseshoe shaped table by placing them side by side. The CO had the center seat at the horseshoe's closed end. He had a gallon sized, stone crock that he passed around the table. Every person had to contribute something to the jar. They emptied ashtrays, ketchup bottles, liquor, salt, and pepper, anything into that jar. The drunken new guy had to stand in front of the CO and recite a poem about how great it was to have a black hat. If he said it wrong, he had to take a large drink from the jar and start again. Throughout this spectacle, the other pilots kept a steady steam of catcalls directed toward the initiate.

Before the ceremony, Zane had time to observe pilots recently returned from Viet Nam. They stayed together and did not have much to say except to those who had been to the place. Individuals sat alone at the bar or found a booth where they sat and downed drink after drink. Many collapsed into a drunken stupor. They were decidedly different. Zane had little idea that he might join their ranks soon. It happened. Three months later, he was on his way.

From Kimpo's flimsy air terminal, he could see soldiers approach the access gate with their yobos. A yobo was a Korean word loosely translated to girlfriend or boyfriend in English.

Gate guards watched their partings without interest. They had seen many in the past. The soldier and yobo would hug, kiss, and say their good-byes repeatedly. With time waning, the soldier would pass through the entrance from which there was no returning. The girl would scream, pull her hair, and roll upon the ground in anguish. She kept this charade going until her yobo entered the out-processing center. The building was windowless and out of view for anyone at the gates. At this event, she would get up; dust off her clothes; and walk away smiling, as she counted the money he gave her. Her destination was the exit gates at the in-processing center. New meat, arriving by air, would enter Korea from that location. The earlier in their tour they could catch a yobo, the more time they had to convince them to marry.

Turning away from the dismal scene, Zane ordered another bourbon and water. These drinks were far more expensive than five cents each. A fifth of Johnny Walker Scotch went for $75.00 on the street. Top of the line bourbon brought the same price. A waiter left his heavily watered drink and moved to wait on senior officers. Lieutenants did not tip well, if at all.

"Three months here and I am on my way to 'Nam," he thought. "What was worse I volunteered. It will be worth it to get away from Scab-in-the-Butt Lendrain."

Staring into his glass, he could not recall a single officer as bad as Lendrain. When Captain Hinson left, Zane's world turned to crap. Hinson's replacement, Captain Newhart Lendrain, was a piece of work. He lived in total terror of higher headquarters. Since he couldn't handle senior officers, he dumped on his men.

At first, he seemed fine. He met him at Osan with an H-23 and flew him to their unit. He remember it like a nightmare come to fruition.

"Hi sir, I'm Lieutenant Zane. I'm your maintenance officer," Zane introduced himself.

"At ease, lieutenant. Grab a bag and let's go," Lendrain said.

That was the unit's high point with Lendrain as CO. It started downhill after their short flight.

The flight from Osan was 15 minutes to Camp Humphries. They made it in ten with a tailwind. Zane got landing clearance and hovered to their parking ramp. A crew chief was in place to direct their H-23 to its parking pad. After engine shutdown, Zane began completing logbook entries for the flight.

"Where's your checklist Zane?" Lendrain asked.

"Sir?" Zane replied with evident surprise at the question.

"Where is your checklist lieutenant?" Lendrain demanded.

"In my right flight suit pocket sir," Zane answered.

"I didn't say anything at Osan when you did a run-up without it. Nevertheless, I cannot condone this total disregard of flight procedures. Get your checklist and use it," he said while climbing from the craft.

Grabbing his baggage, Lendrain stood upright and walked stiffly towards the maintenance building. If the crew chief had not been present, the ship's rotor blade would have struck his head as it was dipping low. The crew chief ran past Lendrain and stopped it before it hit. During the following months, Zane wished it had.

"At ease men," he said. "I am Captain Newhart Lendrain, Transportation Corps. We will be together for the next 12 months."

First Lieutenant Zane, Second Lieutenant Harrellson, and Chief Warrant Officer Laughton leaned against the wall in operations. Captain Lendrain paced back and forth in front of them.

Lendrain walked with his hands clasped behind his back. He would lift his head up and down as he paced and never once looked at his officers.

"Gentlemen," he said. "We are one officer short so I will handle operations. Zane you are next senior so you stay in maintenance. However, you will also be my executive officer and perform appropriate duties. Harrellson you will leave operations and handle the supply officer slot. Laughton, although you are not a commissioned officer, I expect you to conduct yourself as one. You are responsible for personnel. Any questions so far?"

No one made a sound. Lendrain stopped pacing and inclined his head to one side as if listening.

Hearing nothing, Lendrain continued, "Good, I've made myself clear. From now on, unless someone has an early flight, we will have breakfast together. Be prepared to answer pertinent questions for the day. We will meet again at 18:00 hours for chow. After that, we can have entertainment. I understand there are free movies so you can attend those with me after chow. Light's out is 2200 hours. Okay?"

Again, he stopped and inclined his head sideways. Again, there was silence.

"Great, that's it for now. I'm going to Osan to meet the brigade commander and staff. See you at 18:00 hours. Dismissed," he said.

Zane and his fellow aviators came to attention and saluted. Lendrain rendered an off hand salute and never looked up as they left.

Outside, Laughton said, "Wait until WOPA hears about this."

Harrellson looked at Zane and then Laughton, he asked with a wide grin. "Chief, are you going to sic the Warrant Officers Protective Association on his ass?"

"You bet I am. I can't today because I have a flight to Hill 416 and a follow-up to Yong San. I will remain overnight (RON) at Yong San for an O-dark-30 takeoff the next morning. I should be back here by 1600 hours without any complications," Laughton explained.

"Yeah, you will have a couple of hours in your new personnel office," Zane said as he grinned.

"Be sure to check the morning report. We might have some deserters," Harrellson added.

Zane walked the one-mile to his maintenance office. Inside Specialist 5 Rex Tuttle sprang from his seat as he entered.

"As you were Tuttle," Zane said. "Did we get the new pubs in that I ordered?"

"No sir," Tuttle answered. "I checked with 6th Trans and they don't have any yet. They ordered three months before us."

Zane's wool OD uniform felt great. Early November in Korea starts the cold season. Soon it would get downright miserable. He stood by the oil heater to warm his backside before going to his desk.

As he sat, he asked Tuttle. "How is the periodic maintenance coming on 762?"

One of the first things Zane learned about maintenance was the importance of periodic inspections. They were not an option. Every aircraft required a major inspection and repair after 100 flying hours. It was necessary to disassemble, inspect, and reassemble each aircraft.

"Fine sir, it should be out of the hanger for test flight in two days," Tuttle answered.

"Thanks," Zane answered as he reached for the field telephone on his desk.

He lifted its handset from its cradle and turned the set's handle two times very fast. With the handset to his ear, he heard the switchboard come on line.

"Sixth Trans maintenance please," Zane said.

He heard one long growling sound before someone answered, "6th Trans maintenance, Sergeant Bigalow."

"Hi Sergeant, this is Lieutenant Zane. I need to schedule an H-13 test flight for day after tomorrow. Do you have a test pilot available that day?" He asked.

"Sure do L-T. How about Mister Proctor?" Bigalow asked.

"Hey sarge, that's fine. Can you have him here by 0800 hours?" Zane asked.

"You've got it. By the way, how's the new CO?" Bigalow questioned.

"He's the CO. You know how that goes. Later," Zane answered.

"Tuttle, I have a 10:00 hours takeoff for Inchon with H-23 980. They are through with the quarterly on it aren't they?" Zane asked.

"Yes sir. They will have it on the line in time for preflight. This intermediate inspection at Inchon is getting to be a pain. We could do that inspection," Tuttle commented.

"Yeah I know but to inspect the valves, requires removing the heads. We cannot do that nor can 6th Trans. The procedure requires depot maintenance. H-23s are having valve troubles somewhere I am sure. That's why they must inspect them every 25 flying hours," Zane explained.

Zane waved to the waiter and he ignored Zane each time. Finally, he slipped two fingers in his lower lip and placed his tongue against them. He gave an air blast resulting in a sharp, piercing whistle that echoed throughout the lounge. The waiter promptly looked in his direction, as did everyone in the room. Zane gestured with his empty glass at him. He rushed to Zane's table.

"One more of these but make it a double. I want to at least taste bourbon," Zane stated.

Zane lit a cigarette from the one he was smoking. He put the pack into his shirt pocket.

"That's another benefit of Lendrain, smoking," Zane thought. "I had not puffed on one since flight school graduation. Now, I am chain-smoking the damned things," he thought.

In Zane's mind, three events put him in his current situation. Two were near death situations for him. The other was for one of his crew chiefs. Lendrain didn't count because he brought it on himself. The first happened immediately after Lendrain appointed himself operations officer.

"Zane, I need 980, 762, 483 and 030 for flights tomorrow," Lendrain told Zane.

"Sorry sir, 762 is completing a periodic maintenance inspection. It has to go to depot maintenance at Inchon for a valve inspection before its mission ready. I can only clear it for a one time flight to Inchon," Zane explained.

"That's unsatisfactory. Colonel Berdon wants to fly in 762 tomorrow," Lendrain said with an irate tone.

"Sir, 895 is flyable. You can schedule it for Berdon," Zane responded.

"Lieutenant you are not listening. Berdon wants to fly in 762 and he will fly in 762," Lendrain yelled.

"Sir, it's disassembled in the hanger. We're not through with it," Zane now pleaded.

There was a deafening silence as Zane waited for Lendrain's reply. It came too soon and Zane definitely did not like what he heard.

"Lieutenant, get off your ass. Get every man you have on 762. You fly it to Inchon today. Get the valves inspected and have it back here so it can fly Berdon tomorrow. Don't say a word. Do it," Lendrain stated in a slow, cold monotone.

Zane heard the line disconnect. He put his handset down and looked at Tuttle.

"Tuttle go to 6th Trans and find Mister Proctor. Ask him if he can spare two mechanics. I need them until 14:00 hours. I will appreciate it," Zane instructed.

"Right away, L-T," Tuttle said as he left his desk and put on his heavy fatigue jacket.

Zane watched Tuttle leave as he asked the operator to connect him with the 45th Maintenance Battalion in Inchon. Once connected, he asked for Major Kannaday. He came on the line.

"Kannaday," he said.

"Sir, this is Lieutenant Zane at Camp Humphries. I have a big favor to ask," Zane said.

"I'll try. What's up?" Kannaday asked.

"Sir, if I bring H-23 762 there right after lunch, will you have your guys do a valve inspection while I wait for the aircraft?"

"Zane, you know the procedure. Even if I get the inspection done, it will require a test flight and I'm short test pilots. Why don't you leave it overnight as usual?" Kannaday asked.

"I will explain when I get there sir," Zane replied.

"Okay, bring it on but don't make a habit of this," Kannaday stated.

"Thank you sir, goodbye," Zane said just before breaking the connection.

As Zane left the maintenance building for the hanger, Tuttle arrived with two, direct support helicopter mechanics.

Under his breath, Zane said, "Thank goodness for Proctor."

The mechanics rolled 762 onto the flight line in record time. Zane did his preflight and entered a circled red X in the logbook. He made an entry clearing the craft for a one -time flight. He was airborne in 15 minutes.

The coastal route to Inchon was the shortest way and Zane took it. The inlets and bays along the coast were nothing more than mud flats. Korea's massive tidal changes left ships, fish traps, and anything else floating, sitting in mud when at low tide. After receiving a landing clearance, Zane began his approach to the maintenance battalion's airstrip.

On short final, at about 200 feet altitude, Zane heard a loud snap and his aircraft started a sharp right turn. Zane's reaction was as if Flight Instructor Harold Oates was in the cockpit. He had made them practice low level autorotations so often that making one was instantaneous. It is possible, with helicopters, to land them when an engine fails by disengaging the transmission from the rotors. This allowed the rotors to build RPMs so that an emergency landing could take place. Helicopters do not glide like fixed winged aircraft. The glide ratio of most helicopters is the same as a big rock.

At low altitudes, however, there is little time to allow the rotors to increase their speed, which invariably ends in a crash. Oates' training saved Zane and his aircraft. He could not remember slamming his collective pitch lever down and turning off power. Immediately before ground contact, he made a sharp upward movement of his pitch lever stopped his H-23 two feet above ground. He used remaining RPMs to cushion his landing.

Zane sat dazed and unharmed as fire trucks surrounded his H-23. He did not remember any of the control inputs he made.

"Are you okay lieutenant?" A medic asked as he jerked his door open.

Zane sat silent for a moment, trying to think and said, "Yeah, I think so."

The next face he saw was that of Major Kannaday and his red, handle bar mustache. He unbuckled Zane's safety harness and helped him from the H-23 as Zane's hands began shaking.

"Come with me son," Kannaday said as he took Zane to a grassy area by the runway. "Sit here while the medic's check you out. Do not move. I will be back in a minute."

As medic's examined Zane for injuries, he watched Kannaday go to the H-23.

He began examining it when a medic said, "Sir, you need to lay down for a minute."

Zane could no longer see Kannaday or his aircraft. The medics checked him thoroughly and declared him okay except for the shakes.

One of them said, "Damn lieutenant, you are a lucky guy. Don't too many survive engine failure at that altitude."

"It didn't quit," Zane said three times in a row.

Next, he asked for a cigarette. The medic gave him one and lit it. Zane inhaled deeply and began coughing.

"First smoke, lieutenant?" The medic asked

"My first this year," he answered.

Medical personnel helped him to his feet. While he was regaining his composure, Major Kannaday appeared.

Taking Zane by his elbow, he led him away from the others and said, "Son, you lost your tail rotor. The reason you lost it was because one of the pitch change links was not safety wired. How, could you overlook that? Fortunately for you, there's not any damage to the aircraft. However, I will have to submit an incident report. Tell me what happened."

Zane told him about Lendrain's insistence upon having that particular aircraft available the next day.

Kannaday responded by asking. "Who schedules the aircraft in your unit?"

"I used to sir but it looks like that's changed," Zane answered.

"Well, there's one sure thing. That colonel is not going to fly in that machine tomorrow. It is staying here for the night. I will get someone from your unit to pick you up. Meanwhile, come in and have lunch," Kannaday said.

Zane's recollection of his close call required another drink. He waved his glass at the waiter who responded immediately this time.

As he approached, he asked. "The same lieutenant?"

Zane nodded, indicating yes.

"Might as well get smashed. What are they going to do to me? Send me to 'Nam," he thought.

His thoughts returned him to Inchon. Lendrain had picked him up with their L-20 Beaver. He didn't say a word on their flight to Camp Humphries. Zane learned later that Kannaday chewed his ass for not listening when Zane told him the H-23 could not go. Zane had hoped that things had changed. They had not as he shortly learned.

The following month Zane returned from a mission taking their commanding general to missile sites. The brigade CO was visiting nuclear capable units. Zane noticed that their H-13 seemed to have lost power. As the day progressed, he noticed that its spark plugs appeared to misfire.

Zane explained to Brigadier General Welt that they should get another helicopter. Since only one unit remained to visit, General Welt choose to cancel for the day and return to Osan. After dropping the CG off, Zane returned to Camp Humphries. On two occasions, Zane almost decided to land in a rice paddy because of obvious power loss. He decided to maintain a high altitude in case the engine failed. Landing areas were plentiful because the area was mostly rice fields.

"Chief, could I get you to do a test flight on one of our H-13s?" Zane asked CWO Proctor over the telephone after landing safely at his unit.

"Sure thing Dale. I will be right there," Mister Proctor said.

"Zane, you are one lucky SOB," Proctor said as he stuck his head into Zane's office. "Come out here I want to show you something."

Proctor pointed to air vents on the H-13's crankcase. Thick black sludge oozed from them and dripped on the parking area.

"That engine is shot. A new one is necessary. I'm grounding it until you put in a new engine," Proctor stated as he placed a red X in its logbook.

Lendrain pulled the same stunt as before. He wanted that particular H-13 and none other would do. His reason for insisting was that the interior had been redone with leather and fancy, nonstandard accoutrements. He wanted the general to fly in that aircraft.

"Sir, Mister Proctor grounded that aircraft. It needs a new engine. It cannot be flown until depot puts a new engine in her," Zane explained.

"I don't want to hear that shit. I am the CO and I will test fly that ship. I have the authority to override Mister Proctor's red X. Get a crew chief to it. I will be there in ten minutes," Lendrain stated over Zane's continued objections.

Zane recalled how pissed he was. Not because Lendrain almost killed himself but because he had one of his crew chiefs aboard. They were on climb out, at about 300 feet, when the engine threw a rod through its block. Fortunately, Lendrain autorotated into a rice field with no injuries or further damage. He never filed an incident report. Zane did, which did not endear him to Lendrain. Zane had no choice. He had to go to the rice field with a wrecker and tractor-trailer to recover the downed ship. His effort was in full view of the tower. They would have made a report if he hadn't. Nevertheless, it was the right thing to do.

Finally, Zane could tell he had a drink. It took about three to one of a Korean's bar drink to one from an American bar. There probably was good reason for this. It seemed that some Orientals had a low alcohol tolerance. At their prices, that was not all bad.

It was the third incident that really brought matters to a head. It seemed ironic since Lendrain had nothing to do with it. The flight was routine except for the weather. He was flying another H-23 to Inchon for a valve inspection. It was early December and the outside temperature was 18 degrees. Nothing was unusual until he started to tie the rotor blade to the helicopter after engine shutdown.

Securing the rotor on an H-23 meant tying one of its blades to the craft's tail. While holding a blade tip and walking to his ship's rear, Zane saw that the engine deck was awash with oil. He secured the rotor and examined the engine area. He could not find an oil leak anywhere. The ship's engine was spotless.

"Jesus, not you again Zane," Major Kannaday exclaimed. "What is it this time?"

"Sir, you are going to have to tell me. I cannot figure it. Do you have time to come look?" Zane asked.

"Why not," Kannaday left his seat and followed Zane to his ship.

"Good grief, what in the world?" Kannaday asked walking around the H-23.

"Zane, go inside and tell them I want a tech inspector here right now," Kannaday ordered.

Kannaday's technical inspector soon found the problem. The H-23 had a reciprocating engine that used a vertical mount. The rotor blades connected at the same position that a fan would on an automobile. An oil pump pushed oil through the engine and back to its reservoir. On the engine's side there was a receptacle for a hand crank. There was no way to hand crank a helicopter but the receptacle was standard.

The oil, on its way back to the reservoir, passed through a metal line. This line had no cold weather protection. Condensation in the line froze blocking its return. Oil pressure increased until a leak took place at the hand crank receptacle forcing oil past a rubber seal. To the pilot, there was no indication of a problem. However, when the oil supply went to zero, the engine would have seized. This would have been a major, life-threatening situation. Again, luck was on Zane's side.

Captain Lendrain arrived in the Beaver as usual and flew Zane back to Humphries. He was not silent on this trip.

"Listen Zane, you must be a real hard head. Something is going wrong every time you have anything to do with our birds. Rest assured, your efficiency report will reflect this," he told Zane.

"Sir, if you would only let me schedule maintenance like I am supposed too, we wouldn't have these problems," Zane replied.

"Bull shit," Lendrain responded and said no more on the flight.

With a chuckle, Zane remembered Lendrain's nickname of "Old Scab in the Butt." Anytime, he talked to a senior officer, he became nervous. During his anxiety, he picked his neck with his fingers. His neck had pustules covering it. He would pick his neck for a while and then put the same hand behind his back. He would insert his hand into his trousers and pick at his rear.

One day while watching this with Chief Laughton, Laughton said, "You know what he's doing? He's picking scabs off his neck and pushing them up his rear."

The name stuck. However, no one ever dared tell him.

About one week after the H-23 oil incident at Inchon, a mechanic burst into the maintenance building.

He said quite excited, "Hey everybody, come look at this."

Outside, six, 18-wheeled tractor-trailers were pulling into a circle in front of their hanger. Major Kannaday got out of the leading truck's cab and walked toward Zane. Zane saluted.

"Lieutenant Zane, as of this moment, every aircraft in your unit is grounded," Major Kannaday stated.

Dumbfounded, Zane answered after the major returned his salute, "Sir, we have three ships on missions."

"Recall them. They're grounded upon arrival," Kannaday related with a sincere sense of concern. "Also, get every crew chief you have to the flight line now. Understood?"

"Certainly sir but one is on KP at 6th Trans. I cannot get him out of that," Zane explained.

"I know Gerald Garwood the CO. I will take care of that. You get the rest," Kannaday ordered.

Captain Lendrain was flying one of the helicopters on a mission with Colonel Berdon, the brigade's operations officer. Lendrain had to cut his mission short and return him to Osan. By the time he arrived at Camp Humphries, he was in emotional chaos. He went after Zane first.

"What the hell is going on? What have you screwed up now?" Lendrain asked.

"Nothing to my knowledge sir. Major Kannaday is conducting a maintenance evaluation based upon a request by General Welt, the brigade's CO," Zane answered.

For the next three days, Major Kannaday's evaluation team went over unit maintenance procedures with a fine toothed comb. If they found a deficiency, they corrected it. During this same period, Captain Lendrain did not speak to any of the officers. That was a difficult task since they lived, ate, and slept together. On the fourth day, Major Kannaday sent for Captain Lendrain and Lieutenant Zane. They met him in the maintenance office.

"Captain," Kannaday said. "Look at that maintenance chart on the wall. Every aircraft you have is in mint condition. What you are looking at is the means to keep them that way. Aircraft require maintenance at scheduled intervals. Before you took command of this unit, their maintenance schedules looked just like that one. Afterwards, it went to hell. There is no such animal as a "flying periodic inspection." An aircraft is grounded until the designated maintenance is accomplished."

Kannaday continued, "We have updated every maintenance manual you have. Your crew chiefs are good ones and they know their aircraft. In other words, captain your maintenance is again shipshape."

"And, let me tell you this, maintenance schedules aircraft and not operations. This calling for an aircraft by tail number must stop. Listen to what Zane's is telling you. He is correct, "Kannaday stated firmly.

Zane remembered squirming internally at those words. He knew Lendrain. When the major left, Lendrain would have his hide. He knew and he had seen it in Lendrain's' eyes.

An announcement blared from Kimpo's public address system driving Zane's daydreams away.

"Those individuals with boarding passes go to gate six for final checks and boarding," a voice said.

Zane arose and definitely felt the bourbon as he mumbled, "Hey world, I am not going to fall off just yet."

A long line extended from gate six. In it were persons going home, on leave or those like him, Viet Nam. Zane presented his boarding pass to the NCO at the gate.

He took one look and said, "Sorry about that lieutenant. I will take Korea's cold to Viet Nam's tropics any day. You be careful."

Once aboard and seated, Zane leaned against the 707's side and looked across its wing. He was fortunate to have a window seat so that he could get some sleep. He felt drained after three months of total ruin. Nevertheless, it all wasn't a loss; General Welt gave him a good boost.

"You RA Zane?" General Welt asked.

"No sir, I'm reserve. I will have about a year after this tour," Zane answered.

Zane had flown General Welt many times when he visited missile sites. Zane always made sure to give him a thorough briefing before departure. He showed Welt their plotted route with expected flight times for each leg of their flight. Welt was sincerely interested and handled the map when they flew. Frequently, Zane let him have the controls over safe terrain and during smooth weather.

"Zane," Welt said one day. "In the near future, helicopters are going to be very important to the Army. We are going to need many pilots. You got your rating early so you will have an open field upward in rank. Why don't you apply for a RA commission?"

"Sir, if I could stay in aviation, I would do that. However, I am a field artillery officer. Aviation is a secondary specialty as far as my career branch is concerned."

"That is going to change in the near future. I guarantee it. I will favorably indorse your application if you apply," Welt explained.

Two weeks after submitting his application, Zane received word to go before a review board at brigade headquarters. The review took place in the officer's club over drinks. Five senior officers had drinks and asked a few questions. Lendrain could not believe it when his commission came through.

"I do not know who you have stroke with but that's the quickest approval I have ever seen," Captain Lendrain had said. "You are now a first lieutenant in the Regular Army of the United States. Congratulations, Lieutenant Zane."

Those were the only complimentary words his aviation section ever heard him say. However, Lendrain had one more incident in his plus column. Zane wanted to fly H-21s. Lendrain thought he was nuts.

"Jesus Zane, you must have a death wish. Their blades are wood and their engines are renowned for swallowing valves. They are going down in rice paddies everyday. Have you cleared this with the 6th Trans CO?" Lendrain asked.

"Yes, sir. He's approved a local area transition," Zane explained.

"I will have to check and make sure. You have my approval as long as it does not interfere with your maintenance duties," Lendrain said.

Two events in the Pentagon directed attention to Dale Zane. The first was General Welt's recommendation for Zane's Regular Army Commission, which meant a 30-year commitment. The second was his qualification to fly H-21s.

President Kennedy recently authorized additional personnel for duty in Viet Nam. He also expanded an authorization for more helicopters that included H-21s. Zane's file was in the hands of a personnel officer when the requirement arrived. Zane was a warm body already in the Far East. It was simple to send him on temporary duty (TDY) from Korea. He could spend six months in 'Nam and return to Korea with three months remaining on his overseas tour. They promptly sent orders.

Zane felt the Boeing 707 begin its takeoff run. As they accelerated, the passengers grew quiet. When the landing gears came up and locked, a roar echoed throughout the airplane. Those persons on their way home were cheering as loud as they could.

"More power to them," Zane thought as he placed a pillow by his window seat.

He watched Korea disappear through breaks in the clouds. They climbed higher into a sunny blue sky. Zane slept soundly for the first time in three months.

Chapter Twenty Nine

December 1962

A little knowledge that acts is worth infinitely more than much knowledge that is idle.
Kahlil Gibran (1883–1931), Lebanese poet, novelist.

Colonel Jean Danjou focused his binoculars. Lying prone, he rested his elbows in red clay typical of the region known as the Plain of Jars. The Plain was a mystery. Nobody knew who created the huge vessels scattered about this highland plain between Luang Prabang and Vientiane. Nobody knew for sure what they were for. The most likely speculation was that they were funeral urns. The jars dated back some 2000 years and the largest of them weighed six tons. The high plateau region was strategic because it was the juncture of Yunnan Province, China, Cambodia, Thailand, and Vietnam.

To his front, Jean watched parachutes blossom and drift to earth. Overhead, in plain view, he watched what he knew to be Soviet aircraft delivering supplies to Pathet Lao and North Vietnamese troops. He knew they were Soviet because he had monitored their radio traffic for almost two months.

Next to him, Je Ling Boa watched approaches to their position. Boa doubted if an enemy could see them unless they stepped on them. This Frenchman was no novice to camouflage. This very morning he had watched him prepare for this mission. First, he had clothing that matched flora in their region. Next, he took vegetation and covered his body. Finally, he applied camouflage grease to all exposed flesh. It was like watching a person disappear one part at a time.

Boa was a Hmong tribesman. His home village was south of their present position. He remembered when the Viet Minh started coming to his village. They were forming military groups from their people. They were constantly telling how France and the United States were trying to take their country from them. They were imperialist trying to exploit them. However, his leader, Vang Pao, told them they were lies. He believed Vang Pao.

As a child, he had seen people helping his villages. In particular, he remembered a medicine man named Tom Dooley. He healed the sick and would not accept anything for doing it. He only wanted to help.

Another American, a farmer like his father, helped them. His name was Edgar Buell. He trained his sister to be a nurse so she could heal others. He also helped construct schools. Many called him Pop as he asked. Because of him, he could read and write.

The French could not all be bad. They held elections so that Laos' people could manage their country. They removed their military and soon left. The Viet Minh said they had to fight to make them go. Maybe they did but the Hmong didn't. He did not care for the Pathet Lao because they were the same as the

Viet Minh. They were the ones trying to take his country. No, Je Ling Boa believed Vang Pao and would fight with him forever.

Jean saw what he most feared, Regular North Vietnamese Army units working with the Pathet Lao. He watched as columns of trucks streamed south on Route 7. Based upon intercepted radio messages, he knew that Kong Le, the Pathet Lao leader, requested NVA units. However, he had to leave their monitoring too soon. He did not know what the NVA response was.

He had to learn for himself. That's why he did not return to Bangkok with Briscoe. What Briscoe didn't know was that he helped on the mission to provide information for France. He realized that Briscoe was not naïve enough to think his presence was for anything else.

Now, he knew. He estimated at least two battalions of NVA troops. They were well equipped and had supplies for the Pathet Lao. Kong Le was now receiving support from the Soviets and the NVA. This was vital information that he must get to France.

If Briscoe delivered his message and the cylinder, France knew that he would go to Saigon. From his present position, Saigon was his best travel route. He could travel parallel to the NVA as they moved south. He would be able to observe their activities in detail. Of particular interest was whether they traveled through Cambodia or not. With such a long route, they would need service facilities, truck parks and supply depots. His task was to document them.

Information gathered would reveal what the United States and France already suspected. They already knew that there was significant activity along what they called the Ho Chi Minh trail. However, they did not know the extent of it. Whether France would relay his information to the United States was another matter. That decision was not his to make. He was a messenger nothing more.

Jean turned to Boa and made a gesture for them to leave. They crawled backward away from the hill's crest. On other hills surrounding the plain, more Hmong troops watched the Communists. They had Kong Le in a trap on the plain but could not do anything about it. They expected a delivery of supplies from the United States at anytime. During past years, they received supplies from the Royal Laos and Royal Thai military. Yet, it was not enough to engage a force the size of that now on the plain. They needed more, much more. If it didn't come soon, they would lose a decided advantage. Kong Le would slip away to the south with the NVA units.

Away from the crest, the pair rose to a low crouch. They moved rapidly in short bursts. They stopped and watched. Three miles south, they were close to Vang Pao's headquarters. They felt safe enough to stand but remained steadfastly alert. Soon they would be near Vang Pao's outposts. If they did not approach and be recognized, they would die swiftly. The Hmong were deadly.

Boa suddenly stopped and lowered himself to a crouched position. He extended a hand with his fingers spread and palm downward. He made up and down gestures causing Jean to take a prone position while Boa moved forward. Plucking a leaf from a nearby plant, Boa placed it in his mouth to moisten it. Once wet, he stretched it between two fingers and blew across it making a bird's sound. He crouched lower and waited. He blew twice in succession. From amidst trees to their front, two bushes moved towards them. Boa stood upright and signal Jean to do the same.

"I bring the Frenchman to see Vang Pao. He is expecting him. Do we have your permission to pass?" Boa asked.

One of the Hmong raised one hand with his palm facing them. He shook his head indicating that they could not. The other tribesman disappeared into the jungle. Shortly, he reappeared and whispered to the one facing them. Without a word, he turned and started into the jungle. Boa motioned Jean to follow.

Vang Pao's camp was a cold camp. They dared not have a fire because the enemy was too near. After passing through an inner ring of troops, Jean and Boa arrived at a tunnel entrance. It was a portal into a limestone cliff. Looking up, Jean observed an American 50-caliber machine gun's barrel protruding between boulders. He and Boa entered. As their eyes adjusted to the darkness, four Hmong soldiers approached and placed blind folds on them. After numerous turns, their guides stopped and removed the scarves from their eyes. Vang Pao sat in front of them in a squat, Hmong style. He indicated for them to join him.

"I know of you Frenchman. You came through our country many years ago. Why are you here again?" Vang Pao asked.

Jean knew better than to lie. To do so would immediately discredit him. They knew what he was doing but not why. He was French and the French were gone.

"I am here to learn what the Pathet Lao and NVA are doing. It is important that I provide this information to my leaders. It will help defeat the Communists," Jean explained.

"You French, and the Americans, are not very smart," he replied. "The Communists know how to organize and exert control over people. It is a lesson you should learn," Vang Pao replied.

Continuing he said, "While the West was complying with rules established in Geneva, the Pathet Lao extended their influence throughout this region. When they take control of a village, it is different than when Western powers do it. The West thinks in terms of holding terrain. The Pathet Lao think in terms of minds. If they control minds, they have little use for the terrain."

"You are correct," Jean agreed. "We did not learn much until it was too late."

Vang Pao picked up a twig from the cave's floor. He used it to clear an area in dirt immediately to his front. In the cleared area, he drew a circle.

Looking directly at Jean, he continued, "When the Pathet Lao take military control of a village, they immediately begin to take control of minds. They put their people into office with existing civil leaders."

Vang Pao drew another circle inside the larger one.

He said, "This is my district, they installed one of their people as a district chief in the same office of our district chief."

Vang Pao drew another smaller circle inside the other two.

Explaining farther, he said, "They did the same in subdistricts and villages. This formed a hierarchy of political-military structure. The village leaders became part of the Pathet Lao chain of command. They integrated the villagers into their guerrilla organization down to its lowest level.

He drew a smaller circle inside the others and said, "Children became lookouts. Women became cooks and nurses. Western leaders do not think in these terms. All they want to do is attack and kill the Communists. The Westerners say they have won control. They control nothing but dirt. When they leave, the Communists return."

Jean commented, "I have seen this and agree. Since we are Westerners we cannot become district chiefs without causing a revolt against us."

Vang Pao stood upright. He indicated for Jean to do the same. He placed a hand on each of Jean's shoulders. Looking at him intently, he said, "Tell me Frenchman. Why do my men fight the Pathet Lao and NVA? Why do we willing die fighting them?"

Perplexed, Jean did not promptly answer, Vang Pao said, "Because Westerners came to our villages and helped us. They taught us how to care for our elderly and the sick. They helped us build schools and get an education. Our own government never did that for us and we did not fight for them. Yet, Westerners did and we fight for them. If you take no other message than this to your people, you should consider your venture a success. You cannot kill an idea or a faith but you can replace it. You must go now."

Before Jean or Boa could speak, Vung Pao put blindfolds on them again and moved them from the cave. Outside the cave, their escorts removed their blindfolds. They squinted while adapting to daylight. Bao spoke first.

"I am to go with you. From the plains through the valley of the Mekong, people know and trust me. Once I was a trader and traveled throughout the region. My children live in Hmong villages with my four wives. Yes, I will lead you," Boa said.

"This may take months," Jean told Boa.

"I understand. With me, your effort will not take months. I know every stream and canal feeding the Mekong. Many tribes are not Hmong and speak different dialects. In addition, few speak English or French. You will have to take precautions that will slow you. With me, this will not be a problem and you can travel without fear that a tribe might misunderstand your motives. The matter is settled. Come with me. We must prepare for our journey," Boa explained.

For one month, Boa led Jean over rugged mountains and through thick jungle. They left Laos and entered Cambodia. Seldom did they see a Laotian or Cambodian soldier. Often they circumvented outposts and counted those manning it. Jean knew from his experiences at Na Son and Dien Bien Phu that the North Vietnamese accomplished logistical miracles. Yet, what his journal contained few would ever believe. He documented a vast roadway from North Viet Nam to South Viet Nam. Side routes from the main trail provided access to any part of South Viet Nam from the DMZ south. Many parts were rudimentary but required little work to improve them. He could not help but admire their underwater fords across raging rivers. At places, swinging bridges crossed deep canyons for foot traffic. Some distance away there would be a bridge strong enough for armored vehicles. Much work was in the early stages of construction but basics were in place. He counted the stockpiles of weapons and supplies. In

Cambodia, along South Viet Nam's border, he drew sketches of training camps, supply depots and medical units. This was not going to be a short war.

"I will not be a help to you now," Boa said.

"Why is that?" Jean asked.

Jean and Boa were 100 meters from a highway that crossed into South Viet Nam from Cambodia. Other than some bicycle travel by local farmers, they had not observed any NVA forces. However, the day before, five kilometers to their west into Cambodia, they located a Viet Cong (VC) training camp and supply area.

"The highway you see passes into South Viet Nam. It is QL-13 that goes to An Loc, a provincial capitol. There is a small village after you cross the border. Its name is Loc Ninh. I know nothing of these places. You are close to your destination Saigon. Ql-13 will take you there. You no longer need me, besides I must return to my people," Boa explained.

Jean saw the logic in what Boa said. This Hmong tribesman had been of invaluable service. He had responsibilities elsewhere.

Jean asked. "How can I repay you for your dangerous work for me?"

"Destroy the Communists," Boa answered quickly.

With those words, Boa faded into heavy vegetation surrounding their position. It was as if he was never there.

Jean spent the remaining daylight studying the terrain along QL-13. Almost all of it consisted of deserted rubber plantations. At one time, this region produced vast amounts of rubber. Now, it lay idle. Nutrients filled the soil making it productive.

However, rubber did not have the importance that it once did. During the war, synthetic products replaced most of it. Some tried to make a living by harvesting from the rubber trees. Most of them failed. Jean wondered why someone did not try to grow a different crop. He found this thought intriguing.

After sunset, Jean crossed into South Viet Nam. He paralleled the highway and by passed Loc Ninh by moving south and making an arc that returned him to the highway. He used the same method to bypass An Loc. A few kilometers later, he approached a stream. He tried to find a place to cross but the water was swift and deep. He moved north along the stream's bank and located a bridge where QL-13 crossed. It appeared unguarded. He waited.

After an hour, a jeep approached the bridge. Three persons were in it but Jean could only see their outlines. He could not determine who they were. It stopped on the bridge.

"Where are you Bien?" Someone in the jeep asked loudly in Vietnamese.

No response came. The jeep's driver got out and leaned over the bridge railing.

"Are you down there?" He asked, yelling quite loud.

"Yes," someone answered. "I had to relieve myself. I am on my way."

Jean watched a soldier climb the opposite shore to where the bridge crossed. He stopped to retrieve his rifle leaning against the bridge abutment.

The other two soldiers in the jeep got out and waited for the soldier approaching with his rifle.

"We should have left you," the driver said while getting into the jeep. "Hurry, I am hungry."

Jean watched the jeep lurch and its gears growl in protest as the driver and passenger sped away. Silently, he moved closer to the bridge. He stopped in some tall reeds on the stream's edge and listened.

One guard said, "One day Bien will get caught sleeping by an officer. Then he will be in big trouble."

"I do not think he was sleeping," the other guard commented. "He would have taken his rifle with him."

"Ah yes," the first guard replied. "I saw when he got it at the bridge's end. Perhaps he was not asleep."

Jean did not want to cross the river at the bridge. He would have to find another place. Traveling downstream, the farther he went the deeper and wider it grew.

"Damn, I could cross anywhere but my journal might get wet. I cannot risk that," Jean thought. "I must either stay here for the day or cross now."

He checked the straps on his backpack and made sure they were tight. The container was supposed to be waterproof but he did not want to risk it. He eased his feet into the water and immediate felt the swift current. Raising his backpack above his head with his left arm, he began a one-armed stroke across the stream. He completed his task swiftly and silently.

As his feet touched bottom, he began his short climb to dry ground. He tried to lift his left foot but could not. Moving back, he tried to determine what was holding it. Reaching into the water, he felt a fish net tangled around his foot. He unsheathed his knife and quickly cut the net free and climbed ashore. He crouched and waited. He never felt the blow to his head.

As if he was inside a metal tank, he heard voices. He felt an aching throb above his left ear. Remaining still, he opened one eye. Standing over him were two Viet Cong guerillas. One held a flashlight while the other rummaged through his backpack.

The one examining his pack said suddenly, "Ayah, look at this."

The soldier held Jean's gold watch. He immediately dropped the backpack. Both became excited and the one holding the flashlight grabbed at the watch.

"Give it to me. I found him," he said. "I have to examine it."

He took the watch, handed the flashlight to the other man, and said, "Shine the light on it so that I can see."

The VC with the watch pressed its stem and it opened. He looked closely at the cover's picture and then the watch's face.

Looking at his wristwatch he said, "The time is incorrect. I suspect it is worthless."

Pulling its stem outward, he set the correct time as Jean closed his eye. There was a thunderous explosion. Jean immediately grabbed his pack and raced for a levee. He did observe the scene before grabbing his backpack.

The VC holding the watch had no hands or wrists. His cohort had both hands over his face with blood seeping between them. Both were screaming.

Guards on the bridge took cover and began firing in the explosion's direction. One, with an M-1 Garand, emptied one clip and exhausted another. Both took cover on the other side of the road and waited. The two VC lay dead; their bodies riddled with bullets.

Jean, on the levee's other side, hugged its steep bank, and thought, "I must move from here quickly. Others will arrive and begin searching."

Moving over levees and using them for cover, Jean neared the highway. At dawn, he saw two Americans approaching in a three-quarter ton truck. He walked to the highway's edge and waved.

The truck came to a sudden stop as its wheels cried in protest. Two suspicious NCOs opened their doors, resting M-14 rifles on the vehicle's window edges.

One yelled at Jean, "Who the hell are your?"

Jean answered, "Colonel Jean Danjou, Foreign Legionnaire."

Both NCOs laughed aloud and one retorted, "No shit, we thought you were General Harkins, MACV Commander.

Chapter Thirty

July 1961

This is not a jungle war, but a struggle for freedom on every front of human activity.
Lyndon B. Johnson (1908–73), U.S. Democratic politician, president.

Lieutenant Diem felt his enemy watching his team. This was a sense passed down through generations of Tia tribesmen. He knew that Lieutenant Vinh, following his team, would also feel it. Onboard Air America's C-46 enroute to Khe Sanh, Vinh said the NVA would see them land and move to Lao Bao and he was correct.

Their unit's mission was to take positions around Techepone, Laos, and report their observations. Now, Diem was moving his team from Lao Bao to objective Xray southwest of Tchepone. Vinh followed, moving to objective Yankee, due south of Techepone. Lieutenant Bien was moving his team to point Zulu, southeast of their objective area.

Captain Hoi kept Lieutenant Bhan's team at Lao Bao with him. They were a reserve force Hoi could use to help other teams. In addition, they provided security for his command post. Hoi told his lieutenants to avoid contact. Their mission was to observe and gather information. However, if they did make contact and were unable to move, Hoi could send Bhan's team to help.

Diem stopped his commandos and had them take cover. He raised his right hand with his fist clenched. This was his signal to Vinh to move his men. If Vinh's team received fire, Diem would be in a position to provide fire support so that Vinh could move safely. Diem and Vinh agreed upon this leapfrog technique before arriving at Khe Sanh.

Captain Hoi was proud of his commandos. They were Tia tribesmen known for their fighting abilities. Their home had always been the jungle. They were South Viet Nam's elite forces of Airborne Rangers. They each had to complete a rigorous training course to be members. In addition, most of them came from the same villages. They knew each other's strengths and weaknesses. They knew their thoughts. They were of one mind working together in a deadly concert within mountainous jungle shadows.

Each team was in position as darkness cloaked them. Their lieutenants sent one man from each team to probe obstacles surrounding Techepone's airfield. They knew that three NVA companies were in position south of the field. They worked their way past them undetected and began memorizing every tripwire, bobby-trap, and weak point in their assigned sector. With dawn approaching, they withdrew to concealed positions where they could observe. They were certain that someone reported their presence when they departed Khe Sanh. Their task was to remain hidden while the NVA hunted for them.

Vinh, with his radio operator, lay within tangled roots of an ancient tree. They blended into surrounding foliage and were impossible to detect unless stepped upon by someone.

"Snake's head, this is fang, over," Vinh's radio operator whispered.

Captain Hoi's operator at Lao Bao answered, "Fang, snake's head, over."

"Estimate battalion engineers, over," Vinh relayed to his operator who repeated it.

"Snake's head, roger, over," Captain Hoi acknowledged.

At dawn, Vinh watched NVA engineers begin their workday. They moved through a clear zone in their perimeter. Vinh noted the cleared zone on his map and continued his observations. He heard hidden heavy equipment engines start. From beneath camouflaged parking spots, two bulldozers began clearing away debris from beneath the jungle's canopy. Two officers moved through the trees marking those to remove. They were leaving trees that provided thick overhead cover. Observers from the air would not be able to see anything parked beneath them.

While watching the clearing activities, his radio operator nudged him. Vinh turned to look at him. He pointed toward the cleared zone observed earlier. A command vehicle was slowing moving through to avoid mines. Vinh could see three people in it. One was the driver and the other two appeared to be officers. He used his binoculars in an attempt to determine their rank.

As Vinh adjusted his focus settings, he could see the two officers clearly. One was continuously gesturing with his hands while the other watched. He focused on the gesturing officer and saw that he was a colonel of engineers. Putting his binoculars down, he relayed this information to Hoi.

After acknowledgement, he studied the other officer. What once was a fuzzy figure became a clear image that leaped at him. It was as if his heart stopped. He felt perspiration on his forehead and his hands began to tremble. The officer's artillery insignia and colonel's rank were in clear view. It was his brother Anh. He focused again with the same determination.

Lowering his binoculars, he tried to think. While doing so, his radio operator was looking at him in anticipation of another transmission. Vinh said nothing.

His radio operator whispered, "Lieutenant?"

Putting his binoculars to his eyes, he looked again. It was Anh without a doubt.

Without lowering his binoculars, he said, "Colonel, field artillery."

His operator immediately relayed Vinh's information. Vinh continued to watch as mixed feelings coursed throughout him. He wanted to run to him and tell about Minh Thanh. He wanted to hug him as a brother and learn of news from home. Vinh could tell him what happened to their mother. There was so much that he wanted to do. He dared not move.

Noise of an approaching airplane came from the northwest. Vinh and his radioman watched with interest for it to appear. It came into view above the far tree line and loomed larger with time. Over the airfield, the craft turned west to travel away from them. When it was almost out of sight, it made a 180-degree turn and approached the airfield at a higher altitude. Vinh recognized it as a Soviet transport.

Once over the airfield, a large, dark object appeared from the transport and began to fall. Early in its descent, parachutes began opening. There were five chutes connected to a medium-sized road grader. While it drifted earthward, the transport returned to a northwest heading and disappeared. Vinh realized why.

"If they continued to the southeast, they would fly into South Viet Nam's airspace," he thought. "They are delivering supplies and do not want to be discovered. Well, that's no longer deniable."

His radioman quickly relayed the aircraft sighting and its activity. Soon, another transport came into view. It dropped crates and fuel drums. Vinh's radio stayed busy making reports. However, the Soviet planes were of no interest to him, only Anh.

They watched trucks arrive with load after load of fuel drums. Vinh knew they were full because it took four men to unload one drum. Two in a truck's bed would roll it to its edge. From there, they turned it onto its side. Using ropes, they lowered it as two men placed it on a wood platform.

"They are building a truck park and fuel depot," Vinh realized.

Vinh removed a camera from his backpack and mounted it on a tripod. He began taking pictures. He spent considerable time watching his brother through its zoom lens. However, he did not want to make his radioman suspicious. Nevertheless, he only took pictures of the engineer colonel. He did not allow Anh to be in any photo. He would not intentionally put Anh in danger. Yet, he had to document this place.

Slightly before sunset, Vinh moved his team into a defensive perimeter for the night, as did the other commandos. They positioned themselves into a ring-of-rings. Each lieutenant made sure that his automatic weapons could provide fire support for the other two rings. They previously cut firing lanes through the dense foliage. During an attack of any one team, the others moved their light machine guns to a set direction. Holding this direction, they fired down the lanes. Anyone moving through a lane died. Diem learned the technique by watching Japanese build defensive positions. He passed the information to the others.

At night, Vinh's mind drifted to memories of Anh. He remembered how, at Dien Bien Phu, their ammunition supply did not work properly. They were not able to use their artillery at times for lack of munitions. He recalled Anh making trips to determine what the problems were. Now, Anh was here personally overseeing supply route construction. He was remembering his lessons learned fighting the French. Each day Anh appeared once for an hour, sometimes two, to check progress. He would then leave. Vinh was sure that he was inspecting construction elsewhere.

For six days, they had been observing activity at Techepone. Vinh watched as the NVA closed their cleared area from inside their perimeter. He knew every mine, trip-wire and flare's location. The defenders installed them in the same place every night.

Furthermore, Vinh did not understand why the NVA did not find them. They had to know that they were still in the area. They depleted their rations once and a resupply was necessary from Khe Sanh. He knew there would be no more because the weather was getting worse. Low clouds and rain began every day by Noon. Aircraft could not land at Khe Sanh. They would have to leave soon. These factors caused Vinh to do the unimaginable.

Vinh stripped nude during a massive, nighttime downpour. He made a loincloth from a fatigue shirt. His only weapon was his survival knife. He had one small package no larger than a soda cracker. In it, he had compressed pages with information about Minh Thanh, Diem, and him. He sealed the notes with thick wax from a candle. He slipped through his defensive circle and went toward Techepone.

In a full squat, he slowly worked through the defensive wire of the NVA. He would pull aside a single stand of barbed wire at a time and tie it to another. Continuing in this fashion, he created a body-sized tunnel through the wire. He disabled every trip flare, alarm device and mine. When lightning flashed, he froze in position. He knew the NVA felt secure and could hardly see through the massive downpours of rain.

Vinh moved through the interior of the NVA encampment. He found Anh's command vehicle next to a tent. Gently, he moved the tent's flap aside and watched as his eyes adapted. He saw Anh in a hammock sleeping soundly. Once inside, Vinh placed his waxed package in one of Anh's boots.

Backtracking, Vinh rearmed every device he disarmed during his entry. He put every barbed wire strand in place. The rain erased any trail of his ever being in their camp. As he moved through the jungle toward his defensive position, a hand grabbed his bare shoulder. He raised his knife to strike but saw Diem's face staring at him streaked with rain. He smiled and the pair returned to their men.

Captain Hoi ordered them to withdraw. The NVA detected their movement and Lieutenant Bien's team started receiving fire from an NVA patrol. Two members fell severely wounded at first contact. Mortar rounds began hitting his position wounding more. Vinh and Diem moved and provided covering fire for Bien to get his wounded back to Lao Bao. Vinh held his position to allow Diem to move to where he could receive covering fire from Lao Bao. Vinh began taking mortar fire. They knew exactly where his unit was. If anyone tried to move, they received heavy automatic weapons fire. Two of his men died when they moved to return fire.

Vinh's group was the last team to try to return to Lao Bao. He was out of range to receive support from Lao Bao. Mortar rounds kept pounding his position as well as continuous automatic weapons fire. He couldn't stay and he couldn't move. Suddenly, firing stopped. Vinh had his men remained absolutely still. They could hear the NVA withdrawing.

"Why are they leaving," he wondered. "They had us. We couldn't do anything."

Not believing such good fortune, he had his team stay completely still until nightfall. First, he had his dead removed to Lao Bao. Vinh, his radio operator, and two men with machine guns departed last. They encountered no resistance. They stumbled into Lao Bao exhausted and thankful to be alive.

When reports began arriving in Saigon about observations made by Captain Hoi's unit, they were immediately sent to Washington, D.C. President Kennedy became extremely upset that the NVA were trying to take portions of Laos. In the past, they had been sensitive on the subject. However, when they learned the magnitude of the NVA's efforts, they made a decision to expand across border operations in Laos.

Top secret instruction went to the Office of Combined Studies (OSD) in Saigon's American Embassy. OSD was a cover for a small group of CIA operatives. A major portion of expanded operations into Laos became their responsibility. They would have to expand the training program for Vietnamese Airborne Rangers. Colonel Ray Balbeery, Chief of OSD, wanted to learn first hand what happened during the Tchepone operation. He arranged to be present during debriefings when Captain Hoi's unit returned.

Hoi's unit arrived at Thu Duc, north of Saigon, in mid-August. Team NCOs began training replacements, while intelligence personnel debriefed Captain Hoi and his lieutenants. Balberry attended every session.

Colonel Balberry had high praise for Lieutenants Vinh and Diem. He recognized their leadership abilities and individual courage. In particular, their detailed reports gave a vivid picture of the Laotian situation. He also learned that they were Catholics. This would put them in the good graces of President Diem who was wary of anyone not Catholic. Without consulting Hoi, or his superiors, he recommended Vinh and Diem for promotion to captain. In addition, he wanted them to command units to conduct expanded across border operations in Laos. Balbeery's recommendations received approval.

Minh Thanh squealed with delight when she saw Vinh and Diem in uniform with their new captain's insignia, "You look so grand," she said. "Oh Vinh, it seems that just a few days ago we were pulling water from the Nam Youm. Now, look at you, a captain. Uncle Diem I am so proud of you too."

They were in the parlor of the Catholic Church in the Cholon District of Saigon. They sat in the same parlor where they spent time together the last time they visited Saigon. Seated around the room's coffee table, their animated chatter rang with joy for being together again.

"Minh Thanh, I have news about Anh," Vinh said. "I saw him while we were away."

Reacting before Minh Thanh could speak, Diem exclaimed, "You never mentioned that to me."

Embarrassed for not having confided in Diem, he explained, "If I had told you, you might have had to reveal it to the intelligence people during debriefing."

Slightly angered by what Diem considered an affront, he answered sharply, "You didn't tell. What makes you think I would?"

"Please, Diem," Vinh said. "Do not be angry. I did tell them that I saw two colonels. I simply did not tell them that I knew who one of them was."

Continuing, Vinh explained about leaving his unit and putting a note in Anh's boot. He also revealed that he thought Anh had intervened to stop the NVA from destroying them because he knew Diem and Vinh were in the group.

"I believe you are right," Diem said. "It was strange that they stopped their attack when they did."

"What have you two been doing? Why were you in Laos? Who was shooting at you?" Minh Thanh asked filled with fear for their lives.

"I am sorry Minh Thanh. I should not have spoken of our mission. They forbid us to speak of our missions. I beg you not to mention what I told to anyone. Do I have your solemn promise?" Vinh asked pleading.

"You have my promise," she responded.

Continuing Minh Thanh said, "Anh is not the only relative we have in North Viet Nam. We have family from Hanoi to the Nam Youm valley. Many of them are young men who will either join or become conscripts in the NVA. We will be killing our brothers and sisters. In spirit, we are all brothers and sisters. I hate this war. I hate all wars. They are so wrong."

Covering her face with her hands, Minh Thanh leaned forward and began to weep. Vinh and Diem sat beside Minh Thanh in an effort to comfort her.

Her grief spent, she sat upright and looked at Vinh and Diem in turn, and said, "We do not have freedom in the south. President Diem is a dictator and a murderer. Those who oppose him, die. My students tell me these things. At first, I did not believe them. He claims to be a good Catholic. Nevertheless, he uses that to punish, without cause, Buddhists. He is driving our people to the Communists. It is terrible for people in Saigon and getting worse in the provinces."

"Perhaps he will not be elected president when we vote," Vinh commented.

"There will be no vote," Minh Thanh responded.

"He will never give up being president. Those who work for him are corrupt. They steal from the treasury and money that's is supposed to be in the lottery. It is a terrible situation," she continued.

Diem arose and said, "We must go. There is an important meeting this afternoon and we must attend."

Minh Thanh stood as Vinh did. She hugged them both and promised to keep a candle lit for them. She continued to cry as she watched them leave.

Upon their return to Thu Duc, Vinh and Diem learned they were going to command companies. Vinh would command an experienced unit that required replacement training. He had two weeks to get them mission ready for an airborne operation. Diem would have to wait two weeks before there would be enough graduates from Airborne Ranger training to form a company. He would have one month to get them mission ready.

This would be the first time that the pair would fight apart. They lived together in the highlands and trained together at Kontum. After that, they underwent Airborne Ranger training together. The ultimate cement of their relationship was a bond established in combat. It was going to be difficult for them but they accepted the situation stoically. Their consensus was that the situation was one of divine will and who were they to question it.

Vinh moved to his company's unit area on the northwest side of Thu Duc. His unit's personnel were on a short leave after recent operations in Laos. He had a few personnel available to meet and get to know. He was in his command tent after being in his new unit for two days.

A clerk looked through the tent flap leading to his office area and said, "Captain, there is a Captain Hoi to see you," he stated.

"Send him in right away," Vinh said while getting to his feet.

As Captain Hoi entered, it was all Vinh could do to keep from saluting him. As a new captain, he had not yet adjusted to his new station in the military.

Vinh walked forward and extended his hand and said, "Welcome captain, it is an honor to see you again."

Hoi answered, "I had hoped this day would come. You deserve it plus I have a promise to fulfill."

"What's that?" Vinh asked.

Hoi opened his briefcase on Vinh's desk and removed two miniature bottles of Johnny Walker Scotch. Deftly removing their caps, he passed one to Vinh.

"I told you," Hoi said, "that I would have two drinks with you. It is time for the second and I consider it an honor."

The pair quickly emptied the small bottles and disposed of them in a trashcan. Hoi took his briefcase; said his goodbye; and left Vinh's tent without further discussion.

Vinh could only respect Captain Hoi's visit to a junior officer's unit to keep his promise. This was a matter of honor that he had kept. Many would not have. Vinh vowed to maintain an equivalent position of honor with his new lieutenants. They arrived soon and there was little time for preparation.

Vinh received his mission briefing from Major Kinh his battalion commander. In attendance at the briefing was the American Colonel Bayberry. Now it was time to brief his lieutenants. He had only known them for ten days. He did not consider this sufficient but he had to do with what he had. In addition, he had eight lieutenants whereas his previous unit had four. They consisted of 14 man teams each with its own communications.

Standing beside an easel, Vinh pointed to the Se Kamane River in Attopeu province, Laos.

"Your mission is to patrol and gather information," Vinh explained. "Tomorrow morning you will jump at 08:00 hours. First priority is to establish a secure perimeter for following drops. The first teams will be Teams Delta, Echo, and Foxtrot. You have the most experience that is why you are going in first."

Looking directly at the commanders of the three teams, Vinh asked, "If you have questions, ask them now. After you are in the drop zone, it will be too late."

Hearing no questions, Vinh continued, "Lima, Mike, Oscar and Romeo will follow at 15 minute intervals. These jumps will not take place until I provide clearance. I will jump first with Delta team. The last jump will be Victor along with a ration drop. Again, you must have clearance from me."

Pausing momentarily, Vinh gestured with his pointer to the room's rear and said, "With us will be Lieutenant Hanh. Please stand lieutenant."

"He will be our fire support coordinator. If there is a heavy engagement, we have air support sorties. In addition, during a portion of our mission, we will be in range of some artillery units. We can call upon them for support. Every support request comes to me and I will coordinate your requests with Hanh," Vinh continued.

Vinh gave each person in the briefing an inquisitive look and said, "Insertion will be by C-47 from Than San Nhut. Transportation will be outside at 06:30 hours tomorrow. I expect each of you to inspect your men to assure their sanitation. There must be no identification with our country whatsoever.

Vinh jumped first followed by Lieutenant Hanh. Delta, Echo, and Foxtrot teams floated earthward through low hanging clouds. Fortunately, only one person had difficulty by landing in the river. It was monsoon seasons and the river was out of its banks and swift. Team members recovered the man but his parachute floated downstream. Vinh canceled jumps for the remainder of the first day. They would commence the following morning. While establishing a perimeter Vinh found three punji pits. After his experience, he was quick to identify them much to the amazement of his men. Hidden quite well, it was difficult to detect them.

The night was miserable. Constant rain and insects plagued them and few could rest. The new lieutenants, in particular, found their state almost intolerable. Vinh quickly let them know that they were Airborne Rangers and they could expect worse. Unknown to Vinh, it would come sooner than later.

Early the next morning, there were considerable breaks in the overcast. They heard the drone of an aircraft overhead and watched for it. Never seeing it, they still established contact by radio. Vinh advised them the drop zone was secure. Soon they saw chutes descending toward them.

Lima, Mike, Oscar, and Romeo teams landed without incident. Vinh dispersed them around the perimeter while he waited for the final drop. It came within one half-hour and was successful.

Vinh dispersed his teams farther away from their drop zone should someone detect them. He gathered his lieutenants to issue instructions.

"I am forming two groups. The northern group will consist of Mike, Oscar, Romeo, and Delta teams. You will patrol in different directions and report any significant events. The remaining teams will be the South group. Lieutenant Hanh and I will travel with you. Hanh you stay close to me," Vinh instructed.

"The rains will make it hard to find trails. However, when you find one, it will likely be fresh. Use caution for those making it will be near. We're going to stash our rations above ground in trees. If we leave the rice on the ground, it will ruin. Cover it well and protect it for we won't get another drop for a month. Maintain radio contact. Let's go," Vinh ordered.

The north and south groups used their drop zone as a start point. Each individual team traveled compass headings 20 degrees apart. The south group covered a zone extending from 180 degrees south to 270 degrees west. The north group used the same base compass setting of 20 degrees. The southernmost team of the northern group began at 290 degrees moving away from their drop zone. As they moved away, the farther apart they became. Their patrol pattern was much like the spokes of a wheel.

Vinh moved west on a course of 270 degrees. He patrolled with Foxtrot team. Their pace was one slow step and then stop to look and listen. On the second day, they moved into a region of limestone cliffs. The terrain was hard underfoot and, at times, left some persons exposed. One good thing was a cave they found at the base of a high bluff.

"Hanh you stay here. You may not be able to communicate from inside the cave. Lieutenant Ngoc, have your team clear the cave. We will stay here tonight," Vinh directed.

For the first time in two days, they slept dry. Furthermore, they had a fire and hot food. As Vinh suspected, he could not contact his other teams from inside the cave.

"Lieutenant Ngoc have one of your men go with Lieutenant Hanh. Hanh drop a wire antenna from the bluff's top down to the cave entrance. I will connect our radio to it," Vinh ordered.

With guards posted, communication check completed and a hot meal, Vinh began to relax.

"I would have expected to see more by now," Vinh said as Ngoc and Hanh listened intently.

"I agree Ngoc," answered. "There has to be a major trail or small road through this area. The NVA are striking too far south with ample ammunition. They have to be moving some of it through this area."

Looking at Hanh, Vinh asked. "Where did you learn to adjust artillery and control aircraft?"

"American Special Forces taught me. I went to school for four months at a base in southern Thailand," Hanh answered.

Vinh replied, "I like the artillery. I was a forward observer and worked in a fire direction center at Dien Bien Phu."

"For the French?" Hanh asked.

"No, the Viet Minh," Vinh answered.

Talking in the cave stopped and everyone grew quiet. The only sound was an occasional snap from their fire.

Finally, Lieutenant Ngoc asked hesitantly. "Sir, how did you become an Airborne Ranger from a Tia tribe if you fought with the Viet Minh? I would think that you would be with the NVA?"

Vinh told a short version of his experiences over past years. Confidence seemed to flow through everyone in the cave. The men looked at each other and smiled. Their captain was not some new, "out of some school" officer. He was a hardened, combat veteran. They looked at him differently after their night in the cave.

Before dawn, as Vinh and his commandos prepared to leave, an outpost guard reported hearing vehicle noise to the west. He also reported what he thought to be campfires.

Vinh took Hanh and Ngoc aside and said, "Expect forces to our front today. They may be Royal Laotian troops or they could be NVA. We must determine who and what they are doing. If they are NVA in a fixed camp, I want those aircraft sorties ready if I need them Hanh. Get on the radio now and get it done. Ngoc, no matter who they are, we will not make contact. We are observers and cannot sustain an engagement. Brief your men and make sure they understand.

If they discover us, we will return to these limestone bluffs. They provide excellent cover."

As Vinh left the cave entrance, he saw Hanh recovering his antenna wire and asked. "Do we have those sorties for today?"

"Yes," Hanh answered. "We have two Vietnamese, Douglas A-1 fighter-bombers on standby. They can be here in 15 minutes."

"Excellent," Vinh responded. "Ngoc, get your people moving."

After an hour's travel, Vinh saw a commando give a halt hand signal. The commando group halted and moved to covered, firing positions. Vinh moved forward and joined Ngoc. With Hanh following, the pair moved forward as if in exaggerated slow motion. They made no sound and were only visible when they moved. Otherwise, they were part of the jungle.

Ahead, they saw a fortified base camp but could not determine if they were VC, NVA, or Laotian. No one wore shirts and their headgear was straw work hats. Vinh gave the signal to hold position while they observed.

A cleared area surrounded the position. It was about 100 meters on all sides. No one could approach during daylight without the workers seeing them. After two hours of close observation, they determined that the early vestiges of a road entered the clearing from the north. It wasn't certain but every worker came and went to a small opening in the trees. Vinh deduced this to be a new road's entrance into the clearing.

An uprooted tree lay directly ahead of Vinh's current position. Its roots spread in a large arch as if someone downed the tree with force. This would indicate heavy equipment or elephants. Vinh took an hour to move the 20 yards to the tree. He examined its trunk for marks made by machinery. He found none. A hand touched his ankle.

Lieutenant Ngoc followed Vinh to the tree. Vinh had not noticed because Ngoc was directly to his rear. He moved beside Vinh and pointed through a small hole where the tree's roots and trunk touched ground. Vinh saw nothing unusual and gave Ngoc an inquisitive look.

Ngoc's head swelled and instantly became shrouded in a bloody mist. A millisecond later Vinh heard a rifle shot echo through the jungle. Ngoc slumped beside him with a large portion of his head missing. Vinh eased down and became part of the earth. Red dirt, clinging to exposed roots above him, exploded throwing stinging grains into his face. Again, he heard the rifle fire.

Vinh heard excited voices in the distance toward where he had seen the workers. Laying face down, he dared not move. A sniper knew he was there but could not get a shot because of the tree. Easing his right hand upward, Vinh extended two fingers to form a V. He hoped Hanh would understand he meant numeral two for the air support.

Automatic weapons began firing from the fort's direction. Bullets tore through the dense jungle behind him. No one returned fire. It soon became obvious that their attackers did not know where the others were. Finally, the firing stopped. In an hour, rain began to fall.

Overhead Vinh heard aircraft engines. Their sound would grow in intensity and then fade. This continued for 15 minutes.

"They cannot see to attack," Vinh thought. "I will have to get to cover on my own."

As the rainfall's intensity seemed to be at its highest, Vinh sprang from his position and ran to the trees. No one fired at him. Hanh was where he had left him. Vinh indicated for the others to withdraw. Silently, they worked their way to the limestone cliffs.

Vinh watched as two commandos helped a third get to cover. He appeared to have a leg wound. Vinh made his way to where the wounded soldier lay. While his wound wasn't in a vital area, he was losing considerable blood. They couldn't completely stop his bleeding.

Gesturing to Hanh to join him, he continued to administer to his wounded leg. He gave an injection of morphine that caused the commando to become quiet. Hanh arrived with another soldier carrying Lieutenant Ngoc over his shoulders.

"Give me the radio. You take command of the team. Move this wounded man into the cave and have someone stay with him. The rest of us will remain outside. Hide Ngoc and cover him. Take care of it," Vinh instructed Hanh.

Vinh contacted the other teams and advised them of his situation. He ordered them back to the river for rations and to regroup. One team reported that they had one wounded by a punji stake and needed evacuation.

As darkness fell, Vinh ordered trip wire grenades put in place should someone follow them. He ordered everyone to the river.

At dawn, they found their rations destroyed. Someone had found them and split the bags allowing rain to spoil their rice. Someone stole the remaining items. Unable to continue their mission, Vinh called for a medevac of their wounded. The remainder would move overland into South Viet Nam.

A CH-34 arrived and lifted their wounded to safety. They also retrieved Lieutenant Ncog's body. The remaining forces found a ford across the river and continued east toward the border. While enroute, Vinh received a report that another commando group was coming to meet them and escort them from the area. Two days later, they were safely across the border and with their escort force. Vinh considered his first mission as a captain a complete failure.

During his debriefing with Major Kinh and Colonel Balbeery, Vinh sketched a device that he thought would help future missions.

"What I have in mind is this," Vinh said as he began drawing on a chalkboard. "First, we must reduce our teams to ten men. The current size is more than we need for patrol and observation. This is a harness made from parachutes except there will be no chute or cords. By connecting five harnesses together, we can retrieve from an area by helicopter without landing. Two CH-34s could insert or retrieve a full team."

Balberry gazed at Vinh's crude drawing and asked. "How are you going to get inside the ship?"

"We don't," Vinh answered. "We can remain suspended during insertion and retrieval."

Major Kinh chuckled and said, "I can see five of you hanging beneath an H-34 2,000 feet in the air. You won't get anyone to do that."

"Sir, you might be surprised. At least let me see if I can get some volunteers," Vinh said with obvious sincerity.

Kinh looked at Balbeery and asked. "What do you think colonel? Would you do that?"

"Sure would," Balbeery responded instantly. "I think it's a damn good idea. We should try it."

"Fine," Kinh responded, still somewhat amused. "Vinh go to battalion supply and get some parachutes and see what you can put together. You and four others can go first. Frankly, I think, even if it works, the helicopter will have to hover too long. They'll bring it down with small arms if they don't shoot the five to pieces first."

"While we're on that subject," Balbeery added. "There's considerable talk about arming our helicopters. I'm not talking about door gunners. I mean mounting machine guns and even rockets to their airframes. They could provide covering fires during an insertion or an extraction."

"What do the pilots think?" Kinh asked, showing a more serious side.

"They are for it. At least the ones I've talked to. They are tired of not being able to attack," Balbeery answered.

South Viet Nam's commandos continued their Laotian missions. Vinh and Diem documented extensive activity by North Viet Nam and Pathet Lao forces pouring into Laos. They firmly established that the Communists were saying one thing and doing another. By the summer of 1962, an effort to have Laos in a neutral posture became an agreement from talks at Geneva. Despite this, Ho Chi Minh and General Giap knew they must have a transportation network to support military operations in South Viet Nam.

Based upon Colonel Anh's continued persistence, the two leaders agreed that they must also conduct operations in Cambodia. In a memorandum through General Giap to Ho Chi Minh, Colonel Anh reminded them of the devastation wrought upon Dien Bien Phu. He made it clear that they could never achieve this again without a continuous supply network south. General Giap agreed and made clear to Ho Chi Minh that ultimately they would have to use conventional forces to overcome Diem's government. The key was to know when to use them. For the time being, they would continue to organize South Viet Nam's population and to support their indigenous brothers.

By late 1962, it became clear that there was no neutrality in Laos and would likely never be. In late 1962, President Kennedy agreed to provide additional advisers, helicopters, and general support for Diem's regime. However, the United States Department of State and President Kennedy's National Security Adviser, McGeorge Bundy were becoming wary of Diem and his tactics. Plans for continuing without Diem became fact.

Presidents of two nations died at the hands of assassins in 1963. First, President Diem succumbed during an overthrow of his government. A few weeks later President Kennedy died of gunshot wounds from an assassin. These two events plunged the United States into a dark abyss where it would remain over a decade.

Chapter Thirty One

August 1963

To the rulers of the state then, if to any, it belongs of right to use falsehood, to deceive either enemies or their own citizens, for the good of the state, and no one else may meddle with this privilege.
Plato (c. 427–347 BC), Greek philosopher. *The Republic,* bk. 3, sct. 389

Vanessa could see Galag from her second story bedroom at Haughton House. He was definitely a champion Arabian but had not placed in his first three races. Frederick claimed that was due to their loss of Devon's training skills. She did not wholeheartedly agree with him. Devon picked who he thought would be the right man for the job. Devon knew what he was doing when he sent a letter of introduction with Carlos Weaver.

"Weaver needs more time," she thought. "Galag is young but the spirit of Daytran is in him. She could feel it."

"Not finished yet," Frederick said upon entering their bedroom. "Neville is waiting."

"I'm just double checking everything," Vanessa answered. "I do not want to get to Udorn, Thailand, and discover that I've forgotten something we really need."

"Dear, Udorn is nothing like Udon Thani. It is a major air force base. They have schools, base exchanges and the like. What they do not have, you can order," Frederick advised.

Vanessa moved around the bed to an open suitcase. Lifting various clothing items, she examined its contents. She examined a stack of tee shirts thumbing their edges like a deck of cards. Satisfied, she stepped backward a step and placed her hands on her hips. She extended her lower lip and blasted away a hair strand over her right eye.

"Captain Earling, you may advise Neville that these are ready to go," Vanessa said with finality.

"I'm going to tell Neville but you have to promise me that you will not lift anything," Frederick said.

"I won't lift anything. Go," she ordered.

Vanessa moved back to the window to watch Galag. She sat in an antique rocking chair that she had used frequently during her recovery. On occasion, she would get a twinge of pain from her abdomen.

"Don't lift anything he says. Glory be it's as if I didn't have a brain in my head. What does that man think I have been doing in physical therapy for a month, sitting on my duff?" She said aloud.

"Ah, it's a beautiful creature you are Galag," she thought as she watched the stallion grazing. "I'm a gonna be missing yah I am."

She was happy at Haughton House. She did not realize how much she missed it. It was six weeks before she could leave the Bangkok hospital. Air America gave Frederick a leave of absence to get her home. They were not flying enough to warrant keeping a full compliment of pilots. Frederick could have stayed if he wanted but he felt he should be with her.

She had a personal trainer during her physical therapy. Her name was Pearl McClain and a lot of woman she was. How they cursed in their native tongue when a muscle complained because Pearl stretched it. Now, she didn't need Pearl. Her recovery was complete.

"My Lady," Neville exclaimed. "Are you really going to need this many suitcases?"

Looking over her shoulder, she smiled at Neville and answered, "You know the lady folk Neville. One carries enough for an army."

She looked back at Galag and wondered why Frederick had to return to Thailand.

He kept saying, "I'm a flyer and there's flying in Thailand. It is where I need to be."

"Damn politicians," she thought. "It was that blasted man William Sullivan that caused this. He's going to be ambassador to Laos. So, what does he do? He contacts a crony in parliament who requests Frederick. Damn his eyes. That's all the excuse Frederick needed to return to Air America."

"Hey, take it easy. You're going to break that rocker," Frederick said from behind her.

Without realizing it, as her anger grew, she accelerated her rocking. When Frederick came in, she was traveling at a breakneck speed.

Springing from her chair, she ran to him, threw her arms around his neck, and said, "Let's holiday in America. We can stay a month."

"Tell you what," he answered. "We will do that as soon as our job is finished. That's a promise."

"You are a hard headed man Frederick Earling and I wonder why I love you. I guess it's because you need someone to take care of you. I volunteered so I have to live with it. Let's go," she said.

Frederick watched Vanessa doze on their way to London's International Airport. He knew she wasn't full strength yet after three major surgeries but she would not relent. She insisted upon coming with him.

"I would like to tell her about Sullivan but I cannot," Frederick thought. "With her temper, she might say the wrong thing or do something she shouldn't. I have to make this right. She would never have been hurt if it wasn't for me."

William Sullivan was the United States Ambassador Designate to Laos. However, in reality, he would also be the chief of CIA operations. Frederick didn't know if it was Sullivan or someone in the United States Executive Branch that approached parliament. Nevertheless, the Prime Minister summoned Frederick for a clandestine meeting. He went and learned that the request for him came through NSA. Supposedly, NSA needed someone to "fly racetrack patterns." The minister did not understand that part. Frederick did.

Nevertheless, he needed to return. He had unfinished business. Business that he wanted to do personally. It started with one incident. He remembered the first incident with crystal clarity. It was while he and Vanessa were still living in Vientiane, Laos. While delivering passengers to Bangkok, he was on a one-hour break. A Royal Thai Army Major approached him in the coffee shop.

"Mind if I join you Captain?" He asked pulling a chair away from his table.

Without waiting for Frederick to answer, he sat and said, "I am Major Saberrank, logistics officer for Major General Phoulouma of the 45th Royal Panther Division."

Frederick immediately noted that there was not even a minor effort toward the customary Thai greeting. This major was rude and arrogant. Frederick started to cup his hands when Major Saberrank continued talking, which made matters worse socially.

"You are a senior pilot for Air America are you not?" Saberrank asked.

"That's correct," Frederick answered in a not too friendly manner.

"You work for the CIA and they pay you to spy on our country," Saberrank stated.

"Listen," Frederick retorted. "Find another seat."

Major Saberrank remained seated and leered at Frederick with an evil grin.

"God's blood, are you deaf?" Frederick asked with a low, hissing whisper.

Gesturing towards Frederick's large, flight manual case Saberrank asked, "Customs never looks in your Jeppesen manual case do they?"

Jeppesen was a company that supplied aviation literature to pilots on a subscription basis. Their documents included detailed diagrams for approaches to airports, notices to airmen (NOTAM), and critical information needed by individuals who flew on a regular basis. It was particularly important to commercial pilots. Air American supplied the service for its pilots. Their case was the size of an overnight suitcase.

"I do not see that's any of your business," Frederick responded.

"Listen captain. I will say this once. Twice a week, when you file your flight plan at Bangkok, you will receive a booklet of approach plates for Southeast Asia. When you land in Vientiane, you will exchange the booklet for a package containing $10,000 in British pound notes. Kindly note this is not a request. You start today," Saberrank said as he arose and then departed.

Speechless, Frederick watched the diminutive major swagger into the crowd. Two other officers joined him as he disappeared amid the many travelers.

"What the hell?" Frederick mumbled.

The more he thought about the situation, the more he became concerned. This man was not joking; he was certain.

"What do I do now?" He pondered. "Nothing, of course."

Later, when Frederick submitted his flight plan, he pushed it to an operations specialist. The man never looked up from his writing on a form. He reached beneath the counter top and retrieved a package. He placed an unopened, set of new Jeppesen approach charts on the counter and pushed it to Frederick. Frederick stared at it and did nothing. The clerk took his flight plan and moved away.

Holding the packet up, Frederick called to the man, “You there. Come here. I do not want this.”

Looking at Frederick, the clerk smiled and returned. He took the packet from Frederick and feigned reading information written on its cover.

Again, with a smile, he held it toward Frederick and said in a low voice, “Take it or your wife dies.”

Each word pounded into him but seemed not to fit into his life. This wasn’t him. It was someone else and he wasn’t hearing this.

Still smiling, the clerk added, “Before you arrive home today.”

As if some robotic force controlled him, Frederick took the package. He walked toward a ramp exit for flight personnel where he boarded his plane for Bangkok. In a daze, he did not respond to a stewardess’s greeting and went directly to his captain’s seat. He began opening the package.

“She looks good to me,” First Officer Gerard Johnson said as he took his seat.

“Good,” Frederick answered as he shuffled through the approach charts.

“New issue captain?” Johnson asked.

“Uh, no, it’s an extra one from last month,” he answered.

Frederick placed the documents in his “Jepp” case and asked. “Ready for start check?”

Johnson replied, “Sure thing captain.”

At Vientiane, after completing shutdown, Frederick said. “Gerard, if you will get the post flight, I need to go to flight operations (Ops).”

“Glad to captain. See you in the parking lot,” Gerard answered.

Frederick turned in their time sheet at Ops and began completing his after action report. One of their regular clerks, who Frederick knew well, asked. “You have some charts for me Captain Earling?”

Frederick removed the opened package and handed it to the clerk who never blinked. He wrapped some scotch tape around it and handed an identical chart set to him.

“Thanks captain,” the fast-talking, gum chewing clerk said without hesitation.

Frederick met Johnson in the parking lot. Their apartments were near each other so they carpooled whenever they could. Gasoline in Vientiane was $3.00 a gallon American.

Frederick and Gerard were fortunate to be flying. The Laotian neutrality agreement, while tenuous at best, significantly reduced operations in Laos. Only because they were senior pilots did Earling and Johnson get to stay and fly commercial. Frederick did not need the money. He simply loved the type of flying Air America did.

Later that night, while Vanessa slept, he removed the new “charts” from his Jepp case. As the major said, it contained $10,000 in British pound notes. They appeared new.

“They’re probably phony,” he thought.

After a detailed examination, he determined them to be authentic. Before dawn, he made his decision.

Two weeks later, he was in Taiwan at Air America's home office. He had posted a letter to Air America's Director of Operations. Since his encounter with Air America's Operations clerk, who gave him the money, he did not know whom to trust. He decided he should make his request to the top. In addition, he did not say why.

To hide his intentions further, he requested that they temporarily amend his schedule to include flights to Taiwan. He hid all of this from Vanessa. She considered it routine.

Frederick, entering the director's office, found someone's idea of an impressive foyer of rotating mirrors as childish. As soon as he entered the main room, he recognized Redford Willhampton behind a custom-made mahogany desk.

"Willhampton, you're a no good SOB. We thought you died," Frederick said joyfully as he took large strides across the room. "We didn't see any chutes and your ship was a blazing torch."

"Aye, and you're the bloody bloke who left me to the Jerries," he answered while rushing to meet Frederick.

The pair slammed together with considerable back slapping and good-natured bantering. Redford noticed Frederick's escort, Meyers, watching.

"Meyers," Redford said. "Give us an hour. On your way out have someone bring some gin and tonic water."

Frederick, the instant he saw him, remembered Willhampton. Frederick was providing air cover for Willhampton's wounded bomber on a night return from bombing Germany. Suddenly, it exploded and plunged earthward. In the darkness, he could not tell if anyone jumped before it exploded on impact.

"The bloody resistance saved me life ol' man," Willhampton explained after a few drinks.

Others at headquarters would have been amazed to hear his return to his British accent. He had not used it in years.

"This was Earling by damned. He would talk like he pleased," he thought as he removed his shirt.

"Look at this shit," he said. "Just about cooked my goose ol' chap."

Frederick could only wince when he saw the scars. His hand was a wrecked mess.

"That night ended my flying days it did. I spent over two years 'iding from the Jerries. After the war, they cashiered my ass. I went to work for CAT as a simulator instructor. Finally, I ended up in this office. What do you think of my entranceway?" Willhampton asked with a loud laugh.

"It's definitely you," Frederick answered with a chuckle.

"What's with the spooky letter ol' man?" Willhampton asked, his demeanor now serious.

Frederick detailed the situation for Willhampton. He listened intently throughout Frederick's relation of events.

"I figured it would be best to come here," Frederick said as he completed his story.

"Bloody good move ol' man. Bloody good move," Willhampton agreed.

Leaning forward, Willhampton mixed another gin and tonic. He held the bottle up with an inquisitive look.

"No thanks," Frederick answered.

Setting his drink aside, Willhampton began putting his shirt on with some minor difficulty. Frederick noticed that it had snaps rather than buttons.

As he was stuffing his shirttail into his trousers, he said, "That general is a rotten apple. We knew about his dope dealing almost a year ago. However, he is not stupid. We have never been able to get him directly involved in anything. We could have brought down that smart-ass major a long time ago. He is not the one we want. This could be our chance. Come over here."

Willhampton circled around his desk to his chair. He indicated for Frederick to take a seat next to his desk, which he did.

"We are going to move you," Willhampton said. "We're going to have to move all of our pilots. The word is not out yet but you, and some others, will move to Ubon Thani in Thailand. You will have to trust me on this. Keep doing what you are doing until we can determine what those charts mean. They bloody well mean something or they would not give you $10,000 to deliver them. We just do not know what yet."

"What am I going to do with that much cash?" Frederick asked.

"You will give it to one of our guys who will sign a receipt for it. I say he is one of our guys. That's not quite true. He's with Interpol and working undercover. If anyone can figure out about those approach charts, he can. We have a big problem. We must have them in our possession long enough to study them. With such a short time between when you get them and exchange them, we do not have time. We will work something out though. Count on it," Willhampton explained.

A light started to blink on Willhampton's desk. He turned a vase on his desk and Meyers came through the doorway.

"Need more time?" He asked.

"No, not really," Willhampton answered as he stood up and turned to Frederick.

Continuing, he said, "It has been great to see you after so many years. You are a valuable asset to us and we will consider your request. Thanks for letting us know. We will be in touch. Have a safe flight."

"Thanks Redford. I appreciate your consideration. Come visit Vanessa and me if you can. I will be on my way," Frederick answered.

Crossing a speed bump into London's airport jarred Vanessa from her slumber. Stretching her arms, she yawned slightly.

"Are we here already?" She asked.

"We sure are. Would you like some tea before departure?" Frederick asked lovingly.

"Aren't you sweet but you know I can't do that. I will be running to the potty every five minutes," Vanessa said with a giggle.

Their driver unloaded luggage while Neville went to confirm their reservations. Vanessa went to the gift shop and purchased three magazines.

She gave a copy of "Home Electronics" to Frederick and she kept "Harper's Bazaar" and "The Reader's Digest."

"Hon, there's an article in there about the new eight track audio players. Guess your equipment will be obsolete," she commented.

"No way my dear," Frederick replied. "That stuff is for kids."

Frederick looked at her curled in her seat. First Class seats were large enough to accommodate her size with ease. He reached above her head and turned off the reading light. He indicated to a stewardess that Vanessa needed a blanket. He removed her magazine while covering her.

"She is so pale," Frederick thought. "Her skin has always been light but it had a reddish tint to it. Now it is gone. She should be at Haughton House or with Ian. He offered to see to her in Switzerland. She was a McBeal for sure, obstinate and determined."

He had ordered a brandy and now cupped its snifter with his right hand. He gently rotated the pear shaped glass and watched the fine liquor cling as he did so. The last time he had brandy like this was when he met the agent from Interpol. Moreover, a strange meeting it was.

He flew to Pha Khao, in northeastern Laos with William R. Andersevic. The Hmong leader, Vang Pao, had his headquarters at Pha Khao. He recently relocated to this new position along the southern edge of the Plaine of Jars. Andersevic needed to inspect their new airstrip.

Air America brought William Andersevic to expand their short takeoff and landing (STOL) capability at Hmong's villages. Initially called Victor sites, they later named them Lima sites. The flight with Andersevic was a ruse to get Frederick away from Thai surveillance.

Upon landing, two of Vang Pao's staff met them. One took Andersevic to inspect the airstrip. The other took Frederick to a camouflaged, limestone cave.

While outside temperatures soared, inside the cave it was a cool 56 degrees all year. His Hmong escort left him in a domed room hewn from limestone by water over the centuries. A small stream of cold water gurgled its way along one side. Candles provided light.

Frederick saw his escort, carrying a flaming torch, returning with someone. He noticed that he walked with a familiar gait. He felt that he knew this person but could not see who he was in the flickering torchlight. When they entered the cavern, he knew the man. He was Devon Elder.

"Quite a bit different here than Haughton House," Devon said as he approached with a wide grin.

Frederick arose from his seat and went to meet him. As they met, Frederick took his right hand while gripping Devon's elbow with his left.

Shaking Devon's hand and arm vigorously, Frederick said, "So this is what you've been up to Devon."

"Not quite sir. I'm on special duty from MI6, better known now as the Secret Intelligence Service (SIS). They called me to Vauxhall Cross in London for some special work. Normally, I wouldn't reveal this to anyone but I know you can find out if you wanted to. I see no reason for subterfuge with your sir," Devon explained.

"It's good to see you. We miss you very much as I know Vanessa does. Daytran and Galag still look for you. I am sure of that," Frederick added.

"Sir," Devon continued, "I do not want to appear rude. However, we need to get right to it. However, before we do, I have something to kill the chill in this ice chest of a cavern."

Devon walked to a wooden crate stacked with others along the cavern's wall. He pried open its lid and dug amid wood shavings.

"Ah ha," Devon said. "It's still here."

Frederick stared in disbelief. Devon pulled a five star brandy and two snifters from inside the packing material. He sat beside Frederick on a boulder and opened the bottle.

He handed a glass to Frederick, poured a small amount into it, and said, "Well sir?"

Swirling the liquid by rotating the snifter, he tested its aroma. Next, took a small sip and tasted it by swishing it inside his mouth before swallowing it.

"Grand," he said with obvious pleasure.

Smiling, Devon poured for him and Frederick.

"Here's to the ladies," he said. "Long live the queen."

Touching glasses, they both took hefty swallows.

"You are a man of many talents Devon. This would have been the last thing I would have thought existed in this place," Frederick told Devon.

"Anyone can live like animals sir. Someone here must have some bloody class," Devon answered.

"Now, for your situation," Devon continued. "If my information is correct, you've received $50,000 so far."

"That's correct," Frederick promptly replied.

"There is a major opium distribution network throughout Southeast Asia. Eventually, a large portion goes to Great Britain and America. If it makes you feel better, you have not transported any. What you are transporting is time schedules for various locations in Laos, Thailand, Cambodia, North and South Viet Nam. The approach plates reveal minute marks that show places and times. The marked chart is the place. We have not determined their code for times. This does not matter because we watch 24 hours a day. In addition, we monitor every telephone call," Devon explained.

"There's another problem," Devon continued. "The charts that you carry may go through the hands of five other pilots before they get to the appropriate action group. We do not have an answer for this because they change action groups often. An action group is the people who actually get the opium for processing into heroin."

"What can I do to nail these blokes?" Frederick asked.

"Continue what you are doing. Do exactly as they say and you won't have any problem. Muck it up and they will carry out their threat," Devon answered.

Devon, noticing Frederick's brandy was gone, hoisted the bottle and asked. "More?"

"Don't think so. I'm supposed to fly out of this place," Frederick replied with a tone of discouragement in his voice.

"Hey, we will get them. Do not worry. Okay?" Devon asked.

"Yeah, I guess. Can I tell Vanessa?" Frederick responded.

"Absolutely not. Do not mention this. She won't get hurt if you do what they say," Devon emphasized.

Their Hmong escort arrived and indicated for Devon to follow him.

As he left, Devon said, "I will take care of this."

"I've got to go pee," Vanessa said as she wriggled from beneath her blanket. She saw Frederick's snifter.

Vanessa stood with her knees together and her upper teeth biting her lower lip. She moved from one foot to the other.

She mumbled, "I want one of those," as she turned and raced down the aisle to the ladies' room

Frederick laughed aloud as he watched her knot kneed pace between the seats. Passengers leaned into the aisle to watch after she passed their seats.

"What a woman," he thought. "If only they get the bastard who shot her."

Devon had had no explanation for the shooting. Frederick had followed instructions without erring. Still they tried to kill her. There was some speculation that they were making an example of her. Perhaps they had a person of significance to their operation that they were extorting. If that person balked, they could have shot her to prove they would do it. In any case, he wanted the asshole dead.

After 18 hours, Frederick and Vanessa wanted off the plane. They knew their arrival time was close. They completed their custom's declaration forms. The stewardesses had moved up and down the aisle spraying some noxious insecticide as if it would keep bugs from getting into Thailand.

"Ladies and gentlemen, we are beginning our descent to Bangkok International. Please fasten your seat belts and put your seat in the full upright position and close trays in front of you. Please observe the no smoking signs. Thank you for flying with Pan American. We hope you enjoy your visit to Thailand," a stewardess said over the intercom.

Frederick felt the pilot extend flaps and reduce power. He didn't think too much of his control touch as he felt as if he was going to float from his seat.

After going through customs, they saw Gerard Johnson waiting for them with a giant smile. He stood on his toes above the crowd and waved. They walked to where he stood behind a barrier rope.

"I will meet you at the customs' exit. See you there," he half shouted.

Vanessa gave Gerard a generous hug and asked. "How's your better half and that little girl?"

"Mam, they are doing just great. Melissa told me, when I left to come here, that she is looking forward to bridge games again," Gerard replied.

Looking at Frederick, Gerard said with a large grin, "Captain, it is going to be great to fly with you again. I've missed your touch."

As Gerard dodged through Bangkok's traffic, he explained that their flight to Udorn would be in two days. In the meantime, Air America rented a villa for them in the suburbs.

"Air America is hiring as many professional pilots as they can find. If a guy loves to really fly, Air America is the way to go," Gerard chortled.

Vanessa did not realize how much she needed rest. She had no pain but lacked energy and wanted to sleep most of the time. Frederick had room service handle their meals. It was a blissful two days of complete rest. It ended too soon.

When they arrived at Udorn, they had a taxi take them directly to the address that Gerard gave them. Frederick and Vanessa stood together looking at a three floored villa surrounded by a security fence. As Gerard said, the key was under a rock by the gate.

Frederick removed the lock and chain. He pulled on the twin metal doors causing them to open wide. As they did, the courtyard filled with a burst of colored lights. Chinese lanterns danced on an electrical cord strung between metal posts with Tiki torches burning atop them.

Men and women filled the area and they screamed in unison, "Welcome Home."

Vanessa put both hands over her face and began to tremble as the group sang, "For She's A Jolly Good Fellow." She would look at Frederick and then the crowd. Frederick watched her eyes begin to fill.

Turning to Frederick, she laid her head on his shoulder and said between her hands, "Oh Frederick, this is our family."

Every Air America pilot and their family, if they had one, were present. They had a 55-gallon drum cut in half for a charcoal grill. They had hamburgers, hot dogs, steaks, and gallons of various dips.

They carried their luggage inside for them and Gerard showed them their new home. The bottom floor was a combination recreation room and workshop. The second floor had a large living room, master bedroom with bath, guest bedroom with bath and a den. Vanessa loved the kitchen and utility room. The den opened onto a veranda lined with tropical plants and flowers. The third floor was a live-in maid's quarters with bedroom, bath and living area.

"Oh, it is so nice honey. They did this for us," Vanessa said totally bewildered.

"No darling, they did it for you," Frederick clarified.

Their last guest left at 02:00 hours. Frederick and Vanessa climbed the stairs from the workshop to the second floor. He opened their suitcases for her. While she was removing clothing, Frederick remembered that he had to lock the gate.

"Hon, I'm going down to lock the gate. I won't be but a minute," Frederick explained.

Frederick went to the double gates. They opened outward so he walked outside the courtyard to pull it shut. He noticed a Tiki torch to his left that he did not remember being there when they entered. Moreover, it looked strange. There was no flame and something was at its base.

He pulled the right gate closed and walked over to examine the post. Sitting on its top was something in a wool ski mask. He removed it.

"God's blood," he gasped.

Staring at him was Major Saberrank's head impaled on the post. At its base sat an opened bottle of brandy and two snifters. One snifter had a small amount of brandy remaining in it. The other was full.

Frederick, his hand trembling, picked up the full glass and raised it to Saberrank's face.

He held it in position for a moment and said, "Here's to MI6."

Frederick upended his glass consuming its contents. He set his glass beside the other empty one and closed the other gate. He installed the chain and locked it in place.

A calm coursed through Frederick. Whatever it was that had been gnawing at him for past months was gone. He lay beside Vanessa already asleep. Leaning over he lightly kissed her cheek.

"I know you are now safe," he said softly and went to sleep.

Chapter Thirty Two

October 1963

Those in possession of absolute power can not only prophesy and make their prophecies come true, but they can also lie and make their lies come true.
Eric Hoffer (1902–83), *U.S.* philosopher.
The Passionate State of Mind, aph. 78 (1955).

"Hi Mr. Briscoe. This is Lieutenant Colonel Delaney," Briscoe heard, as soon as he answered his telephone.

"Good evening colonel. What can I do for you?" Briscoe asked, curious as to why Delaney would call him at home.

"Sir, I think I may be able to do something for the both of us," Delaney answered.

Growing more curious, Briscoe asked. "What might that be?"

"Sir, remember that recipe mom used to fix when you came for dinner. I still have it if you would like it. You always did enjoy it so much," Delaney continued.

"The kid's trying to tell me something but cannot on the telephone," Briscoe thought.

"I haven't forgotten colonel. To answer your question, I would like a copy," Briscoe said trying to determine what Delaney wanted.

"Sir, mom left me the old home place when she passed away. If you want to get together, we can cook a batch for ourselves. I still have some of the special ingredients. Like to try that tonight?" Delaney asked.

Without hesitation, Briscoe said, "That sounds great. Do you want me to bring anything on my way?"

"Yes sir, if it's not too much trouble," Delaney responded. "Do you remember that Turkish tobacco store on Whitcomb Street?"

"I sure do. How about some Partegas?" Briscoe asked hoping for a specific response.

"Sounds good sir. Get some number eights," Delaney answered.

"On my way colonel. See you in a bit," Briscoe said, trying to keep his anticipation under control.

After replacing the telephone's handset, Briscoe exclaimed, "Jesus, Bryan I knew you didn't commit suicide and you always had a backup. This kid knows something."

Briscoe immediately went to his bathroom's entrance. He opened the hidden compartment and removed his weapons' container. After opening it, he removed a chromed revolver.

He examined the 357 Magnum. It held five, hollow point cartridges. He removed each round and examined it with care. Briscoe made his own cartridges and these hollow points were special. He had filled the hollow points with paraffin. Since the revolver was a snub nose, he wanted to increase its accuracy. By filling the hollow points with paraffin, he retained the projectile's streamlined shape. This enhanced its ability to maintain an accurate trajectory better than regular hollow points. In addition, the bullet retained its explosive-like effect when hitting a target. Satisfied, he put the weapon in an ankle holster on his right ankle.

Reaching into the weapons' container, he removed two, quick change units. Each contained five hollow point cartridges. He inspected each as he did those in the revolver. With the quick-change units, he could reload in less than two seconds. He placed them in a holder and clipped it to his belt.

Next, he removed his 45-Cal., semi-automatic, and his shoulder holster. He slipped the holster's strap around his shoulders and secured it with two snaps under his left arm. Beside the snaps was the pistol's holster. Directly beneath was a spare clip holder. He removed its clip and examined its 20 rounds. After determining each round was in its correct position, he put it back into its holder. Beneath his right arm, he had two additional clips. He inspected both and replaced them.

After pushing the weapons' container into place, he closed the panel hiding it from view. Getting up, he walked to the light above his kitchen's table. Pressing a button, on each side of the pistol's handle, a full clip fell into his left hand. After examining it beneath the light, he firmly struck the table top with one side of the clip. This assured a free flow of cartridges from the clip into the pistol's chamber.

Firmly gripping each side of the pistol, slightly in front of its hammer, he pulled briskly to the rear. This exposed one cartridge in the weapon's chamber. He slowly reduced his grip allowing the barrel to move to its original position and re-inserted the full clip. This gave him 21 cartridges.

While walking to the garage exit, he took a coat from his hall closet and donned it. Washington nights were getting chilly and this coat covered his weapon well. Flexing his shoulders a few times caused everything to fall into place. He entered the garage and checked his intrusion detectors. Each hair was in place.

"It appears who was getting in here before has not been around," he thought.

With accumulated back pay, he had purchased a two-door sedan. His other car's tires rotted while he was away; in addition, various engine seals leaked when put under oil and water pressure.

"Serves me right," he thought. "I could have pickled the thing if I had known I would be away for almost a decade."

After removing the garage's steel locking rod, he pushed the door upwards causing it to remain open. He backed onto his driveway and stopped to close his garage's door. He maneuvered through Washington's crammed streets and entered Maryland.

"Ain't this a pisser," he thought. "I knew Delaney had a kid at West Point back when I was visiting him. I never made the connection when I met Lieutenant Colonel William B. Delaney. His dad, Bryan, often said he wasn't going to name his kid junior. Any kid of his wasn't going to be any junior. He would be his own man. I'll bet my ass that B stands for Bryan though."

Soon, Briscoe had the suburbs behind him. He was traveling deep into Virginia's agricultural country. Although it was dark, Briscoe knew it to be a land of rolling hills, green forests, and beautiful pastures. Delaney's parents had a country place that Bryan went to in order to unload stress from his work.

"Lanny, I can split a piece of red oak trunk with one blow," he would say. "When that axe strikes, all this covert crap blows it apart. I love it here in the country."

Briscoe saw the mailbox shaped like a barn, with Delaney written on its side, ahead on his right. He slowed and turned onto a gravel road winding through heavy timber. At the bottom of a hill, he crossed a wooden bridge and began the final climb to the farm's main house.

What remained of the original structure was one of very few like it. Its construction was from hand-hewn oaks. There was not a nail in it. Wooden pegs held it together. Over the years, other Delaney family members added to it but left the main house untouched. It was a showplace of American craftsmanship.

As he approached the building, Briscoe noticed that the front porch and gate lights were illuminated. He could not see any other lights. He parked at the main gate and walked toward the porch. The porch only covered the original building's front. Behind it, a breezeway ran completely through the structure. Briscoe felt naked because, once past the gate, he could see nothing but the porch. He climbed the steps and walked to the door.

"Over here Lanny," he heard Colonel Delaney say.

Looking to his right, where the voice came from, Briscoe could not see anyone. Squinting, he placed his left hand above his eyes to shield them while at the same time reaching into his coat with his right hand.

"You won't need that. Walk this way. There's another set of steps. We need to go around to the barn," Delaney told Briscoe.

With the porch light to his back, Briscoe could see Delaney's outline at the porch's end. He walked toward the steps that he could now see and went down them to the ground. Delaney greeted him.

"I'm glad you could come Mr. Briscoe. Dad spoke about you often," Delaney said.

Briscoe noted that Delaney looked quite different in civilian clothes. He looked like someone would expect to see at a Feed and Seed Store loading bags onto a pickup truck. He was gangly with not an ounce of fat on him. He towered over Briscoe by at least six inches. He was his dad's son that was for sure.

"Call me Lanny," Briscoe instructed. "Your dad always did."

"You know the military Lanny. After four years at the academy and 12 on active duty, we stay rather formal. I'm sure you understand," Delaney replied.

With his eyes rapidly adjusting to the dark, Briscoe could see the barn. It was a picture postcard barn with its typical roof and double sliding doors. Above the sliding doors, there was a smaller door for access to a hayloft. A post protruded above it with a block and tackle for lifting hay bales. On one side, there was an open-sided, machinery shed with a tractor and hay baling equipment parked in it. The other side had a white, boarded fence surrounding a corral and loading chute for livestock.

Another smaller building was to the right of the barn. It appeared to be a tobacco-drying shed common in this part of Virginia.

"Sir, uh Lanny, step here by me. You are still in the porch's light. Here it is difficult to be seen," Delaney said.

"Damn, I know better than that," Briscoe thought. "I made a beautiful target and I had to have a kid tell me."

"Come with me," Delaney directed. "I need to show you some things. Dad left word for me to do so but you've been gone so long."

"Yeah, I figured that when you asked about the cigars. Few know about that anymore," Briscoe answered.

Delaney thrust his hands into his pockets as they walked side by side to the barn. Briscoe noticed that Delaney followed shadows as naturally as he recalled Jean Danjou doing.

"I knew dad was CIA before I was graduated from the point. Mom knew too and she did not adjust to it. It is a business that doesn't lend itself to marriage," Delaney explained. "You never met mom. Lanny, she was a good woman and mother. She raised me you know. I spent my summers with Grandpa Delaney here on the farm. Dad came and stayed when he was in D.C. That's when we really got to know each other. He was a good man and I know he did not commit suicide," Delaney explained.

At the barn door, Delaney lifted the door's locking board and set it aside. He pushed on the right door enough for the two of them to enter. He took a Coleman lantern from a peg immediately inside the door. He pumped its pressure rod a few times and locked it in place. Next, he raised its globe and lit it with a kitchen match from his pocket. It sputtered and spit a few times with bluish flames dancing around its mantel. Soon, the flame disappeared and the mantel glowed, lighting the barn's interior.

"Lanny, hold this for me please," Delaney said while holding the lantern toward Briscoe.

"Sure," Briscoe answered gripping its handle.

Delaney closed the door and rotated a long board between the doors into a recess. This prevented anyone from opening the main doors from the outside.

Taking the lantern from Briscoe, Delaney said, "Over here."

He walked toward a large container built into one corner. It was a wooden bin that Briscoe found similar to a corncrib. However, to Briscoe, it appeared higher than most. Delaney opened its wooden top that rotated on metal hinges. He moved the cover to the rear until it rested against the barn's wall. Inside, Briscoe saw ears of dried corn as he suspected.

"Lanny, take the lantern again please," Delaney said.

After taking the lantern, Briscoe watched Delaney thrust his right arm deep into the corn. He heard a distinct, metallic snapping sound. Delaney closed the bin's lid and pressed its front with his right knee while holding its sides. The wood front moved inward, exposing steep steps leading down beneath the bin.

"I'll take the lantern. Follow me and watch your step. It's a steep drop," Delaney explained.

Delaney was able to descend two steps before he had to lower his upper body to continue. Briscoe watched as Delaney reached bottom and held the lantern so that Briscoe had a good view of the steps. He entered without difficult and made his way down to stand beside Delaney.

Reaching above his head, Delaney pulled a wood handle connected to a metal cable. Briscoe watched the bin's doors close above them and a metal pin slide into place locking the entrance.

"Pretty slick. What is this place?" Briscoe asked.

"Lanny, as the crow flies, we are not too far from D.C. Gramps and dad built this place as a fallout shelter. There's another secured door a little farther along. Dad figured a nuke would level the barn. Dad knew some inside shit and he insisted on this place. I think you will appreciate his thinking as we go along," Delaney explained.

Looking around, Briscoe saw that the walls were cement. He suspected that they were probably steel reinforced and very thick. In addition, the floor sloped gently toward its middle. In the center, there was a built-in, steel grating serving as a storm drain. With the barn gone, there had to be a place for rain to go. Particularly, if it contained radioactive particles. In the far wall of the ten-foot by ten-foot room, there was a metal door with a handle.

Delaney went to the door and gripped its handle. He pushed up while pulling it. From somewhere, Briscoe heard the release of compressed air and the door seemed to float open with the slightest effort by Delaney. When it fully opened, overhead electrical lights in a tunnel illuminated on the other side. Steel grating covered its walkway. The walkway made a right turn preventing Briscoe from seeing more.

"Jesus," Briscoe exclaimed. "Your dad must have definitely known some shit."

Grinning, Delaney turned a knob on the lantern causing it to quit burning. Again, it sputtered a few times, dimmed and its flame quit.

"Go ahead, Lanny. I am right behind you," Delaney told Briscoe.

Briscoe took a few steps into the tunnel, stopped, and turned to watch Delaney. He entered and used one hand to close the door. The door was anything but ordinary. Its sides were at least eight inches thick. Rather than flat like a normal door, the sides were stepped like stairs. Recessed in its sides Briscoe could see three stainless steel rods. Once closed, Delaney turned a wheel, similar to a car's steering wheel, and Briscoe saw the door tremble as it obviously locked.

When Delaney turned toward him, Briscoe asked. "No one is going to get into this place but how are we getting out of here?"

"I will show you on the way back. Let's continue," Delaney stated.

Briscoe led the way down the corridor. After about 20 meters, he arrived at the right turn. Another set of stairs continued downward. At the bottom, they entered a circular room that Briscoe estimated to be ten meters across. In its center, light blue water churned and bubbled inside a meter wide, terrazzo tiled pit. Briscoe went to it and looked inside. On each side, there was a circular opening. Briscoe guessed that one was an inlet and the other an outlet of an underground, artesian well. Stainless steel shelves lined the pit.

"Lanny, that water stays a steady 39 degrees all year. It never changes. It makes a great refrigerator to keep perishable items cold. Grandma kept fresh milk and butter in it before there were such things as refrigerators and freezers. This was their old well house and tornado shelter until dad and grandpa worked on it," Delaney explained.

"Take a look in one of those lockers on the wall," Delaney instructed.

Briscoe did not notice them when they entered because they blended with the light green, pastel wall color. Each door started about one foot above the floor and extended about five feet toward the ceiling. They were three feet wide. He opened one directly to his front. Shelves contained cartons of dehydrated meals, fruit, and other foods.

Briscoe, examining one package asked. "What's the shelf life on this stuff?"

"Most of it is 15 years. Some are Korean War vintage and only have five years. Of course, the plan was to eat those first," Delaney explained. "I have eaten most of them at one time or another. They are reasonably good. Yet, they would never touch grandma's cooking," Delaney answered.

This room, like the tunnel, had fluorescent lights recessed to provide indirect lighting. Briscoe saw an exit across from where they entered.

"Where does that go?" Briscoe asked.

"We were going there next. I will lead the way," Delaney answered.

Briscoe noticed that this corridor was much longer than the first. On each side, there were standard doors at regular intervals. At the corridor's end, there was another steel door.

As Delaney walked down the corridor, he opened doors for Briscoe to see inside and said, "These are two bedroom units with bunk beds. They can sleep four apiece. Each has a separate bath. Wastewater is recycled through a flocculation tank containing used water, chlorine, sodium hydroxide, and alum. The sodium hydroxide and alum congeal to form a gelatinous, floating layer that filters particles from the water. This water, under pressure, rises to the top of twin towers containing sand. Gravity feeds the water through the sand and into a large cistern for reuse. The sand towers require back flushing every two weeks if the shelter is at maximum capacity. Even without the artesian well, the water system is self sustaining."

Awed by what Delaney's dad had built, Briscoe asked. "How did your dad pay for this place?"

"He has subscribers within the CIA," Delaney answered. "He got the idea when he learned of the secret facility being built for Congress and the Executive Branch. That facility is beneath what most folks think is a regular hotel. It is far from it. Hidden beneath is a facility capable of housing them and their families. They also have available equipment to conduct our government's daily business. They also have a private security force to protect them. Tax dollars paid for theirs. Dad and his friends paid the bill on this. Believe me it did not come cheap. Let's see the rest."

Astonished, Briscoe asked. "There's more?"

Delaney opened the second steel door. It was identical to the first. Beyond the door was a group dining facility with a fully equipped kitchen.

"Directly above us is the old tobacco drying barn. Dad converted it into a smokehouse some years ago. Through that far door is the generator room. It contains four; 2,000-kilowatt generators that use liquefied petroleum for fuel. Currently, exhaust vents to the smokehouse. Of course, if D.C. has an atomic attack, the smokehouse will disappear. There is a throw-over valve to re-direct the exhaust. A pipe would take it under water at the river you crossed driving to the house," Delaney continued.

"What about fresh, uncontaminated air?" Briscoe asked, obviously enthralled.

"Lanny, I could keep going like this for another hour. This is not why I asked you to come. I'll take you to dad's communication and high security room," Delaney said.

Delaney opened a walk-in cooler and stepped aside for Briscoe to pass. Delaney closed the door. The doorknob was a large, wooden disk with a steel rod through the door. To open it from the inside a person pressed the knob. This caused the steel rod to raise a bar on the other side opening the door.

However, Delaney pushed the knob toward the wall and lifted at the same time. He held this position for approximately ten seconds. Briscoe heard a noise behind him and turned to see the back wall move. Delaney released the rod and pushed the wall. It moved enough to leave a narrow entranceway. Briscoe followed Delaney through it.

Inside, Briscoe saw nothing spectacular. There was a standard, metal office desk, chairs, and three file cabinets. However, he knew by now not to believe what he saw.

"Okay, where is it?" Briscoe asked.

"What?" Delaney asked in return, grinning all the while.

"The communications, I haven't even seen a telephone or intercom in this place," Briscoe stated knowingly.

Delaney walked behind the desk. He pressed his chest tight to the wall while placing his finger tips along an almost imperceptible seam. He pulled until the seam grew wider and then put both hands inside the opening. He pulled until both of his long arms extended full length in both directions. He finished by pressing one side with both hands exposing a wall map.

The map showed North American, Central America and most of the Pacific and Atlantic Oceans. In addition, there were insets of major metropolitan areas nationwide. One inset in particular drew Briscoe's attention, Washington, D.C. Various overlays were available on three sides, above, left, and right. Map pins, with plastic heads, held the overlays away from the map. Each overlay set had designations of kiloton and megaton yields.

Briscoe asked, "Colonel, have you examined these?"

"Yes sir, I have," Delaney answered.

Walking around the desk, Briscoe removed the first pin on the megaton yield side. A colored diagram became available to place over Washington. Moving it into place, ever enlarging circles spread outward from the city. It continued into the surrounding states. Each ring was marked in nautical miles.

Briscoe read aloud from the overlay, "Tree blow down. This thing shows how far a five-megaton nuclear device would blow down trees. Jesus H. Christ Bill, he's not supposed to have this stuff here. This is top secret shit."

Briscoe continued reading aloud, "Wood structures, brick, cement, steel-reinforced cement. Man would the Communists love to get their hands on this."

Turning to face Delaney, Briscoe asked. "How long has this been here?"

"Lanny, I do not know. I did not know this room existed until a week ago. Last week I had a flat on my car in the Pentagon parking lot. Someone removed the control stem from the tire's air valve. When I removed the spare, I found directions to this place. Dad didn't put it there. I've only had the car for a little over a year. They found dad's body in 1955. One of the subscribers to this place had to put it there as best I can figure," Delaney explained.

"I still haven't answered your question about communications. Take a look at this," Delaney said.

Beneath the map, there was an inset counter top. Delaney went to its far end and pressed a button. The countertop folded back against the map and a new one rose to take its place.

Radio and monitoring equipment, capable of monitoring or transmitting on all known wavelengths, sat side by side on the countertop. A person, sitting at the desk, could swivel and reach any device.

"Was info about this beneath your spare?" Briscoe asked.

"Yes it was," Delaney answered.

"Colonel, I have to do what you should have already done. I have to go to my superiors about this. The shelter was fine but this! My God, I cannot walk away from this," Briscoe explained as he displayed total exasperation with Delaney.

"Lanny, I did not report this because I was waiting for you. I need to show you one more thing and then you can turn me in," Delaney said.

"First of all, I'm not turning you in to anyone. We will report this together. I cannot believe you have anything to show that will top this," Briscoe said sternly.

Delaney went to the file cabinets and opened their bottom drawers. He removed a plastic container from each and carried them to the desk. He began removing their locking bolts. He lifted the covers revealing their contents.

Looking at Briscoe, Delaney asked. "What is it?"

Briscoe moved close and rearranged the three as his hands trembled. Satisfied with his task, he pressed the two end components toward the centerpiece. There was a distinct snap as the three components became one.

"Bill, find me an electrical outlet," Briscoe said with a distinct need for haste in his voice.

Delaney immediately dropped to his hands and knees. Beneath the desk, he saw a waterproof receptacle.

Raising one of its covers, he said, "Hand me the power cord."

Briscoe handed Delaney a power cord but he disconnected it from what appeared to be a transformer before doing so.

Delaney inserted the three-prong plug and got up from the floor. Now assembled, Delaney could see its design clearly. It sat on a base approximately 12 inches deep and five feet long. Its construction appeared to be mostly burnished aluminum. On the end where Briscoe stood, there was a transformer with an uncovered, female electrical connector. Two grooves, about four inches inboard on the base, ran almost the base's length. Midway of the base, a raised platform with a thick lens had metal feet that fit neatly into the two grooves. This apparently allowed the raised platform to traverse most of the base's length. Above the lens there was a viewing support for a person to peer threw the lens at something beneath it. Two coaxial, flexible cables connected to the viewer. These connected to a black box with three lights on it. On the side nearest Briscoe, there were a variety of gages and control knobs.

"Bill, go to the map and get me coordinates for this location," Briscoe said.

Studying the map, Delaney saw a pin with a red head inserted into it. It was where he would consider the farm's location to be. Beside the pin, written with grease pencil, were coordinates.

"Here they are," Delaney said.

Delaney started to read the coordinates aloud but Briscoe interrupted, "Not yet Bill. Give me a second."

Briscoe turned every control know counterclockwise to their off position. Next, he connected the electrical cord and flipped a toggle switch to its on position. A low, almost inaudible, humming noise came from the transformer.

"It needs to warm up a bit. Did you get an altitude for our location?" Briscoe asked.

"No, I need a topographical (Topo) map for that," Delaney answered.

"There has to be one. See if you can find it," Briscoe ordered.

Delaney, again, went to the map. He could not find one in plain view. Next, he examined the overlays. He saw one with contours on it. He removed its retaining pin and it fell into place covering the inset for Washington, D. D., and vicinity. Lines on the overlay connected altitudes of equal elevation. Again, written in grease pencil, an altitude above mean sea level appeared by the farm's location.

"I have it," Delaney exclaimed.

"Okay, stand by for a moment," Briscoe directed as he moved the viewer to a middle position on its base.

"Now give them to me. Give me a longitude, a latitude and then the altitude," Briscoe said.

As Delaney read them to Briscoe, he saw him input the information with what appeared to be a miniature, adding machine. Each time Briscoe completed an element a light illuminated on the black box. Ultimately, three lights glowed.

Briscoe stepped away and said, "That's it. It is initialized."

Delaney left the map board moving to stand beside Briscoe and said, "This thing looks like what we use to study reconnaissance imagery."

"It can be used for that but it's more important," Briscoe answered. "Remember those photos you brought to us in the meeting?"

"Yeah," Delaney answered.

Briscoe moved a metal platform from beneath the viewer. The platform moved along the grooves in the base.

Pointing to four screws, Briscoe explained, "Mount a high resolution photograph on that platform using the four pins beneath those screw heads. Slide it beneath the viewer and you have a three dimensional view of anything on the photo. Make a few adjustments to center crosshairs over any object in the photo. Next press the calculate switch and the device will provide exceptionally accurate, three dimensional coordinates for that object."

"Hell, we have maps to tell us that," Delaney commented.

"No we don't," Briscoe answered quickly. "You cannot imagine how much of the USSR and Communist China remains unmapped. What maps that do exist are ancient and worthless."

Turning to Delaney, Briscoe pointed at the black box and said, "You cannot obtain coordinates from a map like what that little jewel generates. To help understand, think about this. If you have a ballistic missile to fire at a target, it is necessary to know two basic things. First, you need an accurate location of the missile. Second, an accurate location of the target is essential."

"Visualize the missile leaving its start point. It climbs into space and starts its descent. From the highest point of its trajectory to its target, it is totally passive. That's what ballistic means. It's a big artillery projectile traveling a set course. Remember that this thing is traveling halfway around the world. Suppose it travels through a typhoon on its way to its target. Strong winds will push it off course and it will not impact where we want it."

"Suppose we put an inertial guidance system in it. A system like this has gyros in it to hold the missile on course. If it tries to stray from it initial course, these gyros activate stabilizer fins to keep it on course. Now, it is no longer ballistic. It is a guided system. By activating its gyros with extremely accurate, three-dimensional information, the missile will not stray. It is still passive. You cannot jam it. You must destroy it or it will hit its target."

"If I have an image of a corner street sign in downtown Moscow, in the Soviet Union, I can center this equipment on it. It will give me the information, in three dimensions, that I need to tell the missile to hit that street sign."

"Locating points this way is called photogrametrics. This equipment is an Analytical Photogrametric Positioning System that you heard me refer to as APPS. You are looking at one of two existing prototypes under development. It is highly classified and is supposed to be locked in a vault."

"Are you saying dad was a spy?" Delaney asked, his voice dripping venom.

"No I am not. Frankly, I do not know. The possibilities are endless. I had your dad checking on a contractor for me. That was nine years ago and your dad died. A working prototype did not exist then. Someone either made this one independent of the contractor or the contractor is missing one of the two that exist today. We have to see if Meyers Corporation has its two."

"I suspect Meyers Corporation planned to build an extra one. Your dad learned of it and they killed him. Now, one of his friends brought this one here. He also sent photos to me in Laos knowing I would return. We have to learn who is behind this," Briscoe explained.

"Let's check with the general and get his help," Delaney suggested.

"Not yet Bill. I really cannot trust him. If you can get me one of the photos with holes in it, I can tell if it came from this equipment. Beneath those screws are the pins that hold photos in place. Each APPS leaves a signature on a photo when put on the viewing tray. I can compare the holes to this machine. If there's a match, someone who has access to this place used this equipment. If it doesn't match, we can compare it to the others. We will at least be able to narrow the field of suspects," Briscoe suggested.

Delaney's eyes widened and he snapped his right thumb and middle finger and blurted, "Damn, I think I know where we can get a list of those who helped dad build this shelter. Follow me."

Briscoe followed Delaney into the cooler and watched how Delaney closed the hidden entrance. After that, it was almost a footrace. Delaney's long legs took strides twice as long as Briscoe's. He almost had to jog to keep up with him.

When they entered the bedroom corridor, Delaney said, "I must show you one more thing. It's in here."

Delaney led the way into the first bedroom door on his right. This room did not have bunk beds. It had one king sized bed and a nicely decorated living area. Against the bedroom wall, there was a roll top desk with a chair in front of it.

As Delaney lifted the roll top, exposing a desktop with pigeonhole storage spaces, he explained, "This was mom and dad's room if they had to take refuge here. I do know that mom had this desk here for dad to use. He worked here a good bit. I saw this the other day but it didn't make any sense until now."

Briscoe watched as he removed what appeared to be a standard, bookkeeping ledger. He opened it to a page tabbed as S.

He handed it to Briscoe said, "Take a look at the pages listed in the S section. I would almost guarantee you that dad used that section for his subscribers."

Briscoe thumbed through the pages. Entries almost looked like Egyptian hieroglyphics except that they were alphanumeric. As he scanned the pages, Briscoe's brow became furrowed.

Looking at Delaney, Briscoe said, "This is my expertise, cryptography. Your dad had to keep track of who paid their share and who did not. These must be his accounting records. I need this for a few days."

"I thought you would find that interesting. Now, one more thing and we're gone," Delaney said as he opened a closet door. Inside, various work clothes hung on hangers. Pushing them aside, Delaney opened a sliding panel in the closet's rear area.

"Take a look at this," Delaney said quite excited.

Briscoe counted 28 gas masks, 14 riot shotguns, ten Browning Automatic Rifles and 4 45 caliber, "grease gun" automatics. Cases of ammunition lined the compartment's bottom along with hand grenades, pyrotechnic devices, detonators, and plastic explosives.

"I will give your dad this. He knew how to prepare for the worst. I know he was not paranoid. He had to know something we don't and it scares the piss out of me," Briscoe said. "Let's go. It's late."

On his ride to D.C., Briscoe tried to bring the mind boggling last few hours into focus. Bryan Delaney had to start construction of his survival shelter in the early fifties. He had to suspect a high probability of a nuclear holocaust when the rest of the world did not know about it. He had to perceive a massive strike capability from some country when the only nation thought capable of such a thing was the United States. There were too many holes and not enough information to make a guess. Perhaps, when he decoded Bryan's notes, he would understand better. In any case, he was totally perplexed.

As he approached his driveway to his garage, Briscoe saw a vehicle he did not recognize parked in it. He continued past and checked its license plates. They were Virginia plates but did not help identify whose car it was.

"Hell, there's one way to find out," he thought.

Slightly before turning onto the street where his driveway was, he turned off his car's lights. He slowly approached to within 30 yards and stopped. He removed his 45 pistol from its holster. With his vehicle's door open, he turned on his headlights and rushed to a board fence leading to his garage. Remaining flat against the boards, he approached the strange car with utmost caution. He looked at his apartment's windows, nothing.

Bending low, he ran to the car's fender area that was opposite his headlights. He did not want to outline himself for whoever was inside. Moving swiftly, he went to the driver's side window and pointed his pistol inside. He saw Katherine laying in a fetal position with her hands between her knees. She appeared asleep.

Briscoe yanked the door open. He pointed his pistol at her and asked. "Katherine, are you okay?"

She moved her head, looked straight at him, and asked. "Lanny, is that you?"

Chapter Thirty Three

January 1963

There is nothing strange about fear: No matter in what guise it presents itself it is something with which we are all so familiar that when a man appears who is without it we are at once enslaved by him.
Henry Miller (1891–1980), U.S. Author. The Wisdom of the Heart, *"The Enormous Womb"* (1947)

"Hold on lieutenant. We're not going to be late. We're short pilots and you have to start flying missions right away," Major William M. Barry told First Lieutenant Dale Zane.

As soon as Zane walked through the door into Than San Nhut Airport, near Saigon, his company commander was waiting for him. Major Barry was the CO of the 93rd Transportation Company. The 93rd was an H-21 unit like the 6th Transportation Company in Korea. The only difference was that there were thousands of Vietnamese guerillas wandering around Viet Nam with the sole purpose in life of shooting down their aircraft.

The H-21 was a weird flying machine. It had a set of rotor blades on each end. The ship's body had a distinctive bend in its middle causing many to describe it as looking like a banana. Its power source was a reciprocating engine like that on the H-19 and H-34. The only problem was that it had a propensity for failure at the worst possible times. His instructor pilot in Korea made it clear.

"Zane, if you hear that engine cough, have a place to land. That dude just swallowed a valve," he told him.

One pilot described flying the H-21 as trying to drive a boxcar across a greasy dance room floor on roller skates. The rear rotor blades would try to fly ahead of the front ones. It was a constant battle trying to keep it flying straight. The rear would constantly "fish tail" causing the pilot to have to maintain a delicate control touch. One slip in the H-21 and it could mean serious trouble.

Viet Nam was receiving some of the new turbine powered helicopters made by Bell Helicopter. The models arriving in country were UH-1Bs. Zane bemoaned that he did not get an UH-1 transition at Fort Rucker. Instead, he went through a cargo helicopter checkout and that was what he was going to fly. He didn't stand a chance of getting into an UH-1 unit.

It was 28 December 1962 and Barry's unit had a major mission coming up soon. It was essential to get Zane to his headquarters so that he could at least get a few hours of area familiarization before flying combat missions.

"Watch out for this one it's a bitch," Barry said.

His warning came too late. The jeep's right front wheel hit a pothole bouncing Zane a foot into the air. When he came down, he came down hard. He ached from his tailbone to between his shoulder blades.

Barry was driving south into the Mekong Delta Region of South Viet Nam. Delta country was flat and crisscrossed by hundreds of natural and man made canals. The Mekong River flowed through the region and it simply was what most folks would call a big swamp.

Zane, never before in a combat zone, saw every person they passed on the rugged road as a potential killer. Vietnamese were in every direction. They rode bicycles, pulled carts, and carried packages on their heads. Occasionally, there would be a pair in tandem with a pole over their shoulders. It sagged heavily in its middle from whatever was in a large container. As the pair walked at a rapid pace, the container bounced constantly. Zane concluded that had to hurt.

"Sir, aren't you worried about hitting a mine?" Zane asked.

"Shit no, the Viet Cong (VC) won't waste a mine on two guys in a jeep. Besides, they usually don't use mines on the highways. They will plant an 800-pound bomb in the road during nighttime. They will run electrical wires out to one of those people you see working in the rice fields. When a lucrative target comes along, they blow it to hell. Look out there. There's hundreds working. Which one detonated the bomb? Don't know? What then, kill them all? They are not going to waste something like that on us," Barry said with a laugh.

Continuing Barry said, "Now, when you are flying that H-21 every son of a bitch in the country will shoot at you. You don't get to return fire. Old men wander out of huts with muzzleloaders to shoot at you. You cannot return fire without clearance from the district headquarters. To get a clearance takes hours. Hell, you're shot to shit before you hear a word from them."

"You're not serious?" Zane asked.

"Damned straight I'm serious," Barry responded. "Military Assistance Command Viet Nam (MACV) is trying to get permission to return fire if fired upon. We don't have that yet."

"So, what do we do?" Zane asked incredulously.

"It's not going to be your decision to make lieutenant. You will be flying pilot in the right seat. The aircraft commander in the left seat makes that decision. My unit has mostly crusty old Chief Warrant Officers as aircraft commanders. Although you outrank them, they are the aircraft commanders. You do what they say and you might get out of this place in one piece," Barry answered.

Zane yearned for the comfort of the aircraft that brought him to Southeast Asia. Barry's race to his unit kept him bouncing up and down plus from side to side. It was like being on a bucking bronco without the ability to get off. Now, Zane ached so much he would accept landing once on hard ground.

"There it is. Home sweet home for the next six months," Barry said cheerfully.

Zane looked at tents surrounding by a few strands of barbed wire and was not favorably impressed. Barry blew right through a guard post with nothing more than a wave of his hand. On the other side of the tents, he saw rows of H-21s parked on red clay. The clay was soaking with oil to reduce dust. An unpleasant smell permeated the air.

"What is that terrible smell?" Zane asked.

"Smell? I don't smell anything," Barry answered.

"Damn," Zane thought. "If he cannot smell that, he must be brain dead."

Barry drove through what smelled like diesel fuel but worse. It was a black cloud coming from some 55-gallon drums with fires in them.

"That's where the smell is coming from," Zane said.

"Oh that," Barry answered. "They are burning shit. We use outhouses with cut 55-gallon drums beneath each hole. Once a day, they remove them and soak the contents with JP4. It is a jet fuel. However, it's nothing more than high-grade kerosene. Once soaked, the shit burns. We don't want to create a biohazard now do we," Barry jokingly replied.

Major Barry stopped the jeep in front of a tent with a sign over the walkway to it. The sign was the shape of an arch and held in place by two tall poles.

The sign stated, "Home of the 93rd Transportation Company, Major William Barry Commander."

Nailed beneath the lettering was a lace bra and panties. Some one had written, "Lest We Forget" beneath the lacy lingerie.

Zane lifted one duffel bag from the jeep's rear seat with a grunt. Major Barry grabbed the other.

"Follow me," he said. "We'll get you settled."

Zane made sure to stay on the crushed rock walkway. On each side, red mud waited to sink anyone up to their ankles in goo. Barry entered the second tent on his left. Zane followed, feeling heat and humidity envelop him. He watched moisture forming on his arms.

Barry dumped his duffel bag and said, "Take your pick. You're welcome to any of the empty ones."

As he left the tent Barry said, "Evening chow is at six."

Zane began examining the tent's interior as his eyes adjusted to the dark. On each side of the tent, there were 12 folding cots. Most of them had bedding and mosquito nets covering them. Others were empty and without bedding. At the tent's far end, a warrant officer sat on the edge of his bunk reading a "Playboy" magazine. As Zane looked his way, he raised his hand in greeting.

Zane walked to where he sat and said, "Hi, I'm Dale Zane. I guess I can have any bunk without a net and bedding?"

The pilot stood up; extended his hand; and said, "I'm Jim Manuel from Houma, Louisiana. Go ahead and take your pick."

"Where is everybody?" Zane asked.

"They are out flying," Manuel answered. "They will be back before dark."

Thinking about the large number of aircraft he saw, Zane asked. "What is the deal with those parked 21s?"

"They are broke-dick and waiting parts. There's no supply system in place yet. Our parts come from Korea, the United States, and Hawaii, anywhere that we can find them. Fortunately, we have more birds than we do people to fly them. That's probably why DA transferred you out of Korea. You did come in from Korea?" Manuel asked.

"That's right. I was flying with the 38th Air Defense Brigade at Camp Humphries. I volunteered for a 21 local checkout and here I am," Zane replied.

Manuel sat on his bunk and gave Zane an incredulous look that said, "You must be a dumb shit."

"FIGMO, I'm on my way back to the 6th Trans," Manual replied.

Zane asked. "FIGMO?"

"Yeah, fuck it got my orders. I'm short man. One day and a wakeup and I'm on my way out of here," Manuel explained.

Continuing, Manuel said, "We get a lot of people from Korea on temporary duty (TDY). Another lieutenant arrived three weeks ago. You might know him. His name is Daryl Scott."

Breaking into a broad grin, Zane replied, "Yeah, I know him well. We came into the Army together; went to flight school together; and were in Korea together. But, he wasn't 21 rated. If he had come to 6th Trans for a transition, I would have known it."

"You know DA. In all their wisdom, they sent him here for his transition. Hell, we don't have time for that. This is not a training school. Fly around here and you're likely to get your butt shot off," Manuel observed.

Continuing he said, "Come with me. I will show you the supply tent to get you some bedding. You will need to draw a weapon and ammo also."

As they left the tent, it was refreshing to be outside. Zane noticed that his uniform was soaked with perspiration.

As he and Manuel walked toward the supply tent, Zane asked. "How do you stand this heat?"

"Lieutenant, I told you I was from Houma, Louisiana. That's Coon Ass territory and it's a lot like it is here. I'm used to this," Manuel answered.

"Coon Ass?" Zane asked.

"Yeah, Coon Ass. That's another name for a Cajun. You know, the French who moved into south Louisiana's swamps where no one else would go. I cannot believe you've never heard of a Coon Ass," he answered with a laugh.

"I've heard of Cajuns but not Coon Ass. There was a Cajun in my flight class. His name was Dibennideto," Zane mentioned."

"Just a second," Manuel said as the two arrived at a tent marked Orderly Room.

When Manuel stuck his head inside the tent flap, typewriter noise stopped and he yelled, "Short."

As Manuel ran from the tent, someone threw a large ashtray at him. It impacted in the mud and disappeared into the red muck.

He did a little jig and said repeatedly, "One and a getup."

"This is supply," Manuel said as he stopped and turned to his right.

Zane followed him into another overpowering accumulation of heat and humidity. About ten feet inside, a countertop ran from one side of the tent to the other.

Manuel yelled, "Short," as he leaned over the counter.

As Manuel moved away, a Sergeant Ramsey arose behind it. It was obvious that he had been sleeping.

"Chief, you are a pain in the ass," he said with a yawn.

Seeing Zane, Ramsey began a slow grin and said, "Hi LT. Just get here?"

"That's right sarge. Manuel said you could fix me up with what I need in the way of bedding and a weapon," Zane answered.

"Can I ever," Ramsey said as he reached below the counter.

Zane watched as Sergeant Ramsey began putting items on the counter. He started with an air mattress, some sheets, a blanket, a pillow, and a pillowcase.

"Any preference as to a weapon?" Ramsey asked.

Manuel interrupted and asked. "Sarge, you're not going to stick LT with one of those rusty ass 45s are you?"

"He has a choice of a 38 special, an M-14 rifle or a 45," Ramsey answered.

"You've got my shotgun hidden back there somewhere sarge. Get it and some ammo for the lieutenant," Manuel told Ramsey.

Sergeant Ramsey gave a slight sigh, turned around, and went behind a canvas divider out of sight. Shortly, he returned with a 12-gauge shotgun. He put it on the counter.

"Check it out lieutenant," Ramsey said.

Before Zane could touch it, Manuel raised it from the counter and gave it a loving stroke with his hand. He pulled its pump handle to the rear opening the shell chamber.

He handed it to Zane and said, "Can't be too careful. I just wanted to make sure that it was empty."

Continuing, Manuel explained, "Lieutenant, I carried that weapon with me everywhere I went for six months. I slept with it; ate with it; and flew with it. I had to use it a few times and it never let me down. I recommend you take it."

Zane examined the shotgun. It was a Mossberg pump with its stock cut down to a pistol grip. The magazine held ten shells and its barrel extended slightly past it. He hefted the weapon and noted its weight. An avid duck hunter Zane knew Mossbergs. Normally rather heavy, the Mossberg was a duck hunter's favorite. This one had a good feel about it.

Zane asked. "Chief which shell do you recommend I use?"

Manuel answered, "Nothing smaller than single '0' buck. Frankly, I used double '00' but you can make a choice."

"Chief, you are leaving this place so you had to do some things right. I will go with the double '00' buck Sergeant Ramsey," Zane said.

"You might as well have these too," Ramsey said reaching beneath the counter. He laid a sling and an ammunition pouch in front of Zane.

"Shotgun or not, Major Barry says you will carry a sidearm. Take this 38 Special. It's almost new and is in good shape. Here's you a holster and two boxes of ammo," Ramsey explained.

"Now, let's get your flight gear," Ramsey said.

He handed a white, flight helmet to Zane and said, "Try this on."

The helmet felt as if its sides were going to touch his shoulders so he said, "This is too big sarge."

Sergeant Ramsey took the helmet; reached inside and began ripping out padding. He reached beneath the counter and got new padding of a larger size. He stripped a plastic sheet from one side of the pad leaving an adhesive exposed. He plunged it into the helmet and held it with his fist for a moment. He did this same procedure for side pads that cover a pilot's ears.

Ramsey handed it to Zane and said, "Try it now."

Zane slipped it on his head and it was a perfect fit. He bounced it up and down. There was little movement.

"This sergeant knows his stuff," he thought.

"It is perfect," Zane said.

Next, the supply sergeant put a survival vest and a flak jacket on the counter. After that, he put three flight suits and one pair of gloves.

"That should do it lieutenant. Bring your bed linens by here on Tuesdays for fresh ones. Also, bring your flight suits and personal clothing when you want. I get it cleaned in the local village," Ramsey said.

As Zane and Manuel walked to their tent, Zane asked. "Don't these white helmets make perfect targets in the cockpit?"

"They sure do. We'll have to get you some OD paint. With our supply system, there's no telling when we will get it. As soon as it comes in, you paint that mother," Manuel stated emphatically.

Once inside their tent, Manuel helped Zane setup his mosquito bar to cover his cot. Manuel gave Zane a metal frame to go over his cot from which he could suspend the netting.

Noting that Manuel would no longer have a mosquito net, Zane said, "Hey, I cannot take your frame. You are going to need it."

"I won't miss it at all," Manuel replied. "I used to sleep on bayou banks all night and not get a bite. You take it lieutenant."

"Thanks, I really appreciate it. These nets are worthless without something to tie them in place with," Zane stated.

"L-T, Manuel," said. "You seem a lot like Scott. Scott is a learner and he will make it out of this place. Take this advice. Always listen to your aircraft commanders (AC). Some of them flew during combat in World War II and Korea. They can get your butt through this tour. Get on your high horse with them and you will find yourself alone."

While Zane was thanking Manuel, he heard the distant sound of helicopters. Although they were far away, their distinctive sound was unmistakable. Zane and Manuel walked outside and looked in the sound's direction. In the distance, small specks appeared on the horizon.

"Damn, they make a lot of noise to be so far away," Zane commented.

"You better believe it and do not think that the noise doesn't give the VC advanced notice," Manuel added.

As they watched the H-21s begin their landing approaches, Manuel nudged Zane and said, "Let's go to OPS. The guys will come through there to turn in their flight data," Manuel suggested.

"Fine with me," Zane agreed.

While walking to OPS, Zane watched as maintenance personnel swarmed the H-21s. Mechanics and crew chiefs began opening compartments to make repairs. Walking from the airfield, pilots carried their helmets, maps, and other paraphernalia. Their flight suits were soaked with sweat. Anything they could take off, they did. This provided some heat relief.

As they entered OPS, Zane saw Daryl Scott completing required mission reports. As a junior pilot, he was responsible for completing mission report forms. He was so engrossed in his task that he did not see Zane approach.

Zane grabbed Scott's neck from behind with a firm grip and asked. "Who in the hell ever told you that you could fly."

Scott looked up slowly and initially did not recognize Zane. However, Zane saw something in Scott's eyes that he had seen elsewhere. At Camp Humphries, pilots returning from Viet Nam had the look. It was an eyes half closed, exhausted stare. It only lasted for a second but Zane saw it in his best friend and it caused him deep concern.

Recognition brightened Scott's eyes and he dropped his pen while breaking into a happy grin, "Dale you worthless piece of cow shit. I got word you were on your way. Damn, it is good to see you."

With all the backslapping and good-natured bantering, some of the older warrant officers saw it. They watched the pair with interest.

Finally, one said, "Looks like Scott has a new bunk mate. It looks like true love to me."

Another added, "Hell, he's too cute to be Scott's. I want her."

Scott promptly made an obscene gesture with his middle finger that only provoked others.

"Hey Scott, is that your number of legal parents?" One warrant officer asked.

Scott replied, "No, that's how many dimes it cost to sleep with your mother."

One of the chief warrant officers introduced himself to Zane, "Hi lieutenant, I'm James Welsh. We have really been expecting you. After chow, come by the WOPA tent for drinks."

Zane knew about WOPA, the warrant officers protective association, and answered, "Sure thing."

Manuel excused himself and left Zane and Scott together. When Scott finished his paper work, they walked to the tents together.

"How's Janice," Scott asked.

"The last word I got she was fine. You know that we have a baby due this month," Zane answered.

"Has it been that long?" Scott asked.

"Yes, it has but it doesn't seem so," Zane responded. "And how's your family?"

"Hell, I haven't had a letter from Georgia since I got here. There's not much of an established mail system in place. I guess my mail is still going to Korea," Scott said, sounding quite frustrated.

"I'm sure that's it," Zane assured his friend.

As the two started into the tent area, Scott asked. "Have they put you in the IO tent?"

"What's an IO tent?" Zane questioned.

"An IO tent is for In and Out. Guys who are really short and new guys stay in the IO tent. I see you are carrying Manuel's shotgun so I figured that's where you were. Guys, who are short, have to turn in their gear just before they leave so they only have the essentials. New guys, like you, are not well known. Depending upon who likes you, and whom you like, you will move to another tent. Someone will ask you after about a week," Scott explained.

"That doesn't sound right," Zane said.

"Dale, it works well. We have one pilot who has his own tent because he snores so loud. It is hard enough sleeping as it is," Scott continued. "I will show you where to take a dump and where to wash up for chow."

What impressed Zane was their shower. It consisted of a salvaged, aircraft external fuel tank mounted atop a platform. Around the shower area, there was a three-foot high privacy fence on three sides. By standing beneath the fuel tank and pulling a chain, water flowed through a showerhead. A danger was trying to shower in the afternoon. The tropical sun heated the water to a scalding temperature. It was necessary to shower early or late.

Another item Scott showed him was a pee tube. Located throughout the unit area, there were three-sided enclosures. Inside, a metal, tube-like artillery ammunition container rose from a gravel bed. When the urge struck, duck into one of these and it met the need. Still, Zane wondered what was available should a woman be in the area. Scott told him not to worry about it because they did not allow women on their compound. If they were USO girls, they used the outhouse with a guard posted.

After chow, Zane made his way to the WOPA tent. He knew which one it was because there was a sign outside that stated, "WOPA Officers Enter By Invite Only." Zane hesitated and then entered.

"Over here, L-T," he heard, as he watched CWO Welsh leave a card table and approach him.

Zane immediately saw the difference between the IO tent and this one. Between cots, there were tables with reading lamps and portable radios. Some had fans to help stay cool. Each cot had at least one chair and some two. It was apparent these people were trying to make their quarters as comfortable as possible.

Welsh introduced him to baby faced WO 1s to CW 4s, with gray hair and wrinkled skin. There were so many that Zane could not remember them. He did notice that one end of the tent was clear of cots. There were four card tables, an ice chest, and a refrigerator in the area. Three of the tables had poker games going. In addition, there was a ping pong table. This was their best effort to have a recreation area.

CWO Welsh pointed toward the empty card table and said, "Let's sit over here."

As Zane sat, Welsh asked. "How about a cold brew?"

"Yeah, sure. That sounds great," Zane answered.

Welsh brought two beers from the refrigerator and said, "Hope you're not particular about brands. We take what we can get when we can get it."

Dressed in Bermuda shorts, a tee shirt, and flip-flops, Welsh sat next to Zane.

"At Oh Dark 30 tomorrow morning, the CQ will wake you. I will meet you at chow. Come prepared to fly because we have a maximum of five hours flight time for an orientation and a check ride. You will fly with me, which means I won't be available for missions. With five months here, I do not miss many missions. Major Barry said that, if you are ready in three hours, release you for missions. You will be ready in less than five. We can get the remainder flying missions," Welsh explained.

"Sounds fine," Zane commented and asked. "What kind of missions have you been flying?"

"We fly the usual ash and trash missions. We deliver mail, ammo, food, and general supplies. We have been doing some practice air assault missions hauling ARVN (Army Republic Viet Nam) troops. I don't know the details but we have a big mission in the near future. That's one reason Major Barry wants you ready right away," Welsh answered.

Continuing Welsh said, "L-T, unless you get assigned to OPS, you are going to be a flight platoon commander. You need to know that flight platoon commanders do not command missions. That is the job of the air mission commander, who is normally one of the more qualified CWOs or Major Barry. I think Barry may lead this particular mission. We've been doing some sketchy work with UH-1s flying escort. They are from a unit named UTT and they are good at their jobs. They prep a LZ with rockets and machine guns as we go in to off load troops. I would hate to have to go into one without them."

"Chief, I am in your hands. To my knowledge, no one has ever shot at me. I particularly do not care about not being able to shoot back. In addition, my transition in Korea did not include sling loads. Do you get much of that here?" Zane asked.

"Not many sling loads. The ARVN do not know how to rig a load for pickup. We have to teach them so we're particular about those missions. Unless you have more questions, have another beer and get acquainted," Welsh answered.

Zane spent the next few hours getting acquainted and listening. He absorbed every war story that he heard and stored it for future reference. He excused himself and went to use the shower. He figured the water was cool by now. Showered and shaved, he returned to the I-O tent to find Scott waiting.

"Hi Dale, how did it go with WOPA?" Scott asked.

"I think it went good. I sure felt at ease among them," Zane answered.

Scott said, "We need to go to OPS to see tomorrow's missions. They should have them posted by now. Let's go."

"Let me get dressed," Zane replied.

"Nothing formal around here. After hours, a towel and flip flops is all you need," Scott said.

"Fine be right with you," Zane said as he went to his cot.

He wrapped a bath towel around his waist and tucked it into a holding twist. Next, he picked up his shotgun and an ammo pouch. He put the ammo pouch over his shoulder as he started to join Scott. Directly across from him, CWO Manuel was looking at him and made eye contact. Manuel gave him an approving look and a small smile as if to say, "Okay."

As Zane turned to leave, Scott was standing behind him and said, "You don't need that thing. We're not going elephant hunting."

Turning to leave the weapon, Manuel frowned and made a miniature shake of his head indicating, "No."

"Humor me Daryl. I just want to get the feel of it," Zane told Scott.

"Okay but watch where you point that damned thing," Scott replied.

OPS was nothing more than another tent with a counter in it. Pilots stayed outside the counter and operations personnel were behind it. Two pieces of plywood had maps stapled to them and the whole thing covered with clear vinyl. The mission board listed two pilots, an aircraft tail number, and the next day's missions. Zane was with Welsh and a notation said, "Local Checkout in 497."

Like the supply tent, there was a canvas divider behind the counter. Zane could hear considerable radio noises coming from the area. The conversations were mixed and difficult to understand, as some of it was Vietnamese. While he and Scott were looking at the mission assignments, Major Barry appeared from behind the divider.

"About settled in with us Zane?" He asked.

"I am getting there sir," Zane answered.

"I see in your file that you were a gunnery instructor at Sill. You ever do any aerial artillery adjustment?" Barry asked.

"No sir but I know how to," Zane replied.

"Well, keep it to yourself. MACV is starting a program to teach that to the ARVN artillery people. You are here to fly H-21s. Okay?" Barry asked, to make sure Zane understood.

"Roger sir," Zane replied, feeling a little uncomfortable at Barry's tone of voice.

Turning to Scott, Zane asked. "Daryl, you ready?"

"Yeah, let's go," he answered, as he turned toward the tent's exit.

Once outside, Zane noticed that he and his towel were soaked with perspiration. He walked with Scott until they reached his tent. After saying goodnight, he returned to the IO tent. CWO Manuel grinned as Zane returned to his bunk.

"You did good L-T. Do not get caught anywhere without your weapon. I pulled a Korean tour and folks here are in for a hard lesson soon. There's no damned security. One of these days the VC are going to walk through that skimpy wire and blow those 21s to hell. They will likely try to kill as many in here as they can. I'm ending six months without it happening. I figure that we're overdue," Manuel said seriously.

Zane thought a moment and replied, "When Major Barry and I came in today, I saw one guard. The barbed wire on the perimeter was one strand. I did not see a trench, bunker or anything like a defensive perimeter. Who is protecting the 21s?" Zane asked.

Manuel raised his hand and formed a zero with his thumb and forefinger. He lay down on his cot to sleep but he made sure that Zane saw an M-14 rifle with him. He fluffed his pillow and was soon asleep. At least he appeared to be sleeping. Zane had his doubts.

"Up, up, time to go. Breakfast is getting cold," the CQ yelled.

Awaken by the incessant yelling, Zane swung his legs from his cot and remained seated. He yawned while looking for Manuel. He was not in his bunk and his duffel bag was gone.

"Shit," Zane thought. "I would be out of here too, if I was in his shoes."

After struggling in the dark, Zane finally had his flight suit on and his helmet in hand. He stumbled through the tent and toward the wonderful aroma of coffee. Down the row of tents, he saw one with its sides rolled up to provide ventilation. Incandescent bulbs hanged from a single wire strung along the tent's length. Inside, he saw picnic style benches with people seated having breakfast. As he drew closer, he could see others going along a typical chow line.

As Zane stepped inside the tent and went toward the tray rack, someone said, "Over here lieutenant."

Looking in the direction of the voice, he saw a young soldier sitting behind a small, field table. He beckoned Zane to come to him.

As he approached the young man said, "That will be one dollar and 25 cents sir."

"Pardon?" Zane asked, disbelieving what he had heard.

"Officers pay one dollar and 25 cents, sir," the soldier repeated.

Zane knew that, during field exercises, he paid for his meals. He had difficulty conceiving that he had to in a combat zone. He would have to sort this out later. He began digging through his pockets.

"Here you go," Zane said as he offered the required money.

"Thank you sir," the soldier replied as he placed it in a cigar box.

After getting a tray, Zane began moving along the serving line. There was bacon, powdered scrambled eggs, and toast. The final item was canned milk sitting in a pan which once help ice. Now it was warm water. As he left the serving line, he saw CWO Welsh waving at him. He joined him.

"Morning, L-T," Welsh said. "It's not exactly the Marriott is it?"

Zane replied, "What can one expect at the price. I did not know we paid for our meals in a combat zone."

Welsh laughed and said smiling, "Lieutenant, you are not in a combat zone. We are advisors helping out our Vietnamese friends."

Zane saw the humor in what Welsh said and replied, "I guess I should pay the government for sending me on a picnic to the exotic Orient."

"There it is," Welsh answered. "Now, let's go preflight."

Both the supply sergeant and Manuel forgot an item, a flashlight. As Zane stumbled along behind Welsh, he felt like an idiot. He should have known better. He had to have a flashlight for missions at dawn. Climbing around on a CH-21 in the dark was a dangerous endeavor. However, Welsh had a solution. Rather than one pilot doing the top and the other the bottom, Zane could do both.

Bringing drooping blades of a 21 from full stop to full speed is different. The wooden blades begin to spin and rise. As they do, they transmit a circular motion throughout the craft. In the cockpit, pilots have shoulder harnesses and seat belts to hold them in place. However, their upper bodies begin to rotate as the blades gain speed. This circular gyration begins in the butt and moves upward. The pilots' shoulders and heads began moving in harmony with the blades. If there has been rain, the gyrations are more pronounced. Water, accumulated inside the blades, moves outward and passes through holes in the blade caps. Once the blades are at full speed, the gyration diminishes to almost nothing.

Without a control tower, Welsh announced his intended actions on the unit's assigned FM frequency. He taxied and made his takeoff as stated. He flew one traffic pattern, testing the craft's feel. Concentrating on vibrations and sound, he made sure the ship was airworthy before transferring control to Zane.

"You've got it L-T. Take us around the pattern and do a normal approach. Shoot for the first white square on the runway," Welsh told Zane over the intercom.

"I've got it," Zane replied as Welsh raised both hands to show he was not on the controls.

For an hour, Welsh had Zane do every standard maneuver. Initially, on turns, the aft rotor tried to move forward causing the 21 to fishtail. Welsh shared his wealth of 21 experiences. He explained how to use power and control inputs, in anticipation of turns, to decrease fishtail movements.

"Fine work L-T. Leave the pattern and start a climb to 5,000 feet on a heading of three six zero," Welsh instructed.

Zane complied as Welsh said, "When flying cross country missions always fly at 5,000 feet or above. The VC do not have a weapon that can touch you at that altitude. Your AC will expect this. The rest of this flight is an orientation ride. Enjoy the scenery."

After another hour, Welsh said, "Take us home. We'll shoot some autorotations."

Later, Welsh, satisfied with Zane's performance directed, "Park it unless you want to eat C rations in the cockpit."

After their post flight inspection, Welsh debriefed Zane in OPS. He cleared him for "Peter Pilot" status. This meant he would fly right seat and log pilot time with an AC on board. After lunch, Zane returned to the IO tent and began rolling up its sides. An hour later, he had every side up and tied in place. Next, he borrowed a shovel and dug a trench around the tent to divert water away from its interior. Tired, he lay on his cot and went to sleep.

"Zane, wake up. Wake up," a voice filtered through Zane's mind. Dismissing it, he turned over without opening his eyes.

Someone gripped his shoulder and shook it while saying, "Zane, I said wake up."

Rolling onto his back, he opened his eyes to see Major Barry looming over him. He immediately got to his feet and saluted.

"Uh, sorry sir," Zane said, still groggy with sleep.

"Who told you that you could raise the tent's sides?" Barry asked.

"No one sir," Zane replied immediately with a nervous tone in his voice.

"Well, damned good idea. I will have the rest like this by tonight. By the way, there is a command briefing in the mess tent at 2100 hours. Be there," Barry told him.

At the appointed time, every pilot in the 93rd TC gathered in the mess tent. Major Barry and his Operations Officer, Captain Bigalow, had an easel placed where all could see it.

"Gentlemen," Major Barry began, "We are to provide air support tomorrow for the 7th ARVN Infantry Division. Their mission is to capture a VC communication's center at Ap Bac. We will airlift two ARVN battalions to support their mission. I will be the Air Mission Commander. Captain Bigalow will now provide details."

Major Barry sat at the front dining table as Captain Bigalow walked to the easel. Bigalow reached behind the easel and pulled a sheet of butcher paper over its top. On it were military symbols designating the various combat elements.

Pointing to an aircraft list in the charts lower left corner, Bigalow explained, "We will initially deploy ten H-21s for this operation. They will have five UH-1Bs from UTT flying escort to the landing zone (LZ)."

Continuing, Bigalow pointed to the name of a town on the chart, "Gentlemen, we will stage out of Tan Hiep at this location. We will follow this route to the designated LZ at this location. It is slightly north northwest of Ap Bac. Estimated VC strength is no more than 350. Artillery fire support is available and will be coordinated through the Air Mission Liaison Officer Lieutenant Zane."

"What did he say?" Zane asked himself. "Air Mission Liaison Officer, what the hell is that?"

Zane could hear Bigalow continuing his briefing but it was background to his thoughts. He was dumbfounded and surprised. No one, including his commander, ever mentioned this operational change.

"Damn, Major Barry said that I had to get cleared fast because he was short pilots. We busted our assess getting here and Welsh went out of his way to get me ready for this mission. What is going on?" Zane thought, as questions overwhelmed his mind.

Bigalow's briefing came back into focus with Zane's full attention. He had to know every detail of this mission, if he was going to be on the ground controlling artillery fire requests.

"We, of course, will not be able to make this air assault with one lift. It will require at least four. Be prepared for more if things get bad and ARVN needs to reinforce. Frankly, I do not anticipate this since there will be ARVN, light mechanized infantry available with M113 Armored Personnel Carriers (APC) to reinforce from the south. Senior advisor is Lieutenant Colonel John Paul Vann. We've worked with him in the past so expect an aggressive ground attack. Fuel is available at Tan Hiep and refueling will be hot. Do not shut down to refuel. Any questions?"

Zane stood up immediately, "What is an Air Mission Liaison Officer?"

Those present filled the tent with laughter. Pilots began nudging each other with elbows and snickered. Zane saw nothing funny in the situation.

Mustering his deepest, strong command voice, he asked with a roar, "What the fuck is so damned funny?"

Instant silence swept through the group. Some began to squirm while others looked at anything other than Zane. No one, not even Major Barry, would make eye contact. Immediately, everyone knew not to screw with Zane when he was serious.

Bigalow, nervously said, "Lieutenant Zane I will brief you after this meeting if that's okay?"

"Thank you sir," Zane replied as he took his seat.

After dismissal, Major Barry and Captain Bigalow remained. Zane joined them near the briefing easel. The first one to speak was Major Barry.

"Zane, I guess you've got an apology coming. This announcement was new to me, as it was you. I will resolve that through command channels," Barry said, as Zane watched Bigalow flush red.

"Brief the man Bigalow and then report to my tent," Barry ordered.

An embarrassing silence ensued until Barry was out of earshot and Bigalow said, "I apologize Zane. WOPA set this up as a joke. Obviously, it did not carry much humor."

"That's alright sir. What's my job?" Zane asked.

"You go into the LZ with the first lift. You will have a FM radio on our frequency. You are to work with Colonel Vann and Major Barry. If there is to be artillery missions fired, you will advise Major Barry who will then advise the flight. You will keep Colonel Vann advised of anything that you think should be done regarding the air operation. It is a real job and an important one," Bigalow explained.

Before dawn on 2 January 1963, Lieutenant Zane sat in the rear of their unit's lead aircraft. Around him, ARVN soldiers sat solemnly eyeing him. Their stares made Zane uneasy. There was a sense of dread that Zane could almost touch. He saw it in the ARVN soldiers' eyes. For some reason, they seemed to blame him for it. He was already on board when they loaded at Tan Hiep before dawn.

It was now past sunrise and the UH-1Bs from the UTT were escorting the H-21 flight. Zane had a headset connected to the ship's intercom to hear what the crew was saying. Beside him, he had a steel helmet for use when he unloaded.

"Snake leader this is snake six, over," Zane heard Major Barry say on his radio.

"Six this is leader, over," Zane's aircraft commander answered.

Zane noticed the sound of automatic weapons fire in the background during this radio transmission. He guessed it to be the UH-1 providing suppression fire into the LZ. Suddenly, he saw one of the ARVN soldiers fall forward with blood spreading across the floor beneath his seat. In quick succession, he saw holes appear in the ship's floor allowing light to beam through. Next, came a radio call by the aircraft commander.

"Snake six this is leader. We are receiving heavy automatic weapons' fire. Are we cleared into the LZ over," Zane heard.

"That's affirmative leader, six out," Barry said.

Near Zane's head, he heard two whack sounds and another ARVN across from him fell forward bleeding profusely. Zane could tell from the engine sound, and the craft's attitude, they were near touch down. He took off his headset and put on his steel pot. As he felt the 21 touch down, he held his loaded shotgun close and rose to leave the craft. He hesitated to wait for the ARVN to start unloading. None of them moved.

"I cannot stay here and I do not want to be out there alone. The hell with it, I'm gone," he thought as he bolted to the aircraft's door.

His feet hit the ground and he headed for the nearest cover, which was a small levee across a rice field. He looked over his shoulder once to see ARVN following him closely. He hugged the earth tight, as automatic weapons raked the protecting mound of earth. Looking up and down the levee, he saw ARVN doing the same. Zane pulled his FM radio from his back and extended its antenna. When the antenna went above the levee, earth around it exploded with impacts from projectiles in great numbers.

Overhead Zane saw a spotter plane circling their position. He concluded that it was an artillery forward observer.

After tuning his radio to the artillery frequency, Zane transmitted, "This is snake three alpha. We need some artillery or air support. We're pinned and cannot move. We're receiving extremely heavy automatic weapons' fire. Most of it is 30 and 50 caliber from south of our position, over."

Zane listened for five minutes after making three calls. All he heard was static. He changed to the command frequency and immediately began receiving transmissions.

"Snake six this is snake three alpha. Be advised there is heavy automatic weapon's fire this location. Do you copy over," Zane transmitted.

"Roger three alpha. This is six. Pop green smoke your location, over."

Zane immediately removed a green smoke grenade from his shoulder harness; pulled its pin; and tossed it over the levee. He lay flat as he could to the ground.

"Three alpha this is six. Have your location. Give direction of incoming over," Barry instructed Zane.

"Roger that six. Incoming bearing my location is one four five degrees over," Zane answered promptly.

"This is six. Standby," Barry answered.

The helicopters continued delivering troops in full view of Zane. He knew they had to be receiving hits from the automatic weapons. ARVN left the craft and moved immediately for cover. He saw what he knew had to be their artillery forward observer from the American equipment he carried. He was a lieutenant staying close to an ARVN captain.

With the same unit, Zane saw an American sergeant. He was the only one that Zane could see located with the ARVN. The NCO was talking to the ARVN captain and his forward observer. Whatever the discussion, it was animated. The sergeant attempted to take the radio from the forward observer. The observer and the captain would not allow him to do so.

To the north, Zane saw fighter-bombers rapidly approaching. They passed directly over Zane and unloaded their ordinance based upon subsequent explosions. Automatic weapons fire diminished enough for Zane to dare a look in the explosions' direction. Slowly, he raised his head while lying on his stomach.

To his immediate front, Zane saw a dike similar to his small one but much larger. Smoke billowed skyward from the fighter bomber attack. He inched back to cover and opened his map. He noted that the few huts he saw were a small village named Ap Tan Thoi. Extending from it to the southeast was a canal running to Ap Bac.

"Damn, if those VC are dug into that dike. They have excellent protection from artillery and air strikes. The smoke had to be from burning huts," Zane surmised.

Again, he inched upward to view the scene. A hail of automatic weapons fire erupted from the canal and ripped through the top of his minimal cover. He immediately sought earth's protection by getting as close as he could.

"Jesus God, do not let me die in this place," Zane prayed.

Zane, outwardly, did not show himself much of a religious person. He was now and he was scared.

"Six this is three alpha. We need artillery where those bombers hit. Tell them to use variable time (VT) fuses set for a 20-foot airburst. Those dinks are dug in like ticks on a hound," Zane wailed on his radio.

"Three alpha this six, roger," Barry answered.

Zane saw the fixed wing spotter plane again. It circled high above the action. The last time he called for air support he got it. Zane figured that ship was definitely a FAC.

"Six, this is three alpha. We could use some more bomber support but use napalm over," Zane transmitted.

"Roger three alpha. I will try," was Barry's reply.

Zane felt a tug on his shoulder. He looked to his side and the American sergeant seen earlier was beside him.

"Sir, I am Sergeant Buncombe. Can you get some artillery on your radio," he asked looking desperate.

"I've tried twice sarge without success. I did get an air strike though," Zane answered.

Staying low, Sergeant Buncombe held his steel helmet on by pressing its top with one hand. In the other, he held a 45 pistol. He saw Zane looking at it and put it in his holster.

"Hell L-T, I don't know what I planned on doing with that," Buncombe said. "I cannot get those SOBs down there to do anything. One's the company CO and the other is his forward observer."

Zane replied, "I figured that's who they were. If we don't get some fire support on that canal's dike, we're screwed. Oh, by the way, do you know who is in that spotter plane?"

"Yeah, that's Lieutenant Colonel Vann. He's our senior advisor. He is probably who got those fighter bombers," Buncombe answered, as he winced at repeated whines over their heads.

H-21s continued delivering ARVN troops. Zane watched the fourth lift, for that morning, making its approach. He noticed the third ship, immediately before touchdown, behaved erratically. As soon as its troops unloaded, the pilot was obviously in trouble. When he attempted to take off, the aircraft rose a few feet and its blades began slowing causing a slow descent. The ship struck the ground and rolled onto its side. Both sets of rotor blades began disintegrating, as they struck ground. Parts began flying in every direction.

"Holy shit," Zane yelled as he began running along what small cover their small dike provided.

None of the ARVN he passed seemed interested in doing anything to save the crew. Sergeant Buncombe was close behind Zane. As the two ran, Zane saw the flight crew abandon the 21 and take cover behind its fuselage. The last 21 in the fourth lift emptied its troops and came to a low hover. It headed toward the downed ship. It was apparent to Zane that they intended to attempt to rescue the flight crew.

"Snake six this is three alpha. We need that artillery now. I repeat now, over."

"Roger three alpha. Six out," Barry responded.

Before Zane completed his call, he saw 30 caliber and 50 caliber rounds rake the rescue ship. Parts scattered and cockpit Plexiglas flew in every direction. This ship hit hard causing it landing struts to puncture its main hull. Without wheels, the 21 rolled sideways and began disintegrating.

As soon as Zane had traveled along the protective dike to a point closest to the first downed ship, he sprinted across open ground towards the trapped crew. He threw himself behind the downed 21. One crewman was leaning against the hull with his flight suit open. One of the others had already placed a compression bandage on his chest wound.

Zane moved to the next man. He appeared to have a broken leg. Cutting away his trousers, Zane saw that he had a compound fracture. He was also in shock. Laying him on his back, Zane checked to make sure that his airway was clear. Assured of this he turned to find something for a splint when Sergeant Buncombe pushed by him with two pieces of aluminum tubing from the 21.

"L-T," he said. "You hold these in place while I set this leg," Buncombe directed.

Zane grabbed the two tubes and held them while looking directly into the wounded pilot's face. It was CWO Welsh. He appeared dazed and had a glassy stare. When Buncombe pulled Welsh's leg to set it, Welsh grabbed Zane's shoulders and screamed. Zane dared not move until Buncombe had the leg wrapped. Welsh slipped into unconsciousness. Next, Zane removed his poncho and placed it over him after checking for other wounds. He seemed okay for the moment.

Zane looked in the direction of the second downed 21. He saw every crewmember returning fire. He could see none that appeared wounded so he remained with Welsh.

"Six this is three alpha. We need medevac here soonest, over," Zane transmitted.

"Roger that three alpha. It's on its way out," Barry replied immediately.

Zane took a quick look around the sky. He noticed that the spotter plane was no longer in the area.

"Wonder where the hell he went," Zane thought. "We need him more than ever."

Zane took Welsh's M-14 and scooted on his stomach to get a line of fire toward those shooting at them. He found an opening at the 21s midpoint. He could see directly into Ap Bac. The long canal, running southeast from Ap Tan Thoi to Ap Bac, was ablaze with weapons firing.

"There is one hell of a lot more people there than 350," he thought. "I was told the VC would slip away after being engaged. These are not. They are putting up one hell of a fight."

Zane emptied a clip toward one firing position. He watched his rounds throw dirt skyward with no effect on the VC hiding behind the levee.

"Hell, this is useless. We're probably going to die in this damned mud," he thought.

"Damn you all to hell," he yelled as he emptied another clip against the protecting levee.

Chapter Thirty Four

December 1963

Politics is war without bloodshed while war is politics with bloodshed
Mao Zedong (1893–1976), founder of the People's Republic of China.
"On Protracted War," lecture, May 1938

Colonel Jean Danjou was in Saigon again. The last time he was a lieutenant and the hero of Na Son. Like his comrades, he had to leave because his country's colonial power fell. Its demise took place at Dien Bien Phu. He was one of few escapees and his military career with the Legion did not die.

Over subsequent years, he rose in rank rapidly. There was some resentment because of it but it was no bother to him. Some contemporaries held the view that his name brought him rapid promotion. Being the grandson of probably the Legion's greatest hero, they thought propelled him to higher rank fast. Jean could care less what others thought. He simply did his work the best way he knew how. He was a Legionnaire and a good one.

Nonetheless, this time was different because he was not fighting an enemy as a Legionnaire. He was undertaking a dirty business. He was conducting a covert operation involving the drug trade and he had to become personally involved.

He never knew of his country's use of money from the heroin trade. In 1955, France lost its control over the heroin from Laos and Cambodia. In the past, French control was through their intelligence service. The intelligence operatives allowed certain Saigon criminal elements to market the product. Funds from sales bought daily intelligence to ferret out Communist terrorists in Saigon's streets. While he was an intelligence specialist and covert operative, he never had a need to know. Now, he not only knew of it; he was becoming an active participant.

When France withdrew their undercover, intelligence operations, they no longer controlled the heroin. The suspicion was that the upper echelons of Diem's South Vietnamese government had taken control after France's 1954 defeat at Dien Bien Phu and subsequent Geneva Accords. However, Diem was dead and the drug trade thrived. His government was sure that Diem's death carried with it benefits for certain key officers in South Viet Nam's defense ministry and the county's senior executive officers were controlling the heroin flow.

Jean was certain they were in error. While many senior military officers raced to fill the void left by Diem's death, they did not control the drug trade from its origins. Any control they had in Saigon was at the benevolence of the CIA. Diem's death simply complicated the situation.

Diem's assignation was the result of his dictatorial rule and his religious intolerance as far as Jean was concerned. Jean saw it coming when Buddhists organized after Diem's attacks on them. Diem did not trust any religious organization unless it was catholic. Moreover, he did not trust military leaders who did not practice Catholicism.

Buddhists had a flag of their own. They began displaying it publicly. Diem thought they should fly South Viet Nam's flag. Buddhists brought Diem's wrath when they did not comply. There had to be a confrontation and it came in May 1963.

Jean tried to tell his superiors that the confrontation would take place. He advised France's Ministry of Intelligence when they could expect Diem's downfall to begin. The one at Hue on 8 May 1963 was the first event that began Diem's downfall. This ceremony had Buddhists in the tens of thousands present. Diem's rancor caused him to dispatch troops to assure the Buddhists displayed South Viet Nam's flag. When they did not, Diem halted the event. The Buddhists did not cooperate so troops fired live ammunition to stop the ceremonies. There were dead and wounded Buddhists.

Jean's accurate prediction caused his assignment to Saigon. The Security Minister made his assignment clear. If Diem falls, the French wanted to know who moved to control the heroin trade.

Diem's use of deadly force against a religious group was a catalyst. This caused events, from the White House to the U.S. Embassy in Saigon, to begin his removal from office, by force if necessary.

On 11 June 1963, Buddhist monks began a protest to garner world support. A monk named Quang Duc calmly had himself doused with gasoline and set afire. Pictures of this emulation flashed around the world. In addition, such events began throughout South Viet Nam almost on a daily basis. The world cringed as the Buddhists fought Diem's religious policies.

Message traffic between the U. S. Embassy and the White House increased as particular South Vietnamese officers formed a coup committee. Most were general officers and they intended to take the government by force. These officers organized with White House blessings straight from President John F. Kennedy. Diem had to go and the Kennedy Administration knew it.

If Diem could have picked the dumbest action of his presidency, he did so on 21 August 1963. He had troops loyal to him change into regular army uniforms and attack Buddhist temples throughout South Viet Nam. This drew Kennedy's wrath that he exhibited publicly to the world.

Religious leaders from Calcutta to Rome denigrated Diem. If this dictator thought he had trouble with Buddhists, he now had his own Catholics calling for his hide. It was final.

Not only did Diem have to give up his Presidency; he also gave his life. Those conducting the coup assassinated him and his brother on 2 November 1963. General Duong Van Mingh became South Viet Nam's new president. This meant new leaders at almost every level. Along with new leaders, it would be necessary to establish who were the leaders involved with heroin.

Jean's job was to observe and report drug oriented operations conducted between Laos, Cambodia, and South Viet Nam. There were rumors that the CIA was controlling production and distribution of heroin. This was what the French did when they were in control. Their intelligence agency controlled the drugs.

With Jean's recent detailed reconnaissance of the transportation network from Laos to Cambodia, he knew every trail, hill, and river. In addition, he had a working and friendly relationship with the Hmong. This was particularly important because planting, cultivating, and harvesting from the poppy fields was done mostly by the Hmong.

Jean's current focus was on the role played by individuals in Saigon. He knew that there were contacts doing business in the city. He must identify them and determine their role in the marketing process. He worked from a back office in Cholon's most rundown district. He knew his life was in danger so he used every ploy learned while with the French resistance.

Corsican Mafia members handled drug trafficking for French intelligence in the past. Jean felt sure the same people were involved with the CIA. He needed to make contact with one in particular, Frank Furchi. Reportedly, Frank Furchi was the son of Dominic Furchi, the number three man in the Mafia's hierarchy. The word on the street was that Frank Furchi remained in Saigon to take control of heroin distribution. Jean considered this contact essential to verify his suspicions regarding the CIA.

However, Furchi was not going to divulge to just anyone his criminal activities. Jean's task was to put himself in a position that would cause Furchi to do so as a matter of course. Jean, at a minimum, would have to appear to be either a CIA operative or a criminal in the heroin trade. His controller in France could not build him a CIA identity. However, he could do so as a criminal.

Jean strongly protested his assignment. He was a Legionnaire with explicit military skills of value to France. The process of getting him into his current position started upon his return to South Viet Nam after his month long trek with Boa. The American NCOs, who intercepted him, took him to MACV headquarters. During the trip, he convinced the NCOs of his identity.

The truck driver, Sergeant First Class Leroy Jenkins asked. "What in the world were you doing along that highway? Do you have any idea of your appearance?"

"Sergeant, while I am a Legionnaire, I am also a colonel. I believe that your army does have protocols in place regarding military courtesy," Jean said.

"Uh, yes sir. Sorry, sir," Jenkins replied.

The other NCO was Sergeant Major McKenzie. He had 25 years service. He wore a Green Beret, a ranger tab on his shirt and silver wings on his chest. He not only recognized Jean's status but also deduced where Jean needed to go in Saigon. He had Sergeant Jenkins drive them to the American Embassy.

McKenzie escorted Jean directly to the Combined Studies Division (CSD). This was the CIA organization training Tia tribesmen as Airborne Rangers for intelligence gathering missions. Its new chief was Colonel James Whitaker.

"Colonel Danjou, I have read of your exploits during World War II and at Na Son," Whitaker said. "We could really use your talents. However, I suspect you need to contact your embassy."

"That's correct," Jean answered. "It is best that I not be seen going there unless that is their desire. Can you provide secure communications?"

"Yes I can but not from this office. Would you like to contact them now?" Whitaker asked.

"Yes I would," Jean answered.

"Come with me," Whitaker directed as he arose and started for his office's door.

It was necessary for the pair to go outside the main building onto a walkway. The building's construction was such that an outside wall precluded anyone observing them. The wall was in place for reasons other than decoration. It had multiple openings from which a person could view the embassy grounds and the streets outside. Alternating apertures in the brick façade allowed this.

Whitaker opened a door and they entered the main building. They traveled down a long corridor past offices on either side. About midway down the corridor, Whitaker opened an unmarked door on his right and the two entered.

"I have cleared your use of our secure facilities with Ambassador Lodge. He has contacted your people and they are expecting your call. You can use either of the telephones inside those booths," Whitaker said as he pointed to the enclosures.

"Lift the handset and listen to the dial tone for a second or two. It should change frequency. When it does, press the pound key, and wait for two tones. When you have the two tones, make your call. If you do not hear the tones, do not call. There is a tap on the line. When you finish, press the pound key, and wait for two tones again. If you hear them, your communication was secure. Any questions?" Whitaker asked.

"None," Jean replied as he walked to one of the booths.

Jean entered and closed its privacy door. As the door closed, he heard a mild hissing sound. He knew this was the door sealing into place and making the booth soundproof.

Jean's early arrival surprised France's chief of station. They did not expect him for another month. Word came from their Bangkok embassy that he was on his way. Jean explained how Boa expedited his trip. His controller advised that he not approach their headquarters. They gave him an address in the Cholon district as a reporting in point. In addition, the location would become his living quarters for another assignment.

Through special arrangements, Jean could brief CIA station personnel at the U.S Embassy. According to his controller, a special request from Pierre Salinger, in the name of President Lyndon Johnson, received approval. Jean was almost speechless with the news of Kennedy's assassination. He had been in isolation while doing his detail recon of North Viet Nam's road network. With President Kennedy's death, Pierre Salinger should have nothing to do with President Lyndon Johnson's staff. Jean attributed the arrangement to Lanny Briscoe. Jean closed his call with a secure indication.

Jean joined Whitaker and said, "I have instructions to brief you regarding the operation I just completed."

"Yes, I already knew. However, I knew you would need clearance first that's why we suggested that you call," Whitaker answered.

"Do you have a place where I could take a shower and obtain civilian clothing?" Jean asked.

"Certainly, I'll take you to our executive locker room. You will find everything you need to bathe and shave. While you do that, I will get you some clothes right away," Whitaker replied.

Colonel Whitaker and Sergeant Major McKenzie debriefed Jean in a secure room. They recorded every detail that Jean had to offer.

Jean's information made clear that Ho Chi Minh intended to provide significant support for the National Liberation Front (NLF) forces in South Viet Nam. It was essential that this information get to military leaders in Washington, D.C. as soon as possible. While support was increasing with both troops and aircraft, there were those who would stop the American support for Viet Nam. There were indications that President Johnson might begin withdrawing U.S. Armed Forces. If the U. S. intended to stop Communist aggression in Southeast Asia, they needed to support the ARVN. There was no doubt that North Viet Nam was committed.

The news of Kennedy's death, so soon after Diem, made Jean suspicious. Perhaps it was coincidence but he still thought there was a likely hood of a relationship. If there was one, he could not find evidence to support it. This did not mean that it did not happen. It simply meant that he could find no evidence. Besides, he had his own problems with the Corsicans and did not have time to pursue the matter.

Jean had never failed in an assignment until now. He could not penetrate the Corsican network after a six-month effort. At first, he thought that the CIA was using Air America to transport raw opium from the Golden Triangle. He had left Saigon and backtracked to Laos. He could not find a single instance of knowing participation in drug distribution by Air American crews.

In Saigon, every time he thought he had a reliable contact, that person disappeared. It was as if someone knew his true reason for his activities. During his last contact with his controller, he conveyed that he was sure that his cover no longer existed. The CIA knew his identity. He was not certain about the Corsicans. However, if the CIA were an active participant in Heroin distribution, the Corsicans knew. He requested his return to France. He received approval and permission to end his current efforts.

Without having to maintain his cover, Jean could now visit the Cathedral. Often, he had thought of mother superior and how she knew so much about Operation Vulture. He remembered the beautiful student Minh Thanh. They only spoke but for a moment and he never forgot her. She had to be a nun now. He looked forward to visiting with them after such a long absence.

Standing before the steel door, Jean remembered the first time he and Captain Louis stood in the same spot. Everything looked the same except that it was ten years later. He gripped the heavy cord and pulled twice. Inside, he heard the expected sound of a bell ringing. The small steel door opened and he looked directly at Mey Ling. Her features remained fixed as if frozen. She blinked a few times and tears came. She did not speak but stared.

"Mey Ling, it's Jean, Jean Danjou. Don't you remember me?" Jean asked.

Her expression did not change as she closed the opening without speaking. Confused, Jean reached for the rope but the aperture opened. A nun looked at Jean through the opening. He did not recognize her.

"I am Sister Marie. May I help you sir," she asked, obviously upset for some reason.

Jean explained his reason for visiting. He told Sister Marie of his previous contact with mother superior. He expressed his desire to visit.

"Sir, I do not think that is possible. Mother superior is gravely ill. She has been for a month and there is little hope for her," Sister Marie explained.

"I need to speak with her only for a moment," Jean pleaded in desperation.

"I do not think that would be wise. She needs to rest," Sister Marie responded.

Thinking for a moment, Jean asked. "Would you give her my name and ask if she wants to see me?"

Sister Marie hesitated and Jean spoke before she could answer.

"Please do this little thing for me sister?" Jean asked with obvious, deep emotion.

"Wait here sir," Sister Marie said as she closed the opening.

Jean paced back and forth in front of the steel gate. As time passed, it seemed an eternity to him.

"I must see her," he kept telling himself.

He heard the big, steel door squeak on its hinges. He looked up to see it move and open enough for him to enter. Sister Marie met him on the inside.

"Mother superior wants to see you. You must not stay but a moment. She is extremely weak. Kindly follow me," she explained.

They passed the small chapel and Jean saw Mey Ling prostrate before the Tabernacle. She was sobbing as she held a rosary tightly in her clenched hands. Her forearms extended up towards the large crucifix. Soon they arrived at mother superior's quarters. The rooms were dark with only candle light as a light source. Sister Marie stopped outside a door.

"Sir, I remind you, do not remain long," Sister Marie whispered as she slowly opened the door.

Inside, Jean's eyes adjusted to the darkness. He was amazed at her Spartan bedchamber. She lay on a small bed with a crucifix above it. There was one table and a chair. Beside her bed, a nightstand held various medications and a rosary. Two candles on tall holders flanked her bed. Jean walked quietly to her bedside where he could see her better. She must have sensed his presence for her eyes fluttered open slightly.

"Lieutenant Danjou how wonderful to see you again," she said with labored breaths between words.

She raised her trembling hand and Jean took it while kneeling on one knee. He kissed it and noticed that it was without warmth.

Looking at her, Jean said, "Mother superior it has been many years. I never forgot how you tried to help me and Captain Louis."

Now on both knees, Jean took mother superior's hand and placed it with her other one. Jean felt her move and looked into her peaceful face with a little smile at the corners of her lips.

"Will you give me my rosary please?" She asked.

Jean removed it from her nightstand and placed its crucifix in her crossed hands. She smiled and looked at him with a loving gaze.

Whispering she said, "Thu Duc. She is at Thu Duc."

Leaning closer, Jean asked. "Who?"

Mother superior did not answer. She made trembling movements with her hands to move a bead between her fingers. Her lips moved but Jean could not hear the words.

Turning her head to look at Jean, she whispered, "Minh Thanh is at Thu Duc. Go to her my son."

Jean could tell that it took every ounce of what strength she could garner to tell him this. He arose and leaned forward to kiss her hands.

After standing straight, he said, "Thank you mother superior."

She continued moving the rosary's beads but now her eyes closed. Jean turned and left the room to meet Sister Marie outside the door.

"Sir, you must be a special person. That is the most mother superior has spoken in a week," she said with tears streaming. "It's as if she was waiting for you. I think she is gone."

Jean turned and looked to see that mother superior's rosary was not moving. It hung loosely from her hands. He could see no evidence of her breathing. Sister Marie went to her and felt her cheek and then her throat for a pulse. Sister Marie's shoulders began to shake as she tucked the bed covers neatly around her neck. After a few moments of prayer, she came to the door and closed it behind her. She did not speak.

After having the steel gate locked behind him, Jean heard the Cathedral's bells slowly ring their message to all that could hear, "Mother superior is dead."

Jean hired a taxi to take him to Thu Duc. Despite a full day's questioning, he did not learn of Long Thanh's whereabouts. Finally, he realized what he must do. He had to keep watch on the market. Everyone living in Thu Duc had to come to market eventually. There was a problem. Thu Duc had three. While he was watching one, she might appear at one of the others. For one week, he moved between the markets at various times of day. Time for him to depart for France was overdue. He requested, and received, a month's leave to continue his quest.

He saw a blue ribbon. It was not the first blue one he saw but this one moved a certain way. Shouldering his way through the crowd, he kept the ribbon in sight. Suddenly, it disappeared.

In a panic, Jean shoved villagers aside. He arrived where he thought her last location was before she disappeared. He scanned the area section by section, looking intently. His search stopped at a woman filling a water jar. She had her back to him. Somehow, she did not stand like the others. A gracefulness made her stand apart. She was leaning over a water spigot, filling one of two jars. He stared as she arose. She wore the blue ribbon. Slowly, she turned and her eyes met his.

It was the same sensation that he had as she walked away from her language class. He could feel emotion growing inside, gripping his chest and his throat. He tried to speak but the words did not come. A demure smile lingered at the corners of her lips as she looked toward the ground.

Walking close, he extended his right hand while placing his bent forefinger beneath her chin. She did not move away, resist, or speak. With a gentle pressure, he raised her chin. Again, their eyes met.

"Monsieur Danjou, it is good to see you again," Minh Thanh said softly again lowering her head.

Jean's voice cracked like that of a teenager when he replied, "Mademoiselle, the pleasure is most certainly mine."

Continuing, he said, "Please, let me help you with your water jars."

"If you must monsieur," she replied.

By this time, other Vietnamese ladies became aware of the two. Some giggled while older ones knowingly clicked their tongues. Jean noticed that he and Minh Thanh were in a circle of an increasing number of village women. He quickly lifted one filled jar and reached for the other before Minh Thanh stopped him.

"Please Monsieur, your actions are becoming embarrassing. I will take the other jar. Feel welcome to come with me," she said.

Jean prided himself on his composure. However, this situation was quickly causing him to lose it. He felt his palms becoming moist and his hands began to tremble slightly.

"I apologize for any embarrassment. Show me where you want me to go," Jean almost pleaded.

"This way," she said as she started toward a street exiting from the market area.

As the crowd grew thin, Jean wanted to speak but the words did not come. He followed silently. When completely away from the crowd, he moved forward to her side. They continued their silent walk.

After a few minutes, Minh Thanh asked. "What do you know of Monsieur Louis?"

"I don't know," Jean replied. Even if he did know, he could not remember.

"After he had to leave, I began teaching his classes," Minh Thanh commented.

Finally regaining some measure of composure, Jean asked. "What do you do here?"

"I teach English three nights a week. I also care for my brother and uncle. They are Airborne Rangers with the ARVN," she answered.

Jean watched her long remembered movement. She did not walk but flowed with grace. While others bounced carrying their water jars, Minh Thanh glided.

"She is so beautiful to watch," Jean thought. "Her feet cannot be touching the ground."

Remembering her comment, Jean asked. "You have close relatives in the South Viet Nam military. Aren't you from North Viet Nam?"

"Yes," she answered. "I did tell you that I was from Muong Valley and my ancestors were Thai. However, I have since learned that they were Tia."

"How did you learn this?" Jean asked.

"My uncle from Hanoi told me and my brother. My brother, Vinh, lived with them for seven years before joining the Army. They are at a training base near here. Both are lieutenants," she said with pride.

Jean did not mention mother superior for fear of ruining the beauty of their meeting. They arrived at a single dwelling with a typical suburban wall around it. She unlatched its entrance gate and put her water jar inside. She gestured for Jean to hand her the one he carried. She placed it beside the other one.

Looking up at Jean, she said, "I would ask you to honor our home. However, Vinh and Diem are not here and it would not be proper for us to be alone. They will be here before sundown."

"May I return this evening?" Jean inquired with a fear that she might say no.

"Of course. You are welcome and we will gladly share our humble fare with you. I will see you then," Minh Thanh said, as she stepped through the gate. She gave a broad smile and closed the entrance.

Jean stood transfixed. The reality of his final success was the reality that it was not final.

"Stupid, how damned stupid," he thought. "She is taking a brazen chance inviting me to her home. She has to get her brother's permission for me to visit. She invited me anyway. In addition, she has an uncle from Hanoi. They hate France. Now, she has to try to convince them I am acceptable before I arrive. She is in one hell of a fix."

Jean returned to his Cholon apartment. He showered and shaved. He spent an hour trying to select proper attire for the evening should they decide to let him visit. It was necessary that he obtain a proper gift. It must not be too costly but still of a value to warrant notice. Moreover, he needed a meal gift, perhaps a wine. He had no idea what kind to buy. He needed help from a professional. He knew exactly who to see.

"Sir, you cannot go. I must although you're invited. It was not her place to invite you," Phat Van Bien said.

Bien was a professional go-between, an arranger. Many Vietnamese used them to arrange marriages, courtship, and other matters of the heart. He had to be good because Sister Marie recommended him.

"Can't we speed this along? We can go together," Jean blurted with frustration.

"Absolutely not. They cannot speak freely in your presence. If you want to lose this girl, come along. However, if you wish any chance of progress, stay away until I obtain approval," Bien stated in earnest.

Bien began consulting ancient astrological charts. He grilled Jean for an hour about his background, personal traits, financial status, and a dozen other things. Jean quickly recognized that he made a wise decision. If he appeared that evening, any chance of seeing Minh Thanh again would have been finished.

Jean gave Bien money to buy gifts, clothing, and other necessities for that evening's visit. Bien did not return until the next morning. He appeared glum.

"It was necessary for me to obtain lodging," Bien said. "It is too dangerous for travel at night."

"Okay, I will pay for your lodging," Jean agreed. "Tell me about the evening."

"I had to tell that you are a French Colonel and you fought at Dien Bien Phu," Bien said. "Lieutenant Vinh also fought at Dien Bien Phu."

"That's great," Jean exclaimed.

Giving Jean a stern look, Bien said, "He fought for the Viet Minh."

"Jesus, I'm dead," Jean cried aloud.

"Not so," Bien replied. "He sees the error in the Communist way. However, I must overcome the stigma of your being French. This will take longer and cost more."

Jean spent 12 days in agony while Bien shuffled back and forth between Saigon and Thu Duc. Each time he paid for new gifts and for Bien's expenses. Added to that was Bien's professional service fee.

"You may join me this evening," Bien said to Jean.

"Great, that's wonderful," Jean said excitedly.

"You may not see the girl. The brother and uncle will share a meal and wine. You may not speak unless asked a direct question. The gift for tonight is white soap," Bien explained.

"White soap?" Jean asked. "Why?"

Bien answered, "It is a useful household item. It also signifies purity and cleanliness. You must have at least a dozen bars. I will present them. Remember that you must not speak. It is necessary that you wear your full dress uniform with all decorations."

"My sword too?" Jean asked.

"Particularly your sword. Are you not a famous warrior?" Bien asked.

"If you are not, I have been lying to them for a week," he continued.

Trying to sit on the floor while wearing a sword was difficult for Jean. There is simply no comfortable or convenient place to put it. If he placed it forward, it would prod Minh Thanh's uncle. Placing it to his rear, caused it to bind his belt and place consider strain on his midriff. He felt ludicrous without his boots. Finally, in desperation, he removed the sword and laid it across his legs. He sat idly by while Diem, Vinh and Bien made small talk.

That evening, in their hotel, Bien said, "You did well. It is now permissible for you to have dinner with Diem and Vinh without me present. Follow my advice and eventually they may consider you worthy. Frankly, if it were I, I would never allow my daughter to marry you. Your feet are too big."

Vinh sat at the table's head in formal, Vietnamese attire. Diem dressed the same, sat directly across from Jean. Jean, wearing a suit and tie, watched as Vinh poured warm rice wine into their cups. Jean waited until Vinh placed the ceramic pot on the low table. As instructed, Jean took his cup with two hands. He first bowed toward Vinh and then Diem. He then drank the entire contents.

As advised, Jean took the pot in his right hand. Bracing his right elbow with his left hand, he filled their cups. This process continued until each had served the others. Vinh spoke first.

"I am deeply concerned about Great Britain's new Prime Minister. I do not think he understands the Orient very well. What is your opinion colonel?" Vinh asked, looking directly at Jean.

Jean felt the glare of their looks and thought, "Who the hell is the Prime Minister of Great Britain?"

"I cannot think that any westerner could ever understand the Orient very well," Jean answered.

Vinh took the wine container; and hefted it as if it was empty; and said loudly, "More wine this is empty."

Minh Thanh, dressed in formal, native attire entered the room. She removed the ceramic pot and replaced it with another. Her presence lasted no longer than a few seconds. Jean, feeling the wine, could not focus well but he knew pure beauty, drunk or sober.

While Jean stared, Vinh filled Jean's cup as he did Diem's. Finally recalling Bien's instructions, Jean lifted his cup; bowed toward Vinh; and drank its contents. This process continued for an hour. Vinh and Diem tore at Jean with question after question but he always provided a diplomatic answer.

Eventually, Vinh poured more wine on the table than in the cup. Jean and Diem did not do well either. Vinh arose, as did Diem.

Swaying, Vinh said with a distinct lisp, "It is too late to return to Saigon. Follow me, colonel."

Jean followed Diem and Vinh to the back of the building where they began relieving themselves. Jean joined them eagerly. Returning inside, Diem took Jean's elbow and led him to a room with a straw mat on its floor. Once inside, Jean saw that Vinh held a large piece of sackcloth that he spread on the mat.

"Lay down colonel," Vinh sputtered while still swaying.

Again, he followed his professional's advice and lay down atop the sackcloth. Diem and Vinh each grabbed a side of the material and brought it together around Jean. Vinh began stitching the cloth together until it encased Jean.

"Good night colonel," Vinh and Diem said in unison and left the room, extinguishing the room's candle on their way.

Jean was in total darkness. He began experiencing vertigo. It was a combination of too much wine and not being able to focus in the dark room. As his eyes adapted, the spinning waned and he felt better. Considerably drowsy, he drifted in and out of sleep. He dreamed of Minh Thanh. He watched her remove her ribbon, allowing her sleek black hair to tumble to her waist. He detected an aroma of orchids that enveloped his senses. She was always just out of reach.

"Get up colonel. Get up, your taxi is waiting," Vinh ordered.

Jean awoke to see Vinh and Diem standing over him. They were in field uniforms except for their boots. Vinh removed a survival knife from its sheath and deftly sliced through the threads holding him within the sackcloth. He attempt to stand but the room tilted.

Sternly, Vinh said again, "Your taxi is waiting colonel."

The three donned footwear in the foyer. Jean, wearing shoes, finished first.

As he started to stand, Vinh, still lacing his boots said, "Colonel Danjou, you have my permission to marry Minh Thanh. Treat her badly and you will die. Catch your taxi. You will receive details soon."

Jean stumbled through the door and to the taxi. He collapsed in its backseat.

"He sure said that in a matter of fact fashion," Jean thought. "Shit, one would think he didn't care."

Jean was deliriously happy the entire ride to Saigon. He lunged into his apartment removing clothes as he went. He never saw who hit him.

Fortunately, it was a glancing blow causing him to stumble and fall. Instinctively, he immediately rolled sideways to avoid another strike. He heard a knife plunge into the floor. His "flee or fight" response was instantaneous. He was astride his attacker's back in one swift movement. Simultaneously, he plunged his ballpoint pin into his neck. The man died instantly.

Without slowing, Jean sprang into his bathroom. He pushed aside a tile and grabbed his nine-millimeter pistol, falling into the bathtub in the process. A pistol fired from the direction of the doorway. Jean heard a bullet strike the iron-cored tub. Not hesitating, he pushed toward the tub's opposite end; put his pistol over the tub's side and fired twice toward the door. He heard a groan and a body fall to the floor. Quickly rolling over the tub's side, he was on one knee with his pistol pointing toward the doorway. It was empty.

Jean jumped up and lay flat against the wall. He could see into the bedroom by looking into a mirror mounted on the open door. He saw someone dash through the apartment's main door. He remained still and listened. Soon, he heard sirens and footsteps pounding up the outside stairs. Three Vietnamese policemen, in their white shirt uniforms, eased through his doorway with drawn weapons.

In a loud, calm voice, Jean explained who he was. He threw his identification into the room. Next, he placed his pistol on the bathroom's floor and stepped over a body past the doorway. He had his hands in the air.

Chapter Thirty Five

February 1968

The whole LSD, STP, marijuana, heroin, hashish, prescription cough medicine crowd suffers from the "Watchtower" itch: You gotta be with us, man, or you're out, you're dead.
This pitch is a continual and seeming MUST with those who use the stuff.
It's no wonder they keep getting busted.
Charles Bukowski (1920–94), *U.S.* author, poet. Tales of Ordinary Madness, *"The Big Pot Game"* (1967)

"Off with the power 20 percent; that's good; now give me 25 degrees flaps and a little left pedal," Frederick Earling instructed.

Frederick, as standardization pilot for Air America, was responsible for qualification of pilots for duties with the organization. Having considerable time flying commercial routes, he asked to perform missions requiring more direct flying skills in 1964. Now he was qualifying a new pilot for flights to Lima landing zones. These were nothing more than dirt strips allowing access to Hmong villages in Northeastern Laos. He was the most qualified pilot for Short Takeoff and Landings (STOL) with Air America. His primary aircraft was the Helio Courier.

"But I don't see the strip. How do you expect me to land when I cannot see the strip?" Marvin Bolger asked quite nervously.

"No sweat Marvin. You are doing fine. Slow her down a bit and hold this heading for one minute," Earling stated calmly as he checked landmarks.

"Slow it down, we're almost hovering," Bolger commented somewhat calmer.

"Coming up on one minute, turn left to a heading of three five zero degrees. Now, 20 more degrees flaps. You're looking good. Add some power. That's it. Look straight ahead," Earling told Bolger.

Directly ahead wispy cloud bottoms stroked a dark green hillside. A clay red gash lay in its middle climbing toward the hill's top.

"I'll be damned," Bolger said, as he added a touch of power.

"Just a tad more back pressure. You are doing excellent," Earling commented as he watched tree tops flash by their Helio Courier on both sides.

Bolger continued his approach and terminated with a gentle touch onto the strip. As they traveled uphill, their craft's speed dropped dramatically. The Courier came to a halt as Hmong children surrounded it, filling the air with laughter. Behind great billows of red dust swirled outward to trees on either side.

"Marvin, hold it here. I'll unload," Earling said as he opened his door.

Four Hmong tribesmen approached displaying large smiles. They circled around the Courier to where Earling was stacking boxes. Whatever they said, Earling did not understand but he returned their smiles. Obviously finished unloading, the Hmong each shook Earling's hand with great up and down movements. He returned to the Courier and climbed aboard.

"Okay Marvin, I see you already have the flaps set. Run her up and let's go," Earling said as he fastened his harness.

Bolger made a superb takeoff. With no load, it was easy as he climbed above the low hanging clouds and set course for Udorn, Thailand.

"Marvin, you did fine. For that strip, always look for two things before turning base. On the left, there is a distinctive saddle between two hills. On the right, there's a valley ending at a waterfall. Start your turn and go one-minute at 70 knots then turn to three five zero degrees. It's not too bad now but when the Hmong start burning, visibility is tough," Earling noted.

"Burning, I've heard about that but never understood why," Bolger stated with interest.

"Yeah, they can only get a few years growing time for rice in any area and they have to move. First, they burn the forest creating massive fires and lots of smoke. It's hard to navigate in the smoke. When they have an area cleared, they plant rice among other things," Earling commented.

"Oh, you mean poppies," Bolger said.

"Yes, they can get more growth time growing poppies. They harvest the juices and it's opium. It is refined somewhere else into heroin. It's a rotten business but it is their only decent cash crop," Earling continued.

There was a considerable period of silence. Bolger wanted to ask the question but did not. Earling did not want to hear the question and Bolger knew it. Therefore, they both avoided the issue of whether Air America crews hauled opium or not. Finally, Bolger changed the subject.

"You and Vanessa going to be at Ed's tonight?" Bolger asked.

"Wouldn't miss it for the world. Ed has been here seven years and he hates to leave. Nevertheless, he can't pass a deal like the one he has," Earling answered while checking the Courier's needle, ball, and airspeed.

"I heard that. Can you believe it? His father-in-law is putting him in charge of his company's fleet in Alaska," Bolger added. "They have eight of these Couriers flying hunters and fishermen into the back country. Moreover, no one will be shooting at him. Man, that's great."

"Well, I am not too sure that he's that hot to go. Ed feels like he's making a difference. It's Shirley, his wife, who really wants him to go. If it came down to Air America or Vanessa, I would take Vanessa every time," Earling added as he searched the sky for aircraft.

Vanessa fanned through her mail until she found the regular letter from Ian. Of late, she was becoming concerned about her father. She detected strong leanings toward support for the Irish Republican Army (IRA). He was getting too old for such nonsense.

Laying the other mail aside, Vanessa sat at their dining table to read Ian's letter. She quickly opened it and unfolded the pages.

January 20, 1968

My wee bonnie lass,

I worry so much about the reports I see on the telly. It is a great thing that Frederick is doing but it is so dangerous. I have my sources and I know that there is a major war in Laos. There is little use trying to hide it. It's obvious the North Vietnamese will continue to fight until they gain their goals no matter the price.

The same is true in our beloved Ireland. There is a major conflict within the IRA. One group is fighting the other for how they will free our native land from the British boot. I am thinking there is enough fighting for the lot of them. Instead of fighting each other, they need to focus their efforts on the enemy and not their friends. I watch what the NLF is doing in South Viet Nam and it reminds me of Tom Barry's Flying Column in Cork

They fought for a united country just as we have for hundreds of years. I am doing what I can to help. I am too old for the fighting but I will not hesitate to support Sinn Fein. They are our political party and represent us as best they can.

If it is money they need, I can help and will continue to do so. I have made two trips to America to raise money for the party. We have many friends in the United States and they always help.

It is my deepest hope that you will soon return. I am not getting younger and I miss my girl.

Love you forever,
Da

"I have never known Ian to be at a loss for words. His letters are getting shorter and shorter," Vanessa reflected. "Surely, he is aging faster than it seems. He is my father and I love him so much but I must stay with Frederick."

Vanessa had been home to Haughton House twice since her recovery. Galag finally found his stride and is showing the others his rear in most of his races. It was necessary to put Daytran to sleep because of his age and associated ailments.

"Oh lord it almost broke my heart it did when I watched the light go out in those brown eyes," Vanessa recalled. "He raised his head when I entered his stall as if to tell me goodbye. Weaver said that he had not raised his head for three days as if waiting for my arrival."

Weaver was every bit as good as Devon said he would be. She had not heard of or seen Devon since the day he left Haughton House. She thought she would have but she hadn't. She prayed that he was safe.

"Oh, Devon. If it were not for Frederick," she thought.

Udorn grew so fast once the Americans came. Their skies roared night and day as they flew in support of forces in South Viet Nam. She and Frederick were so fortunate to have the home they did. Air America got it for them before the influx of so many people.

She never understood why Frederick stopped flying commercial flights. He said it was the same as he was at home flying commercial. He felt too much like a truck driver flying those routes. His job now was truly flying. For three years he flew regular missions to God knows where. He never said.

Now, he spends most of his time teaching others. He liked to think that everything he did was a secret. That was impossible when other wives gathered twice each week for bridge. She knew that Frederick checked other pilots because their wives told her. She would let him think that his comings and goings were secret and she did not know a thing.

There had been no more threats and she and Frederick never heard any more about her attacker. The police think that he fled the country. In any case, she was happy.

As Bolger taxied to Air America's parking ramp at the Royal Thai Air Force Base at Udorn, Earling saw an unexpected friend waiting. Redford Willhampton, from Taiwan, watched as they parked. He had not seen him since he reported the Thai major four years earlier. Seldom did Willhampton leave CAT headquarters. Earling deduced that something important was at hand.

"Marvin, would you mind taking care of post flight and our paper work?" Earling asked.

"Sure thing Frederick. Oh by the way, am I cleared to fly the Lima sites?" Bolger asked, as Earling was loosening his seat belt.

"Absolutely Marvin. I will take care of the paperwork in Ops," Earling answered in a hurry to see Willhampton.

Earling took long strides to see his old friend. His debt to Willhampton was gargantuan for taking care of the mess with Major Saberrank and his cohorts. He and Vanessa never heard another threat or word after he found Saberrank's head outside his Udorn villa. While Devon did the work, he knew whom the driving force was behind getting the job done. It was Willhampton for sure.

"Redford, who ran you from your burrow on Taiwan?" Earling asked as he gripped his old friend's gnarled hand.

"Oh, I say ol' man. Sometimes I have to see what the natives are about now don't I," Willhampton replied with a broad grin. "How's Vanessa?"

"Thanks to you, she could not be better. We owe you a lot my friend," Earling shouted in attempt to be heard above the sounds of aircraft landing and taking off.

Leaning forward, close to Earling's ear, Willhampton asked. "Do you have some time to go next door with me?"

Next to Air America's parking ramp at Udorn, was the 4802nd Joint Liaison Detachment, the CIA's command center for military operations in Laos. Earling had never been inside and could not imagine what Willhampton could possibly want to talk to him about in the CIA Command Center.

Prop blast from a taxing aircraft caused Earling to grab for his hat. The powerful blade wash also sprayed them with grit from the tarmac.

"Sure, lead the way," Earling answered still holding his hat and squinting against flying sand.

Earling followed Willhampton through the doorway and outside noise dwindled. Earling removed his hat and began using it to brush down his trousers.

"This way ol' man," Willhampton said as he started down a short corridor.

Opening a door, Willhampton gestured for Earling to enter. Once inside, Earling noticed that there were no outside sounds. In addition, the air was downright cold and dry.

Shivering his shoulders, Earling asked. "It's like a meat locker in this place. Why so cold?"

"It's the equipment. The Company couldn't care less if we baked but they make sure their equipment stays cold," Willhampton answered as he started for another door.

"The Company? That's the first time I've heard him use that term. Does he work for Air America or not?" Earling thought.

As they approached, Earling noted a person he did not know sitting at a desk near the door. He looked up and nodded in recognition to Willhampton but gave Earling a concerned stare.

Willhampton stopped and, nodding his head at Earling, said, "He's Earling, Frederick."

Removing a ledger-like book from a desk drawer, the man scanned through pages and then stopped. He looked back and forth between the book and Earling. Seemingly satisfied, he pressed a hidden switch that opened the door.

"Thanks ol' man," Willhampton said as he led Earling through the door's opening.

Inside, Earling saw that the left wall had a large map of Southeast Asia on it. A thick piece of Plexiglas covered it. As if floating inside the glass, multicolored symbols glowed and moved. Above the map, sweep second hand clocks indicated times for zones around the world.

In front of the large display, there was a rostrum and seating for ten people. The seats were plush easy chairs and obviously intended for high-ranking individuals to receive briefings.

Directly ahead, a wall formed the outside of another room. Its length was one half that of the room in which they were. A four-foot high, glass window provided a view inside for almost its full length. The remainder was for a door.

Inside, he saw individuals seated at consoles. Some were radar screens while others displayed information that he could not discern from his position. Facing outwards, he could see individuals wearing headset microphone combinations. One person paced back and forth between the group. He wore a headset with some sort of device clipped to his belt. He held a switch of some sort in one hand.

Where this room ended, the wall indented for about six feet. Along its remaining length, Earling saw a row of six-foot high machines. The top third contained large reels moving tape at rapid speeds back and forth. He could not help but compare them to his AKAI recorder a home. Except they were on a massive scale.

On top of each machine, he saw what he knew to be a thermite device. They were about two inches thick and two feet long. On their ends, there were pins similar to those one would find on a hand grenade. Attach to the pins were bright red strips of cloth with a warning written on them. Earling knew, if pulled, the pins would activate a detonator. The thermite would melt straight through anything below it.

On his right, a series of doors appeared to provide entrance to offices. Every office had windows with Venetian blinds. On the far right door, a sign stated, "Director."

The place was alive with activity. People were agitated and moving swiftly. The man, inside the room directly ahead, was constantly mouthing words. At times, he would stop and appear to yell into his microphone. His pace back and forth was rapid.

Every few moments, an individual would tear a piece of paper from a printer. He would show it to the man with the microphone. After reading it, he would nod "yes" or shake his head indicating "no." If "yes," the individual would take the paper to the office marked director. What transpired inside was not visible, as the blinds were not open.

Leaning toward Earling, Willhampton whispered, "Follow me ol' chap. We'll have a seat in the front row."

Once seated where Willhampton indicated, Earling had an excellent view of the large display. He immediately noticed that South Viet Nam was alive with red indicators. Moving about were blue symbols. Some of the symbols were unknown to him.

"Take a look at the map area around Khe Sanh in South Viet Nam," Willhampton said. "On the 21st of January, General Giap sent three NVA divisions against the place. Some think that the ol' boy was trying another Dien Bien Phu maneuver. According to our information, two of those divisions fought the French at Dien Bien Phu," Willhampton explained.

"There it is again," Earling thought. "He's talking as if he routinely monitors the tactical situation in South Viet Nam. There's no need for that in his job."

Continuing, Willhampton said, "I think the ol' boy has gone daft. There's enough surveillance equipment there to let us know if one of his men farts. He's getting one hell of a pounding with air power despite the bad weather. The Yanks can put their ordnance within inches of their troops through the clouds. Originally, we thought this attack was his best move but now it looks like a diversion."

"One hell of a diversion," Earling said. "What's he trying to hide?"

Willhampton answered, "Today is the first day of the Chinese New Year, Tet as you well know. Early this morning, NLF forces struck South Viet Nam's entire length. They're attacking every provincial capitol and most cities. Sappers are in the American Embassy in Saigon. The Company's tit is in a bit of a wringer right now. We didn't see this coming. The media is having a field day on the telly and in the press. You have been flying Lima sites all day and haven't heard about this."

"There it is again. 'We didn't see this coming.' I feel sure he's CIA now," Earling concluded.

"God's blood man. Where did all the bastards come from without us knowing it?" Earling asked.

"Frederick, it's damned glad I am that I don't have to answer that question. The poor bastard in that office marked 'Director' has some tall explaining to do later. Right now, everyone's responding to the attack," Willhampton answered, still whispering.

Earling had noticed that there was not a single Search and Rescue (SAR) helicopter parked on the ramp when they arrived. Also, there were no fighter-bombers. While he made a mental note of it, he attached no significance to it. He wondered what this had to do with him and Willhampton.

"Redford, you want something. What is it?" Earling asked.

"Take at look at the area near the valley north of Luang Prabang. As you know, there is a major navigational facility at that location. It is for American craft bombing North Viet Nam. I have it on good authority that the NVA are pissed at the Pathet Lao's poor performance against Vang Pao. Additional NVA divisions are gathering to invade that region. Their attack has a link to what is happening right now all over South Viet Nam. We're right at the dry season and I figure the NVA is going to increase operations significantly across all of Northeastern Laos," Willhampton answered.

Lowering his voice, he continued, "The last four years have been quiet for us. We've lost few people and aircraft. Things are going to get worse, much worse. Vang Pao is doing what the NLF is in South Viet Nam. He's fighting a guerilla war against conventional, NVA units. There's too damned many NVA up there. Vang Pao is going to catch hell ol' man and we have to support him. However, that's the least of my worries."

"What's got you so worried Redford?" Earling asked.

Willhampton ground his stump of a hand into his good palm, obviously concerned he answered, "Lair, the man in that director's office, will leave soon. His deputy Lloyd ("Pat") Landry will take his place. Landry is a fine bloke and knows this job better than most. He will do a good job. Nevertheless, the chain of command will change. They are pulling our main man out of Saigon damn it."

"They're pulling Ed Blair out of Saigon. God's blood Redford, he is the heart of that operation," Earling exclaimed.

"I know it damn it," Willhampton said raising his voice. "I'm going to have to replace him with my best man. I do not want to but I have to."

"Who?" Earling asked with sincere concern.

"You," Willhampton blurted. "You Frederick."

Earling fell against the large cushioned chair's back in disbelief. He was a pilot not some paper pusher.

"Willhampton's lorry was running on three wheels to think such a thing," Earling surmised.

Willhampton sat giving Earling a most bewildered look, as he said, "You have the most experience of anyone in Air America. You have flown from the Battle of Britain to here. You've flown and mastered everything but helicopters. You have more time getting in an aircraft's seat than most blokes have in the air. Jesus Frederick I really need you now and not in a cockpit."

"Redford, I owe you my wife's life and probably mine but you cannot mean what you're asking," Earling pleaded.

Willhampton sat with his forearms on his thighs with his head bowed. He stared at the floor shaking his head left and right.

"I don't want to do this Frederick. I really don't but I have no choice. Vanessa can go with you and I will provide the finest villa in Saigon," Willhampton said with despair.

"Redford, you have lost it. You are telling me that NLF troops are inside the American Embassy and I am going to take Vanessa into that," Earling said as he arose and headed for the door.

Willhampton jumped up and followed close wailing, "Frederick, think about it. I do not want to lose you. If you don't take this, I do not have a choice. Think about it for a few days."

Earling flung the door aside with such force that it startled the man outside. He jumped from his desk and had his sidearm out of his holster as Willhampton passed. Willhampton gestured for him to sit and continued following Earling.

Once outside, noise and heat enveloped the pair. Earling and Willhampton stood almost nose to nose yelling but could not hear. It was a comical situation to watch. Both men argued with hand gestures and lip movements but no sound. Earling's face flushed and he whirled away and left Willhampton standing on the tarmac.

As Earling drove toward home, his mind whirled through years of flying and his love for it. For him it was an obsession. An obsession that was insurmountable as far as he was concerned. Station chief at Tan San Nhut for Air America was prestigious. Yet, he felt sure now that his duties would be for the CIA and not Air America. From an Air America perspective, the job was significant. He could see Air America flying in a direct support mode against the NVA and NLF forces.

At home, he slammed his car door and rushed inside through the recreation room entrance. He took stairs two at a time. He threw his hat and brief case at the sofa and went directly to the bar. He filled a water glass with gin and added a minute trace of tonic water. He downed the lot in two gulps. As he poured his second glass, Vanessa entered from their bedroom.

With one glance, Vanessa knew that something was amiss.

"What's wrong Frederick?" She asked.

She watched as he yanked his tie from around his neck and opened his collar button with one hand. He did this while downing half of his drink. The look on his face Vanessa had seen only once. He had the same expression when she awakened in the hospital with her gunshot wound.

"Leave this alone," she thought. "When he gets ready, he will release whatever furies roaring within and I must be there."

"Mind if I join you?" Vanessa asked as she stepped behind the bar.

"Of course not," Earling answered as he brushed by her.

She was able to get a quick kiss on his cheek as he passed. Opening the freezer, she removed an ice tray and placed ice cubes in a bucket. She repeated this twice. Next, she filled her glass with ice, leaving little room for gin. She made her drink and picked up the ice bucket. She made her way beside Earling where he gazed out a window.

Vanessa sat her glass down and used tongs to remove an ice cube. She put it in Earling's glass without asking.

"Another," she asked.

Earling held his glass forward and Vanessa added two more cubes as she said, "Let's go out on the deck."

After retrieving her drink, she tugged his elbow and said, "Come on Frederick. It's nice today."

As they walked toward the door leading to their veranda, she felt him relax. As soon as he opened the sliding doors, the howl of aircraft activity grew louder.

"My," she said. "They sure are busy today."

Earling put his arm around her shoulders and said, "Come sit down. You know exactly which buttons to push. I will tell you everything."

After listening to his rendition of events, she commented, "Frederick, it would not break my heart for you to be behind a desk. The lads in Saigon could learn a lot from you. It is about time that you shared your expertise with others. Nevertheless, I will support anything that you decide. You know that Hon."

Earling returned to the bar and prepared a sensible drink. He asked Vanessa if he could prepare her another but she declined. He went outside and sat close to her. Having unloaded his tensions, he felt better and began rethinking the situation.

He held his drink between both his palms, rolling it back and forth. He stared into it in deep thought.

Finally, he said, "I will not go there unless it is safe for you. Now, it looks as if the question may be moot. If South Viet Nam falls, there will be no need for a station chief. However, if the situation changes, I will consider it," Earling stated.

As he spoke, their telephone began ringing.

"I will get it," Vanessa said, as she left her seat.

Earling watched aircraft's lights fill the sky, as it would soon be sunset. He knew the situation was bad when all the SAR ships were gone.

He heard Vanessa say, "Oh hi Redford. It has been a long time. How are you?"

There was silence as Vanessa listened. Frederick turned to a position from which he could see her. He gained eye contact and nodded his head to indicate agreement.

"I would love to see you. You know where we are. Join us, please," she said while smiling at Frederick.

Concluding her conversation, she walked to where Frederick sat. She slipped her left arm around his shoulders while gazing at the aircraft activity with him.

"Hon," she said. "You would not have it any other way and that's why I love your noble, British arse."

They both began laughing and Earling said, "That's my girl. Shanty Irish to the core."

Vanessa returned to England while Earling went to Subic Bay, in the Philippines. Both events served their purposes. Their separation would last six weeks.

Ian McBeal's health was in a massive state of decline. The cause was mostly exhaustion. Vanessa arrived to find him deeply immersed in IRA operations. On the surface, he was a spokesperson for Sinn Fein, the IRA political arm.

Meanwhile, he continued obtaining funds and weapons to support military operations. When he collapsed, Vanessa was there to nurse him back to health. If he had not been so ill, she would never have convinced him to stay a month at Haughton House. With daily nursing care and professional medical help, he began a slow recovery. Vanessa coordinated all of it.

Furthermore, it was time for Galag to become a full time stud. Innovations with in vitro fertilization had allowed him to continue his racing success while providing his superb genes to continue Daytran's bloodline. Age was the driving force leading to his becoming an in-house stud. Their trainer, Weaver, was bringing along a young, Galag descendent.

Vanessa soon learned why Galag did not do well initially after Devon left. Weaver had his own training style with Arabians. It was difficult for him to overcome some of the methods used by Devon. Now, with a colt, Vanessa saw that Weaver was a superb trainer. Dandure, the new colt, was thriving with Weaver. She knew what to look for and Weaver met every expectation that Vanessa had.

Vanessa major disappointment was being away from Frederick. He put her on a flight home while he made final preparations for his new position in Saigon. They parted with her understanding that matters had to improve before she could join him. He would never agree to her being in Saigon if it was not safe. He would contact her when he did whatever it was that the CIA wanted before moving to Saigon.

Earling went to Subic Bay, in the Philippines, after giving his replacement an orientation on his required Air America duties. Considerable time in Subic Bay was waiting for a final clearance. Meanwhile he went through an intense indoctrination procedure that the CIA liked to call in-briefings.

He gained a new perspective regarding his previous job. He was now able to see how his Air America missions tied into an overall plan. Before, his flights were simply that, flights. Daily, he received tactical updates on the battles now raging in South Viet Nam.

Various intelligence sources became aware in late 1967 that Giap was planning a Khe Sanh action. Reconnaissance and surveillance sources identified two NVA divisions; the 325th and the 304th were moving within attack range. In addition, they located another division moving along Route 9. As best they could figure, this division's purpose was to stop any attempts to reinforce from Quang Tri. A source they would not identify let them know that the two NVA divisions fought at Dien Bien Phu.

Signal intelligence revealed a rising star among Giap's generals. He was General of Artillery Nguyen Van Anh. They knew that he was an artillery officer at Dien Bien Phu and played a major role devastating the French. Anh released a massive artillery bombardment against Khe Sanh just like Dien Bien Phu. It appeared, based upon signal interceptions, that Anh would move his artillery to high ground at Khe Sanh, and repeat his artillery success.

These briefings confirmed Willhampton's observations. Intelligence allowed Westmoreland to move heavy reinforcements to Khe Sanh. Moreover, he was able to resupply with helicopters and flying columns up Route 9. Once they dug in, the NVA couldn't blow them out of their positions. Estimates of NVA forces approached 40,000 troops. They died in massive numbers with air power that the French did not have at Dien Bien Phu.

During January, Giap had NLF and NVA forces straggle into major cities and towns. They launched their attacks expecting support from the local population. They got practically none. At Hue, the NLF slaughtered thousands of civilians as they withdrew. Advancing forces through the rubble found mass graves throughout the area. When the smoke cleared, the NLF was no longer an effective fighting force. There was no doubt in the CIA's mind that Giap would be a long time trying to recover from their force's being so decimated. However, the media was not convinced.

Battle scenes flowed into American homes day and night. Newspapers and magazines extolled the superiority of Giap's forces. They deemed the Tet Offensive a major NVA success. Nothing could have been further from the truth.

In early March, Earling received his clearance. He arrived in Saigon one week later and reported to his new assignment as Air America's Director of Saigon Operations. True to his word, Willhampton had a posh villa ready. It occupied the entire top floor of an apartment building. The roof served as an entertainment area. Convinced it was safe, he sent for Vanessa and arranged a welcoming party for her.

At Than Sanh Nhut, Earling met Buff Winslow. Winslow was the Chief Technical Representative for Boeing Vertol Corporation, supplier of the CH-47 Chinook and CH-46 Sea Knight helicopters, for the Army and Marine Corps respectively. Winslow had a similar villa directly across the street from Earling. Their meeting was by accident.

Earling was on the tarmac at Than Sanh Nhut when a burly, barrel-chested man approached and said, "Hi, I think that we are neighbors. I'm Buff Winslow with Boeing. I have a villa directly across from yours downtown."

Winslow had a ferocious grip when Earling shook his hand. He estimated him at a solid 250 pounds and six feet five inches.

"My pleasure," Earling said. "I'm just getting my feet wet here. I'm with Air America."

Releasing Earling's hand, Winslow replied, "Yes, I know. Sorry your missed all the fun a month ago. It was too much for the guy who had your place. He transferred back to the states. I kind of had my eye on the place but you outbid the crap out of me."

"So sorry but my former boss got it for me. I have no idea what he paid," Earling answered.

"Damn, that must be nice. I wish I had a boss like that. I understand you're throwing a bash soon," Winslow said with a friendly grin. "I can get you some good deals on food and entertainment. If you would like, I will drop by this evening and fill you in on what's available."

"Quite a pushy lout," Earling thought. "Yet, he seems sincere."

"Where's your office?" Earling asked.

"Office, if I have an office I guess it's back at the villa. I spend most of my time visiting Hookers all over the country," Winslow said with a loud laugh that Earling found infectious.

"Hookers?" Earling asked with a curious look while grinning slightly.

"Yeah, you know, Chinook pilots. They do a lot of sling load work and there's a large hook suspended beneath the ship. Someone stuck them with the moniker 'Hooker' before I got here," Winslow explained.

"We're supposed to be getting some Chinooks at Udorn real soon. I'm not helicopter qualified but I understand the Chinook is a versatile aircraft," Earling related.

"Hell, don't feel bad about not being qualified. I can take them apart and put them together in the dark. Yet, I cannot fly one," Winslow said as he gave Earling a hefty slap on his back. "See you tonight."

Earling watched Winslow walk away down the tarmac and thought, "It is great that he is a friendly sort. I wouldn't want him angry. He bears watching though. At Subic Bay, they warned me to be wary of his type. We'll see how it goes. Hookers, huh."

Chapter Thirty Six

March 1968

Evil is unspectacular and always human,
And shares our bed and eats at our own table.
W. H. Auden (1907–73), Anglo-American poet. Herman Melville, st. 4.

"This is what I've been trying to do since my first meeting with Ike," Lanny Briscoe thought as he rewound the tape. "I've wandered around Southeast Asia chasing navigational beacons and the like long enough. It's about time they finally have me doing something in my field."

Briscoe pushed his chair rearward while opening a recording tape canister marked "CEFLIEN LION." The tape he put inside was the first of four from a new unit deployed to Southeast Asia. This organization used Army pilots to fly Navy P-2V Neptune aircraft. Now referred to as RP-2E ships, they pinpointed transmitter locations with ease. In addition, they added an all weather capability and a significantly longer on station time.

NSA had collected tapes from an RP-2E flying a mission covering the DMZ between North and South Viet Nam. The collection time was early January just before General Giap's Tet Offensive. The NVA began using a new code that local cryptographers were unable to decipher. Rather than send the information to Briscoe, NSA sent him to the tapes.

"Well, at least they think I can break this stuff without their equipment," he thought. "So far, I have not lived up to their confidence."

Getting up, he entered a storage vault barely large enough for his body. Briscoe placed tape 1 inside the vault and removed tape 2. He returned to his desk and opened the tape's container. Sitting down, he turned his chair to his right and placed the tape on a spindle. Next, he threaded it through some rollers, across a capstan, and onto a take-up reel. After assuring that the tape was tight, he put on headphones and activated a switch. The reels began turning as he watched an oscilloscope.

Sound filled his ears. He listened to what most people would consider static. By manipulating various controls, he changed the tape's speed, isolated different frequencies, and compared them to known cryptographic modes. Finally, he isolated the sound that he found on tape 1. As soon as he did, he pressed a toggle switch next to the display and removed his headphones.

"Go to it honey," he said aloud.

Leaning back in his chair, he continued watching the oscilloscope. According to his records, others did the procedure in progress before his arrival. Nevertheless, he had to stick to protocol. It could be that the others overlooked something. If none of this worked, he had an idea of something that might break the code.

Intelligence personnel in the Pacific region simply did not know these methods. There was no need for them to know because everything he had related directly to the Soviet Union. He did not believe the USSR would share their encryption process with Ho Chi Minh's forces.

"Hell, who knows?" He thought. "They damn sure did some strange stuff four years ago. They could do it again. The APPS debacle proved that. Hell, they gave me a promotion and a medal. I wonder if they will take them back if I don't bust this one."

He remembered what they asked him, "Mr. Briscoe, what was the name of Neil Burnum's secretary?"

They knew what her name was because they had her letters. It was so obvious that it never entered his mind. Moreover, he knew that they read them.

Briscoe remembered finding her in his driveway after his meeting with Lieutenant Colonel Delaney.

"What are you doing here," he asked as he removed his jacket.

As she sat up, Briscoe slipped his coat around her shoulders as she shivered. Once he had her inside, he fixed a hot rum and cinnamon tea for her.

"Feeling better?" he asked.

"Yes, Lanny. Thank you," she answered.

She sat on his sofa with her legs pulled beneath her. Briscoe had added a blanket to his coat for additional warmth. She held her rum with both hands as she sipped the warming beverage.

"You should have called," Briscoe said.

"I did," she replied. "I called a lot but there was no answer. I absolutely had to see you so I came to your place. When no one answered the door, I decided to wait," she explained.

"Why would she wait," he thought. "She knows my job and she shut down our relationship. For all she knew, I might be gone for a year. Why would she wait? It made no sense."

Briscoe added some rum to her cup and fixed himself one. He sat beside her and saw that she was no longer shivering.

Leaning back, Briscoe commented, "You know that I never expected to see you again."

"Yes, that's what I thought. However, I couldn't get you out of my mind. I had to see you Lanny," she explained.

Katherine explained again about her letters, her marriage, and her divorce. She told about her daughter.

"She's with my mother in North Carolina for two weeks. Her grandmother spoils her rotten. It will take a month after she returns to get her back to normal," Katherine said.

Removing a snapshot from her purse, Katherine showed it to Briscoe and said, "She's special Lanny. My life wouldn't be much without her in it."

The two chatted until after dawn. While she did not say it, it was clear to Briscoe that she wanted to continue their relationship. He fixed breakfast and afterward offered to drive her home. She declined. Yet, she did ask him to call her the next evening. He walked her to her car and watched her leave.

After a shower and shave, Briscoe returned to his office. He spent the day reviewing files on R. L. Meyers Corporation. He initiated a background check on McNeese. They found Delaney dead after he did the same from the CIA. Briscoe made a mental note to stay particularly alert.

His next step was to get an appointment to see Doctor Jenkins at MIT. Jenkins was at the heart of APPS' development. He's the one who turned theory into a working device. Briscoe figured he might as well start at the beginning and Jenkins was that. He arranged an appointment through Jenkins' secretary for the following day.

Back tracking mentally, Briscoe reviewed events. First, he went to see McNeese about research and development on new cryptographic equipment and its interface with data processing equipment. He saw classified APPS documents on McNeese's desk to which he should not have had access. Then he says he was working with another contractor who wants to bid on APPS. This was a conflict of interest. Someone rigged his brakes to fail, which almost got him killed. He sees Colonel Delaney's dad at the CIA for a background on McNeese and Delaney ends up dead. The entire trail smelled and Briscoe knew that somewhere he could find an answer.

That evening he went to Katherine's new apartment. Their evening was pleasant enough with a fine dinner at a local restaurant and some wine at her place.

She walked to where he sat with a fresh bottle of Chablis and said, "Do the honors and remove the cork for me Lanny."

"Sure, I can do that," he said getting to his feet. "Where's a corkscrew?"

"You will find one in the drawer below the wine rack. Please excuse me I will be back in a moment," she answered as she left the room.

Briscoe removed the cork and took two glasses from the wine rack. He took them to the coffee table in front of the sofa. He took a seat and waited for her to join him.

Briscoe began having a sensation of someone watching him. He glanced around the room until he saw Katherine standing in the doorway. Her negligee left nothing to one's imagination. She crossed the room and sat beside him.

"Say when," Briscoe said, as he began filling her wineglass.

"Now," she answered, slipping her arm around his neck and pulling him ever so slightly.

Leaving the next morning, he returned the glasses and wine to the wine rack unused. If he hurried, he could get to his place; change clothes; and keep his appointment with Jenkins.

"Pleased to meet you Doctor Briscoe. I will tell Doctor Jenkins that you are here," Jenkin's secretary said as she left her desk.

She returned in a moment and said, "Go on in doctor. He's expecting you."

Briscoe thought, "It has been so long since anyone addressed him by my title that it sounds strange."

"Thank you," Briscoe said and entered Jenkins' office.

Jenkins was already standing when Briscoe entered. He came from behind his desk and greeted him.

"Finally, I get to meet you," he said gesturing toward a bookcase. "I have everything you've written in my special library."

"Thanks," Briscoe replied. "I've not published that much."

Shaking Briscoe's hand, Jenkins continued, "Yes, but what you did publish is priceless. I've used every algorithm in my work. Please, sit down," Jenkins said, while leading Briscoe to an easy chair.

Jenkins was short and wore thick glasses that made his eyes appear unusually large. Obviously, he was not remotely interested in appearance. His clothes looked ancient and worn. His demeanor was cheerful and friendly which made Briscoe feel at ease.

"How can I be of service doctor?" Jenkins said as he sat in a chair next to Briscoe.

Briscoe reached into his inside coat pocket and removed his credentials. He handed them to Jenkins who stared in awe.

"My, why are you wasting your talents with these people?" Jenkins asked.

The way he said "these people" made NSA sound dirty. Briscoe retrieved his documents and looked at Jenkins for a moment. Jenkins sat looking somewhat ill at ease.

Briscoe asked. "My interest is your work with APPS. How many prototypes do you have at MIT?"

"Two of course, would you like to see them?" Jenkins asked looking rather concerned.

"Yes I would but we can do that later. I need some information first," Briscoe replied.

Jenkins sat staring waiting for Briscoe to speak.

"Do you know a person named V. L. McNeese?" Briscoe asked.

Jenkins smiled and answered quite cheerfully, "Yes, I do. He works for the Meyers Corporation. He has been a big help with APPS."

"In what way?" Briscoe asked quickly.

"Oh, he has provided special components that I needed. He is very helpful as I said," Jenkins responded.

"Do you have some of those components at MIT?" Briscoe continued, becoming most interested in what Jenkins had to say.

"Yes, oh yes, follow me. They are in the next room," Jenkins answered getting to his feet. "Come this way. I will show you."

Jenkins walked to his desk and gestured to a door behind it.

He said, "I do my work in here. It is most handy to have my lab adjoining my office."

As Briscoe walked to where Jenkins stood, he noticed a picture sitting on a shelf behind his desk. It was in an ornate frame.

Pointing to the photograph, Briscoe asked. "Who is the lovely young lady?"

"That's my daughter. She's only three but sharp as a tack. She has a head on her shoulders," Jenkins bragged with pride.

Briscoe moved closer for a better view of the picture. Jenkins, noticing this, retrieved the picture and gave it to Briscoe.

"Isn't she just like a baby Barbie?" Jenkins chortled.

Handing the picture to Jenkins, Briscoe said, "Let's take a look at the prototypes."

For three hours, Jenkins demonstrated both prototypes. He was particularly proud of his work and Briscoe agreed that Jenkins was brilliant when it came to hardware. In addition, he showed Briscoe some capacitors and relays that McNeese gave him. Briscoe noted that they were functional but of an inferior quality.

"Doctor, I must go," Briscoe announced. "Your work is exceptional. Now, it is time to get the items into production."

"It has been my pleasure sir," Jenkins replied. "It has been a joy working with your ideas. I hope to continue making refinements."

On his return drive to Washington, Briscoe telephoned Colonel Delaney. He arranged for him to meet 40 miles north of D.C. at a bed and breakfast inn. Briscoe reserved adjoining rooms. Briscoe knew he should not return to Washington that night.

Delaney was there when Briscoe arrived. He greeted Briscoe and asked him if he would like a drink. On the room's coffee table, there was a fifth of Black Label Jack Daniels, glasses, and ice.

As Briscoe removed his coat he said, "Bill, you are just like your dad. He planned just as you have. I get here to find you knew exactly what I wanted before I did. That's damned spooky. Pour me a drink."

Briscoe made himself comfortable. He removed his tie and shoes. Next, he pulled his shirt from his trousers to let it hang free. He positioned an easy chair where he could sit and prop his feet on the sofa. Delaney sat directly across from him on the sofa's end.

Briscoe sipped his bourbon while looking intently at Delaney.

Delaney returned his gaze and asked. "What?"

"Bill, you are not telling me everything. You are holding back when you shouldn't. It may cost you your career or your life if you don't tell me all you know," Briscoe said, using a tone of voice implying hurt feelings.

"When did you figure it out?" Delaney asked.

"Your dad made contingency plans for you to contact me if something happened to him," Briscoe said.

Looking at his feet, Delaney blushed slightly and replied, "You are correct but you did not answer my question."

"When I figured it out doesn't matter now. Your dad died in 1955 and the Cuban crisis took place in October 1962. There is no way he could have foreseen that event. However, he gave you instructions to let me know about APPS should an event like it take place. You sent those photos," Briscoe stated with assurance that comes from being right.

"That's correct," Delaney answered in a subdued voice.

"Damn son, if your dad trusted me that much, why couldn't you?" Briscoe asked.

"Honestly, I was afraid," Delaney answered.

"Well, you are only human. There is nothing wrong with being afraid. Hell, there's a reason for being afraid. It's called self preservation. Being afraid is what makes heroes do what they do. Let's put this behind us and get the dirty bastards," Briscoe explained.

"Yeah, McNeese deserves the worst that can come to him," Delaney stated with vengeance in his voice.

"McNeese is small fry. He's a gofer. It took someone in a position of high authority to get your dad to allow him to become a subscriber. I was able to decipher the subscriber's list and found McNeese listed. However, he was never in the CIA and did not fit the profile of those you said that your dad allowed to join," told Delaney.

Continuing, Briscoe said, "McNeese had to have access to the third APPS your dad had in the bunker. In fact, McNeese got it for him. That protective shelter was the ideal place for McNeese to do the calculations and provide data to the Soviets. He would still be able to provide information after an attack. McNeese knew about that room didn't he son?"

"Yes sir, he did. I showed him how to get in and allowed him to use the bunker whenever he wanted. Dad said that he was okay," Delaney blurted almost in tears.

"Hey, don't blame yourself. I would have done exactly what your dad did. When a Special Assistant to the President of the United States asks a person to do something, they usually consider it an order in our business. The kingpin in this mess is Neil Burnum. There are a couple more but Burnum has to go down first and soon.

"What are we going to do?" Delaney asked.

"We are going to the Federal Bureau of Investigation (FBI) first and give them details. As soon as Ike left office, Burnum became Chief Executive Officer (CEO) for R. L. Meyers Corporation. That organization was supposed to be a cover for the development of cryptographic equipment working with data processors. Next, he and his Soviet friends planned to form a venture capital operation to provide startup funding. Later, after they had details on APPS and our surveillance gear, they would leave the cover organization as it was. They would then split with the technology to the USSR. However, if the FBI will go along with my plans, they are in for a surprise," Briscoe told Delaney.

Continuing Briscoe said, "Let's get some sleep. Tomorrow is going to be a busy day."

"Yeah, it was a busy day all right," Briscoe thought as tape 2 neared its end. He removed the tape stored it and got tape 3 from the vault. He set it up for analysis and watched the scope for any peculiarities. Not seeing any, he let the analysis equipment do its work. He would give 20 to one odds that nothing would appear on this tape either. He felt sure that he knew what Ho Chi Minh's intelligence people were doing. He just had to prove it. He had to prove it just as he did with Burnum, McNeese, Katherine, and Jenkins.

"Doctor Jenkins was used by the bastards," he thought. "For almost four years they led a brilliant man around by his nose. They planned to do the same with me."

Over breakfast the next day, Briscoe explained to Delaney, "Bill, the first thing today we have to go see General O'Conner. You must tell him every detail.

He's my boss and yours. Probably the only way you are going to keep your commission is to convince O'Conner that you have integrity. To do that it is your professional duty to tell him everything you know. I will be there to help."

"You are right Lanny. I let it go too long and I really feel like an ass," Delaney replied.

Briscoe waited for an hour outside of O'Conner's office. Delaney insisted that he had to tell the general on his own. If O'Conner wanted to talk to Briscoe after he had his say, that was fine. Briscoe knew that the general would respect Delaney. He did.

General O'Conner's secretary answered her intercom. The general said that he wanted to see Briscoe.

Once inside, O'Conner motioned Briscoe to sit. Delaney sat straight with his chin up and his shoulder's straight. Briscoe was sure that O'Conner knew that Delaney was a fine officer. He had made a small slip but so does everyone at one time or another.

"Lanny, I contacted the FBI. Their man is on his way. In addition, I alerted Benjamin Phillips so he could tell the White House. We have to let the President in on this. Initially, the FBI wanted the lead on this operation. However, you've made a favorable impression on Phillips. He insists that you take this action. In addition, he wants you to brief the National Security Advisor and possibly the President. He will let us know when as soon as we make this case. Phillips has a man from the Attorney General's office joining us," O'Conner explained.

"Anything you want to add Lanny?" General O'Conner asked.

"Uh, yes sir," Briscoe replied. "Can we meet in this office? Your conference room will not hold this many people."

O'Conner chuckled and answered, "Sure thing. I can live with that."

McNeese cut a deal. For his testimony, he got immunity. At first, the FBI did not agree. However, Briscoe made sure that they understood that McNeese was a nothing, an errand boy at best. They needed Burnum and his associates. The Attorney General's representative made the decision. With that, everyone else fell. The hardest part was Katherine.

Briscoe asked that he inform her of the situation. For some reason, he felt duty bound to do so. The FBI could monitor their conversation and make the arrest after Briscoe talked with her.

Briscoe recalled that she knew something was wrong as soon as he entered her apartment. It was in her eyes and she asked.

"What's wrong?" Katherine asked.

"Let's sit over here," Briscoe said, as he pointed to her kitchen table.

He pulled her chair back for her to take a seat. He took a chair directly across from her.

He took her hands in his and asked. "What makes you think something is wrong?"

"Lanny, you did not take your coat off and you look different. There is sadness in your eyes," she answered.

Clearing his throat, Briscoe looked directly into her eyes and said, "Burnum and McNeese are under arrest. There will be more arrests of Burnum's cronies."

Briscoe felt a hard knot growing in his chest as he saw her chin begin to tremble. She was hurting and it hurt him.

"We know you married Jenkins. Our heart goes out to your daughter. He will obtain full custody unless you want to fight it. I would recommend that you do not," Briscoe explained.

Briscoe watched a horrid transition take place. One moment Katherine was a beautiful lady with a gracious loveliness in her face. Slowly, her beauty disappeared as the tears came. Her face turned from beauty to a profound morass of guilt.

Briscoe continued holding her hands as Katherine directed her gaze at them and said, "Lanny, please do not hate me. I will not make any excuses for what I've done. My deepest hope is that my daughter will not be destroyed because of what I have done."

Katherine lowered her forehead onto Briscoe's hands. Her shoulders heaved with body shaking sobs.

Tears filled Briscoe's eyes as he said into his hidden microphone, "Come on in, it's okay."

The tape's loose end continued to flap as its take-up reel spun faster. Briscoe continued to stare unaware that tape 3 had reached its end. His only feeling was a revived old hurt deep within that he had not felt for sometime.

"Are you going to turn it off or must I," a voice cut through his remorse.

"Uh, what?" Briscoe answered.

"The tape. Are you going to stop it?" Captain Haldron asked.

"Oh yeah, sorry. I was way away from here," Briscoe answered.

Haldron closed the door on the mobile van for crypto analysis. Outside the South Viet Nam sun caused runways to appear like lakes from heat wave mirages. Briscoe was attached to the First Army Security Agency Company (Aviation) located at the Naval Air Facility at Cam Ranh Bay. As far as Briscoe knew this was the only unit with Army Aviators flying Navy P2Vs. Crammed with electronic gear, the unit's aircraft could stay on station up to 14 hours. Equipped with four engines, two reciprocating and two jets, the organization was spewing raw data for analysis.

"Any luck?" Haldron asked.

"Not yet but I think I might know what they're using. I am going through the basics first," Briscoe explained.

"What tape do you need next?" Haldron asked with a tinge of sarcasm in his voice.

Putting tape 3 into its canister, Briscoe replied, "Get me tape 4."

Haldron and Briscoe exchanged tapes and Briscoe threaded tape 4 while saying, "If this is what I think it is, the USSR is providing Uncle Ho with some heavy duty crypto equipment. We may have to send this to Arlington Hall for processing."

Arlington Hall's location was Washington, D. C. Nevertheless, the facility took the name of its headquarters' home in Virginia.

"That's unsatisfactory. We need as close to real time as we can get. That's why you are here," Haldron said with obvious disdain.

Briscoe flipped off the analysis device with a swift move and turned to face Haldron.

"Listen captain, if you have a problem, spit it out," Briscoe said with obvious irritation.

"There's too damned many civilians over here now. I do not have much use for civilians to start with," Haldron threw his heated words at Briscoe.

"What's your mother?" Briscoe asked sharply.

"Keep my mother out of this. What's she got to do with this?" Haldron asked as his word carried even more dislike.

"She's a civilian isn't she?" Briscoe quipped.

"Shit," Haldron said as he whirled and exited the trailer, slamming the door behind him.

Briscoe thought as he stared at the door, "Damn someone must have slit his foreskin and put his foot through it."

After working the four tapes thoroughly with usual procedures, Briscoe decided that he needed more information to support his suspicions. He locked the vault and left the trailer. Standing on the bottom step, he gazed at the facility. It was massive spreading across thousands of acres. Cam Ranh Bay was the primary supply facility for combat units deployed throughout South Viet Nam. Its construction and operation was the responsibility of a Texas based engineering company. The word was that the initial construction contract was for nine billion dollars. With President Johnson's Texas heritage, this raised many eyebrows. Republicans shouted outrageous and to hell with raised eyebrows.

Briscoe crossed the tarmac enroute to MACV's communication center. Before crossing a taxiway, he saw a Chinook helicopter on approach. He crossed in front of the approaching, twin-rotor helicopter. It was necessary that he run because he had misjudged the ship's nearness. Once across, the leviathan passed immediately behind him. Hurricane force winds blasted him causing him to stumble forward. His prized bush hat disappeared in a gust of grim that stung his hunched body.

Once the winds dissipated, he turned to see the helicopter taxing on four wheels with its blades at flat pitch. Its aft pylon had a large yellow patch with a black line across it. Above the line, there was a black imprint of a horse's head. The CH-47 made a 90-degree right turn to park in a designated area. On its nose, there was a painted crest with a depiction of Pegasus on a blue field. On its forward pylon, there was a large letter C within a circle. During the turn, Briscoe saw that the craft had gunners. On each side, near its forward end, there were two, square openings. In each, a helmeted soldier manned an M-60 machine gun.

As the ship's speed slowed, a ramp at the helicopter's rear lowered and a crewman stepped onto the tarmac. He wore a standard flight helmet and one of the new Nomex flight suits. He held a device in his right hand that connected to the helicopter. Briscoe guessed it to be a device for communicating with its crewmembers.

Briscoe began looking for his bush hat. Having a bush hat seemed to be a mark of distinction among those stationed at Cam Ranh Bay. He had paid a tidy sum to get his. The more he looked without finding it, the more he became pissed. He started for the parked Chinook.

As he approached, a captain stepped from the ramp, now in a full down position. He was not tall but had a National Football League build. With broad shoulders and a large chest, he had a sawed-off, pump shotgun hanging by his right side from a strap across his right shoulder. He wore a mesh, survival vest, and a 45-Cal., semi-automatic pistol in a shoulder holster by his left arm. The closer Briscoe got, the more intimidating the captain appeared. He glared at Briscoe with cold eyes. And, he never blinked.

Before Briscoe could speak, the captain said, "You are one stupid son of a bitch. We almost had to abort our approach when you ran in front of us. Are you brain dead? We had a clearance to land when you ran across. What do you have to say for yourself, mister?"

Not only was Briscoe taken aback by the captain's frontal assault but he looked familiar.

"Where have I seen this guy," he thought.

"Well?" The captain asking again, still without blinking.

"My hat, you," Briscoe tried to say before he was interrupted.

"I know you. You're that dumb ass who thought Turks sold cigars in Hong Kong and screw your hat," he said, stepping menacingly closer to Briscoe. "You don't fuck with the Cav."

During their confrontation, Briscoe saw a Chief Warrant Officer step from the ramp. With him were the two door gunners. They watched developments with the hint of a smile on their lips. In addition, Briscoe was close enough to see the captain's subdued name on his uniform. It showed his name to be Zane.

Keeping on eye on Briscoe, Captain Zane turned his head slightly toward the crew, and ordered, "Get this guy a hat."

One of the door gunners disappeared into the ship. He promptly returned with a large, cardboard box. He set it on the ramp and opened it. Inside, Briscoe saw what he estimated to be hundreds of bush hats.

Looking at Briscoe, the gunner asked. "What size?"

"Christ," Briscoe thought. "I paid $20.00 for my hat. They've got a case of them."

"Seven and one-half," Briscoe answered.

The gunner entered the ship and returned with another cardboard box. He opened it and removed a hat. He promptly threw it to Briscoe.

"Hell, they have cases sorted by size," Briscoe thought.

Briscoe caught the hat and put it on as Captain Zane asked. "We square?"

Adjusting his hat, Briscoe answered, "Yeah, sure. It's a perfect fit. I remember you now. You were at the terminal at Hong Kong in December 1962."

Captain Zane stepped forward, almost causing Briscoe to stumble backwards, until Zane extended his hand and said, "Good to see you again."

Relieved, Briscoe grasped Zane's big hand and replied, "Yeah, me too. How did you like this place?"

"About the same as now. It sucks. Want to come aboard and see what almost cut you into pieces?" Zane asked.

"Follow me," Zane said as he returned to the ship's lowered ramp. Briscoe noticed that the other crewmembers stepped away as they exhibited broad grins.

As he came to the CH-47s ramp, he looked up to see three large blades, atop a high pylon, drooping toward the tarmac. On either side of the pylon two, turbine engines made clicking sounds as they cooled. At the pylon's base, just above the entrance, there was another outlet port of some type.

As Briscoe started to step onto the lowered ramp, a sergeant stepped from the group and grasped his elbow saying, "Watch your step sir. It can be slippery."

Briscoe looked down as the NCO helped him aboard. The ramp was wet with a red fluid that seemed to come from somewhere above his head. Looking up, he gazed into a morass of tubes, cables, wire bundles, hydraulic cylinders and items he did not recognize. Looking forward, he saw fold-down, red nylon seats extending the craft's length on either side. On and beneath the seats, he noticed cross bows, Viet Cong flags, flip-flop sandals, and other miscellaneous items, to include more boxes of bush hats.

Captain Zane beckoned him to proceed forward toward him. Briscoe noticed that aluminum tubing extended along both sides of the ship with multiple wire bundles and solenoids. He could not fathom the craft's complexity. He had been inside B-29s, 17s, and 24s. They were nothing compared to the CH-47.

Zane climbed into the cockpit and sat on the left side. He extended his hand and helped Briscoe take a seat in the pilot's right seat. After Briscoe entered, CWO Scott lowered a small seat in the cockpit's entranceway and sat watching.

"Chief, keep me straight here," Zane said to Scott.

"Roger," Scott answered.

Even with Scott's assistance, Briscoe soon became lost in Zane's brief explanation of the CH-47s components and capabilities. One thing he did remember. It was big, powerful and carried a shitload of people or cargo.

It became apparent that the CH-47 crewmembers were proud of their ship. The gunners and flight engineer were quick to explain their duties. As he left the cockpit, Briscoe saw a winch and cable mounted inside the Chinook's cargo compartment.

He asked the flight engineer, Sergeant Randall. "What do you use that for?"

Randall explained that he could winch vehicles or other items into the cargo compartment with it. The cable was long enough to reach from the cargo compartment's forward area to outside the ship. Using a hand operated switch; he simply pulled cargo aboard.

With his interest in electronic components, Briscoe noticed a map mounted between rollers in the cockpit. Zane explained that it was the display for a Decca Navigational System. Three antennas located far apart in country, transmitted radio signals that onboard equipment received. This equipment computed the time for each signal to arrive and drew the aircraft's course on a tactical map for the pilots to follow. Zane made sure that Briscoe understood that it was an experimental device and not a primary, navigational means.

Once outside the Chinook, Briscoe asked about antennas mounted in a zigzag fashion along its length. According to Randall, the antenna was for an ARC 102, Ultra High Frequency radio capable of transmitting around the world at high altitudes. Their unit used it to transmit daily reports to their operations people when located far from their main base.

"Can you operate in the same frequency bands that HAM operators use?" Briscoe asked.

Randall promptly replied, "Yes."

Zane grasped Briscoe around his shoulders with his right arm. His massive hand dug into Briscoe's shoulder.

"Lanny," he said. "When you see one of these mothers coming get out of the way. Winds from those blades reach 125 mile per hour. They could blow your puny butt away."

Pulling loose, Briscoe thanked each crewmember and shook his hand.

Looking at Zane, he asked. "What's all that stuff you've got in there for?"

Zane answered, "Trade goods," as he walked away with Scott toward a large warehouse.

Briscoe continued his trek to MACV's communication center. Along the way, he examined his hat while putting it on and taking it off numerous times.

"Hell, this dude is comfortable," he thought as he neared a security gate.

Once cleared, Briscoe entered and went to the facilities Officer-In-Charge (OIC). He explained that he needed a top secret, secured communication channel to Arlington Hall. While getting clearance, he prepared his message.

It stated:

"Ref.: VENONA – Urgent need this location – signal source device and source containing THE BANK AND ARSENAL raw data for comparative analysis to assist current effort. Signed RAMPART."

Briscoe watched as his message left in an electronic burst lasting less than a nanosecond. Next, he had the OIC witness the original document's destruction.

After leaving the building, he saw Zane's Chinook making a takeoff. Swinging slightly beneath it there was a CONEX container. The ship's blades almost seemed bowed upward and the takeoff was agonizingly slow.

Briscoe thought, "If I had to make a guess, they've got that ship loaded."

As he returned to his van parked on the tarmac, he made sure to keep his hat in his hand. He climbed the steps and unlocked the van's door. Once inside, he unlocked the vault and removed tape 1.

As he threaded it onto its spindle, he thought, "Uncle Ho, if I am right, I've got you by the balls."

Chapter Thirty Seven

March 1968

All men think all men mortal, but themselves
Edward Young (1683–1765), English poet, playwright. Night Thoughts, *"The Complaint: Night 1*

Captain Dale Zane sat in the CONEX container's shade waiting for sling gear from his Chinook. He still had a humorous recollection regarding his recent encounter with the civilian Briscoe.

"They simply do not understand the winds that a Hook generates," Zane thought. "He will remember the next time."

It had taken him a moment to remember Briscoe from his short stopover in Hong Kong. He wondered at Briscoe's inquiry about "Turks selling cigars."

"Time can be a betrayer of one's mind. After joining the 93rd TC Company in late 1962, it seemed to stand still. These past six years seem mere seconds and here I am watching days become week-long events again," he thought.

Continuing his reflections, he remembered his first combat at Ap Bac, "What an Ethiopian jug screw that turned into. The ARVN got their asses kicked and so did we. Four 21s shot down and six more damaged. The guys from the UTT didn't fare much better."

"Later that day a rescue 21 made it into the LZ. We loaded the wounded and other downed crewmen. During our climb to altitude, they raked us with 30 and 50-cal. machine gun fire. We went down less than a mile from the LZ. Finally, after Lieutenant Colonel Vann raised enough hell, the ARVN got us out aboard some Armored Personnel Carriers (APC)."

"Jesus, six months of hell and fear. I sure was glad to get back to Korea," he remembered. "One thing good came of that tour. I learned one hell of a lot from those CWOs who took me under their wing. Those guys knew how to fly with little or nothing."

The order, to attend the Officers Career Course at Fort Sill, Oklahoma, was a surprise to Zane. He arrived to be the only lieutenant in the class. Most of the other students were captains and majors. As junior officer, he drew the shit details but that was fine. He had his wife, his daughter, and his newly born son.

Someone at Department of the Army (DA) took pity on him and sent him home early from Korea. It was definitely for the best because he was in no mood for any of the former, Mickey Mouse, horse shit. Old Scab In The Butt's raving would have only got him a court martial.

The people at Sill had to find something for him to do until class started. When they saw that he was a former gunnery instructor, they assigned him to the Department of Instruction. Initially, his primary duty was to attend and evaluate classes given by other instructors. However, when he learned that there was a special project underway involving firing rockets from helicopters, he went to his supervisor, Colonel Riker "Bull" Malone.

"Come on in Zane. What's up?" Malone asked.

Zane stood at ease before the colonel's desk and asked. "Sir, I request permission to work on the CH-34 project?"

"Wish I could Zane but we're over committed on that program. The commandant would have my ass. Every guy working there is special duty from another unit on base. That means they come out of their hides. They have no authority to be doing what they are doing," Malone explained.

"Yes sir, I know but I am excess. I am a snowbird. I'm killing time for over a month waiting for class to start sir," Zane said almost pleading.

Malone thought a moment and replied, "Tell you what Zane. You can observe, review data, and submit a report to the commandant. We need someone who knows gunnery but can give an unbiased report on how that system stacks up against conventional artillery. That's the best I can do."

"Thank you sir. That's great," Zane answered as he immediately came to attention and saluted.

Malone smiled and returned his salute saying, "Get out Zane before I change my mind."

Overjoyed, Zane rushed into the office to announce his new assignment. As he entered, he saw secretaries crying openly. Other personnel clustered around a television set.

Perplexed, Zane asked a weeping secretary what was the matter.

She forced out her words between gasps, "Someone assassinated President Kennedy."

Zane stared as the words refused to register in his mind as he asked. "What?"

"Somebody killed President Kennedy. They killed Kennedy and wounded the Texas Governor," she wailed from deep, emotional pain.

This could not be. The nation idolized John F. Kennedy. He was the guiding light for a nation deep in need for it. It was his time. It was his Camelot. He was a beacon amid darkness and his was a new age. Zane began openly blubbering like a baby.

"Oh my God in heaven," he cried as he found an empty chair.

He heard a loud ringing in his ears and numbness enveloped him. He could not focus on those around him or where he was as his mind tried to register a tragedy of such a magnitude. Then the anger came.

During following days, he watched Jack Ruby kill Kennedy's murderer. He agonized with the nation as they put his Commander In Chief to rest. He cried as Kennedy's son saluted his fallen father. In addition, like the rest of the nation, he began to think, "Why?"

Kennedy's death was the antithesis of another president's murder only a few weeks past. South Viet Nam's President Diem was a hated dictator. Kennedy was a revered leader of a democratic nation. Diem was a hysterical Catholic trying to impose his faith upon a nation. Kennedy was a Catholic vowing not to allow his faith to interfere with his leadership. Diem's religious leaders were killing themselves in protest of his regime. Kennedy's religious leaders were embracing him because of his religious courage.

Zane agonized with his nation trying to find reason where there was none. He had nightmares of Jackie Kennedy standing aboard Air Force One in her blood stained dress. Beside her, her husband's presidency slipped to now President Lyndon B. Johnson. Haunting visions of black artillery caissons draped with America's flag tore at his soul. It was a hurt unlike that of any he had ever experienced and he was not alone, for a nation grieved with him.

"Sir, I have my first report on the H-34 tests," Zane told Colonel Malone without enthusiasm.

"Dale, have a seat," Malone said.

Zane watched as Malone swiveled his executive chair to his right. He stared through his large office window at the headquarters' flag at half-staff. Seven rows of decorations filled his left chest. At the top was the Medal of Honor.

"Son, during World War II this nation lost its leader at a time when we needed him the most. At the time, I was certain that his death meant the failure of our nation's effort to preserve freedom. I learned what made the country worth dying for when President Roosevelt left us. Another stepped forward and took the reins in our darkest hour and we continued the fight. So, I ask that you remember this as you serve your country," Malone said not taking his eyes off the flag.

Turning to face Zane, he continued, "Lieutenant give me your report tomorrow in writing. If there's nothing else, you're dismissed."

Zane came to attention and his eyes locked with Malone's for an instant. During that moment, a great understanding passed from senior to junior.

"Thank you sir," Zane said as he saluted; did an about face; and left Malone's office.

"Daryl, where the hell have you been?" Zane asked as he saw his best friend, Lieutenant Daryl Scott, approach.

The pair lunged together slapping each other's backs as Scott answered, "I've been in the land of the morning calm. Whose ass did you kiss to get home early?"

Zane answered with a loud laugh, "I'm not sure but I would kiss it again if I had the chance."

Scott looked around Zane's small office and commented with a strong tone of sarcasm, "Looks like you've been kissing some ass here too."

Zane backed to his desk and placed both hands on it. In one swift movement, he lifted himself to land sitting on it.

"Hey, some office. You get to sit in the only chair in here. By the way, how's your wife?" Zane asked.

"Compared to what?" Scott responded gleefully.

"Mine. If you answer that, you're a dead man. Damn, it's good to see you," Zane answered mocking Scott.

"We are doing just great. You know how Georgia feels about Fort Sill but we're together so she doesn't complain. I understand you are the father of a baby boy," Scott said.

"That's right. He's a heart breaking stud too," Zane replied with pride. "We named him Steve after you asshole."

"You would use my middle name. What kind of friend is that?" Scott asked, while continuing to jest with Zane.

Continuing Scott added, "There are now two lieutenants in this class but you are junior. You still get the shit details."

Zane remembered that he submitted his H-34 reports to Colonel Malone that morning. In addition, he had a practice run to watch that afternoon.

"Hey, I want to show you something you are not going to believe," Zane told Scott.

"What's that? Proof that you have a father," Scott hurled back.

"No, I am serious. Here's what's going on," Zane said with a sober tone.

"Would you believe firing 4.5-inch rockets from an H-34?" Zane asked with excitement.

"Get out of here. I would have heard about that," Scott answered dubiously.

Zane explained that the H-34 project was not official. It was an experiment outside of normal research and development channels. He told Scott that the artillery school took World War II vintage, 4.5-inch rocket launchers and modified them for attachment to an H-34. There were 24 tubes on each side of the helicopter. The tubes were a group fitted with a mounting point for a gunner's quadrant.

Scott knew that a gunner's quadrant was a device used to measure angles of elevation. A gunner set a desired number of degrees on it. This caused a bubble, like that in a carpenter's level, to offset. By placing, the quadrant on a firing device and raising the device until the bubble centered caused the firing system to achieve a precise elevation.

"Wait just one minute. A gunner's quadrant is for indirect fire weapons not direct fire. Are you saying that someone is firing 4.5 inch rockets from a helicopter in an indirect fire mode?" Scott asked.

"That's right. They're sitting on the ground and firing just like regular artillery," Zane said with excitement.

Now Scott said with interest, "Tell me more. A 4.5 inch rocket is one big rocket."

"Tell you what. Call Georgia and have her visit with Janice. I'll give you our address. If you're interested, you can come with me and see for yourself," Zane said as if a challenge.

Zane drove west on Fort Sill's South Boundary Road. He turned north toward a firing range used for demonstrating artillery-firing demonstrations for visitors.

As they neared some bleachers, Scott asked. "Isn't this where they have the MAT 102 demonstrations?"

"That's right," Zane answered as he parked beside a sign bearing a notice "No Civilian Vehicles Beyond This Point."

The two crested a hill with seating for 600 on its top. As they went around the bleachers, they had a panoramic view of prairie against a backdrop of small hills. Parked a few hundred meters in front of the bleachers, they saw two H-34s surrounded by troops. They were busy putting rockets into pods on each side of the helicopters. Zane indicated for Scott to sit on the bleachers' bottom row.

Zane explained, "There are two things a gunner needs to know when firing artillery, direction and elevation."

"Yep," Scott agreed.

"Imagine this," Zane continued. "The H-34s land after receiving a fire mission from a forward observer. On-board, FDC personnel compute a direction and elevation to the target. Troops unass the H-34s and place rollers beneath the tail wheels. In the cockpits, the pilots read direction from their radio magnetic indicators (RMI). They tell the crew when the ship is pointing in the correct direction. The gunner sets elevation on the quadrant and places it on the rocket pod. He then elevates the pod until the bubble centers. The elevation is now correct. They fire two rockets and tell the forward observer, 'On the way.'"

Zane ended his explanation by saying, "From there on, it's a simple adjustment onto the target. When the FO says 'Fire-for-Effect,' they fire the remaining rockets."

"What kind of accuracy are they getting?" Scott asked.

Without hesitation, Zane answered, "As good as a standard 105-mm howitzer unit. The burst radius of a 4.5-inch rocket is 35 to 50 meters. If you can get two rockets that close, that's when the FO has them unload their tubes. They don't have to worry about counter battery fire. They engage their rotors and fly away. I have seen the data and checked it. This shit works."

Thinking about what Zane said, Scott commented, "Yeah that's the beauty of the H-34. You can shut down the blades and leave the engines running. They can shoot and scoot. I like it."

While listening to Scott, Zane saw two Air Force Lieutenant Colonels arrive and take seats in the bleachers. They were at the far end, a considerable distance from Zane and Scott.

"Damn," Zane said.

"What?" Scott asked.

Nodding his head toward the new arrivals, Zane answered, "Those two have been here for every firing. They should mind their own business."

Looking at the two colonels, Scott asked. "So what?"

With a disgusted look, Zane replied, "They do not want us putting weapons on our aircraft. They claim that we are invading their roles and missions. They report our tests to D.C. The Air Force Chief of Staff complains to the Joint Chiefs that we're trying to steal their show. What a crock."

Looking at the helicopters, Scott asked. "They ever fire those things in direct fire?"

"Yes," Zane promptly answered. "They are deadly. Remember how the 2.75-inch rockets on the UH-1s in 'Nam hit all over the place? Well, these 4.5-inch killers do not. Some Tech Reps designed a pyrotechnic gyro for the rocket. When the pilot pushes the fire button, a tiny gyro begins spinning. If there is a crosswind, the gyros keep the rocket on course. These guys claim an accuracy of three meters of where the pilot was aiming when he hit the fire button."

"Must cost like hell," Scott stated.

"Not so. The cost is less than $3.00 per rocket. That's cheap," Zane said with enthusiasm.

Scott glanced at his watch. He stood up and started from the bleachers.

"Where you going?" Zane asked.

"My friend, it is late. Those girls are going to kick our butts. Let's go," Scott explained.

"You're right. Remember what you've seen here today. When a chance comes in the future to arm our birds, we know that it works," Zane said as he joined Scott toward Zane's car.

The next nine months were a combination of serious hard work and many good times. There were 40 pilots in their class of 600 artillery officers. The aviators were a clique not appreciated by their artillery contemporaries. Many begrudged their flight pay and proud attitude that only served to drive them closer together. As aviators, they had to be bright to get in flight school. With the high washout rates, only the brightest of them graduated. They had reason to be proud of their silver wings.

For the first two months, their classes took place in high security classrooms. They learned the skills of a nuclear weapons employment officer. Those completing the course had a numeral five put into their military occupational specialty designation. This "prefix five" meant they qualified to advise senior commanders on use of atomic weapons. Because of its serious nature, this course was the hardest of their nine months' training. Daily, and weekends, Zane and Scott studied into early morning hours. Their wives complained that they saw more of their husbands when they were overseas. At least they got to read their mail.

After completing seven months training at Fort Sill, they went to Fort Bliss, Texas, for two months. Fort Bliss was the Air Defense Artillery (ADA) School. This was a gentleman's course, which meant there were no examinations. In anticipation of the Bliss school, the 40 aviators pooled resources to send two officers to Fort Bliss one weekend. They located and reserved the finest motel available for 40 families. They reserved rooms on the ground floor facing the motel's swimming pool.

The following two months were a blur of parties, dog races, water polo (combat rules), and general good times. Zane and Scott received their promotions to captain. The pair reserved a room at the Lone Star Brewery for a bachelor party that ended up in a run through every burlesque show in nearby Juarez, Mexico. A number of threatened divorces followed to include Zane and Scott. There were no more bachelors' parties. Their long awaited orders for their new assignments arrived. Most expected orders to Viet Nam.

Since Zane and Scott already had tours in Viet Nam, they went to the Army Aviation School at Fort Rucker, Alabama, to share their combat knowledge. They were returning to Mother Rucker where only a short time before they were students. Both were overjoyed for they knew what awaited their classmates. The friendly pair had no remorse about their assignments.

After reporting to Fort Rucker, Zane and Scott met their wives for Happy Hour at Fort Rucker's Officers' Club. Zane and Janice saw Scott and Georgia enter the crowded bar. Zane arose and waved them to their table.

"Hey you two," Zane said as he remained standing. "We had to fight to save you seats. Can you believe this place? They are starting to pump aviator students through this place like cattle."

As Scott seated Georgia, he asked. "Looks like I will have to fight my way to the bar. What are you two having?"

"A Black Russian for me," Janice answered and then looked at Zane.

"Bourbon and ginger," Zane added.

The three watched Scott elbow his way into the mobbed bar. Student pilots stood four deep to order drinks. They had good reason because drinks were 15 cents each during happy hour on Fridays.

Scott returned trying to juggle four drinks without spilling them and said, "It can get violent up there. They need to have at least three more bars open. Where's Zane?"

"He's getting us some goodies," Janice answered.

Scott glanced toward the room's middle. He saw Zane with two paper plates filling them with cold cuts, fried chicken wings, and other assorted snacks.

"Look at that bull," Scott said. "If they do not move, he knocks them out of the way. When they see what hit them they don't dare say a word."

The trio laughed while they watched Zane muscle his way back to their table. He had two plates with an ample supply of treats.

"Dinner is served," Zane said as he put the plates on the table. "Now, I will get some more drinks."

As Zane plunged into the crowd, Scott noted, "He hasn't touched the drink I brought."

"That's my Dale," Janice said laughing. "Always have a reserve."

Later, at dinner, they discussed their new assignments.

"I don't guess I will ever get away from it," Zane said. "They've got me teaching artillery again. I have to show these guys how to adjust artillery from the air. I wanted to be an instructor pilot and they put me in a platform instructor's job."

"Hell, me too, except I don't have a platform," Scott related with a smirk. "I'm teaching survival, escape and evasion out in the woods. The school has a prisoner of war (POW) camp in the swamp. We catch students and put them through interrogation and shit."

"Is it true that you feed those guys rattlesnake, ants and grasshoppers?" Zane asked.

"Sure do. Moreover, we make them skin live rabbits and cook them over fires they make. Two guys fainted when we killed a rabbit in front of them. What they hell are they going to do when they have to kill a human?" Scott asked cynically.

"Wait a minute," Zane said. "You ever kill anybody?"

The ladies stopped talking and turned to stare at Zane. Scott placed his knife and fork on the table.

After some obvious thought, Scott answered in a slow, deliberate manner, "No, not that I know of directly."

"Me neither," Zane answered. "I've tried but I'm sure I didn't. Here I am, teaching these guys how to blow people to hell with artillery. I've called artillery fire in 'Nam. Did I kill the guys that the artillery hit or did the gunners firing the weapons? How about air strikes that I called?"

"Dale, let's talk about something else," Janice suggested.

There was no more enjoyment that evening. Their togetherness carried a formal aura until they parted later.

"Hon, why did you say that?" Janice asked, as they drove to the post nursery to retrieve their children.

"It needed saying," Zane answered.

One of Zane's fond memories was an officer's revolution against the installation commander. Various departments at the school had individuals attending weekend parties at their homes. When Zane's group became too large for their quarters, they reserved the Officers' Wives' Club building for weekend gatherings. It was free plus large enough for them to dance.

However, the installation commander noticed that attendance at the Officers' Club was beginning to dwindle. He issued a directive that future departmental social functions had to be at the Officers' Club that charged a substantial fee. In addition, he decreed that the Officers' Wives' Club building was not available for such functions. This was a direct challenge to the ingenuity of Zane's fellow aviators. Thus, the Fort Rucker Discotheque Society was born.

An officer, selected at random, went to the Wives' Club and reserved it in the name of the Fort Rucker Discotheque Society. The Wives' Club granted the reservation because no such department existed. Word spread by word of mouth of a Halloween Party. Individuals decorated the facility with corn stalks, pumpkins, black, and orange crepe paper. The party took place and selected individuals cleaned the facility spotless after the function. Various parties continued for months.

The installation commander noted that use of the Officers' Club continued to decline. He began an investigation to determine why. He immediately learned of the Fort Rucker Discotheque Society and demanded a membership list. No such list existed and Wives' Club personnel could not identify who made the reservations other than the club's name. The installation commander banned the phantom organization. Nevertheless, parties continued at facilities in surrounding communities. With no leverage over civilian facilities, the installation commander became more frustrated. He implemented a formal inquiry to determine the membership of this rogue group. He never succeeded.

Nevertheless, the ghost group died. Major developments were underway that allowed little time for social pursuits. Zane and Scott learned of them at a top-secret meeting at the Post Theater.

"Gentlemen, what you hear today is classified top secret. You are not to discuss this with anyone except those with a need to know," Major General Hollifield said from the theater's stage.

"Lights please," he continued.

The theater darkened and an aerial photo appeared on the screen. A relatively large, single peak appeared amidst surrounding jungle.

"This is An Khe in Viet Nam's Central Highlands. Starting next week, you will begin helping form and train a new organization for deployment to this region. This organization is the first of its kind in the annals of warfare. No such unit has ever existed on this planet. Slide please," Hollifield said.

An organizational chart appeared on the large screen. On the surface, the organization structure looked similar to any other division except there was an aviation brigade shown on the slide.

"This is an airmobile division. Its aircraft will total 440. It will be a lean, mean, fighting machine dependent upon helicopters for maneuverability. It will move fast and strike hard. In coming months, we will work closely with elements at Fort Benning, Georgia. The organization will be the 11th Air Assault Division. There is one hell of a lot of work to do. We must have this unit ready for combat in six months," Hollifield explained.

A murmur rolled throughout the theater. Statements like "It cannot be done." "No way." And, "I'll be damned," traveled between attendees.

Later, Dale and Janice went to Scott's home. While their wives chatted, Zane and Scott went into his study to talk about their new task.

"You know that President Johnson had to approve this," Zane said excited at the prospect.

"I know but that's not what he is telling the public. He keeps saying that he's going to bring the troops home," Scott added. "This thing is costing billions of dollars. How is he getting around congress with this?"

"Beats me but this is serious shit. We're talking almost 14,000 troops in this unit alone. Do you realize the size of the logistical tail to wag this dog? My God, aircraft parts alone will cost a fortune," Zane added.

Scott's brow furrowed in thought slightly before he asked. "How is he going to justify sending this unit into combat?"

After considerable thought, Zane answered, "It is over my head. However, this unit is going to 'Nam. You know it and I know it. It won't be this month or the next but it is going and we know exactly where. Unless, things change, he is going to have to create a reason to convince congress."

The tempo of events at Fort Rucker raced. There were clandestine trips to Fort Benning and late night planning sessions. Meanwhile, aviators were streaming into Fort Benning along with tons of equipment. In addition, they were receiving the latest aircraft in the Army's inventory.

Zane recalled the first event in his involvement. He received word to attend a meeting with Hollifield and his deputy, Colonel Nelson Beam.

"Zane," Hollifield said. "We've received word that our fixed wing pilots don't know how to adjust artillery fire. They are having a big problem with this in 'Nam."

Colonel Beam interjected, "We know you only teach rotary wing students on a puff board without any live firing. We need you to teach fixed wing pilots coming through Rucker."

"Beam's right," Hollifield agreed. "Put a program of instruction (POI) together with live firing exercises for fixed wing students. When do you think you can be teaching the first class?"

"Sir, I can teach the platform stuff but not the live firing," Zane answered.

In unison, Beam and Hollifield asked. "Why?"

"I am not fixed wing qualified," Zane answered.

Hollifield looked at Beam and said, "Fix this."

Beam replied, "Yes sir," and turned to Zane.

"Get to work on the POI. You will hear from me soon," Beam said.

Zane threw himself into the task. He had to compute ammunition requirements, aircraft, weapons, classroom schedules, lesson plans, and a myriad of other details. In the midst of his endeavor, word came from Beam to report to the next fixed wing qualification course the following Monday.

"Jesus," he thought, "I'm tickled shitless to learn to fly fixed wing but now. I need help."

Zane's supervisor assigned him a lieutenant to work details while Zane was at class. When classes were over for the day, he could come in and work nights. Workdays became 18 hours or more. He saw little of his family and practically nothing of Scott. What the installation commander could not destroy by edict died of natural causes. Thus, the Fort Rucker Discotheque Society was no more.

After being graduated, Zane began teaching fixed wing aviators to adjust artillery. In addition, he continued teaching rotary wing students through simulated fire missions. While the hours were long, he found the work rewarding. Beam presented him with an Outstanding Instructor award along with an Army Commendation Medal, his first service award.

Colonel Beam telephoned at work, which was most unusual. Deputy Commanders followed the chain of command. They did not go directly to junior officers but Beam did.

"Zane, you're going to instrument school," Beam stated.

"Sir?" Zane asked.

"Did I stutter captain? You are going to instrument school. Orders will be on your desk tomorrow," Beam said sternly.

As soon as he got off the telephone with Beam, Zane exclaimed, "This is too damned much."

He immediately contacted Scott and pleaded for him and Georgia to join him and Janice at his quarters that evening.

"Dale, I can't man. I have too much on my plate. How about some other time?" Scott asked sounding tired.

"No," Zane said, "We need to talk. It's been too long."

Scott agreed with his reasoning. He needed a break and wouldn't turn down a friend.

Zane and Scott sat on Zane's carport on Galt Lane. They had a metal table between them with bourbon and ice.

"Can you believe this?" Zane asked. "Instrument school is six weeks of hell. Those guys do their best to flunk you. In addition, when you're not flying blind in an UH-1, you're inside a simulator flying instruments. Man, I am tired," Zane said.

"Well, misery loves company. I got word before coming over here that I'm going to the same class. Someone thinks you and I are joined at the hip," Scott said lifting his drink skyward.

"No shit. You're joking," Zane replied with disbelief.

"Dale, I'm not joking. There's too much going on around here," Scott said with assurance.

Immediately after Scott spoke, Janice jerked the kitchen door open and said excitedly, "Get in here. President Johnson is on the TV. It's about the Gulf of Tonkin business."

The pair scrambled indoors to join their wives. They listened intently as Johnson announced the deployment of the 1st Cavalry Division, Airmobile, to Viet Nam.

"I told you. Damn it, I told you. He had to have a reason. He's using that Gulf of Tonkin crap to send them to An Khe," Zane blurted.

Scott sat still staring at the screen as a moderator explained the news. His shoulders slumped; he barely held his drink, as he seemed to shrivel with dread.

"Oh my God, the long eared son of a bitch has gone and done it," Scott said with a deep sadness in his voice.

Zane's son, Steve, starting crying from his bedroom. Janice retrieved him and returned. She held the young boy over her shoulder gently patting his back. She hummed a nursery rhyme while looking at Zane. Her tears came and she left the room.

Fort Rucker became an aviator gristmill. Escalating combat operations required more pilots for more aviation units. Airmobility became the conflict's byword. Southeast Asia's skies filled with ever more helicopters. New airmobile divisions became realities.

The other services had their demands. Navy, Air Force, and Marine's began ever-expanding operations against an ever-increasing intent by the North Vietnamese to drape a cloak of Communist ideology over the south.

Department of the Army's Aviation assignments officer contacted Zane and Scott. He explained that the new Chinook units were taking too many losses. They need commanders with experience to lead the new CH-47s in their combat missions. Their experience with H-21s would add to their effectiveness. He was sending them to the Chinook transition course as soon as they finished instrument training. They could expect orders to Viet Nam soon afterwards.

That was almost 12 months ago. Now, here he sat at Cam Ranh Bay on a scrounging mission. Scrounging was an art without which units did not survive. The Army's supply system was in such a mess that units traded for what they needed. In the end, it worked. However, in the interim, considerable time was lost trying to cope.

"Damn, they should be here with those slings by now," Zane thought as he repositioned himself.

With the day's advance, his protective shadow from Viet Nam's tropical sun moved. Zane recalled an old phrase he had heard in school.

"Only mad dogs and Englishmen go out in the midday sun," he said aloud.

"Well, I am neither so I'm moving," he thought.

"Sir, come see what we have," he heard his flight engineer, Sergeant Randall, say.

Arriving at his aircraft's rear, he peered into its cavernous darkness. Glistening inside, he saw sparkling new, stainless steel, commercial blenders. In addition, there were sheets of tin, bags of cement, two stainless coffee urns. Mixed among the equipment were cases of various office supplies. He saw cases of magic markers, legal pads, paper clips and reams of typing paper.

"Hell sarge, you guys have been busy. You're going to make the mess and supply sergeants' happy folks with all this. Anything left to trade?" Zane asked.

"Not a bit sir. These guys in the rear have warehouses full of good stuff with no one picking it up. They'll trade for anything that they can send home and say they took off a captured VC officer," Ballard said laughing.

Continuing he asked, "Do we still get the CONEX?"

"Sure do," Zane answered. "We have to sling load it out of here so let's get it rigged."

"Right away sir," Ballard answered, as he motioned the gunners to follow him.

"It's amazing," Zane thought. "The supply NCOIC here has been bugging me for months to let him jump out of a helicopter. He's a frustrated paratrooper stuck in the rear. I could not turn down 500 cases of beer and whiskey."

Earlier they had climbed to 10,000 feet. They watched as the guy jumped out the rear. He wasn't bragging when he said he would touch down in the supply yard. They spiraled earthward watching as he fell. He waited until the last moment before pulling his ripcord but he made it. Later, he had a forklift move the CONEX to a convenient place to snatch it from the supply yard.

Ballard and his crew returned running, as they gave Zane a "thumbs up." He walked up the ramp and hit CWO Scott on his foot where he slept.

"Off your ass and on your feet. Let's get this Hook in the air," Zane said. "I'm getting short."

Zane climbed into the left seat as he arranged its "chicken plate." A chicken plate was an inch thick, ceramic plate inside a vest. Its design was to wear it as a chest protector. While both he and Chief Scott wore one on their chests, they also sat on another. They claimed something about protecting the "family jewels."

Their seats' construction included armor plating. On his left, a heavy armor plate extended forward past his left arm and torso. Scott had the same arrangement on his right.

Starting a CH-47 was a coordinated, and somewhat complex, process. In the aft pylon, there was a small, turbine powered auxiliary power unit (APU). It was necessary to start it with a powerful, nickel-cadmium battery. Once started, the APU had enough power to drive the main, twin turbine engines. These connected to the fore and aft rotor heads through a series of complex, direction changing gearboxes and shafts. It would be humanly impossible to manipulate direct control mechanisms. Therefore, hydraulic powered controls were necessary.

The CH-47 had dual systems for most everything. There were dual hydraulics, generators, instrument panels, and controls. This was a two-man flying machine. What Zane liked best about it was its stability augmentation system (SAS). Unlike the H-21s, this ship's aft blades were not always trying to overtake the front ones. The SAS was a blessing. Nevertheless, they had to demonstrate regularly that they could fly it without the SAS engaged.

As aircraft commander, Zane read the startup checklist to CWO Scott who was training to become an aircraft commander. Safety dictated that they handle the CH-47 by the book. Otherwise, they could overlook something that would kill them.

As Chief Scott worked through the startup, Zane watched his flight engineer through a rearview mirror. He stood outside the craft to monitor the blades and engines. At the same time, he peered inside for signs of trouble.

With startup completion, Zane asked. "Ballard?"

Ballard answered, "Six turning, two burning, ramp's up, clear rear and up."

Ballard connected his monkey harness to an overhead cable running the aircraft's interior length. Ballard's harness was much like that of a parachute's. Its purpose was to provide a safety line for him should they have to make unusual maneuvers which might cause him to fall from the ship's rear.

Zane said, "Clear left. I've got the beep trim."

Chief Scott applied power with a thrust lever. This handle supplied power by lifting it.

"Clear right," Chief Scott said.

"Cam Ranh Tower, Pegasus four five seven. Three six right for hover, over," Zane said over is radio.

"Cam Ranh Tower, Roger. You're cleared hover your location, over," the tower operator answered.

"Cam Ranh we have a pickup at 12 O'clock, 100 meters over," Zane continued.

"Cam Ranh, roger. Cleared for pickup, depart your discretion, heading two seven zero over," the operated said.

"Four five seven," Zane replied.

Slowly they ascended sending dirt and debris flying in every direction. At the correct altitude, Chief Scott moved the craft forward and above the CONEX. Flight engineer Ballard began calling instructions over the intercom.

Earlier Ballard propositioned a heavy duty, multi-layered, nylon ring atop the container. He gave directions until the ship's hook connected through it.

"Hooked up, pick it up," Ballard said.

"Rear clear," he continued.

Zane monitored the instrument panel for engine torque and temperature. He watched closely for any indication of an overloaded condition. Everything was in order.

"Take it out Chief," Zane said.

Chief Scott added left pedal causing the ship to rotate 180 degrees to a heading of 270 degrees. He gradually let the aircraft accelerate forward as it gained altitude. Each door gunner, in turn, said, "Clear right." "Clear left."

As they climbed, Zane saw Briscoe standing near a fence gate watching their departure.

"I wonder what the shit that guy is up to," Zane thought.

"Take us home Chief," Zane said.

Chief Scott turned to the north northwest toward Viet Nam's Central Highlands. His destination was An Khe and Charlie Company of the 228th Helicopter Battalion.

"Fifteen minute fuel check, 450 pounds," Chief Scott said.

This check allowed the monitoring of fuel to determine its use rate. It was a standard checklist item on every takeoff. With their current load, they could project their available flight time.

Remembering an old CWO's advice, Zane said, "Take her to 10,000 Chief."

During their climb, Zane had a grand view of Viet Nam's China Sea coast. It always impressed him with its beauty. Aquamarine waters against snow-white beaches lined with coconut palms gave a vision of paradise to him. However, he had to face the reality of a paradise lost. Along its shores and inland to Cambodia and Laos, humans hurled themselves together in death throes over an idea.

"It is surely a madness unique to mankind," he mused.

The Central Highlands was a grand plateau like region at South Viet Nam's midsection. As the terrain rose, they added power to maintain an altitude above ground level of 10,000 feet. At this altitude, they were clear of the VC's ability to hit them. Their AAA capability was severely limited. The best they had seen so far were some quad .51 caliber, AAA weapons. They were high above their top range.

In the last year, Zane learned considerable about how military professionals built their careers. He did not have the remotest idea that General Hollifield and Colonel Beam had an agenda while at Rucker. He soon learned that was not so. He heard about it when he met Daryl Scott in Oakland on their way back to 'Nam.

They had taken a taxi into San Francisco. Zane had heard from others that The Forbidden City Oriental restaurant was a necessity when visiting the area. He and Scott were having drinks in the bar when Scott told him what was going down.

"Would you believe this?" Scott asked. "General Hollifield is on his way to the 1st Cav as their commanding general. He's bringing Colonel Beam along as commander of the 2/20th Aerial Rocket Artillery."

"Well hell that explains his working our asses off getting them into shape. Moreover, it explains Beam's being constantly on my ass about artillery. Just one problem, I had nothing to do with ARA. All my work was with conventional artillery," Zane answered.

"Damn Zane, you still don't get it. As far as Beam is concerned, convention artillery doesn't count. He wants everything airmobile," Scott continued.

Zane raised his glass toward a waiter, indicating him to bring refills. He thought about what Scott said.

"He is dreaming. The airmobile artillery he has is the new lightweight 105-mm howitzer. He still needs heavy stuff like 155s, 175s and 8-inch mothers that can kick ass. Those tiny 2.75-inch rockets will kill many friendlies. Count on it," Zane said bitterly.

Continuing, Zane added, "You do know where his airmobile artillery is don't you? Our primary mission is moving artillery and that's his mobility. Screw the ARA."

Their waiter delivered two more drinks. Neither Zane nor Scott had eaten any dinner. The alcohol was doing its work.

"Dale, listen to this," Scott said, leaning forward and whispering. "Hollifield sent orders to pull every writer and photographer from subordinate units and attach them to his headquarters for special duty. Those guys are in those units to keep unit histories and do administrative work. Hollifield is forming his own PR agency. He wants that third star. I have this info in a letter from their headquarters company commander. How about that shit?"

Zane felt the room move and Scott became a blur as he said, "Let's eat before we're both on our butts."

The next day they reported to the processing center for overseas movement. As they entered the building there were signs stating, "All 1st Cav Personnel Follow the Red Arrows." They twisted their way through a quagmire of soldiers wandering about the building. In the distance, above the heads of a gymnasium full of people, a large sign stated, "This is it. All 1st Cav Personnel Report here."

Six NCOs sat behind a long table. Each wore a vinyl armband with a 1st Cav Patch on it. In front of each NCO, different signs indicated where officer, NCO, and enlisted personnel were to show their orders. Zane handed his orders to the NCO processing officers. He never looked at Zane but simply read the orders.

Still looking down, the NCO said, "Sir, follow the blue line for shots. Then report back here for your boarding pass."

He thrust Zane's orders at him and Zane broke, "Goddamnit sarge, look at me when you speak."

The NCO slowly raised his head, looking directly at Zane and said, "Sir, follow the blue line for shots. Then report back here for your boarding pass."

Later, Zane learned people assigned to the 1st Cav were not arriving in their units. When they got to Viet Nam, they contacted friends and had their orders changed to other units. To correct this, all personnel assigned to the 1st Cav had to travel on planes that went directly to their unit. This stopped people from changing their assignments through the buddy system.

Zane and Scott sat beside each other on their Tiger Airlines' flight. There were no alcoholic beverages served and the stewardesses looked like senior rejects from a nursing home.

"Daryl, can you believe this crap?" Zane said.

"Hey, my friend. It's mass transit. I have a feeling it is going to get worse before it gets better," Daryl said with a wide grin.

Zane had to laugh aloud. Scott joined him laughing as others watched the pair. Some of the onlookers wondered where they had their booze stashed.

After a short refueling in Anchorage, Alaska, they flew nonstop to Pleiku in Viet Nam's Central Highlands. It took considerable skill for the pilot to land a Boeing 707 on Pleiku's poor excuse for a runway. As they off loaded, Zane and Daryl stared in awe as military personnel stood beneath a forward hatch begging for milk and bread. At this point, they both knew that Daryl's forecast was going to be accurate.

"Sir, you can bunk here until the CO, Major Treadway, comes in from the field," First Sergeant Miller told Zane. "Chows at six and the CQ will get you up for breakfast."

"Damn that sounds familiar," Zane thought as he looked at his miserable surroundings. The CO had his own CP tent with a dirt floor. One piece of furniture was in the tent, a canvas, folding cot.

"First Sergeant, is the supply sergeant or supply officer available?" Zane asked.

"Yes sir," Miller answered. "It's the third general purpose (GP) tent from this one. It has a place to empty weapons in front. I'm going that way. I will show you which one."

"Thanks Top," Zane told Miller. "I'm right behind you."

"At least someone is on the ball," Zane thought. "It's smart to require people to test their weapons before they enter a supply room. It's the unloaded gun that kills most folks."

Charlie Company's supply room was typical of most. Sergeant Tenroy gathered Zane's gear. Zane encountered his first problem when he asked about weapons.

"Sir, you must take an M-16. That's the CO's requirement," Tenroy said.

"Fine, he's the boss," Zane said as he took the rifle from Tenroy. "I need a cleaning kit."

Sergeant Tenroy gathered bore cleaner, gun oil and an ample supply of patches. He put them with the rest of Zane's gear.

"Sarge, I will need a cleaning rod," Zane noted.

Tenroy immediately looked uncomfortable with the question and replied, "I do not have one to issue sir."

"Fine," Zane answered. "When will you be able to issue me one?"

Now, obviously embarrassed, Tenroy said, "Sir, I have no idea. There is one M-16 cleaning rod in the company. The guys swap it around among themselves."

Zane stood staring in disbelief. His look intimidated Tenroy who stated, "I'm sorry sir. It's like that in the entire division."

"Sarge, there are over 200 people in this unit and the CO requires everyone to have an M-16. You are telling me that I have to take a weapon that I cannot clean. That's absurd Sergeant," Zane said, as his voice became cold with indignation.

Sergeant Tenroy started to speak but Zane interrupted him by saying, "That's okay sarge. I will discuss the matter with Major Treadway. Let's get the rest of my gear."

Zane expected some sign of relief from Tenroy but he appeared more disturbed.

"Sarge, I need a 45-cal. pistol. Is that a problem?" Zane asked, lowering his voice.

"No sir, I can issue you one but I do not have any ammunition for it," Tenroy said now being quite apologetic.

"How about a .38 revolver?" Zane asked.

"Same thing sir," Tenroy replied.

"Just where do I get some ammunition?" Zane asked, now finding the situation sadly humorous.

"In the Vill, sir," Tenroy replied, almost wincing as he told Zane.

"Sarge, don't worry about me. You obviously have no choice here. There is no supply sergeant in the Army who would willingly let a situation like this develop. Let's try one more," Zane explained.

"What sir?" Tenroy asked.

"A 12 gauge pump shotgun with buckshot ammo," Zane said.

Sergeant Tenroy broke into a broad grin. He became obviously jubilant and overjoyed. He disappeared behind the tent's divider and soon returned carrying the requested weapon. He placed it on the counter along with three boxes of powerful, high-brass, 00 buckshot.

Tenroy took one step backward and asked. "How's that sir?"

"Sarge, you have made my day. I need an ammo belt and sling for the shotgun. In addition, I want another chicken plate. Is any of that a problem?" Zane asked.

"Absolutely not sir. They're coming right up. I suspect you will need a hacksaw. Right?" Tenroy asked.

"Right, let's get this barrel cut down. I will redo the stock later.

Sergeant Tenroy cut the shotgun's barrel for Zane. In addition, he related a rumor he heard about the M-16s.

"Sir, when I went through logistics training, our instructor warned us about the M-16 problem. He said that McNamara purposely did not allow a cleaning rod for every weapon. He said we could share. It was not cost effective to have that many cleaning rods," Tenroy said.

Zane returned to the CO's tent and stowed his gear. Next, he went in search of other pilots. He found none. He crossed the dirt road between Charlie Company and the battalion headquarters. The headquarters area was in much better shape than his company. There were raised walkways leading to every tent. The first one on his right had a sign showing it to be the S-1, Personnel Tent. He stepped inside.

Two clerks, Specialist Four Gilcrest, and Butterworth came to attention when he entered.

"Can we help you sir?" Butterworth asked.

"Yes, I need the correct mailing address for Charlie Company," Zane answered.

"I will write it down for you sir," Butterworth said as he reached for a pad and pen.

Handing the address to Zane, Butterworth asked. "Anything else, sir?"

Zane thought for a moment and asked. "Where are all the officers?"

"Sir, they are flying missions. There are no pilots in the area today," Butterworth explained.

"Just one more question and I will get out of your hair. Aren't you authorized a specialist for unit history and photos?" Zane asked.

"Yes we are sir but they are not onboard. They are on special duty (SD) assigned to division headquarters. We're missing two men," Butterworth explained as he looked at Gilcrest for confirmation.

Gilcrest added, "He's right sir. We are the only admin clerks remaining at battalion headquarters."

"Thanks for the address. Looks like you two have plenty to do. I'll catch you later," Zane said as he turned and left the S-1 tent.

Zane returned to Charlie Company and walked through the area. He checked inside tents and found one that had pilot's gear on cots. Most of the cots were empty and without any bedding. He removed his equipment from the CP tent and move into what was obviously a pilot's tent. At least this one had ammunition boxes for a floor. In addition, someone had foresight enough to put in a tent liner. This provided insulation from the day's heat. Once situated, he decided to visit the one place that would have people, aircraft maintenance.

A red clay road ran adjacent to his tent. Across it, he saw a three-hole outhouse, an ammunition bunker, and the end of a perforated steel plate (PSP) runway. Having worked aerial photos, Zane had an idea of where most major facilities were. For example, there was only one fixed wing runway on the base. In the distance, he saw one, lone hill standing prominently overlooking the entire area. He knew that the forces deployed initially named it Hong Cong Mountain. Adorning its side was a massive, 1st Cavalry patch.

Zane crossed the road to get a better view of the installation. From his new position, he could see the runway's entire length. To his left, alongside the runway, sandbag revetments provided some protection for parked aircraft. He recalled The First Team's, also known as The Boat People, name for the area. They were the first personnel to arrive and began clearing away jungle growth. From atop Hong Cong Mountain, thousands of personnel were using sling blades to remove undergrowth. From their view, they looked like golfers swinging clubs. The area forever bore the title "golf course."

While viewing the area, a camouflaged, C-130 transport was on approach to the PSP runway. The pilot touched down with maximum flaps extended. He landed as close as he could to the other end of the runway from Zane. Soon after touching down, the pilot reversed thrust on his four engines to slow his speed. In addition, Zane watched the craft's nose dipping as the pilot applied brakes. For a moment, it appeared that the aircraft was going to overrun the landing strip. Prudently, Zane moved across the road to be clear of the C-130. Finally, the airplane stopped but it took every inch of the runway to do it.

The first two CH-47s that Zane approached looked peculiar. As he came closer, he saw why. The ships carried heavy armament. He counted five, 50-cal. machine-guns, two 20-mm cannons, 2.75-inch rocket pods on each side and an M-40 grenade launcher beneath its nose. He had heard of these aircraft when going through CH-47 transition. They were the "Go-Go," armed; Chinooks named ACH-47s the "A" indicating attack.

He almost ran to the first one. As he walked around the ship, he gawked at its configuration. There was two, 50-cal. machine guns on either side, mounted fore and aft. On the lowered ramp, another .50 cal. pointed aft. Kneeling at the ship's rear, he looked forward. The two 20-mm cannons looked fearsome. Continuing around the craft's right side, he saw a name painted on the ACH-47's side, near its nose. The ship was "Birth Control" which brought a chuckle to Zane. Standing in front, he did a detailed examination of the grenade launcher. A pod, attached beneath the nose, had a short launch tube. The pod could move allowing the firing of the grenades in multiple directions. Near the top of its forward pylon, someone painted an insignia. There was a white human skull on a circular, blue field. Two, black, three blade rotors crowned the skull. From its darkened eye sockets and its mouth, red flames emerged indicating firing. As he completed his circuit around the ship, he stepped up the ramp to examine its interior.

Before he could get inside, a voice came from its dark interior, "That's far enough sir."

Zane heard approaching footsteps on the craft's metal floor. As the person came even with the aft, 50-cal. ports, exterior light made him readily visible. He wore fatigue trousers and boots. Bare above his waist, he wiped grease from both hands as he stopped and asked. "You looking for someone in particular sir?"

"No, I was admiring the ship," Zane answered. "I arrived in Charlie Company today and was finding my way around."

"Sorry about that sir. I am Specialist Five Gaines with only 92 days and a wakeup. Come aboard, I will show you my ship," Gaines said.

Zane immediately liked the way he said, "my ship." Pride was a major attribute of a successful, flight engineer. He followed Gaines forward. Gaines showed where armor plating protected critical flight components. Even with the extra weight, the ACH-47 still had room for extensive amounts of munitions. Gaines explained that he was finishing an intermediate inspection. Two other armed Chinooks were away on a mission. The remaining one was being flight-tested.

"Impressive Gaines," Zane said. "Pleasure meeting you. Thanks for the tour. You're a busy man so I will be on my way."

With dusk fast approaching, Zane knew where he could find pilots. There had to be officers' club somewhere in the area. He returned to the S-1 tent and asked. They sent him past their tent to a wood building on his left. He entered and the first thing seen was a slot machine next to a bar. Once fully inside, he found it empty. There were card tables, Ping-Pong tables, and magazine racks. He was sure all he had to do was wait. His wait was short.

From a room, with an entrance behind the bar, a CWO-1 entered carrying four stacked boxes. With the boxes obstructed his view, he never saw Zane. He set the boxes on the floor and stood up. When he saw Zane, he jumped and yelled, quite frightened.

"Shit captain, you scared the hell out of me," he said wiping his brow.

Zane arose and walked to the bar and said, "Hi, I am Dale Zane. I arrived in Charlie Company today."

"My pleasure," the young warrant officer said. "I'm Don Gates, your club officer. Can I get you something to drink?"

"Sure, do you have any Jim Beam?" Zane asked.

"Plenty, how do you like it?" Gates answered.

"Put some ginger ale in it with some ice," Zane instructed.

"Coming right up. So, you got here today. I am no longer the guy with the most time to go. I arrived two days ago," Gates said while preparing Zane's drink.

While Gates worked, Zane took a seat on a barstool. He watched Gates adeptly put his drink together.

"You've done that before I see," Zane commented.

"Yes I have and I made the mistake of saying so. I used to tend bar before I enlisted. After that, I went to warrant officer and flight school. Here I am in glorious Viet Nam," Gates explained.

"Where is everyone?" Zane asked.

"Well sir, they are either flying or at a fire base somewhere. The guys do not get to spend many nights at An Khe. I know that Charlie Company is at a firebase near Qui Nhon. They are operating in the Korean's sector in support of their mission. The only time someone can return here is to bring a ship in for an intermediate inspection after 25 flying hours. Maintenance knows when they are coming so they have a bird ready for them. They return to Qui Nhon. Now and then, maintenance does not have a replacement. The incoming ship's crew may get to spend the night. However, the next morning they are out of here. If it's flying you want, you will damn sure get it in the 228th," Gates told Zane.

With his drink in hand, Zane asked. "How do they get around the 100 hour limit per month?"

"That Reg. is a joke. Most guys have a 100 in less than ten days. They see the flight surgeon and he asks how they feel. If they say okay, he clears them for another 25 hours. Sir, these guys fly 16 to 18 hours a day," Gates answered.

Zane recalled a television interview with Secretary of Defense McNamara on his way to Viet Nam.

"On my way here, I saw McNamara on TV. He said that there was no shortage of pilots in Viet Nam. There was an overage of aircraft," Zane said, scoffing the report.

"That's bullshit," Gates said. "The only reason I am here is every check pilot is flying combat missions. As soon as I complete my flight checks, I will be flying missions."

"Who is the CO?" Zane asked.

"Sir, our CO is Lieutenant Colonel Delaney. He is one fine commander. He's new to Army aviation and older than most that are battalion commanders. The word is that he missed a promotion list. He had some minor problem in his past. You know how promotion boards are. What's sad is that command positions are only available for six months. Hell, a CO hardly has time to learn the ropes before headquarters transfers him to a staff job. This is a policy to get as many officers as possible command time. It sucks," Gates said in a derisive manner.

Continuing Gates asked. "What's your job sir?"

"I don't have the slightest. If someone ever shows at S1, I guess I will find out," Zane answered.

"I think I can help with that. I'm also the assistant S-1. Have you been to personnel yet?" Gates asked.

"Yes, but the two clerks didn't mention anything," Zane replied becoming curious.

Zane started to ask another question when the club's main door opened. Lieutenant Colonel Delaney entered the club as Gates immediately said, "Good evening, sir."

Zane left his barstool and stood in a relaxed attention stance as he said, "Good evening colonel, I' m Dale Zane reporting for duty."

Delaney burst into a broad grin obviously quite delighted to see Zane. He stepped in front of Zane and extended his hand that Zane immediately took.

Shaking Zane's hand, he said, "Captain Dale Zane, damned glad to see you. You flew with the 93rd TC Company in 1963."

"Yes sir. I spent six months with them TDY from Korea," Zane replied.

Delaney looked at Gates and said, "Give Zane another of what he is having and fix me my usual. Dale, come with me."

Zane followed Delaney to a nearby poker table. Delaney threw his cap on the table and took a seat. He motioned Zane to sit beside him.

"Dale we need you in Charlie Company big time. You will be a platoon commander where combat experience is priceless. Most of the First Team is back in the states training others. We're getting pilots that complete flight school; go through instrument training; and then a Chinook transition course. They have no experience and they are flying their asses off. Major Treadway needs you in the worst way. He extended his 'Nam tour for six months to get a Chinook command. They had him working in G-2 Intelligence for a year despite his Chinook training. He has some sort of special Intel experience and training. The division commander pulled him from the pipeline to us. He has had the Circle C Cowboys for three months and he's learning fast. Nevertheless, he needs someone like you. With your date of rank, you could be Company XO but I want you in a command slot," Delaney explained with excitement.

"Sir, I appreciate that. I was just talking to Gates about what my assignment might be," Dale said.

"I've assigned Captain Scott to Bravo Company as a platoon commander. He served with the 93rd at the same time you did. Right?" Delaney asked.

"That's correct sir. We came here together on the same plane," Zane related.

"It's a damned shame you two didn't come with the First Team. When the Air Cav first got here, they got the shit kicked out of them. They lost Hooks at Ia Drang Valley by flying them loaded with troops into hot LZs. That's bullshit. We cannot afford to lose a $12,000,000 helicopter with an infantry combat platoon on board. That's changed. This is for your benefit so listen. I do not care who is on your ship that ranks you. You never go into a LZ until the ground commander says that it is green. After he does that, do not make any approach until five minutes after it is declared green," Delaney stated with a forcefulness that impressed Zane.

"This is a leader," he thought.

"Sir, I am familiar with that operation. The Hooks flew in artillery at its beginning. No one in the 7th Cavalry realized they were facing a NVA force until it was too late. We learned at Ap Bac about hot LZs when we lost so many H-21s. I understand the situation," Zane said.

"Good, we need to get you up to speed. Come with me to operations. Normally, I would have Treadway do this but he's not here and I need you tomorrow. Let's go," Delaney said, almost leaping from his seat.

Zane followed close behind and gave Gates a wink as they left the club. The 228th Operations Center was a short distance from the club and underground. It had excellent overhead protection with layers of PSP, steel drums, and sandbags. As they descended, Zane felt a pleasant temperature change to coolness. After two 90 degree turns, Delaney led Zane into a room filled with chattering radios, marked maps, and people at work. He had walked right by the 228th nerve center without seeing it.

As they entered, a major sitting in front of a bank of radios arose and said, "Good evening sir. We just about have all of tomorrow's missions. Would you like to see them?"

"Sure thing Jake. This is Dale Zane he is the new Alpha Platoon Commander in Charlie Company. Zane this is Major Jake Fedders. He is our operations officer. You will be seeing a lot of him. Go ahead Jake and fill me in," Delaney directed.

"Welcome aboard Dale. Glad to have you with us," Fedders said as he set a map on an easel in front of them.

"We're spread all over the highlands sir. Charlie Company is supporting the Koreans near Qui Nhon. Bravo Company moves tomorrow to LZ English from their present position near Phu Cat Air Force Base. By the way, Captain Scott is already with Bravo. He went out on a Command and Control (C & C) Huey earlier today. Alpha Company is near Dak To close to Pleiku. They are in support of 3rd Brigade. Practically all of their sorties are artillery moves in support of Division Artillery (DIVARTY). Former commander of the 2/20th ARA, Colonel Beam, is now Brigadier General Designate Beam. He took command of DIVARTY this afternoon," Fedders explained.

"Jake, since we're in a TET cease-fire, do you have any reports of VC trying to improve their positions?" Colonel Delaney asked.

"Yes sir I do. I was going to cover that next. The Koreans have located a VC Regimental Headquarters in these hills near LZ Uplift. The place is a major tunnel complex coexisting with natural caverns," Fedders said while pointing to an area northeast of Phu Cat Air Force Base.

Continuing, Fedders defined the next days missions for Charlie Company, "Charlie Company will move two batteries of 105-mm howitzers into these infantry controlled LZs. They're our infantry not Korean. The 229th Aviation Battalion is going to lift an infantry battalion into these LZs near the caves. Once secured, Charlie Company will bring in reinforcements for the original battalion lift. We have 25 sorties on the reinforcement lift. There's a potential problem communicating with the Koreans. We have their C & C frequencies but we have no one to translate should they get too close. We have a Navy Cruiser prepping the LZs. They will fire Willie Peter (White Phosphorous) when they're through. That's when the 229th starts their insertion. When declared green plus five, that's when our Hooks go in."

Delaney stared at the map, deep in thought. He gave Zane a quick look and then turned to Fedders.

"Jake, do you have any of that poor excuse for coffee around?" He asked.

As Fedders left for coffee, Delaney asked Zane. "Do you speak any Korean?"

"Only gutter talk sir. I only spent about four months in Korea," Zane answered.

Delaney waited until Fedders returned and said, "Here's the deal. Zane you will go in with the first 229th ships as our Air Liaison Officer. Monitor those frequencies for any indications that the Koreans might decide to move into the area. We could get into a bad situation."

"Not again," Zane thought. "That was my first mission in 'Nam the last time."

"Dale, I know what you're thinking. You did this at Ap Bac. I saw the recommendation for a Distinguished Service Cross by Lieutenant Colonel Vann. You would have the award if Vann were not a burr under General Harkins saddle. I need your on-the-ground-experience," Delaney said.

"Yes sir," Zane replied.

"Just one more thing before we get you to the 229th tonight. Treadway will likely tell you this but I will also. If there's an aviation mission where the safety of the crew and aircraft are secondary, that's a Tac-E (Tactical Emergency). A Tac-E requires an order from a general officer. This unit does not accept Tac-Es unless I personally receive the order. So, don't let some staff officer, other than a general, send you on a Tac-E mission. Do you have any question about this procedure?" Delaney asked.

"Absolutely none sir," Zane answered.

"Fine, get your gear and meet me by the S-1 tent in 15 minutes. I will give you a ride to the 229th. Jake get the 229th on the Lima-Lima (land line) and tell them about Dale," Delaney ordered.

"Yes sir," Fedders replied.

At dawn the next morning, Zane sat in a Huey with his feet on its skids. He watched terrain passing beneath as they approached their LZ. Sitting next to him was Lieutenant Colonel Breedmore, Infantry Battalion Commander of the lead unit into the LZ.

"I can remember when I envied guys in these things. It's probably different if I was at the controls," he thought.

Zane felt a nudge in his side from Breedmore. Pulled from his thoughts, Zane looked in Breedmore's direction. Breedmore leaned close and shouted, "You let me know about any Korean traffic."

Zane replied by giving him an affirmative nod and a thumbs-up. From his position, Zane could see copious white smoke drifting away from an area to their front. It was a narrow opening in heavy jungle. Elephant grass looked to be about waist high that filled the LZ. Huey gunships were strafing the place furiously ahead of them. Zane prepared to jump as soon as he detected the pilot's deceleration while ending his approach. From about five feet above the ground, every passenger leaped into the tall grass.

Zane hit the ground with such force that his knees buckled causing him to fall forward. When he hit ground, he made a grunting sound.

"Perhaps that's why infantry troops are called grunts," he thought as he crawled to his knees.

He understood why the Huey pilots would not touch down. Charlie liked to place mines in potential landing zones to take out landing helicopters. In addition, it was impossible to see the ground through the tall grass. Hidden stakes could easily puncture a ship. If the stake got one man that was better than a helicopter full.

From Zane's position, his head barely cleared the elephant grass. He looked for Breedmore and saw him walking east standing upright. Remaining low, Zane ran toward the tree line. As he ran, he heard the familiar whine of bullets cutting through the grass. He saw stalks falling around him so he fell face forward and crawled to the trees.

In every direction, he began hearing calls of "Medic." They were taking casualties but he could not locate the firing's source. He sought refuge behind a massive anthill near the trees and listened. There was considerable noise from the LZ, from helicopters, and some small arms fire. He turned his radio on and listened. There was no Korean radio traffic. He immediately changed to Breedmore's C & C frequency. He was amazed at the lack of radio discipline. Every now and then, he heard Breedmore trying to make others not use his frequency. He failed.

Next, he heard a thump sound and said aloud, "Shit, mortars."

The landing rounds were far away and their noise weak. Another sound drew his attention. From inside the trees, he heard mortar shells fired. Seconds later, he heard the shell hit on the other side of the LZ. Realizing that he was close to the firing mortar, he dropped his gear except his shotgun. Remaining low, he used the tall grass to hide his movements. He moved from anthill to anthill. They were mostly three feet tall and had a large base. It was enough to conceal his position. As he moved, he heard mortar shells sliding down their launcher and then the propellant ignite with a "whump" noise. They were close.

Looking around an anthill's base, he saw three VC manning a mortar. They were in a spider hole, a small pit with a camouflaged cover. One guerilla dropped shells into the launcher while another made adjustments. The third VC was receiving firing instructions on a radio. Zane realized he had to get the radio operator first. Inching his 12 gauge forward, he got it into a firing position. However, he could not pump in a new shell after firing the first one. He would have to rise to a kneeling position.

They never saw it coming. Zane took the radio operator down and wounded the gunner with his first shot. He quickly fired twice more and saw the others fall as he took a prone position behind the anthill and waited. No one shot at him for ten minutes so he moved back to his gear.

He checked his radio and heard Breedmore declare the LZ green.

"It's too damned soon. There's too much automatic weapons fire," he thought. "I've got to find him."

Breedmore answered Zane's call and gave his position using a shackle code. Shackle codes were nothing more than substitution of letters and numbers for other letters and numbers. They changed daily and were meaningless to the VC unless they had the key sheet for that day.

Breedmore never saw Zane until he tugged his trousers. Breedmore looked down to see Zane at his feet.

"Sir, get down," Zane said as Breedmore ignored him.

Finally, Zane gave Breedmore a two-handed blow to the back of his knees. Immediately, Breedmore fell to the ground land on his knees.

"Captain, you want your ass court martialled," Breedmore yelled.

"Sir, you won't be around to press charges. It's too early to bring in the Hooks," Zane yelled into his ear.

Breedmore gave Zane a dumbfounded stare and said, "Bullshit, I need reinforcements."

Zane explained about the mortar crew. He told Breedmore that the VC were in an "L" formation with the "L's" stem parallel to the LZ. The "L's" base ran across the LZ exit route.

"Sir, that was part of a VC weapons company with the mortar. You can bet there are another three VC infantry companies in the area. They are waiting on the Hooks, sir," Zane explained.

"Damn Zane that's why I need reinforcements," Breedmore replied appearing frustrated with the situation.

"Just a minute sir," Zane said as he changed radio frequencies.

"Cobra Six, this is Cowboy Six Alpha, over," Zane said into his handset.

"Cowboy Six Alpha this is Cobra Six, over," the gunship commander answered.

"Roger, Victor Charlies, I shackle Alpha Alpha Tango Xray to Zulu Tango November Lima, 200 yards my red smoke, over," Zane said giving map coordinates of the VC's main line.

Reaching onto his chest, Zane removed a red smoke grenade. As he was about to pull its pin, heavy automatic weapons fire cut through the elephant grass. Breedmore, who had got to his feet, fell beside Zane with a low moan and a sigh. Zane threw the armed grenade as far as he could east of his position and turned to Breedmore.

A light, bloody foam was at the corners of his mouth. He stared skyward with a glazed stare. Zane saw blood soaking through the front of Breedmore's shirt. Ripping it open, Zane saw a small purple bruise with some blood around it but not much. First making sure Breedmore could breath, Zane rolled him over and saw an every widening blood stain. Cutting the shirt open, he found what appeared to be an exit wound. He could hear air sucking through the opening.

"Shit, a sucking chest wound," Zane thought as he tore open a bandage from his belt.

Ripping apart a cigarette package, Zane removed the metallic insert and placed it over the hole. Next, he put the cellophane wrapping over it. He placed the bandage's large center section over these and stretched the gauze-like, bandage ends around Breedmore's chest.

Pulling the bandage tight, he yelled, "Medic."

Zane updated the unit's executive officer that now commanded the unit, while gunships attacked the main VC position. The automatic weapon's fire stopped. After 30 minutes, the new CO declared the LZ green. Zane agreed and called the Hooks in five minutes later.

With reinforcements, the infantry cleared the area to the LZ's East. Zane's job over, he ran to the last CH-47 bringing in troops and climbed aboard. He took his steel helmet, put it on the seat's nylon webbing, and promptly sat on it.

"Got to keep the family jewels protected," he thought, as he leaned against the Hook's side exhausted.

Within 15 minutes, Zane's hands began to tremble and a clammy perspiration covered his forehead. He sat forward to place his head between his knees to fight oncoming nausea. He felt a hand on his shoulder and looked up to see the ship's flight engineer.

Leaning down to yell in Zane's ear, he asked. "Are you okay captain? We will be at Qui Nhon in a few minutes."

Zane nodded that he was and smiled. The flight engineer gave him a thumb up and returned to checking the aircraft's interior parts for leaks.

Qui Nhon is a large city on South Viet Nam's Southeast Coast. Charlie Company's base camp was slightly north-northwest and in the countryside. Zane walked down the Hook's ramp and immediately saw a sea of red mud. Remaining on the ramp, he looked for walkways through the mud. There were none.

"Well shit," he said and stepped into the red goo, sinking to his ankles.

He saw tents grouped along some barbed wire strands and began walking in their direction. Zane had not eaten in two days and his stomach began protesting. He saw the mess tent. As he approached, he noted that someone had the sense to raise the tent walls to allow ventilation. As he entered the mess tent, the mess sergeant saw him and brought a steaming cup of coffee.

"Welcome aboard sir. I'm Sergeant Alverez Charlie Company's Mess Sergeant. We've been expecting you. Chows at Noon and coffee's on anytime," Alverez said as he handed the cup to Zane.

"Thank you sarge, I appreciate this coffee. By the way, where is your headcounter? I need to pay up for lunch," Zane explained.

"Not in the Cav sir. We have a headcounter but we do not collect money for meals. That comes out of your pay each month. You don't pay as long as you eat in a Cav Mess Hall," Alverez told Zane.

"That makes sense," Zane replied as he stumbled toward a table.

Within a few minutes, a stream of pilots and crew began gathering in the tent. The pilots were a friendly group and everyone stopped to introduce themselves. While he was eating, Major Treadway arrived in a C & C Huey. He spotted Zane and headed in his direction. Everyone seated at his table arose at his approach.

Treadway said, "At ease, carry on," as he came to Zane.

Treadway welcomed him warmly. Zane now knew why the others were friendly and hospitable. They obviously reflected their commander's values. It was easy to tell when a unit had an asshole commander. Unit members were always sullen and irritated. Zane liked Treadway immediately.

"Colonel Delaney told me this morning where you were. That's a bitch the first day in a unit. Glad to see you made it okay. Hook drivers are hard to find," Treadway said.

Continuing, Treadway asked. "By the way, what happened this morning? Our Hooks got a green and then an abort. They circled for 30 minutes waiting to bring in their troops."

"Sir, the LZ was too hot. Charlie had an ambush waiting. Some trigger happy VC gave it away by firing too soon. Also, they started using a mortar that is only found in VC weapon companies. The Huey gunships took care of the situation," Zane answered.

The mess sergeant brought Treadway a food tray and refilled Zane's coffee. Treadway explained that he and Colonel Delaney just left the LZ.

Pointing at Zane's 12 gauge, Treadway said, "Someone with one of those blew away a mortar crew. The battalion XO told me that none of his men carried shotguns. Did you take those guys out?"

"Yes sir. That's how I knew they had a weapon's company in there. That mortar was too big for a smaller force," Zane answered.

"The infantry XO is putting you in for a Combat Infantryman's Badge. There are not many artillerymen or aviators with one of those. Sounds like you did a fine job up there," Treadway said while he ate. "Also, one of our guys found your flight gear at An Khe. They will bring it this afternoon. I want your local checkout over with today. You will be on tonight's mission board. It's only the fifth of the month and some of our pilots are close to 100 hours. I hope you like flying because you are going to get plenty."

"That's fine with me sir. I'm not a grunt," Zane replied. "Sir, I need you help with something. The supply sergeant said that you require that I have an M-16. He also said that there was only one cleaning rod in the company. I've lugged that M-16 with me all day and it is useless. It is so dirty that it won't safely fire. If I did not have the shotgun, I would be defenseless. Is the supply sergeant pulling my leg?"

Treadway put his eating utensils beside his tray, as he looked straight ahead. He slowly wiped his lips with a napkin. Zane placed him in an embarrassing situation with others present who could hear his response.

Turning slowly to Zane, he said, "Captain, the sergeant is not pulling your leg. The infantry units have priority. We are lucky to have the one rod. There are infantry platoons with only two or three cleaning rods. I'm sure you know the M-16's reputation for jamming unless maintained properly. When rods become available, every person with an M-16 will receive one. Improvise captain; I'm sure you can rig a substitute."

"I certainly can sir. When I was a kid, I used a piece of string with a weight on one end and a rag on the other. Simply pull the rag through to clean the bore. However, this does not get powder deposits like a wire brush. But sir, I don't care how clean the weapons are; they are not much use if I do not have ammunition." Zane said.

Before Treadway could respond, Zane said quietly with a firm resolve, "Sergeant Tenroy said for me to buy it in the Vill. I know about the Black Market. Give me four men and I will go to the Vill and confiscate all government property in view. If they have government ammunition and are selling it, that's illegal and I have a duty to take that ammunition away from them sir."

Treadway's cheeks began turning red as he replied, "Zane, this is my final say on this matter. General Hollifield is a staunch supporter of the 'Hearts and Minds' philosophy. We must gain the spiritual and mental support of the Vietnamese if we expect to win this war. What you propose is the legal thing to do. Yet, it is not the right thing to do. It will only cause trouble and turn the village people against us and we need their support. Stay out of the Vill. Now, go get your checkout."

It was dark when Zane returned from his local area checkout with CW4 Elliot, Charlie Company's most experienced aviator. The check flight was a trip to An Khe and return. As they left the coastal plain, they climbed toward An Khe Pass. This was a low point between mountains leading onto the Central Highland's area. Elliot explained how many ships had crashed in the pass trying to fly through heavy fog and clouds. An Khe had Ground Controlled Radar and a directional beacon. It was a cinch to climb under radar control and then descend to Ah Khe. Unfortunately, light observation and Huey pilots did not have instrument qualifications. Flying into weather meant a pilot would experience vertigo within 60 seconds if he were not instrument qualified. The result was a crash.

Elliot made the two-hour flight a tough one. He required completion of every emergency procedure. They did autorotations at An Khe and instrument landings back at Qui Nhon.

"Captain I recommend you visit operations the next time you are at An Khe. Study the flight records of every pilot in your platoon. Know their strong and weak points. This will serve you well when you begin assigning missions," Chief Elliot explained.

Stumbling into his tent at Qui Nhon after dinner, he found his other gear on an empty bunk. None of those present said who had brought it. Nevertheless, Zane was glad to see it. He needed his entrenching tool. Surrounding the tent, there were sandbags stacked four high. This provided little protection. Also, the perimeter was only a few feet from the tent. Along it, someone had placed one skimpy strand of barbed wire. What protection they had, was what they provided. There were no infantry units available for security.

Beside his cot, next to the sandbags, Zane began digging. Soon others in the tent displayed an interest. Some gathered to watch. Before long, Zane had a hole four feet wide and four feet long. He continued digging, hurling mud outside over the sandbags. He heard the others wondering among themselves what he was doing. With his pit now chest high, he stopped for a smoke break and some water. Covered with mud, he sat on the edge of his cot.

One of the bystanders, First Lieutenant Melvin Whitaker, asked. "Captain, what are you doing?"

"I'm digging a hole. What else?" Zane replied.

With a gesture of frustration, Whitaker continued, "Sir, you know what I meant."

"I am digging a foxhole. This tent is within hand grenade range of that flimsy wire. If attacked, I can roll from my bunk into the foxhole. Pretty much standard procedure in a combat zone," Zane answered.

Putting out his cigarette, Zane climbed into his pit and began shoveling. When he was deep enough that the rim was above his head, he constructed a standing step from wooden ammo boxes around its bottom. When he wanted to look out or return fire, he could step onto the boxes. This also kept his feet above water standing in the bottom. In addition, he provided boxes on one side to climb from the hole. Satisfied, he climbed from his pit.

To provide a clean place for his feet, he dug in three ammo boxes parallel to his cot. He could keep his boots dry by setting them on it. Looking around him, he saw the others digging pits. With a chuckle, he grabbed a towel and headed for the shower.

The first mortar rounds struck while he was standing nude in the middle of a mud field.

Chapter Thirty Eight

March 1968

The general who advances without coveting fame and retreats without fearing disgrace, whose only thought is to protect his country and do good service for his sovereign, is the jewel of the kingdom.
Sun Tzu (6th–5th century BC), Chinese general. *The Art of War,* ch. 10, axiom 24

"Chief, if I had as much time to do in 'Nam as you, I would slash my wrists," Zane said over the intercom to CWO Scott.

Pressing his intercom button, Chief Scott answered quickly, "OK, Aircraft Commander captain and revered leader, you get us into An Khe."

Zane immediately grabbed the controls as Chief Scott threw both hands above his head with palms skyward as if worshiping some deity.

"Damn Chief, when we get back I hope your mother runs out from under the mess hall and bites you on your leg," Zane said, his voice filled with merriment.

They were approaching An Khe Pass with a load of scrounged goods from Cam Ranh Bay. What they had aboard was priceless to a unit like the 1st Cav. By design, their unit lacked many of those things that other units took for granted. Ground transportation was not a consideration when organizing their unit. Zane had not traveled in a ground vehicle in almost a year. The CO had a jeep and that was the sum total of their unit's ground vehicles. The Cav was an airmobile unit with significant emphasis on airmobile. Nevertheless, that did not mean that they intended to live like animals. If they could lay their hands on useful gear, they either purchased it by trade or were not above making "midnight requisitions" to get it.

With dark fast approaching, they saw An Khe Pass ahead. Its border mountains flanked a narrow passage that was the demise of numerous aviators. However, Zane had an advantage. The CH-47 had dual instrumentation of those instruments required for flight without visual reference to a horizon. Aircraft lost in the pass most often was the result of a pilot trying to slip through without being able to fly on instruments.

Zane made the transition to instruments. From this point forward, he would ignore any outside visual references. In addition, he would ignore any body sensations suggesting that he was doing any maneuver. He believed what the instruments told him about his ship. To do otherwise invited disaster.

"Chief, get me Hong Cong GCA," Zane said.

"Roger, Chief Scott," answered.

From this point forward, they were professionals. Their procedures almost required perfection. Horseplay ended when Zane started flying on instruments.

Chief Scott tuned the ship's radios to the proper frequency and said to Zane, "You're up sir."

"Hong Cong GCA this is Pegasus Four Five Seven, An Khe Pass, Ten Thousand request GCA over," Zane said through his headset.

"Roger Pegasus Four Five Seven, turn right, heading three one five, maintain ten thousand over," An Khe's ground control radar operator answered.

"Four Five Seven, roger," Zane responded.

Zane began a turn to his right to the required heading. As he rolled his ship level on the correct heading, he transmitted, "Hong Cong GCA, Four Five Seven, heading three one five, over."

"Roger Four Five Seven, radar contact. Turn left heading two seven zero descend and maintain five thousand, over," the radar operator instructed.

The ability to operate the CH-47 throughout the 1st Cav's Area of Operations (AO) during adverse weather gave them a tactical advantage. In bad weather, their helicopter could fly with a minimum ceiling of 300 feet and one quarter mile visibility without needing instruments. However, with GCA's available, their ships were able to fly through inclement weather and deliver vital supplies to units. At the time, helicopter school graduates were not qualified to fly on instruments. Most pilots in the Cav could not get through because their crews were not instrument trained. To fly a CH-47 required an instrument-qualified team in the cockpit. Thus, the Hooks played a vital role delivering vital supplies when no other craft could.

"Four Five Seven, Hong Cong GCA we have a C-130 inbound with wounded. Hold over the outer marker, standard right turn, maintain five thousand, over," the GCA operator advised Zane.

"Four Five Seven, roger," Zane replied.

After Zane received an electronic indication that he had crossed a point on the ground, he began a right turn to a heading 180 degrees opposite his inbound heading. Once on the new heading, he would fly for one minute and then initiate a right turn to his original heading. This resulted in a race track pattern at specific altitude. The GCA operator could now bring in the C-130 ahead of Zane's ship.

"Hey Chief, join the fun. Take her for a while. I've got the radios," Zane told Chief Scott.

"I have the aircraft," Scott replied.

This was Zane's signal to get off the controls. He immediately raised both hands to show that he was clear. From this point, his responsibilities were to be ready to take the ship if Chief Scott developed vertigo; monitor all instruments; and, respond to requests from Chief Scott.

Zane enjoyed flying with Scott. While he recently made CWO 2, he had maturity beyond his years. Moreover, he was a superb pilot. He had a sensitive control touch that was the envy of many.

He remembered when he first met the man. Zane jumped into a pit nude to find Chief Scott in his foxhole. Zane became particularly upset because he just completed his shower. He was on the way to his tent when mortar rounds began landing in their area. He ran across the open field; jumped the tent's sandbags; and grabbed his shotgun as he plunged feet first into his new foxhole.

"What the hell are you doing in here," Zane screamed above the sound of exploding mortar shells. "I didn't build this for two."

"I'm just visiting," Chief Scott said. "Don't be so damned stingy."

Illuminating flares floated earthward, providing enough visibility to see beyond the barbed wire outside their tent. Zane could see that Chief Scott had a mud coated M-16 in his hands.

"What do you intend to do with that?" Zane asked, while nodding toward the weapon.

"I can use it as a damned club. There's no ammo for it," he answered, obviously frustrated.

The pair watched the wire less than 30 yards in front of them. Looking around the tent, Zane saw others in newly dug foxholes while some hid behind sandbags. As best he could determine, Zane was the only person with a useful weapon with one problem. Its range was limited. To hit a target, it had to be close. In these circumstances, they would be through the wire before he could shoot.

From outside the wire, they heard screams in English yelling, "Don't shoot damn it. Don't shoot, we're coming in."

From the darkness, two soldiers emerged running at full speed while holding their helmets on. They jumped the wire with ease and Zane raised his shotgun.

"Don't fire. They are our guys," Chief Scott said as he pressed Zane's shotgun barrel toward the ground.

"What the hell were they doing out there?" Zane screamed.

"They volunteered to man listening posts to warn us of a ground attack," Chief Scott explained.

As suddenly as it started, the incoming mortar rounds stopped. In the distance, they could see tracers from automatic weapons flaring through the night. The green tracers Zane knew were VC. The red ones he figured to be U.S. troops firing. Mixed with the automatic weapons firing, they heard numerous grenades explode.

From outside their perimeter, they heard someone yell, "Anh yah hass sayo. Anh yah hass sayo."

"Screw me, they're Koreans. Anh yah hass sayo," Zane yelled in return.

"If any of you jerkoffs have ammo, don't shoot. They're Koreans," Zane yelled loud to assure the others heard him.

Nine Korean soldiers appeared within a circle of light from an overhead flare. They waved and disappeared from view.

"Cam saam nee da," Zane yelled three times.

"What the hell was that about?" Chief Scott asked.

"They were yelling, 'Hello.' I told them 'Thank you or you are welcome. I'm not sure which,'" Zane explained.

Zane climbed from his muddy pit covered from head to foot with red clay. The others seeing this did the same. Finally, they noticed that he was nude and began laughing.

"Laugh you dumb shits. I'm the only man in this tent with two guns that work. Those Koreans just saved your impotent asses," Zane yelled as he grabbed a clean towel and headed toward the shower.

The laughing stopped immediately as they looked at each other. They knew that death had come to call and they owed their lives to the Koreans. They were not able to defend themselves.

During the night, Zane heard a CH-47 takeoff. It returned before dawn. When Zane went to breakfast, Major Treadway stood beside stacked cases of ammunition of various sizes. In addition, he had ten cleaning rods. As Zane approached, he handed Zane a bandoleer of M-16 ammunition and a cleaning rod.

"Zane, we got the ammo. I'm sorry about the cleaning rods. I have enough for five in each platoon. You can pickup another four after chow," Treadway said as if nothing unusual had taken place.

"Division ship come in?" Zane asked.

"Let's say there was an ample supply found among indigenous personnel," Treadway responded.

As Zane walked away, he thought, "I knew I liked this guy. He's not too damned proud that he won't listen. He's going to be a fine leader."

Zane laughed to himself as he recalled the event. Their GCA approach put his mind on the business at hand.

"Four Five Seven, Hong Kong GCA, over," their ship's controller transmitted.

"Four Five Seven, over," Zane answered.

"Four Five Seven continue right turn to two seven zero degrees. Descend to two thousand and five hundred, over," An Khe's GCA instructed.

"Four Five Seven, roger," Zane replied.

Chief Scott continued his aircraft's turn to the correct heading and continued a 500-foot per minute descent to the directed altitude. Zane reported reaching their assigned altitude. Next, their original controller transferred control to a final controller who gave precise instructions as to heading and position on a glide slope angle. He requested they report when the runway was in sight. Zane saw four dim lights directly ahead and reported them. They received instructions to take over visually and complete their landing.

"I've got the lights Chief," Zane said.

Zane directed powerful search lights so that Chief Scott could locate the closest open revetment to park their helicopter. They shutdown and completed entries in the ship's log book.

"Chief, if you will get the post flight, I will go by Ops and turn in our mission data. I will also drop by supply and let them know about our goodies. They will scrounge a truck from maintenance and pick them up tonight. They will need this ship tomorrow I am sure. The maintenance people will complete the intermediate inspection tonight," Zane said.

Lying in his bunk that night, Zane used a blanket. The Central Highlands became quite cold during the monsoon season. He listened to Charlie Company's pet singing its song. He recalled the first time he heard it and insisted that someone had a hidden tape player near his tent. With one week to go, he had the pleasure of conning new guys for almost 12 months with their pet.

No one had a name for their tree lizard. Its home was a hollow place in a large tree in their company area. At night, it would emerge and begin prepping for its nocturnal melody. The reptile inhaled vast quantities of air, swelling a pouch beneath its head. As it ballooned outwards, the lizard made a sound like, "Dega, dega, dega." With its air sack filled, it exhaled making a clear and distinct sound. It said, "Fuck you, fuck you, fuck you." Zane once counted 17 iterations of this phrase.

The lizard's sound was so distinct that the pastor of a nearby chapel complained to their company commander about the Circle C Cowboy's pet. Their CO explained that the lizard was making a natural sound bestowed upon it by nature. It was neither good nor evil. Any such perception was in the mind of the person hearing the song. The chaplain left talking to himself about hellfire and damnation in Charlie Company.

"Damn, that was centuries in the past it seemed," Zane thought. "That's when we lived in tents and walked through mud ankle deep everywhere we went until CW4 Dennis Yates arrived."

CWO Yates was an engineer before he became an aviator for the Army. He was appalled at our living conditions and insisted we change them.

"You are a sorry ass bunch," he said. "There are enough materials lying around this place to build a city. It makes no sense to keep living like this."

Tired of his bitching, someone challenged him by saying, "If it is so damned bad you tell us what we can do about it."

That was music to Yate's ears. He spent every spare moment he had drawing plans. When he finished, he gave copies to the two platoon commanders.

"You are the leaders of this route step, sorry ass outfit. I've prepared the plans and I will supervise construction. You two must get the materials. I have some contacts," Yates explained.

His drawings showed a complete rebuild of the unit area. There would not be a tent remaining. He designed long buildings with apartment like cubicles for two men each. The walls were six-inch thick, steel reinforced cement and the roof was tin. He had cement walkways through the area with recreation rooms, showers, and other amenities.

"Chief, where are we going to get the stuff to build all this," Zane asked.

"Easy," Yates said with confidence. "You guys haul hundreds of tons of empty ammo boxes back here every day. The artillery shell boxes have a steel rod in each of them. Instead of taking those boxes to the dump, drop them in the company area. We can use the wood for formers, doors, rafters and more. We will put the steel rods in the walls for strength. We can start as soon as you guys get the stuff here."

"Where's the cement coming from?" Captain Hamilton, Bravo Platoon Leader asked.

"There is a Special Forces camp in the Valley East of here. They can get all the cement they want but they do not have anything to haul it. We have CH-47s that can carry 10,000-pound loads. Special Forces will order the cement. We will pick it up and deliver. Every other load comes to us," Yates explained, as he became more excited about the project.

Continuing he said, "You guys can think of more reasons for not doing something than anyone I've ever met. How about thinking of reasons to do things instead? I will supervise this project and provide material lists. You guys get it and I will rebuild this place."

Deadhead flights ended that night. Anytime a Charlie Company ship delivered something, it never returned empty. Chief Yates had them go by a particular place and scrounge supplies. Soon Charlie Company had hundreds of cement bags and ammo boxes hidden beneath tarpaulins. Chief Yates talked an artillery unit out of a broken aiming circle. This was a device, similar to a surveyor's transit that measured angles. He repaired and used it to align foundation slabs for their new buildings. With the foundation formers in place, they were ready to pour cement. However, a simple wheelbarrow would not work because it was too small. The unit needed a cement mixer and this was the genesis of the "Great Phu Cat Raid."

"I saw a motor pool full of cement mixers over at Phu Cat Air Force Base," Captain Hamilton said.

"I don't doubt," Yates answered. "You know how the Air Force operates with its money. They budget to build an airfield and state their cost way below what it really will cost. They use their money to build comfortable, air conditioned quarters and officers' clubs. By this time, they only have half of their required runway completed. They apply for an additional appropriation because they know that they will get the money. They cannot takeoff and land without a runway," Zane told Hamilton.

Continuing Zane asked. "When is the next dark of the moon?"

Hamilton checked with battalion operations and found it to be in one week at 02:00 hours. He told Zane.

"I will carry my camera on every mission and you do the same. Get as many photos as you can in the next few days," Zane said. "I will get with maintenance and see which bird will be coming out of its 100 hour inspection. We want one that is not out on an operational mission," Zane explained. "It is essential that the maintenance officer be in on this."

At 01:00 hours, a CH-47 with all exterior markings taped, took off for a 45-minute flight to Phu Cat Air Force Base. At Phu Cat, the Air Force Engineers, known as Red Horse, were asleep in their posh quarters. The next morning they went to their motor pool to start work. Their ten feet high, 8,000 pound commercial cement mixer was missing. They never found it.

Meanwhile, the same morning, Charlie Company's CO walked from his tent and saw a ten-foot high tarpaulin covered object sitting in his company area. He walked around the huge, hidden item amazed at its size.

He lifted a corner of the tarpaulin and looked inside. He screamed, "Zane, you and Hamilton get your asses out here this minute. You are going to have me in Fort Leavenworth Prison."

By the time Bravo and Alpha companies finished their building projects, the shell of a worn out cement mixer found its way to the bottom of the South China Sea. No one at Phu Cat ever knew what happened to their mixer. They could have cared less. They had a new one in less than a week. The Air Force had money to do things like that.

In February 1967, Charlie Company's CO held a briefing for Operation Pershing. He gathered his platoon commanders and senior maintenance personnel.

He began by saying, "Gentlemen, starting tomorrow the 1st Cav is going to do something it has never done before. General Hollifield is going to mount a three-brigade attack on the Bong Son Plain in northern Binh Dinh Province. One Hook Company is already at LZ English. We will join them tomorrow. We are finally going to clean out An Lo Valley."

An Lo Valley was an NVA and VC stronghold. On all tactical maps, it had red hash marks across it showing it to be a No Fly Zone. Ships, straying into the An Lo, always drew heavy AAA fire.

As their operational briefing was in progress, Lieutenant Colonel Delaney entered their operations bunker. Their company CO called everyone to attention.

"At ease, gentlemen. Carry on," he said.

It was rare for Delaney to attend a company briefing. He left that to his company commanders. However, there he was.

Major Treadway pointed to his map display and said, "LZ English is on the coast south southeast of the An Lo. North of English, the terrain is coastal. To the immediate west, the terrain rises rapidly to a mesa covered with elephant grass. Farther west, this mesa descends into An Lo Valley. The An Lo is wide at its base and narrows rapidly to the north."

Treadway placed an overlay on his map showing a racetrack like drawing. The long, east side of the track went due north along the coast. Once past the apex of An Lo Valley, the track made a turn and traveled south directly over the An Lo. Once this track portion left the valley to the south, it made another turn and resumed its original course north.

Treadway, pointing to the race track pattern, said, "Tomorrow every aircraft in the 1st Cav will fly in formation. That is more than 400 ships. Their original course will be up the coast. After that, they will follow the overlay on the map. As the ships fly north, they are not visible to NVA or VC in the An Lo. The south leg of the pattern puts all aircraft in full view. However, after making the turn south of the valley, back to the original course, they are no longer visible. Every aircraft will fly this pattern repeatedly. To the enemy, it will appear that we have thousands upon thousands of ships. Any questions so far?"

CWO Wellford arose from his seat and asked. "Sir, that's a no fly zone. What's to keep them from wasting our aircraft?"

"Good question, Chief. The enemy in the An Lo, in the past, has only fired at one or two aircraft. Intel is certain that they will not dare fire at the number of aircraft coming down the valley. We're hoping they will be scared shitless."

Major Treadway pointed to a military symbol for Bravo Company and explained, "Your sister company has spent today moving artillery onto the plateau above the An Lo. The artillery will be able to place heavy fire upon every inch of the valley. There are some special plans for them that I will explain later."

"During the formation flying," Treadway continued. "Psych Ops will be dropping Chu Hoi passes up and down the valley's length. These special passes tell the enemy that they have 24 hours to leave the valley. If they come to the south end, we will buy their weapons and ammunition. In addition, they will receive hot food and will not go into a POW camp but will move onto land that will be theirs. Mixed with the passes, there will be playing cards. On one side of the card, there is the ace of spades. The Vietnamese are superstitious and consider the ace of spades a bad omen. Many of them consider it a death card. On the other side of the card, there will be a human skull. Around this skull will be the words 'The Blue Eyed Corpse Makers Are Coming.'"

Mumbling and comments moved through the assembled soldiers. Major Treadway told them to be at ease.

Treadway continued, "As I speak, there is an armored brigade moving into position across the valley's base. They will seal it so that nothing can pass to the south. Twenty-four hours after our flyby, artillery will begin firing into the valley's northern apex. We will have 105, 155, 175 and 8-inch artillery pounding the northern escape routes. The Air Force is going to carpet bomb the valley from north to south. Once they finish, the armored unit will start moving north. They are to destroy any living creature in the An Lo. We will have our gunships and Air Force air strikes constantly bomb in front of the armor as it advances. Gentlemen, we will clear that damned valley of every NVA or VC in it."

Colonel Delaney arose and asked. "Major, may I say a few words?"

"Certainly sir," Treadway answered.

"Gentlemen," Delaney began, "General Hollifield told me that this mission will not succeed without our Hooks. To sustain this operation with ammunition, fuel, food, medical supplies and aircraft recovery depends solely upon you. The artillery alone will expend hundreds of thousand of rounds. That many aircraft will burn millions of gallons of JP4 fuel. The only way to get it there is with your Hooks. Let's make ourselves proud tomorrow."

Zane remained seated as the others jumped and cheered. He watched young warrant officers, not yet 20, cheering that they were flying to their possible deaths. Zane would go and he would lead his men well to save their lives. However, he found no happiness knowing what may happen. He had not forgotten CWO Welsh dying in his arms. He never wanted that to happen again.

The next day, as Zane watched, hundreds of helicopters departed An Khe traveling northeast toward LZ English. He had his flight platoon flying a formation of "Vs." Seldom did CH-47s fly formation and Zane admitted to himself that he had goose bumps as they joined the other ships at arranged rendezvous points.

"I'll give General Hollifield credit," he thought. "He has a flare for the magnificent. This would likely be the only time that a full airmobile division would fly formation. Those who lived would never forget the sight."

The flyby lasted one hour. Zane could not imagine what went through the enemy's minds as they watched aircraft overhead for an hour. Twenty-four hours later, the attack began. The An Lo became a charnel house. Firepower devastated the place. Artillery closed the valley with exploding steel on the north. B-52s carpet-bombed the place into one large cultivated field as if being preparing for planting. Tanks rolled up the valley destroying every structure. The Go-Go ACH-47 pilots told of seeing cave openings on hillsides like cutting through an anthill and watching ants squirm from within. They had a free fire clearance. NVA, and VC alike, stumbled around in shock bleeding from their ears and noses. It was a turkey shoot.

Hollifield made the front page of the "Stars and Stripes." The article told how a projectile hit his C & C Huey, missing his head by six-inches. Division's PR team had a field day writing articles and taking photos.

Hook pilots ate meals in flight. Flight engineers would pass a can of concentrated grease mixed with beans and ham into the cockpit. One pilot gulped it down while the other flew. Their ships flew hundreds of sorties to artillery units on the plateau overlooking the An Lo. Their day was a round robin of aircraft recovery as UH-1s and OH-13s succumbed to ground fire. They took their hits going to and coming from the valley. AAA fire did not exist in the An Lo.

After the initial attack, Cav units settled in for a sustained fight on the Bong Son plain. LZ English was too small to allow many Hooks to remain over nigh (RON). This meant a few hours sleep on a cot. The company that was the RON unit slept on the ground in mud and rain. When they first arrived at the cramped base, there was one large tent next to a 175-mm artillery battery. It had a floor made from ammo boxes and there were folding cots. Flight crews collapsed onto the cots fully clothed for they were on emergency standby. Every time the artillery fired, dirt flew from the floor three feet into the air. It fell into a sleeping person's hair and ears. The artillery weapons were so close that tent sides sucked in and then flew horizontal from muzzle blasts.

Zane would never forget one of General Hollifield's visits. He saw the folding cots and asked who used them. When he was told that CH-47 crews did, he ordered them removed and said, "The infantry does not sleep on cots so no one will sleep on cots."

After receiving permission from his CO, Zane went to the Division Safety Officer. He was Lieutenant Colonel Lionel Kingsley and an acquaintance from Fort Rucker.

"Sir, my men fly a 12 million dollar aircraft. They frequently have entire infantry platoons on board after only a few hours sleep. Pilots have to take naps while on missions and in flight. We're going to have a major accident," Zane explained. "If the general won't let us use cots, we can sleep in the ships."

Kingsley saw the division commander and brought his reply, "They cannot sleep in the hooks and they cannot sleep under them. The Hooks are a prime target. They could get killed sleeping in them."

Zane gave up in disgust and joined his friend Daryl Scott. They dug a foxhole, put their shelter halves together, and slept standing up in a pit.

For morale purposes, each soldier in Viet Nam was entitled to one Rest and Recuperation (R & R), 14-day leave after being in country six months. The Department of Defense paid transportation costs to various destinations. Among married soldiers, Hawaii was a favored choice. They could pay their wife's costs and she could meet them in Hawaii. Since Zane and Scott arrived in country about the same time, they were able to travel to Hawaii together.

While waiting for their Hawaiian flight at Cam Ranh Bay, Zane said, "Daryl, I do not want to see your grubby butt the whole two weeks. I've slept in a hole with your for four months and that's enough for anyone. It's time to sleep with Janice for awhile.'

"Oh, you're so cute when you're angry," Daryl answered, while extending his lips as if to kiss Zane.

Zane lay back in his chair, inter-linked his fingers on his chest, and said, "The second thing I want is fresh milk in a frosted beer mug. Damn, it will be great to be back to the land of the big PX."

Grinning Scott asked. "Dale, did you hear about the guy that Pam Am rushed to the hospital after landing in Hawaii?"

Giving Scott a disgusted look, Zane answered, "No, I didn't hear about it. I guess I'm going to."

"Well," Scott started, "As they were unloading passengers in Hawaii. This stewardess found this GI still in his seat unconscious but staring at the ceiling with his eyes open. He was so anxious to see his wife that he didn't have enough skin left to close his eyes. So much blood ran to his groin, that his brain went dead for lack of oxygen," Scott related between laughs.

"That's probably what's going to happen to you. Let's get our butts to the boarding area. We don't want to miss this flight," Zane said, as he arose from his seat.

Again, time seemed to cheat Zane. The 14 days were gone in seconds. Their children were with grandparents so they had every moment to devote to each other. After two days, he and Janice left the hotel to see the sights. He rented a car but refused to drive. He rode in total fear of an accident not having been in traffic for so long. He had three beer mugs of milk the first day. They drove the entire island and visited the landmark showplaces, Don Ho, Sea World, Blowing Rock and the historical monuments at Pearl Harbor.

Zane chartered a boat for big game fishing. They shared it with civilian newlyweds from Canada. The guy was a wealthy stockbroker with a young wife. They were in Hawaii for as long as she wanted to stay. He had a penthouse apartment where they had breakfast. The broker had his BMW shipped from Canada for their honeymoon. They had been in Hawaii for a month. Janice was green with envy and Zane wondered what he was doing in the Army. Walking aboard his returning aircraft was the hardest thing he did in his life. Janice saved her tears until after Zane's departure.

Operation Pershing was still going when Zane returned. Subsequent events made it the longest operation in the 1st Cav's history, almost 11 months. Zane became quite upset with his friend CWO Scott.

"You did what you stupid shit?" Zane raged.

"I extended for six months," Chief Scott answered. "I get a paid, 30 day leave to anywhere in the world. After that, I return to the Cav."

Zane heart fell. So far, he had not had a single casualty in his platoon. He wanted it to stay that way. However, he salved his conscience with the knowledge that he would not be Chief Scott's platoon commander when he returned. Zane would be home with his family.

While platoon commander, he had a few rules for success. Fly from point A to point B at 10,000 feet. Never take off in the same direction as your approach. When low, remain over thick jungle. Do not fly across open rice paddies when low. It was basic stuff but it worked.

Zane was giving people in his unit a hard time. His return date was getting close, less than ten days to departure. He took great joy using phrases like, "I'm so short I could walk under a snake's belly and not knock my hat off."

Ho Chin Minh almost destroyed Zane and Daryl Scott's plans. The NVA military leader, General Giap, hurled his forces across the DMZ on 21 January 1968. Both Zane and Scott had their equipment returned to supply and were counting minutes when the Tet Offensive of 1968 began, almost ending their chances of returning home.

Giap's first major thrust was across the DMZ toward Khe Sanh. The Marines were taking a heavy beating but they returned ten fold what the NVA threw at them with their three divisions. Word of the major assault filtered south.

Their An Khe base came under attack but Zane and Scott weren't particularly concerned. Scott was visiting Zane in Charlie Company. The pair had two lawn chairs and were sitting outside when the attack started. An Khe had three defense rings named A, B, and C. Their battalion was inside C ring. If Charlie got to them, the entire base would be theirs.

"Isn't this grand Daryl," Zane quipped. "Here we are watching the war in Vista Vision with stereo sound. The Army is actually paying us for watching the show."

"I know Dale," Scott replied, "I am almost tempted to stay and see it twice. However, I heard Georgia is getting pregnant and I thought it would be neat if I was there."

In the next few days, the 1st Cav Division moved to Camp Evans. General Westmoreland suspected that General Giap was going to make a major attack across the DMZ. On 31 January 1968, he did and the Cav was there to fight.

Colonel Delaney sent for Zane and Scott. The Division was on its way north to the DMZ and Zane and Scott expected to move with them.

"You two have orders and it is time for you to go home. Here's the deal. One of our ships, Four Five Seven, has a replacement coming for it. It needs to go to Saigon for a major over haul. Buff Winslow will arrive with the replacement while we are on our way north. He will take Four Five Seven south. You two will be on it. I'm leaving Chief Scott and another pilot here to fly the replacement up north. I'll be damned if I will have you two on my conscience. Good luck and get out of here. I have work to do," Delaney explained.

"Captain Zane, are you awake?" Someone yelled from outside Dale's room.

Grumbling, Zane pulled his blanket over his head and tried to sleep.

"Dale, wake your butt up. This is Buff Winslow and I am here to pickup Four Five Seven," Winslow said as he shook Zane.

Rubbing his eyes, he swung his feet onto the floor. Looking up, he saw Buff Winslow, Boeing Vertol's Chief Technical Representative from Saigon.

"What time is it?" Zane asked.

"It is seven A.M. civilian time and 07:00 hours Army time. We've already done our preflight and are ready to go," Winslow said.

"Okay, okay. Where's Chief Scott?" Zane asked.

"He's bringing some coffee and will be here in a minute," Winslow said.

"I'm surprised he found any. This place is as empty as it was the day I arrived," Zane said. "With most of the folks up at Camp Evans, there's not much here."

CWO Scott opened the door and pushed it aside with is shoulder. He held a large thermos and some stacked coffee cups.

"I'll give you a hand," Winslow said as he took the thermos from Chief Scott.

After Winslow poured, Zane took his coffee and walked to his screen window. He looked at the banana trees along the cement walkways they built with scrounged equipment. The place was an estate compared to 12 months before when he first came to Charlie Company.

CWO Scott said, "They have the replacement Hook ready. I did the preflight. I will be leaving for Camp Evans in an hour. I will be taking the GCA crew with me. There's not much activity around the base. It is pretty deserted."

Zane and Chief Scott had come to An Khe with a load of scrounged goodies to take to Charlie Company up north. The Boeing people arrived the previous day with a replacement aircraft for Four Five Seven. Chief Scott was going to fly it to the 1st Cav with the pilot brought by Winslow from the Replacement Depot in Saigon. Zane would fly to Saigon with Buff Winslow on Four Five Seven and catch his flight to the U.S. He had orders to Fort Rucker.

"Buff, excuse me and Chief for a bit. We're going to take a walk across to the old battalion headquarters," Zane said as he put his hand on Chief Scott's shoulder.

As the pair left Charlie Company's old area, Zane pointed to the Battalion Headquarters' sign and said, "Chief, when the First Team built that sign they put a six pack of Falstaff beer in its rock base. The thinking was that there would always be a beer available for a Hooker should he wander through here again. Perhaps, some day we can meet here and drink those beers. What do you say?"

Turning to face Chief Scott, Zane said, "I am not much on good-byes. I have a tendency to blubber. Let's shake. You have my greatest respect as a Hooker Chief. It has been an honor to fly with you."

The pair shook hands when Zane said, "Screw it."

He pulled Chief Scott forward and slapped his back with his other hand.

"I have to go sir," Chief Scott said as he came to attention and saluted.

After Zane returned his salute, Chief Scott did a smart about face and walked away.

What took many by surprise was Giap's coordinated attack throughout Viet Nam. They used General Giap's "Gnat Swarm" technique that failed miserably. The VC never recovered from massive losses. When Giap's defeat was firm, he no longer had a NLF to fight in the south. It was necessary for him to replace them with NVA troops. The NVA and VC lost 32,000 killed and 5,800 captured. Zane and Scott missed the action by one day.

The two made their flight to Saigon with Winslow as a passenger on Four Five Seven. Zane and Scott caught their flight to the U.S. for another tour at Mother Rucker.

Zane took with him a prize from his second tour. He relished in the knowledge that he had not lost a single member of his unit to hostile action. In addition, he formed unbreakable bonds with fellow Hookers that would serve him well in the future.

"If I can show future Hookers at Rucker how to survive, my time in this war will have been worth it," he thought.

Chapter Thirty Nine

December 1967

Valor is common but great souls are rare.
Bernard Joseph Saurin (1706–81), French dramatist. Spartacus, in *Spartacus,* act 3, sc. 1

"Hurry darling," Minh Thanh called as she placed gifts in their Land Rover. "We will be late for Christmas Mass. Sister Marie will never forgive us."

"I am," Jean Danjou answered. "She won't forgive us if we forget the macadamia nuts. You know how she likes to bake pies. Macadamia nut pie is her favorite."

Jean lifted a 25-pound bag of the expensive nuts onto his shoulder. He turned and walked through the double glass doors and onto their veranda. He continued across it to the drive of their plantation known locally as Peace Retreat.

Minh Thanh placed Anh Vinh Danjou, their young son, in a prepared cradle between the vehicle's front seats. The satin lined container fit nicely behind the Land Rover's floor mounted gearshift lever and Christmas gift packages in the rear.

Starting to call again, Minh Thanh saw Jean coming across their veranda.

"Oh, I love him so much. We have finally made our home and my prayers have been answered," she thought.

Opening the driver's side door, Jean placed the large sack behind the driver's seat. Little space remained in the cab as they had gifts for each of the sisters at the Cholon Cathedral. In addition, there were gifts for her younger brother Vinh and her Uncle Diem.

After Christmas Mass, she would remain at the Cholon Cathedral and await the Tet New Year. It would be an extended visit but she needed to help her replacement prepare for future French classes. Jean would return to the plantation to oversee its operation until Tet when he would return for the celebration.

Jean sat in the driver's seat and asked. "Do we have everything?"

"I think so," Minh Thanh answered.

Jean started the vehicle and drove through their main gate saying, "It's dry enough to take the short cut to An Loc. I will take the back road to Highway LTL-17 and then go to QL-13. We can avoid going through Loc Ninh and save time."

Peace Retreat Plantation was ten miles west of Loc Ninh. Two roads provided access to it. One went directly east to Loc Ninh and then south through An Loc to the Cholon District of Saigon using QL-13. Traveling this route, it was about 65 miles to their destination. By taking the south road, the distance was about 60 miles.

Jean preferred the south road because he could inspect their newly planted trees. However, during the monsoon season, the south road was impassable to any vehicle except their Land Rover.

"They are doing well," Jean said as he gazed across rolling red hills filled with saplings held in place with stakes. "This is ideal soil for them. We will be harvesting these in about seven years. They require fertilizing next month."

Minh Thanh admired the results of their hard labors. She and Jean had hand planted each of the young trees. It was hard work but worth it. They had land and she had not forgotten the lessons taught her in Muong Valley.

"Land is the greatest wealth there is," her father had said.

"I know that he was wise," she thought. "The earth returns its gifts to those who love it."

They arrived at Highway LTL-17. Perhaps, "highway" was an overstatement. It was rugged but much better than their road joining it. They soon arrived at QL-13 and turned south toward Saigon.

"This is a good highway," Jean commented. "We will be in Saigon in less than an hour."

Their young son began to cry. Minh Thanh removed him from his cradle and held him in her arms to breast-feed.

"He is an eating machine," Jean thought, while taking an occasional glance at his son. "I am indeed a fortunate man. However, being a civilian and a family man takes some getting used to. It was worth it despite the cost."

Jean remembered paying a high price.

"I could never serve again," he thought. "Fellow Legionnaires would no longer respect me after the lies I told to cover the intelligence service's operations."

A court martial would have been a disgrace to the French intelligence agencies. They trusted him like no other and they thought that he had turned against France. To them, it was an offense crying out for the guillotine.

Nevertheless, they could say little for fear of making public their intricate world of lies, deceit, and deception. They would remain silent but supply information that would convict him in a military court. Murdering a fellow officer was enough to assure his conviction.

Jean recalled pacing his cell in Paris. He was in the infamous maximum-security prison on Treaudeaux Street. The dank facility had scrawls, made by revolutionaries in 1776, adorning its walls. Scratched deep into stone, paint could not remove them.

"Step back Danjou," the guard had said. "You have a visitor."

His visitor was a personal representative of de Gaulle, Major General Prejean. Prejean was chief adviser for Military Affairs to de Gaulle.

"Danjou," he had said, "you are going to put our nation through a trial that will expose our most sensitive operations. De Gaulle does not want this to happen. If you will accept a Letter of Reprimand, you can retire with a full pension at your current rank of colonel."

"I fired in self defense," Jean remembered telling Prejean. "They were trying to kill me. The one I killed was Prudhomme's protégé. My initial thought was that he was trying to seek vengeance for some misguided affront. I now know that he was working for the Corsicans. They were afraid that I was going to reveal their drug activities."

"That is your word against a dead man. His fellow officer, Hebert, says different and will testify that you were in the drug business. He will also testify that they were arranging a drug deal to expose you," Prejean explained.

"That is a damned lie," Jean said with steadfast earnestness.

"Maybe so," Prejean replied. "However, Hebert has a corroborating witness who was on the fire escape. I am certain of your conviction. For the sake of France, you should take de Gaulle's offer. I know you do not want to expose our Southeast Asia operations. Many of our operatives will die."

It took Jean two weeks of agonizing introspection to make his decision.

"You are doing what is right for France," Prejean had said. "We have provided a passport as per your request. Also, you have two years back pay coming upon retirement."

"Jean, you are daydreaming. Be careful, you almost ran off the road," Minh Thanh said excitedly.

"I'm sorry," Jean said becoming alert.

"You are in one of your moods. I wish you could forget what happened. You have not dishonored your name," Minh Thanh said with her usual understanding. "I am proud to have it as mine. Your son will also one day know that his father is a special person of honor and character."

While keeping his eyes on the road, Jean leaned to his right to receive Minh Thanh's kiss. As he straightened, he looked down at his son.

"She's right you know young man," he thought. "One day you will learn of your great grandfather's exploits. You will make a fine Legionnaire."

They entered Saigon's suburbs on a route that was most familiar to them. Cholon's Cathedral was their wedding place and their center for social activities. Minh Thanh maintained a strong bond with the sisters for she knew them well. They were her sisters and she loved each of them. After mother superior's death, the Vatican replaced her with a senior nun from a Catholic Church in Hue. She loved Viet Nam and its people. Viet Nam was her birthplace before the country's division in 1954. She, like most, wanted to see Viet Nam whole again but not under a Communist regime.

After her brother and uncle gave permission for Jean to marry her, Jean disappeared for a year. It was only through her brother's contacts that she learned of his imprisonment. When he did return, her wedding was grand. The sisters organized the event and showed her their love through making it a dream-like event. Their Bishop performed the ceremony. Jean looked handsome in his black tie and tails. Her brother and uncle wore their dress uniforms. Her many friends and in-laws, who had fled to the south, attended her ceremony. Often, when at home, she would remove her wedding dress and relive the most joyous moment in her life.

Jean had said, during their brief engagement, that he planned for them to have a plantation near Saigon. By the time he paid various officials their bribes; he obtained title to 500 acres on the Cambodian border near Loc Ninh. The former owner had left Viet Nam in 1954 as most French landowners fled the country. Considerable taxes were due and the state held its title. The state could not find a buyer because it was not good rice land. In addition, it was a dangerous location.

Mother superior approached President Thieu about Jean buying the estate for back taxes. He readily agreed after receiving a special blessing from their Bishop.

After their wedding in 1965, they moved to and named their plantation "Peace Retreat" to correspond with their strong desire for an end to hostilities. The site was in considerable disarray and the nut trees were almost dead. Jean diverted water from a small steam and recovered most of the nut bearing trees. Next, they put in new saplings on 200 acres. It was hard, backbreaking work. Nevertheless, they prevailed.

"I will ring the bell for Mey Ling. Stay in the Rover with Vinh until I can get the gate open," Jean said as they arrived at the Cathedral.

Mey Ling never recovered from the death of their former mother superior. She seemed to age rapidly after her loss. Mother Superior found her on Saigon's streets and raised her as if she was her child. Now, it took a major effort for her to open the facilities' double steel gates. She refused help from anyone. It was her task and she would continue doing it without help.

As Mey Ling closed the gates behind them, Sister Marie ran to greet them with a joyous, "Welcome loved ones. We were worried that you had problems. There are ominous rumors in abundance. I am so glad to see you."

As Minh Thanh exited the Rover with Baby Vinh, Sister Marie took him into her arms as she crooned, "Oh my little man, you grow everyday. You are going to be a big man some day."

Other sisters helped Jean unload gifts from the Rover. They carried them to a parlor in the nun's living area. A Christmas tree almost touched the vaulted ceiling. Beneath it were many packages for exchanging gifts on Christmas Eve after mass.

Sister Marie held Baby Vinh to her ample bosom with her left arm. She kept making baby sounds and tickled his stomach with her index finger. She was oblivious to those around her, pressing to look at the child.

With a squeal, Sister Marie exclaimed, "He can be baby Jesus tonight during our Christmas Eve play. We've never had a real baby before this. Oh, how wonderful."

Every Christmas Eve, the sisters had a Nativity play. They dressed as Joseph and Mary in a manger with Jesus. Three wise men came to visit bringing gifts. It was open to the public and always drew a large crowd. They used live animals in an area on the Cathedral's front lawn. They had never had a baby for Jesus so they had used a doll. This time they would use Baby Vinh. Other than their Easter play, the Christmas rendition of Christ's birth was their favorite celebration.

Earlier in the month, Minh Thanh's brother, Major Nguyen Van Vinh confirmed he could attend the Christmas festivities. His unit, the 23rd Ranger Group, was in Saigon to help bolster defenses in case of a holiday season attack. Rumors were running rampant about an impending, major offensive by VC forces. President Thieu was not taking chances and ordered Vinh's unit to Saigon.

Minh Thanh's uncle, Major Nguyen Van Diem, could not visit during the Christmas season. His unit, the 33rd Ranger Group, was providing security in Hue. It was too far and his commander did not support celebration of Christian holidays. He did indicate that he could come for Tet.

Jean sat in the parlor beside Minh Thanh on a sofa. He was admiring the tree erected by the nuns.

"Their decorations are individual works of art," he said admiringly. "Some of those decorations are over 100 years old. They are precious. I particularly like their tree because it has no lights. Lights seem to add a gaudy look to a tree," he said to Minh Thanh.

"I agree. The sisters allowed me to place that carved angel on it four years ago. I made it from pure ivory. Mother superior said it was one of her favorite pieces. I miss her Jean," Minh Thanh replied.

"Me too. We must say a special prayer for her," Jean agreed/

Jean placed his right arm around Minh Thanh's shoulder and drew her close as he said, "I must go back to our home before it gets dark. I will return on Christmas Eve. I also have some errands to run."

"You be careful," Minh Thanh said, as she kissed his cheek.

Jean left the Cholon District and drove to the headquarters of Major General Nguyen Van Hieu. Jean knew General Hieu from files kept by the French. His reputation for honesty, integrity, and character were well known. He had the respect of his soldiers because they knew that he had their interest always foremost in his mind. It was necessary that Jean see him today because he would soon return to his unit, the 22nd ARVN Division.

"Hello Colonel Danjou," General Hieu said, as Jean entered his office.

"Good morning sir. I am no longer a colonel. I am retired," Jean replied.

"I know about your 'retirement,'" Hieu stated. "I also know that you retired under pressure. Your intelligence agency used you and then thrown into the street. This is no way to treat the hero of Na Son," Hieu observed.

"Thank you sir. I need to speak to you about a matter of national security, if you have the time," Jean said.

"I always have time for such matters. Please have a seat," Hieu said as he pointed to a chair beside his desk.

Jean took the offered seat. As he sat, he removed a map from his rear pocket. As he did so, he exposed his sidearm.

General Hieu noticed the weapon immediately and said, "You are wise to carry a weapon during this time."

"Sir, I agree. That is part of why I am here," Jean said as he opened his map.

Holding the map so that General Hieu could see it, Jean pointed to his plantation's location and said, "Sir, I have 500 acres at this location near the Cambodian border. That is my home now and I have named it "Peace Retreat." When I was on active duty, I did a reconnaissance extending from Northeastern Laos through Cambodia along the Ho Chi Minh Trail. I exited Cambodia at OL-13 near my home. I know every inch of the Ho Chi Minh trail. I know where every refueling point, service area, river ford and weapons cache is along it."

General Hieu leaned forward to see and hear better for Jean's statement drew his interest. Hieu used his index finger to trace the Ho Chi Minh trail north to where it was near South Viet Nam's Central Highlands.

"Tell me about this area colonel," Hieu directed.

Jean detailed every facility that the NVA had on the trail across the border from Dak To, Kontum and the Central Highlands region. While Jean talked, General Hieu took notes.

When Jean finished, Hieu asked. "Can I have that map colonel?"

"Certainly sir. You are the only one with whom I would share the information. My only hope is that you and South Viet Nam's ARVN forces can put it to good use," Jean said as he handed the map to General Hieu.

"Rest assured that I will see that it is put to good use. This is very valuable information and it will help us immensely," General Hieu replied.

Jean continued, "I use only Vietnamese workers on my plantation and I pay them a good wage for their work. If I do well, the families at Loc Ninh do well. The workers, and their families, are my friends. They report things to me that they would not tell anyone else. There will be a major attack by the VC and NVA forces in the near future. I do not know the exact date. I do know that NVA forces are gathering across the border in Cambodia. If I hear more I will see that you get the information."

Jean arose and said, "General I must get back to Peace Retreat. I look forward to working with you in the future."

General Hieu arose and extended his hand to Jean, and said, "Thank you colonel. I appreciate this very much. You are doing the right thing for our country."

Jean resisted the urge to salute before leaving. It was a habit he found hard to break.

As he drove along QL-13, he reached behind his seat and removed an AK-47 assault rifle. He laid it on the seat beside him. Reaching to the rear again, he removed two additional clips and put them with the rifle. He knew that, from time to time, the VC would establish checkpoints along highways to intercept travelers. He had to be prepared because his workers told him that the VC were going to get the "Frenchman who works our land."

Jean stopped in Loc Ninh to deliver medical supplies to a Vietnamese nurse who supervised a small clinic. Her husband, who worked at Peace Retreat, told Jean that US AID shipments were not going to the people who needed them. The VC were confiscating some supplies while corrupt government officials were selling the remainder.

"I need to let Major General Hieu know about this. He will put a stop to it," Jean thought.

Jean stopped at his home to deliver food supplies that he bought in the market at Loc Ninh. He had two ladies from Loc Ninh working as inside help for Minh Thanh. When she was away, they prepared his meals. During past years, they grew close and they considered them as family members. Jean trusted the pair explicitly.

Jean drove to the north orchard to see about harvesting that was underway. This was Jean's second full crop since moving to the plantation. If this crop was unsuccessful, he would have to borrow money to keep the plantation. He used his life's savings to purchase it. He did not owe anything to anyone. He did not want to go into debt.

As he approached the trees, he saw his foreman Nguyen Van Ngoc helping load bags of nuts onto a trailer. Ngoc was responsible for outside operations. He had Jean's confidence and trust.

Jean parked and walked toward Ngoc who watched his approach with a broad smile. Jean saw that the trailer was almost full.

After their polite greeting ceremony, Jean asked. "How much of the orchard is left to harvest?"

While loading another sack to the trailer, Ngoc answered, "This load is not quite 50 percent. It is a grand harvest this year."

Jean noted that the workers were bringing filled bags faster than Ngoc could load them. A large stack of bags sat behind the trailer. While Ngoc loaded another, Jean stepped beside him and began lifting bags onto the trailer. Soon he was sweating profusely. As he and Ngoc worked, they exchanged stories and local gossip. Any observer could see that the workers considered Jean different from previous owners. All they ever did was ride horses and give orders. Seldom did they ever receive a living wage.

An hour before sunset, Ngoc stopped harvesting for the day. Men, women, and children began walking to their homes in Loc Ninh.

Ngoc remained with Jean and said, "Your harvest this year is a good one. The water from the stream helped when it was so dry. The trees are healthy. When the younger trees begin bearing, we will have to have extra help. I sent three workers to the young trees today to trim them. They will now grow taller because they had too many low branches that retarded their upward growth."

"Thank you," Jean replied. "You are a wise man. I could not operate this place without you. Come to the house with me."

Jean parked beside the veranda and asked Ngoc to join him for a cold drink. The two entered and Jean brought a cold beer for each of them. They sat at the kitchen table and made general conversation.

After a polite wait, Jean explained, "I will attend mass with Minh Thanh in Saigon again this year. I will not be here on Christmas Eve. I want you to do something for me on Christmas Eve."

Ngoc replied, "I will be honored to do what you wish."

"Since the crop is good, I want to share with the workers. Will you distribute a bonus to them for me on Christmas Eve?" Jean asked.

Ngoc, obviously pleased, answered, "You sir are most kind. Not many of the workers are Christians though."

"That does not matter," Jean said. "See that every worker gets an even share. This includes everyone, especially the children."

"They will be joyous of your generosity. Can I tell them now?" Ngoc asked.

"No, this is a surprise. Wait until Christmas Eve," Jean explained.

Laughing, Ngoc commented, "It will be a grand surprise indeed."

Jean looked outside and then turned to Ngoc saying, "It is almost dark. I will drive you to Loc Ninh."

As they entered the Rover, Ngoc saw Jean place his weapon between the seats within easy reach. As Ngoc entered the passenger's side, his demeanor changed to a somber one.

Ngoc said, almost whispering, "Sir, you must get your harvest sold and delivered before Tet. Do not remain here for the holidays. You and your family must find a safe place before Tet begins."

Jean's facial expression became concerned. He knew that Ngoc was telling him something that he should not tell. He was placing his life in danger.

Jean replied, "Thank you Ngoc. We will not be here."

The pair did not exchange words during their short ride to Loc Ninh. When Ngoc left the vehicle, he pointed to Jean's weapon.

"Get more," he advised as he departed.

Before Christmas Mass, Minh Thanh lit candles for her mother Xuan, her brothers Vinh and Anh and her Uncle Diem. She prayed that one day they could be together and share their love as they did in Muong Valley. On Christmas day, they gathered with the sisters and exchanged gifts. The gifts consisted of items made by each person for the other. Father Cicero visited with them for a while. He had to leave North Viet Nam and now had a church near Xuan Loc, slightly east of Ben Hoa.

The group missed Uncle Diem but his unit was on alert at Hue and he could not join them. Vinh talked to him at considerable length by telephone. Minh Thanh noticed that Jean and Vinh were having animated discussions but grew silent when she approached. She knew she would get the subject of their discussions later from Jean. They had no secrets.

Jean entered the sisters' parlor the afternoon of Christmas day and removed his son from his cradle. He held him above his head and gently rolled him from side to side.

"That's my little man," Jean said as he hoisted Anh Vinh Danjou above his head. "Before long you will be joining me in the fields. What fun we will have together."

The child clearly enjoyed his father's antics for he would cry when Jean stopped lifting him. With a large swoop around the room, Jean held him at arm's length as if he was an airplane. The youngster muttered unintelligible happy sounds as he flew through the air.

"This child fears nothing," Jean said proudly. "What a Legionnaire he will make."

Minh Thanh immediately arose from her seat and took Baby Vinh from Jean. She placed the child over her left shoulder with her right hand firmly on his back.

"That is one thing he will never be," Minh Thanh said with finality as she left the room.

Jean, surprised at her actions, detected a tone in her voice that he had never heard. It was one of cold determination. It made clear to Jean that he was never to make such a suggestion again.

Jean turned to Vinh and gave him a questioning look. He stood still with his palms upward as if say, "What did I do?"

"She means it," Vinh told Jean. "I recommend you never mention it again."

Thinking for a moment, Jean asked. "When do you have to return to your unit?"

"Tomorrow morning," Vinh answered. "Why?"

"There is a friend that I want you to meet. He is in Saigon for his weekly joint staff meeting," Jean replied.

"Who is he?" Vinh asked.

"Major General Nguyen Van Hieu," Jean said. "We need to tell him what Diem said when you talked to him. In addition, I have some other things that he needs to know."

"You know General Hieu?" Vinh asked.

"Yes. I met him a long time ago. He is an honest man who is trustworthy," Jean responded.

"That's what I hear. He is the CG of the 22nd Infantry Division. Right?" Vinh questioned.

"That's him. There's not much going on right now. I will drive us to see him," Jean stated.

As they entered Hieu's office, Vinh came to attention and rendered a crisp salute. General Hieu promptly returned it and then shook Jean's hand.

"At ease, Major," Hieu said.

Jean had forgotten that Vinh was an ARVN officer. However, he appeared to be comfortable in Hieu's presence.

"Gentlemen, how about some tea," Hieu said, as he arose behind his desk.

It was obvious to Jean and Vinh that this was not a request. They followed him into a small, adjoining room. Once seated, an aide brought them a tray and the general poured first.

"What is on your mind colonel?" Hieu asked Jean.

"Sir, Major Vinh has an uncle who is a Ranger Group Commander at Hue. He relayed some information that I thought you should hear," Jean explained.

Turning to look at Vinh, Hieu asked. "What is it major?"

"Sir, my uncle relayed information to me regarding a major attack in the near future," Vinh answered.

"Yes, I have heard the same thing but I have not found anything to substantiate the reports," Hieu stated.

"Sir, one of my uncle's long range patrols reported that there would be a major offensive throughout the county during Tet. We have heard of a possible attack in the Khe Sanh area but this offensive will be nationwide. They captured a senior NVA staff officer who told them of their plans. They are infiltrating groups into every provincial capital. They will make a coordinated attack on the night before Tet," Vinh stated in the most serious fashion that he could muster.

General Hieu, obviously surprised at the information, was giving Vinh's report much thought.

"Colonel, Major Vinh, I must leave now. My concern is Qui Nhon. I will launch intensive patrolling in an attempt to verify this information. As soon as I can verify this, I will make sure that the G-3 of the General Staff hears of this. This causes considerable concern. Thank you," Hieu said as he started to rise.

"Just one more thing general if you will allow me sir," Jean said.

"Certainly colonel, go ahead," Hieu said, as he relaxed into his seat.

"I can verify what Major Vinh says. There are forces, as we speak, filtering into Saigon and other cities. In addition, you are the only person I can trust with this information. US AID supplies, destined for people living in An Loc's province, goes to VC forces. Someone in the ARVN supply chain sells it to them. You know much better than me what to do about it," Jean added.

"Thank you colonel. I certainly do. Now, I must return to my unit. We have much to do," Hieu said as he took his hat from a table and started for the door.

Vinh never had an opportunity to salute General Hieu. It was obvious to the pair that General Hieu took their reports with the most serious intent.

During their return to the Cathedral, Vinh said, "General Hieu has a reputation of being honest and straight forward. He has the respect of his officers and men but these traits could possibly present a political problem. As a Major General, he is in a position of high visibility. I sincerely hope this does not affect his career. We need more senior officers like him."

Minh Thanh and Baby Vinh remained at the Cathedral when Jean returned to Peace Retreat. Jean would oversee the remainder of the harvest and then return to celebrate Tet at the Cholon Cathedral.

Jean arrived in Loc Ninh on 28 December on his way to his home. As he drove through Loc Ninh, he noticed that many older men and women bowed deeply as he passed them in his Rover. He knew that they were doing so as a sign of respect but he did not understand why. Ngoc explained when he arrived home.

As Jean exited his vehicle at the North Orchard, he saw Ngoc standing beside a filled trailer. Jean realized that without the rover the trailer was useless. It was too heavy to pull to the storage building.

"How stupid," Jean thought. "I wasted two days. I should have returned on the 26th."

Ngo bowed deeply as Jean approached and said, "Welcome home sir. This is all that remains of the harvest."

"This is it?" Jean asked obviously concerned. "I expected at least 15 trailer loads."

"Actually sir, it was 18 trailer loads," Ngoc answered with a wide smile.

Jean, confused, asked. "How did you get them to storage?"

"We carried them one bag at a time sir," Ngoc explained. "The workers are having their mid-day meal in the orchard beneath the trees for shade. They will return in 30 minutes to begin carrying these."

"My God, Ngoc. It is one-quarter mile to storage. They carried the bags that far?" Jean asked befuddled.

"Yes sir. They were glad to do it. The Christmas bonus was almost two months pay. They felt that they should carry them for you," Ngoc explained further.

"Well, they will not carry any more. Help me hitch the trailer to the Rover. We will take this load in one trip," Jean directed.

Jean parked the Rover, with the full trailer attached, beside his home's veranda. He and Ngoc exited the Rover and walked to the storage bin. Jean opened the door and saw that it was full.

"Ngoc, leave the bags on the trailer. While I was in Saigon, I arranged for the exporter to provide trucks to move what's in storage. They can load directly from the trailer. They should be here soon," Jean explained.

"You are wise for making this arrangement. This way your crop will be to market before Tet," Ngoc noted.

"Come Ngoc; let's sit on the veranda until the trucks arrive. It is much cooler there," Jean suggested.

As they took seats at a wrought iron table, Ngoc asked. "Are you going to use the swimming pool?"

Jean looked toward an area behind his home. He could see one end of a deep, tile-lined, dry swimming pool. The previous owners had an Olympic size pool built for swimming but it did not interest him or Minh Thanh.

"I don't think so Ngoc. It is a useless luxury. I do not have time for such recreation," Jean answered. "Besides it is too much trouble to maintain."

"Here they come," Ngoc said.

Jean looked toward the North Orchard. He saw the workers walking single file, toward where he and Ngoc sat. The usual departure route to Loc Ninh was behind the storage building and not by the house. Jean and Ngoc arose and walked to the veranda's edge.

As the first person neared, he stopped and bowed deeply while thanking Jean for their bonus. Jean paid the customary compliment in return. He did this for every worker that thanked him. It took two hours before the last worker departed.

"Whew, I am tired," Jean said. "I am ready for something cold to drink."

Before he could go inside, a large Mercedes truck arrived. Close behind it, three others followed.

Ngoc said, "Sir, you get something to drink. I will see to this."

"Are you sure? Don't you want something cold?" Jean asked.

"No sir, you go ahead. This will not take long. I will bring you the tally sheets when we are finished," Ngoc answered.

As Ngoc went to meet the incoming trucks, Jean left the veranda and went to his Land Rover. He was particularly fond of it because of its exceptional all terrain qualities. It was an F102. An F102 was a military vehicle. He purchased it from an Australian salvage yard in Saigon and rebuilt it.

Jean made sure that no one had tampered with its locked cargo compartment. He had followed Ngoc's advice to 'get some more of those.'" Through his Saigon contacts, he purchased additional weapons should he have need for them. He placed half of them in the Rover and the remainder in catacombs beneath the Cholon Cathedral. If mother superior knew about his cache, he felt sure she would try to have him excommunicated.

In the Rover's compartment, he had two M-60 machine guns, five light anti-tank weapons (LAW), five M-16s, two cases of fragmentation grenades, two 40-millimeter grenade launchers, six nine-millimeter side arms, and ample ammunition for each. Originally, he had considerable concern about the Rover being able to handle the load and still pull his heavy trailer. The Rover's military specification suspension and engine handled both with ease.

Jean, using workers from Loc Ninh, began fertilizing his young trees in the South Orchard. He had two, four-inch wide, plastic pipes driven inside the drip line of each tree. Each pipe had one-half inch perforations starting three feet beneath the surface. The pipes went to a depth of seven feet. Into these, workers poured a mixture of water and high ammonia content fertilizer.

The plantation's soil was red clay. It did not percolate properly so Jean devised this method to feed each tree's roots. As the trees grew, their roots received nutrients and rainwater from the pipes. This caused the trees to develop a deep root structure. The roots followed the pipes to their maximum depth.

"Sir, you are a wise farmer," Ngoc said. "The people before you always had poor crops and their trees fell prey to insects because of their weak condition. I am amazed that a soldier knows these things."

"I am not a soldier Ngoc," Jean replied. "I am a farmer. In Morocco, the farmers had to conserve water and use it to its best advantage. The desert is fertile but lacks water. This is a method they used."

Jean worked with four teams of two men each installing the pipes. They used hand augers to prepare holes for inserting of the pipes. Following them, Ngoc worked with 40 villagers mixing the water and fertilizer. Once mixed, they pumped it into the pipes until they overflowed.

Ngoc had left his team to ask Jean how much longer he thought it would take to complete the orchard. The workers wanted to finish in order to celebrate Tet starting 1 February.

"Sir, when do you estimate we will finish this orchard?" Ngoc asked.

While helping another worker turn an auger, Jean answered between breaths; "We will finish about one week before Tet. Is that enough time for everyone?"

"Oh, yes sir. Some workers will travel to home villages to join their relatives. Others will have their relatives coming here to visit a day before the celebrating starts," Ngoc answered.

Continuing, Ngoc said, "I will tell everyone after work today. I must return to my workers now."

Before Ngoc left, Jean said, "Ngoc I noticed that fertilizer in the storage building was getting low. Take the Rover and start using the bags stored in the cellar."

The South Orchard work ended on 19 January as the final tree received its fertilizer. The next day Jean and Ngoc sat at a pay table on the plantation's veranda. Workers were gathering to receive their pay. They were joking and in a joyful mood. Tet was soon and they had ample time to prepare as Jean said.

Plus, they would have money to make their holiday more enjoyable than in the past.

As Jean opened a leather pouch to remove its cash, he said to Ngoc, "After Tet, my plan is to start another section with saplings. My hope is that I will have them before the end of February. In the meantime, as soon as Tet is over, we can start clearing the land. Next, it will be necessary to terrace it to avoid erosion. Surely, by the time that is completed, the saplings will have arrived. It was necessary to order from Costa Rica. My Hawaiian source will not sell any more to other countries."

"The villagers will be happy to know that there will be work available. Their land is not adequate for rice growth so they must have an income to purchase it," Ngoc commented.

After paying the workers, Jean and Ngoc drank a beer. Jean thanked him for his valuable help and the two parted until after Tet.

"I will check the trees until the 29th and then leave for Cholon," Jean thought as he went to bed that night. "I miss Minh Thanh and my son."

Before dawn, an incessant pounding on his door awakened Jean. Checking his watch, he saw that it was 05:30. Armed with a pistol, he opened a small observation port to see Ngoc. At first, it was difficult to determine who he was because he remained hidden in shadows.

Working quickly, Jean opened the door and asked. "Is there an emergency? What is wrong?"

Ngoc whispered, "Turn off the lights."

As soon as Jean turned the lights off, Ngoc entered and said, "Leave here now. Take your valuable possessions and go. It has started. Go quickly."

Jean detected raw fear in Ngoc's manner and voice. H was extremely nervous and would not remain still. He was constantly looking out different windows. Finally, Jean gripped Ngoc's shoulders firmly, just enough to immobilize him.

"Ngoc, please, what has started?" Jean asked with deep concern.

"The NVA started their attack across the DMZ this morning. All week VC, in twos and threes, have been traveling through Loc Ninh. Many have families in Loc Ninh, An Loc, and Saigon. I thought they were on holiday leave. They are not. They are here to attack. You must get your loved ones to safety," Ngoc babbled between gasps for air.

"What about the cease fire?" Jean asked.

"There will be no cease fire this Tet. I am sorry to say that there are many VC sympathizers in Loc Ninh. They will join the Communist guerillas during their attack. Please go now," Ngoc answered almost in tears. "Do not go through Loc Ninh. Take the short cut," Ngoc added.

Leaning close to Ngoc, Jean whispered, "You go now. Get home before light so that no one will see you. Thank you Ngoc. You are a good man. I will be out of here in ten minutes," Jean told him.

Jean watched Ngoc leave for a moment. He then closed the door and dressed. He closed storm shutters on the house's windows; disconnected electrical power, and went directly to the Rover. Opening the locked compartment, he removed an M-16 and four clips. He put on a sidearm and ammunition belt. He locked the compartment and started the vehicle without lights.

With dawn now near, he raced as fast as possible south to Highway LTL 17. Once on better ground, he disengaged the Rover's four-wheel drive and increased his speed. A few moments later, he turned south toward Saigon on QL-13. He arrived at the Cholon Cathedral 45 minutes later.

"Oh my," mother superior said. "The rumors must be true. Some of our church members warned us that there would be an attack on Saigon soon. We didn't know when but now I guess we do. We must prepare."

Cholon's Cathedral, throughout its history, provided nursing care to anyone asking for it when there had been battles fought in its vicinity. The sisters vacated the first floor leaving their rooms for wounded. The sister's parlor became a main reception area. Jean helped them remove furniture and place beds along the walls.

Jean saw that the sisters knew what they were doing. They gathered candles, canned foods, bandages, lanterns, and other vital supplies. They placed these inside walk-in cupboards in the kitchen. The cupboards were inside walls three feet thick. The main building walls were six feet at their bases and three feet at their tops. Exterior walls surrounding the cathedral's grounds were five feet thick. They had considerable protection.

Minh Thanh's brother, Major Vinh, brought additional information. ARVN and American units received notice of an impending attack.

"General Weyand, the U.S. Commander for the Saigon area, has recalled infantry battalions from the Cambodian border," Vinh said. "However, ARVN forces are responsible for the cities defense. I have three companies in the Cholon District. One of them is near the Cathedral. I am using the Cathedral's Administration Building as my command post. Mother superior was difficult to convince. She finally realized that they need protection if they are going to treat wounded."

Vinh continued, "My units are not at full strength. Senior commanders are continuing to authorize Tet leave for those who want to celebrate the Lunar New Year. Fortunately, my men are airborne rangers and they understand the problems of a fight in Saigon. I have far less people on leave than other units."

"Is Diem still in Hue?" Jean asked.

"Yes, his airborne group is in the Citadel. They are at full strength because they received sporadic attacks before his people left on leave. The Citadel is a fortress. The Communists will pay dearly to take it," Vinh answered.

Jean continued his questions. "Have you heard anything about what the Americans are doing?"

"Westmoreland still believes the main attack is at Khe Sanh. He was not totally wrong. Fortunately, he deployed 6,000 Marines to Khe Sanh before the NVA attack. The 1st Air Cavalry Division is moving to the Khe Sanh area to help," Vinh explained.

Vinh stated a major concern saying, "I have many reports that the Cholon District is going to be a main staging area for NVA/VC attacks. We have arrested

NVA troops dressed like ARVN. They have told us that they were to meet others here in Cholon. That is why my group is here."

"Vinh," Jean said, "You and I know the sisters are not going to use force to defend themselves. Someone must protect them so that they can care for the wounded. I have enough weapons to provide security for them. However, I do not have anyone to fight."

"Talk to the grounds keeper. His name is Hoa. His son is an airborne ranger of considerable renown. Hoa was once a Tia tribesman. He has five sons. One of them is an airborne ranger but his unit is at a Special Forces camp near the DMZ. The other four attend school here like their elder brother. Hoa is a devout Catholic," Vinh advised Jean.

"I will see him now. Advise your troops to approach the Cathedral with caution. We will man the outer wall. No one will get past us unless they are wounded," Jean explained.

Jean located Hoa pruning shrubs along the Cathedral's side. He explained the situation and the elderly man said that he, and his sons, would help. In addition, he had six nephews that would also help. He left to gather his relatives.

Jean made his way through the wine cellar where he opened a door leading to the catacombs. He descended stairs to another door that provided access to sacred burial sites. He went past vaults on each side to where vault covers were stacked. Pulling aside discarded crates, he located his weapons cache. He opened one container and removed three claymore mines.

Claymores were not typical mines. About two inches thick, they were 12-inches wide. They were concave explosive devices intended for placement above ground. They were for perimeter protection. When detonated, they threw razor sharp metal shards in an ever expanding blast zone.

Jean chuckled as he read aloud a notice stamped into each of the claymores, "This side toward enemy."

As he was exiting the wine cellar, mother superior confronted him, she asked. "Jean, what are those things?"

"Mother superior, 'The Lord helps those who help themselves.' They are for the sisters' protection. Please excuse me. I have much to do," Jean answered as he swept past her almost at a run.

Outside, Jean saw Hoa waiting with 11 of his male relatives. As he approached the group, he estimated the oldest youngster's age as 16.

"Holy Mother, they are children," Jean thought, as he approached the group.

"What do you want us to do?" Hoa asked, while staring at Jean's three mines.

Jean expressed his concern for the youngsters by asking Hoa. "Are you certain you want to risk the lives of these young men?"

Hoa pulled himself erect as he could. The others with him did the same.

"Sir," Hoa answered, "We have a deep obligation to the sisters. My family wandered into Saigon as refugees from North Viet Nam. We had nothing, not even our dignity, as we were beggars on the streets. The sisters cared for us and educated our children. Now, it is time for us to help them."

Continuing Hoa asked. "What do you want us to do?"

Jean hesitated a moment before saying, "Go to the wine cellar. Remove the wine from every rack. Bring the racks outside and place them along the exterior walls."

Without speaking, Hoa went toward the wine cellar with the others following him. Jean watched as they disappeared into the building.

Jean went to the Cathedral's main entrance. A wide, paved walkway extended from the Cathedral's entrance to twin, steel doors in the exterior wall. On each side, shrubs and flowering plants lined the pavement. Momentarily, he looked at the garden and fishpond that he saw the first time he visited in 1954. Jean went to the steel doors and walked toward the church. He measured the blast distance of a claymore as he walked. He hid one on each side in the shrubbery. He began pacing again when he saw Hoa approaching.

"Every wine rack is out of the cellar. What do you want us to do next?" Hoa asked, breathing heavily from his previous exertion.

"Put three racks in each corner of the exterior wall. Use two as a base and put another on top of them. Place them diagonally across the corners. Midways of each sidewall place three more. Put them tight against the wall for support. When you have finished, return to the cellar. Go into the catacombs and you will find vault covers at the far end. Beside them are some OD containers. Bring them outside and I will tell you what to do with them," Jean directed.

With his one remaining claymore in his hands, Jean studied the Cathedral's front. At about 30 feet up the bell tower, he saw a three-foot square ventilation cover. Jean made a mental note of it as he proceeded to install his remaining claymore. He paced the blast radius distance from the other mines toward the church. In the shrubs on his left, he hid the third mine. Satisfied, Jean started toward the wine cellar exit.

As he rounded the church's corner, he observed ten of the youngsters placing wine racks according to his instructions. Beside the cellar exit, he saw two OD cases stacked. He went to the stack and removed the top two, placing them on the ground. Quickly, he released their cover retaining clamps and opened the cases. He began examining their contents as Hoa exited from the cellar entrance.

Hoa was backing up the cellar steps while using both hands to grip the last case's handle. On the case's other end, the biggest youngster struggled with his heavy load. Jean went to his assistance.

"Take it to where the others are," Jean directed.

As they set the container down, Jean told Hoa, "Gather the others. I need to talk to everyone."

In a few moments, Jean stood in the middle of a circle consisting of Hoa and the 11 young men. He removed the cover from the remaining container. Reaching inside, he removed a portable, two-way radio and handed it to Hoa.

"Do you know how to use that?" Jean asked.

"Yes I do colonel," Hoa said.

Jean gave Hoa an inquisitive look and asked. "How do you know that I once was a colonel?"

"Sir, everyone here knows who you are. I saw you and Captain Louis the first time you came to the Cathedral. My relatives and I prepared the grounds the day of your wedding. Minh Thanh is a gracious lady and she often shared her dreams with me. Her brother Vinh served with my son Captain Hoa who is also an airborne ranger," Hoa answered.

Continuing, Hoa said, "I was at Na Son in 1954 when the Viet Minh attacked us. I served with an airborne company as a first sergeant. During a jump into a drop zone a year later, I cracked my spine. I had to leave the military. Yes, we knew that Captain Jean Danjou was the hero of that battle. Yes colonel, I know how to operate this radio."

Jean reached for Hoa's hand to shake it. Hoa took it and noted Jean's firm grip.

While shaking Hoa's hand, Jean said, "It is my honor to serve with you again First Sergeant Hoa. If you squeeze any harder you will cripple my hand for life."

The group began laughing oblivious of what was to come. They found joy in each other's presence and the merriment of the moment. For a minute, their fear of what the future held was no longer on their minds. The thought soon returned and the group became somber.

Jean turned slowly looking into the eyes of each person. In the younger ones, he saw innocence and excitement. He felt sure that they could not comprehend what was to come. In the eyes of Sergeant Hoa, he saw the hurt left by seeing friends die. The light in his eyes did not burn bright like those of the young.

Pointing to his parked Land Rover, Jean said as he removed keys from his trousers' pocket, "There is a compartment inside that vehicle. Sergeant Hoa will unlock it. The rest of you bring the weapons to this location."

Handing the keys to Hoa, Jean asked. "If you will First Sergeant?"

While the group went to his vehicle, Jean thought, "This is a sickness not worthy of a single soul belonging to one of those young men. Yet, many may lose their souls because of man's folly. What a stupid creature man is."

With all of his equipment in front of him, Jean said to the others, "What you see here is everything. You must conserve ammunition. I will be in the bell tower. You are to follow my instructions. Do not fire unless I tell you. First Sergeant, stay in contact. Relay my instructions. If something happens to me, you take charge."

Waiting for someone to speak, Jean stopped giving instructions. No one spoke.

Continuing, he said, "I will place one more claymore in the shrubs in front. First Sergeant you install the other four to cover the rear gate. I will install control wires for those in front and you do the same in the rear. Run the wires to me in the bell tower. One man on each wall will have an M-60. One of you will handle ammo for him. Everyone will have an M-16 and one bandoleer of ammo. I will have an M-60 in the tower plus the LAWs. First Sergeant evenly distribute the grenades to those manning the walls. Does anyone have a question? Now is the time to ask it."

Again no one spoke and Jean said, "Okay, let's do it."

From his position in the bell tower, Jean had an excellent view. Each side of the tower had a ventilator cover made of slats. By looking between them, he could see into a nearby, government housing project. The administrative building, Vinh's headquarters, was next to the west wall with a narrow street separating them. Vinh's soldiers were already moving equipment into it. To see other areas, he moved to another ventilator. Doing this gave him a clear view for two blocks on streets surrounding the Cathedral. Also, a ladder provided access to a small, overhead room that housed the bells. From this location, his view was better but the bells restricted his movement. There were no covers over openings in the bells' room.

Satisfied with arrangements, Jean left the tower and went into the church to find Minh Thanh. Mother superior directed him to the wine cellar. Because it no longer contained wine racks, she had the wine moved into the catacombs. This provided additional space for living quarters. Being underground provided extra protection. He saw Minh Thanh, with their son, as he came down the stairs and waved to her.

"Oh Jean," she cried as he approached. "I am frightened. For some reason, I believe this Tet will be a disaster to our people."

Jean sat beside her on one of the spartan beds from the nuns' living quarters. He took Vinh into his arms and held him close while rocking him back and forth.

"Honestly, I do not know how bad this will be," he answered. "There are so many rumors. I will be in the bell tower where I can see. Sergeant Hoa and I will stand watch in the tower. If there are many troops, we will see them."

Minh Thanh leaned her head on Jean's shoulder as she sat beside him. He saw that she was wearing her favorite blue ribbon in her hair. She wore the same ribbon the day he found her in the market.

Jean moved Vinh to his left arm and placed his tiny body on his shoulder. He slipped his right arm around Minh Thanh's waist, pulling her closer. He continued his fore and aft rocking with the two most important people in his life beside him.

"When I left the Legion I thought my fighting was over," he thought. "Now, that I have everything I want in this world, I still have to fight. Dear Lord give us peace and protect these people who only want to do good."

An ache settled into his heart as he thought of his loved ones and their danger. Despite clamping his jaws tight, his eyes began to fill and his ache became almost overpowering. As a distraction, he began humming as he rocked. His mother sang an old French song to him when he was a child. He now hummed it to his loved ones.

Soon Vinh and Minh Thanh slept. Jean gently lowered Minh Thanh's upper body onto the bed. Arising slowly, he placed Vinh into his cradle. After lifting his wife's legs onto the bed, he kissed her on her forehead. Turning to his son, he brushed back a wisp of hair on his head. He gazed thoughtfully at him for a moment and then kissed him. He left the cellar for the bell tower. It was early evening 30 January 1968.

"Good evening colonel," Sergeant Hoa said. "We're getting some activity."

Immediately attentive, Jean asked. "What kind?"

Sergeant Hoa, still looking between the slats, said, "For the past six hours, many strangers entered that housing project. I know they are strangers because I have been here for ten years. I watched those buildings during construction and I watched as people occupied them. At one time or another, I have seen every one of them at our market place. The one's going into that project do not belong there."

"Have you heard anything from Major Vinh?" Jean asked as he looked at the administrative building.

"No sir, I haven't. They have not moved over there for two days. I suspect they are trying to keep their presence unknown to outsiders," Hoa responded.

Suddenly Sergeant Hoa said whispering, "Sir, look here quick."

Jean moved beside Hoa and looked outside. He saw a building's door open. A soldier, wearing an NVA uniform and carrying an AK-47, rushed out and immediately ran into an adjacent alley. He disappeared into darkness. Soon, another one did the same.

"Sergeant, alert Mother Superior and your people. Keep your radio close," Jean ordered.

Hurriedly, Sergeant Hoa disappeared down the tower's ladder.

Jean began loosening and removing slats from the lower part of every window. He removed enough so that he would have a clear field of fire in every direction. He returned to the window from which he had seen the NVA soldiers. He lowered himself to a prone position with his M-60 muzzle barely protruding outside the opening. For an hour, he watched over 50 NVA soldiers leave various doors in the housing project. However, every one of them entered the same alley. He relayed this information to Sergeant Hoa and Major Vinh.

"There is at least an infantry platoon in that alley," he thought. "Now, if they will only come out this way in a group."

At 03:00 hours, Jean saw two NVA soldiers. Each moved slowly to where the alley joined the main street and stopped. One was on each side of the alley. In unison, they quickly looked around their corners and pulled back into the shadows.

"That's their point men," Jean thought as he reached for an M-40 grenade launcher. "They will exit anytime now."

Whispering, he relayed his observations to Vinh and Sergeant Hoa. He moved his launcher into position and aimed for a spot 20 feet outside the alley. An eternity passed as he waited.

"Come on. Come on," he whispered. "Come on."

The point men appeared first. They hesitated for a moment and both turned left toward downtown Saigon. Within seconds, a steady steam of soldiers appeared moving quickly in the same direction. When what Jean estimated to be 20 soldiers reached his selected aiming point, he fired. Saigon descended into chaos.

As the 40-millimeter grenade exploded, Jean already was firing his M-60 with short, aimed bursts. Within ten seconds, no one was standing in the street. Jean counted 18 bodies. The others had returned to the alley. They had no idea where their attacker was.

Jean could hear explosions in every direction. Green and red tracers filled the night. Soon he could hear men's voices yelling commands.

"Easy, easy. Hold your fire until you have targets," Jean whispered to Sergeant Hoa. Major Vinh did not answer. Nevertheless, Jean knew they were okay. During the initial firing, Vinh's soldiers never fired.

"Wise soldier," Jean thought. "The NVA are not sure where we are but they do not know that Vinh's force even exists."

Jean watched a hand grenade fly from the alley's darkness. It left a firefly like trail as it flew through the air. It bounced twice in the street and exploded throwing tiny shrapnel against the wall's steel doors. No one fired.

"Trying to draw fire?" Jean considered.

"Sure thing but it didn't work," he answered.

To the East, Jean could see the night sky becoming light. He knew that the pinned platoon had an objective to take. They were not getting it done. They will come out of there soon. Jean steadied his shoulders and sighted along his M-60's barrel.

A loud cry came from the alley and the soldiers rushed out and turned left as they did the first time. Jean fired, as did the young men manning the wall below him. Over 40 NVA lay dead or dying in the street.

Jean heard men singing. He recognized the song. It was a Viet Minh victory song coming from his left. Sliding his body around, he looked down the street through another opening.

Marching up the street, he saw at least 200 NVA in formation. The ones in front carried VC flags and waved them wildly. The song they sang was about how the people rose and destroyed their oppressors.

"They're having a damned victory parade," Jean whispered aloud. "They are trying to get the locals to join them."

Jean radioed for Hoa and Vinh. Both of them answered.

"Sergeant Hoa, let them pass. Some will stop when they see the bodies. The others will disperse along the sides of the street. Do not fire. Wait until the first group gets past Vinh. We will engage the second group's rear. Hang tough," Jean said calmly. "They do not know we are here."

It was now full daylight and the bodies in the street were in plain view. The singers stopped and then dispersed as Jean predicted. They were fully alert and moving ahead in good battle order. The ones across the street searched rooftops and Jean's position repeatedly. Jean felt sure that they could see him but his mind knew better. Let them go. The ones on his side of the street searched above their comrades' heads. They moved one squad at a time while the others held to provide covering fire.

"Those are hard core NVA veterans," Jean thought. "They know what they are doing."

The intensity of explosions throughout Saigon grew to an almost unending roar. Automatic weapon's fire sounded almost as one continuous burst. In the distance, Jean saw groups of helicopters flying in formation toward the Presidential Palace. Beside them, Cobra gunships provided covering fire. Green tracers streaked toward them. One Huey aircraft crumpled in flight and fell in flames to the ground. Two of the Cobras attacked ground targets in the city with rockets. Buildings began to burn.

Suddenly, Hoa's youngest son began firing at the NVA across the street. Jean could not see the NVA on his side of the street. They were holding tight to cover. Jean held his fire while the others starting firing every weapon. In a few minutes, Jean saw a grenade come over the wall where the young man fired. It exploded destroying the wine racks and sending those on them to the ground. Hoa's youngest son did not move while the others got to their feet. Another grenade came over the wall and they scattered throwing themselves onto the ground. Shreds of hot steel flew across the courtyard whistling a death song as it went. He heard a cry from the back wall. Another youngster grabbed his leg and fell to one knee with blood pouring from between his fingers.

A third grenade came over the wall. It rolled a few feet and exploded harming no one. No one fired.

After a few minutes, Jean heard a whistle blow three blasts. He immediately recognized this as an NVA captain's whistle used to send commands. He was telling the others to move in a hurry.

"He figures the grenades took out their attackers," Jean thought as he rolled to his right.

From his new position, he could see up the street near where Vinh had his troops. Jean still could not see the NVA on his side of the street. They would have to get past the wall's corner before he could see them from his position. As instructed, the others did not fire until the first group was past Vinh's position. When the second group appeared, his men started firing. Almost simultaneously, Vinh's troops began hitting them with 40-millimeter grenades and machine gun fire. With the second column in view, Jean began firing. The NVA were in crossfire. Those who stayed died. Some of those who ran to cover lived.

As Jean fired, a rocket-propelled grenade (RPG) struck the steel gates. The explosion bent one side so that only one hinge held it in place. It was twisted and torn. As Jean moved to see where the RPG came from, a rifle round struck a bell in the upper room. Soon three more struck. He lay completely still.

"They believe I am up there," he thought as a crescendo of projectiles ricocheted among the bells.

Jean had two choices. Remain were he was and not fire for a long time or climb down and join the others. He remained where he was. Firing into the bells stopped.

One month later firing continued. The Cathedral's bell tower was gone. It lay in a pile of timbers on top of the courtyard's fishpond. Bodies of the first NVA platoon they first engaged still lay in the street. Both steel gates no longer existed. The housing project lay in smoldering ruins. Thousands of civilians lay dead in the smoking debris. Death's smell permeated everything.

Fortunately, Major Vinh was able to get supplies into the Cathedral. Jean watched as he and his men came in the back gate. They brought wounded on stretchers and other wounded hobbled along as best they could. They arrived in armored personnel carriers (APC).

Jean, unkempt and haggard, walked slowly toward Vinh. In his right hand, he carried an M-16. It was the only weapon with any remaining ammunition. Exhausted, Jean fell into a seated position on an empty crate. Vinh sat beside him.

"How are Minh Thanh and Vinh?" He asked.

"They are alive. Otherwise, they are in hell. We lost water the first week. We dumped human waste in the catacombs. The stench in the cellar is horrid. Those the sisters could not save we burned behind the cathedral. Eventually, we ran out of fuel so we kept dumping and covered them with what lime we had. I still hear firing. What is the situation?"

"We're cleaning out pockets of resistance. Apparently, the Cholon district was their main staging area. They got 16 sappers inside the embassy. They died the first day. You probably heard the B-52 strikes near the city. Once the NVA and VC did not get support from the locals, they began a staged withdrawal from one housing project to another. To get at them, we had to destroy the projects. Headquarters estimates that there are over 15,000 civilians killed and 1,000,000 homeless in the Saigon area," Vinh explained sounding exhausted.

Jean started to speak but Vinh raised his hand and stopped him. Vinh removed his canteen and handed it to Jean. Jean took it and ran to the cellar stairs. Working his way among the refugees and wounded, he found Minh Thanh with their son. They lay on the floor beside an elderly woman on their bed. The woman had a blood soaked bandage on each leg. Neither Minh Thanh nor his son moved.

Jean took a bandage from a pouch on his belt. He removed it from its sterile covering and poured water onto the gauze, soaking it. Kneeling, Jean placed the gauze against his son's lips. He immediately began to suckle. Minh Thanh's eyes fluttered as she moved and felt for Vinh. She touched Jean's hand.

Startled awake, Minh Thanh rolled onto her back and saw Jean. She gasped aloud at his appearance. Climbing to her knees, she entwined him with her arms.

"Oh Mother of Jesus, when will this end?" She moaned.

"Its over for now," Jean said. "Here, take this. You need it for Vinh."

Since Vinh was getting water, she put the canteen to her lips. Her split lips rebelled at the metal's touch and sent pain throughout her jaw. Nevertheless, the water tasted like the finest water from the finest spring. She began to cough and Jean took the canteen.

"Easy," he said. "I will help you outside. Your brother is there. I saw a Red Cross truck arriving when I left to come here."

Jean lifted Vinh with his left arm and helped Minh Thanh stand erect with his right. When they reached the stairs, others were beginning to leave. Jean helped her climb the stairs. As sunlight struck her eyes, she squinted and threw her arm over them for protection from the glare. She had not seen sunlight in four weeks. She thought she saw her brother as she fainted.

Chapter Forty

January 1968

Communism has never come to power in a country that was not disrupted by war or corruption, or both.
John F. Kennedy (1917–63), U.S. Democratic politician, president. Speech, 3 July 1963, to NATO

General of Artillery Nguyen Van Anh mourned losing his mother. She was the most important person alive with whom he could share every thought, problem, and dream. With her gone, there was no way to fill the void in his daily life. She was waiting when he returned from his office and long missions away from home. She was his conscience, adviser, and confidant.

"Yes," he thought, "She, on occasion, treated me like a child. Invariably, because I acted like one."

Over the years, he had lovers. One of them was special and he had considered marriage. However, she set about trying to change him to something he was not. Their love spoiled like milk exposed to a contaminate. He did not need changing.

"Perhaps I am self centered," Anh considered. "Nevertheless, I could not live a life that was not mine. She wanted me to live a life that existed in her mind. It was a fantasy with me as a person I was not. It was good that we never married. It would have been a disaster. Yet, with mother gone, I am truly alone."

He knew that his sister Minh Thanh, his brother Vinh, and Uncle Diem were somewhere in South Viet Nam. According to the message found in his boot, they escaped to safety. However, that was long ago and the war exposed his loved ones to death at any time. They both could be dead and he would not know.

He found little pleasure with his promotion to Brigadier General. He had no one with whom to share it. He had the recognition of his colleagues but that carried the taint of professional jealousy. He came from the rice paddies of Muong Valley while many of his peers were graduates of major universities in the USSR and PRC. He gained his knowledge from experience in combat. Most of the others gained their knowledge in a classroom. They were not pleased when he became the officer in charge of artillery operations for their upcoming attack.

"Pardon me sir. You have a General Staff meeting in 30 minutes," Second Lieutenant Phong said.

"Thank you. I will be along in a moment," Anh replied. "I need to check two more items."

"Yes sir," Phong said from the doorway of Anh's underground quarters.

Getting up from his field table, Anh took his candle with him to see his maps. He crossed his small room to a map mounted on a wooden frame.

"Surely they will allow generator use again soon," he thought. "Every time there is a report of a suspected reconnaissance aircraft, they stop using every generator. They cannot detect our generators 50 feet underground."

Arriving at his map, Anh lit two candles on each end of the map board. The flickering flames danced reflections across the acetate, making map reading difficult.

He studied the disposition of two, newly arrived divisions, the 325th and the 304th. The Chief of Staff had not yet made a decision as to which division he would use to cover Highway 9. Anh's position was that they needed a third division to close the highway.

"We must deny that highway to the enemy," Anh reflected. "If they can move freely on it, they will be able to reinforce easily. Hopefully, I can convince them today."

Anh recalled a major problem he had at Dien Bien Phu. He remembered how difficult it was to keep enough artillery ammunition on hand to support operations.

"That really infuriated Vinh," he remembered. "Well, if he was here now, that would not be a problem. For six months, logistical units have been pre-positioning artillery ammunition. The Americans have found some of it but not much. I am confident that there is enough to support a sustained offensive for five months if need be."

Anticipating his aide's return, Anh rolled down his sleeves and buttoned them. He put on his plain tunic void of any decorations. With it buttoned, he took his hat from his field desk just as Phong entered.

"Ready to go general," Phong asked.

"Yes, yes. Do you have my copies of the artillery plan?" Anh asked.

"Yes sir. They are in the next room. I will retrieve them as we leave," Phong answered.

"Turn out the lights," Anh said with a chuckle. "We don't want to overwork the generators."

Phong grinned and snuffed each candle as Anh left the room. Phong hurried to stay with the general. While his temples were gray, he was quick of foot and mind. There were few generals with his understanding of combat tactics. He had fought at Dien Bien Phu with the 325th as an artilleryman. General Giap personally selected him to coordinate fire support for their entire attack.

Phong took position ahead of Anh to light their way with a flashlight. As he moved, he made sure that the general was close. Their passageway footing was poor with two boards to keep their feet clear of the ever-present muck. Its ceiling was low for the general and his head often brushed unlit light bulbs strung overhead.

"The first turn to the right is just ahead general," Phong advised Anh as he walked even slower.

As they turned, Phong moved his flashlight from side to side so the general could stay in the passage's middle. Its weak light showed supporting timbers every ten feet along its sides. Overhead beams alternated every ten feet for additional support. From each of these beams, a light bulb dangled from an electrical wire.

"The last turn is to the left and coming up now sir," Phong advised as he lighted the tunnel's left side. "The meeting room will be on our left after we make the turn sir."

Phong almost bumped into the guard at the meeting room's entrance.

"Watch where you are going idiot," the guard chastised Phong.

Before Phong could answer, the overhead lights flickered and gradually illuminated. With the additional light, the guard saw Anh behind Phong and immediately came to attention.

"I am most sorry general," he stammered.

"Don't worry about it son. Who could possibly expect you to see in the dark?" Anh commented.

As soon as Phong went through the entrance, he stepped to his right to allow Anh to enter.

As Anh passed, he said to Phong, "Turn off the flashlight. We will probably need it before this meeting ends."

Tobacco smoke floated in layers above the heads of officers in the meeting room. They sat on two rows of bench seats with a small aisle between them. The first row was immediately ahead of Anh. Commanders of subordinate units sat on the first two rows. Staff officers occupied the remaining 15 rows. General's aides lined the walls standing.

To Anh's left, there was a step up to a platform about two feet higher than the rest of the room. Four tables, placed end to end, formed one table that ran its width. Behind the table, seated in individual chairs, was the NVA General Staff.

Anh stepped up and took a seat behind a small nameplate that read, "General of Artillery." As he sat, he turned to the officer seated next to him.

"I thought we were supposed to have ventilation by now. It's almost impossible to breathe in here," Anh said.

The officer spoken to, also a brigadier, hunched his shoulders up and replied, "Perhaps Giap will make them quit smoking."

Other officers wandered into the meeting. Soon the front table was full except for one seat in the middle. Behind the middle chair, there was another like it.

Anh saw General Giap's aide step through the entrance as he announced, "Gentlemen, the commanding officer."

In unison, every person in the room came to attention. General Giap entered and went to the platform's middle seat and stopped behind it. His aide stood behind his seat directly to Giap's rear.

"Please extinguish your cigarettes and pipes. The smoke burns my eyes," he said at almost a whisper.

As General Giap took his seat, there was a rush to dispose of smoking materials. As Giap looked around the room, he nodded to some familiar faces and rendered a slight smile.

Giap turned to Lieutenant General Whinh Van Noc, Chairman of The General Staff, seated to his right, smiled, and said, "General."

Anh looked closely at Giap; this was the first time that he had seen him close since Dien Bien Phu. He was a frail man, small in stature but always appearing pleasant. His crossed hands, on the table, appeared almost translucent. Blood vessels ran across them in tiny blue streaks.

"He appears extremely tired," Anh thought. "Yet, other staff members say that he works 20 hour days."

As General Noc arose, two of his staff members went to the far wall and retrieved a large map. They remained at the table's far end and turned the map for everyone to see.

Turning to General Giap, General Noc said, "Thank you sir."

Next, Noc directed everyone's attention to the map and said, "This is the last operations meeting before our attack on the 21st of January. On General Anh's recommendation, I am putting the 388th Light Armored Division in place to control Highway 9. Their mission is to intercept and destroy any attempt to resupply or reinforce units in the Khe Sanh Area."

General Noc gave Anh a quick glance, as did many of the seated commanders. Anh could feel some of their jealousy cutting into him with stares.

General Noc continued, "We will commence the attack with elements of the 304th crossing the river. There will be an intense rocket attack against Khe Sanh forces while they cross. They will eliminate small units around Khe Sanh's main base with one regiment. The 2nd Regiment of the 304th will pass through units occupying these positions to strike the main base. If, for any reason, the 2nd Regiment stalls, the 3rd Regiment will join their attack."

Anh laughed to himself as he watched commanders of the named units pretend to take notes. Others stared with grim looks and then would write some more.

"If after six month's preparation, they do not know what their jobs are, they should not be here. If they are trying to impress General Giap, they are definitely giving the wrong impression. Giap never takes notes. He has everything in his head," Anh thought.

"This first phase of our attack is to locate every defensive location around Khe Sanh and assess its strength. Every attacking unit will withdraw across the river no later than 15:00 hours to prepared positions. Report every detail about enemy dispositions and strengths to this headquarters immediately after your withdrawals."

Noc glanced around the room for anyone indicating they had a question. None did so he continued.

"The 388th will make a secondary attack against the Special Forces Camp at Lang Vei. Remember the primary mission is to control the highway. I will discuss the Hue attacks in a moment but first I want our communications officer to give a short talk about communications security," Noc said as he took his seat.

A nondescript lieutenant colonel, standing against the wall near the map, stepped forward and said, "Since our last meeting, I distributed new crypto procedures to each unit. This is a major change to keep the enemy from decoding our sensitive transmissions. Any classified information transmitted must use this method. Our comrades in the USSR assure us that the enemy cannot decode it. They have validated this system in World War II, Korea, and against NATO. So please use it."

The colonel stepped back to the wall and looked at General Noc. Noc got to his feet and gestured toward Anh. Noc sat while Anh arose and went to the map.

Turning toward the group, Anh explained, "There are three divisions of artillery available not counting rockets and mortars. For the initial attack, there will be a rocket barrage against all positions. Artillery regiments will support their division's fire requests. After 15:00 hours, every artillery unit will revert to my temporary control. There will be a time on target (TOT) firing mission against Khe Sanh's ammunition stores, fuel supplies, and airfield on my command. Every artillery piece will fire in a timed fashion so that every projectile will arrive at the targets at the same moment. This amount of concentrated firepower will destroy every target."

As Anh spoke, he pointed to each target. After this, he made eye contact with each commander in the two front rows. His purpose was to make sure that they understood their artillery would be his.

Anh continued, "When I release control to the individual units that is the signal for the main attack. You can expect it take place in the early morning hours of the 22nd. After you have control of these hills, you will move your artillery to them. This is the highest ground in the Khe Sanh area. You will be able to dominate the battle from these positions. There is an ample ammunition supply so do not hesitate to use this firepower. The enemy will certainly use theirs. Thank you."

Anh walked the length of the front row to return to his seat. As he did so, he came abreast of General Giap. From the corner of his eye, he saw Giap smiling with obvious pleasure. He was a strong advocate of artillery firepower. He made that clear at Dien Bien Phu."

The meeting lasted another 30 minutes. General Noc gave an overview of the Hue attack. To end their meeting, General Giap explained how he was using the Khe Sanh attack to draw General Westmoreland's forces from the south. Nine days later NVA and NLF forces would strike hard across South Viet Nam. Opposition would be minimal. In addition, people across South Viet Nam would join their cause to bring down Thieu's corrupt government.

General Noc closed the meeting. Everyone came to attentions as General Giap left the platform. As Giap passed behind Anh, Anh felt two gentle pats on his left shoulder. Anh stared ahead without moving.

After General Giap was clear of the room, General Noc asked that Anh remain. The others filed out through the narrow exit talking excitedly among themselves. This was to be their second Dien Bien Phu and they looked forward to bringing the Americans, and their allies, to their knees.

In a few moments, General Noc dismissed his aides holding the map. Anh indicated for Lieutenant Phong to go with them. General Noc gestured for Anh to sit beside him.

As Anh sat, Noc said in a low voice, "General, we are depending on your artillery. We must inflict as much damage as possible in a short time on the enemy. Forget moving artillery units onto the hills around Khe Sanh. The Americans would soon destroy them with B-52s. We cannot afford the losses. So be prepared to either remain in the DMZ or withdraw to prepared protected positions. This situation is not the same as Dien Bien Phu. General Giap knows it as both you and I do. The French had no aerial support. The Americans have massive resources."

Anh, not surprised, answered, "Yes sir."

"In addition," Noc continued, "There will be no second, massive offensive attack. Units on the river's south side will begin making trenches. This is going to be a siege situation. This part of the operation will be much like Dien Bien Phu. This is the only way we can attack with minimal damage. Attacks in the open will be few. The only time I see it happening is if a unit takes an objective and needs to maintain momentum. We must convince Westmoreland to commit major units to this area."

This information did no take Anh by surprise. He did not understand why the unit commanders did not receive the information. If they knew, they could enhance the mission by being prepared. This way the surprise might cause some to make mistakes. There was little room for mistake without disastrous results.

"Sir, why were the unit commanders not told," Anh asked.

Noc responded, "General Giap wants the unit's morale high with hope of a major victory. If they knew, they would not attack vigorously and could destroy our intent. Our intent is to convince the enemy that this is our main thrust."

Anh nodded agreement and said, "I understand sir."

General Noc turned his chair a half turn toward Anh and asked. "Didn't you oversee our supply route development through Laos and Cambodia?"

"That's correct, sir," Anh answered.

"General Giap is extremely pleased with your work. Those routes are essential. If, for any reason, the enemy should decide to move major combat units astride it, our effort would be lost. To keep this from happening, General Giap is counting on political pressure against President Johnson. Our sources tell us that Johnson wants out and he has told General Giap so in writing. If we can convince the American People that we are getting stronger, they will force Johnson to remove his forces. That's what General Giap wants from this offensive. Your artillery can deny support to Khe Sanh and cause many more casualties than our infantry," General Noc said, as he stood erect.

Continuing, he said, "We're a short distance from the DMZ. Come with me on a quick look at the situation."

While Noc spoke, light bulbs began to dim indicating that they would soon quit working. Noc and Anh's aides turned on their flashlights to illuminate the room's exit.

"Shit," Noc said. "Let's get some sunlight."

Noc and Anh exited their command bunker beneath trees on the north side of a mountain. Extensive camouflage kept their compound relatively secure from aerial attacks. Since occupying the new complex, there had not been a single attack in six months. This was unusual since they were only five miles north of the DMZ.

Anh attributed their success at avoiding detection to a number of things. While it required considerable effort, their communications array was remotely controlled. The NVA made sure that antennas remained away from communication complexes. In addition, they moved them on an erratic schedule so that reconnaissance aircraft could not get a fix on them.

Furthermore, they required that vehicles disperse. Vehicle movement took place beneath trees so that vehicle wear on the terrain would not reveal positions. Mechanics took parts to individual vehicles for repair rather than having them gather in motor pools.

General Noc's vehicle was an American Jeep parked at a large tree's base. It had no windshield or rearview mirrors. Commanders made sure that reflective surfaces did not exist on every vehicle. This precluded Forward Air Controllers (FAC) from seeing a reflective flash.

Noc's driver took a circuitous route to the DMZ. He parked beneath overhead cover at Noc's direction. Noc and Anh left their vehicle and proceeded on foot to a knoll overlooking the DMZ. From their location, they had an excellent view of unit positions.

General Noc said, "It is time for weather in this area to get worse. It is my hope that it comes soon. With our AAA units in position, and poor weather, it will be difficult for resupply of Khe Sanh. At best, they might get some things in by helicopter but not enough to affect the outcome. What do you think?"

"General, I agree but I have major concerns," Anh answered. "The American units have ground surveillance radar equipment. Their artillery has target acquisition radar. They have placed seismic detection devices throughout approaches to their positions. They will detect our advancing troops no matter what the weather is."

"I agree," Noc replied. "That's some of the reasons we will be using trenches."

"General," Anh began, "I must advise that there will be carpet bombing with B-52s. It does not matter what the weather is. They will bomb our positions with considerable accuracy. We will have major losses. I sincerely hope that the sacrifices made here bring rewards in the south. If we can get a general uprising, we will prevail. I think we can do that sir."

"General Giap believes so," Noc commented. "I have advised him of everything you mentioned. You have an excellent grasp of firepower and its use. Giap's faith in you is well founded. You ready?"

"Yes sir," Anh said as he turned to leave.

Slightly before dawn on 25 January 1968, Anh watched as the sky to the south glowed as thousands of rockets launched from units within the DMZ. Ground units, under the cover of this barrage, started advancing across the river. Almost immediately, the enemy detected them and hit hard with artillery and mortars. As planned, they started their withdrawal across the river to the north.

Anh, in his fire support coordination center, already had every NVA artillery unit under his direct control. He had three TOT missions already computed. The first mission was the main base at Khe Sanh. The second was the ammunition and supply storage area. His final TOT would be the airfield.

Anh watched the second hand on the wall clock and said to the telephone operator, "Fire mission one."

Every NVA artillery unit fired at different times based upon their particular firing data. The result was that every projectile fired from every weapon hit Khe Sanh' main base at the same time. Some projectiles burst in the air to rain shrapnel upon personnel. Other shells were white phosphorus to start fires and burn through protective cases to ignite explosives. Projectiles with delay fuses penetrated bunkers and exploded inside protected areas.

Anh continued to watch the clock. At the artillery units, crewmen were traversing and elevating their weapons. Other crewmen were setting their fuses to achieve desired effect against their next target.

When every unit reported ready, Anh commanded, "Fire mission two."

Khe Sanh's supply dump erupted with massive explosions. C-4 plastic explosives, by the tons, began to explode. Artillery shells, small arms ammunition, grenades, anti-tank rockets and jet fuel sent blazing clouds tens of thousands of feet into the air.

Fifteen minutes later Anh said, "Fire mission three."

As the NVA shells hit the airfield, pieces of blazing hot, perforated steel plate whistled across the area. Its razor sharp edges cutting through most anything it touched. Craters appeared in the runway. Aircraft exploded and burned.

Anh nodded to the telephone operator and said, "Return control to the Division Commanders. Take damage reports for target analysis. I will be in the intelligence bunker if you need me."

Anh traveled through the command bunker's passages until he came to the intelligence section. He entered a room with three walls lined with radios and telephones. Operators were taking messages and passing them to other soldiers who were posting reports on a battle map. It was almost possible to feel tension racing around the room. Everyone worked at a hectic pace. Moving through the group, Anh went into a separate room.

When he entered, a Teletype operator started to get up but Anh told him to stay seated. Taking a pad from the operator's desk, Anh wrote a message to General Noc in Hanoi.

Anh handed the message to the operator and said, "Send this."

Sliding the message to his left, the operator began typing. In less than a minute, he finished. He turned and gave Anh a questioning gaze.

Anh nodded to indicate, "Yes."

The soldier folded the message so that it had a small point. He lit the message with a match and held it above a metal trash container, as the flames grew larger. When it became too hot to hold, he dropped the flaming paper into the container. Anh and the operator watched it curl and turn into one black mass. Using a nearby poker, the operator reduced the remainder into a pile of ashes.

"Thank you son," Anh said as he left the room. He followed his former path through intelligence and out where he had entered. As he walked along the dim passageway toward his fire support center, he thought, "I damn sure hope that Soviet equipment works or the Americans are reading our mail."

As Anh entered his work area, he took a pile of messages from his telephone operator. He went into his private room and sat at his field table. He began reading reports from forward observers as to the effectiveness of their TOT missions.

After reading the last message, Anh clasped his hands behind his head. He leaned back and gazed at the ceiling deep in thought.

"Khe Sanh is an inferno. Their ammunition storage area is destroyed and continuing to explode. The airfield cannot is useless. Great," he thought. "Now, we are going to catch hell."

At Khe Sanh, a continuing flight of CH-46 Sea Knight helicopters began bringing supplies to its Marine defenders. The attack against the Special Forces base was a success with its defenders deserting it. Nonetheless, the NVA lost a number of PT76 armored vehicles in the process.

NVA AAA began taking its toll on supply helicopters. They returned with fighter-bomber escorts that suppressed their antiaircraft unit's effectiveness.

However, the weather turned to General Noc's liking. It got much worse.

C-130 aircraft began trying to supply the base using a low altitude extraction method. The aircraft flew down the runway only a few feet from the ground. From inside, parachutes attached to supply pallets deployed from the craft's open cargo ramp. The parachutes jerked the supplies out and onto the runway. Upon impact, many of the pallets exploded into useless pieces. Other loads continued in motion for considerable distances after leaving the airplanes. Finally, one went into a group of Marines killing some and injuring many. This attempted method of resupply stopped. They returned to conventional drops from altitude.

General Westmoreland reinforced with almost 10,000 Marines. This provided considerable defensive strength. On the hills surrounding the main base, there were constant attacks and counter attacks. As predicted, the B-52s struck with carpet bombing within a few hundred yards of the Marines.

In late February, Anh sent his aide to arrange a private meeting with the General Staff's Intelligence Officer, Brigadier General Kohan Van Biep. They met in Biep's private room in the command bunker.

Biep slowly poured rice wine into a small cup in front of where Anh sat at a field table. Biep, sitting directly across from Anh, filled his cup next. Biep lowered his head slightly and Anh returned the gesture. Anh held his cup with both hands and took a small sip. He complimented Biep for his good taste in wines. Biep returned Anh's ritualistic gesture in kind. The pair made appropriate small talk before Biep ended their social requirements.

"How can I be of service?" Biep asked.

"What have you heard from the southern operation?" Anh asked.

Biep thought for a moment and said, "The initial effort looked very good. In particular, Hue was a standout with popular support. The Hue Buddhists were tired of the regime in Saigon. They were ready to remove the corrupt politicians and bureaucrats. However, we did not get the desired support in other areas. Saigon, in particular, was a major disappointment."

"I hear many rumors," Anh replied. "My sources tell me that the NLF is lost as a fighting force."

"I think that is a hasty judgment," Biep responded. "It is much too soon to tell. They are still fighting in Saigon and other areas," Biep commented.

Before Anh could speak, Biep put one finger in front of his lips indicating for Anh to be silent. Getting up, Biep went to the entrance to his office and looked into the other room. Satisfied that no one was paying them any particular attention, he lowered a canvas covering over the doorway. Almost in total darkness, Biep lit a candle and placed it in a holder that he set on the table in front of Anh. He filled their cups and sat.

"Anh, senior members of the Central Committee are saying good things about you. It is important that you speak of matters in a way that reflects favorably upon the party and its strategy for the Central Committee determines what and how the party functions," Biep said.

Biep stopped speaking for a moment and took a small sip of his wine. All the while, he watched Anh across the rim of his cup. Unable to discern any reaction from Anh, he continued.

"Keep in mind that every military action has a political objective. A military objective may fail but a political objective may prevail. The NLF, as an effective fighting force, no longer exists. They have suffered a major defeat across the south. Nonetheless, our political objective is a resounding success,' Biep explained.

"How so?" Anh asked.

"The United States imperialist leaders are in total disarray. They are confused at how we were able to mount such a major effort throughout South Viet Nam. Their media keeps our cause before their people and erode any indication of success made by President Johnson. As a national leader, he is a failure," Biep said with a wry smile.

"I understand," Anh said. "There can be only one response to Johnson's regime. Replace it with one that will end their participation in the conflict; thus, we will have succeeded politically."

"Exactly," Biep responded enthusiastically. "What they say about you is true. Your future is bright comrade Anh."

Anh arose and bowed saying, "Thank you. I hope I can count on your support with the Central Committee. Your wise counsel makes clear what I suspected."

Biep responded in kind adding, "You are welcome. It is always my pleasure to see that our leadership always has the counsel of those who understand our cause. You have my support."

Anh explained that he must return to his fire support center. The Americans had reinforced the Marines at Khe Sanh with the 1st Cavalry Division. In addition, they were helping at Hue. It was important that he assure that artillery units made maximum use of their capabilities against these new arrivals.

During his return, Anh thought, "I know Biep loves the idea of my kissing his ass. However, it was necessary to confirm what I already expected. Our attack was a failure and it's time to save as much of our artillery as we can. As for his political meandering, his perception of America's desires for this conflict is in error. The American attitude is 'win the damn thing and get out.' With Johnson gone, they may provide a leader to do just that. All they have to do is sever our supply route to the south."

Anh, using their new USSR encoding equipment, sent a message to Chief of Staff Noc. He requested permission to begin bringing artillery units north of the DMZ. Anh knew that, if Noc approved his request, they would begin withdrawing ground units. It would be impossible for them to remain without fire support.

Furthermore, Anh continued his daily practice of scanning prisoner of war (POW) reports. During the last days of the Hue battle, he recognized a name, Major Nguyen Van Diem an Airborne Ranger unit leader. Anh read the name with an ominous foreboding.

"Is this my father's brother?" he wondered.

"There is only one way to learn if it is," he thought. "I will have to take the chance."

Chapter Forty One

July 1971

Valor is of no service, chance rules all, and the bravest often fall by the hands of cowards.
Tacitus (c. 55–c. 120), Roman historian. The Histories, bk. 4, sct. 29

"What the hell?" Major Zane wondered as he opened his eyes.

Red and blue light reflections moved around the walls and ceiling of his guard post in a repeating circular fashion. From outside, he could hear a loud chanting by male voices.

"Let it burn. Let it burn," they said, interspersed with handclaps.

Zane arose to a sitting position. He looked around the recreation room of the Reserve Officers Training Corps (ROTC) at Saint Mary's University. Between slats in venetian blinds, he saw flashing lights atop emergency vehicles. They appeared to surround the building.

Putting his two-way radio to his head, he pressed its transmit button.

"Security, you there?" He asked.

"Yes major we are here," a campus policeman answered, sounding disgusted and perturbed. "Some idiot knew you were in there and called in a false alarm."

Getting up, Zane walked to a window and raised the blinds. As he did, the singing increased in volume.

"Let it burn. Let it burn," they cried.

Responding to a knock at the door, Zane opened it. A fireman, axe in hand, stood in full fire fighting gear.

"Everything okay major?" he asked.

Zane replied, "I think so."

"I had better check," the fireman said, sounding weary of the situation.

He entered and left the recreation room to examine the rest of the building. Returning shortly, he passed Zane to exit.

"Everything is fine," he said. "When are these kids going to learn?"

Zane stepped outside into the glare of blinding spotlights. From outside the lights, he heard a resounding roar from what sounded like a crowd at a football game. Away from the lights, his eyes began to adjust and his vision improved. On a hillside near a dormitory, he saw the school's drill team standing and cheering.

"Way to go Major Z. He's our man. If he can't do it no one can," they chanted.

"Jesus," Zane thought. "It's the whole drill team. What a bunch of clowns they are. Except this time they have gone too far."

Zane walked to an area away from the crowd and motioned the drill team to join him. They ran down the hill dressed in Bermuda shorts and tee shirts, laughing as they came.

As the first of the group neared Zane, he asked. "Arty, who did this?"

The group gathered around Zane, their merriment replaced with a somber demeanor. They sensed that Zane was not amused.

Zane turned in place while looking into each man's eyes and asked. "Who did this?"

In unison, they replied, "Not one of us sir."

Their leader, Cadet Colonel Arthur "Arty" Artearga, said, "Sir, we heard the sirens. We could see that there was no fire so we watched the show. No team member would do this."

Zane placed his right hand on Arty's shoulder and said, "Good enough. I have to return to guard duty. You guys sleep well. I will."

Zane returned to the R.O.T.C. building. Waiting to meet him was Chief of Campus Security Mathon.

"Sorry for the trouble major," Mathon said. "We will learn who did this. You rest easy tonight. We have the building covered."

"Thanks sergeant major. You don't have to apologize for some kid's antics," Zane answered as he entered the building.

"Goodnight major," Mathon said.

"Goodnight sergeant major," Zane answered.

After locking the door behind him, Zane returned to the sofa to retrieve his radio. He made a communications check with campus security as he sat. With the emergency vehicle's departure, the recreation room became dark. An outside security light provided some light but only enough to see large pieces of furniture. It was now quiet as Zane's thoughts turned to St. Mary's and his current assignment.

"I should not be here," he thought. "According to DA assignment policies, helicopter pilots had 18 months between Viet Nam assignments. I was supposed to return to Nam from Fort Rucker. Instead, they sent me to this lucrative assignment. I think I know why."

Zane arrived at Fort Rucker on schedule. As soon as he reported, he went to a Method of Instruction (MOI) course. The course's purpose was to teach him how to train others to fly Hueys, which came as a surprise. He had little experience with the utility helicopter. He expected Chinook training.

Nevertheless, he found the training a challenge. It was necessary that he increase his piloting skills to precision flying while at the same time talking a student through every maneuver. Regardless of what situation an inept student might place him in, he had to recover his aircraft. Accordingly, his instructor, CWO Filtzer, put extensive emphasis on emergency procedures.

Chief Filtzer had completed his second Viet Nam tour as a medevac pilot. Members of his group earned respect because of their dedication and flying prowess. They did not fly in groups following other ships. They flew single ship missions into hot LZs, night or day, and in any kind of weather. Each was a hero in the eyes of ground unit members. If they became a casualty, they knew that a medevac crew would get them to a hospital or die trying.

"Major," Chief Filtzer said. "You have MOI down pat. It's time for the precision flying phase."

The pair had entered a stage field's traffic pattern and were traveling the downwind leg. To their right, narrow runways ran parallel to their course. On the runways, three foot, white squares appeared every 200 feet along its length.

As Zane started to turn their Huey on the pattern's baseleg, Filtzer said, "Do not descend on base. Maintain this altitude on final. Hang loose; I want you to do something for me."

Zane maintained 2,000 feet as they flew immediately over a runway. He watched the white squares disappear behind them.

After they passed the last square, there was no more runway. Filtzer turned off engine power and Zane immediately started an autorotation, as if they had an engine failure.

"Put us on the square we just passed," Filtzer directed.

Zane immediately pulled the craft's cyclic control (joystick) to the rear and watched the ship's airspeed drop to zero. In order to land safely, it was necessary that the rotor blades remain optimum revolutions per minute (RPM). Zane watched as RPMs began falling rapidly.

"Jesus Christ," he thought, "We're falling like a brick."

Next, the Huey began to vibrate and make loud sounds of metal hitting metal. He had pulled the cyclic so far to the rear that the engine's overhead shaft to the rotor blades was banging against the ring holding the blades to their ship. Immediately, Zane pushed the cyclic forward to gain airspeed and RPMs. Meanwhile their altitude loss was significant.

Zane had decided that he had to add power or they would crash when Filtzer said, "Take it to the ground."

"The damned fool wants an autorotation to the ground. I cannot add power. Bullshit," Zane thought as he added power and recovered to normal flight.

Filtzer said, "I've got it," and took control of their helicopter.

As Filtzer continued climbing to 2,000 feet, he asked. "Major, what are you going to do when you loose an engine and the only landing area is behind you?"

Zane answered, "Pick the best spot I can and hope that I don't crash and burn."

"Major, you could have made it to where I said and landed with enough rotor RPMs to have made another landing," Filtzer explained.

"No way in hell," Zane thought but said, "I will have to see that."

"Coming up," Filtzer said.

After flying the traffic pattern, Filtzer came to the same place that he initiated an engine failure for Zane. He reduced engine torque to idle and entered autorotation. He pulled the cyclic as far as possible to the rear as Zane had. However, unlike Zane, he held it there and the mast began banging.

"Damn, we're falling backwards," Zane observed with sincere concern.

"Look between your legs," Filtzer directed.

Zane looked between his legs to see through the Huey's plastic nose. He saw the white square appear but they were falling backward with zero airspeed and few rotor RPMs.

"Now, full forward on the cyclic to get our airspeed. Watch the RPMs so that we don't exceed their limit. They are going to climb like hell. When you see a normal landing sight picture approaching, place the ship in a landing attitude. At about three feet, level the ship and give a firm upward pull on the collective to cushion our landing," Filtzer explained.

Zane watched each event take place exactly as Filtzer described. He knew that when Filtzer said, 'upward pull on the collective' he meant the control in his left hand. The collective was the same as a thrust lever on a Chinook. It changed the rotor blades' angle of attack. By pulling up, the blades would bite into the air and stop their descent. Without engine power, the pilot used energy stored in the rotor blades to stop a descent. Normally, it was a one shot deal. Pull at a high altitude and the ship would slam hard on landing.

Filtzer landed gently and precisely on the white square. The runway's yellow centerline bisected the Huey from front to rear.

"Now there's this," Filtzer said as the Huey went airborne; made a 180-degree turn, setting down pointed in the opposite direction.

"I'll be damned," Zane said over the intercom.

Filtzer directed, "Now, you do it."

During the next two weeks, Zane learned to fly as he never had in the past. The craft seemed to become part of him. He was sensitive to every sound and movement. He knew what they were and what they meant. His confidence soared with every flight. Having flown Chinooks, he held some disdain toward the Huey. It disappeared and a sincere appreciation for the craft's capabilities grew.

After passing his final check ride, Zane received instructions to report to the training flight's commander. He knocked on Major Linstrom's office door, which was open.

"Come on in Zane," Linstrom said.

Linstrom was a balding, big man with large shoulders. He was much like Zane with an athletic build. In addition, Zane knew that Linstrom was on the promotion list to lieutenant colonel.

"Sit down Dale," he said. "You did well on your check ride. However, I expected it with Filtzer as your instructor. He's one of our best."

"Thanks. I enjoyed flying with him," Zane commented, as he wondered why he was to see Linstrom.

"I will get to the point. You are not supposed to be here. Someone screwed this up big time at personnel. General Beam saw orders assigning you to a Huey class as an instructor and he threw a shit fit," Linstrom stated.

Zane knew that Major General Nelson Beam was the new Commanding General of Fort Rucker and The Aviation Training Center. He was the same Nelson Beam who went to Viet Nam as a full colonel. He returned a major general with the distinction of being the youngest major general to command the post. He was 41 and an aviator in an aviator's war. It was a sure thing that he would get his third star at Rucker. After that, he would return to 'Nam in some senior aviation position. Unless he screwed up, he would get his fourth star. The scuttlebutt was that he would be the youngest chairman of the Joint Chiefs of Staff in its history.

Continuing Linstrom said, "You are to report to Chinook MOI to become a CH-47 instructor pilot (IP)."

"Tell me you're kidding," Zane replied. "I expected that assignment when I arrived. Personnel would not listen. They insisted that I go to the Huey IP course."

Linstrom added, "You need to go by personnel and get a copy of your orders. For the next eight weeks, you will be flying a Hook."

Zane thanked Linstrom and departed. He went to where CWO Filtzer sat at his desk.

Extending his hand, Zane said, "Chief, thanks for the superb instruction. I have an appreciation for the Huey that I did not have before flying with you."

Filtzer arose, shook Zane's hand, and said, "Major, it was my pleasure. You will make a fine Huey IP."

Zane asked. "Do you have time to drop by the club and let me buy you a drink?"

"You got it major. You need to spend some of that enormous flight pay on us poor Warrant Officers," Filtzer quipped.

"Don't give me any of that WOPA shit. Let's go. I have a sad tale to tell," Zane said laughing.

Sitting beside Filtzer on a barstool, Zane asked. "What' yours?"

"Bourbon and water," Filtzer answered.

"My kind of man. Barkeep two bourbon and waters in tall glasses," Zane told a nearby bartender who was wiping down the counter.

"Coming up," he answered.

"Chief, listen to this shit," Zane said.

After listening to Zane's news, Filtzer shook his head in bewilderment and said, "There goes my chance to save some more lives. I figure every IP I train will know enough about Hueys to save some rookies ass."

"Major," Filtzer asked, "Do you know what the wash out rate is these days? Don't answer. Let me tell you. How about ten percent? Would you believe ten percent?" Filtzer asked in disgust.

Continuing, Filtzer explained, "I was an IP teaching guys going through flight school before I went to MOI as an instructor. If you put a guy up for a check ride because he lacks proficiency, the standardization people pass the guy and send him back for five more hours. It is almost impossible to flunk anyone. I have given pink slips to students that read 'a danger to himself and to others. This man should not be flying.' The check pilots send them back for more training. The situation is serious major."

"Damn, I had no idea it was that bad," Zane replied. "I guess I should be thankful. The Chinook students will have considerably more experience than guys going through flight school for the first time."

Filtzer started laughing and said loudly, "Barkeep another round for my naïve friend."

"I predict," Filtzer said, "Students will go directly from Hueys into Hooks while at Rucker after completing flight school. Want to bet?"

"No thanks. I don't bet into pat hands. You've been here long enough to know more than I do," Zane answered.

As Zane started to speak, someone behind him clamped a hand onto his neck and began to shake him.

"Dale, you sorry sack of shit. What damned lies are you telling now," a familiar voice said.

Zane turned to see Daryl Scott, and immediately clamped him in a bear hug. Patrons turned to watch two field grade officers acting like kids.

"Where have you been?" Zane asked, beaming with joy at seeing Scott.

"First I took a month's leave and then dad passed away. I've been on emergency leave," Scott answered.

Zane turned to Filtzer, and then back to Scott saying, "Daryl meet the finest Huey driver this side of Shit City. This is CWO Filtzer. Chief this is Daryl Scott."

Scott shook hands with Filtzer and asked. "Have you been flying around with this dirt bag of your own free will?"

"No major. I had orders. Otherwise, there's no way," Filtzer answered.

Scott suddenly threw his arms wide. He gave Zane and Filtzer a shocked expression.

"Huey, what are you doing in a Huey? You are a Hooker to the bone Dale," Scott said loudly, again attracting stares.

"You didn't go to the Hook IP course?" Scott asked.

"No, I didn't but I am," Zane answered.

"What kind of politician's pussy answer is that?" Scott asked as he laughed.

"Barkeep do it again but three this time," Zane said.

Zane explained the situation. He told Scott that he was on his way to personnel for orders to the Hook IP course.

"Been there done that," Scott replied. "Got my orders today to the same course. Wouldn't it be great if we were stick mates again."

Zane checked his watch and said, "Uh Oh, I'm in trouble. Janice will be pissed. I usually don't hang out in bars. She is used to me being home on time."

"Are you living on base?" Scott asked excitedly.

"Yeah, on Red Cloud road. How about you?" Zane asked.

"Me too. I bet the gals are already together. You know how everybody snoops when a moving van starts unloading. They have to know who the new neighbors are. Hot damn, this is great," Scott exclaimed as he climbed onto a barstool next to Chief Filtzer.

As Zane turned to leave, he asked. "You coming Daryl?"

"No man, me and the chief are going to have a drink," Scott answered.

"What do I tell your old lady if she's at my house?" Zane asked concerned.

"Don't tell her anything. She knows where I am," Scott answered somewhat indignantly.

"Okay, it's your butt," Zane said as he departed.

Zane passed General Beam's quarters as he drove along Red Cloud Road. His house was a nice, five bedroom, ranch style home set back from the street.

There was considerable distance between it and the other homes. A moving van came into view. Moving personnel were unloading it. As he passed, he saw Janice with Scott's wife Georgia. They were having an animated discussion and did not notice him pass. Nevertheless, the pair spotted him as he parked in their carport, two houses farther down the road. They waved and he returned the gesture.

"Thank goodness I don't have to go through a grilling sessions about Daryl's whereabouts," Zane thought.

Susan, now six, came toward him on her tricycle and screamed, "Daddy, daddy, daddy. I start first grade next week."

Zane swooped her off the tricycle and spun her around saying, "Now aren't you the big girl. Where's Steve?"

"He's with Mom-ma. He doesn't know how to tie his shoes and I do," Susan said pouting.

Zane nuzzled her neck and said, "Go ask mommy if I have to light the grill."

After Zane put Susan down, she ran up the street yelling, "Mom-ma, does daddy have to light the grill?"

Removing Susan's tricycle from the driveway, Zane entered his quarters through the carport door. It opened into the kitchen and Zane saw pork chops marinating on the kitchen counter.

"It's light the grill time," Zane said, as he went through the living room and down the hall.

Their bedroom was the last one on the left. Inside, he sat on the bed and began unlacing his boots. With his boots removed, he unzipped his flight suit at the bottom of each leg. Standing up, he unzipped the front down to his groin and removed the garment. After stowing his flight gear, he put on shorts, a tee shirt, and some Jesus shoes. He was ready for some serious grill time.

During dinner, Steve put a spoon of green peas in Susan's milk. A fight promptly ensued that Janice resolved with sending the feuding pair to bed. One of the big benefits of a field grade officer was three bedroom quarters. This separated Susan and Steve, which provided a measure of peace. Janice joined Zane at the dinner table.

"I have some news," Zane said.

"Yes, I know. You are going to the Chinook IP course," Janice said, as if proud of her advance knowledge.

"How did you know that? I didn't know until a few hours ago," Zane said as he placed his knife and fork on the table.

"We wives stick together Dale. The personnel officer's wife told me at the Wives' Club meeting today," Janice answered with a giggle. "I also met Marsha Beam, the CG's wife. She's nice."

"Was Georgia there?" Zane asked cautiously.

"No. She had to wait for the movers. Daryl didn't stick around to help either," Janice said in a tone that Zane recognized. There was more to come.

"Mister Daryl Scott better get his act together or he's going to have long stays in the dog house," Janice continued. "And, by the way mister, you were late today."

"I know. I took my IP by the O-club for drinks. He is a great pilot and he restored my confidence in the Huey. I think I am going to miss its agility. There's no such thing as a backup autorotation in a Hook," Zane explained. "I hope my IP in the Hook MOI course is half as good."

"By the way," Zane added. "When are we supposed to make our call on the CG?"

Janice withdrew her attention from dinner and gave Zane a perplexed look as she answered, "You know it's strange that you should ask. I had the same question on my mind today. Marsha told us that there would be no individual calls made. They will announce in the daily bulletin when new arrivals should call in a group."

"That makes sense," Zane responded. "This place is growing so fast they would stay busy every day doing nothing but receiving new officers. This will work much better."

"I guess I am used to the old ways," Janice stated. "It is hard to believe that we have been in the service for eight years."

Janice's statement reinforced Zane's firm belief that the military was a way of life and not a job. Theirs was one large military family that included the wives and children. Each served their country in their own way. It was difficult for a civilian to understand. Zane didn't when he first entered service at Fort Sill and he had four years enlisted time when he came on active duty.

A small room adjoined the living room. It had two doorways, one from the living room and the other from the kitchen. The living room door was doublewide with an expandable, sliding door. The kitchen entrance was standard size but did not have a door to open and close. Too small for a den or bedroom, it was a nuisance for the wives. Every family used it as a TV room.

Zane, a sci-fi buff, said as he turned on the TV. "That new show, Star Trek comes on in 15 minutes. You going to join me?"

"In just a minute Dale, I haven't checked the mail box today. Have you?" Janice asked.

"Nope," Zane answered.

A short while later, Janice entered the TV room. Zane noticed her clinched jaws immediately. She held a piece of crushed paper in her hand.

"What's wrong?" He asked.

Janice threw the crumpled paper at Zane. It was light and didn't travel far. Zane picked it up from the floor and opened it.

"Crap," he said aloud. "There goes tonight."

Janice, totally infuriated, cried out, "Those damned Post Engineers. They could have painted this place before we moved in and settled. No, the assholes wait and put us through a three-day nightmare.

Zane read the notice. "Your quarters are scheduled for interior painting. Move all furniture away from walls and into the room's middle. Empty cabinets and drawers. Painters will arrive promptly at 07:30 hours. Have preparations complete before their arrival.

Janice said through clenched teeth, "You just wait until the next wives' meeting. I am going to give Rebecca Gibbons a piece of my mind. I bet because her husband is the Post Engineer they had their quarters painted before they were settled."

"Uh Hon," Zane stuttered. "Her husband is a lieutenant colonel. Watch what you say."

"I have changed my mind. I am going to dump this on Marsha Beam. This is a pain in the ass," Janice said vehemently. "These quarters have to be in immaculate condition when we leave. The Post Engineers require that we pass a 'White-Gloved' inspection before they clear us for departure. By damned, they should have to be in the same condition when we move into quarters. They can paint them when they are empty."

Zane sat quietly for a moment before he said, "Now you are going to raise hell with a major general's wife. Jesus think what he can do to me. I'm not saying another word. Next you'll be calling The First Lady."

Janice began to laugh. She ran and jumped sideways into Zane lap and hugging him around the neck.

"Dale you are nothing but a big old Teddy Bear," she said before giving him a long, passionate kiss.

When Janice released him, he said, "To hell with Star Trek. Let's go play doctor."

Janice got to her feet and pulled Zane's arm as she said, "You've got it Dr. Zane. Come show me your stethoscope."

Zane stopped at Scott's quarters on his way to Hanchey Army Airfield the next morning. They had agreed to carpool so the girls would have a car for their use during the day.

"Dale, this is like old times isn't it," Scott said.

"Yes but we have a few miles on us since we started. I'm looking forward to flying the Hook again," Zane replied.

"Me too," Scott agreed. "She's a forgiving ship. I predict that Hooks are going to be around for a long time."

Much to the pair's disappointment, they did not have the same instructor. Though they tried, the training flight's commander would not approve a change.

Zane met his IP, Mr. Jerry A. Kilborne. Kilborne was a Department of The Army Civilian (DAC). He had a GS-13 rating with the Federal Government, which was a lucrative assignment. In addition to his base pay, he received hazardous duty pay.

Captain James R. Darlington was Kilborne's other student. Kilborne introduced Zane to his new stick buddy. Darlington recently returned from a Chinook assignment with the 101st Airmobile Division. Formerly the famed 101st Airborne Division, their new combat structure was the same as the 1st Cavalry Division Airmobile. They traded their parachutes for helicopters.

The three sat at a table on the second floor of the administrative building at the famed heliport. There were 12 students in the room with them. The instructor's first step was to get to know their students. They had already done an extensive review of their flight records, which was the reason the flight commander would not let Zane and Scott fly as stick buddies.

After Zane and Darlington explained their backgrounds to Kilborne, he gave them a brief description of his.

"Gentlemen, I am a retired CW4. I gave the Army 26 years before my retirement. During those years, I flew during World War II, in Greece, the Korean Conflict, and the early stages of Viet Nam. Zane, you and I just missed each other flying H-21s. I left a few days before you arrived. Those were hard times," Kilborne explained.

"You bet," Zane replied.

"Mister Kilborne, do you draw retired pay and full salary as a GS-13 plus flight pay?" Darlington asked.

"Yes, I do," Kilborne answered.

"Damn, you are knocking down some coins," Darling said with a tone of disbelief.

"It's not bad," Kilborne commented with grin.

Kilborne pushed Zane and Darlingon's flight records aside and said, "Here's the deal. I am sure you both know this but I have to say it. The aircraft is my responsibility and I am in charge. What I say goes. When I tell you that I have the controls, release them immediately. Raise your hands in the air and tell me, 'You've got it.'"

"Chinook maintenance at Hanchey is probably the worst in the world. A civilian contractor has a maintenance contract. His maintenance people come from the local work force. From personal experience, I am telling you to watch your ass. Preflight the crap out of your ship because it may be a flying death trap. These peanut farmers don't know a Chinook rotor blade from a go-cart. They will kill you."

"On bad weather days, we will preflight. I don't care if it's raining like a cow pissing on a flat rock, you will preflight. There are two reasons why. First, the weather may break and we can get some time. Second, the contractor is paid by how many Chinooks he has flyable daily. On bad weather days, they report any Chinook at this facility as flyable. When you go to inspect, you may find our ship sitting in a hangar without rotor blades or engines. I am a taxpayer and I will not put up with that crap. Let's go fly," Kilborne said as he got to his feet.

Two weeks into the course, their IP Flight Commander held a meeting after their morning flight.

"Gentlemen, do not pay attention to rumors. Also, do not believe everything you read. There are those who would defame and destroy a person for sensationalism purposes. We are officers and it is necessary that we put our faith in each other. As leaders, it is essential that we have each other's trust. Thank you, dismissed," he said and left the room for his office.

Zane and Darlington looked at each other with an expression of "What was that about?" Zane glanced across the room at Scott. He returned his glance with humped shoulders and palms up body language.

Kilborne leaned forward and asked with a low voice, "Don't you guys read the paper?"

"Of course, I read the pictures and laugh at the words. What the hell is going on?" Zane asked.

Removing his wallet, Kilborne said, "You guys read this and draw your own conclusions."

Taking a tightly folded piece of newspaper from his wallet, Kilborne handed it to Zane. Zane unfolded it to find a newspaper column written by a renowned, newspaper columnist. After reading it, he handed it to Darlington.

"Are we through for the day," Zane asked.

"Sure thing, see you in the morning," Kilborne replied.

Scott joined Zane as they started down the stairs.

On the way down, Scott asked. "What was all that about?"

"You really don't know?" Zane responded.

"No," Scott said in frustration.

"I will tell you in the car," Zane answered.

As Scott drove, Zane explained, "A newspaper columnist wrote an article about a major general. In it, he says that this general's former Chief of Staff retired as a full colonel. As soon as he retired, he went to see the Chief of Staff of the Army. This colonel gave the Chief of Staff a packet of letters written to his wife by his former commander, this particular major general. They were love letters."

Scott said, "Damn."

Continuing, Zane said, "It gets worse. This colonel says that the general used Army aircraft to fly to rendezvous with his wife. In addition, this general invites the colonel's wife to visit him at his quarters on base. The colonel's wife moves in, while the general's wife is at home, under the pretense of painting his portrait. He's banging his chief of staff's wife while the chief of staff is working for the general. This article said that the colonel asked the Army Chief of Staff if this was the type of general officer that the Army wanted."

Scott whistled and asked. "Holy crap, who was it?"

"There's more," Zane said. "This columnist quoted lines from letters the general wrote to the colonel's wife. If this is true, that colonel was a cool customer. He nailed the general and his old lady while protecting his retirement benefits."

"Damn it, who the hell is it?" Scott yelled.

"One each Major General Beam," Zane answered.

"Don't screw with my head Dale," Scott stated sternly.

"I'm not. Think about this a minute. The youngest major general in the Army, and an aviator, throws his career away over a piece of ass. I absolutely refuse to believe this," Zane said with total disbelief.

Scott stopped in front of Zane's house and said, "I will be back in an hour to go to maintenance class. My old lady is going to shit when she hears this."

Janice had lunch ready when Zane entered. He put his flight gear away and sat down for lunch. Steve was in his high chair. Susan was at school.

As usual, Janice asked. "How was your morning? What's going on?"

Zane told Janice what he had told Scott. She sat silent with her eyes getting wider with every word. Here and there, she injected an "Oh my God."

When Zane finished, Janice retrieved the "Daily Bulletin." She sat down and opened it.

"What you said explains this I guess," Janice said pointing to a feature article.

Zane read the headline, "Retirement Service for Commanding General."

After reading the article, Zane put the document on the table and said, "I guess he did it. What a crying shame this mess is. This guy was sort of my mentor. We were in the Cav together. Damn, damn!"

Subsequently, a retirement ceremony did not take place. Beam's household goods left post quarters immediately. They remained in storage in vans for a month by the post tennis court. One day he was there and the next he was not present. The Deputy Installation Commander assumed command until a replacement arrived.

One week, before completing the Chinook IP course, Scott received instruction to report to the Chinook Transition Division as a Chinook IP. Zane received a memo to report to Lieutenant Colonel Gibbons, Fort Rucker Personnel Officer.

"Just a moment Major Zane. Let me check. I think Colonel Gibbons is free," Gibbons' secretary said.

After knocking, she opened Gibbon's office door and said, "Major Zane to see you sir."

"Send the major in," Zane heard Gibbons say.

During Zane's meeting, Gibbons said that he knew his office looked stupid when they sent him to the Huey IP course. He also said that it looked like his office did not know what they were doing when they sent him to the Chinook course later.

"Major, here's why," Gibbons said. "General Beam told me that you were to attend those courses in that order. Your next assignment is Chief of The Standardization Division. You will be responsible for checking the instructor pilots in Hueys and Hooks. Your office will not be in the Instruction Division's chain of command. Your pilots will be checkers of the checkers so to speak. If an IP has an accident, your people will administer his check ride. Anytime that an instructor's abilities come into question, your job is determine his qualification. It is not a popular job. Some pilots refer to your division as the 'Rat Squad.' The reason I am doing what General Beam said is that we have spent too much money training you for the job. In addition, the new CG concurs that you are the best person for the assignment. I hope you can live up to General Beam's confidence in you."

Later, Zane told Scott that they would not be instructor pilots together. Scott also had news to deliver. They were grilling steaks at Zane's house. The pair watched their steaks while drinking beer. Whenever they could, Saturday cookouts were a ritual.

"Dale, I just got word that the former Field Artillery Branch is being reconfigured into two branches. There will be a separate branch for Air Defense Artillery officers. The former Field Artillery Branch will remain. DA sent me notice that I will be in the new branch. Looks like our career paths are going to split old buddy," Scott explained.

"Man, I am so sorry but think about this," Zane said. "We have been together since flight school. We have served in the same countries and units. Hell, we've even been on the same set of orders. You will admit that this was quite unusual. At least we will be together for this tour."

"I tried to tell those numb nuts in DA that I fly airplanes. I do not shoot them down," Scott said exasperated.

"Daryl, one day there will be an Aviation Branch. It is stupid to expect us to be Field Artillery or Air Defense first and aviators second. Hell, I will probably never get an artillery command. Anytime there are so many officers dedicated to a skill like flying, a de facto Aviation Branch exists," Zane commented.

"Hey man, you better get some water on that fire or those steaks are going to burn," Scott said with apprehension.

"I'm on it," Zane said as he departed for his kitchen.

As Zane removed a glass from a kitchen cabinet, he saw Janice and Georgia sitting together in the TV room. While filling the glass with water, he looked again and saw that Janice appeared to be consoling her. Tears were pouring down Georgia's cheeks and she had her hands clasped tightly in her lap.

"I wonder what that's about," Zane thought as he returned to the grill.

Later, during dinner, Zane perceived coolness between Scott and Georgia. It was difficult to notice unless someone knew them both a long time. They seemed ill at ease. Zane didn't like it. Nevertheless, he never mentioned personal affairs with Scott and he wasn't going to start now.

Zane reported to the Deputy Installation Commander, Colonel Byron L. Charron, for duty as Chief of the Standardization Division. Charron was a hard-nosed, to the point officer who didn't quibble about small stuff.

"Zane," he said, "If you haven't figured out how to read a job description by now, we're in trouble. If I need you, I will call. Otherwise get to Hanchey and get to work."

On his way to his new job Zane thought, "I like Charron. He is my kind of boss."

The Flight Standardization Division was in the same building where Zane reported for Chinook IP training. He had a reserved parking place in front of the building. As he went toward the building's entrance, he saw his name on a large sign at the entrance.

"Hey, that looks pretty damned good," he thought as he entered.

His office was straight ahead on the first floor. He passed some restrooms and came to his office door to his front. Written on the door's frosted glass pane was his name again. He entered a large room with tables and chairs. No one was present. He continued across the room to another door with his name on it. Looking inside, it had a desk, a chair, two file cabinets, and a telephone.

He turned and looked around the room. On the opposite wall, there was a listing of nine aviators. Beside each name, there was the name of a person designated for a check ride. The person listed for a check ride had an aircraft type written beside their name.

Looking closer, Zane saw a clipboard hanging beneath the name list. He removed it and looked through its attached documents. The documents were individual referrals for check rides. It had the IP's name, type of aircraft and reason for the check. All of the referrals were routine annual checks.

As he was looking through the documents, Zane heard loud talking from outside the room. There was considerable laughter and it grew louder. The door suddenly opened. A skinny second lieutenant with acne stopped through the doorway. Zane figured his weight at about 160 pounds. He had a crewcut with sun bleached hair.

He stared at Zane for a moment, obviously perplexed, and finally said, "Oh shit."

The young man dropped his flight helmet and came to attention so quickly that the man behind him crashed into him. He saluted.

"Lieutenant Ludlow, sir," he stammered. "You must be Major Zane."

"That's correct lieutenant. We do not salute indoors while wearing headgear," Zane replied.

Ludlow rapidly removed his baseball cap with his right hand and tried to salute holding the hat. Realizing his mistake, he dropped his hat and saluted again. Meanwhile, the man behind him was trying to see over his shoulders.

Zane returned his salute and said, "Come on in Ludlow and bring your friend with you."

A CWO 4 Engram followed Ludlow inside and said, "Good morning, major."

"Good morning Chief," Zane replied. "You two carry on with your business."

"Yes sir," they both replied in unison.

Zane went to his inner office with the clipboard. Inside, he went to the file cabinets. Examining the contents, he found flight records for each assigned pilot. He found test results from their required annual written examinations filed alphabetically. Zane removed the flight records and took them to his desk. He sat and began studying them.

As the morning progressed, Zane studied every man's records in detail. While doing so, he heard persons talking outside his office. Most of it was standardization pilots briefing individuals as to how they did on their flight checks. Slightly before Noon, someone knocked on his door.

"Come in," Zane said.

As the door opening slowly, Lieutenant Ludlow's face appeared in the widening space. He had a concerned expression on his face.

"Sir, can I come in?" He asked.

"Sure can Ludlow. What do you need?" Zane replied.

Ludlow entered and said, "Money sir."

Zane directed, "Close the door and tell me what for."

"Sir, I need money for your going away plaque. I am the junior officer and I am in charge of the slush fund. We collect for plaques in advance because people come and go around here so fast. It's $25.00, sir," Ludlow squeaked.

"Jesus, did I look like that when I was the junior officer at Sill?" Zane asked himself.

"Sit down L-T. I need to chat with you a bit," Zane told the nervous lieutenant.

Ludlow sat in a chair beside Zane's desk and waited.

"You've had an unusual aviation career Ludlow. First, the Selective Service drafted you. You went through Infantry Basic Training at Benning. After that, you came to Rucker for Advanced Individual Training (AIT) as a crew chief. I see that you were a crew chief and door gunner on Hooks in 'Nam for a year. While there, you applied for the Warrant Officers Rotary Wing Aviators Course at Wolters and they accepted you. You graduated at the top of your class and went back to 'Nam for 12 months. DA offered you a direct commission as an Infantry Second lieutenant as a Reserve Officer and you obviously took it. In addition, you accumulated over 3,000 hours of combat flight time. You aced the Hook IP course. How did you get here?" Zane asked.

"The IP Course Flight Commander recommended me, sir" Ludlow answered, his eyes opened wide.

"Your IP was?" Zane asked.

"Mister Kilborne, sir," Ludlow replied rapidly.

Zane relaxed and thought, "Hell, the kid's got the juice. Why not?"

Leaning across the desk's corner, Zane extended his hand and said, "My pleasure lieutenant."

After shaking Ludlow's hand, Zane said, "Let's see if my wife left me any money."

Removing his wallet, Zane found it empty and told Ludlow, "Sorry, lieutenant. Do you think I might last a day in this job? I will pay you tomorrow."

"Sir, that's fine sir. Really, you will last. Don't worry about it," Ludlow stuttered.

"Thanks," Zane answered. "When will everyone be here at one time?"

"After lunch, sir. The morning rides are over for today. The afternoon checks will be here at 13:00 hours," Ludlow told Zane.

"Fine, let's get some lunch and I will be here 30 minutes early. You can introduce me to the flight," Zane directed.

Knowing that their talk was over, Ludlow arose and saluted.

Zane said, "Lieutenant, if we keep that up every time we see each other, we will never get any work done. Here's the drill. When we are inside, salute the first time we meet. Outside, salute every time we meet and depart. Okay?"

"Yes sir," Ludlow said as he left Zane's office.

Zane watched the officer door shut behind Ludlow. He watched the door for a moment.

"We are sending these kids to kill people. Why? What for? Orders, that's what for," Zane thought.

"He will do fine," Zane said aloud as he arose and exited the building.

The following months were bittersweet. Zane had the best group of professional aviators with whom he ever served. He was proud of them. The problem was contract maintenance.

Zane had a taste of it when he flew with Kilborne. Now, he had a group of pilots not able to do their jobs because of it. When they arrived at their assigned aircraft, they were unsafe to fly. Often, they would preflight over three ships to find one that was even safe to start. His flight had aircraft making emergency landing in cornfields at night.

One of his pilots summed up the situation when he said, "I have made so many emergency landings that I know the firemen, their kid's first names. Hell, I know the ambulance drivers' nieces and nephews. I spend more time riding back to the office with them than I do flying."

The situation on the flight line was becoming hostile. Flight foremen began arguing with pilots. One offered a bribe for him not to ground a ship. He approached the wrong pilot who almost punched his lights out. Zane had to do something. He called a special meeting with his pilots.

"Here's what we are going to do," Zane began. "I want a chart on the wall with the tail number of every Hook on this airfield. Each day, if you have one of those ships to fly, you will write on the chart if it is unsafe to fly. Write on the chart why you grounded the aircraft. I will collect the information daily and post it to a form I am preparing."

"This form will list every write-up on every ship by day. For example, if you have to ground a ship, put the exact reason for grounding it on the wall. Use the same words you put in the ship's logbook. Each day, before going to fly, check the form for your assigned ship. There will be a list, for the past 30 days, of every write-up grounding a specific ship. You will know in advance of any previous grounding conditions. Make sure the grounding condition no longer exists. If it does, ground it again."

CW4 Milsap, Zane's most experienced pilot, raised his hand at the back of the room. Milsap was an older, quiet person who seldom became involved in controversy. He could tap dance his way through most any unpleasant situation. However, this time, he looked different.

Zane pointed to Milsap and said, "Yes, Chief."

"Major, I know our flight has the cream of the crop at Rucker. However, I am finding things that I think are not getting attention. Day before yesterday, I grounded 857 for excessive vibration in flight. Anytime a grounding condition takes place during flight, and is written up, there must be a test flight to assure the vibration does not exist after maintenance fixes the problem."

"This morning I had to ground 857 for the same reason, excessive vibration in flight. Yesterday, a pilot in here now, took off in that ship. He wasn't in the air ten minutes before making an emergency landing because of excessive vibrations. I checked the logbook on that Hook. The maintenance action taken was 'ground checked and found okay.'"

"That ship should have been grounded simply by reading the logbook. A test pilot did not fly that Hook and sign off on it as okay in flight. We're letting this mess get the best of our better judgment. That's all I have to say sir," Milsap said and took his seat.

"Milsap's right guys," Zane agreed. "The forms on each ship will alert you to a previous condition that could get you killed. Stay alert out there. I have some other actions in mind that might help. Thanks for coming in on your day off. I appreciate it. Let's hang it up for this evening."

Zane went to his office and removed a blank Army Disposition Form (DF) from his file cabinet. As he sat down to write, he remembered what Master Sergeant Blake told him at Sill.

"L-T, when words don't work, put it on paper through command channels. Commanders cannot ignore a DF signed by another commander, even if the commander is a subordinate. They either have to correct the problem or indorse it to a higher commander explaining why," he told Zane.

Zane began writing. He addressed the DF to the Commander of the Army Center for Aviation Safety. The Safety Center was not in the Commanding General's Chain of Command. The Safety Center was a tenant unit on base. Any aviator for any safety reason could correspond with its commander. Safety personnel instituted the procedure to allow an open conduit to save lives. Zane, as he wrote, wished such an organization had existed his first tour in Korea. Now, there was one.

Nevertheless, Zane was smart enough not to circumvent his immediate superior. He prepared a carbon copy for the Deputy Installation Commander. This way, someone would have to act to correct the problem. If they did not, they would be explaining to the Safety Center as to why they didn't.

In the DF's body portion, Zane itemized instances of maintenance safety procedure violations. He listed the aircraft tail numbers, the dates, and the violations. On his way home, he put the original in the Safety Center's drop box. He also delivered a copy to the headquarters' drop box.

As Zane pulled into his driveway, he thought, "Tonight is a two double night. Tomorrow the shit will hit the fan."

Two days passed with no contact from either of the two addressees. Zane could not understand why. He would allow another day and then go in person. Meanwhile, he had check rides to give.

On the tarmac, Zane and his assigned IP approached the Hook he was to fly. Standing beside him was Neil Bookerman, the contractor's line foreman. Beside him was Ralph Golden, the contractor's technical inspector.

"Good morning major," Bookerman said. "You can't find anything wrong with this Hook. We just did a Safety of Flight Inspection on her.

A Safety of Flight Inspection was a special procedure for a thorough examination of an aircraft by a highly qualified individual. Often, it was an inspector assigned by a higher headquarters for a readiness evaluation or other operational examination. Zane was quite knowledgeable regarding the inspection.

"Well, good morning Mister Bookerman. I am pleased to hear that. We will get airborne in no time," Zane replied as he turned to the IP sent to him for a check ride.

"Chief Lee, you get the top and I will get the bottom," Zane said, stepping onto the CH-47's ramp.

CW4 Lee climbed the side of the ship to examine the engines, shafts, gearboxes, and rotor blades. Zane went to the ship's cockpit and began examining its logbook. Immediately, he noted that there were no previous write-ups. The only entry was for the completion of a Safety of Flight Inspection. Behind the entry was Ralph Golden's signature and special technical inspector's (TI) stamp. The TI stamp was a special mark assuring that the aircraft met every requirement for flight. Zane returned to the ship's rear. He began examining hydraulic lines and electrical wiring in the aft pylon. Bookerman and Golden remained outside and watched with smirks on their faces.

The pair immediately noticed Zane making entries in the ship's log. The more Zane wrote, the closer they came to see what he was doing. They backed away as Zane walked down the ramp and outside the Hook.

Shading his eyes from the sun with his hand, Zane looked up at Chief Lee and asked. "How's it coming Chief? Are you about finished?"

"In a little bit sir, I'm almost through," Lee answered.

After ten minutes, Lee climbed down the Chinook's side. He walked over to Zane with a small notebook in his hand.

As he approach Zane, he said, "Sir, I need the log book."

Zane promptly handed it to him and he began making entries. Bookerman kept inching closer to see what Zane and Lee were doing. However, Golden remained where he was and appeared nervous. He kicked at non-existent rocks on the tarmac and kept moving in small circles. He obviously was concerned about something.

CW4 Lee returned the logbook to Zane who turned to Bookerman and said, "Here's the write-ups. We will need another ship."

Bookerman bolted forward and grabbed at the book saying, "No damned way."

As Bookerman read, his face became flush. Obvious anger began to overcome him.

Glaring at Zane, Bookerman said, "This is bullshit. There are 27 red X write-ups in here. That's not possible. Golden get over here."

Golden joined the group as Bookerman said to him, "There cannot be 27 grounding conditions on this ship. Take a look at these write-ups."

Before Golden could examine the logbook, Zane challenged Bookerman by saying, "Tell you what Bookerman. I will take this ship if Golden will sign them as 'checked and found okay' and puts his TI stamp by each entry."

"Well," Bookerman said, as he stared at Golden who now held the logbook.

"I will have to examine the deficiencies before I will sign them off," Golden replied as he entered the Hook's rear.

The group watched as Golden went to each place that Zane said there was a condition that made the Hook unsafe to fly. As he exited the aircraft, Bookerman asked for the book. Golden handed it to him.

"You didn't sign these off as okay. Do it now," Bookerman ordered.

"I can't. They are all grounding condition boss," Golden responded. "They have to be repaired before I will put my stamp on them."

Before Bookerman could react, Zane very politely said, "Mister Bookerman, I need the tail number of another Hook so I can conduct an IP check ride. If I don't complete his ride today, his students will not be able to fly with him. That means his students will fall behind in their flight schedule which screws up everything."

"There aren't any aircraft available," Bookerman said, as he slammed the logbook shut. "Golden, you come with me to my office."

Zane turned to CW4 Lee and recommended that they conduct the oral examine portion over coffee in the snack bar.

"If a Hook becomes flyable, they are supposed to contact us there," Zane said as he gathered his flight equipment.

While Zane was questioning Lee, a snack bar attendant came to their table and said, "Major, there's a telephone call for you. You can take it in the manager's office."

"Major Zane, this is Colonel Charron. You be in my office in 20 minutes," Charron directed.

"Yes, sir," Zane replied.

Zane took his tongue lashing from Charron. He knew that Charron would eventually listen to his side of the story. While Charron was hot tempered, he was fair. Zane felt secure, knowing that his actions were correct.

Charron ended his ass chewing by telling Zane; "You have the screws turned down so tight that the flight foreman and his mechanics cannot do their job. They say your unrelenting pressure is the cause of the maintenance errors. What do you have to say for yourself?"

Zane removed a manila folder from beneath his left arm and answered, "Sir, I have the maintenance records for that aircraft that Bookerman said they did a Safety of Flight Inspection on. The Quality Assurance branch allowed me to copy the logbook pages for the past month on that ship. Will you take a look at them?"

"Certainly, give them to me," Charron directed.

Zane stood in front of Charron's desk in an "at ease" stance with his legs spread and his hands clasped in the small of his back. He watched Charron read a few pages and then stop.

Looking up from the records, Charron ordered, "I will keep these. Zane you are dismissed."

Zane returned to Hanchey and completed CW4 Lee's oral examination. He told him to return the next day to complete his check ride.

Arriving home late, Zane was tired and disgusted. The constant fight to have safe aircraft to fly began to take its toll. He did not figure that things could be worse. They were.

Janice met him at the kitchen door with a grave expression on her face. It was a look seldom seen by Zane and he immediately wanted to know what the problem was.

"It's Daryl," she said. "Georgia is divorcing him."

"For God's sake, why?" Zane asked.

"It has been building for some time now. After flying he always goes to a bar somewhere and hangs out until after dinner. He comes home half drunk. When questioned, he won't talk. He broods a lot. Twice he never came home until the afternoon of the next day," Janice, quite dejected, explained.

Zane sat in his recliner and began unlacing his boots as he said, "I haven't talked with him in two or three days. Since we no longer car-pool, I don't get to talk to him very often. When I have, he seemed the same Daryl that I have always known. I believe, if he was having problems, he would tell me."

Janice explained that Daryl was already living in the Bachelor Officer Quarters (BOQ) and that Georgia had already left post for her hometown. Scott was responsible for clearing quarters and getting their household goods shipped.

Zane telephoned the BOQ but Scott was not in his room. Concerned, Zane made the rounds of the Officers Club and local bars. He could not locate Scott. He returned home tired, morose, and upset.

"Damn, what a mess this is becoming," he thought. "I cannot imagine what Daryl's problem is. He is a cool head. I simply do not get it."

After dinner, Janice answered the telephone. The person calling was the DA Aviation Assignments Officer, Colonel Billwell. She called Zane to the telephone.

After some chit chat, Colonel Billwell said, "Zane, we are recommending that you go to the Presidential Flight Detachment."

"Sir?" Zane responded.

"The Commander of the Presidential Flight Detachment needs an operations officer. This job requires that the individual be multi-engine and tandem rotor qualified. In addition, the individual must have over 5,000 flying hours and have an instrument rating. You meet every one of those qualifications. The duty station will be Key Biscayne, Florida, for President Nixon. Do you want us to submit your name?" Billwell asked.

Without hesitation, Zane answered, "Yes sir. Go ahead and submit my name."

"You have a pleasant evening. I will be in touch a few days from now. Goodnight," Billwell said.

"You too sir," Zane answered and placed the handset in its cradle.

"Janice," Zane yelled. "You are not going to believe this."

With summer fast approaching, it was close to Zane's 18th month at Fort Rucker. He could expect orders to Viet Nam. This assignment would be for much more than 18 months. Zane heard from friends in the unit that their assignment was for five years.

"Viet Nam will be over by then Hon," Zane told Janice as they went to bed. "This is absolutely great."

The pair talked to almost dawn about a Key Biscayne assignment. How it would be flying the President and its exposure to senior officers. An assignment like this could destroy or make a career. Make one mistake, in the President's Flight Detachment, and it would result in a relief from assignment. However, make no mistakes; it would be a bright star in an aviator's file. It would cinch promotion to lieutenant colonel.

Things did not improve on the flight line at Hanchey. The same problems continued and Zane looked forward to leaving the mess. However, he would like to see the problem solved before he left.

Colonel Billwell called him three days later. Zane knew something was dreadfully wrong by Billwell's tone of voice.

"Major, I hate this more than you will ever imagine. My section worked hard to get them the best man Army Aviation had to fill the requirement," Billwell said obviously frustrated.

"Get to the point," Zane thought.

"The White House declined our recommendation. They stated that the position is one of 'high visibility.' Their reason for declining was that 'your appearance was not right for the job.' You are too big. I guess they want someone who is slim and stupid. I am sorry Zane," Billwell said.

"No sweat sir. We cannot win them all," Zane replied as disappointment started to consume him.

"Dale, let's do this. You are near reassignment. How would you like to go to a university as an Assistant Professor of Military Science?" Billwell asked.

"R.O.T.C. sir?" Zane asked.

"Yes. Dale, I will give you a list of available assignments. You and Janice go through them and pick the one you like. I suggest you two go to a public library and research each school. Give me a return call and let me know what you decide. How's that?" Billwell asked.

"Sir, that is absolutely wonderful. Let me get a pen and paper," Zane replied, as he waved frantically at Janice.

Dale and Janice studied every university on the list. They spent three evenings in the local library going through anything they could find. Before they could return Billwell's call, another officer called them.

"Dale, I'm Major Victor Lanston, Colonel Billwell's assistant. We've decided to send you to Norwich in Connecticut. It is a military academy on the order of The Citadel, Virginia Military Institute and Texas A & M," Lanston said.

"What happened to my choice Victor?" Zane asked.

"Dale, you know the needs of the service come first. Norwich is an excellent career choice. Only our best people get that assignment," Lanston replied.

"Let me make a suggestion," Zane said. "From my research, every university is changing to General Military Science from branch related training. One university still teaches Field Artillery. I have been a gunnery instructor at Fort Sill. I taught artillery at Fort Rucker and I am a Field Artillery Officer. What's wrong with sending me to Saint Marys University in San Antonio, Texas?"

After an extended silence, Lanston said, "Just a moment Dale."

Lanston asked. "You still there Dale?"

"Yes," Zane answered.

"Be at St. Marys by 29 July this year. The assignment is yours. Keep up the good work. We feel bad about the Nixon crap," Lanston told Zane.

"Count on it and thanks," Dale said before breaking his connection.

Janice, who had her head beside Zane's as he talked, hugged Zane, and cried, "We got it. We got it."

The pair wanted St. Marys because it came highly recommended for academic excellence. It was a private Catholic University operated by Jesuits. San Antonio was a military town with five major military installations. With Susan and Steve going through childhood illnesses, Brooke Army Medical Center was in the heart of San Antonio. The Army had a flight detachment, stationed at Randolph Air Force Base, where Zane could keep his flight requirements current. They were pleased. However, Zane grew suspicious.

The assignment was too good, too soon and unreasonable. It was a set policy of 18 months between tours in Viet Nam. Suddenly, personnel offers him a presidential assignment. When it flops, they send him to a university. Zane would not complain but there had to be other forces at work.

Since sending his first DF, Zane had sent two more without a response. The Center for Aviation Safety and Colonel Charron were not talking to him. The situation broke on 10 July.

Zane was in his office completing aircraft forms when Chief Milsap opened his door. He did not knock.

He put his head inside and said as his voice broke with emotion, "Major, you had better come with me to Base Operations. It is urgent. Let's go sir, now."

Zane grabbed his hat and had to run to catch Milsap who ran out the front door. Zane ran to Milsap's side as he rounded the building's corner. Milsap stopped and grabbed his head with both hands. Bending his knees, he fell to the ground and began cursing, as he raised and lowered his head. Zane saw the reason.

On the far side of the tarmac, flames swirled skyward. A column of black smoke rose above Hanchey's control tower.

"Son of a bitch," Zane screamed, as he removed his hat and began running toward the flames. He ran up a small incline before reaching the tarmac. From this position, he could see through the parked aircraft to the other side of the airfield. He ran faster.

As he approached the crash site, he saw ambulances and fire trucks surrounding a Hook's burning remains. Zane stopped running. There was no need for he had seen this in the past. No one survived a crash like the one he saw.

Twisted metal, burned black, lay in a pile. Extending around the pile, ripped and torn rotor blades lay in a circle. He turned away from the crash site and ran to Base Operations. CW4 Milsap met him at the door.

"I have them, sir," Milsap said as Zane approached.

"You have what?" Zane asked.

"Copies of the maintenance records on 857 from Quality Assurance," he answered.

"Damn the records. Who was on the ship?" Zane cried as tears began gathering in his eyes.

"Ludlow, sir, and an IP on a check ride," Milsap answered, as he gripped one arm around Zane's shoulders.

"Holy Mother of God," Zane screamed as he turned toward the maintenance hangar. "I am going to kill Bookerman."

As Zane started to run, he felt a sharp pain in his neck. His vision began to fade and he felt his knees hit the cement.

Gagging, Zane struggled to move. He could not see but he was choking. His eyes fluttered open and he saw a medic's face above him. He kept trying to put a crushed ammonia capsule under his nose. When he tried to move to push the capsule away, he felt heavy pressure on his shoulders. Pushing his head back, he saw Milsap holding him to the ground.

Milsap said to the medic, "You can take that away now."

"Let me up chief," Zane ordered.

"Not unless you stay with me major. You are about to make the biggest mistake of your life. Promise me you will stay with me. I have the means to handle this shit," Milsap insisted.

"Okay chief, okay," Zane answered, feeling calmer but his neck hurt.

Milsap released Zane, allowing him to stand. Zane rubbed his neck and turned to look toward the crash. The fire and smoke were gone.

"Come inside with me, sir," Milsap said in a sad and understanding voice.

As they sat in the snack bar, Milsap apologized for hitting Zane. He explained that he knew no other way to stop him. He couldn't allow Zane to get to Bookerman.

"Your career would have been over sir," Milsap said.

"You are right. What did you find in those records you had?" he asked.

"Last night's records show that maintenance replaced a hydraulic link in the aft pylon. It was in the control linkage for the aft rotor blades. Golden signed it off and stamped it okay. However, there was no test flight. That link was a primary flight control. Replacing a primary flight control component requires a test flight. It never took place," Milsap explained.

Continuing, he said, "I assure you that they did not replace the flight control linkage. They left the old one in the Hook that gave us the vibration problems. If they had a test pilot take the ship, he would ground it immediately because the serial number of the linkage did not change. I guarantee you that the serial number on that link is the same as the one replaced. If they had replaced it, there would be a different number on it."

"Before coming to get you, I saw that ship takeoff. It was about 200 feet in the air when the aft rotor blades went to full pitch. This caused the aft rotor to move up and over. The Hook went inverted with its nose facing in the opposite direction of the takeoff. The accident board can find that link and verify its serial number," Milsap stated.

"We have to move on this Chief. We have to make sure that the board knows this," Zane said.

"Sir, I am a witness. I saw it crash. They will have to take my statement and I will tell them about the link, the vibrations and the rest of the crap around here," Milsap replied.

"Chief, I know you will. I have sent DF after DF to the Center for Aviation Safety without a response. They form the accident board. We don't know who will be on it," Zane added.

Milsap leaned across the table and whispered; "That board will have a Warrant Officer on it who is Hook qualified. Do not forget about WOPA. Lieutenant Ludlow was a warrant officer before he got his commission. We take care of our own."

Zane leaned back and looked around the room. He noticed that the snack bar was almost empty. He figured practically everyone went to the crash site. With one of his men gone, personnel would be screaming for details. He had to return to his office.

"Chief, one more thing before I go. The sad part is someone had to die. If a test pilot took that bird last night, he didn't stand much of a chance. Perhaps he would check the serial numbers and maybe not. I know those test pilots are straight and professional. No one told them that 857 needed a test flight. Our man died when no one should have. I have to go. See you later," Zane said as he arose and left the snack bar.

Zane escorted Ludlow's widow during his burial. He helped cut red tape to see that she received every benefit that her husband's death brought.

Two days before the accident board was to begin its hearings, personnel moved Zane's departure to an earlier date. They said that he needed to be in San Antonio in time to attend R.O.T. C. summer camp at Fort Sill with St. Mary's cadets. Zane had to get his information before the accident board. Mother Nature provided his answer.

On Zane's departure date, Hurricane Camille roared ashore directly across his travel route. He called St. Marys Professor of Military Science and explained the situation. He approved Zane's change in arrival date. In addition, he told Zane not to start until it was safe to travel through Mississippi and Alabama. Janice added the final touch.

"Daryl, the Post Engineers will not allow us to clear post until we pass inspection. You know what a bunch of assholes they are about the gas range. I will not clean it and they will set a later date for another inspection. Honey, you do what you have to do," Janice explained.

Zane telephoned Colonel Charron for an appointment. He reported to Charron that afternoon.

"You wouldn't leave it alone would you Zane. I told you that you had the situation in a mess because of your pressure on the maintenance people. Now, we have dead pilots," Charron said livid with rage.

When he finished, Zane replied, "Sir, I am going before that board. They will hear what I have to say. You can cream my ass on my efficiency report and I can live with that. I cannot live with Ludlow's life on my conscience. Yes, his death was my fault because I did not persist. My faith was on those to whom I reported. I will take whatever is coming."

The following Friday Zane reported to the President of the Accident Investigation Board. The meeting room was full. The board members sat at a wide table with the president at its middle. Zane stood beside a lone chair opposite the president. Zane noted that, along the room's walls, civilians in three piece, pinstriped suits watched.

After taking his oath, Zane testified. He also presented his copies of the forms he made to track each ship's maintenance from day to day. Board members questioned Zane at length. One CW4 paid close attention to every word. When the president started to dismiss him, he asked to make a statement.

"Go ahead major," the president said.

"Mister president and members of the board, this meeting today was avoidable. It never would have existed if Lieutenant Ludlow's leaders had not failed him. That failure starts with me. I let him down and failed to do my job. When I leave Fort Rucker today, I will take with me the burden of knowing I could have saved a man's life. Mister President, you, and your board can save untold numbers of lives by correcting the maintenance situation at Hanchey Army Airfield. I pray that you do so. That's my statement sir," Zane said.

"You are dismissed, major," the board president responded.

Zane and Janice left Fort Rucker the next day. They drove through devastation remaining after Hurricane Camille came ashore near Gulfport, Mississippi. In a motel near Houston, Texas, they stopped early to relax at a motel. Sitting safely beside the motel's swimming pool, Zane examined his farewell plaque. He received it at his going away party. However, foremost in his mind was the young lieutenant who first asked money to buy it.

He watched Susan and Steve splashing in the kiddy pool with Janice beside them. He made a personal vow to never lose another person serving under his leadership. As far as he was concerned, Ludlow was the first and the last.

Chapter Forty Two

July 1971

How does one kill fear, I wonder?
How do you shoot a spectre through the heart,
slash off its spectral head, take it by its spectral throat?
Joseph Conrad (1857–1924), Polish-born English novelist. Marlow, in *Lord Jim*, ch. 33 (1900)

Major Zane gazed at the young man seated in front of his desk. He looked vigorous and in good health. According to his medical file, his problem was mental. He had complained of severe back pain on six different occasions in the past two months and had seen doctors at Brooke Army Medical Center for the stated ailment. The last doctor recommended a psychiatric evaluation.

The entry stated, "This is a healthy, young male adult 20 years of age. He has received evaluations on six occasions with complaints of lower back pain. Extensive workups with MRI, Xray, and Catscan fail to reveal any basis for the complaint that he presents. Dr. James Whitting, a board certified orthopedic specialist (see attached report), states that he cannot find any anomaly associated with bone structure in the sacra lumbar regions Electromylograms (2) show no neurological damage."

"It is the opinion of this office that the patient be seen by a psychiatrist for a possible determination that the present complaint is psychosomatic, the result of a neurosis, or the patient is lying for reason/s unknown."

Zane placed the file on his desk and said, "Mr. Bradley, I cannot get you another appointment with Brooke except for a psychiatric exam. They will not see you for a back complaint. I have exhausted every option with the medical community at the installation. At this point, I suggest you see a private doctor. If you want an appointment, you can ask the Professor of Military Science (PMS). I strongly feel that Colonel Connelly will tell you the same thing that I have."

Bradley grimaced, rubbed his back with his right hand, and whined, "The damned Army is supposed to take care of me. There is no way I can go to Rot-C (Reserve Officer Training Corps – R. O. T. C.) drill on Monday. My back hurts. I can hardly walk."

Incredulous, Zane asked. "You received a draft deferment when you signed for R. O. T. C. didn't you?"

"Of course I did. You know that," Bradley snapped.

Continuing Zane asked, "Out of curiosity Mr. Bradley, what number did you get in the recent draft lottery?"

"That's got nothing to do with my back. What difference does it make?" Bradley blurted, still rubbing his back and grimacing.

"You do know that I can make a phone call and the selective service will tell me," Zane stated.

"It's 315, so what?" Bradley challenged.

"Mr. Bradley your effort is transparent. You joined advanced R. O. T. C. to get a draft deferment. You also signed an agreement to serve two years on active duty as a commissioned officer when you graduate. With a damaged back, you will not qualify for active duty. With the high draft number, you have practically no chance of the draft enlisting you. It looks to me like you are trying to obtain a release from your agreement," Zane said emphatically.

"Who wants to be a damned lieutenant? Look what the Army is doing to Lieutenant Calley. They trained him to kill people and that's what he did. Now they are going to court martial him," Bradley said as he swiftly came to his feet.

Zane, noticing that Bradley no longer grimaced, slowly said, "Mr. Bradley, the charges against Lieutenant Calley include murder. The charges allege that he shot defenseless women and children. Murder is a crime in any segment of society."

Bradley reached onto Zane's desk and pushed his file toward Zane, as he said, "Keep your appointment. You are nothing but a damned bigot."

Slowly standing, Zane towered over the young man and said coldly, "Mr. Bradley leave my office before I throw you out. Do you understand?"

Bradley whirled and swiftly went through the opening in Zane's partitioned office space. He heard the main office door slam, causing its Venetian blinds to rattle loudly.

Staff Sergeant James Allen appeared in Zane's doorway grinning and asked. "Do you want me to put that file away, sir?"

"Sure thing Sarge," Zane replied.

"Sir?" Sergeant Allen said.

"Yes," Zane responded.

"Sir, the Army does not need that guy as an officer. I would not want to serve with him," Sergeant Allen commented.

"You're right, the Army doesn't. We know he lacks integrity and his character is wanting. I will make my observations a part of his record. I cannot imagine him getting a commission," Zane told Allen.

Allen removed the file from Zane's desk and took it into the outer office. In the wall, next to Zane's desk, there was a small, sliding door. It allowed Colonel Connelly to push it aside and talk directly to him. Zane knocked on the small door to get the colonel's attention. The door opened.

"Yes, Dale, what can I do for you?" Connelly asked.

"Sir, I just had an incident with a cadet, Mr. Bradley," Zane explained.

Zane told Connelly details of the event with Bradley. He asked if the colonel wanted to see Mr. Bradley's file.

"There's no need Dale. Forget about it. We know what Bradley is," Connelly said as he closed the door.

Zane noted that it was Thursday. Thursday afternoons, the university faculty had an informal gathering. It was more of a social event than business. Those attending could discuss any subject. It was a way for faculty members to know each other better and to exchange ideas.

Colonel Connelly, newly arrived at St. Marys, arranged for two officers to attend the group sessions. Connelly always attended with one member of his staff. He desired a better understanding between the university faculty and the R. O. T. C. instructors. University President, Father Linder Flowers, thought it a good idea and agreed. Some faculty members did not.

The university's faculty was a mixture of Jesuit Brothers and civilians. Some of the civilians had stated that Army officers, without advanced degrees, should not enjoy faculty status. The Brothers had no objection. In addition, the only status that officers had was the listing, of their names on a variety of documents issued by the university. Some of the younger faculty members took strong objection to this.

Zane tried to tell Connelly that he had been attending the meetings for most of his tour. For one reason or another, the opportunity never presented itself.

The NCOs did not appear as faculty members on university documentation. None of the faculty objected to their teaching on campus. To the NCOs liking, they did not attend the Thursday faculty meetings.

Colonel Connelly looked into Zane's office and asked. "You ready for some coffee and Danish Dale?"

"As they say in the artillery, 'On the way,' sir," Zane answered as he closed his file cabinets and donned his hat.

The pair walked toward the Administrative Building without seeing a student. It was 13:00 hours and classes ceased at Noon. Most students were at work. St. Marys was a private school and expensive. Most students had full-time jobs to help pay their college expenses. Those who could afford not to work were either scholarship students or from wealthy families.

Most students were from San Antonio's West Side Barrio near St. Marys. They were young Hispanics. The university arranged classes to help them obtain a degree. The school maintained high academic standards but was also expensive. These young people had to work.

Major Zane held the building's side entrance door open for Colonel Connelly. They removed their hats upon entry. Zane and Connelly's footsteps echoed in-unison through empty halls with shining tile floors. They entered the faculty lounge.

Along one wall, the brothers had a long table covered with various pastries and drinks. Sofas and easy chairs lined the other walls. The room's interior had large comfortable seating with nearby tables. Thick carpeting covered its floor. Faculty members chatted among themselves throughout the room. Father Flowers saw Connelly and Zane enter.

Breaking into a wide grin, Father Flowers came toward them. He wore traditional black of a Catholic priest.

"Good afternoon Colonel, Major. It is a pleasure to have you with us," Flowers greeted them. "Idea exchange is always healthy for any institution."

"We're glad to be here, Father," Connelly replied. "I am sad to say that Major Zane will be leaving us soon."

Father Flowers immediately became visibly concerned, as he turned to Zane and asked. "Why are you leaving us? What about your Masters?"

"Father, DA wants me on another Viet Nam tour. They have a command assignment for me. As for the Masters, I will have to wait. DA assured me that they would assign me to Fort Sam Houston after Viet Nam. My family will be able to stay in the home we've bought while I am away. When I return, I will start work on the degree again," Zane explained.

Flowers listened intently and then replied, "The Graduate School Dean will be here any moment. You must let him know about this."

"I already have, sir," Zane replied.

Flowers stroked his chin and appeared in deep thought. He asked, "I distinctly remember DA telling us that you would be here for three years. Why did they break our agreement?"

"Sir, I do not have any idea. They told me the same. I guess withdrawing from Viet Nam is taking longer than originally planned," Zane answered.

Suddenly, Flowers' face filled with recognition. He was looking over Zane's shoulder toward the room's entrance.

"There's Doctor Miler now. You go ahead Major. I will keep Colonel Connelly occupied. I have an offer for him," Flowers said.

"Thank you, sir," Zane said as he turned to look for Miler.

At six foot six inches, Doctor Miler was easy to see among the others. He wore his shoulder length hair tied into a ponytail. His full beard had gray wisps in it although he was younger than Zane. Miler saw Zane and gestured for Zane to join him.

A year before Zane would avoid the company of any person with Miler's looks. His appearance set the standard of the Hippie culture. His shirt was a crumpled tee shirt, which looked unwashed in weeks. Torn jeans covered his skinny legs and his rope sandals exposed unwashed feet. He wore a denim vest covered with ironed on images of marijuana plants. Under his left arm, he held two large books.

As Zane came near, Miler asked. "Dale, I received your memo. You are really leaving?"

"I'm going back to 'Nam, Bill," Zane said.

"What a crock of shit. Nixon is supposed to be getting you guys out of there," Miler, showing anger, commented.

"Someone must cover the rear while others leave. I am overdue another assignment to 'Nam," Zane said.

"When are you leaving exactly?" Miler asked.

"I will be out of here in a week," Zane answered.

Miler removed a book from under his arm and handed it to Zane saying, "Dale, read through this and we will talk about it on Monday. You can meet with me on Monday?"

"I will make it a point to do so," Zane said as he examined the book's cover.

"Communism and the World Arena by Nathan Brewwilder, Ph. D.," Zane read its title, while listening to Miler.

Zane watched as Miler glared at a professor sitting in a corner nearest them. The professor, obviously uncomfortable from Miler's stare, arose and left his seat.

"Come on Dale. Let's get started," Miler said as he began walking toward the empty seat.

As they worked their way through standing attendees, Zane realized that he had been meeting on Thursdays with Miler for close to 24 months. This was before Connelly had the idea of their attending the gathering. Neither he nor Father Flowers wanted to take away from the colonel's originality.

Zane's first meeting with Miler was far from pleasant. It happened in the same room at the same function. St. Marys School of Law's Dean, Dr. Bellington Whiteshear, was a retired Army Colonel. He arranged for Zane to attend. It was the first time that an APMS ever came to the faculty meetings. Some of the Graduate School's top professors did not welcome Zane's presence. Miler, in particular, challenged Zane's attendance immediately.

Zane had just entered the lounge when he saw Miler's upper body shoving through other attendees toward him. He physically pushed them aside if they didn't instantaneously respond to his touch and move from his path.

"I believe you are new here colonel. This meeting is for faculty members, sir," he said, looking down at Zane.

Zane smiled and said, "You are correct sir. I am new to St. Marys. My name is Dale Zane and I am a major. It is my pleasure to make your acquaintance. To whom am I speaking?"

"I am Doctor William Miler, Professor of Political Science and Dean Designate of St. Marys Graduate School. This gathering is for faculty members. I do not believe you are a faculty member and suggest that you leave," Miler said indignantly.

Zane continued smiling while extending his right hand and said, "It is a pleasure to meet you. I have read some of your writings. While I totally disagree with your premise regarding North and South Korea, your work is stimulating."

Very flustered, Miler took Zane's hand and gave a hearty handshake. Zane's demeanor was disarming. He didn't know whether to thank Zane for a compliment or be argumentative.

Stumbling for words, Miler responded, "Major Zane, you do not hold an advanced degree. To the best of my knowledge, you are not pursuing one. You cannot be a faculty member without an advanced degree. It is incumbent upon you to depart the lounge."

"Doctor, I am the personal guest of Dr. Bellington Whiteshear, Dean of the Law School. Do you not allow guests?" Zane asked.

"Well of course," Miler answered immediately.

"Actually, I was hoping to meet you. My intent is to obtain a Masters in Political Science. I'm sure that's your field, is it not?" Zane questioned, as he watched Miler hostile attitude melt.

"What degrees do you hold?" Miler asked.

"I have a Bachelor of Science in Biology and a minor in Chemistry," Zane answered.

Miler scoffed and said, "My God man. You have to have some background in Political Science before you can enter graduate school in that field. And, I want to know what it is about my publication that you do not agree."

"Doctor, I see an empty chair in the corner. Would you mind if we went there to discuss that? By the way, please call me Dale," Zane said as he pointed to the empty seat.

Once seated, Zane asked. "What training courses do faculty members have to complete before they start teaching?"

"None," Miler answered. "Their credentials speak for themselves."

"Doctor, do you mean that you are not qualified to teach a grade school class?" Zane asked.

"I beg your pardon?" Miler blared.

Zane feigned deep thought and said, "I think that Texas requires a teacher's certificate before a person can teach in their school system. To obtain this certificate requires successful completion of numerous training classes. Since you said that faculty members do not attend such classes, I can conclude that you are not qualified to teach in the Texas school system."

Miler's dour expression began to fail. An upward turn appeared at the corners of his mouth.

"Major, you are nimble with words and twist them to your own ends. I would think you to be a politician or an attorney," Miler finally said with laughter.

The barrier between them fell that day. When Zane explained his teaching background, Miler became enthralled with the military's education system. He admitted that most professors never prepared lesson plans. They seldom defined goals for each hour's instruction. Some went to their rostrums, opened their textbooks, and did little else. They asked for questions. If the students hand none, they dismissed the class. Students had to guess what the instructor considered important.

Zane made a significant point. He submitted that few faculty members had outside experience in their fields. They graduated with their undergraduate degrees and went directly into graduate studies. When they obtained their masters, they began work on a doctorate. Many, after receiving their doctorates, stayed in the system as professors. They talked their field but few ever lived them.

It was necessary for a security guard to let them out of the building that day. Zane remained at Miler's request. He was deeply interested in Zane's personal experiences in Korea and Viet Nam. Miler considered Zane's experiences more than any undergraduate could ever learn in Political Science. Miler made a graduate degree program proposal.

Miler went to the library and returned with a book that he gave to Zane saying, "Read this before next Thursday. I will discuss it with you at our faculty meeting. We will see how you do. I suspect that you will do well. This way we can get you enough credits for a BA in Political Science. After that, we can start on a master's program for you in the same field."

Now, almost 24 months later, Zane needed to complete his thesis for a master's degree. He tried for a six month delay on his assignment date to 'Nam. DA's response was that he could complete it when he returned from his tour.

"Bill, I will miss our Thursday sessions. I now have a much better understanding of how government systems should work and why many do not. I deeply appreciate your personal assistance," Zane said.

Miler handed Zane the second book that he brought to the meeting. It was a leather bound volume of "War and Peace" by Leo Tolstoy.

"This is for you," Miler said. "Consider it a going away gift. I only wish some of my contemporaries had an experience as we had. It would give them a better understanding of the current situation in Viet Nam. It is sad for it was not that long ago that I believed as they do. While I still maintain that we have no business in Viet Nam, I see where responsibility lies. You take care of yourself Dale. Lisa and I look forward to your safe return to Janice and your children. In addition, we want to continue our friendship while you are away. Write when you can. We will take care of your family. I must go now."

Miler almost leaped from his seat and rushed from the room. Zane saw Miler's eyes begin to get misty before he left. Zane felt the same because of their close friendship.

The next morning Colonel Connelly received a telephone call from Father Flowers. When they finished speaking, Connelly opened the sliding door between them.

"Dale, stick around. Cadet Bradley's mother is in Father Flowers' office. She is making a formal complaint against you for assault," Connelly said looking grim. "If I need you, I will call."

After 30 minutes, Connelly called and asked Zane to come to Father Flowers' office. Flowers' secretary ushered him into the University President's office. Sitting in front of Flowers' desk was a dumpy woman in her early fifties. She was incessantly tapping one foot in apparent emotional distress.

"Good morning, major. Mrs. Bradley this is Major Zane. Major Zane meet Mrs. Bradley, Cadet Bradley's mother," Father Flowers said.

Zane nodded his head in the lady's direction and said, "Pleasure to meet you, mam."

Mrs. Bradley scoffed and ignored Zane. Father Flowers moved from behind his desk to a position at its corner nearest Zane. Crossing his arms, he leaned against the desk and looked at Zane.

"Major, tell us what happened yesterday with Cadet Bradley," Flowers directed.

Zane explained every detail of his meeting with Bradley, concluding with his threat to "throw him out."

Zane added, "Mrs. Bradley if I frightened your son I apologize. I would never touch a student for any reason. I am not foolish enough to destroy my career over such a trivial matter."

During his telling of the event, Zane noticed Mrs. Bradley's foot tapping faster and faster. She almost seemed to swell as he told details. When he added the part about scaring him, she lost control.

"Major Zane, my baby is not afraid of you. He is a grown man and can take care of himself thank you," she shrieked.

"I still apologize," Zane said, as he looked at Father Flowers.

Mrs. Bradley came to her feet and advanced toward Zane. Father Flowers intercepted her and placed one arm around her shoulders while guiding her toward the door.

"Mrs. Bradley, if it is any consolation, Major Zane will leave our faculty in less than a week," Flowers said with a soothing tone.

Mrs. Bradley shook her head back and forth while saying, "My baby is not afraid of him. My baby is not afraid of him."

Father Flowers returned from his outer office and closed his door. He leaned his back against it and began laughing quite loud. Realizing that Mrs. Bradley might hear him, he quickly placed one hand over his mouth to stifle his laughs. His face began to turn red from the effort.

Looking at Zane, Father Flowers walked to him and began shaking Zane's hand. He chuckled a few times.

"Dale, we see Mr. Bradley's problem. What grown man has his mother fight his battles? Go about your business and we will see you and Janice at your farewell party tomorrow night," Father Flowers said.

During his tenure at St. Marys, Zane gained perspective regarding the Hippie Movement. While he did not understand some intellectuals who participated, he felt he understood the younger members. The "Flower Children" were just those, children. They wanted to belong to a group of their peers. Their life style wasn't any different than others before them. For one generation, it was "zoot suits." For Zane's, it was pegged pants and pompadour haircuts.

As far as the intellectuals were concerned, Zane saw them as adults trying to regain their youth. What he despised about some of them was their introduction of drugs. In particular, he found the use of mind-altering drugs, such as LSD, as insidious and destructive. He had counseled students while at St. Marys. Too often, he found uncaring parents and irresponsible adults as the root causes of many young people's problems.

Zane's third departure for Viet Nam was a family affair. Janice held Steve while Susan tugged at her skirt. He kissed each of them, promising to try to get leave for Christmas. Janice had to be father and mother again. It was a heavy burden to see to everything. It was a sacrifice made before and she would do it again.

On his flight to Viet Nam, Zane missed Daryl Scott. He had not seen, or even heard from, his old friend since his divorce. Despite his efforts to find Scott, it was always the same. He had just left or his telephone was busy. He wished the best for him and hated to know that he lost Georgia and two children. It happened to many soldiers on continuing overseas tours.

The chartered Tiger Airlines flight from San Francisco was full. Most of those on board were career soldiers returning for a second or third tour. Sprinkled among them were draftees who recently completed their advanced individual training. The mood on board was sullen and bitter. Usually, flights like this had joking and laughing among the younger soldiers but not on this flight. The air felt thick with dread and foreboding. Not a person on their flight wanted to be the last person killed in Viet Nam. Up and down the aircraft's aisle the question screamed, "What the hell am I doing here?"

It was 04:00 hours when their flight landed at Tan Son Nhut airport near Saigon. A line of buses awaited them on the tarmac. Military Police oversaw their transfer to the buses and provided an armored car escort to the Replacement Depot. The depot processed individuals for transfer to units. It was a filthy place with rats scampering between buildings and in the dirty rooms. Red dirt coated everything and no one seemed to care. More than likely they didn't.

"Major Zane, Major Zane, report to the main office with bag and baggage. Your unit is here with transportation," the depot's PA system blared.

Carrying his duffel bag over one shoulder, Zane walked to the headquarters. He entered a large room the size of two basketball courts. Its design was to process thousands of troops at a time for assignment to their units. Now, it was in disrepair, unkempt, and bleak. Other than one young soldier, Zane was alone. The soldier walked toward him.

Wearing a khaki uniform, he was the sharpest soldier he had seen in country. On his epaulets, he wore the insignia of the 3rd Brigade of The 1st Cavalry Division. His wore a freshly pressed uniform and his shoes gleamed.

Stopping in front of Zane, he saluted and said, "Sir, I am Specialist Four Carswell. I am your driver for your trip to the 3rd Brigade."

Returning his salute, Zane asked. "Which way Carswell?"

"I will take your bag, sir. Follow me to the side exit," Carswell answered.

Lifting his bag onto his shoulder, Zane replied, "Thanks Carswell but I can handle it. Lead the way."

As they exited the building, Zane stopped dumbstruck. Sitting by the exit was a four-door sedan. He watched Carswell open its nearest rear door and stand at attention.

"As you were, son," Zane said. "This is a 1st Cav vehicle?"

"Yes sir. I drive Commanding General Burton. In addition, I provide transportation for VIPs. It is air-conditioned, sir," Carswell answered, smiling and obviously proud.

Zane looked at his duffel bag covered with red dirt, after seeing the car's interior, and said, "Let's put this bag in the trunk. I don't want to be the one who gets the general's trousers dirty."

With his gear stowed, Zane climbed into the sedan's rear. As he entered the door, he felt the air conditioner's dry, cold air flow over him. He could almost hear moisture, which soaked his uniform, sucked from it. He sat back and relaxed against the comfortable seat.

"Damn, this is not the unit I once knew," Zane thought. I can get used to this."

Carswell drove through the depot's main gate and traveled east as Zane asked. "Where are we headed?"

"We are going to the 3rd Brigade's Headquarters at Ben Hoa. Are you familiar with the area, sir?" Carswell asked.

"Yes, this is my third trip," Zane said. "I am not used to air conditioned sedans. Things have changed in the Cav," Zane answered.

"What's going on, Carswell," Zane asked.

"We are going home, sir. Two thirds of the 1st Cav has already left. Supply yards are brimming with equipment for shipping to CONUS. That's how I obtained this car. The supply people in Saigon did not have a place to put it. They just gave it to me for asking," Carswell answered.

Continuing, Carswell explained, "There is considerable confusion, sir. Two months ago, MACV put together a provisional brigade for the Cav. Their mission is to protect Saigon while other units go home. However, their area of responsibility is extremely large. The scuttlebutt is that we have too much area to cover. There are less than 65,000 American troops remaining in country."

"Sixty five thousand," Zane thought. "It was not long ago that there were over 500,000. I guess the ARVN have to fight."

As it became light enough to see well, Zane noticed deserted buildings and installations. They were in shambles. He recognized the highway to Ben Hoa. It stood stark black against undulating, red terrain. Power lines lined the roadside. Few vehicles were about other than Vietnamese riding bicycles. Occasionally, they would see a military vehicle. He recalled traveling this road in the past. Traffic was bumper to bumper and diesel fumes choked those who traveled it. There had been an incessant roar of helicopters passing overhead. Now, they saw three on their way to Ben Hoa.

When Carswell stopped the sedan at brigade headquarters, a Second Lieutenant Ramsley stepped from a doorway. He saluted and opened the rear door for Zane. While exiting the vehicle, Zane noticed that the lieutenant wore a golden citation cord. This indicated that he was a general's aide.

When Zane went to the car's trunk area, Lieutenant Ramsley said, "Sir, we do not have time for that. Specialist Carswell will get your bag. The morning briefing starts in five minutes. General Burton wants you present. This way sir."

In San Francisco, Zane had showered, shaved, and put on a fresh uniform. After 23 hours aboard an aircraft, his ride in a filthy bus, and unshaven, his appearance was decidedly poor. While following the lieutenant, he attempted to brush dirt from his trousers and clean his shoes with a handkerchief.

Lieutenant Ramsley stopped and opened a door, stepping aside he said, "Your seat is up front by the general sir."

Stepping inside, he saw a familiar scene. To the direct front was a small stage with a rostrum and a large viewing screen. Two rows of chairs, six wide and ten deep, extended away from the stage. Nearest the stage, and in front of the other chairs, two empty chairs sat. Zane walked the narrow aisle toward the front. He watched as seats filled with officers and senior NCOs on both sides of him. There was considerable low mumbling by the gathering group.

When he reached the front row of seats, Zane saw name plates on the rear of the two lone chairs. On the back of the left one was the brigade's commanding general's name, Burton. Beside it, the other plate had Major Zane inscribed upon it.

"I can grow to like this," he thought. "This place is cold. I was expecting the usual tent. Things have really changed."

Stepping in front of his designated seat, Zane began another unsuccessful attempt to clean his uniform. As soon as he sat, Lieutenant Ramsley stepped through a side door.

"Gentlemen, the commanding general," he announced.

Everyone arose at the general's rapid entry and sat when Burton said, "Seats, gentlemen."

Zane remained standing to greet Burton. He said, "Major Zane reporting, sir."

Zane took Burton's offered hand and gave it a quick shake as the general said, "Zane you cannot know how glad we are to see you. Sit and listen. Colonel Baines?"

Lieutenant Colonel Baines, obviously the Brigade Operations Officer, stepped behind the rostrum as the room's lights dimmed. He started to speak when Burton interrupted.

"Milton, fill Major Zane in on our current status," Burton directed.

"Yes, sir, Colonel Baines answered, "Let's have the organization slide first please."

Someone, behind the stage's screen, placed a transparency on an overhead projector and turned on its lamp. It appeared crisp and focused on the screen.

"This is all these guys do is make presentations," Zane thought. "I bet every visiting bigwig to 'Nam receives a briefing at Ben Hoa. Its proximity to Saigon is a blessing and a curse."

"In accordance with our Commander-In-Chief's plan to withdraw forces, one brigade remains of the original three assigned to the 1st Cavalry Airmobile Division. This brigade, the 3rd, is a separate brigade with a provisional structure. Our mission is to interdict enemy infiltration and supply routes in War Zone D."

"The 3rd Brigade is equipped with helicopters from the 229th Assault Helicopter Battalion. There is a battery of Cobra gunships, known as the 'Blue Max,' to provide aerial fire support. In addition, there are two air cavalry troops."

"Our organization includes a quick reaction force (QRF) designated as "Blue Platoons," They support air assault actions. They have three missions. First, they form a protecting unit around any downed helicopter. Second, they reinforce Ranger patrols that make contact. Third, they search for enemy trails, caches, and bunker complexes."

"To keep our artillery assets airmobile, we depend upon the newly formed 362nd Aviation Company. Once a World War II transportation company, it is now a provisional Chinook company. Formerly B Company of the 228th Assault Support Helicopter Battalion, it has 24 CH-47 helicopters, 1 Command and Control Huey and over 500 personnel. Attached to it is a depot maintenance unit, making the 362nd capable of major helicopter rebuilding. It is smaller than a battalion but much larger than a company."

General Burton leaned toward Zane and whispered, "That's yours."

Looking back at Colonel Baines, Burton directed, "Milton give me the tactical situation. We have to go."

Baines completed his briefing by providing details of unit locations, any engagements, attacks, and future plans. He ended his presentation by asking for questions.

"Let's go," Burton said as he bolted from his seat toward the exit.

Caught unprepared, Zane almost had to run to stay with Burton. They traveled down a hall and to an exit opening near a helipad. A Huey, with its blades turning at full speed, sat on the pad. Holding their hats, the pair boarded the ship. Zane felt out of place dressed in khakis when everyone else wore combat fatigues. Burton didn't seem to mind so Zane forgot about it.

Burton's Huey was as a command and control ship. Two pilots manned the cockpit area as usual. The passenger area had significant modifications. Behind the pilot's seats, there was a wide radio console. It ran from side to side inside the ship. The console gave a commander the capability of talking to many different units on differing frequencies. One wide passenger seat was behind the console. It had seating for four. On each side, a door gunner manned an M-60 machine gun.

Burton gestured for Zane to put on a headset he thrust at him. Zane put it on and listened.

Burton pressed his talk switch and said to Zane, "You stick with me for one week. You eat with me in the general's mess. You have quarters attached to mine at Ben Hoa. That is where you sleep. Attend every briefing with me. You will meet every commander in the brigade and many outside of it. Ask questions. I must rely upon your judgment to get your job done after that. I do not have time to wet nurse commanders. Is that clear?"

"Affirmative, sir," Zane answered.

During the following seven days, Zane traveled Burton's entire operational area. It covered thousands of square miles in one of South Viet Nam's most critical areas. If the NVA had plans to take Saigon, they would likely attack from their Cambodian sanctuaries nearest the city. Highway QL-13 coursed through the border near Loc Ninh and led to its provincial capitol at An Loc. A scant 60 miles from Saigon, QL-13 offered the best and shortest attack route.

After dinner on Zane's seventh day, General Burton asked Zane to join him in his quarters for drinks. While the general's mess had a full bar, he wanted to speak with him alone.

Sitting in the general's receiving room, Burton asked, "Zane, there are two, classified missions that you must give special attention. One is the evacuation of the American Embassy in Phnom Penh, Cambodia. The other is the evacuation of our embassy in Saigon. You control the greatest lift capacity in South Viet Nam. Your Chinooks can get the job done in one sweep while it would take hundreds of Hueys to do the job."

"Keep foremost in your mind that we cannot shoot, move or communicate without your Chinooks. We depend upon them for ammunition, fuel, and every thing we need to fight this war. As you saw, land resupply won't get it. The enemy can cut our land routes any time they want. We cannot stop them. Soon there will not be another American ground combat unit remaining in Viet Nam. General Abrams does not want to see another American soldier die in this hellhole. In addition, you will be doing medical evacuation missions for ARVN forces and us. We are depending on you."

Continuing, Burton added, "My tour ends in three months. A new commander takes over then. You make me proud when he arrives. I do not want any casualties."

"Sir, that is one thing I intend to accomplish. Every man of mine is to go home unharmed," Zane said with determination.

Burton got up and said, "My driver will take you to see the 229th Commander in the morning. I purposely did not take you to visit his unit. You work directly for him. He will give you his guidance and get you to the 362nd tomorrow by Noon. Goodnight and good luck, son."

"Major, I figure General Burton told you most everything about our operations," Lieutenant Colonel Wilson R. Smith, Commander of the 229th Aviation Battalion said. "I have a couple of items to cover and you can be on your way. There will be no change of command ceremony. We do not have the time."

Colonel Smith, like Zane, was a field artillery officer. This was his second 1st Cav tour and his first aviation battalion command. One disturbing thing for Zane was that Smith knew nothing about Chinooks and said so.

"Burton told you how important they are. I am telling you again. You must have as many ships combat ready daily as possible. The 362nd readiness rate is unsatisfactory. They have yet to top 75 percent. That is unacceptable. Can you fix that situation, Dale," Smith asked.

"Absolutely sir," Zane answered. "Seventy-five percent is way too low. I will give you textbook maintenance for the CH-47. You will get nothing less than what's expected of the Chinook."

"That's great, Dale. I am anxious to see that, as I know General Burton is," Smith responded.

"Your unit is at Camp Martin Cox at Bear Cat. Bear Cat is the headquarters for the 45th Thai Panther Division. Their commander is a major general. The installation belongs to him. You are a guest. There are no infantry available to defend your unit. You must man your own defense perimeter and still get your job done. I suggest you coordinate defensive zones with the Thais. Unless you have questions, your C & C Huey will pick you up at our helipad in ten minutes," Smith said getting up from his seat.

Reaching across his desk, he shook Zane's hand and wished him luck. Smith called for Specialist Billerman. He entered the room from a side office.

"Sir?" Billerman said.

"Take Major Zane to his waiting ship," Smith ordered. "Also, tell my crew to get mine ready."

Zane followed Specialist Billerman to the helipad where Zane dismissed him. Zane looked at his C & C Huey and saw on its side door a painted likeness of a longhorn steer. Above it someone had painted, "B Company." Beneath, words appeared that said, "The Longhorns."

A door gunner ran from the ship and grabbed Zane's duffel bag. As he climbed aboard, the two pilots gave him a big grin and a "thumbs up" signal. The other gunner checked Zane's seat belt for tightness. As he returned to his M-60, he gave the aircraft commander a tap on his shoulder. Zane could see the commander talking through his mouthpiece. Zane knew that he would be requesting takeoff instructions. No one offered him a headset on his C & C ship.

"Looks like an attitude adjustment is necessary," Zane thought, as his ship went airborne for Bear Cat. In less than ten minutes, they were on approach to his new command.

Chapter Forty Three

October 1971

Men with secrets tend to be drawn to each other, not because they want to share what they know but because they need the company of the like-minded, the fellow afflicted.
Don DeLillo (b. 1926), U.S. author. Walter Everett, Jr., in *Libra*, pt. 1, "17 April" (1988)

Lanny Briscoe was correct. The USSR supplied the encryption method in use by North Viet Nam. The VENONA project was the key. After World War II, Susan Fillers, cryptography expert, suggested NSA begin trying to decode Soviet messages intercepted during the war. On the surface, the messages appeared to be routine transmissions of little worth. However, Fillers suspected otherwise. NSA chief, Erwin Bruenwylor, approved an initial investigation and assigned Fillers to the project. For two years, she worked alone. When she made a breakthrough, that changed.

Bruenwylor received funding to continue the project. He assigned four other cryptographers to work with Fillers. He gave NSA's highest priority to their work and code-named their effort VENONA. It was tedious work, which required immense patience. Mundane messages received intense scrutiny. It was three years before their team decoded their first, one paragraph message. However, it provided a foundation for future efforts. The most significant of which began at Harvard in 1968.

A Harvard University group tried to send digital messages over standard telephone lines. MIT, with Dr. Jenkins heading the effort, joined Harvard to help. The thrust of the work was to reduce messages to minute parts. They would send these digital parts across the country to USC at Berkley. Upon receipt, data processors would reassemble the messages into their original digital forms. After this, they converted the message to a text file for printing.

Jenkins received Briscoe's request for analysis of digital data recordings. The VENONA group applied their digital processing techniques to recordings supplied by Briscoe. They disassembled them and applied their decryption algorithms. Only digital data processors could achieve success. The messages often used over 1,000 characters to represent one letter of the alphabet. The result was a printed copy of the decoded transmission. The next chore was to translate the message into English. This was the easiest part of the process.

NSA assigned Briscoe to MACV headquarters in Saigon to oversee decryption of North Vietnamese messages. He arrived in Saigon in early October 1971. It was necessary that he work with various collection agencies to assure recordings at a particular frequency and type. The code was so immense and fast that it could easily escape detection. The primary collection agency was an Army aviation unit stationed at Long Thanh North near Ben Hoa. The cover for the unit was the 224th Aviation Battalion (Radio Research). Briscoe checked with MACV operations to determine who commanded the unit. Operations advised him that the current commander was Major Daryl Scott.

MACV Operations had to schedule a flight with the 1st Cav Division to provide transportation to Long Thanh North. Normally, MACV had ample aircraft assigned to their headquarters to use. However, with the intense unit withdrawal underway, they frequently had to task subordinate units for aircraft. In addition, they advised Major Scott of Briscoe's impending visit.

"That's Long Thanh North straight ahead, sir," the Light Observation Helicopter (LOH) pilot, CW3 Bendinger, said over the intercom.

Briscoe noticed when he boarded the LOH (Loach) that it was a 1st Cav ship. The CWO3 pilot wore a Cav patch on each shoulder.

"Chief, is this your second tour?" Briscoe asked.

"My third, sir," Bendinger answered.

"Jesus, DA sure gives you guys a workout with tours," Briscoe commented.

"I volunteered," Chief Bendinger responded.

"From what I hear," Briscoe said, "The life span of Loach pilots is not long in this place."

"Sometimes it gets tough. I didn't mind getting this milk run today," Bendinger said with a chuckle. "We're close enough to Long Thanh North for a better view now sir."

Briscoe had a panoramic view of the installation. The base had an excellent fixed wing runway. In revetments on both sides of it, he saw various aircraft parked. On the right side, he saw Army Mohawks. This twin turbine aircraft was the Army's fastest fixed wing. It had a pod attached underneath that housed a Side Looking Airborne Radar (SLAR). It could identify objects through their infrared signatures. It also could intercept electronic communication signals for later analysis.

After the Mohawks, there were shiny, new, twin engine aircraft parked in neat rows.

Pointing to them, Briscoe asked. "What unit uses those airplanes?"

They belong to the Command Airplane Company. They fly admin missions for the brass at MACV. That unit is a dream assignment for Viet Nam. They routinely fly to Bangkok and other exotic places.

Farther down on the right, there were numerous Army U-21 and U-8 ships parked. They were from companies subordinate to the 224th. By 1969, the 224th had six subordinate companies stationed from Da Nang to Can Tho. One of the units Briscoe worked with was the 1st Radio Research Company at Cam Ranh Bay in 1969. It used Navy aircraft flown by Army pilots. The first transmissions Briscoe received that started his VERNONA request were from the 1st Radio Research Company. At that time, the 224th had over 1,000 assigned personnel.

Nixon's withdrawal resulted in the battalion having two aviation companies remaining. They were scheduled to leave Viet Nam in the near future. A major reason for Briscoe's visit was to gain information to stop the withdrawal of these units. There was a significant need for them. Normally, this battalion required a lieutenant colonel as its commander. With its size reduction, Major Scott filled the position.

Turning to his pilot, Briscoe asked. "What unit is that on the runway's left side? It's the one that has a gate leading into the main base.

"That, sir, is a Special Forces base. They like to remain independent. See those ships with the large wings on the left. They are STOL ships used to conduct secret operations," Bendinger explained.

"I am very familiar with those," Briscoe replied, recalling his long nights over Laos.

Continuing, he asked. "See that fenced unit at the right corner of the base. Can you let me off close to it?"

"Hell sir, I will put you inside," Bendinger bragged.

"No, no, don't do that. In front of their main gate will do," Briscoe replied. "You could get shot doing that."

"No sweat, sir, I can get shot bringing you here. What's one more bullet," he said with a grin.

Briscoe watched the Loach depart after leaving him by the unit's gate.

"Sounds like a bee," he thought, as he turned toward the guarded entrance to the 224th.

Briscoe gave his credentials to one of the two guards and said, "I'm here to see Major Scott."

The guard entered a small shack and twisted the handle of a field phone. Briscoe watch him talk to someone.

The guard put the phone's handset in place and returned outside to where Briscoe waited.

"Major Scott will be with you right away," the guard said.

As Scott approached, Briscoe noted the numerous ribbons below his silver wings. He had learned that the second and third tour veterans had the most rows. He had no idea what they meant.

"Hi Mr. Briscoe, I'm Daryl Scott. How was your flight?" Scott asked.

"Great, this trip was my first in a Hughes OH-6. It provides quite a view," Briscoe answered.

"That's their main mission, looking. They make great reconnaissance ships," Scott commented.

Scott asked Briscoe to follow him. They entered a long hall extending in both directions. On the inside wall, there were doors without markings.

Scott stopped at one of them after making a right turn into another long hall. Scott opened it and motioned Briscoe to enter. Inside, Briscoe noted that the room was like the halls. They were bare. Usually, units had some sort of pictures adorning their walls but not this one.

"Major, why the bare walls?" Briscoe asked.

Scott replied, "Great places for bugging devices."

"Did not think of that," Briscoe said.

Briscoe discussed the possibility of adding data processing equipment to Scott's aircraft. He explained that doing so would reduce their decoding time.

Scott agreed to try the procedure and would give an answer later. During the next two hours, Briscoe explained in detail about VERNONA and what came of their crypto effort. He maintained that, with Scott's help, they could intercept and decode every message sent to or from North Viet Nam's political and military headquarters. Scott, excited about the concept, agreed to accelerate his evaluation.

"Major, I have one more question you might be able to help me with," Briscoe stated.

"What' that," Scott answered.

In 1969, at Cam Ranh Bay, I meet this captain built like a fire hydrant. He carried a pump 12-gauge shotgun. He was a bad looking hombre. I convinced him to show me through a Chinook. I noticed an antenna on the aircraft's side. Its configuration was like a series of Vs. I'm sure it was an ARC 102 radio. Do you have any experience with Chinooks?" Briscoe asked.

A knowing grin crossed Scott's face as he replied, "Yes, I have considerable experience. Was the name of the pilot, Dale Zane?" Scott asked.

"That's him," Briscoe answered. "I'm to visit his unit for a mission proposal and I don't want to get on his bad side by not doing my homework."

"Visit his unit?" Scott asked. "The last I heard he was in San Antonio, Texas."

"No, he's in Viet Nam. He is CO of the 362nd Aviation Company at Bear Cat," Briscoe explained.

"Bear Cat," Scott, responded, obviously excited. "Hell, that's almost across the street from here."

"Oh really," Briscoe commented.

"Yes, really. I guess it's less than a mile. I would love to see the ol' shit. I'll drive you over there," Scott said as he turned to exit the room.

"I did not know it was that close. It would be great if I could get this done today," Briscoe replied.

As soon as he approached the gate at Bear Cat, Scott saw that there were no Chinooks on the airfield. He questioned the Thai gate guard about the 362nd. He did not speak English. Dejected Scott drove Briscoe back to Long Thanh North.

Along their way, Briscoe commented, "If his unit is in Viet Nam, I can locate it."

"They may have sent them to CONUS. They're leaving everyday. Nevertheless, if he's in country, I can find also find him," Scott added.

"I will check as soon as I get to MACV. Do you want me to let you know his location?" Briscoe asked.

"There's no need. When we get to my unit, I will tell you where they are," Scott answered.

"That's great, thanks," Briscoe said.

Scott checked with his Operations Officer to determine the 362nd's location. They recently moved from Bear Cat to Phu Loi, west of Ben Hoa.

"I'll have to visit soon," Scott thought.

He gave the information to Briscoe before the Loach picked him up for his return trip. Briscoe return flight lasted 15 minutes.

Briscoe arrived at Tan Son Nhut near sunset. He was in base operations requesting ground transportation. He saw a man with a familiar face talking to an Air Force weather NCO. It appeared that the person was getting a weather briefing for a flight.

"Who is it, damn it? Who is it?" He asked himself.

"Thailand, that's where I met him. He flies for Air America," Briscoe remembered.

He made his way through passengers awaiting flights. Engrossed with his briefing, he did not see Briscoe approach.

"Sir Frederick Earling I presume?" Briscoe asked, his voice brimming with friendliness.

Frederick turned and immediately recognized Briscoe and said, "Briscoe, I figured you were in Thailand. What on earth are you doing here?"

Donning a coy grin, Briscoe answered, "I will answer that if you will truthfully answer the same question."

Frederick smiled and shook Briscoe's hand as he said, "I am Air America's Operations Officer for Saigon and that's the truth. Now, it's your turn."

Briscoe raised his hands with their palms facing Frederick. He swung them back and forth, as he shook his head indicating "No."

Laughing, he stated, "I guess I stepped into that one. You know I can't say."

Continuing, Briscoe asked. "This is your permanent station now. You don't work in Thailand anymore?"

"That's right. I've lived here for a good while now. On occasion, I have a flight to Thailand but not often. I live in Saigon," Frederick explained.

When Frederick learned that Briscoe was living in the BOQ, he asked. "Hey, do you want a topnotch meal? I am talking about first class. Join Vanessa and me at a party Thursday night. Will you come?"

Briscoe was tired of his room and the BOQ. It was a lifeless place and boring. He decided he would enjoy a party.

"Tell me when and where," Briscoe stated.

Frederick took a page from a pocket notebook and began writing. He handed the note to Briscoe.

"Take this and show it to any taxi driver. The address is where the party is. I live directly across the street on the top floor. Come by early and have a drink before we go," Frederick suggested.

Briscoe checked the time on the paper given to him by Frederick. The stated time was 19:00 hours.

"I would like that, Briscoe replied. Is 18:30 hours okay?'

Frederick noticed the Air Force NCO staring at him. He seemed perturbed.

"That's great. Please excuse me but I have a flight. I will see you tomorrow night," Frederick said.

As Briscoe departed, he said, "Until then. You be careful out there tonight."

The next morning Briscoe waited at MACV's helipad for his scheduled flight to Phu Loi. He was in a waiting room set aside for VIP use. Five minutes before his scheduled pickup time, a Chinook landed on the helipad. On its side, was an emblem of two white ducks mating in flight. The topmost duck had a leering expression on its face. The ship's nose was marked with one large word, "UNITED."

Briscoe watched the Flight Engineer lower its ramp. From inside the CH-47, someone drove a jeep down the ramp and onto the helipad. The driver waited while two full colonels and a brigadier general left the ship and climbed into the jeep. They immediately sped away. However, the Chinook remained with its ramp down and the flight engineer outside the ship. Almost five minutes passed.

"Mr. Briscoe, your flight to Phu Loi is waiting," some one said over speakers.

"I can't believe they sent a Chinook," Briscoe thought as he exited the waiting room.

As he ran toward the Hook, Briscoe removed his bush hat and stuffed it in his pocket. He was making sure that the Hook's rotor blast did not blow it away. As he ran, he saw the flight engineer (FE), raise his clenched right fist above his head. He moved it up and down indicating for Briscoe to hurry. He ran faster and did not slow, as he went up the ramp. His feet slipped from beneath him and he sprawled face first onto the floor. He felt the FE grab him beneath his arm and begin pulling him to his feet.

As Briscoe straightened, the FE yelled, "Grab a seat and fasten your belt."

The noise level inside the Hook was overwhelming. It was necessary to scream to communicate. He chose a seat on the ship's right side near its door gunner. As he was fastening his seat belt, the FE tapped him on his shoulder. He looked up to see the FE thrusting a headset toward him.

Briscoe put it on and immediately heard the FE ask. "Do you want a chicken plate?"

Not knowing what a chicken plate was, Briscoe raised his hands palms up and mouthed the word, "I don't know."

"Sir, there is a talk switch near your right leg. It is part of the cord going to your head set. When you must talk, press the switch. We prefer that you not use it unless you absolutely have to. I will get you a chicken plate," the FE said.

The FE went to a cabinet on the ship's left side. He removed a rigid plate, slightly larger than a man's chest. Its exterior had an OD covering with straps to wear it on a person's chest.

As the FE returned with it, he said, "Slip this beneath your ass. You will have to adjust your seat belt. This might just keep you from becoming a tenor during our trip. Welcome aboard United 490."

Briscoe felt overwhelmed by the Hook. The one he examined at Cam Ranh Bay was not operating. This was an entirely new perspective of the CH-47. It was one thing to walk around one sitting on a ramp. It was a totally different world to fly in it. The noise was horrendous.

He could see through a narrow doorway into the cockpit. He had a limited view of the pilot in the left seat. The person in the right seat was out of his view. The doorway was through a metal divider separating the cockpit from the ship's cargo area. Immediately behind the wall, a door gunner manned an M-60 on each side. He noticed that they continually kept their attention focused outside the ship. From the gunners to the ship's rear, he estimated the cargo area as 40 to 50 feet in length. He was never good at estimating distance

The FE was constantly making visual checks at the craft's rear area. He looked up into the aft pylon repeatedly. On occasion, he would use a rag to wipe something and then watched with obvious interest. Briscoe's attention focused on what the FE wore. He had a chicken plate covering his chest like the one upon which he sat. In addition, he wore a harness. It was almost identical to a parachute harness. Trailing behind the harness, a long nylon strap attached to an overhead steel cable. Briscoe deduced it to be a lifeline of sorts. Later he learned that the crew called it a monkey harness.

Gradually Briscoe felt the Hook slow and begin descending. Its nose began to rise and the FE went to an opening in the Hook's floor. He fell to his knees and then to a prone position where he could see outside through the opening.

"Hook us up James," someone said over the intercom.

"Roger that, sir," he heard the FE answer.

Briscoe heard the FE giving a series of command to move the ship in various directions. The FE's upper torso disappeared through the opening.

In less than ten seconds, the FE said, "Hooked up. Pick it up."

Briscoe heard a decided change in engine noise. It became louder and higher pitched. The ship shuddered slightly and began to accelerate forward and climb.

"Looking good," the FE said, while continuing to watch through the floor's opening.

"Clear right," someone said.

"Clear left," another voice stated.

Gradually, Briscoe felt cooler. He figured they must be at a much higher altitude. The air temperature continued to drop and he became cold. Engine noise became less noisy and stabilized. The FE arose and began making his rounds checking various parts of the aircraft.

The FE looked at Briscoe and said, "We have to drop this load then we will head for Phu Loi. This ship is due a 25 hour check."

Briscoe gave him a thumb up and smiled. The FE continued with his duties.

"James?" Someone asked.

"Yes, sir," James answered.

"Drop site coming up. We have six paxs (passengers) for Phu Loi," someone said.

"Roger that," James answered, as he moved to his prone position at the floor's hatch.

FE James began to chant, "Level at ten. Down, down, release."

The ship moved forward away from whatever it had beneath it. James went to the ship's rear and lowered the ramp until it was level with cargo compartment's floor. Briscoe could see a massive, red dirt cloud billowing behind the Hook. Next, he felt the aft tires touch and then the front ones. The engine and rotor noise diminished as James lowered the ramp to the ground. He exited the ship.

Soon, six soldiers ran up the ramp into the cargo area. They removed their steel helmets and placed them on a chosen seat. Each helmet's interior faced upward. Each man sat on his helmet and fastened his seatbelt. They looked around to see who was on board and then almost immediately went to sleep.

At Phu Loi, the pilots taxied into a revetment with sides almost as high as the rotor blades. The cement and steel structures extended well beyond the ship's nose and rear. James told them it was clear to unload. The six paxs left first with Briscoe close behind watching his footing.

James stopped him and said, "Sir, transportation is on its way. We're over a mile from the company area. Just hang loose."

Shortly an Army mule appeared. Briscoe had seen one before but never rode one. It had a flat deck about two feet above the ground. A low railing went around the vehicle's bed. A Specialist Four drove the odd contraption.

"You Briscoe?" He asked.

"Yes," Briscoe said with apprehension.

"Climb aboard. I have others to pick up. It's almost chow time," the driver said.

Briscoe sat on the flooring where he could see the mule's engine. It looked like the type found on lawn mowers. His driver sat behind a steering wheel on the platform's right corner where foot pedals were available.

The mule's first movement was a lurch as the driver put it into gear and applied power. Bouncing up and down, the hard floor was extremely uncomfortable. The lad driving knew one speed, fast. He raced along a dirt road running parallel to the airfield's parking area. Briscoe saw L-19 Birddogs, a small two man fixed wing aircraft and a variety of helicopters.

At the road's end, the driver made a fast left turn almost throwing Briscoe from the mule. They bounced up a steep hill and into a Quonset hut area. They stopped next to one with a large sign by its entrance. It displayed the two ducks seen on the aircraft. These were on a blue oval. Across its top, the words "362nd Aviation Company" appeared. In an arc, below the oval the words "Fly United" appeared in white. Across the sign's bottom, in large letters, was an inscription, "Major Dale Zane, Commanding."

The driver revved the mule's engine and yelled, "This is it, sir."

Stepping from the strange vehicle, Briscoe stood erect. Pain pulsed in his lower back and legs.

"They can have that damn torture machine," Briscoe said as he rubbed his buttocks.

Opening a screen door, Briscoe entered the building. Typical of most orderly rooms this one had a counter running from side to side. At its rightmost end, there was an entrance available by lifting a portion of the counters' top. Behind the counter, clerks were typing at six desks. In the far right corner, Briscoe saw an infantry first sergeant studying documents. He never saw Briscoe enter.

A clerk nearest the counter snatched a document from his typewriter. He removed the carbons and put them in a box on his desk marked "Hold." He placed the original in another box marked, "CO." After doing this, he looked at Briscoe and arose from his seat.

As he approached the counter, he asked. "Can I help you, sir?"

"Yes, my name is Lanny Briscoe. I have an appointment to see Major Zane," Briscoe answered.

The young soldier turned to look at the first sergeant and yelled, "Top, Briscoe to see the major."

"Send him back," the sergeant said, as he arose from his desk.

As the young man opened the counter for Briscoe to enter, he saw the first sergeant knock twice on a door by his desk. He heard some unintelligible response and the sergeant partially opened the door. Briscoe suspected that he was announcing his arrival.

When he arrived at the first sergeant's desk, he introduced himself as First Sergeant Byron Kubble and asked Briscoe to have a seat. Briscoe saw that the first sergeant wore a 1st Cav patch on each shoulder and airborne wings. Near the wings, he wore a Combat Infantryman's Badge. Briscoe thought this unusual for an aviation unit first sergeant.

"Sir, Major Zane is on the telephone right now. Can I get you some coffee?" Kubble asked.

"Sure thing first sergeant. I like it black," Briscoe answered.

"Me too," Kubble said, as he went to a small table and filled two cups.

After ten minutes, a deep voice from behind the door said, "Top, send him in."

Kubble opened the door wide for Briscoe to enter. On his right was a long conference table with 12 chairs around it. On his left, he recognized Major Zane standing behind his desk with a curious look upon his face. He wore standard combat fatigues.

Behind him, an American flag and a 362nd Unit Guidon crossed with the American flag on Zane's right. Directly behind Zane, and between the two flags, a Southeast Asia map filled a large frame. Briscoe noted that the room's walls had a woven bamboo lining beginning about three feet from the floor. It was unusual to see a Quonset hut this tastefully decorated.

Zane extended his muscular right arm across his desk toward Briscoe and asked. "Have we met?"

"Yes we have major," Briscoe answered. "You gave me a tour of a CH-47 at Cam Ranh Bay a few years ago.

Recognition filled Zane's face as he smiled and said, "The hat. You're the guy with the hat problem. Yes, I remember you," he answered, while crunching Briscoe's hand.

Zane released Briscoe's hand and said, "Let's sit at the conference table. We will be more comfortable."

Briscoe went to the conference table. He took the seat that Zane indicated.

Zane sat next to him and asked. "Coffee?"

"No thanks. First Sergeant Kubble already gave me some," Briscoe answered.

"What can I do for you?" Zane asked.

"I would like you to help me with an operation. Major Scott has already agreed," Briscoe said, watching for a reaction from Zane.

"Scott? Daryl Scott?" Zane asked obviously interested.

"Yes. I met with him yesterday. He said that he knew you and would get in touch," Briscoe explained.

"Where is he? What is he doing," Zane asked excited.

Briscoe explained his meeting with Scott and his desire to use some special equipment with their SIGINT aircraft.

"Long Thanh North, I will be damned. I saw those fixed wing ships coming and going from that location. I never had any idea that Scott might be flying spook missions," Zane observed.

Briscoe asked. "Do you still have ARC 102 radios on your Hooks?"

"We only have two. The others are in storage awaiting shipment. We do not have a need for them. Why do you ask?" Zane asked.

"Major," Briscoe began, "What I am going to tell you is on a need to know basis. I have you a clearance from NSA. What I tell you, you must not repeat to anyone without my approval. Is this clear?" Briscoe asked.

"Certainly, proceed," Zane responded.

Briscoe explained that he would like to use their radios to transmit high speed, and encoded, signals to Virginia. He would furnish the necessary interface between his equipment and Zane's radios. He said that he remembered Zane mentioning sending reports from 10,000 feet.

Zane thought for a moment and answered, "Lanny, my guys would love this mission. However, there's a rub. I would have to get permission from my CO who would have to get permission from brigade. Chinook flight time is at a premium. We have to guard every second to assure each hour is worthwhile."

Hoping to counter Zane's statement, Briscoe said, "Your unit must have time to spare to send a Hook to get me."

"I hate to burst your ego bubble but we did not send a Hook to get you. That ship only had a few hours until it went through a 25-hour inspection. We had a MACV mission already plus an artillery load to move. Since you were at MACV, we picked you up. Otherwise, you would have had to come another way," Zane explained.

"What do you recommend I do?" Briscoe asked.

Zane replied promptly, "Get the elephants to speak."

"What?" Briscoe asked.

"You work at MACV. That is where the elephants are. By elephants, I mean high-ranking officers with power. Get them to schedule your mission as a classified, high priority requirement. Brigade will comply as will the 229th. If you cannot convince the MACV brass, the mission must not be important," Zane explained.

"You are right Dale. I'm jumping channels. At least I know you and Scott want to help. This could be damned important. Think about being able to know the contents of every message going to and coming from Hanoi's headquarters. That is tremendous stuff," Briscoe said.

"I agree," Dale answered. "We have a company of Left Bank aircraft here at Phu Loi. They like to think that no one knows what they do but it's obvious. They are Hueys carrying direction-finding equipment. With all the equipment they have hanging, I don't see how the damn things fly. They appear to be near, or outside of, their center of gravity limits."

Zane rubbed his hands together and asked. "What else do you have?"

"That's it," Briscoe answered.

Zane placed his left hand on a desk telephone and asked. "Do you mind riding backseat in a Birddog?"

Briscoe said, "I will take what I can get."

Zane called Major Bunks, CO of a light fixed wing company. He asked him if they had anything headed for MACV. After a few moments, Bunks explained that he had one going in an hour. Zane thanked him and explained the situation to Briscoe.

"Let's have some lunch and I'll get you on your way. How's that?" Zane asked.

"Fine," Briscoe answered.

Zane reached to a through-the-wall air conditioner next to his desk. He reduced its speed and increased its temperature setting.

Finished Zane said. "There's not much use for that thing to run when the office is empty. It is a lifesaver when we have meetings. With 12 people in here, it's tough. Let's ride."

As Zane and Briscoe stepped outside, a driver awaited with a jeep. Zane pulled the right front seat forward so Briscoe could use the back seat.

Zane dropped his seat and sat while telling the driver, "Let's go to chow MacMilland."

"I hope you like hare," Zane said. "That's for lunch. Hell, we like it so much we will have it for dinner."

Briscoe asked. "You mean hare like in rabbit?"

"Yep. The withdrawal has our supply lines really screwed up. One time we had fried chicken for ten days. Some of us took to eating C-rations. When a freighter arrives in 'Nam with a load of chicken that's all the supply point has. Troops remaining in country do not get anything else until that shipload is gone. It gets interesting. Once all we had were T-bone steaks. Have you ever eaten a deep-fat fried steak? They are not bad. We got sick of the things so the mess sergeant tried various ways to cook them. After our maintenance people walk three miles for lunch, they have big appetites. Unfortunately, most of the pilots spend most of their time in the air. They eat C-rations mostly," Zane explained.

After lunch, Briscoe returned to MACV, as scheduled, in an L-19. After riding in a Hook, the Birddog seemed like a stealth aircraft. However, he felt that the small aircraft was flimsy compared to a Hook.

That night at Phu Loi, Zane sat in his office writing a letter to Janice. He sat at the conference table with his 12-gauge shotgun near at hand. It was for his protection from some disgruntled members of his unit. When he arrived at Bear Cat in August, he plunged into an environment totally unexpected. He should have known from the discord in CONUS. In particular, some young people like Mr. Bradley found themselves in the military. They did not like it and they hated being in Viet Nam.

He recalled his flight to Bear Cat aboard his C & C Huey. Executive Officer, Captain Terry Greenletter, met him at the 362nd helipad near operations. He had two other captains with him.

Zane stepped from the Huey and the three officers gave a crisp salute. Zane returned it and walked to Captain Greenletter.

"Captain Terry Greenletter, Executive Officer, welcome to the 362nd Longhorns, sir," Greenletter said.

Zane noted that Greenletter seemed old for a captain. He wore dual 1st Cav patches on his shoulders. Near his aviator's wings, he had a Combat Infantryman's Badge. Zane made a mental note to ask him about that later."

"Thank you Terry. Who are your friends?" Zane asked.

Greenletter turned and stepped to the right front of the first officer and said, "Sir, this is Captain Earnest Caldwell, Operations Officer.

Zane shook Caldwell's hand and said, "My pleasure Caldwell."

Stepping to his right, Zane accepted the second captain's hand as Greenletter said, "This is Captain Chris Mullins, sir. He is our admin officer."

Zane said, "Nice to meet you Mullins."

Greenletter said, "Sir, if it is okay, we have some light refreshments in operations. We are prepared to brief you at this time."

"That's fine captain. Let's go," Zane said, while watching the Huey's crew chief bringing his duffel bag.

Captain Greenletter fell in beside Zane and began walking rapidly toward a sandbag bunker near the airfield's parking area. Zane examined the area as they walked. His overall impression was that Bear Cat was a dirty place. Water stood in ditches with high weeds growing along them. He saw loose packaging materials lying about on the airfield. Greenletter crossed a ditch on two, rusty PSPs placed across it. They crossed a pot-holed road and then another footbridge like the first. Greenletter stopped at an entrance to the bunker and pulled aside a canvas covering for Zane to enter.

When Zane stepped through the door, Greenletter announced, "The Commanding Officer."

Five young men, bare to their waists, came to attention. Two had been sitting at switchboards taking messages. One was posting missions on a vinyl-covered chart. The fourth stood behind a desk where he had been typing. The fifth stood in front of a chair where he had been playing with a yo-yo. He had a kerchief wrapped around his forehead and his long hair had a part down its middle. Around his neck, he wore peace beads that he had seen Hippies wear.

Zane turned to face Captain Caldwell and asked. "Are these men assigned to you?"

"Yes, sir," Caldwell answered promptly.

"Get them into uniform. I will return in 20 minutes. Captain Greenletter, you come with me. Mullins you do whatever you are supposed to be doing," Zane said as he pulled aside the door's covering.

As Zane stepped outside, he stumbled over his duffel bag sitting in a mud puddle. He picked it up by its strap.

"Where is my hooch captain?" Zane asked Greenletter.

"This way sir," he answered.

Zane followed him to another footbridge across a weed filled ditch. Muddy water filled it as far as Zane could see. They crossed another road, which made a T intersection with the first road they crossed. On the other side, they crossed another footbridge like the others. Straight ahead, Zane saw another sand bag bunker. Compared to operations, it was small. On the side facing them, there was an entrance without any covering.

In front, there was a large cement pad running the bunker's length. In cement, directly in front of the bunker's entrance, there was a large circle painted red. In its center was an indentation with jagged edges. Around the outside of the circle, someone had painted some words.

"At this spot on 1 July 1971, SP4 Hinson reupped for LBJ," Zane read aloud.

Zane looked at Greenletter and asked. "What is this captain?"

Greenletter appeared nervous. Zane found this odd in an older man.

Greenletter answered, "Sir, on the date painted there, SP4 Hinson threw a live hand grenade at our last CO. LBJ is an acronym for Long Binh Jail where they took Hinson for confinement. Hinson had one day left in country. He's at Leavenworth Penitentiary by now."

Zane scoffed and went into the bunker's entrance. It was midday and Zane had to allow his eyes to adjust for the dark interior. While he waited, he heard a steady whine of mosquitoes. Inside, he saw an army cot in the room's far corner. Next to it, a worn and beaten nightstand held a lamp. Zane turned its switch but it would not illuminate.

"Uh sir," Greenletter mumbled. "There's no power to the bunker. The last CO used a flash light."

Zane snapped, "I saw a power line leading into the bunker. Why does it not work?"

"It is PA & E sir. We cannot get them here to fix it," Greenletter answered.

Zane restrained himself. However, his cold words visibly jarred Greenletter.

"Captain this company has electricians galore. Personnel assigned can practically rebuild the most complex helicopter in the world. Yet, you cannot find anyone to fix one electrical wire," Zane said slow and deliberately.

Zane stood his duffel bag on its end. He began loosening its top to gain access to his gear.

"Where's the nearest shower?" Zane asked.

"Right here," Greenletter said proudly as he pointed to a dark doorway.

Zane leaned his duffel bag against his cot and walked to where Greenletter indicated there was a shower. He stopped at the entrance and peered into its dark interior. A few openings, between overhead sandbags, allowed light to pierce the interior's darkness.

Finally, able to see, Zane saw a cubicle about four feet square. It had a cement floor covered with algae. In its center, there was a metal covered drain. A chain hung down about three feet. Beside it, there was a showerhead. The walls had algae growing from sandbags.

Zane turned away and asked. "Where's the john?"

"Outside and across the main road," Greenletter said.

"Captain, I will see you at operations in ten minutes. You are dismissed," Zane said.

Greenletter came to attention and saluted. He said, "Yes, sir."

Zane felt grimy and did not have hope that this place would help. Nevertheless, he removed fresh fatigues and boots from his duffel bag. He stripped and entered the shower. From experience, he knew to test the water. He stood aside and pulled the chain. Water came through in small streams but it was not too hot. He wet himself and lathered. With his eyes closed, he pulled the chain. Slowly, the water began washing away the soap.

Suddenly, he felt something on his feet. Opening his eyes, he looked down to see three large roaches, running back and forth across his feet. Kicking at them, they finally retreated between the sandbags.

Zane returned to operations exactly 20 minutes after leaving. He pushed aside the curtain.

As he stepped through the door, Captain Caldwell yelled, "Attention."

"As you were," Zane responded.

Every man had on his shirt. The soldier who was wearing the peace beads was not present.

Zane asked. "Where did our guru go?"

"Sir, I don't know," Caldwell answered.

"Is he assigned to your section?" Zane asked.

"No sir," Caldwell replied.

Zane realized that he must stop. He did not want to degrade Caldwell before his men. He decided to obtain his gear from supply and visit every place in his unit's area. He would withhold questions and directives for later.

Zane turned to find Greenletter standing behind him. He had not heard him enter.

"Terry come with me please," Zane said.

Zane left operations with Greenletter following through the door. Outside, Zane stopped and turned to Greenletter.

"Do you mind my calling you Terry?" Zane asked.

"No sir. Of course not," he answered.

"Okay Terry, here's the deal. First, I want to go through our maintenance buildings and meet every soldier. After that, I want you to show me every Hook that's here. After that, take me through the men's living quarters. I want to see every place where we have soldiers sleeping. Next, we will go by supply and get my gear. Where's the largest place where we can have a sit down meeting with the senior NCOs?" Zane asked.

"The NCO club would be best for that sir," Greenletter answered.

Zane asked. "I knew there was something else. Where is the first sergeant?"

"We do not have one, sir," Greenletter answered.

"When can we expect one?" Zane asked.

"Sir, I do not know. Our personnel office is at 229th Headquarters in Ben Hoa. I have been there at least six times but senior NCOs are not coming into the country they say," Greenletter replied.

"Okay, no sweat. Who is our senior NCO?" Zane asked, sounding concerned.

"That would be Staff Sergeant Woodring, our maintenance NCO," Greenletter answered.

Zane would not consider pulling a maintenance NCO from his job. He had rather do without a first sergeant.

The afternoon went swiftly. He found knowledgeable and skilled young men in his unit. However, there was something wrong. The men were reluctant to mention whatever it was. They would not say in the presence of their peers. Zane understood this but he had to determine what was happening.

Furthermore, he was almost nauseous at some living conditions he found. One building in particular burned into his brain. It was a wood structure about 15 feet wide and 100 feet long. Ten separate cubicles ran down its length on one side. Each cubicle opened onto an open walkway extending its length. As he neared the walkway entrance, he smelled a horrible odor. It caused his stomach to knot and he almost wretched.

"Damn Terry, what the hell is that?" Zane asked.

"Sir, I do not know," Greenletter said.

Zane stopped and glared at his Executive Officer. Greenletter wanted to say something but was holding it.

"Spit it out captain," Zane directed.

Greenletter seemed to think for a moment before he answered, "Sir, I have been in the unit three days."

"No damned wonder," Zane thought. "He was being totally unfair with his XO. He was learning as they went."

"Fine Terry, we will whip this bear's ass together," Zane said smiling.

Zane watched Greenletter relax and take on a look of determination. His demeanor changed before his eyes.

"Sir, let's go see what that smell is," Greenletter said.

Zane stepped through the walkway door, followed closely by Greenletter. The mysterious odor was overpowering. Zane looked to his right and could not believe what he saw.

The left side of the walkway was rooms with doors. The right side was a low wall with upright boards extending to the roof every few feet. Normally, this type building should have screens stretched its length and doors on each end. However, this one did not.

In the corner, where the two entered, a debris pile extended to the wall's top. In it were C-ration cans with partially eaten food in them. Green fungus covered rotted food. Mixed with these were human feces. It lay in piles on urine soaked boards. Green flies buzzed around the pile and maggots worked in unidentifiable goo. It appeared that those living in the rooms used this spot for a trashcan, urinal, and outhouse.

Zane turned away and went to the first door. He knocked twice hard. There was no response. He pushed on the plywood sheet and it moved aside. Inside, he saw a room in total disarray. Clothing lay about as did various beer and liquor bottles. Hearing a noise Zane looked beneath a cot. To his surprise, he found a wide-eyed, frightened dog with a puppy litter. Zane backed outside and stopped.

Working his way from room to room, Zane found the same situation. At one door, he heard movement inside when he first knocked. He knocked again and heard more so he pushed the door aside. Inside, he found an oriental woman pretending to sweep the floor. Lying on a cot was a man in his shorts. He did not move when Zane called to him.

As Zane walked across the room, the woman cringed in a corner jabbering something he did not understand. He nudged the man but he did not move or make a sound. Quickly he grabbed the man's chin and turned his face where he could see his eyes. He could not do an examination because his eyes were not open.

Lifting an eyelid, Zane noted that the pupil was widely dilated. Next, he checked his breathing and pulse. While his breathing was shallow, his pulse was normal.

Looking farther, Zane found a small vial on a nightstand. In its bottom was a white residue. Opening the nightstand's drawer, he found surgical tubing and a burned, bent spoon. This was beyond Zane's experience.

"Let's go outside," Zane said.

Greenletter looked appalled. Zane mind raced to determine what to do.

"This guy is on drugs," Zane said. "I think its heroin. He is not turning blue; his pulse is good; and he is breathing. Let's get the flight surgeon in here."

Greenletter said, "We don't have a flight surgeon. There is one at Ben Hoa. We're the only Americans on the installation. The rest are Thai soldiers."

"Hell, they've got medical personnel. You go to Ops. Have them contact the Thais and get a doctor in here. We are not qualified for this. I will see to him until you return," Zane said.

Greenletter did not hesitate and ran down the long walkway toward operations. He disappeared with a leap through the far away entrance.

Zane continued checking the young man's breathing and pulse every few minutes. The woman continued to cower in a corner. Occasionally, she would babble something that he did not understand. He knew enough Vietnamese and Korean to know this woman was not speaking those languages.

Looking around the room, Zane found some identification. He located dog tags laced into boots beneath his cot. Zane removed them and read the inscription. The young man was Specialist Four Lindmeyer.

About one-half hour after Greenletter left, Zane heard someone running down the walkway. Leaving the room, he saw Greenletter and an unknown NCO running toward them. They stopped in front of Zane and put their hands on their knees, bent over gasping for air.

Between gasps, Greenletter said, "This is Sergeant Killinger. He was a medic for two years. He can help until a medevac gets here from Ben Hoa. It's on its way."

Killinger stumbled past Zane and began checking the young soldier. Zane and Greenletter watched from outside.

Finished, Killinger joined them and said, "He is going to be okay. However, he came close to an overdose (OD).

Before Killinger finished talking, two soldiers came running down the walkway. One carried a folded stretcher. The lead man pushed past them and went into the room. He began examining the unconscious soldier. While doing so, he told the one with the stretcher to have their Huey land next to the building. The medic ran from the scene. In less than two minutes, a Huey hovered beside the building with its side doors open. It displayed the red cross of a medevac ship.

The three watched the medics placed Lindmeyer aboard their Huey. They made their takeoff directly from their position beside the building. Zane began to feel the adrenaline and his hands began to shake slightly. He recognized it for what it was and tried to ignore it. It had been awhile since being in combat and he knew he would adapt. He had to or fail his men.

By 22:00 hours that first day, Zane was exhausted. He had met his NCOs and liked them. They were veterans and professionals. They had major concerns about the unit's overall health and welfare. They agreed to help him improve the situation. He stumbled to his cot by the light of a flashlight. As an afterthought, he tried the electric light. To his amazement, it illuminated. He also noticed that someone erected a mosquito bar over his cot.

"How about that. Things are looking up," he thought.

Too tired to stow his gear, he placed it next to his cot. He was able to get his preferred shotgun and ammunition. The supply sergeant had an ample supply of anything a person could want. He explained that warehouses brimmed with equipment. Withdrawing units were unloading it far faster than depots could pack and ship. This equipment was that portion remaining after ARVN forces collected most anything they desired. After a shower, he lay on his cot in the dark and began to doze when he heard it.

After pulling the pin on a grenade, and releasing its handle, there is a distinctive snap. Following this, there is a minute sputtering sound a few seconds before detonation. Zane had his shotgun firing at a dark figure at his bunker's entrance. He fired three rounds before taking a fetal position to avoid the oncoming blast. Instead of a blast, he heard the fizzing noise of a smoke or tear gas canister. Zane put his gas mask on and leaned against his duffel bag with his shotgun pointed at the entrance.

In a few moments, he heard a meek voice ask. "Major Zane are you okay?"

Numerous flashlight beams penetrated the darkness. He heard men mumbling phrases.

"Is he okay?" Someone asked.

Another said, "Be careful. He's got a shotgun."

Zane turned on the light, to see Caldwell and Greenletter rubbing their eyes and trying to see through the tear gas. Zane walked toward them.

As Zane passed the pair, he gave a muffled command for them to follow. Outside, he pushed his mask up from his face. Now, a rather large group stood in a semi-circle around Zane's entrance. It occurred to Zane how he must look to them. He wore jockey shorts, a tee shirt, dog tags, and a gas mask pushed atop his head. In his right hand, he carried a shotgun. He began to laugh. Nervous laughter came from the group.

Captain Greenletter went inside and swiftly returned saying, "Sir, you blew the shit out of two sandbag rows. Did you see who it was?"

"Not really," he lied.

Zane had a good recollection of the person's stature and size. He wore a GI haircut with a flattop. He felt sure he could identify the attacker's silhouette. Few soldiers wore their hair in the flattop style popular in the early sixties. In the surrounding group, Zane saw one man with a smug grin. Next to him was a smaller soldier talking to him excitedly. He made a point of remembering their faces.

At 05:30 hours the next morning, Zane's first stop was operations. Again, Captain Caldwell announced Zane's entry and everyone came to attention. Every soldier was in full uniform. The general appearance of the bunker's interior was better than his first visit.

As Caldwell explained the day's missions, Zane told him to dispense with announcing his arrival. It wasted time and distracted the men from their duties. If they wanted to recognize his presence, the senior person present should report without disturbing the others.

"What is the availability rate today?" Zane asked.

"Sir?" Caldwell said, looking perplexed.

"He doesn't know what an availability rate is," Zane thought.

Asking again, Zane rephrased his question. "Of our 24 Hooks, what percentage of them are mission ready?"

"Eighty five percent, sir," Caldwell answered quickly.

"Good. Let me know if it ever drops below 85," Zane directed.

At 06:00 hours, Zane arrived at his headquarters orderly room. Captain Mullins called the orderly room personnel to attention. Later he would explain not to do this in the future.

"What time is formation?" Zane asked.

"Sir, we do not have formation," Mullins replied.

Surprised, Zane asked. "How do you keep track of personnel?"

"Each platoon commander let's me know," Mullins answered.

"Captain that only accounts for two thirds of our people. What about the mechanics in the Avionics, Hydraulics, and Depot Maintenance Attachment?" Zane asked.

Obviously trapped, Mullins did the correct thing. He told the truth.

"Sir, I do not know," he said.

"Okay, we will fix that. Where is the XO?" Zane questioned.

"He's flying today, sir," Mullins said.

"Captain, I want to have an officers' call at 19:00 hours. Where is the best place to have it?" Zane asked.

"The Officers' Club, sir," Mullins answered.

"Are you telling me that this unit has its own Officers' Club?" Zane asked, incredulous.

"Yes sir. Each officer contributes $20.00 a month. We pay for its operation from personal funds," Mullins explained.

"Private slush funds are illegal," Zane thought. "I will have to see about this tonight."

"Thank you," Zane said. "I will be in the company area. If you need me, send a runner. I will meet you here at 18:00 hours. We will go to Officers' Call together," Zane explained.

The rest of the day Zane spent meeting and talking with every unit member. He examined every building in his company area. He studied their defense perimeter in detail and found it in dire condition. The one bright spot he found was the mess hall. There was ample food and the mess sergeant was imminently qualified for his job. However, his tour ended in 30 days and there wasn't a replacement. Zane wrote this in a small notebook he kept in his hip pocket.

That evening Captain Mullins escorted Zane to the 362nd Officers' Club. The building did not appear in the 362nd's Company building's list. Otherwise, Zane would have inspected it earlier. Captain Mullins announced Zane's presence as they entered. What he found was surprising.

The nondescript building belied its interior. Most of the room had tables and chairs similar to those found in a nice restaurant. The room's front had a full stage for floor shows. On one side, running half the room's length, was a full bar that would do justice to any nightclub in CONUS. A divider separated an area that had a pool table, stuffed chairs, a television set, and a ping-pong table. Zane quickly realized the significant resources expended to build such a facility. He told the officers to be at ease.

"Gentlemen, be seated and listen up," Zane said. "In the next few days I will get to know each of you personally. Meanwhile, I have general guidance for you as a group regarding this unit's operations. Our first priority is mission accomplishment. Everything we do and say must focus on that one element. We have a profound responsibility to our unit and its members. We meet that obligation because we take care of our people. That is not happening in the 362nd and it is our fault. We are not meeting our leadership obligations. We start doing that tomorrow morning at 06:00 hours."

Zane asked a CW4 behind the bar for a glass of water. Talking with the unit's members during the day had taken it toll on his throat. After a few swallows, he continued.

"Company formation is in front of the orderly room at 06:00 hours. Platoon commanders and section leaders will attend and account for their unit members to me. This includes those who are flying missions. While they may not be present, they will still have an accounting given."

"At this point, no one has a lock on any leadership position. I do not care what your date of rank is. I will relieve anyone of their duties who is not getting the job done."

"Furthermore, I learned something today that deeply disturbs me. I learned that a clique exists among the officers with title of 'the animals.' Leadership of this group goes to the person who does the grossest act. The current leader holds his title because he ate a urinal cake from a pee tube," Zane said, as laughing and knowing looks at each other rippled through the group.

"At ease," Zane roared, his deep voice echoing through the building.

Silence fell upon the group and some appeared nervous. Others stared in disbelief.

"Knock off the chit chat when I am speaking. I demand your total attention. Is that clear?" Zane demanded.

"Yes sir," the group replied instantly.

"If this group exists, it is now disbanded. Any officer found conducting himself in a manner detrimental to his position as an officer will receive an Article 15 from me. A second offense will result in a court-martial for conduct unbecoming an officer.

Zane waited a moment as he made eye contact with every officer, before he said, "Alpha Platoon leader, you are responsible for perimeter defense. Those in your platoon will rebuild the perimeter when not flying or performing maintenance."

"Bravo Platoon leader, tomorrow your platoon will remove weeds from ditches in our area. In addition, you will clear the ditches of obstructions that cause standing water. Spray any stagnant water with used oil. Report to me when these assignments are completed. Does anyone not understand?" Zane asked.

No one spoke as Zane looked at each officer. He finished his glass of water.

"Gentlemen, the first drink is on me," Zane said as he stepped from the stage toward the bar.

"Bourbon and water," Zane said to the CW4 behind the bar.

Someone at the end of the bar rang a brass bell and yelled, "The drinks are on the major."

Zane motioned Greenletter to join him. Moving aside, Zane made room for him at the bar.

"Have the C & C ready for takeoff at 07:00 hours in the morning. Have Ops list it for a flight to Saigon. In addition, I want our Huey IP on board so I can get my local checkout. Take care of that for me please," Zane directed.

Greenletter started to leave to do Zane's bidding but Zane stopped him by saying, "Wait a minute. I have a few questions," Zane stated. "Barkeep give Greenletter another of what he is having."

Continuing Zane said, "I noticed that you've had a previous tour with the 1st Cav. What was your unit?"

"Sir, I was an infantry company platoon leader for 12 months from March 1968 to March 1969. After returning to the states, I applied for flight school. After graduation, they sent me through instrument school and then Hook transition. This is my first aviation assignment," Greenletter answered.

"Damn, Scott said that one day this would happen and it has. These guys don't know jack shit about flying a Hook in combat," Zane thought.

"How many like you are there in the company?" Zane continued his questions.

"As of today, we have eight that went through school with me. More will arrive soon from the class behind ours. To be honest sir, we have no idea what to do on a mission. I've been here three days and I'm scared shitless. I thought it was bad in an infantry company. This is worse because of the responsibility," Greenletter conceded.

Zane told Greenletter, "Finish your drink. You come with me. We have work to do."

The defense perimeter was Zane's first stop. He and Greenletter approached a sandbag bunker. Zane called to those on guard. He heard no replies.

Zane entered first using a flashlight in order to see. Greenletter followed close. Moving his flashlight beam around the bunker's interior, he found five men asleep. Two lay by M-60 machineguns intended for defensive fires. The other three had M-16s with 40-mm grenade launchers mounted on them. Zane grabbed one man's leg and shook it.

"Wake up soldier," he said and received no response.

He repeated this twice before taking the man's M-16 and giving it to Greenletter. Continuing around the bunker's interior, Zane removed every person's weapon. He could not get any of them awake. Some mumbled but what they said made no sense.

Using the bunker's field phone, Zane contacted the 362nd Command Bunker. There was an immediate response from the Sergeant of the Guard.

"Sarge, this is Major Zane. Put the Officer of the Guard (OG) on the line," Zane ordered.

"Lieutenant Wilcombe, sir," the OG said.

"Lieutenant, contact Ops. Get me five new men for bunker number four. Bring them in our three-quarter ton truck. Also, contact the Military Police (MP) and have them send an arrest team," Zane directed.

"Sir, we do not have any MPs on base," Wilcombe advised.

"Okay, you come with the truck. Captain Greenletter and I will man this bunker until you get replacements here," Zane advised. "Do it now."

Searching the bunker, Zane found three small, plastic vials. Each had a minute amount of what he knew to be heroin in them. In addition, he located three pipes that he felt sure the five used to smoke the heroin. When the truck arrived, Zane had the replacement guards help load the groggy guards onto the truck. Zane rode in the truck's cab with Lieutenant Wilcombe, while Greenletter watched the five former guards in the truck's rear.

"Lieutenant when did you check the bunkers last?" Zane asked.

"I haven't checked them at all," he answered.

"Why not?" Zane continued.

"I didn't know I was supposed to sir," he answered.

"Fine lieutenant," Zane said with disdain.

"Wait a minute," Zane thought. "This lieutenant was not at Officer's Call. He was on duty on the perimeter. Perhaps I shouldn't come down to hard on him. However, he should know to check the perimeter. They received training on that in the basic officers course."

The sleeping guards remained at operations under armed guard after Zane read them their rights. He told them that he was charging them with sleeping on guard and recommending them for a general court martial.

"Let's go Greenletter. We need to check the barracks," Zane said. "Check your sidearm and be sure it is loaded. Someone is selling this shit and he is likely dangerous."

With his shotgun hanging upside down from his right shoulder, Zane led Greenletter to a row of barracks. One of them still had the repulsive debris pile he found earlier. He had walked through the others during the day and all was quiet. However, this was normal as everyone was supposed to be at their duty stations. Barracks at night would be a different situation.

Everything was normal at the first barracks. The men were writing letters home; listening to music; playing cards; and, sleeping. As he and Greenletter left the last room, Zane was sure he saw someone run from the building at the end already visited.

Approaching the second barracks, they saw what appeared to be two females run from it. They disappeared into the darkness. Once inside, everything seemed normal until they entered the fourth cubical. A soldier leaned against a cot nude to his waist. He had multiple black and blue marks on his back, face, and arms. Zane and Greenletter helped the man onto his cot. While doing this, Greenletter saw a wallet on the floor and retrieved it.

"What's your name son," Zane asked.

"Speck Four Barnfield," the injured soldier answered.

Zane turned to Greenletter and said, "Get me a wet towel Terry."

Taking the towel, Zane cleansed Barnfield's head and asked. "What happened?"

Barnfield became evasive. He would not reveal how he became injured. His injuries were superficial but obviously painful.

Zane sent Greenletter to operations to determine who was this soldier's NCO. He gave Greenletter specific instructions.

"Bring this man's NCO to him. Have him remain with Barnfield and not let him go to sleep. I will take him with me in the morning. We will have the battalion's flight surgeon examine him. He could have a concussion," Zane explained.

Events in the remaining barracks were normal. In Zane's mind, they were too normal. He felt sure that someone was moving ahead of them giving a warning. He saw someone run from the first barracks and figured that person was sounding an alarm.

Nevertheless, Zane saw something that a warning would not help, peculiar openings in screened windows. He did not know if Greenletter saw them or not. In any case, he did not mention them. Every cubicle had screening along its top edge. The screen strip was four feet high. At the bottom, where the screen joined wood, he saw a finger sized hole. Practically every cubicle's screen had a similar hole. He suspected what they were but he would have to check during daylight.

Furthermore, it was 01:30 hours. He knew that he must rest. Operations received instructions to wake him at 05:30 hours in order to oversee formation.

Zane watched his men gather the next morning. He observed from the orderly room while having coffee. He noted that Captain Greenletter was an old hand at handling troops. He was a good soldier and an asset. He must review every man's file soon. His pilots had little experience and he must know which ones. He knew that inexperienced pilots were flying as aircraft commanders with CWOs with much more experience. The rush to get him in command should have made alarm bells ring. It appeared that his superiors knew more than they were saying. Perhaps they were testing him.

When Greenletter had his reports, he gave an "At ease." He turned to face the orderly room and stood at ease. He saw Zane approaching and called the company to attention. Zane received his report and told him to prepare the troops for inspection. Zane did his inspection and told his XO to dismiss the troops.

Returning to his orderly room, he thought, "My God, it is worse than I expected."

Captain Mullins met him as he entered saying, "Sir, your C & C is ready when you are. If you have time, I put a document on your desk that I think you need to see soon."

"Thanks Chris. I'll take a look at it," Zane said, as he entered his office.

Sitting down, he read the document's cover. It was marked "Confidential Contains Sensitive Information." Inside was a directive from Battalion Headquarters making him an Article 32 Investigating Officer. It stated that he was to conduct an investigation into charges that the previous commander was guilty of conduct unbecoming an officer demonstrated by drunkenness and fighting in the company street with enlisted personnel.

Zane felt his anger rising as he thought, "They knew this when they sent me here. I refuse to do their dirty work."

"Chris, come in please," Zane said loudly.

"Yes, sir?" Mullins said as entering his office.

Zane directed, "Return this to battalion headquarters without action. You tell their personnel officer that I cannot conduct an Article 32 Investigation without the charged party present with counsel. This is the dumbest crap I have seen. This action is in total disregard of every tenet of military justice. If they complain, tell them to put it in writing and have the Battalion Commander sign it. Clear?"

Mullins broke into a wild smile and took the offered document as he said joyously, "Yes sir."

Zane could not avoid hearing someone say, "Cajones, finally someone with cajones."

Captain Greenletter came to Zane's door and knocked and said, "We're ready to go, sir."

"Come on in Terry. There's a minor chore before we leave," Zane said, as he removed his wallet. "Take this $10.00 and use my jeep to go to the Vill. Buy as many VC flags, sandals, and crossbows that you can. I will meet you at the C & C. I will have your flight gear. Now go."

At operations, Zane found Specialist Four Barnfield waiting, and asked. "How are you feeling this morning?"

"Sleepy sir. I haven't had sleep for 24 hours," he said weakly.

"No sweat. When the flight surgeon clears you, take the day off. Get some sleep. How's that," Zane asked.

"That's great, sir. Thanks," Barnfield answered.

Across the room, Zane saw the guards he relieved of duty. They appeared sullen about their current predicament. Zane did not intend to speak to them. He motioned Caldwell to join him outside.

Speaking quietly to Caldwell, Zane said, "Earnest, call battalion. Have them dispatch a Huey to pick up the men under guard. Be sure that they send Military Police to oversee them. Get with Chris in Admin and make sure that the charges are properly prepared. In addition, send this message to the Battalion Commander."

"Keep the men out of my unit. Under no circumstances, return them to me. I will explain as soon as possible. Put my name on the signature block. Any questions?"

"None, sir." Caldwell replied.

"Where is my IP?" Zane asked.

"He is preflighting the Huey sir," Caldwell answered. "You helmet, survival vest, and chicken plate are also at the ship."

"Give me another chicken plate," Zane directed. "Let me have Greenletter's gear. I will take it to the ship."

"Uh, yes sir," Caldwell replied.

Zane arrived at his Huey with his extra armor. His IP was on top inspecting its rotor head. Zane noted that he saw him at Officers' Call. The reason that he remembered him was because he was the only African-American present. Zane recalled that he was a first lieutenant.

Zane called to him asking, "Have you done the bottom lieutenant?"

"Yes sir," he answered. "However, I would appreciate it if you would check it again."

"You've got it," Zane replied.

On the aircraft commander's seat's right side, Zane draped his 12-gauge's sling. He placed his extra chicken plate in his seat. While checking the aircraft's lower portion, Zane opened an access panel to the engine area. He noticed that a quick release connector for the fuel system's wiring bundle did not have a tight connection. He pressed it to its receiver and locked it in place. He found three other faults, which he corrected.

While Zane continued, the lieutenant IP returned to the tarmac. Zane, now finished, saw him and headed in his direction.

"Hi lieutenant, I understand you're a standardization pilot," Zane said.

"That's right sir, Sam Robertson at your service," he replied as he saluted.

Zane returned his salute and extended his hand, which Robertson accepted and shook.

"Tell me," Zane began, "I wonder about this ship. There were four loose connectors. Are my people maintaining this Huey like they do Hooks?" Zane asked.

Robertson, wiping grease from his hands, began to grin. He named the four loose connectors before Zane divulged them.

"Sir, they were part of your check ride. So far, you're 100 percent. I loosened them to see if you really knew how to preflight a Huey. As for our maintenance, it is topnotch," Robertson explained.

"Aren't you the clever one. This flight is a combination check ride and personnel trip. As soon as Greenletter gets here, we can be on our way to Saigon. We need to make a brief stop at Ben Hoa on the way to drop a pax," Zane explained.

Greenletter arrived with a cardboard container filled with the items Zane requested. He loaded it inside while Zane and Robertson went through the startup checklist. Barnfield came with Greenletter and boarded at the same time. Barnfield still did not appear well.

"Sir," Robertson said, "The Repo Depo (Replacement Depot) helipad is no longer operational. We will have to land at Tan Son Nhut and get a ride. Is that a problem?"

Zane answered using the intercom, "Not at all. It's not far. I'm sure I can get us a military taxi."

"Okay sir. You call for clearance. Give me a 500-foot per minute climb out and 60 knots. Bring her level at 2,000 feet. You have the aircraft. I've got the radios," Robertson directed.

Medics met Barnfield at Ben Hoa's pad. Zane and the others continued to Tan Son Nhut. On their way to the Repo Depo, Zane spoke with Lieutenant Robertson about their flight.

"I noticed you used the call-sign Longhorn Six when talking to towers. Any particular reason for that?" Zane asked.

"Longhorn is B Company's call-sign. We kept using it after they deactivated," Robertson answered.

Zane considered Robertson's reply and said, "B Company does not exist. We should not use their call-sign. That's part of their history. We need a new one. Think about it and let me know you ideas."

At the Repo Depo, Zane examined the contents of Greenletter's container. He removed a particularly dirty and worn VC flag. He stuffed it into the lower pocket on the right leg of his flight suit, leaving a portion hanging outside in view.

"It's barter time," Zane said. "We need a new mess sergeant. Ours leaves soon. Greenletter, you and Robertson visit with the officer in charge of NCO inbound processing. See what you get for a crossbow. I'm going to visit with the facility commander. I will meet you here in one hour to compare notes," Zane directed.

"Come in major. How can I help you," Lieutenant Colonel Gilbert, Commander of the Repo Depo, said.

Colonel Gilbert wore tiger striped jungle fatigues. These were fatigues used by a few elite combat units. It was also the uniform of Viet Nam's National Police Force. Its colors made it distinctive among those who wore standard combat fatigues.

Gilbert was an Adjutant General (AG) officer and wore that insignia. It was difficult to see his AG insignia since it was subdued to make it difficult to see by the enemy. AG officers specialized in personnel and administrative functions. Seldom did they hear a shot fired in anger.

The decisive factor came when Zane saw that he wore a survival knife strapped to his left leg. This guy was the proverbial "wanna be." On the street, onlookers would think him to be some badass killer in town from the boon docks.

"Sir, I have a personnel problem and I hoped that you could provide some advice," Zane said.

Gilbert motioned Zane to have a seat in a posh easy chair while he sat across a coffee table from him. Zane made sure the VC flag was in clear view.

Continuing, Zane said, "I recently took command of the last Hook company in 'Nam. The personnel pipeline is not providing qualified personnel for aviation units. We have to take potluck from units leaving for the states. I do not have a first sergeant. Perhaps you can provide advice on how I can solve that problem."

Zane knew the moment that Gilbert saw the flag. He couldn't keep his eyes from straying to it throughout Zane's request.

"Perhaps I can Major Zane. Personnel replacement is a mess and I understand your problem. Would you be willing to accept a first sergeant with a different military occupational specialty (MOS) than aviation?" Gilbert asked.

"If you think that is the way to go sir," Zane replied.

"Okay, hang loose a minute. I will bring in some personnel records for our inbound first sergeants," Gilbert said as he arose and left the room.

Gilbert returned with a pushcart filled with personnel files. He moved it near where Zane sat.

"Feel free to look through those and let me know if you see someone you like," Gilbert offered.

As Zane arose to examine the records, Gilbert warned, "Be careful major. You have something hanging from your pocket. It could cause you to trip and fall."

Zane looked down and removed the flag saying, "Thank you sir. A crew chief found this on a dead VC we were hauling from a hot LZ. I stuck it in my pocket to get it out of the way."

"Mind if I have a look?" Gilbert asked.

"Not at all, sir," Zane said, as he handed the flag to Gilbert.

Zane examined file folders while Gilbert admired the flag. One in particular caught Zane's attention. The individual was First Sergeant Byron Kubble. He had orders to the 101st Airmobile Division as an Infantry Company First Sergeant. He was a second tour veteran who served his first tour with the Cav as a Platoon Sergeant. He spent 12 months in the bush chasing Charlie. Zane removed his file from the cart.

Zane offered it to Gilbert as he asked. "Is this man available for interview?"

Gilbert stuffed the flag in his pocket as he took the file from Zane. He glanced through it for a moment.

"This man is outside being processed. You may use my office to interview him if you like," Gilbert responded.

"First sergeant, my name is Zane and I am CO of the 362nd Aviation Company. I have examined your file and I have an offer. You can take what these people assign and start humping the bush again. There is a better alternative. Instead of walking, you can fly. How does that sound?" Zane asked.

"Sir, that sounds absolutely wonderful. However, you must understand that I don't know the first thing about helicopters or airplanes. I am an infantryman to the bone. If you can live with that, I am your man," Kubble answered.

After touchdown at Bear Cat, Zane's passengers unloaded. First Sergeant Kubble and Mess Sergeant Gooding removed their duffel bags as Greenletter chatted with Maintenance Sergeant Lansdow about his new assignment with the 362nd.

Still in the cockpit, Robertson asked Zane. "Sir, weren't you the Standards Division Chief at Fort Rucker?"

"Yes," Zane answered, as he made entries in the craft's logbook.

"Major may I shake your hand again? Lieutenant Ludlow and I received our commissions the same day. Everyone in our class knows what you did at Fort Rucker. I want to thank you for hanging those rotten bastards out to dry," Robertson said, thrusting his hand toward Zane.

"You're welcome L-T. I'm sorry I was too late. Ludlow was good people," Zane replied, saddened at the memory.

Robertson began removing his shoulder harness as he said, "You should have been giving me a check ride. Admin didn't get your flight records to Ops in time for me to examine them before the flight. Shit, you flew 21s here when I was in high school."

Finished with the aircraft, Zane and Robertson met with the others who were nearby. The unit's mule and three-quarter ton truck arrived. Close behind them Zane's driver arrived with Zane's jeep. The NCOs placed their duffel bags on the mule and started for the truck.

Zane stopped them. He told the drivers to take their gear to Ops and secure it. Next, they were to drive the new NCOs to the orderly room for processing. He went to each new NCO and welcomed them to his unit. He said that he would have a personal meeting with them the next day. First, he wanted them to get settled.

Zane said, "Terry, you and Kubble come with me."

In Zane's office, Greenletter and Kubble sat facing the CO's desk as Zane said, "The birth of the 362nd starts now. Our call-sign is 'United.' See that this appears on the nose of every aircraft. When a person answers a telephone, the first statement is 'United sir.' For our unit insignia, I will give you a basic sketch. Get me some drafts made for my selection. Here's the basic idea," Zane said.

Using a page from a legal pad, Zane drew an oval. Inside of it, he drew two ducks mating with their wings spread in flight. Following the oval's contour, he sketched the words "Fly United" across its top. Around the oval's bottom, he wrote, "362nd Aviation Company." He turned the pad for the others to see.

"Gentlemen," he said, "I, obviously, am not an artist. From some of the artwork on our ships, someone in this unit is. Find him and put him to work. By morning, the day after tomorrow, I want every Hook in this unit changed to our insignia. These two ducks, depicted as I have shown you, are not my idea. I have seen it somewhere in the past. The 362nd is a group of individuals from various units thrown together. They have no unit identity. Let's give them one. Other than a Cav patch and tail number of each ship on its aft pylon, no other markings are authorized."

Zane tore the sheet from its pad and handed it to Greenletter. Next, he opened his desk's lower right hand drawer. As he did so, he told Kubble to close his office door. Once closed, Zane set a pint of Black Label Jack Daniels on his desk. He removed three shot glasses from the same drawer and set them beside the bottle. He filled the three shot glasses and handed one to each of them.

Zane said, "Twelve months from now, the three of us will make this toast together when we arrive in CONUS. That is my personal vow. Here's to the 362nd."

The trio touched glasses and simultaneously swallowed their contents. They returned their empty glasses to the desk.

"Now, let's get to work. You two will run this unit. Captain Greenletter, as my XO, you have my permission to speak on my behalf to anyone. Considered yourself armed with my authority with one exception. If we receive a Tac-E mission, I must approve its implementation. Let Ops know that I approve them and no one else. Consult me when you consider it necessary to keep me informed."

"First Sergeant, you are in charge of the day-to-day operation of this unit. You have my command authority within the unit but not in outside matters. Any person desiring to see me for any reason at any time may do so. I prefer they use the chain of command first. However, if they persist, I will make myself available."

"I must free myself from the routine in order to see that our mission succeeds. I want to welcome every new man to this unit. This guidance remains in effect until I tell you otherwise," Zane explained.

Looking at each man, Zane understood the major concessions he made. He entrusted these two with his career and the lives of his men. However, to restrain them and try to do their jobs was unacceptable. They would cease to be an asset. He had enough liabilities on his plate for now.

"Captain Greenletter, see to this unit insignia action for me. On your way out have Captain Mullins send for our maintenance officer. I need to see him as soon as he can get free," Zane directed.

As Greenletter left the room, Zane said, "Top, take 24 hours to get organized. After that, arrange a group meeting between me and the enlisted men who are not NCOs. I want to see them in one place at one time."

Zane walked Kubble to his office door. As Kubble departed, Zane told a clerk to bring him the Maintenance Officer's personnel file.

Soon after studying Captain Wellington's file, Zane heard a knock at his door. He looked to see a freckle-faced, big man with blazing red hair standing in the doorway.

When their eyes met, the man asked. "I'm Captain Wellington sir. You sent for me?"

"Yes, come on in captain," Zane replied.

Zane greeted the fair skinned maintenance officer and had him take a seat. Zane opened Wellington's file.

"Captain, how many aircraft is operations scheduling you for each day?" Zane asked.

"None sir. I schedule the aircraft," Wellington answered.

"Good answer. How many did you let him have today?" Zane questioned differently.

"Twenty Hooks and your C & C Huey, sir," Wellington responded.

Zane continued, "I see you have three senior warrant officers working for you. Did any of them attend test pilots' school?"

"Yes sir, two have and I have also. The remaining one is a graduate of the Army's Aviation Safety Officers' Course. He also doubles as the Unit Safety Officer," Wellington explained.

"Captain, do you mind if I call you Richard?" Zane asked.

"Not at all," Wellington replied.

"I have a couple ideas I want your input about before I put them into effect. Whether I do or not is up to you. First, before a pilot becomes an aircraft commander, I want him to work with one of your maintenance teams. Specifically, I want him to work as a mechanic until he completes a 100 hour inspection," Zane explained.

Wellington threw his head back while slamming his right fist into his left palm and said, "Finally."

Continuing, Wellington said while grinning, "That is an answer to my prayers. I concur wholeheartedly."

"Good," Zane said. "The second item is the formation of Quick Reaction Teams (QRT)."

Appearing not to understand, Wellington asked. "I'm Transportation Corps major. I know little about infantry combat tactics. What specifically did you have in mind?"

Leaning forward, Zane answered, "Richard, what I meant by a QRT is a group of aviation mechanics. The team will have specialists in avionics, hydraulics, engines, and airframe as members. They will be on duty around the clock. They will have a vehicle with spare parts and tools on board. For example, when an aircraft is inbound, he will contact your office by radio. They will specify any deficiencies they intend to place in the aircraft's logbook. You will dispatch the QRT to meet the ship at its parking spot. The team will begin repairs immediately by assisting the flight engineer. There will be three teams with each pulling rotating, eight-hour shifts."

Wellington leaned back in his chair obviously thinking the idea through. He scratched his neck and closed his eyes while considering what Zane suggested.

"Sir, if you can get me one more Technical Inspection, I will assign one to each of the teams. He will be available to inspect work and approve it on the spot. I like it, sir," Wellington stated.

"Great Richard, let me know when you are ready. In the meantime, I have to shit you a vehicle," Zane replied.

Wellington roared with laughter and said, "Sir, I knew I didn't have one so I figured you knew. I intended on your getting me one. Hell sir, this will work great. Nevertheless, we must have at least a three quarter ton truck."

"By the way Richard," Zane began, "Check with the XO. He has the action on another project. To help him, remove any painted insignia or drawings on ships now in maintenance. The only markings you can leave are the Cav patch and tail number on the aft pylons. Terry will fill you in on the rest. That's all I have for now Richard. Thanks for coming."

After Wellington left, Zane phoned Ops and asked Caldwell, "Earnest, do we have any ships passing through here this afternoon on their way to LZs along QL-13 near the Cambodian border?"

"Yes sir, we do. Hook 295 is on its way to Vung Tau. It will stop here to refuel in about one hour. It will sling two 500-gallon containers (blivets) of aircraft fuel (JP4) from Ben Hoa to Quon Loi. Quon Loi is at An Loc. It will sling empty ammo containers to Ben Hoa and then return to Bear Cat for the day. It will be almost dark before returning," Caldwell answered.

"That's great Earnest. Call maintenance and get an aircraft recovery sling set. Load it on 295 when it stops to refuel. I will replace the person flying first pilot. I am going to the mess hall if you need me," Zane explained.

On his way to the mess hall, Zane saw soldiers with sling blades cutting weeds from ditches around the company area. At one location, they were dumping used oil into a ditch and setting it ablaze. Taking a circuitous route, Zane went to the building where he found the putrid debris. Two soldiers were scooping it into the back of the unit truck. None of the soldiers appeared to like their duties.

At the mess hall, Zane found Mess Sergeant Gooding already at work. He was learning from the man he was to replace. Zane had some soup and a sandwich. He had completely forgotten lunch. Since he missed breakfast, he wasn't about to go on a mission without something to eat. After chatting with the two NCOs, he returned to Ops.

"Your ship is 15 minutes out sir," Caldwell said. "The sling harness is already at the refueling point with your flight gear. If it's okay, you can exchange pilots during refueling to save time."

"Good thinking captain. In addition, your Ops crews look like soldiers. Keep up the good work," Zane said as he left for the refueling point.

On the flight to Quon Loi, Zane felt strange in the right seat. He had spent years flying left seat as a Check Pilot, IP, and Aircraft Commander. However, since there was little difference between the two, he adjusted rapidly. His aircraft commander was CW4 Winnota from Nebraska on his second 'Nam tour flying Hooks.

"Do you want to drop off the blivets?" Winnota asked.

"Sure thing. I have the aircraft," Zane answered.

Zane placed the blivets with ease and began his climb out from Quon Loi's refueling area. He turned the Hook toward Loc Ninh, slightly northwest of An Loc.

"Sir, we're supposed to sling a load of empty ammo boxes to Ben Hoa. They are in the other direction," Winnota said.

Zane continued on his current course and replied, "The boxes will be there tomorrow. We have something more important to do."

Somewhere to the west of Loc Ninh, Zane had seen a Land Rover sitting on blocks at a plantation. He remembered it from his trips in the area with General Burton. Zane pressed his intercom switch.

"Gunners, listen up. We're looking for a vehicle sitting on blocks at a plantation. If you see it, let me know. Stay alert. There's NVA and VC all over this place. Do not hesitate to return fire," Zane said.

Continuing, Zane directed, "FE have the sling set ready if we need it. You and the crew chief be prepared to rig the Land Rover for a sling load and do it quick. Get back to the ship and we will yank it out of there."

"Sir, I have the vehicle at ten o'clock, two miles," Winnota stated.

Above weapons' range, Zane began a high reconnaissance to determine the best approach direction and look for obstacles. While doing so, he saw people exit the plantation's main building and gather to watch them.

"Chief, I'm going to talk to those people. You keep this ship hot and ready to go. If you get incoming, leave without me. Don't you dare wait. Get out and do not take the route I used to land. Do you understand?" Zane asked.

"Yes sir," Winnota answered.

Zane ran toward the group watching their landing. One was a Caucasian and the others Orientals. Zane went to the Caucasian.

"Pardon me sir. I am Major Zane. I apologize for our abrupt visit. I have a request," Zane said breathing hard.

"My name is Jean Danjou major. I own this plantation. How can I be of service?" Jean asked.

Zane removed his helmet and shook Danjou's offered hand. He turned toward the Land Rover.

Pointing to it, Zane asked. "I saw that vehicle and wondered if we could purchase it?"

"No major. It is not for sale. However, I will give it to you. Its transmission is shot and it is an eyesore. As you can see, it also needs tires. It is yours sir," Jean responded.

"Pardon me a moment," Zane said, as he turned to face the Hook. He raised his right arm above his head and pumped it up and down twice. The FE and crew chief ran to the vehicle and began installing a sling.

Returning to face the Frenchman, Zane noticed a beautiful woman standing next to him. She had her arm around Jean's waist. Zane bowed gallantly.

"Is this lovely lady your wife? If so, you are indeed a fortunate man," Zane said with a broad smile.

"Thank you major. I am indeed fortunate. This is Minh Thanh," Jean replied.

Zane took her extended hand and kissed it saying, "My pleasure Madam."

Turning back to Jean, Zane said, "My ship and crew are a lucrative target. I know that the enemy saw us. I must leave before they have time to arrive and fire. Please understand my haste."

"Your perception is correct. Leave now. It has been our pleasure," Jean answered.

Zane saluted and ran to his aircraft, never slowing as he went up the ramp. His feet slipped twice but he was expecting it and kept his footing. Close behind him, the FE and crew chief boarded.

In the cockpit, Zane told Winnota, "Get that sucker and let's get out of here."

At sunset, Winnota set the Land Rover next to the 362nd Motor Pool. For the powerful Hook, the Land Rover was a minute load.

The next challenge was to get it operating. With the skills available in his unit, Zane had little doubt.

Putting his aviation experience and leadership skills to good use, Zane watched his unit become a cohesive, proud group. He called upon his NCOs for support and they gave it. In two "Rap" sessions with his troops, he explained why and how they could get through their Viet Nam tour using their heads. Most realized that the unit was theirs and they had to make it a decent place to live.

The Rap sessions were frank, honest, and open discussions. First Sergeant Kubble had sincere concerns when Zane walked into a room surrounded by 500, pissed off soldiers. At times, Zane became nervous as hostility poured out against "Lifers." Lifers were the establishment. They were the career NCOs and officers. They did not trust Lifers. They did not trust Zane.

It was incumbent upon Zane to earn their trust. He listened and corrected those things that he could. When they met again. They knew that their CO and NCOs were with and for them. It was after the second Rap session that Zane learned what happened to Barnfield. Barnfield's injuries were a symptom of his men's nervousness and evasive responses.

A young crew chief and gunner, Specialist Four Gunter, was with Zane while he inspected his Hook before a mission. It was before dawn the day after his second meeting with his men.

"Sir, I want to tell you something but I need your word that you won't let anyone know where you heard it," Gunter said.

Zane kept checking his ship as he replied, "You have my word Gunter."

"Sir, there is a group of ten men in the 362nd who are causing most of the trouble. They beat the hell out of a guy and take his valuables. When finished, they say that they will kill you if you report them. Sir, these are bad people. They will frag you in a heartbeat," Gunter explained.

"Thanks for the warning Gunter. I will take care of these people but I must know who they are," Zane responded.

Gunter was quiet for a few minutes as Zane continued to preflight the Hook. When Zane was almost finished, Gunter whispered to him.

"Check the back flap in the logbook after today's flight sir. My life is in your hands," Gunter said with fear permeating every word.

"Rest easy Gunter. You are doing your friends a great favor. None of you will have to fear these jerks again," Zane vowed.

Taking down the ten troublemakers was easy and a pleasure. Zane arranged a sting with an MP guard dog platoon commander. One of the MPs came to the 362nd as a new arrival. He displayed considerable cash while processing into the unit. He also had an expensive, stereo tape player that he put in his cubicle for others to see. Zane made sure that the MP's bunk was with six of the ten extortionists.

Two truckloads of MPs, with guard dogs, remained hidden while their man prepared for bed. When attacked, the MPs struck with their dogs. Trainers teach guard dogs to attack a person's groin. Those arrested individually were cowards of the worst sort. They readily ratted on their conspirators. The ten shackled troublemakers left the unit in full view of a morning formation. Zane could almost see terror leave his soldiers.

Meanwhile drugs continued flowing into the 362nd. Most of the dealers were Thai soldiers and prostitutes. Zane tried for weeks to obtain a meeting with the Thai Division Commander without success. He never understood why he could not achieve a lasting working relationship with the Thais. He learned later that it was his continued persistence to keep his unit drug free. Someone in the Thai unit was bringing in the drugs and Zane was powerless to stop it. Nevertheless, he could do something about their prostitutes.

Initially, some soldiers did not understand why he barred Thai females from the unit area. Once they saw the ravages of syphilis chancres and other venereal diseases, they came to understand. It took a short arm inspection to drive his point home.

At morning formation, XO Greenletter saluted Zane and reported, "Sir, all men present and accounted for."

Returning his salute, Zane directed, "Prepare the unit for inspection."

Greenletter's "Open Ranks" command provided room for Zane to move through the assembled soldiers with ease. Two medics from Ben Hoa joined Zane as Greenletter reported the unit ready for inspection.

Zane unbuttoned his fly and exposed his penis. A medic stepped in front of Zane and began making a visual examination of his sex organ. The second medic observed and held a notepad and pen.

Since Zane had no circumcision, the medic directed, "Skin it back, sir."

The medic looked to find external evidence of venereal disease. He did not find any and continued with an internal examination.

"Milk it down, sir," the examining medic directed.

With his thumb and index finger, Zane gripped his penis at its base. Next, he moved them forward along his penis' length. The medic watched closely for any discharge.

Not seeing any, he said, "That all sir, next man."

After moving in front of Greenletter, Zane inspected him as in a normal, daily inspection.

Zane directed that Greenletter present his penis for inspection and took two side steps to his left.

Obviously befuddled, Greenletter responded, "Sir?"

The examining medic stepped in front of Greenletter. Greenletter stood rigid and had not moved.

The medic directed Greenletter, "Present your penis, sir."

Following Zane's lead, he exposed his penis. The medic did his inspection and asked for the next man.

From their position in the assembled group, platoon commanders, NCOs, and the first rank could see what was happening. The officers appeared stunned while the NCOs grinned and nodded their heads knowingly. The others who could see began to laugh aloud while others giggled. It was necessary for Zane to command, "At ease."

Zane, Greenletter, and the medics inspected the entire formation. For those found to have venereal disease, the second medic recorded the man's name, serial number, and rank.

With the inspection complete, Zane returned to his position as CO of the formation. The group was silent.

Zane said to them, "Gentlemen, I know many of you have heard of a short arm inspection. I am sure some senior NCOs may have had one early in their careers. This inspection was necessary for the health and welfare of your unit. Since some of you chose to obtain medical treatment, it was necessary to have this inspection. Those found to have a venereal disease will receive treatment. To help prevent more disease, condoms are available from the medics. After this formation, get as many as you think you need. One size fits all so you 'big guys' need not ask for extra large," Zane stopped speaking as the unit roared with laughter.

Finally able to continue, Zane said, "There will be no punishment for those with a disease. Having the ailment is punishment enough. After successful treatment, there will be no record kept of those being treated."

Pausing, Zane commanded, "Company, attention."

Zane told Greenletter to dismiss the company. The XO saluted and did an about face. He dismissed the unit.

It was clear to Zane that he had probably violated a dozen regulations by having the inspection. Nevertheless, he was ready to take the heat. His men came first. There were no complaints.

Venereal disease was a problem that Zane could control. However, holes in screened windows were a sign of Zane's biggest problem, heroin. He checked behind sandbags around the buildings. Beneath the holes, he found an accumulation of heroin vials.

Before long, Zane began bringing charges against those found distributing drugs. Defense attorneys were successful at getting charges dropped. The predominant reason was lack of probable cause for a search.

He had his officers and NCOs attend classes given by the Army's Criminal Investigation Division on substance recognition. This was necessary so that his leaders could testify in trials with authority about drugs. If they detected an odor from a closed room, they could say that it was marijuana. If they tasted powder in a vial, they could say it was heroin. He personally removed the empty containers and began checking beneath the windows daily. When he saw vials beneath a window, he concentrated his efforts on those who lived in that particular cubicle. It was two months before users discovered how Zane knew who they where.

Nevertheless, he did not prosecute casual users. First, he sent them to rehabilitation centers. If they stayed drug free, they remained in the unit. He sent known distributors to prison. His philosophy was to heal the users and destroy the distributors.

When orders came in late September to move his unit to Phu Loi, Zane considered it a blessing. His maintenance facilities at Phu Loi were superb compared to Bear Cat. Every unit at Phu Loi was American and the commanders were cooperative. They had an excellent defense perimeter with interlocked fields of fire. Drug use and distribution dropped drastically.

Furthermore, individuals provided information to help. Zane received reports that two individuals intended to kill him. One of them Zane already suspected. He was the one who threw the tear gas grenade. He had a friend who kept him company. Usually, when you saw one, you saw the other. It wasn't long before Zane had a strong indictor of his foe. He found it during a barracks inspection at Phu Loi.

Each soldier had a cubicle to himself. He could call it his and decorate it as he saw fit. While cubicles did not have doors, Zane allowed curtains for privacy. However, they had to be fire retardant for safety.

Zane, accompanied by First Sergeant Kubble, came to Specialist Four Bredermeyer's cubicle. Bredermeyer stood at ease while Zane inspected. He noticed an official looking document stapled to Bredermeyer's wall. Reading it Zane saw that it was a copy of an Article 15. A former commander administered it to Bredermeyer for striking a lieutenant.

While inspecting Bredermeyer, Zane asked. "Are you proud that you received an Article 15?"

"Yes, sir," he answered.

"You do know that the next time you will receive a court martial," Zane explained.

Bredermeyer answered in an insolent and disrespectful tone; "I don't give a shit, sir."

Zane's eyes grew cold as he moved closer to the disgruntled soldier.

His words were chilling as he said, "You will screw up. Touch an officer in this unit and you will deal with me."

Bredermeyer blinked a few times. His face exhibited a sneer but he did not speak. Zane moved to the next cubicle.

Zane put Bredermeyer out of his mind as he completed his letter to Janice. In his mind, he reviewed the day's events. He liked the guy Briscoe.

"I would love to fly that mission," Zane thought. "That guy can get what he wants if he knows the ropes at MACV. He has to be NSA or CIA. He has access to every senior officer at MACV. All he has to do is drop a few words in the right places and they will direct that the 362nd perform the mission."

Zane checked his watch. It was 01:30 hours. He yawned and arose from his desk. He placed his shotgun by his bunk and turned the covers back.

"Tomorrow is Thursday," Zane recalled. "I'm to attend the Hook party in Saigon. What a relief that will be. It has been almost three months without a break. I'm ready for one."

Chapter Forty Four

December 1971

Those who love to be feared fear to be loved,
and they themselves are more afraid than anyone,
for whereas other men fear only them, they fear everyone.
Saint Francis de Sales (1567–1622), French churchman, devotional writer.
Quoted by Bishop Jean-Pierre Camus in: *The Spirit of Saint Frances de Sales*, ch. 7, sct. 3 (1952)

Lanny Briscoe was not convincing anyone of a major, impending, NVA attack. Finally, he and his contemporaries agreed on something. The evidence was plain to see and they saw it. Why wouldn't the senior commanders listen? From the DMZ to the southern tip of South Viet Nam, he sent repeated predictions that fell upon deaf ears. It was Tet 1968 all over again. Now, he was running out of time.

Heretofore, he received raw data from Daryl Scott's unit and sent it to Fort Meade for analysis. It was three weeks before they returned decrypted messages. His only option was to contact Dale Zane for help. He could no longer afford the time delay associated with sending data through regular channels. He must have a direct link and Zane's Hooks gave him that capability. Briscoe realized that, had he not gone to Winslow's party, he might not have made his much-needed arrangement. Frederick and Vanessa Earling were Godsends.

"Hi Lanny, Vanessa and I hoped you would come early. Come on in and make yourself at home," Frederick said.

The Earlings followed Oriental tradition requiring visitors to leave their shoes in their foyer. Briscoe removed his and placed them on a convenient rack. His feet immediately felt lush Oriental carpets underfoot as he entered their living room. It was gargantuan and tastefully decorated. Placed throughout black lacquered, folding dividers bore tranquil outdoor scenes in Chinese script. Rattan furnishing provided ample seating. Along one wall, sliding doors provided access to their rooftop suite.

"Damn Frederick," Briscoe exclaimed. "I am working for the wrong outfit. What kinds of openings are available with Air America for burned out bureaucrats?"

As Frederick escorted Briscoe to a nearby sofa, he called to Vanessa, "Lanny is here."

Continuing, Frederick asked what Briscoe would like to drink.

"This has been a double martini day," Briscoe answered. "With an onion if you have it."

"Sure thing," Frederick answered. "Excuse me for a moment."

Frederick passed Vanessa as she came from behind a divider. She carried a wide, glass tray trimmed with woven bamboo and bamboo handles. On it, she had numerous delicacies pierced with silver slivers topped with colorful Oriental umbrellas.

"Good evening, Lanny. I have heard so much about you. I feel as if we are close friends," she said as she placed the tray before Briscoe.

Briscoe came to his feet the moment that he saw her appear. She was the picture of an ideal, social hostess. She walked with grace across the room exhibiting a pleasant smile below her sparkling eyes. Around her neck, she wore a single strand of pearls.

"Now, that is class. Should I kiss her hand," he thought. "After all, she is nobility."

"It is my pleasure, mam," Briscoe said as she extended her hand.

"While the hell not," he thought as he took her delicate fingers and kissed the back of her hand.

"How gallant for a colonist," she giggled, as she turned her head toward where Frederick disappeared.

"Frederick, she called, "Americans are gentlemen."

Continuing, she said, "Please sit sir. I will join you."

As Briscoe sat, Vanessa sat beside him on the sofa and said, "Lanny, I am likely more American than I am British. My family is from Ireland, sometimes to my husband's chagrin."

Frederick heard Vanessa and his heart hurt when she mentioned Ireland. It was only two months since she returned from burying her father, Ian McBeal. His loss was tragic and personally decimating for Vanessa.

According to the British, Ian was aboard a lorry loaded with explosives. They maintained that Ian worked with the IRA and was positioning the vehicle for a terrorist attack in London.

Vanessa maintained that they could not be correct. He may have been taking a shipment to the IRA but he would never place a bomb to kill innocent bystanders. She had wept over his grave as bagpipes echoed through Irish hills of their family's burial site. He rested beside the wife who he had lost two years earlier. Vanessa was the last in the McBeal line. She remembered the stories of their hard years. Now, she was heir to a fortune beyond her wildest suspicions. Ian had been a staggeringly wealthy person.

"Don't be flirting with Lanny dear. You do know that he is single in a far off land. I do not know if you can trust him," Frederick said as he entered the living room with drinks.

"Tell me about the gentleman who is hosting the party tonight. I believe that you said he had a villa across the way from yours," Briscoe commented.

"Oh indeed he does. I met him a few years ago when I first came to Saigon. He is the Chief Technical Representative for Boeing Vertol's Chinook aircraft in Viet Nam and a few isolated places. At one time, he had technical representatives throughout the country. I think he said that they had over 500 Chinooks in country at their peak. That was a major responsibility."

"As a result of President Nixon's withdrawal, there are few Chinooks remaining. The VNAF has most of them. There is one American unit remaining in country I think," Frederick continued.

"We have become good friends over the years. He is a jolly fellow. You can see his villa from ours by going outside. Bring your drink and I will show you. Please join us Vanessa," Frederick requested.

Frederick opened a sliding door leading to their rooftop veranda. They could see most of Saigon from their position. Frederick pointed toward Chinese lanterns on the rooftop across the street. They could hear a musical group rehearsing a song.

Briscoe asked, "Do you still fly Frederick?"

"Of course, certainly. I must fly or I would be somewhere else where I could," Frederick answered.

Vanessa slipped her arm around his waist and looked up at him saying, "I've tried to get the lout to retire but he's having none of it. I think, if airplanes did not exist, he would sprout wings."

Frederick noticed that Briscoe's glass was empty and said, "There's time for another drink. In addition, we need to consume some of those delicious tidbits."

West of Saigon, Major Zane prepared for his trip to Buff Winslow's party. Armed with a weekend pass from his battalion commander, he was almost ready to depart. First, he had a task to perform.

On his desk were three, unsigned Article 15s. It was necessary that he destroy them. They were the first that he had ever administered to officers. In truth, they were in abeyance pending a probationary period ending after three months. In some respects, he felt partially responsible for the incident leading to them. It took place at the end of his first month as commanding officer. He remembered the day too well.

"Sir, don't forget the 'Hail and Farewell' tonight at the club," Captain Gardner stopped by to remind him.

Captain Gardner was a holdover from B Company. He had nine months in country and over 1,500 combat flying hours. Zane looked to him for leadership as an aircraft commander to teach younger pilots how to survive in combat.

During his first two weeks as commanding officer, Zane started debriefings after missions. It was informal and aircraft commanders shared their experiences on the day's missions. On this particular day, Zane led a flight of three Hooks relocating ARVN troops from an R & R area to fire bases along the Cambodian border near Song Be. It was an ARVN Special Forces' base and known for antiaircraft (AAA) fire. Zane briefed the crews.

"The Cambodian border is a short distance west of Song Be. There are reports of NVA triple A sites around the base. Most of them are to the west. You must do two things. Make your departures in a direction different from your approaches. Make your takeoffs in a direction other than west. If you violate these procedures, they will be waiting for you when you depart. Use the heavy jungle for protection. Avoid flying over open rice paddies. You are a beautiful target from the tree line," Zane told the three crews.

During the missions, there were no incidents until their third troop delivery. Gardner was in the lead aircraft. He made an excellent approach and off loaded the ARVN troops. He made his departure over his inbound route. Zane, and the others, saw green tracers streaking toward Gardner' Hook. Zane ordered him to make an immediate left turn to a heading of 360 degrees. This maneuver would take him over the trees. He did not acknowledge and he continued on the same course. Luckily, his ship was empty and he soon was above the NVA's range.

On their trip to pickup another group, Zane took the lead position. He was able to make radio contact with Gardner. Zane hated to admonish Gardner over the radio but he could not take the risk of him making the same mistake.

Zane made the first approach on the return trip. He approached from the south and departed to the north. Gardner, in the second aircraft, circled to the west across the border. Immediately, he drew AAA fire. Fortunately, he took no hits. After unloading his troops, he made his departure to the east over open paddies. He used the same route the last time. Zane had to order him over the trees.

During that day's debriefing, Zane used Gardner' flight maneuvers as examples of what not to do. Gardner became argumentative. He maintained that he had flown the east departure route for months without drawing fire. He claimed that the day's events were a fluke.

It was necessary to have a private counseling session with Gardner that night. Gardner was a platoon commander because of his date of rank. He continued to be argumentative during his counseling session almost to the point of insubordination.

"Captain Gardner," Zane said, "We have young, inexperienced pilots looking to you for leadership. You do not exhibit it by defying proven flight tactics. Moreover, you defied my direct instructions. Now, you want to argue about it. I will not tolerate your risking the lives of your crew and the safety of your aircraft. As of now, I am relieving you of your duties as flight commander. In addition, I am instructing Ops to withdraw your aircraft commander orders. Dismissed."

Zane heard rumors that Gardner was a member of the group known as "the Animals." Zane ignored rumors and hearsay. It was worthless. However, the first Hail and Farewell confirmed them.

The officers gathered in their club for the festivities. Zane was intimately familiar with such events. He attended them at every duty station.

For the "Farewell" portion, the command officer gave a short speech about each individual leaving his unit. He would then present the man with a plague as a memento. The departing officer often said a few words and took his seat.

The "Hail" portion welcomed new officers to the unit. Sometimes, there was an initiation of some sort. Zane went through his first one in Korea with 6th Transportation Helicopter Company. After its completion, the individual could wear a distinctive baseball cap. Since Zane was a new arrival, he could not officiate at his own Hail ceremony. Captain Gardner took the stage to welcome Zane.

Gardner asked. "Major are you familiar with a flaming hooker?"

"Not really," Zane said with a smile.

"Then sir, it is time for you to complete the rite of a flaming hooker. Please take a seat at yon table," Gardner said, as his words slurred from too much alcohol.

Other pilots, who had been through the ritual, began to laugh and joke. They gathered around the table where Zane sat. Gardner stood at the table's edge.

Pointing toward the bar, Gardner said, "Bring me a receptacle for the challenge."

CW2 Aims, the unit jock, had a shot glass at the ready. He walked across the room with the glass sitting on a purple cushion trimmed in gold. It was regal in appearance.

Aims set the cushion on the table's middle and withdrew, laughing.

Removing the shot glass, Gardner said as he placed it in front of Zane, "Herein the spirits of the flaming hooker will emerge. Now, the challenge."

Pointing to the glass, Gardner continued, "Chief Aims, Longhorn, excuse me, united member, makes this challenge. After filling of this cup, Aims will drink from it until not a single drop remains. He will demonstrate this by inverting the receptacle to show that nary a drop shall fall from therein. Next, initiate Zane will complete the same event and show that nary a drop remains therein. If either Aims or Zane should have a drop remaining, they must attempt the event again. They must consume until they can demonstrate that nary a drop remains. Then, and only then, does the receptacle pass back to Aims."

Gardner stopped talking momentarily, looked at Aims, and asked. "Art thou ready Sir Aims?"

Aims responded, "Yes."

After asking Zane the question, he answered, "Yes."

Gardner raised his hands above his head and cried, "Bring forth the spirit of the flaming hooker."

Captain Burlington, another holdover from B Company, said from behind the bar, "I present the spirit."

Burlington gripped a bottle of Southern Comfort high above his head. He gazed at it as if it were some sort of religious icon. Lowering his arms, he placed the bottle on the purple cushion and marched slowly to the table.

By this time, some were laughing so hard that tears streaked their faces. The other new pilots were not laughing.

Gardner took the bottle from the cushion and removed its seal. He opened it and filled the shot glass.

Between stifled laughs, Gardner said, "In the true spirit of the flaming hooker. Chief Aims will consume the first drink."

Aims marched to the table's side, while Gardner filled the shot glass. Zane saw Burlington come from behind the bar with a pitcher filled with beer. Close behind, CW2 Carlton carried an identical pitcher.

Gardner announced loudly, as if giving a command, "Fire guards post."

After Gardner' command, Burlington and Carlton took positions on opposite sides of the table. They stood at attention with their pitchers centered in front of their chests. They had a somber look.

The room became silent as Gardner said, "Ignition."

Removing a butane cigarette lighter from his pocket, Gardner leaned forward. He lit the lighter and touched its flame to the Southern Comfort. A blue flame swirled one foot above the shot glass.

Chief Aims immediately retrieved the flaming shot glass. He tilted his head back and poured the flaming liquid into his mouth. Flames rose from Aims' open mouth, creating an awesome sight. He continued to pour until the glass was empty. He shook the glass above his mouth and one, small flaming drop fell down his throat.

Aims placed the glass in front of Zane's face and inverted it once more. No liquid fell from it.

He set the glass on the table and said, "Your turn, sir."

Zane sat staring wide-eyed at the glass, while the room filled with laughter.

Continuing to stare, he thought, "I have been to many initiations but I have never heard of this one. Damn, I have to drink one."

Yelling above the laughter, Zane said, "Fill the receptacle."

During his first attempt, he touched the hot shot glass to his lower lip. Upon contact, it burned his lip causing him to spill its contents. Flames went down his chin, his throat, and onto his chest. Almost immediately, Burlington and Carlton hurled pitchers of beer to put out the flames. At that moment, Zane knew why they were "Fire Guards."

After two more attempts and dousing with beer, Zane began using his head. Aims made sure that his head leaned almost perpendicular to the floor. He held the glass well away from his lips. He poured slowly and deliberately to assure the flaming fluid went directly into his mouth. He dared not let any hit his face.

Zane finally completed consumption without spilling a drop. He inverted the shot glass and nothing fell from it. Relieved, he set the glass on the table.

When he started to turn away, Gardner said, "Sir, you have consumed the spirit of the flaming hooker and are entitled to respect for your success. However, you are not qualified for carrier landings under emergency conditions."

Zane started to say that he was carrier qualified. During his first Chinook tour, he had to pickup and deliver supplies to Navy carriers offshore. To do this, he had to pass a check ride to qualify for carrier landings. This qualification appeared in his flight records. He did not say anything for he knew this to be another part of the initiation.

"Foam the runway," Gardner yelled.

Three pilots, Aims, Carlton, and Burlington each had an open can of beer. They placed their thumbs over the openings and began vigorously shaking their cans. Next, they sprayed the bar from end to end with beer foam.

Before Zane realized their intent, five pilots grabbed him by his arms and legs. They lifted him from the floor and carried him to one end of the bar.

Once there, they began swinging him back and forth while reciting, "He's on downwind. He's turning base. Now, he's on final and touchdown."

They released him and he began sliding through the foamed bar top. Since he was husky, they did not apply enough force for him to travel the entire distance. The group obtained more people and repeated the process. This time he went the entire distance.

Once completed, the pilots formed a line to Zane. Each one shook his hand and said, "Welcome aboard, sir. You are now a true Hooker. You are also one of the last Hookers."

After shaking hands with everyone except the new pilots, Gardner said, "Sir, you are now in charge."

As commanding officer, it was now Zane's responsibility to bring the other new pilots into the Hooker fold. They had an advantage because they had seen the technique needed to deal with the flaming hooker. Nevertheless, overcoming the psychological impact of drinking a flaming beverage did not come easy. None made it the first try.

Drenched in beer, with burned faces and chests, they had a miserable sight. Yet, the initiation made a final link in a life time bond. Zane was comfortable with the current situation until it turned ugly.

Gardner proposed a toast to the 362nd. Everyone held their glasses high; drank their contents; and, threw the empty glasses into a corner destroying them. With that, Zane considered festivities complete. He started to leave when Burlington proposed another toast to the ladies. Again, the glasses crashed into the corner. Zane said that the evening's celebrating was over when he started for the door.

Carlton proposed a toast. Standing in the door, Zane called to Carlton. He did not respond. By this time, Mullins, Caldwell, and Greenletter joined Zane to depart. The others followed Carlton's lead and drank a toast to some outlandish thing not remotely relevant to the 362nd. More glasses crashed into the corner.

Realizing that he was dealing with drunken minds, Zane left. The other new pilots went with him.

As the trio came to Zane's bunker, Zane said, "Terry, the situation is out of control in the club. Before formation tomorrow morning, check the club. Let me know what conditions you find. Report to me before you assemble the troops.

Gardner, Burlington, and Aims stood at attention in front of Zane's desk the next morning. They appeared to have slept in their uniforms. They smelled of alcohol.

"Gentlemen," Zane began, "When I first arrived I told you that 'the Animals' no longer existed. I know that you three are key members. However, that's not why you are here. Every furnishing in the club is a wreck. Tables chairs, lamps, and liquor bottles lay destroyed in a corner. I hold you three responsible. When I said it was time to leave, you ignored me."

Reaching into his desk drawer, Zane removed three documents and said, "These are Article 15s. If I administer them, your careers end. You will never advance in rank. Each of you will sign that you received them. If you do not want to do that, you can request Special Court Martials. That is your right as a soldier."

The three, obviously shaken, trembled and looked pale. Zane feared they would be sick in his office. He placed a pen on his desk.

"Gardner, you sign first," Zane ordered.

In turn, the three signed the Article 15s. Each stepped backward to their former attention position after signing. Zane retrieved his pen and the documents. He placed them in his desk.

"I am not going to sign these today," he explained. "You are on a 90 day probation. If during those 90 days, one of you gets out of line, I will sign them. This evening, after duty hours, I am going to the club for a drink. I expect it to be in its original condition. You three will put it that way. You're dismissed."

At day's end, Zane debriefed his crews. Afterward, he went to the club as promised. It was immaculate with new furnishing throughout. He did not know, and did not care, how they did it. They complied with his directive.

Today, the probation period ended. The 90 days were over without incident involving Gardner, Burlington, and Aims. He tore the disciplinary documents into shreds and put them in the trash. It was time to leave for Saigon.

Zane took advantage of a scheduled flight to make his trip. A flight to Tan Son Nhut stopped for refueling. Its load was small so Zane decided to take his jeep in the Hook. He drove it up the ramp and the FE strapped it in place so it could not move in flight.

When he drove from the Hook at Tan Son Nhut, Buff Winslow greeted him. Zane, with a powerful build, found Winslow's size intimidating. He was far from fat. His height and weight were a good match. Zane figured him at around six foot six and 275 pounds.

"Hi Major Zane, I've been wanting to meet you for months. For one reason or another, we have missed each other. I'm Buff Winslow, Chief Technical Rep for Boeing. You have one of our guys in your unit," Winslow said.

"You mean Ralph Cortez. We would have a hard time without him," Zane replied.

Cortez was a civilian working in Zane's company. He worked in maintenance to advise on matters relating to the CH-47. If someone needed technical help, Ralph always solved the problem.

"Hop in," Zane said. "I don't know the way to your place."

"Glad to. Let me tell my driver to go without me," he replied.

Looking in the direction that Winslow waved, Zane saw a man standing by a black Mercedes. He nodded his head and entered the luxury car. He drove away toward the South Gate.

Winslow sat in the jeep's right seat. His head pressed against its canvas top.

"Follow him, he will lead you to our place," Winslow said. "I wanted to talk with you alone."

"Fine," Zane said, "What's on your mind?"

"You need to take another look at your contingency plan to evacuate Phnom Penh's ambassador's staff," Winslow suggested.

"Why? What's the problem?" Zane asked.

"The embassy does not have a refueling point. You cannot rely on their airport. If things get bad enough that you must evacuate the embassy, the airfield will not be safe," Winslow explained.

"I wonder what happened. When we ran our rehearsals, they had a fine refueling area," Zane commented.

Winslow, trying to find a more comfortable way to sit, replied, "Their supplier kept raising fuel prices. They got so high that one could call it extortion. Anyway, the ambassador cancelled the fuel contract. I thought you would want to know."

"I wonder how Winslow even knew a mission existed," Zane thought.

Winslow said, "I know what you are thinking major. You wonder how I knew about the mission. I'll tell you. Some people in your unit talk too much. They say things in front of Ralph that they shouldn't and he let's me know. The information stopped at me."

Ahead, Winslow's driver made a left turn into a driveway at a large hotel. Zane followed until the vehicle stopped at a large steel gate. He watched as the driver unlocked it and pushed its two doors open. He reenter the Mercedes and drove through. Zane drove through the gates and parked next to Winslow's car.

"It seems about every place in Saigon has these huge, steel gates," Zane commented.

Winslow left his contorted position and exited the jeep. Zane joined Winslow in front of Zane's jeep.

"It's like this Dale. These people have fought battles in Saigon for centuries. The walls and gates are self-defense measures. Each is almost a fortress. If you enter their homes, you will find a picture of this area's commanding general where all who enter can see it. This lets them know they are under his protection. It's a service that they pay for," Winslow explained.

Continuing, Winslow said, "Let's head up to my place."

As soon as Zane entered Winslow's penthouse, he knew that he was a party animal. Placed throughout the living area Winslow had mini-bars stocked with a full beverage line. Numerous poker tables were in the rooms. Outside Zane heard a band tuning their instruments and testing their amplifiers.

"I see that you live well," Zane observed.

"Its nothing like it used to be. In 1968 and 1969, the place boomed. Hook pilots made a point of coming by whenever they came to Saigon. They could stay a day or a week. Now, my friend, your unit is about it. The "Black Cats" at Phu Loi is the only unit besides yours in country. They have already turned in their ships. Most of their people left weeks ago. I do not envy you Dale. Your mission load is going to become a bitch. Count on it," Winslow predicted.

Winslow gave Zane a tour of his penthouse villa. The most impressive thing he saw was a sunken tub with water jets. It was Winslow's private Jacuzzi. Taking second place was a bidet. Having never seen one, Zane deduced its purpose. Such luxury and opulence seemed out of place in a war zone.

"Please excuse me," Winslow said. "I have some chores. Make yourself at home. I will be with you in a moment."

Zane sat at a corner mini-bar. He sat on one of its four stools after mixing a bourbon and water. He munched on macadamia nuts from a bowl on the bar. From his position, he could see the entrance doorway and the exit onto the rooftop veranda. He watched caterers arrive with tables of delicacies.

One man entered and went directly to Winslow helping set a table. He had a short animated discussion before he and Winslow left through the main door. Soon the door opened and Zane saw Winslow's huge back coming into the room. He had both arms wrapped around the base of a heavy object. With Winslow in the room, Zane saw a five-foot high ice carving. Two Vietnamese strained at the other end. After a struggle, they placed the carving on a long, empty table. Zane became awestruck when he could see the full ice carving.

The carving depicted a Chinook helicopter in minute detail. Its length was at least six feet. Its nose pointed up at an angle. Below the left door gunner's window, the 362nd emblem appeared. Zane left his seat and went to the carving. Walking around it, he marveled at its accurate depiction. He looked around the room for Winslow.

Zane spotted him by the veranda door with his hands on his hips. He was watching Zane with a huge grin. Zane set his drink down and clasped both of his hands together. He raised them above his head and shook them while beaming at Winslow. Winslow gave Zane a thumb up sign and returned to his work.

Back at his corner seat, Zane watched guests arrive. Some were Vietnamese generals and others appeared to be wealthy Vietnamese civilian couples. He immediately recognized Lanny Briscoe but he did not know the man and woman he arrived with.

Zane watched Briscoe examine the room and their eyes met. Briscoe immediately smiled and gave him a recognition nod. Evidently, the man with Briscoe saw the Chinook ice carving because Winslow took the trio to it. They walked around it and appeared enthralled.

Winslow looked at Zane and said something to the man. He also looked at Zane, as did the lady with him. Winslow led them to him. As they approached, Zane set down his drink and left the barstool.

"Lady Earling, this is Major Dale Zane," Winslow began, "Major Zane met Lady Earling and her husband Lord Frederick Earling. I believe you already know Lanny Briscoe."

Zane bowed when meeting the lady. He took Earling's offered hand and shook it. He also shook Briscoe's hand.

Frederick quickly said, "It is my pleasure Major Zane. Ignore the Lord and Lady business. That's Winslow's attempt to impress someone. Call me Frederick and my wife Vanessa."

"Certainly," Zane replied, "Call me Dale."

"Isn't that ice carving a grand piece of work. How sad it is that it will soon melt," Frederick commented.

Continuing, Frederick said, "I'm with Air America. We are bringing some Chinooks to our Thailand fleet. I would certainly appreciate any advice you can provide regarding their operation. Perhaps we can chat later?"

"I am always willing to talk about Hooks," Zane answered.

"Please excuse us Dale. I see someone that I need to speak with now. We will definitely get together this evening," Frederick said as he turned to leave.

Briscoe added, "I hope you do not mind me chatting with Major Zane. You two go without me."

"Are you keeping busy Lanny?" Zane asked.

"Yes, very much so. I am pleased that you are here. I was going to visit with you in the next few days," Briscoe related.

"You will soon receive a mission from your headquarters regarding my earlier request. Your advice about elephants was on the mark. I finally got the MACV

Intel people to cooperate. They relayed the mission to your 3rd Brigade first. They returned it," Briscoe explained.

"Why?" Zane asked.

"Soon there will be no 3rd Brigade. They are withdrawing. A new unit will replace them. It is Task Force Gary Owen. The 229th will remain as will the 362nd," Briscoe answered.

"This is news to me. I have to get this second hand. Damn what is the matter with those jerks?" Zane erupted.

"I wouldn't mention that you know this. It is something that is not common knowledge. You will receive official notification tomorrow along with my approved mission request," Briscoe explained.

Later than evening, Frederick and Zane talked on Winslow's veranda while enjoying Saigon's view.

"Dale, what do you considered the most important aspect of Chinook operations?" Frederick asked.

"Maintenance without a doubt is most important. The ratio of maintenance hours to flight hours is about 12 to one. Sloppy maintenance will increase that. It costs about $1,200 per flight hour to operate a Chinook. A lot also depends on the model. What models are you getting?" Zane asked.

"They are C models," Frederick answered.

"That's great," Zane responded, "Mine are all A models. They are the oldest ones in the field. You will have a considerable lifting capacity compare to mine. We're limited to 10,000 pounds. The C will handle 18,000 without a problem. Where are you getting your pilots?" Zane asked.

"We already have retired Marines flying most of our ships. They started with H-19s and then we upgraded to H-34s. We're looking forward to getting the Hooks. We will need more pilots soon," Frederick responded.

"Some of my people will retire at the end of this tour. They may want to continue flying. If one applies and he has aircraft commander in his flight records, grab him. He will be our best," Zane stated.

At Zane's first chance, he advised Winslow. "I need to hit the sack. This trip is for rest not partying. Show me where my bunk is. I have to meet a Hook at Tan Son Nhut early tomorrow?"

"Just one moment and you can rack out. Stay where you are," Winslow directed.

Winslow elbowed his way to the bandstand and stopped their music. He called for attention with little response.

Finally he yelled, "Ladies and gentlemen, your attention please. The reason for my presence in Viet Nam rests mostly with one man. He is the Commanding Officer of the 362nd Aviation Company. He is our honored guest. His name is Major Dale Zane. He's tired and must depart. I want everyone to know who he is. Please stand Dale," Winslow said.

Winslow pointed to Zane and the crowd looked in his direction. They began applauding, which embarrassed him among so many strangers.

"Hell, I'm an Army aviator. I must do something," he thought.

Zane began bowing deeply in different directions while smiling at everyone. He went to the ice carving and gave it a big hug and kiss.

Next, he turned to the group and said, "Reminds me of a young lady I used to date. She's now a spinster."

Among the laughter, Winslow took Zane to his bedroom and said, "This is yours for tonight. I recommend the tub for an hour and then to bed. You will have the most relaxed sleep you've ever known."

On his return flight to Phu Loi, Zane received word to meet with Colonel Smith, his Battalion Commander. As the crew shutdown their ship, Zane walked to Smith's office. Smith saw him through his open door and signaled Zane to enter.

With a dour demeanor, he directed Zane to sit as he said, "Major, when you came aboard I told you of my dissatisfaction with your unit's availability rate. I am still dissatisfied. You have to improve it."

"Sir," Zane said, "I agreed that 75 percent was unsatisfactory. I told you that I would provide text book availability and I have. These ships are old and worn. They require close attention or they will start coming apart. These are not Hueys Colonel."

Obviously displeased with Zane's reply, Smith directed, "You will report 22 ships available daily."

"Sir, that's 92 percent. That means I cannot have more than two ships in maintenance at one time. We can get away with that for a short period. After that, the number of flyable ships will decrease way below what you now have. In addition, this will be an open invitation for material failures. You will lose ships and their crews," Zane stated firmly.

"Major, you are not listening. I said you would report 22 ships flyable daily. I do not want to hear your problems. My interest is your solutions. You're dismissed" Smith directed.

Zane immediately came to attention. He saluted and did an about face before exiting Smith's office. He walked toward his waiting Chinook.

"Okay colonel. I will report 22 of my ships available daily. However, I will not let you kill my people," Zane said to himself.

Zane backed his jeep from within the Hook. He began driving toward Ops when he saw a familiar figure near an aircraft hanger. Upon closer inspection, he saw his long time friend Daryl Scott.

Increasing speed, Zane raced towards Scott. When near him, he exited his jeep and crushed Scott in a powerful bear hug.

"Damn Dale, you're going to kill me. Let go," Scott pleaded.

After releasing his grip, the pair exchanged greetings with merry horseplay. As usual, they drew stares from on lookers.

"You know what. These people must think we're homos," Zane exclaimed with a loud laugh.

Continuing, Zane suggested, "Let's go to my orderly room. It's hot out here."

Scott answered, "I wish I could. I've been waiting an hour. I have to return to Long Thanh North. I will try to coordinate a longer visit later."

"That sucks," Zane replied, "You can at least let me know about Georgia and kids."

Zane watched Scott wilt. Grief descended upon him and. tears gathered in his eyes.

"Dale, I've lost them. We're divorced and she got the kids. It was my fault and I should have seen it coming but I didn't," Scott said sadly.

Sympathetically, Zane replied, "That's tough man. Damn, that's really tough. I'm so sorry."

"Don't worry. I will be in touch soon. Catch you later," Scott said as he ran to a waiting U21.

Zane watched Scott's aircraft takeoff before he entered his jeep. He drove to Ops and entered to find Lieutenant Robertson talking with one of the switchboard operators. As soon as Robertson saw him, he called the group to attention.

"As you were," Zane directed.

Zane asked, "Where's Caldwell?"

"He's flying sir. I fill in when he's not around," Robertson answered.

"That's a smart move Robertson. Every commissioned aviator needs an additional duty, if he plans on an Army career. Show me a captain with 10,000 flying hours, dual rated and instrument qualified in both. I will show you a captain who will not make major. All he knows is how to fly. He's worthless for anything else," Zane commented.

"Do you really mean that, sir?" Robertson asked.

Zane answered, "Absolutely."

Zane continued, "Remember that Cambodian rescue mission we rehearsed?"

"Yes sir," Robertson replied.

"Compute its fuel use rate under optimal conditions but do not include refueling," Zane directed.

Zane added, "I will be at maintenance if you need me."

Along his way, Zane stopped and loaded soldiers who were walking to work. When he arrived at maintenance, he had the jeep's tires almost flat. He had soldiers riding everywhere they could find a seat.

"This is bullshit," he thought. "These men bust their asses on 12 hour shifts and then have to walk two miles one way for chow and sleep. This situation has to end."

When Zane didn't find Captain Wellington in his office, he went searching among the aircraft. He found him inside a ship showing a NCO how to assemble a hydraulic servo. Zane listened and learned that Wellington knew Hooks.

"May I speak with you a minute Richard?" Zane asked.

Outside, on the tarmac, Zane said, "Starting in the morning, report 22 aircraft available."

Captain Wellington immediately replied, "Sir, I cannot do that. We have four down at all times."

"Look at it his way, Richard. I said report 22. I did not say to have 22 flyable did I?" Zane asked.

"No sir, you didn't," Wellington agreed.

"You let me worry about the report. You are simply following orders," Zane explained.

Lowering his voice, Zane asked. "How many Quick Change Assemblies (QCA) do you have for our engines?"

Wellington's face almost turned as red as his hair as he answered, "Sir, you must know we are not authorized any. However, I have two."

"See if you can assemble enough parts for three," Zane directed.

QCAs are aircraft components constructed with parts from the Army's supply system. The 362nd did not have authorization to stock spare engines. Therefore, the maintenance officer could not requisition one. However, he could requisition enough individual parts to build one. When a ship went down somewhere because of a malfunctioning engine, one was available without having to wait for one from supply. With the withdrawal of so many units, Chinook engines were difficult to obtain. The 362nd could not risk having a ship down in a hostile situation while awaiting an engine that may not arrive for days. By having spares on hand, they could replace an engine in less than 15 minutes and get the ship airborne.

"One more thing Richard," Zane said.

"Do you have a ship coming out of maintenance for a test flight?" He asked.

"We have one for in the morning. All it needs is a safety of flight inspection," Wellington answered.

"If you don't want to be involved in my next proposal, do not hesitate to say so. I will not think less of you if you decline," Zane said mysteriously.

Curious, Wellington said, "I will have to hear it first sir."

"Do the safety of flight this afternoon before dark. After sunset, spray paint over all exterior markings. Next, there will be a 'test flight' to a supply yard in Saigon's Cholon District. The ship will return about 15 minutes on the ground. Its cargo will be a new three-quarter ton truck. Repaint the markings and give it another test flight tomorrow as planned," Zane explained.

"Jesus sir. You're really looking for trouble. First, regulations prohibit test flights at night. Second, if we get caught without markings, you will be in deep shit," Wellington said, appalled at Zane's proposal.

"It's my ass Richard. I am tired of seeing my people waste valuable maintenance time walking back and forth to the company area. The XO knows a Vietnamese major he met on his last tour. He owes Greenletter a big favor. He has a motor pool filled with trucks on their way to Cambodia. Our people need a truck more than the damned Cambodians. They are not even fighting in this war," Zane stated resolutely.

"Major, those people are my maintenance people. I need them here working not walking. Have Captain Greenletter here shortly after sunset," Wellington directed.

After formation the next morning, Zane watched his soldiers climb aboard a new, three-quarter ton truck. It displayed new unit markings and serial numbers. Others boarded the old one, cutting transit time in half.

As Briscoe said, a classified mission arrived from MACV. It tasked the 362nd to have three Hooks with ARC 102 radios installed. They had to be fully operational on every frequency. Other information would follow. He contacted maintenance and had them turn the task over to their Avionics shop.

Zane could see his unit steadily improving. Yet, one thing continued to plague his unit, drugs. The major problem was still heroin. While he was at battalion headquarters, Zane confirmed use of a new weapon, urine testing.

Battalion's new Operations Officer, Major Rapheal Gonzales, was a St. Mary's graduate and former member of the Marion Guard Drill Team. He arranged with Zane procedures for unannounced urine tests. It was an absolute necessity to keep a urine test a secret. If a switch board operator heard one being arranged, he alerted drug distributors for a handsome fee. The dealers then alerted their users.

There were ways to beat the urine test. With advanced warning, a user would report to the dispensary complaining of diarrhea. The standard treatment was a medication named Lomotil. Lomotil contained an opium derivative and caused a positive result on a urine test. The detected users then could say that he had been taking Lomotil. A check of his medical records showed that he had. By this time, detectable heroin did not appear in his system.

Another method did not last long. Users bought urine from those who were straight. They kept the safe urine in a small plastic container. The user placed the container under his arm and connected a small, flexible tube to it. He then directed this tube to his groin next to his penis. When he took the test, he simply squeezed the bag in his armpit forcing straight urine into the test container. However, test procedures now required an individual to strip to his waist. A medic had to watch urine pass from the individual into the test container.

Zane's arrangement with Gonzales consisted of a message with a code word. When he called, Zane would say the code word in a mundane message. When Gonzales received it, he dispatched the test team by Huey. From receipt of Zane's call to the test team's arrival, was one hour.

Three days after his arrangement, Zane awoke at 03:00 hours unable to sleep. He sent a message to Gonzales who acknowledged its receipt. Next, Zane had the XO and first sergeant meet him in the orderly room.

"Terry, you and Top come in," Zane said. "Have some coffee. It's fresh from the Mess Hall."

While the two drank their coffee, Zane explained, "Wake the officers and NCOs. Have them help you muster our troops in the motor pool. In addition, have two of our drums used in the outhouses moved to the motor pool. Get two that are unused. I will meet you when you arrive."

On his way, Zane saw the test team's Huey arrive. He escorted white-jacketed soldiers, with their collection equipment, to his motor pool. They set up two tables. On one, they placed collection test tubes. On the other, a medic had the 362nd current personnel roster.

The XO arrived, marching unit personnel through the motor pool's gate. When the troops saw the medics, three broke formation and ran. It was too late. First Sergeant Kubble had the gate closed. The three looked for another escape route, while the other soldiers watched from their formation.

A ten-foot high cyclone fence surrounded the area. Along its top, three barbed wire strands ran the entire length of the fence. The three panicked soldiers tried to climb it without success. Finally, exhausted, they returned to formation. They received considerable heckling from their friends.

The XO called the formation to attention and made his strength report. All were present except for five who were on R and R.

Zane commanded, "At ease."

"Good morning," Zane said, which brought forth some grumbling?

"I am sure by now you know why you are here. Every member of this unit will undergo a urine test. You will form a line at the table to my right. The medic will provide you with a collection tube with your name, serial number, and unit printed on it. Next, you will proceed to one of the two drums you see. You will remove all garments covering your upper body. The medic standing there will observe you urinate in the tube. When finished, proceed to the seated medic who will strike your name from the list. After that, you are free to leave. No one leaves without providing a urine sample. I will go first," Zane explained as he removed his clothing to his waist.

By the time Zane obtained his collection tube, there was a line on his right. He attempted to urinate in the tube without success. The more he tried, the more difficult it became. His soldiers seeing this began making catcalls and laughing. This made matters worse. He had a severe case of "bashful kidneys."

Totally flustered, he stepped away with the hope he soon could fill his tube. Meanwhile others came to the barrels. Most, without difficulty, filled their collection tube.

Zane continued trying without success. Soon, he had others standing with him. Zane told the first sergeant to move mess personnel through before the others.

"Top, have them bring coffee, soft drinks, beer and any other liquid that might work," Zane directed.

First Sergeant Kubble wore a mild grin throughout Zane's instructions. Zane gave him a dirty look in return. Two hours, and six cups of coffee later, Zane succeeded with great relief. However, there were others who had not made their first try. Furthermore, the three who tried to scale the fence wet their trousers rather than use their collection tubes.

Slightly less than 24 hours later, the three holdouts finally gave urine samples. Not surprisingly, these three's results were positive. However, nine more were positive. The 12 went to a rehabilitation center for ten days. Those who participated in therapy sessions, and failed no more tests during the ten days, returned to the 362nd for duty. Four would not cooperate. They returned to CONUS and received Administrative Discharges for the Good of the Service.

Zane met with his senior officers and NCOs to discuss their first urine test. The consensus was that urine testing was effective for identification of users. However, it detracted severely from unit operations. Key personnel, the CO included, were away from their major duties for too long. They had missions to fly and standing around in the motor pool wasn't getting the job done. The ultimate decision of the group was to focus on the dealers. Get them and the use rate would likely decrease. Zane scheduled a meeting with Colonel Smith.

Incredulous, Colonel Smith asked. "You want to do what?"

"Sir, whenever I have a person arrested for possession with intent to distribute, I want him sent to Long Binh Jail to await trial. He is to disappear without a trace. Under no circumstance is he to return to my unit," Zane explained.

"Damn Dale, that tells me what you want but not why," Smith commented.

"Perhaps a hypothetical scenario will help. Imagine this. I arrest a dealer who has a large quantity of narcotics. I have arranged for the Phu Loi MPs to lead him from my orderly room to their jeep. They will frisk him across the hood of their jeep in the company street for all to see. They will handcuff him. Next, they take him from our area and he is never seen, or heard of, again."

Continuing, Zane said, "Rumors run rampant in a unit. I want potential dealers to worry when they make a decision to sell drugs. It is psychological, sir."

"Okay Dale. If you think that will help, I will support you," Smith agreed.

"Just two more items, sir," Zane added.

"Go ahead," Smith instructed.

"I am going to start having health and welfare inspections on a random basis. This allows my people to search anywhere they like without having to show probable cause. Any illegal substances found we can keep as contraband. If we link it to a person, it is legal evidence in a trial. The key is having them regularly and randomly. I must do this in order to implement my second item," Zane explained.

"Okay, what is it?" Smith asked.

"When I receive information that a dealer has a large stash, First Sergeant Kubble will contact the dealer. He will tell him to report to the orderly room for transfer to another unit. Sir, a dealer is not going to leave his stash behind. When he arrives at the orderly room, he will have everything he owns. At that time, I will begin a health and welfare inspection. I will have the dealer where it hurts, sir," Zane explained.

"You are telling me that you will inspect your entire unit to catch one man," Smith observed.

"That's correct sir. I am finding drug stashes but I cannot connect them to a person. This way the dealer will have his stash in his possession," Zane added.

"You are determined major," Smith said. "Oh, by the way, congratulations. I see that your readiness reports are up. That's great. Keep up the good work. If there's nothing else, get back to work," Smith said.

"Thank you sir. I am out of here," Zane replied as he saluted and left.

When Zane arrived at Phu Loi, he went to Ops. He needed the results of the Cambodian mission.

Caldwell said, "Sir, Robertson did the analysis. Without a refueling point, we will barely make it to the Cambodian border on the return trip. At that point, we will have exhausted our reserve fuel. We cannot do this mission without secure refueling in Cambodia."

"Fine Earnest, pass that to Battalion Ops. Let's hear what they have to say," Zane instructed.

Caldwell added, "Sir, there is a Lieutenant Colonel Hillcrest at your office. He's from the Inspector Generals' (IG) Office at MACV. He received a report that we have a stolen truck in our unit. I told him that you would arrive soon so he chose to wait."

"Thanks, I will take care of it," Zane replied and drove to his office.

"Hi major. I'm Colonel Hillcrest from the IG's office at MACV. We received an anonymous tip that there is a stolen truck in your unit. Have you seen any new three quarter tons in your area?" Hillcrest asked.

"Yes sir, I have. I will take you to it at our maintenance area," Zane replied.

Along the way, Hillcrest asked. "Are these your people walking?"

"Yes, sir. They are returning from lunch. We have a mule, this jeep, one three quarter ton, and one two and one half-ton truck. The two and one half-ton makes our daily supply trips to battalion and our supply unit in Saigon. It is away most of the day. The mule, and one three quarter ton truck, shuttles personnel at meal times. However, with over 400 people in maintenance, they hardly dent our need. Most walk rather than wait," Zane explained.

As Zane parked near Captain Wellington's office, the new truck arrived filled with troops. When the troops unloaded, it departed to get others. As he and the IG started to enter the hangar, Zane saw Wellington supervising an engine installation on a Hook. Zane took the IG to meet Wellington.

After introducing the two, Zane said, "Wellington, fill Colonel Hillcrest in about the new truck."

"Sir, when I came to work one morning, my maintenance NCO asked me to accompany him to an abandoned revetment behind this hangar. When we arrived, I found a truck sitting on wooden blocks with its transmission removed. I immediately contacted the MPs. They came and investigated. They left and said they would contact me later. When I heard nothing for three days, I had supply put the vehicle on our property books as 'found on post.' Any time government property remains unclaimed, I must, by regulations, take charge of it. We assigned it a unit designation and a serial number. I have not heard from the MPs about it," Wellington explained.

"I've heard enough here. Take me to the MP station," Hillcrest directed.

Zane thanked Wellington and drove to the MP station. They confirmed Wellington's story. The MPs did not have a storage area and could not secure it. Therefore, they left it at the 362nd. They said they had an ongoing investigation.

While returning Hillcrest to the orderly room, he asked. "Why don't you use a Hook for supply runs and use the two and one half ton to transport your personnel?"

"Sir, I am prohibited from using Chinooks for routine in-unit purposes. They must be available for external missions. General Burton issued that directive," Zane replied.

At the orderly room, Colonel Hillcrest said, "I do not need to see more Zane. You keep the vehicle. You damn well need it more than a bunch of Cambodians. You return to work. I can walk to the airfield. My pilot is waiting."

Zane watched Hillcrest walk away and thought, "He damn well knew when he got here where that truck came from. He could have nailed our butts. We need more lieutenant colonels like him."

Inside his orderly room, First Sergeant Kubble said that he had an "eyes only" message for him. He held the sealed envelope for Zane to take.

"Come into my office Top. Open the thing. You have my permission to open such documents in the future. After that, if I'm not around, get the XO and show it to him. You are the ones that are going to have to do the work anyway," Zane said.

Sergeant Kubble shut Zane's door and removed another sealed envelope. He glanced through it and handed it to Zane.

Zane read it thoroughly and said, "Well, how about that. The 3rd Brigade is no more. We are now officially part of Task Force Gary Owen. In addition, we are getting a new Commanding General. I've never heard of Brigadier General Hamlet. Sure hope he's not a pain in the ass," Zane said.

Continuing Zane said, "Top, bring me the Op plan for evacuating Saigon's Embassy. I want a close look at that again."

"Sir," Top said. "I need you to counsel two soldiers. Both received seriously low efficiency reports. They are headed for trouble. Perhaps you can help them get straight."

"Always glad to help Top. Let me see that plan and then I will see them one at a time," Zane directed.

First Sergeant Kubble removed Operation Plan Glad Tidings from the safe. He took it to Zane.

As Zane reviewing the document, he thought, "Since we last rehearsed this thing, we've rotated 30 percent of our pilots out of here. One in three has never heard of this mission much less fly it. It's time to work this again."

Zane contacted Sergeant Kubble by intercom and said, "Okay Top, bring me the files on those two that you wanted me to counsel. Give me 15 minutes and I will see the first one."

Zane read the top file's label and thought, "Bredermeyer, I should have known. I hope he takes a swing at me."

He glanced through Bredermeyer's file. Zane noted that he received the lowest possible efficiency rating from his immediate supervisor. In addition, his reviewer did the same. First Sergeant Kubble's name appeared as the approving authority.

Zane read the supervisor's rating again. It showed Bredermeyer insubordinate and unable to work with fellow soldiers without getting involved in altercations. On two occasions, his supervisor counseled him and gave Bredermeyer a copy as evidenced by his initials.

The other man's file, Private First Class (PFC) Merrill L. Haddock, showed that Zane did an initial interview with him. He recalled the young man and his recollection was a good one. He seemed to have an excellent attitude. Next Zane read the supervisor's portion. On two occasions, he had gone on a rampage at their club. He was in the company of Bredermeyer at the time. However, Bredermeyer was not involved. Twice he was late for formation in the company of Bredermeyer. The pair claimed to have overslept. On another occasion, his supervisor went to his bunk and found both him and Bredermeyer asleep.

"Sounds like this young man is traveling in bad company," Zane thought.

Someone knocked at Zane's door. He told the person to enter. It was Bredermeyer.

Bredermeyer marched straight to Zane's desk; stood at attention; saluted Zane; and said, "Specialist Bredermeyer reporting as ordered sir."

Zane returned his salute and directed him to sit but Bredermeyer said, "I would rather stand sir."

Raising his head from looking at Bredermeyer's file, Zane ordered, "Bredermeyer, take a seat."

Bredermeyer fell into the chair and sat slouched with an insolent expression on his face. Zane turned Bredermeyer's file around so that Bredermeyer could read it.

Zane asked, "What do you find in error in your latest evaluation?"

Glancing through the report quickly, Bredermeyer answered, "The supervisor."

"In what way?" Zane asked.

"He is a dumb ass. I fix hydraulic lines and he's always saying they are not repaired correctly," Bredermeyer snarled.

"I find no mention of that in your report. Most of it has to do with insubordination and getting along with people," Zane noted.

Bredermeyer came erect in his seat and leaned toward Zane's desk and said, "I don't take shit from anyone."

"Come on and take a swing," Zane thought as he said, "I find that the evaluation is a correct reflection of your attitude. You are insubordinate. You may file an appeal with the IG's office," Zane said.

Bredermeyer arose quickly while pushing his chair aside. He whirled and started for the door.

Zane boomed, "Stand where you are specialist."

Bredermeyer stopped and turned to face Zane. At that moment, Zane clearly recognized his outline. He saw the same one during the gas attack.

"Come to attention, soldier. I haven't dismissed you," Zane said through clenched teeth.

Bredermeyer hesitated until Zane left his chair and walked around his desk toward him. He came to attention as Zane neared.

Walking around Bredermeyer, Zane said, "Take a swing, please. I will kick the shit out of your sorry ass. Then I will pull your unconscious body on top of me and yell for help. You will see how bad you are in Leavenworth Penitentiary.

Zane returned to his desk while Bredermeyer stood at attention. Taking his time, Zane leafed through his file again. Then he ordered, "Dismissed."

Bredermeyer saluted and Zane returned it. The upset and furious soldier did an about face and left Zane's office. Zane sent for the next man.

PFC Haddock seemed to be nothing more than a misguided young man. His ratings were not as low as they could be. Zane explained to him that he could overcome his poor rating with some effort on his part. Haddock conducted himself well during the interview. Zane advised him of his right to appeal to the IG and dismissed him.

Zane put thoughts of the pair aside and focused on his mission to evacuate the American Embassy and ARVN senior staff in Saigon. He contacted Captain Caldwell in Ops.

"Earnest," Zane said, "We need a pilot update for Op Plan Glad Tidings. Remember that we have to keep flying our regular missions at the same time. They have priority. Arrange another ground recon for our pilots in Saigon. After that, schedule all new pilots to fly a rehearsal with aircraft commanders. Include me, I will brief the crews and fly the mission with one of the new pilots."

Zane felt as silly as he did the first ground recon of their LZs in downtown Saigon. Their transportation was a tourist bus. Each man wore civilian garb expected of tourists. The bus delivered them to the American Embassy where they walked around the building taking pictures. Each man went inside and up to the Embassy helipad to gauge its size and analyze various approach paths.

Their next stop was ARVN headquarters. The building housed Saigon's Commanding General and his senior staff. In the event, of an attack, such as Tet in 1968, the 362nd had the mission to evacuate them if they requested it. They must do it on short notice day or night. As an added feature, the assumption was that there would be extensive use of tear gas. This meant the pilots had to do their rehearsal wearing gas masks. The same applied for the American Embassy.

The ARVN headquarters did not have a rooftop helipad. The only area to land was a small lawn immediately in front of their headquarters. In the LZs center, the ARVN had three tall flagpoles. On his first rehearsal, Zane told the ARVN commander that his Hooks could not land with the flag poles in the LZ. Zane advised that they move them closer to the building. If they could not do that, they had to use explosive charges to drop the poles before the Hooks could land. The ARVN commander assured him that they would relocate the poles. They were still in place.

The following week Zane was briefing his pilots for their rehearsal. He received a frantic call from Ops.

"Sir, our new CG, Brigadier General Hamlet, is here to see you. He says for you to come ready to fly," Caldwell excitedly said.

"Tell the general that I am on my way. Find Captain Greenletter and tell him to fly lead on these rehearsals today," Zane said.

While on the way to the flight line, Zane told his driver, "Go to my C &C and get my flight gear. Bring it to me at the CG's Huey."

Zane stepped from his jeep in front of Ops. Standing by the entrance, he saw an African American Brigadier. He was BG Hamlet.

Zane stepped in front of him, saluted, and said, "Major Dale Zane, sir."

Hamlet returned his salute and then extended his hand as he said, "Nice to meet you Zane. How many Hooks you got flying today?"

"Twenty, sir" Zane said without thinking.

"Can you do that everyday?" Hamlet continued.

"Yes sir," Zane answered.

"That's exceptional. The A model is a tired machine. I don't see how you do it," Hamlet said. "I need you to ride with me to Long Thanh North. You must get out of Phu Loi. I've heard that PA & E gives you a hard time."

"That's correct sir. When we left Bear Cat, they required a complete renovation of every building. Every light switch had to work. New paneling and repaint. We had to put everything in topnotch condition. I find that acceptable except for what happens later," Zane said.

"What's that?" Hamlet asked.

"My C & C was the last to leave Bear Cat. On climb out, I saw our company area attacked by hordes of Vietnamese and Thais. They were ripping out wiring, paneling, doors, and windows." Zane explained.

Continuing, he said, "When we arrived at Phu Loi, our assigned area was stripped clean. Wiring hung from bare ceilings; there were no panels or insulation. Someone decimated the area. When I told PA & E to rebuild it, they said that was my problem. I reported this but never received a response."

As Zane's driver arrived with his flight equipment, Hamlet said, "You have a response this time major."

Upon landing at Long Thanh North, Hamlet led the way to the Command Airplane Company (CAC) Commander's Office. The CAC commander was a full colonel. His unit flew missions in direct support of MACV headquarters. They had the latest fixed wing aircraft available in country. All of their ships were twin engine and only flew administrative flights. They had been at Long Thanh North for almost ten years.

While walking to CAC headquarters, Zane saw his C & C Huey on approach. They began hovering toward Hamlet's ship.

Hamlet saw Zane watching them and said, "Major I commandeered your C & C ship and your available pilots. You will learn why in a minute."

With their greetings finished, Hamlet told Colonel Garrington, "Colonel, you have 24 hours to be out of Long Thanh North. Your new location is Tan Son Nhut. I have with me an inventory team. They are going to inventory your installation property. If so much as a light bulb is missing when my people arrive, I will see that you receive a Statement of Charges for the items. You will pay for them out of your pocket. I have already advised PA & E headquarters of this. They are going to assure that your clearance goes as I have stated."

Zane watched Garrington, while Hamlet explained what his expectations were. He watched his face grow pale as the significance of his words took affect. Zane knew deep inside that Garrington inherited the unit and had no idea that he would ever have to move. It was likely that he had no field gear and his men would be standing on a hot tarmac at Tan Son Nhut with no provisions.

"Nice meeting you colonel," Zane heard Hamlet say.

"Let's go Zane," Hamlet said.

Outside, Hamlet said, "If you have the slightest problem from these people. You call me direct."

Zane replied, "Thank you sir."

"Don't thank me yet son. You return to Phu Loi and get your people moving. You must close on this station by sunset tomorrow. I am suspending Hook support to other units so that you can use your ships to help make the move. Any questions?" Hamlet asked.

"Yes sir. I have one. Why?" Zane asked.

"Phu Loi is too close to Cambodia. Your unit is out on a limb. You are an exposed flank so to speak. We have to get you east of Ben Hoa for protection. Certain Intel leads me to believe you are in danger. So get moving," Hamlet said as he saluted and departed. Zane never had a chance to salute in return.

Zane saw Greenletter approached with eight pilots. They were supposed to fly rehearsals. That was out now for sure.

"Terry, organize your guys and inventory the shit out of this place. Send one man to the Installation Commander's office and get a plat showing the C & C area. Write down everything you see and get serial numbers. While you get started, I am going to do a quick check of their revetments to see if our Hooks will fit," Zane explained.

Zane went to the aircraft parking area. While on the way, he realized that he would now be on the same base with Daryl Scott.

"I'll be damned. We're back together. That's almost spooky," he thought.

At the first revetment, Zane saw that it was steel reinforced cement two feet thick. They extended high enough to cover a Hook's body and the blades were clear. However, they were too narrow. Looking closely, he saw that the huge cement slabs were moveable.

"We can make them wider but it's going to take one powerful crane to move them," Zane thought, as he moved toward the fixed wing landing area.

As he went around the last revetment, he came upon a Special Force's captain. Sitting on the ground in front of him were ten Montengard tribesmen in jungle fatigues. Each wore a parachute. Someone had parked a STOL aircraft behind them. Standing beside it was Frederick Earling, the Air America guy he met at Winslow's party. He nodded in recognition.

Somewhat startled, the captain said, "Sir, you cannot remain in this area. It's restricted."

"Captain," Zane began, "In 24 hours from now, this entire half of the airfield will have Chinooks parked on it. Sorry I interrupted your presentation."

Zane turned and headed for his C & C ship. He found his flight equipment lying inside.

Thinking a moment, Zane pointed toward the CAC area and told the ship's crew chief, "Find Lieutenant Robertson. He is with the other pilots inventorying property in that direction. Bring him here so we can return to Phu Loi ASAP."

Upon landing at Phu Loi, Zane said, "Robertson, take care of the post flight and write ups. I must go."

Zane ran to Ops and telephoned the orderly room. He got Captain Mullins on the line.

"Chris, get with First Sergeant Kubble. We must have our unit at Long Thanh North by tomorrow afternoon," Zane directed, as he heard a sudden and loud explosion. Simultaneously, he lost his connection with Captain Mullins. Zane's repeated efforts to establish another connection failed.

Next, he saw Phu Loi's fire trucks race from the airfield toward his company area. Zane ran from Ops and looked toward his orderly room. A black smoke column rose above where his orderly room should be.

While running toward the orderly room, he thought, "I didn't hear any incoming rockets. There were no other explosions. Something is wrong, big time."

As he passed the final Quonset blocking his view, Zane saw a smoking pile of debris where his orderly room used to be. He slowed to a walk. It was evident that there was little that he could do. If Mullins, First Sergeant Kubble, and clerks were inside that, they were dead.

Zane pushed his way through a gathering crowd. On the other side of the smoking mess, he saw his orderly room personnel. They looked like they had taken a ride in a coal truck. Black soot covered them. However, he saw no wounds. He ran to them.

"Is everyone okay?" Zane asked.

First Sergeant Kubble replied, "Yes sir, only because of the wall between your office and the Admin area."

"What happened Top?" Zane asked with profound concern.

"Captain Mullins was talking with you when there was a massive explosion in your office. CID is on its way. They probably can determine the exact cause. No one has been in your office since you left. I do not understand it," Kubble stated.

While listening to Kubble, Zane saw Bredermeyer standing among the onlookers. He had a knowing grin on his face. When Zane made eye contact, he lowered his head and left the crowd.

"That's two you son of a bitch. First, the gas and now this," Zane thought.

Zane gathered his men around him and said, "This is a bitch of a time to tell you this. We have to have the unit on station at Long Thanh North by late tomorrow afternoon."

Captain Mullins turned away and placed his hands on his knees as he leaned forward. Zane thought he might become ill.

"You okay Chris?" He asked.

"Sir, I was fine until you said that," Mullins replied.

"Look on the bright side," Zane said. "We don't have to move the Orderly Room."

His men started to laugh and Kubble said, "I will put Snuffy on this."

Snuffy was Staff Sergeant Walter A. Wallace. He arrived in country for MP duty. After hanging around the Repo Depot for three days without an assignment, he began to complain. The replacement Noncommissioned Officer in Charge (NCOIC) contacted Kubble.

First Sergeant Kubble kept Repo Depot Admin personnel supplied with war trophies. In return, they kept a lookout for quality people they could send to the 362nd. Sergeant Wallace wanted an assignment to the 362nd and Kubble grabbed him. He also tagged him with the nickname Snuffy. No one knew why, not even Wallace.

Snuffy became Kubble's "Field First." A Field First expedited things. He accomplished the impossible stuff. Furthermore, he specialized as a scrounger.

Many described him as adroit because he produced best under pressure. For the tough jobs, call Snuffy.

Kubble told Snuffy that he needed 15, heavy-duty tractor rigs with 30 low boy trailers. Zane signed a trip ticket authorizing him to travel to Ben Hoa and Saigon. In addition, he gave him his jeep to use. He had radios to keep contact with the 362nd.

Zane established a command post in Ops. He had field gear flown to Long Thanh North for his XO and pilots. They were to remain as an advance party to oversee incoming traffic. As soon as a Hook completed its assigned missions, Zane recalled it to Phu Loi.

By dawn, Snuffy had 15 tractor-trailers loaded and ready to travel. In addition, he had 15 additional trailers on hand to load. When the loaded ones got to Long Thanh North, they would drop their trailers and race back to Phu Loi. By the time they arrived, the second set would be loaded.

Zane arranged MP armored car escorts for the caravan. There were two leading the column. Two at its middle and two following behind a tow truck in case a vehicle had mechanical troubles. Zane was short pilots so he manned a Hook and controlled the operation from it. While they carried loads from Phu Loi, he would check the convoys enroute to Long Thanh North. Upon delivering their load at Long Thanh North, Zane checked operations with Greenletter. When Zane delivered the first load, he contacted Greenletter.

"United Six Alpha, this is United Six, over," Zane transmitted.

"United Six, Six Alpha, over," Greenletter answered.

"Six Alpha, Six, The space between the revetments is too narrow for our Hooks. The revetments are moveable but extremely heavy. See what you can do, over," Zane instructed.

"Six, Six Alpha, roger out," Greenletter replied.

On Zane's return trip to Long Thanh North, he saw a tank pushing the cement revetments apart. The operator kept the tank's main gun pointed away from a revetment. He then pushed the tank between them, forcing them apart.

"United Six Alpha, this is United Six, over," Zane transmitted.

"Six, this is United Three, over," Captain Caldwell answered.

"Three, this is Six. Where's Alpha? Over," Zane asked.

"Six, Three. He's driving the tank. Over," Caldwell said.

"Three, Six. What unit provided the tank? Over," Zane asked.

"Six, Three. It's our tank. Over," Caldwell answered.

Zane thought about the situation for a moment. He didn't want any long explanations.

"Three, Six. Roger, Out," Zane acknowledged.

Zane's last load of equipment arrived at 15:00 hours. There were no incidents and no injured.

"Damn, I'm proud of those guys," he thought.

Captain Mullins came to Zane on the tarmac where he was watching his Hooks unload. Noise was almost unbearable with so many Hooks in one place. It was necessary for Mullins to yell.

"Sir, follow me to our new orderly room," Mullins said.

Sitting next to the tarmac, directly beside his aircraft's parking area, there was a long, narrow building of recent construction. There was one entry door midway of the structure's length. Mullins held it open for Zane.

Inside, Zane saw a wall on his left. It extended across the building. It had one entrance. The right side had the same arrangement. Above the left door, the words "United States Air Force Weather Station" appeared. Zane opened the door and entered.

Chilled air immediately engulfed Zane. His sweat soaked flight suit became cold as it began to dry. A waist high counter divided the room similar to most weather facilities in CONUS. Behind the counter, numerous Air Force personnel in crisp, pressed uniforms attended to various electronic devices.

An Air Force sergeant approached the counter and asked, "Can I help you major?"

"I don't think so sergeant. At least not now anyway. Are you folks planning on leaving anytime soon?" Zane asked.

"Oh no sir. We're here as long as the Radio Research Unit stays. I do not think they are leaving anytime soon," he answered.

"You mean the unit that Major Scott commands?" Zane asked.

"Yes, that's the one sir. Are you with those Hooks coming onto the field?" He asked.

"Sure thing. That's the 362nd Aviation Company. We're taking the CAC area. I'm the CO," Zane responded.

"Glad to have you with us. I'm Sergeant Fillinger, this shift's supervisor. We have around the clock weather services. Feel welcome to obtain weather briefings from us," Fillinger said.

"Thank you Sergeant Fillinger. We will do that," Zane replied.

Continuing, Zane added, "Excuse me. I have some work to do."

Once outside, Captain Mullins said excitedly, "Sir, that's our orderly room across the hall. Come look sir."

Zane noticed that Mullins was like a kid with a new toy. He brimmed with joy and excitement.

"He should damn it. These guys have worked in junk heaps long enough. It's time they had something decent," Zane thought.

Mullins threw open the door and ran inside. The place was huge. Plush desks and chairs were already in place. File cabinets and storage lockers lined the walls. Zane noted that the file cabinets had thermite destruction devices still in place.

"None of this stuff could have been on CAC's property book. If it were, they would have taken it with them. These guys have been trading favors for almost a decade. No wonder they can live like this," Zane thought.

Mullins' jabbering broke through Zane's train of thought. He looked for him. He emerged from a center door on the back wall.

"Sir, come look at this. You will not believer it. Come on sir," Mullins exhorted.

Zane stepped through the counter's opening and moved a position where he could see into the middle door. Inside, Mullins stood beside a flush toilet.

"Watch sir," Mullins exclaimed.

Mullins kept his smiling face toward Zane as he pushed down the toilet handle. As water gushed into the bowl, Mullins nodded his head up and down.

"See sir, it works. Can you believe this?" Mullins cried.

Continuing Mullins said, "There is a separate posh office for you and one for the XO. Both have private entrances to the toilet. Isn't this the greatest place."

Zane said, "Chris, I think you should watch for what little we could salvage from our other Orderly Room. Our last Hook is here and they are probably unloading now. Go take a look," Zane directed.

"You're right sir. I'm gone," Mullins said as he raced from the room.

Before Zane left, he flushed the toilet once.

Zane had no idea that an aviation unit in Viet Nam enjoyed such plush living conditions. However, everything being relative, the facilities far exceeded any the 362nd had in the past. It was with considerable regret that he had to begin an investigation so soon after his troops arrived.

The CID examined remains of his previous Orderly Room. According to them, the explosion took place outside of the building. They traced its point of origin to the air conditioner next to Zane's desk. The attackers used a plastic explosive known as C4. The wall, separating Zane's office from the rest of the building, adsorbed the blast. Shrapnel imbedded in the wall, rather than striking personnel. CID stated the person or person's intent was to kill Zane. His air conditioner was less than three feet from the explosion.

Two nights after arriving at Long Thanh North, someone knocked on the door to Zane's quarters. He retrieved his shotgun and walked to his door. He stood against the wall with his shotgun pointed at the door's latch.

"Yes?" Zane asked.

"Sir, it's Specialist Dietrick," the person whispered. "I need to talk to you sir."

Zane used his shotgun barrel to release the door's latch. He slipped the barrel between the door and the wall. With an easy nudge, the door opened into the room.

Seeing the gun barrel, Dietrick said nervously, "Sir, don't shoot. I'm here to help."

"Come in," Zane answered.

Dietrick stepped through the door while keeping his eye's on Zane's shotgun. He held his hands even with his shoulders and their palms facing Zane.

Zane directed, "Close the door and latch it."

When Dietrick complied, Zane lowered his shotgun. He nodded toward a sofa.

"Sorry about the shotgun Dietrick. I hope you understand," Zane said as Dietrick sat.

Dietrick worked in the motor pool. He arrived the same time that Zane did. He was one of the first persons he interviewed when he took command.

Dietrick's body was almost a copy of Zane's, except that he was ten yours younger. One of his amazing feats, for a man his size, was his ability to do back flips. He could stand directly in front of a person and do a complete back flip from a flat-footed start. It was impressive to watch.

He had massive forearms and was the reigning arm wrestling champ of the unit. During many of Zane's informal meetings with his soldiers, individuals called for a match between Zane and Dietrick.

Ultimately, they had to arm wrestle. Dietrick challenged Zane when they were alone in the motor pool at Bear Cat. Ultimately, Zane defeated Dietrick but his arm and shoulder ached for a week. Zane never mentioned the contest to a person. Dietrick remained the unit champion and he became a friend to Zane thereafter.

"Want a beer?" Zane asked.

"Thank you sir. That would be nice," Dietrick answered.

Zane opened two, giving one to Dietrick. Two easy chairs faced the sofa across a coffee table.

Zane sat and asked Dietrick. "How can you help?"

"Sir, I watched the sons of bitches do it. I would have told you immediately but we began moving from Phu Loi right after they destroyed your office. I had to drive the wrecker so I was on the road all the time. I saw Bredermeyer place C4 around your air conditioner. He embedded a detonator in it. Next, he ran wires across the ground to the barracks nearest your office. He pushed the wires through one of those holes that drug-heads use to dispose of their vials."

Dietrick stopped talking and took a long drink from his beer. He appeared apprehensive about something.

"Sir," Dietrick continued, "I did not see what happened in the barracks. However, another person who did see it said that Bredermeyer and PFC Haddock used a battery to set off the explosion. This person, who saw this, is scared. He is afraid to come forward because of what Bredermeyer might do to him. I told him not to worry that I could handle Bredermeyer. Nevertheless, he will testify as a witness if you guarantee his safety. He wants protection away from the unit. What it amounts to is this, send him away and he will appear in court when you need him."

Zane promptly replied, "I guarantee his safety. He will be out of here tonight and no one will know where he is."

"Sir, he is hiding outside. I will go get him. Please do not show that shotgun. He will run," Dietrick stated.

Dietrick returned with PFC Lundrum, who worked in the same shop that Bredermeyer did. He appeared panic stricken.

With both of them on the sofa, Zane asked. "Dietrick, do you want to go with PFC Lundrum?"

"No sir. I seldom cross paths with Bredermeyer. We live in separate barracks and he doesn't have a clue about me. Lundrum has to work with him and might give himself away. That's why he wants to leave."

Looking at Lundrum, Zane asked. "Do you mind telling me what you saw?"

"No sir. I saw Haddock give a large battery to Bredermeyer. It was a six-volt battery. You know the kind that fits a big electric lantern. Bredermeyer tied one wire to its negative terminal. Next, he touched the positive post and the C4 exploded. Haddock helped Bredermeyer pull the wires into the barracks. They hid the battery and wires in Haddock's wall locker. That' where they keep their C-4," Lundrum explained.

Zane interrupted and asked Lundrum, "Would you like a beer?"

"How about you Dietrick? Do you want another?" Zane continued.

"Yes sir. I appreciate it sir," Dietrick answered.

Zane could see Lundrum begin to relax and feel secure. He didn't think that Dietrick feared anything.

Lundrum said, "Sir, there's more."

"Like what?" Zane asked.

Lundrum told how Bredermeyer and Haddock had a personal arsenal. Over past months, the two gathered claymore mines, hand grenades, and detonation cord. They hid their contraband as soon as they arrived at Long Thanh North. They placed it between sandbags that surrounds the officers' quarters. They also had three fragmentation grenades in a bag with a string attached. They removed a filter screen from a pee tube and lowered the grenades into the tube. They tied the string to a screw protruding into the tube and replaced the screen.

"Dietrick you can leave any time you like. Lundrum, you stay with me tonight. I will have you out of here while Bredermeyer and Haddock are at formation. I'm going to plant a story that you were caught using heroin. That will explain your absence from work. Please don't worry son. You are safe with me," Zane said.

After formation the next day, Zane contacted CID and told them of the night's developments. They advised Zane that they would arrest the pair that night after duty. It was necessary for them to form an arrest team since the pair could have weapons. They would meet Zane at their barracks at 18:00 hours.

Zane, with his shotgun, stood in shadows near the pair's barracks as six jeeps and a truck arrived. Zane stepped into the open when they stopped. Drivers trained their headlights on the barracks. From the truck, four MPs dismounted with attack dogs. Two CID agents, in civilian clothes, left one of the jeeps while uniformed MPs dismounted from the others.

The attack dog teams plunged through the barracks' door first. Close behind them, MPs brandishing batons followed as the two CID agents remained with Zane behind the others and watched. Alarmed soldiers scattered from the onslaught. The dogs, restrained by leashes, leaped and snarled at any person in their way.

PFC Haddock, hearing the noise, stepped from his cubicle. He had a boot in one hand and a polishing cloth in the other. He made a grab for his wall locker but two dogs pinned him to the floor. The others began looking for Bredermeyer. He was not in the barracks.

One of the men told the MPs that Bredermeyer volunteered for perimeter duty that night. According to the guard roster, he occupied a bunker on the 362nd perimeter. This caused the arrest team concern because Bredermeyer would have an automatic, M-60 machine gun. He could do considerable harm if he resisted.

Zane contacted First Lieutenant Wheeler who was Officer of the Guard at the 362nd Command Bunker. According to Wheeler, Bredermeyer swapped duty with another soldier. Instead of being in a bunker, he now manned a guard tower.

At his disposal, he had a 40-mm grenade launcher, an M-60 machine gun, a night scope, and numerous hand grenades.

Further complicating matters, an innocent soldier was in the tower with him. If Bredermeyer resisted, the other soldier could receive wounds or die. Bredermeyer was capable of holding the man hostage. Lieutenant Wheeler had a solution.

"Sir, he knows I am Officer of the Guard tonight. Have one of the MPs drive our truck to the tower. I will ride with him and have a replacement for Bredermeyer. I will tell Bredermeyer that there is a Red Cross, emergency telegram for him at the Red Cross office. The weapons he has remain in the tower. When he comes down, I will let him in the truck first. That will put him between the MP and me. We will drive to the Red Cross office. As we pull into their parking area, we will subdue him. You and the others can hide behind the building and place him under arrest," Wheeler explained.

"That's good thinking Wheeler. I believe he will go for it," Zane commented.

The two CID agents agreed. The arrest group drove to the Red Cross building by traveling around the opposite side of the installation. Following this route, they would not be visible from Bredermeyer's tower. They watched from their hidden position as the guard vehicle approached. It slowed and suddenly stopped. The MP driver pulled Bredermeyer from the truck as the others handcuffed him.

Agent Malcomb said, "Major, we will hold the two overnight in the post stockade. Early tomorrow morning, we will take them to Long Binh Jail while you prepare charges. We found the hidden explosive and Bredermeyer's prints are on the battery. In addition, each of the pair had pieces of your air conditioner in their lockers. With the eyewitnesses, we have a solid case for attempted murder. I recommend that you prepare charges to that effect. It is important that you read them the charges as soon as possible."

"Thanks Malcomb. You and your men did a fine job tonight. This unit is a lot safer for it," Zane said.

"You're welcome major. It's a bitch when you have to fight the NVA and malcontents at the same time. Sleep well tonight," Malcomb said, as he departed.

Two days later, Zane and First Sergeant Kubble arrived at Long Binh Jail to file charges. Military law required their reading charges to them and providing each a copy. When an MP admitted Zane and Kubble to Bredermeyer's cell, they found a changed person. His false, hard outside shell no longer existed. Underneath, a scared teenager existed.

"Sir, I am so sorry. I didn't mean to hurt anyone," he wailed as tears flooded his eyes. "My defense attorney said that I could get 40 years in jail. My God, I will be 59 when I finish my time. This is the end of my life."

Zane sat beside him on a steel plate that served as a bed. He reached around his shoulders and felt the young man's body trembling with fear.

"Son, there were people almost killed by your actions. If I had been at my desk, you would be facing murder charges. My family would no longer have a husband and father. In the next room, there were others. You choose to take their lives because of a petty rating on a piece of paper. In less than two years, that paper would have no affect on your life."

"However, by what you did, others would have died and death is permanent son. Each person is responsible for their own actions. No one endowed you with the right to deprive people of their lives. A few days ago, I could have helped you. Now, it is out of my hands. I must read the charges to you," Zane stated as he arose.

Zane doubted that Bredermeyer heard the words as he read the charges to him. He sat with his face buried in his hands with his body constantly convulsing with sobs.

Finished reading, Zane place his hand on Bredermeyer's shoulder and asked. "Is there something I can get for you or do?"

Bredermeyer wiped away his tears with the back of his shirt's sleeve and mumbled, "Sir, my dad is a full colonel in the Air Force. I wrote him last night and I wrote another letter."

While removing a paper from his shirt pocket, he asked. "Sir, this is the other letter. Will you please read it at formation? Please," Bredermeyer begged.

Zane took the neatly folded, yellow page and answered, "I will read it first. If I believe it is appropriate, I will read it to them."

Grabbing Zane around his waist, Bredermeyer fell to his knees pleading, "Read it now. I must know if you are going to read it at formation before you leave me. Please, sir."

Zane unfolded Bredermeyer's letter and began to read,

Major Zane,

At this time, I want to extend my most sincere apology to you personally for the inconvenience I caused you. Not just with the bombing but for all of my actions. I realize now how very immature it all was and how ridiculous it must appear to you. I thought that I had all the answers and I was going to set the Army straight.

I am ashamed of how I acted and am actually very embarrassed. I hope that you can understand how I really feel about this and I hope some day that you will forgive me. I want you to understand also that my actions do not reflect that of my entire family because they don't. I guess I've always been sort of the black sheep. I wrote my parents the first day I was here and it was the hardest thing I've done in my life. I hope that no one else in the company has to go through this themselves. I ask you that, if people come to turn in anything not to do anything to them because I told Larry Vickey and Dough Larsen to spread the word to turn everything in or throw it away. In any case, they are to get rid of it. I would appreciate your

I am hoping that when I go to trial I don't get too much time because I want to try and make something out of myself. I was planning to get married next fall to one of the best women in the world. But now that is gone down the drain because I will be in prison.

I want you to believe me when I tell you we didn't want to hurt anyone. I have never been one to want to hurt or kill anyone so please believe me. Thank you for taking the time to talk to us at the MP station.

Sincerely,
Specialist Bredermeyer

Zane refolded Bredermeyer's letter. He gave a questioning look at Kubble who gave an affirmative nod.

Placing a hand on Bredermeyer's shoulder, Zane said, "Son, Top says okay and he hasn't read you letter. Therefore, you see that people do have faith in you. I will read your letter to the company at our next formation. After that, I will make sure that no one has access to it but me. Your letter is an incriminating document. A zealous prosecutor could use it against you as a confession. I will make sure that does not happen."

Zane called for an MP to unlock Bredermeyer's cell. As Zane, and the others, started walking away, Zane glanced back toward Bredermeyer's cell. Bredermeyer was standing at attention and rendering a salute. Zane stopped and turned to face him. He returned his salute and left LBJ.

As the 362nd began occupying their unit area, everyone found facilities exceeded their greatest expectations. The Mess Hall had the latest equipment to prepare food for large groups. One item, a stainless steel, refrigerated milk dispenser was the most popular. Soldiers stood in line to get a glass of cold milk. They sat in air conditioned comfort while eating. The gargantuan building had a commercial grade, air conditioning systems capable of cooling even the usually hot kitchen. The Mess Sergeant was ecstatic.

The installation was large enough to warrant a separate installation commander. As such, the base qualified for non-appropriated funds to operate three clubs. They were the Lower Four, NCO, and Officer's clubs. Non-appropriated funds are not tax dollars. They are funds earned from service members spending their money in base facilities such as a Post Exchange. Slush funds became non-existent.

The installation commander, Lieutenant Colonel Neal A. Gray, appointed Major Zane custodian of the central post fund and the operation of the three clubs. An accountant, WO1 Weyland Phillips kept records for the fund and the clubs. Upon Zane's appointment, he sent for Mr. Phillips.

"Come in Mr. Phillips and have a seat," Major Zane said.

Phillips, with his arms piled high with ledgers, stumbled into Zane's office. Phillips placed the ledgers on Zane's new conference table. The other one did not survive the Phu Loi explosion. Zane moved from his desk to the conference table where Phillips had current ledgers opened.

"Mr. Phillips, I need you to confirm something for me. I've examined the post fund's balance sheets. They indicate that there is $240,000 in the base's fund. Is that correct?" Zane asked.

"You're correct sir," Phillips replied.

Continuing, Zane asked. "Hypothetically, if this installation closes, what happens to that money?"

"It reverts to the central fund in Saigon sir," Phillips answered.

What Phillips did not know, as did few others on the installation, was that the installation would close by next August. Zane already had a warning order to start training VNAF personnel to fly Hooks. In August, Zane would turn his Hooks over to the Vietnamese Air Force.

Zane said, "Mr. Phillips, since the fund belongs to the soldiers, I want them to benefit from it. I want a live band in each club Monday through Friday evenings. On Saturdays, schedule a floorshow in each club. These men are flying their butts off and need a place to relax when they get a chance."

"Yes sir, I will get right on that," Phillips said as he started to gather his ledgers.

"One moment please," Zane said. "Do you have a club menu handy? If not, I have one you can use."

"Uh, sir, I have one," Phillips replied.

"I have examined your inventory list and club prices. Why do we have almost $500,000 worth of food and beverage products in inventory?" Zane questioned.

"Well sir, its buildup took many years. Previous fund officers did not show an interest," Phillips said as he developed a concerned look.

"Here's what we are going to do," Zane began. "Open the clubs at 04:00 hours, seven days a week. Have a hot meal for any crewman who wants it. A full breakfast will cost no more than 50 cents."

Phillips gasped and promptly replied, "Sir, that will cause a drastic reduction in inventory."

"You're getting the idea now Phillips," Zane commented. "Sell beer at 20 cents a can. Cut wine prices by 50 percent. Report to me in one month with the balance sheets. That's all I have."

Phillips left the room mumbled phrases. Some of them Zane could discern.

"We will be broke in a year. He's going to wipe us out."

Optimistically, Zane hoped to do just that. His troops earned it.

When General Hamlet insisted that capital properties remain behind, he could not have known what the 362nd would inherit.

The most powerful and significant item was a fully operational M48A3 tank. Captain Greenletter used it to organize the extremely heavy aircraft revetments. No one claimed the vehicle and it had no unit markings.

"Sir, it was setting behind the mess hall. It was there during our inventory. No one listed it because they figured it belonged to a nearby armored outfit. Sir, there are no American armored units in Viet Nam. It had a full diesel fuel load so I took it," Greenletter explained.

"I used it to gouge a pit midway in our defense perimeter and drove the tank into it. Now, only its turret remains above ground. On the turret's top, there is a 50-cal. machine gun mount with a protective shield for its operator," Greenletter continued.

"Sir, there's more," he said. "When supply personnel moved into the vacated supply building, they found over 200 rounds for the tank's main gun. In addition, they noticed loose ceiling boards. When they tried to repair them, one of the boards fell. A 50-cal. machine gun fell with it. When they checked farther, they found four more 50-cal. machine guns in the overhead crawl space. They're rusty but work fine. Top has a crew cleaning them. Snuffy is already scrounging ammo from the ARVN. They have plenty."

"Hidden among crates in another building, our guys found a 4.2-inch mortar. Hidden with it were high explosive ammunition and illumination flares. First Sergeant Kubble plans to train a crew to operate it during ground attacks. First, they will fire illumination rounds to expose advancing forces. With the perimeter illuminated, they can begin firing high explosive shells. With support from the tank, and the 50-cal. machine guns, the area in front of the 362nd will be a massive killing zone."

A persistent worry for Zane was a ground attack. His people were crew chiefs, flight engineers, avionics, and other skilled personnel. They were not infantry and he had no artillery. It was essential that they stop the enemy before they get to the Chinooks. At Long Thanh North, he began to feel more at ease. The arrival of one man let him sleep at night.

CW4 Robert Davenport was an airborne, ranger, and former Special Forces member. He went through flight school as a senior CW3. He received a promotion soon after his graduation. He volunteered to install a new perimeter when he wasn't flying missions.

"Sir, the NVA and VC watch every move we make. I want them to watch me install our defensive position. Once they know, they are less likely to hit us," he explained.

At considerable risk to him and his workers, Davenport began his defense perimeter over 500 meters from the nearest bunker and tower. He had to remove numerous mines to install defensive equipment.

He examined the terrain with care. He looked for low places where an attacker could obtain protection. He placed a small flag on each. Next, he went to the mortar and determined firing data to hit each flag. He wrote these settings on a placard and waterproofed it. He left it with the mortar so that firing personnel could put rounds into the protected area. He did the same for the tank's main gun.

In the bunkers, he determined the best direction and elevation for machine guns to provide grazing fire. Grazing fire was about 18 inches above ground. He drove a stake into the bunker's firing port. When told by the command bunker to use final defensive fire, the machine gun operator only had to turn his weapon to hit the stake and pull his trigger. He interlocked grazing fires by adjusting stakes in each bunker. With his basic work done, Davenport began installing obstructions.

He seeded the outmost area with antipersonnel mines. These looked exactly like golf tees. Filled with high explosives and a pressure activated detonator they were mean devices. Davenport pushed them into the ground with his thumb. Maintaining pressure, he made a one-half turn clockwise, which released a spring and activated the mine. When a person stepped on it, the concave face directed the explosion's force into a narrow, forceful beam. It did not kill. The device shattered a person's shinbone to his knee.

Overlapping the miniature mines, Davenport installed razor wire. Razor wire replaced barbed wire. Instead of barbs, it had miniature razors to cut and maim. It came in rolls that unrolled to form coil-like rows about three feet high. He put down a base of three rows. Atop these, he placed two rows. A single row topped the barrier.

Inside the wire, nearer the perimeter, Davenport constructed a ditch three feet wide and three feet deep. In the ditch, he placed napalm drums end to end. Each had an electrical detonator with a ten second delay. He strung wire from the detonators to the command bunker. Slightly below the bunker's main view port, he made a detonator switch panel.

While crude, the switch panel proved simple and effective. Davenport drove nails through a six-inch wide board in pairs opposite each other. He numbered them one through 25 with each pair representing one napalm drum. He interconnected one nail row with copper wire. This wire he hooked to a heavy duty, 12-volt battery's negative terminal. He rigged the other nail row the same way and connected it to the battery's positive terminal.

A person in the command post could detonate a single drum or the entire row. All that was necessary was to make contact with a conductive material between two facing nails. A piece of wire would do fine.

Next to the napalm row, Davenport constructed another razor wire barrier like the outer one. In the bottom row, he placed claymore mines. He placed 80 claymores and made a detonation panel in the command bunker like the one for the napalm. Davenport's skilled, hard work would benefit the 362nd more than they could have ever anticipated.

Flight operations did not stop because of defense perimeter construction or any other project. Hook missions always came first. Zane completed the delayed rehearsal for evacuation in Saigon. Each pilot did practice approaches day and night, while wearing gas masks.

Battalion headquarters canceled the Cambodian mission. Zane never asked what their alternate plan was. He had enough to do.

Cockpit time was not as long as it was in 1967 and 1968. They saw few 16-hour days. Nevertheless, 12-hour days were common.

In addition to transporting ARVN personnel, there were numerous relocation missions. These consisted of transporting entire villages to more secure locations. The NVA, and the few remaining VC, conducted terror missions at night. They gathered village and province officials, church leaders, and teachers and marched them into the jungle. They summarily executed them for cooperating with the South Vietnamese government.

Wherever Task Force Gary Owen went, the 362nd kept them supplied. Hueys, Loaches, and Cobra Gunships needed fuel, ammunition, and everything needed to fight a war. The Hookers got it to them.

While at Long Thanh North, the 362nd received its first attack mission. Captain Greenletter and Captain Caldwell brought details to Zane.

"Sir, we have a mission tomorrow that I know nothing about," Caldwell said.

Greenletter shrugged his shoulders indicating that he was at a loss. Caldwell handed the mission request to Zane. He flipped through its pages.

"Nothing new about this," Zane thought. "To get this mission done we will have to work all night."

Their mission was to napalm NVA positions. A company sized NVA infantry unit was dug in and putting mortar fire on Tay Ninh. Tay Ninh was a major rearm and refuel base near the Cambodian border. Weather was so bad that the Air Force couldn't make their runs.

"Gather around, I will show you how we need to do this," Zane said.

Using a legal pad, Zane turned it sideways for a landscape view. He began sketching. When finished, he turned it 180 degrees so the others could see it.

"Terry, I suggest you use Snuffy to help us get some of what we will need," Zane said. "Here's what we need."

Using his pencil as a pointer, he indicated a wide rectangle that he drew and explained, "This is a rack with rollers to handle napalm canisters. You saw the ones we put in our perimeter. This device will allow the crew to safely control canisters like those."

Continuing Zane said, "We need rollers in a metal platform four foot wide. I saw CW1 Phillips helping unload some beer cases at the club. The guy on the truck pitched the cases onto rollers and they traveled with ease to Phillips. These rollers look like those on roller skates. I'm sure you've seen them."

"Yes, I know exactly the kind you mean," Greenletter answered.

"Build the platform about two thirds the length of a Hook's cargo compartment. Weld one-half inch uprights to the roller base. Place them four feet apart. Along the top, weld angle iron to the uprights. This will keep the canisters from sliding off the rollers and make them travel in a straight line," Zane explained.

Using his pencil, Zane sketched a rod attached to the device's upper railing. It extended upward and toward the ship's front.

"Gents, this is a critical item. It's small, no longer than six inches. This is what arms the drums as they leave the ship's rear. Each canister uses a Mark 10 detonator, which activates in ten seconds. You will have to make lanyards for the detonators. I will bet you a $100 that Ordnance will show up without lanyards so make them."

"Attach a metal, D ring to a nylon rope or strap. Make it six feet long. Attach a snap ring on the lanyard's other end. The Mark 10 activates by removing a pin. Attach the snap ring to the Mark 10's activation pin. Place the D ring over the six-inch, rod at the delivery rack's rear. When the canister goes out the Hook's rear, the lanyard pulls the pin so that the thing doesn't arm inside the ship. Any questions so far?" Zane asked.

"I have one sir," Caldwell said.

"How high should the hook be to obtain maximum effectiveness on the target?" Caldwell asked.

"Good question Earnest," Zane replied. "The Hook must be level at 1,500 feet above ground level. I don't mean 1,500 feet as indicated on the altimeter. That's above mean sea level."

Greenletter asked. "How do we determine that?"

"Look at your map. Determine the target elevation and add 1,500 feet. That's as close as you can get with a SWAG," Zane explained.

"A SWAG, sir?" The pair asked at the same time.

Grinning, Zane answered, "A scientific wild ass guess."

Zane interrupted their laughter and said, "Get on this right away. I will fly the lead ship. Make sure the FE gets a detailed briefing on this. Sometime at the club I will tell you a war story why."

The next day, Zane approached the target area in the lead Hook. He kept a close watch in the cargo compartment by using his rear view mirror.

"How's it going back there Randy?" Zane asked his FE.

"Fine sir, except for one of the strap hangers," Flight Engineer (FE) Randy Cone answered over the intercom.

"What's wrong with him?" Zane asked.

"I get no respect sir. He just barfed all over my ship," Cone answered.

Zane, flying as aircraft commander, looked at his First Pilot, CW3 Billy Curls, and grinned. Curls was another 101st Airborne pilot transferred to the 362nd when the 101st withdrew from Viet Nam. With his experience, he would soon make AC.

Curls had little use for straphangers. Usually these people flew along on a mission for pleasure or to oversee some mission. Usually, they got in the way and were a nuisance.

"Make him clean it up," Curls told Cone.

"Sir, I can't. He's an Ordnance captain," Cone replied. "He says he is in charge of this mission."

"Oh, that's different. How about we incapacitate him?" Curls asked.

FE Cone replied, "Have at it sir."

Gently, Curls began to move his cyclic in small circles, which caused the Chinook to begin a slow, rolling movement from side to side and fore and aft. It was much like being aboard a ship at sea with a steady swell moving the ship. It was hardly noticeable but would usually induce nausea in persons not used to it.

"Chief, you are a mean man," Zane said grinning.

Through a rear view mirror, Zane could see into the cargo compartment. Napalm drums sat in a neat row on his left. On the other side, he saw a captain retching into his helmet.

Chuckling, Zane said, "Chief, those clouds do not look good."

Traveling west toward Cambodia, Zane expected low ceilings Air Force Personnel provided a weather briefing before they departed Long Thanh North. They predicted low ceilings and rain.

"Roger that," Curls replied. "I'm at 4,000 feet. Looks like we have to go lower."

"Try to skim the cloud bottoms. Let's stay out of the weather. There are no radar facilities in this area," Zane instructed.

Zane relayed instructions to the Hook following them, "United four eight seven, United five four three, over."

"Five four three, four eight seven, over," the other AC answered.

"Five four three, skim the cloud bottoms but keep me in sight, over," Zane instructed.

"Five four three, roger," the other AC acknowledged.

"Chief, that's Tay Ninh at 12 o'clock. I'll try and get our controller," Zane said.

Zane changed his FM radio frequency to that of the ground commander and transmitted, "Lizard six, United five four three, over."

Zane continued his efforts to contact the ground commander without success. After each transmission, he only heard static. After passing over Tay Ninh, Chief Curls started to circle. Zane stopped him.

"Chief, we're too low. Do not establish a pattern. Who knows what may be tracking us," Zane said.

"Roger, sir," Curls replied. "We're down another 1,000 feet sir."

Zane's FM receiver blared, "Hook over Tay Ninh, this is Lizard Six, over."

"Roger, Lizard Six, United five four three, flight of two over," Zane answered.

"This is Lizard Six. The target has moved. Use coordinates 3389 6714, over," the ground commander advised.

"United five four three, standby," Zane answered as he began checking his map.

At the specified coordinates, Zane found a road junction. Looking from his window, he found the junction on the ground. A village surrounded the road crossing.

"Lizard six, United five four three. Can you mark with white smoke? Over," Zane asked.

"Lizard six, roger that, standby," the ground commander advised.

White smoke erupted in the road junction. This confirmed Zane's concern for the village. He pressed his intercom switch.

"Okay, everyone listen up. We're going to see if we can make a run. We may be too low. Cone, watch that Ordnance guy. Do not allow him to remove a detonator pin," Zane instructed.

"Four eight seven, five four three, over," Zane transmitted.

"Four eight seven, over," came the reply.

"Remain clear. We will try to make a run. If we dump, you try it. Do not use our flight path, over," Zane instructed.

"Okay chief, bring it around to a heading of 260. Try to maintain 2,500," Zane told Curls.

"Roger," Curls answered.

As they approached the road junction, Zane saw that Curls had to descend to maintain visual contact. Even then, they flew in and out of clouds.

Suddenly, Cone cried, "Tracers at six o'clock. One thousand yards this side of the road junction."

"Bring her around hard right to 360 Chief," Zane ordered.

As Chief Curls complied, Zane started receiving unusual background noise on his FM radio. The noise grew in volume and then faded. Lizard Six was trying to contact him but the noise overpowered his transmissions. Able to see the road junction, Zane saw green tracers moving in an apparent arc but falling short of their aircraft. They were coming from a tree line where Cone reported them.

Furthermore, Zane saw women and children watching from the village. The children waved as the older people watched.

"Lizard Six, Five four three, over," Zane transmitted.

"Five four three, this is Lizard Six. Do you have a fix on the target? Over," the ground commander asked.

"Lizard Six, five four three, roger, be advised that location has women and children. West of their location, there's a AAA weapon, over," Zane replied.

While waiting for a response, Zane contacted the other Hook, "Five eight seven, five four three. Did you get a fix on the AAA? Over."

"Five eight seven, roger. This weather is putting us too low. Advise, over," the other AC transmitted.

"Five four three, we're taking the AAA site. Do not hit the road junction and village. Stay as high as you can. We'll go first on a heading of 310. If our load doesn't blow, we'll try tracers. You use a different heading and try the same if necessary," Zane directed.

"Here goes Chief. You heard and understand?" Zane asked.

"Roger that," Curls answered.

"Door gunners, when we break, pour as much as you can where you see the drums hit. FE watch those Ordnance guys," Zane instructed.

"Chief, red line the airspeed as we cross," Zane said.

"Will do," Curls answered.

Zane saw green tracers streaming skyward in front of them. He knew they could not see his ship, they were guessing based on sound. Nevertheless, to get the napalm on target, they had to go over the position. He judged their altitude to be 500 feet low.

Slightly before reaching position, Zane said, "Start pushing them out Cone."

Continuing to watch in his mirror, Zane saw the last drum exit his ship and the FE yelled, "Clear."

Curls made a hard right turn so the right door gunner could see the target. This put Zane where he could not see the target area. When he pushed his intercom switch, he could hear the right M-60 firing.

After turning 180 degrees, Zane saw no tracers but there was no napalm either. Immediately after five eight seven dumped its drums, it broke to its left. Directly behind it, massive balls of fire began billowing upward. Suddenly, secondary explosions began to erupt. Zane could see rocket motors burning as they flew in various directions. They had to be Rocket Propelled Grenades (RPG) exploding from the fire.

Lizard Six was screaming obscenities over his radio. He kept yelling that they had not hit the target.

Ignoring Lizard Six, Zane transmitted, "Five eight seven, four five six, over."

"Five eight seven," came the reply.

"Five four three. Let's piss on the fire and call in the dogs. This coon hunt is over," Zane transmitted.

"Sir, this Ordnance captain is raising hell because we didn't put the drums on the road junction," FE Cone said.

"Okay, fine. Don't worry about it. Curls, rock the man to sleep," Zane said.

Within five minutes, Zane saw the captain with his head over a steel helmet. He could see his shoulders tighten with every retch.

The next morning, after formation, Mullins stuck his head inside Zane's office door and said excitedly, "Sir, General Hamlet, Lieutenant Colonel Smith, and a Lieutenant Colonel I don't know just landed. They are headed this way."

"Damn, guess I'm in deep trouble about that mission yesterday," Zane thought. "I might as well see how much trouble that I'm in."

Chapter Forty Five

March 1972

The nation, which forgets its defenders, will be itself forgotten.
Calvin Coolidge (1872–1933), U.S. Republican politician, president.
Speech, 27 July 1920,
Northampton, Massachusetts, accepting the
Republican vice-presidential nomination.

Supreme Commander of the Southern Front, Nguyen Van Anh, watched as his four year effort would soon free South Viet Nam and unify his country. Few Americans remained. Their estimate was 70,000 but they were mostly advisers and support units. It was time to take control. After South Viet Nam lost the National Liberation Front fighters in the Tet Offensive of 1968, his North Vietnamese forces had to shoulder the burden. Meanwhile, it took three years to form units capable of defeating South Viet Nam' ARVN force. It required another year to move them into position.

Anh recalled General Giap's words, "It is time to use conventional forces against the South. We have enough artillery, tanks, infantry, and antiaircraft units to overcome them. With over 120,000 freedom fighters and 1,200 tanks, we can defeat them. There will be three major fronts. We will attack Quang Tri and Hue in the north, Kontum in the Central Highlands and An Loc in the south. I am making you commander of the southern invasion. It has the strongest political objective. I am relying on you to establish a Communist capital in Binh Long Province. Next, we will proceed along QL3 and take Saigon."

"I do not think we will have to take Saigon by force. President Thieu will abdicate or leave the country. Those remaining will recognize our new government," Anh contemplated.

"By the time we destroy his military forces, we will control Quang Tri and Hue in the north. Kontum will be ours in the Highlands. After destroying his forces protecting Saigon, there will be a Communist capital city in An Loc. Thieu's government will fall with us a scant 60 miles from Saigon," Anh thought.

Nevertheless, Anh's confidence had one bothersome factor. His uncle, Major Nguyen Van Diem caused it. Nagging in the back of his mind was a memory. It was a recollection of the ferocity with which some ARVN fought. In 1968, when Hue fell to their attack, an ARVN unit in the Citadel continued to fight. Eventually, they succumbed but with terrible losses. The leader of this small group was a Vietnamese Airborne Ranger who continued to lead despite life threatening wounds. Finally, he lapsed into unconsciousness and became a prisoner. He was the same person that Anh saw on the prisoner list.

Anh had staff members search until they found him. He was in a POW holding area north of the DMZ. By the time Anh got to him, he had undergone a week of horrendous interrogation. He hardly recognized the man who he used to visit in Hanoi as a young man. Now, he was a wasted shell of a human much less that of a man. He was near death. Only through his intervention did he survive.

Anh had him moved to Hanoi under the pretense of obtaining valuable information. He instructed POW facility operators to treat his wounds and return his strength. No one knew they were relatives. After three months, Anh met with him in an interrogation chamber. Their reunion was bittersweet.

Seeing Diem in shackles hurt Anh deeply. He lived with this man as part of his family. He ate from his table and listened to his advice. Diem taught him how to prosper and provide for a family in the city. He played with his children as if they were brothers and sisters rather than cousins.

"How could Diem fight so hard against us," Anh had wondered. "He lived through the Japanese and French occupations. He protected my mother and hid her. Many times his mother, Xuan, told how Diem cared for her. She also told of Diem bringing Minh Thanh to her."

Diem confirmed most of what Anh learned from the note in his boot left by Vinh. Furthermore, he gave details of Minh Thanh's marriage and the happy days Diem, Vinh, and Minh Thanh had together with her husband. Diem was supposed to meet them in Saigon to celebrate Tet in 1968. The North Vietnamese invasion trapped him at Hue. Diem explained that Vinh was now an Airborne Ranger Regimental Commander with the rank of Major. Anh could not visualize his young brother in this capacity. His remembrance was a skinny boy who distributed rice seedlings during planting. Now, he was the enemy.

After six months as a POW, Diem was one of few allowed to go to a reeducation camp. Once there, he was beyond Anh's help. Anh hoped that he was well and cooperating. However, Anh found it hard to believe that Diem would change. He fought too hard at Hue and never revealed anything during his interrogations. Perhaps, he might feign reeducation as a means to survive but he would forever remain a staunch anticommunist. The loss of his family fired his resistance.

"Sir," Anh's senior aide said, "Your commanders are waiting."

"Thank you. I will join them in a moment," Anh responded.

Opening his notebook, Anh read the designations of his units. He found their titles somewhat amusing.

"Two VC and one NVA division, who do we think we are fooling? The 5th and 9th VC Divisions have mostly NVA soldiers manning them. We keep trying to convince the world that this is a fight by South Vietnamese to reunite our country. We might as well designate the 7th NVA Division as a VC Division," he thought.

On his walk to meet with his subordinate commanders, Anh found it difficult to believe that they remained undetected. In one year, he gathered over 60,000 troops, and their equipment, in eastern Cambodia.

"They must know we are here but they have not reinforced Tay Ninh or Bien Long Provinces," he thought. "We can expect ARVN forces to start reinforcing at any time."

Anh's headquarters was less than three kilometers from Tay Ninh's northeastern border with Cambodia. To the north and east four kilometers was Binh Long Province's border with Cambodia. Despite many ARVN probes, its presence remained undetected as far as Anh knew.

"Take your seats please," Anh stated as he entered his underground briefing room.

Anh sat in a homemade, mahogany chair that he liked. He asked those in the room to gather near his front in a semicircle. This was his preference when talking with his commanders. This let them know that he was one of them.

His protégé, Artillery General Nhog, sat on his right. He commanded the 69th Artillery Command. He had three regiments. One consisted of standard artillery while the other used rockets. The third was an antiaircraft (AAA) regiment.

Nhog would make air support for the ARVN extremely costly. He had a variety of AAA weapons never before used during an organized attack in the south. One weapon held great promise, the SA7, heat seeking missile. An individual fired it from his shoulder. There were few on hand but many were on their way. Anh precluded their use during their initial attack. When more arrived, he would allow their deployment throughout his units. He expected these heat seekers to stop close air support completely.

Seated directly to Anh's front was General Bien, Commander of the elite 9th VC Division. Of the three division commanders, Bien was the only one to attend senior command training in the USSR. He was an assistant division commander in the advance against Quang Tri in 1968. Repeatedly decorated for valor, he was also a Central Committee Member of the Communist Party. After the 1968 Offensive, he went for two years training in the Soviet Union. Subsequently, he was a Special Advisor to General Giap for a year. After that, he commanded the 9th Division and trained it to become a premier unit. An Loc became his unit's objective. Once taken, it would become a provisional Communist Capital in the south. In addition, it would provide a staging area for attacks to take Saigon.

General Thong, 5th Division Commander, sat at Anh's left front. He fought at Dien Bien Phu where he received a promotion to lieutenant from sergeant for bravery. Of the three commanders, Thong had less formal education. However, he had innate leadership abilities. Soldiers sought his unit because of his excellent reputation as a wise commander. He did not sacrifice troops to gain objectives. He demonstrated a flair for using firepower and maneuver to take objectives with minimum troop loss.

Thong had the mission to take Loc Ninh. Subsequently, he would move south to attack An Loc. With the 9th on the south and the 5th on the north, An Loc would soon fall. The 5th Division would also secure the 9th Division's left flank.

The 7th NVA Division Commander, General Hieu, sat at Anh's left. Hieu was a Na Son veteran and fought at Dien Bien Phu. His family's lineage contained many great commanders. His son, an infantry captain, was part of the Quang Tri force. Some considered Hieu suspect because he did not readily embrace Communism. He defended his position that military professionals should not adhere to any government's politics. His desire for reunification drove him to continue their fight. His proven combat record attenuated everything said to his detriment.

Hieu's 7th Division would attack from Tay Ninh Province and proceed south of An Loc to QL-13. His forces would stop any resupply or reinforcement from the south along QL-13. He would take Chon Thanh, south of Tau O Bridge, and interdict any supply or reinforcement attempts from Lai Kai farther south. His position would secure 9th Division's right flank.

Anh began, "Our advance started this morning to take Quang Tri and Hue. ARVN opposition was light and unprepared. ARVN units surrendered rather than fight. The situation there is promising."

Continuing, Anh said, "Our diversionary attacks will begin the night of 4 April to the south of our main attack. The next morning, you will proceed as planned. Within the next 48 hours, have your attached armor elements in place. I expect attacks to be fierce. This is our opportunity to overcome what few units are in Bien Long Province. They do not expect large scale attacks. Heavy artillery fire and armor have a significant shock effect. They have never seen it and they will crumble."

Anh arose and began moving from general to general, shaking their hands. He gave each commander a prolonged look with a soft smile of confidence.

While moving among them, he explained, "This is our last group meeting until we establish a provisional capital in An Loc. I expect every unit to continue our attack to Saigon if the situation permits. Return to your units. There is little time remaining."

Anh returned to his office and sent for his intelligence officer, Colonel Biap. He arrived in ten minutes.

"Have a seat colonel. Did the patrols find what I asked about?" Anh asked.

Biap sat on a folding field stool and replied, "Yes sir, they found the orchard that you mentioned. With so many rubber plantations, it is surprising to discover one dedicated to macadamia nuts. A considerable number of people from Loc Ninh work for the owner and like him even though he is French."

Anh thought for a moment and asked. "This Frenchman, does he have a family with him?"

"Yes sir, he does. He has a Vietnamese wife and two children. They have been there over five years," Biap replied.

Biep added, "Their main house received major damage during the Tet Offensive. They have not completed repairs because working their trees takes so much time."

Anh arose and examined a map that showed Tay Ninh and Binh Long Provinces. Rubbing his chin, he appeared to be in deep thought.

Returning to his field table, he asked. "Would it suffice as a forward command post?"

Colonel Biep responded immediately, "It would make an excellent one when Loc Ninh is under our control. I would not consider it until then general."

"Good, contact General Thong. Advise him to by pass the main house and do no harm to its occupants. Depending upon how soon he secures Loch Ninh, I will move my forward command post there."

Smiling, Anh said, "Thank you Colonel Biep. I will inform the Chief of Staff so that he can make preparations."

Anh reflected upon what Diem told him about Minh Thanh. He could hear him say the words that lifted his heart after searching for so many years. If only Xuan could have heard them.

"Minh Thanh is alive and happy," Diem said. "She married a retired French Legionnaire and moved to a plantation near Loc Ninh. She loves her husband and son. You should see them together. Minh Thanh glows with joy when she is with them. She has land and helps work it. There was nothing left for her in Muong Valley."

"Hopefully, if all goes well, I will see her in less than a week. I do not think they will have time to flee. The plantation is too close to the border. General Thong's forces will bypass it in less than an hour when they attack," Anh thought.

Anh contacted his Chief of Staff, Lieutenant General Hiep. He related his desires regarding the plantation. Hiep gave assurance that Anh could occupy it as soon as Thong's forces passed. Loch Ninh would not be a hindrance to their advance.

With little sleep for the last ten days, weariness descended upon Anh and he began to doze. While in twilight sleep, he doubted that Minh Thanh would remember him with his white hair and aged appearance. As he slept, he saw Minh Thanh and Vinh swinging a water basket between them bringing life from the Nam Youm to their fields.

"What the hell was a 37-mm, radar controlled AAA weapon doing near Tay Ninh?" Major Vinh asked. "How can you be certain? The place burned to a crisp."

The Montengard patrol leader rolled his eyes to the U.S. Special Forces captain for help. Vietnamese often misunderstood his dialect. He hoped that Captain Riley, who sent him on the mission, would help. He didn't.

Trying again, he said, "We found the barrel and the gun's undercarriage. Napalm melted the rest. Also, there were two trucks loaded with RPGs hidden near it that exploded. The entire area burned. The only human remains were charred teeth."

He could see no signs of recognition on the man's face. Fraught with frustration, he tried a seldom-used dialect from the northern tribes. As he explained about the AAA weapon, instant recognition flooded the Vietnamese officer's face.

Major Vinh was at Tay Ninh when they started receiving mortar and rocket attacks. Parts of his Airborne Ranger regiment were conducting long-range patrol operations in the area. He was there to debrief them as they returned. One team said they heard an AAA weapon firing and then a helicopter. Next, there was a large explosion and tremendous heat. They did not stop to investigate because they would miss their pickup ship. Later, he learned that Montengard patrols, controlled by U.S. Special Forces, requested napalm missions in the area. The request originated from a report by their Montengard patrol. Vinh flew to Long Thanh North to meet with U.S. Special Forces to try and learn more about the event. They allowed him to talk to their Montengard patrol leader for that mission.

"Thank you Captain Riley," Vinh said. "We had a small language problem until he changed to a Tia dialect. I need to know more about this situation. I suspect that it is significant."

"Perhaps you would like to talk to the pilots who flew the mission?" Captain Riley asked.

"That might help," Vinh replied.

"The Chinook unit across the airfield flew it. I can get you a ride over there if you like," Riley suggested.

"Thank you. I would like to do that," Vinh answered.

The Long Thanh North Special Forces' Base had a back gate that allowed direct access to the main base. Vinh went to the 362nd Orderly room and asked to speak with their Operations Officer.

"I am sorry major," Captain Mullins said. "The CO, XO, and Ops Officer are in a meeting with General Hamlet. I have no idea when they will finish."

Disappointed, Vinh left instructions on how to contact him. Captain Mullins watched him depart for Tay Ninh.

"Top, how long have they been in there now?" Captain Mullins asked.

"First Sergeant Kubble answered, "Over two hours. Hell, they must need coffee by now. I will check."

Kubble knocked on Major Zane's Office door and waited.

He heard Major Zane's familiar, "Yes?"

Kubble opened the door wide enough to lean in and glance around. General Hamlet sat at Zane's desk and the CO and XO sat to his front in metal folding chairs.

Looking at General Hamlet, Kubble asked. "Coffee General? Anyone?"

Hamlet glanced at Major Zane, Captain Greenletter, and Captain Caldwell and said, "I don't know about the others top but I could use the latrine."

As Hamlet arose, Kubble said, "Right this way sir."

Once Zane's door closed, Zane said, "Damn, Hamlet knows some shit."

Greenletter added, "Guess that's why he's a general, huh?"

"When I saw them arrive, I thought sure it was about that napalm mission," Caldwell said. "I had no idea that it was an Operational Readiness Evaluation (ORE). I didn't think anyone did OREs in a combat zone."

Zane also believed it was the napalm mission until a few moments after the group arrived. General Hamlet gathered him, the XO, and Ops Officer in Zane's office.

The unknown lieutenant colonel was Lieutenant Colonel Marion L. McDougall, Transportation Corps. He was a Master Aviator and headed a MACV inspection team inbound to inspect the 362nd. McDougall asked for the maintenance officer and left with him for his office.

Lieutenant Colonel Smith departed, saying that he would return that afternoon. He would provide transportation back to Ben Hoa for Hamlet and McDougall. Zane thought this unusual. Lieutenant colonels are not taxi drivers.

General Hamlet explained, "Gentlemen, this is an ORE. By now, every aspect of your unit is under a microscope. We will look at how many rolls of toilet tissue you have on hand and how many you used. To say the least, this is a thorough evaluation. Let's get started."

Hamlet conducted an intense questioning session for over two hours without letup. He thoroughly examined every aspect of aviation unit operations, management, maintenance, and communications. Keeping a poker face throughout, Zane had no idea how well their answers satisfied him.

Hamlet returned, holding a fresh cup of coffee, and asked. "Are you ready to continue?"

"Hell," Zane thought, "He's refreshed and ready to do it again. I'm taking a break."

"Sir, if you don't mind, I need to hit the latrine," Zane said.

Hamlet sipped his coffee and said, "Have at it."

The XO and Ops Officer followed Zane to the latrine. Zane unzipped, as did the others.

While the three stood beside each other at the urinals, Zane asked. "I wonder why it is I can stand here and see my career going down the drain but I can't take a whiz during a drug test?"

After washing up, the trio returned to Zane's office with coffee. Hamlet smiled at them from behind Zane's desk. He continued his interrogation.

Hamlet started his questioning at 07:00. Four and one half hours later, someone knocked on Zane's door. It was Captain Mullins.

"General," Mullins said. "Colonel Smith and Colonel McDougall say they are ready when you are, sir?"

"Smith," Zane thought, "He said he wasn't returning until afternoon. It's 11:30 hours now."

"Thank you Captain Mullins. Tell them we are on our way," Hamlet stated.

Turning to face them, Hamlet asked Zane? "What's for lunch major?"

"Beef liver sir," Zane answered.

"Not you too," Hamlet exclaimed. "That's all the task force has had for a week. That's what's at my mess today. I figured you guys would have something better."

Zane noticed that Hamlet smiled for the first time since his arrival. He arose and exited with Zane close behind with his men.

"Gentlemen, it's liver," Hamlet said to Smith and McDougall.

The colonels responded by giving a disgusted look. Zane looked outside for his jeep.

"Gentlemen, if you will come with me, I will drive you to lunch," Zane said.

Colonels Smith and McDougall rode in the rear while General Hamlet rode in the front passenger seat. On the way to the Mess Hall, Smith began asking questions about the ORE.

Colonel McDougall said, "Let me sum things up without a lot of detail. Colonel, you have absolutely nothing to worry about in this unit. It's probably the best I've seen in country during two tours."

General Hamlet added, "Amen."

Accumulated tension flowed from Zane when he heard the words. From the corner of his right eye, he could see a broad smile on McDougall's face.

Zane said, "Lunch is on me."

The others began to laugh as Zane drove into the Mess Hall's parking lot. Zane felt like an accused that had just heard a jury say, "Not guilty." He often wondered who brought the charges.

At 02:00 hours the next morning, Zane's field phone rang. He switched on his bedside lamp and answered, "United Six."

"Sir, this is PFC Gredleck in Ops. We have a TAC-E mission sir. I was told to contact you if we ever received one," Gredleck said nervously.

"You did good Gredleck. I will be there in a moment," Zane answered.

Zane put on his poncho for protection. Outside a major thunderstorm sprouted lightening and poured rain typical of monsoon season. He drove to Ops and ran from his jeep to get inside quickly. Once in, he stamped his feet and removed his poncho. He reached outside to shake it free of water before hanging it on a nearby coat rack. He entered Operations' radio room. Captain Caldwell was talking on the phone line to Battalion Headquarters. Finally, he slammed the handset onto its cradle.

"Idiots," Caldwell said before seeing Zane.

Looking up, he saw Zane and said, "They are idiots, sir."

"What gives?" Zane asked.

"We have two Hooks at Vung Tau. They were to pick up two rifle platoons and take them to Xuan Loc. When the storms started this afternoon, they elected to wait for them to clear. They didn't. The two aircraft commanders say it is too dangerous to fly since they do not have radar coverage. They maintain they could not find Xaun Loc if they wanted to."

"So, what's the problem?" Zane questioned.

"Battalion S-3 says that those two platoons have to be at Xuan Loc before morning. At first, he demanded that the pilots fly the mission. That's when Gredleck called me. I talked to the pilots and they say it is too dangerous to fly and will not take off. I informed Battalion's S-3 and he said that this was a tactical emergency. He had to have those two platoons at Xaun Loc right away. He declared a TAC-E sir."

Zane knew all too well about TAC-Es and ambitious operation officers. On his first tour, he flew with another ship to Cam Ranh Bay through severe thunderstorms to get vital supplies. Their cargo was 20,000 pounds of toilet tissue.

However, it was the second one that really made him angry. Under similar circumstances, he had a lone TAC-E to Cam Ranh Bay. His entire load was cleaning rods for M-16 rifles. He flew the load to LZ English through terrible weather. It was a horrible flight and he had radar coverage to help him.

When he arrived at LZ English, he learned that Secretary of Defense McNamara was arriving the next day to visit with the troops. One of their major complaints was the M-16 reputation for jamming in field conditions. The solution was to keep it clean. However, they did not have cleaning rods. He had the same problem in his company when he first arrived.

Now, here was another Ops Officer saying that the safety of the aircraft and lives of the crew were secondary to accomplishment of the mission. He did not believe it.

"Earnest, let's visit the weather folks," Zane said.

Caldwell went with Zane into the Air Force Weather Center. The senior NCO allowed them to look at their radar scopes. Vung Tau was in the middle of a major low-pressure area. The route to Xaun Loc was solid storms. Zane and Caldwell returned to Ops.

"Earnest, get me the Battalion Ops Officer on the line," Zane said.

Zane heard Caldwell say, just before handing Zane the telephone, "Major please hold for our CO."

Zane took the handset and said, "United Six."

"Major Zane, this is Major Roy Hillenger, 229th Battalion Ops. We must have those troops at Xuan Loc right away," Hillenger stated.

"Where's Major Rodriguez?" Zane asked.

"He's rotated to the states. I'm the new S-3," Hillenger answered.

"Welcome aboard Hillenger, I've checked the weather and talked with our aircraft commanders. They say that it is too dangerous to fly. My aircraft commanders have authority to refuse any mission they consider unsafe. You do understand that you could get two platoons killed and lose two Hooks?" Zane asked.

"I told the CO that they would be there. That's why this is a TAC-E. So, tell them to launch," Hillenger said.

Zane restrained himself and replied, "Major, you get General Hamlet on the line. When he gives me an order to launch under the provisions of a TAC-E, I will do so. Otherwise, do not mention this mission again. My crews will deliver their troop cargo as soon as possible after dawn."

There was no return call. Zane's crews delivered their passengers to Xaun Loc early the next morning. While there, they loaded two more platoons to go to Vung Tau. Companies were seeing that their men got as much R & R time as they could. With few U.S., ground units remaining in country, they were not actively pursuing enemy contact. A rumor making the rounds was a quote by MACV's Commander, General Abrams. Supposedly, he stated that there would be no more U.S., ground unit casualties in Viet Nam. Zane hoped he was correct.

Nevertheless, Zane thought, "March is becoming a troublesome month. It started with the napalm mission and steadily got worse. Long Thanh North seldom received many attacks. The enemy would throw in a few 122-mm rockets and mortar rounds every so often. They never amounted to much. Daryl Scott had been at Long Thanh North far longer than Zane, he consider the current attack level to be extraordinary."

In March alone there had been two, serious ground assaults. Those attacking the 362nd perimeter never made it to the second wire set. Zane remembered his disappointment at not getting to detonate the napalm drums. The attackers never got close enough to use them. Their mortar crew lit the place up like daylight. They watched sappers with satchel charges try and get through but ended up hanging in the razor wire. Between the tank's main gun, the 50-cal. machine guns, and the mortar's high explosive shells, they didn't stand a chance. Across the airfield, some had more success. Nevertheless, they didn't breach the inner perimeter. Troops in the towers ate their lunch with 40-mm grenades.

Five days later, they attacked again. This time they used rockets and mortars during their assault. Normally, they targeted the hooks. This time they placed them on the perimeter in an effort to blast their way onto the base. While they were extremely determined, they never made it. Their attackers proved to be young locals fighting as VC and not NVA. Zane felt something brewing. He didn't like not knowing what.

The third week of March Zane entered Ops to complete his mission reports. While he entered information as to tons carried, locations, and such, Captain Greenletter approached him.

"Sir, we have a new Battalion Commander," Greenletter said.

"Oh really, I heard that Smith was going to extend his tour six months," Zane replied.

"He did. He's taking command of the only U.S. artillery battalion remaining in the Cav. It belongs to Task Force Gary Owen," Greenletter explained.

Zane stopped writing and said, "He's really wanting full bull colonel isn't he? I knew he was Field Artillery but I never thought for a minute he would extend six months in Nam to get an artillery command. If he makes it, it will look good on his records."

"Sir, you will never guess who his replacement is," Greenletter commented.

"No I probably won't so please tell me," Zane responded.

Greenletter, smiling widely, leaned over and said, "One each Lieutenant Colonel McDougall."

"You mean the TC Colonel that headed the ORE team?" Zane asked.

"The one and the same, can you believe it?" Greenletter asked.

Thinking a moment, Zane answered, "Yes I can. The guy is a real fox. If the 362nd bombed, he would never have tried for the command. He has a free ride with us. His boss, General Hamlet, knows we're in fine shape. McDougall does not have to worry about us. He can concentrate on his other units. I bet you two double bourbons that he never visits us again."

"No sir," Greenletter replied. "I would lose that one. He's not even having a change of command ceremony."

"Frankly, I do not care who our CO is. We continue the way we have," Zane stated.

"Sir, I have one other message. The CO at the Special Forces Compound across the field called. He wants you to attend a steak cookout and a floorshow. I told him you would return his call," Greenletter explained.

"Shit, who is the CO over there?" Zane asked.

"He is Major Joe Gustafson. I might mention that he also is an infantryman, which entitles him to a special order of respect, sir," Greenletter said displaying a smug look.

Without a second's hesitation, Zane replied, "He cannot be too bright. He jumps out of perfectly good airplanes."

"Touché," Greenletter said as he walked away.

That evening, a Green Beret captain met Zane at the Special Force's gate into Long Thanh North's compound. To the Special Forces, it was their rear entrance, which they kept locked. Zane could hear music and loud talking coming from a Quonset hut.

Inside, he met Major Timothy W. Ragsdale, Commanding Officer of the Special Forces unit.

"Pleasure to finally meet you Zane. Sorry, we haven't become acquainted sooner," Ragsdale said while shaking Zane's hand.

Returning the gesture, Zane replied, "Please call me Dale. I figured you folks might be pissed the way we suddenly descended upon your operation. I knew nothing about it until the day I interrupted one of your training sessions."

"No sweat Dale. How do you like your steak? How about a beer?" Ragsdale asked.

"Rare on the steak and I will have a Blue Ribbon," Zane answered.

Ragsdale asked that Zane join him at a picnic type table away from the others. Ragsdale poured their beers into a paper cup.

"Frankly Dale, I wanted to discuss some things. These are things that you and I know never happened. Are you game?" Ragsdale asked.

"Sure shoot," Zane answered.

"There is a Vietnamese major that I want you to meet tonight. He is CO of an Airborne Ranger Regiment. He tried to meet with you a short while ago but you were having some kind of inspection. It involves a napalm mission that you led near Tay Ninh. If it's okay, I will go get him."

Raising his beer cup, Zane nodded his head indicating that he wouldn't mind. He watched Ragsdale enter a door marked "Authorized Personnel Only." In less than a minute, Ragsdale returned with a Vietnamese major.

With introductions out of the way, Zane asked. "What can I do for you major?"

Vinh explained about what a Montengard Ranger found at the target site. In addition, he told of finding other weapon remnants. He asked Zane if he saw anything unusual.

"I sure did. There were major secondary explosions after we dropped the napalm. Furthermore, I suspect that there was a radar controlled 37-mm AAA weapon at the location. My wingman reported seeing airbursts above us that appeared to be flak. This is my second tour and I've never encountered a 37-mm weapon," Zane answered.

Vinh's demeanor changed from concerned to deadly serious. He drew closer and lowered his voice.

"I did not come to you by chance. A person known to you as Lanny Briscoe suggested I speak with you. First, he asked that I tell you he needs to start flying the missions you two discussed. He will contact you tomorrow," Vinh explained.

Ragsdale interrupted and asked. "Major Vinh, would you like a beer?"

Declining the beer, Vinh continued, "You landed one of your Chinooks at a plantation to obtain a broken vehicle. How do you know those people?"

"That was a long time ago," Zane said. "I do not know those people at all. We needed a vehicle and they agreed to let us have their Land Rover. That's all."

Vinh explained the relationship he had with the plantation owners. He stated a deep concern for their safety. He could not convince them to leave. He wanted to know if Zane could evacuate them on short notice.

"No way, major. If I received a scheduled mission to move them, I would do it. However, I cannot make a special arrangement with you to do something like that. I'm sure you understand," Zane answered.

"Yes, I understand," Vinh answered. "Major, brief your pilots to remain on high alert for more AAA fire. My teams are reporting major concentrations of NVA forces opposite Tay Ninh and Bien Long provinces. They have many AAA weapons. We are sure there will be a significant invasion by the end of this month. The place that you hit was part of that force. They were attempting to preposition forces before their attack. They withdrew units like it across the border into Cambodia for fear they would lose the element of surprise. Mr. Briscoe can explain more."

Now, Zane grew concerned and asked. "Doesn't your superiors know this? Surely, Briscoe has alerted MACV?"

"Yes, he has. He has sent prediction after prediction but your leaders put no stock in what he says," Vinh answered.

Continuing, Vinh said, "I must go now. It is a long drive from here to Loc Ninh. You be careful major."

What Vinh said sounded incredulous to Zane. Nonetheless, what Vinh said with his eyes caused Zane to believer him. Ragsdale vouched for Vinh's creditability and honesty.

Ragsdale said, "I believe him but I'm sending a team to confirm. A STOL aircraft will leave here in the morning. They will be on the ground in Cambodia before daylight. They will let us know for sure. Enough work, the rare steaks are ready."

Zane had not had a steak like the one from the Special Forces since leaving home. A New Your Strip, it weighed at least 20 ounces. The Special Forces lieutenant doing the cooking prepared it to perfection.

After bragging about how wonderful it was, Zane asked Ragsdale. "Where did you come by this jewel?"

"We have a source in Bangkok who diverts them from the Embassy's supply. When the CAC was here, we had all we wanted. Now, we can still scrounge a few. Most of them we trade with Daryl Scott for lobster. His Nha Trang unit keeps him supplied," Ragsdale explained.

Zane had seen little of his friend since moving to Long Thanh North. For one reason or another, he missed invites to dinner and unit parties at the club.

He always said, "He was too busy."

Zane worried if it was true. Daryl had changed in ways that Zane did not like.

Before dawn the next morning, Zane used his flashlight to inspect the forward rotor head of his Hook. While doing so, he watched an Air America STOL ship make its takeoff run and climb into the night's dark sky. When finished with up top, he climbed down to join his First Pilot CWO Bruce Nettles. Nettles was new to the 362nd but not new to 'Nam. He was another pilot transferred from another withdrawing unit. Nevertheless, he had to qualify for aircraft commander orders like the others.

Taxing to the runway, Nettles' asked. "Captain Greenletter said that the 362nd held the record for MACV's Safe Flying award. He showed me certificates lining his office walls. With these older A models, I don't see how you do it. Before coming over here, I transition at Rucker. Hooks there are death traps. Why can you do it and they can't?"

Nettle's statement immediately grabbed Zane's attention and he asked. "You mean to tell me that they are still putting up ships that won't fly?"

"That's right. It's scary," Nettles commented.

The day's missions were a minor distraction to Zane's reaction to Nettle's news. Lieutenant Ludlow stayed in his mind throughout the day. That night at the club, he drank more than usual. He left his men and went directly to bed.

From a sound sleep, he awoke to the sound of singing. It sounded like a group of men in the distance but it grew louder. Finally, it came from directly out side his door. Drunken voices howled an old Cav drinking song.

"Sing a little bit, fuck a little bit, follow the Cav; follow the Cav."

"Sing a little bit, fuck a little bit, follow the Cav; follow the Cav."

"Come on out and join us major. You're a Cav man," Zane heard someone call.

Wearing flip-flop sandals and shorts, he opened his door. Outside he saw a long line of his pilots with their arms extended over the shoulders of the man on either side of him. They swayed back and forth, as they sang their song. Realizing there would be no rest until he joined them, he ran to the group's middle and joined the swaying line.

The group worked their way along the row of sleeping quarters. This continued until every pilot was in the line. Somehow, they kept passing a half gallon bourbon bottle up and down the line without interrupting their out of tune, risqué tune. They continued until the bottle was empty. Each aviator drifted away to his bed to await another day in the air.

As Zane returned to his bunk, he realized the meaning of their special bond. Each day they put their lives into the hands of each other. Each had total faith that their contemporary would give his life rather than fail a fellow aviator. This knowledge was the cement that held them together in the face of any adversity. This was a life long bond for the ages.

Even in Viet Nam, it is cold at 10,000 feet. Zane continued to circle his Hook while Briscoe operated his equipment in the cargo compartment. Before dark, Briscoe carried aboard data processing equipment that he called "IMPs." With these connected to the ARC 102 radio, Briscoe somehow obtained decrypted messages from recorded NVA radio traffic. The tapes came directly from RRU ships that delivered it to Long Thanh North.

While Briscoe installed his equipment, Zane asked. "Why don't you use fixed wing aircraft?

Jesus Lanny, there must be hundreds available."

"Everyone I went to for help made some damned lame excuse. Their ships' designs did not allow for my equipment. I had to submit a Statement of Need so they could work it into a Research and Development project. I didn't have time for that kind of crap," Briscoe said.

Over the intercom, he heard Briscoe say, "I've got it. You can take us down."

After shutdown, Lieutenant Robertson did the post flight inspection with their FE. Zane sat in the Hook with Briscoe. Zane shined his flashlight so that Briscoe could read. Every now and then Briscoe would spit out an expletive and continue reading.

He had teletype-looking printouts in a plastic binder. According to Briscoe, they were decrypted messages.

Briscoe slammed the binder shut and asked. "Can you fly me to MACV in your C & C?"

"Sure thing. We have to go to Ops first and file a flight plan," Zane answered.

Briscoe looked around at his electronic gear and said, "You go ahead. I will get this stuff packed and we will take it with us. I cannot leave it here."

As Zane entered Ops, the Ops Sergeant asked. "Sir, we have a request for a ramp search. There is a STOL fixed wing missing that they are trying to locate. Have you seen it?"

"I don't know. What is its tail number?" Zane asked.

With a strange look, the sergeant said, "That's just it sir. It does not have any markings."

Zane replied immediately, "Yeah, I saw one yesterday morning before dawn. I watched it take off. If the time and place is correct, I saw it."

After contacting MACV, the NCO handed Zane the handset and said, "They want to talk to you, sir."

Zane said into the handset, "Major Zane."

"Dale, this is Buff Winslow. That ship's point of origin was Long Thanh North. It was a Dornier flown by Frederick Earling. You met him and Vanessa at my place. Did you see it?" Winslow asked.

Zane explained, "I saw a Dornier take off from here before dawn day before yesterday. It had no markings. I believe it picked up some Montengards for a mission around the Tay Ninh area."

Zane heard Winslow talking to someone in the background. There seemed to be some sort of argument taking place.

An unfamiliar voice came on the line and asked. "Major, how do you know where that bird was going and its contents?"

"Begging your pardon sir but I have no idea who you are. I will not discuss the matter with you. Put Buff back on the line," Zane directed.

"Yeah Dale, Winslow here," Buff Winslow said.

"Buff, I have said all I am going to say. Tell the other fellow to come to Long Thanh North and identify himself. When I'm satisfied with his credentials, I might answer his questions," Zane firmly stated.

"I'm calling on Vanessa behalf. This jerk is trying to cover his ass. They've been looking for that ship midday the day before yesterday. They couldn't learn anything their way so I tried mine," Buff explained.

"Have them contact Major Ragsdale at the Special Forces' base here. He can likely answer their questions," Zane suggested.

There was a prolonged silence before Winslow said, "He was on the ship Dale."

Zane replied, "Buff, check to see that Earling's assistant has activated Air America's Search and Rescue (SAR) procedures. They have assets available that you and I do not. Other than that, there's little I can do."

"The guy you spoke with says they've already implemented their procedures. Nevertheless, I understand. I will make sure they have. Be sure and let me know when you might be in Saigon. If you have to remain overnight, there's a room reserved for you. See you later my friend," Buff said, as he broke their connection.

Zane purposely did not mention his impending flight to MACV with Briscoe. He did not have time to visit in Saigon. He had to return and make sure that his people began preparing for what he expected would soon take place.

After taking Briscoe to MACV's helipad, Zane and Robertson returned to Long Thanh North. Before landing, Zane sent their maintenance report when they were within 25 miles. During engine shutdown, their international orange, Land Rover met them. Zane had reported an intermittent problem with a hydraulic pressure warning light. They would have the problem resolved within minutes.

While making entries in the ship's logbook, Zane could only marvel at the capabilities of the young men in his unit. Most were barely more than teenagers. Yet, they took a decimated, British vehicle and restored it. They modified a Jeep transmission and installed it. They changed the wheel drums to standard Jeep brakes. They made its engine more powerful than the original by boring out the cylinders and making new pistons for it. With the equipment in their shops, they could build a completely new Hook if they had a mind to do so.

Zane thought what a waste it was for Bredermeyer and his buddy. They had an opportunity to become anything they wanted in life. Yet, they threw it away because of a low rating on an efficiency report. Now, their lives lay in tatters.

Prosecutors plea-bargained attempted murder charges to destruction of government and personal property. The two would be killers received six months at hard labor, a bad conduct discharge, and loss of pay. They would leave prison young men marked for life.

"How sad," Zane thought, "They could have been any one of the young men now working on his Huey. It was a pitiful waste for which he had no answer."

Zane's thoughts returned to the Land Rover. He made a mental note to look at the plantation whenever he was in the area. Major Vinh wanted so much for him to come to their aid as a matter of course. He could not do that. Nevertheless, if he was in the area and saw help needed, there was nothing to keep him for giving it.

Captain Greenletter brought Zane's jeep to meet him. He waited for Zane to join him.

"L-T, I've finished the logbook. Is there anything I need to enter other than the warning light?" Zane asked.

Robertson answered, "No, sir. They've fixed that and I found nothing on the post flight."

"Come on," Zane replied, "I will give you a ride to Ops. You need to attend the pilot's meeting."

"On my way sir," Robertson said, as he gathered his flight equipment.

While returning to Ops, Zane noticed unusual activity across the airfield where "Blue Max" parked its Cobra gunships. Their unit identification was F Battery 79th Aerial Rocket Artillery (ARA) and they were part of the 229th Aviation Battalion as was Zane's unit. These sleek armed gunships provided vitally needed protection for Hueys when doing assaults into LZs. They could rain fire on ground units trying to bring down the Hueys. In addition, they were deadly against enemy positions with their 2.75-inch rockets.

Suspicious, Zane told Greenletter to take him to Daryl Scott's Battalion rather than Ops. He needed to see if Scott had any idea of what might be happening. He doubted F/79th would reveal any special missions.

"Terry, wait for me. This won't take long," Zane said.

Anxiously, Zane waited outside Scott's unit guard gate for Scott to appear. Soon, he saw him approaching.

When he was close enough to hear, Zane said, "Daryl, I don't need to come in. We can talk outside."

Scott agreed and walked with Zane away from the guardhouse, as he asked. "Daryl, I need to know what the hell is going on. I think you know."

Scott hesitated before answering but finally replied, "Dale, I cannot reveal anything. Even though our friendship started in flight school, I cannot tell you a thing directly. Even if I suspected that your life might be in danger, I could not tell you. Everything must go through channels. I hope that you understand."

"Thanks Daryl, I understand. I hope you do not mind but I have to go. My pilots are in a meeting waiting for me," Zane explained.

As Zane and Greenletter entered Ops, Caldwell met them. He held a classified folder with the unit's daily decryption codes.

"What's up Earnest?" Zane asked.

"Sir, I just decrypted a message from Battalion Ops. They said that a major NVA attack took place this morning across the DMZ toward Quang Tri. The rest is garbled with a lot of unknowns," Caldwell said.

"Thanks Earnest. Come with us to see the others," Zane instructed.

As Zane entered the meeting room, Captain Mullins called attention. Zane told them to be at ease and pay attention. It was the time of evening when his aviators had their showers and relaxed. Most of them wore tee shirts, Bermuda shorts, and flip-flops. They, he knew, were anxious to write letters home and take care of personal chores.

"Gentlemen, I am approaching the end of my third tour in 'Nam. Many of you are looking forward to going home. However, to accomplish that you may have to face another trying time."

"Captain Caldwell just gave me a message that the NVA launched an offensive this morning from the DMZ toward Quang Tri. Every fiber of my being tells me that they will attack here. They will attack soon. This time it will not be VC but hard core NVA forces with considerable armament. Recently, we destroyed a radar controlled 37-mm, radar controlled, antiaircraft weapon. I believe it is an indicator of what may come. We must get ready. We must change our tactics or we will lose."

"Here are my instructions. At the first sign of coordinated AAA fires, we will use nap of the earth (NOE) flight techniques. The days of flying high to avoid AAA will end with the introduction of conventional weapon systems. We are too big and slow to survive a conventional warfare environment."

"You will get on the deck. I mean low. Do not hesitate to put your Hook's fuselage into treetops. I do not care if you have a howitzer sling load get down in the trees or die. You must not fly over open terrain. Restrict your routes to jungle areas. Never fly the same route twice. If you land one way, depart in another."

"Aircraft commanders, the responsibility is yours. More than ever, the lives of your crew and passengers depend on your decisions. Most of you are two tour veterans so use your experience."

Zane stopped for a moment and asked. "Any questions so far?"

"I have one sir," a new arrival said.

"Go ahead," Zane replied.

"When we go into an LZ with a howitzer, usually there is a guide. He directs us where he wants the weapon put. On occasion, they take considerable time. Do we still follow their instructions?" He asked.

"If what I suspect happens, you will not have a guide. He will be in a bunker somewhere talking to you by radio. Do not spend more than five seconds delivering a load. Stop it, drop it, and get out fast. Artillery positions are prime targets. The enemy will take you out with a mortar or a sniper. Five seconds, gents and then go. If you can do it quicker, do it," Zane answered.

Mummers spread throughout the group. Some aviators began discussing techniques using their hands as simulated helicopters.

Zane, raising his voice, said, "Gentlemen, you will not survive developing techniques through idle chit chat. If you have something worth knowing, share it."

The group became silent realizing that Zane's comment was valid. They had to work as teams to survive.

Zane continued, "Ops has tomorrow's missions posted. After we dismiss, check the mission board and get with your crew tonight. Make sure every first pilot, FE, crew chief, and gunner knows exactly what the mission is and what procedures to follow in case you're engaged with AAA."

"Furthermore, check every item in your survival vests tonight. Test your survival radios. Draw an additional set of batteries from supply. Every person on flight status will wear a survival knife. Make sure that it is sharp. Clean your firearms and get additional ammo clips from supply. In addition, put an extra case of C rations aboard your ships."

"Give me your complete attention on this item. If you make a forced landing, door gunners will find the nearest best cover they can find. Make sure that an M-60 is on each side of the downed aircraft. When a recovery ship arrives, M-60 gunners will provide covering fire until other crewmembers are aboard the rescue bird."

"The nine o'clock gunner will withdraw first. The rescue ship will provide covering fires for this gunner. Next, the three o'clock gunner will withdraw. As before, the rescue ship will cover him. Wounded personnel have first priority to the rescue ship."

"Now comes the hard part. If a rescue ship is on approach to your location, do not take time to carry out your dead under fire. Do not stop firing to save a lifeless body. If you do, you will lose fire support of two, yours and that of your lost buddy. He gave his life for nothing. He would not want you to jeopardize the rescue ship and your remaining brothers in arms."

"When the shit hits the fan, forget the Hollywood bullshit. Taking out the dead is fine, if you are not in a hostile situation. The decision as to what to do rests with the chain of command. When it comes to Hooks, the top of that chain is the aircraft commander."

"I hope you are scared because I sure am. I have to get with my crew. Thank you. You are dismissed," Zane said, as he turned and left the room.

Chapter Forty Six

April 1972

I gave my life for freedom—this I know:
For those who bade me fight had told me so.
W. N. Ewer (1885–1976), British journalist. *Five Souls*

Jean Danjou moved through night shadows as if a part of them. He had not seen so many destined for combat since Dien Bien Phu. He had slipped through North Vietnamese positions as a child's whisper on a summer's night, soft, quiet. Now, he traveled his land toward those who gave his life meaning. He traveled over terrain that was more than familiar. It was his life's blood.

The NVA were already crossing the Cambodian border toward Loc Ninh. Soon they would be at Peace Retreat Plantation. He knew he barely had time to get to those hiding in the tunnels. Their chance for escape was no more. Moving from column to column, he crossed the veranda. He slipped through the double doors closing them behind him slowly. He waited and watched for what he knew would come next.

Slightly before dawn, Jean heard the familiar whine of artillery shells passing overhead to end in a thunderous crescendo at Loc Ninh. Between explosions, squeaking metallic noise from tank treads grew louder as they passed. The ones passing through the orchards splintered and crushed young trees.

As the sun crested the horizon, he watched thousands of helmeted North Vietnamese troops advancing with their armored leviathans. Some stooped low behind them for protection as ARVN began defending Loc Ninh from their onslaught.

With the morning's light, Jean could not remain by the glass doors for fear of detection. He swiftly moved through the house to its cooking area. In the rooms' middle, a four-foot high butcher's block rose from the floor. Putting his left shoulder hard against the heavy wood furnishing, he pushed hard until his feet began to slip on alternating black and white floor tiles. The rigid structure moved slightly and Jean renewed his effort. Slowly, it began moving, leaving an ever widening opening in its wake.

Jean started to put his feet into the black void when he heard a soft voice ask. "Jean?"

With his eyes growing accustomed to the dark, he could see the outline of an AK-47's muzzle pointed at him from below. He stopped, not daring to move.

"Yes," he answered.

When the muzzle lowered, he continued through the narrow opening in the floor. His feet felt the first step. With the step for support, he rolled onto his stomach pulling the rest of his body through. He backed down the stairs two more steps. Reaching above his head, he felt the metal bar bolted through the floor and into the overhead butcher's block. He pushed forward causing the aperture to become smaller as the overhead block moved. When he felt it stop, he felt for another metal bar. Finding it, he strained to turn it to his right. As it turned, two heavy, steel rods moved forward locking the block in place. Now, no one could move it from above with the bolts set.

Exhausted, Jean turned and lay against the stairs while regaining strength. For three days, he traveled along the well-known Ho Chi Minh trail. Other than being much improved, it used the same route he studied years earlier. This time it was crowded with tanks, armored personnel carriers, antiaircraft weapons, and thousands upon thousands of North Vietnamese soldiers. He found vast stockpiles of artillery ammunition hidden beneath netting interlaced with vegetation. He found it inconceivable that it was happening without detection from aircraft overhead. Yet, the massed equipment and soldiers traveled relatively unmolested.

With his eyes completely adjusted, Jean could see Ngoc's oldest son Nanh. Only 17, he knew the rigors of fighting with the VC. They inducted him as a conscript at age 15. He trained and fought with them for a year. After witnessing the killing of a village's elder and nurse. He could not equate freedom with the killing of innocent civilians. He deserted as a Chu Hoi.

Using a Chu Hoi pass, he went to the nearest ARVN outpost. They accepted him and gave him food and clothing. For awhile, he served with ARVN forces as a scout. However, when National Police arrived things changed. The National Police, wearing their distinctive tiger striped uniforms, questioned him about his home village at Loc Ninh. They demanded to know those in his village who consorted with the VC. He tried to explain that many villagers either cooperated with the VC or they were killed. They had no choice. The police refused to understand or accept his answers. Having seen what they did to others, he escaped and returned home.

Ngoc came to Jean for help. Nanh could not remain in Loc Ninh. The VC would kill him for deserting. It would not be long before the National Police would come to find him. Two evils pursued him, the VC and the National Police. Jean agreed to hide Nanh in the underground shelter he and Ngoc were building at the time.

"We worried that they caught you," Nanh said. "Minh Thanh has not slept in two days."

Jean moved past Nanh with difficulty since the passage was narrow. He opened curtains covering the entrance to a larger room. At present, it contained nothing but tools for digging and large buckets. This was where they brought earth for hauling to the surface. After their experience during Tet 1968, Jean knew that they must have a haven at their plantation. He realized that they were fortunate to get to the Cathedral in Cholon. This time he would have a place where they could stay during hostilities.

The tons of soil removed to build their sanctuary went into the orchards. It was a backbreaking ordeal but Jean knew the plantation house was vulnerable. It could never survive a major battle. Underground, they had a chance.

Moving to another curtain-covered doorway, he entered. This was another narrow passage with rails and cross ties. It extended down a gradual grade for 200 feet. On each side, at regular intervals, other curtain covered doorways appeared. Workers from Loc Ninh slept in these small rooms. For various reasons, they sought refuge. Some were orphaned children cared for by their grandparents while others were elderly couples who lost their children during the conflict. Other rooms provided sleeping space for young men who had no use for killing on either side. Teenaged girls stayed in rooms farther down the passage.

After passing the rooms, the passage opened into a large communal area. Sitting on the rails in this room was their dirt cart. Workers would fill the cart while others pulled it to the furthermost dirt room near the stairs. Villagers squatted around the room performing various tasks. Some prepared food for cooking while other repaired broken equipment.

"Where is Minh Thanh?" Jean asked.

An elderly woman smiled and pointed to another curtained covered doorway. Nanh remained behind when Jean entered the passage. It led to where Jean and Minh Thanh slept. Jean found Minh Thanh and his two children asleep on straw mats. He backed away rather than disturb them.

At the communal area, Nanh squatted while meticulously cleaning his rifle. He wore nothing but a straw hat, a black loincloth, and sandals. He was exceedingly thin but it was a sinewy strength that lay beneath his skin. Coiled beside him on the floor, lay two bandoleers filled with ammunition clips. He looked up and smiled when Jean entered.

Jean said, "Gather the others. We must talk."

Nanh arose lifting his two bandoleers, as he became erect. He slipped his right arm through one bandoleer and his left through another. The two crossed on his chest. He waited while Jean went into the passage leading to the sleeping areas. Once inside, Nanh followed.

Jean continued past the sleeping area as Nanh stopped at one doorway and pulled its curtain aside. At the last curtain on his left, near the dirt room, Jean removed a candle from a recess next to the doorway. He lit it and pushed another canvas curtain aside. He had to stoop to travel this narrow tunnel. After 20 yards, the passage widened into another room with its floor covered with rice straw. He could now stand erect. In addition, he heard explosions clearly at this location. In the other sections, they were muffled thuds. Here they were sharp and clear.

Raising his candle, he looked around the room's walls. Wooden crates sat stacked one upon another. Clearly marked in English, they contained various United States Army weapons. Most contained ammunition while others contained assorted grenades, light antitank weapons (LAW), pistols, and rifles.

Jean heard movement and raised his candle toward the entrance. Nanh appeared with seven, young men. Each of them had relatives in the tunnel complex. Lifting an empty crate, Jean placed it near another covered opening and sat. The Vietnamese squatted around him.

"As you know by now, the invasion is in progress. The sounds you hear are NVA advancing upon Loc Ninh. They are a strong force equipped with armored personnel carriers, tanks, and what look's like regiments of infantry. They are not making any effort to hide their advance. The small force at Loc Ninh cannot defend against these organized units. We have planned for this day for a long time. However, I think that it is necessary to review some things," Jean said as he looked at each young man with him.

Continuing he said, "Our families are relatively safe as long as we remain undiscovered. To reduce the chance of this happening, no one may leave without my permission. The stairs behind me provide the only exit point. They lead to an opening inside the main storage bin. A raised, metal, tunnel extends into the bin. There is a ladder built into its walls. Covering the tunnel is a trap door. I replaced its hinges with leather straps to reduce noise. Nevertheless, be careful opening and closing it as it could expose us due to noise."

"The bin has no doors. The only points of entry are two chutes, one at the top and the other at the bottom. Two small panels are available for viewing. From one, a person can see the main house and surrounding grounds. From the other, there is a view of the road to Loc Ninh and the south road leading to QL-13."

"One person will observe from the bin. Observers will change every four hours. If there is activity that needs reporting, find me. I will come and determine if there is need for us to do anything."

"If an occasion arises that requires outside activity on our part, I will take one of you with me. Each of you has my complete trust and confidence. Who goes with me is my decision and there are no favorites. We will only go outside at night and only if the house is clear. We cannot enter the house with anyone in it."

"We have enough provisions for three months. There is a gravity feed line from the well into the communal area so we have plenty water. The best thing we can do is stay where we are."

"The NVA are making a major mistake. They cannot sustain their attack. While the U.S. has few military personnel in country, they possess massive firepower. The northern troops are in the open and trying to fight a conventional war against a country whose power thrives on conventional warfare. The NVA massed their forces too early. Three months from now, they may have had a chance but not now."

"Hiep, you take first watch. I must rest because I am not the young man that I used to be. I am tired," Jean said, as he arose from his seat.

At Ben Hoa, Headquarters of Task Force Gary Owen, Lieutenant Colonel McDougall briefed his subordinate commanders of the 229th Aviation Battalion.

"Gentlemen, yesterday at about dawn, a major NVA force attacked Loc Ninh north of An Loc in Binh Long Province. The attackers used mortars, rockets, and massive artillery fire to support advancing armor and infantry units. Army advisers, at Loch Ninh, coordinated the use of U.S. tactical fighters and Specter C-130 gunships to fend off their attackers."

F Troop of the 9th Cav responded to a distress call with six Cobras and two OH-6s. Reports show that NVA infantry moved openly around Loc Ninh in considerable numbers. They did not seem the least bit concerned about doing so. Hunter killer teams engaged the NVA force. Later in the day, 'Blue Max' arrived and became heavily engaged."

"AAA fire is intense. Reports are coming in that reveal 57-mm AAA canons firing. The NVA force came prepared to repel air attacks. We lost one OH-6 and one Cobra. This morning tanks continued their attack at Loc Ninh. Defenders split into two groups, one north, and one south of Loc Ninh proper. The tank force today is much larger that yesterday. Air support assets from our aircraft carriers, Thailand, and Ben Hoa are arriving in the area. It now appears that this is a major invasion in strength. This is no hit and run operation. There are too many well-equipped forces using conventional tactics. It appears that An Loc is their initial objective. Intel believes their ultimate objective of this attack could be Saigon."

Zane, listening intently, heard the phrases "AAA intense" and "57-mm." This made it clear that a Chinook could not survive without using nap of the earth (NOE) flight techniques.

"My guys are already on edge waiting for the other shoe to drop," Zane thought. "Our initial alert arrived 30 March and here it is 6 April. They've been tense on every flight. At least we now know where the enemy is."

McDougall continued, "According to reports, an entire ARVN Battalion surrendered without any resistance when the NVA attacked across the DMZ. Making matters worse, the unit commander began making broadcasts for other ARVN units to surrender. This leader is the worst kind of coward. His soldiers would fight with leadership but he failed them. ARVN units will be watching us. We must set an example for them to follow. If we fail, they will fail. I am depending upon you to see that the ARVN do not fail. This battle is mostly theirs and they will win or lose it. We must help them win. Missions are steadily going to your units. Let's kick some NVA ass."

After McDougall dismissed the group, Zane ran to his waiting C & C Huey. Once airborne he immediately contacted his Ops and alerted them to dangers in the An Loc region.

Turning to Lieutenant Robertson in the right seat, he said, "L-T, let's keep this ship parked next to the back entrance to my office. Have it ready to go on a moment's notice. Give it a good post flight. Go ahead and complete the startup checklist so that we can fire her up right away."

"Roger that sir," Robertson answered.

Zane burst through Ops telling Captain Caldwell, "Get the XO and come to my office ASAP."

As Zane passed First Sergeant Kubble, he said, "Come with me Top."

Zane went into his office and around his desk, pushing his chair back as he went. Swinging his right arm across his desk's top, he pushed everything onto the floor. Yanking a folded map from his flight suit pocket, he spread it on his desk.

Seeing Caldwell and the XO enter, Zane said, "Around here gents. You too Top."

The three gathered beside Zane, as he took a felt-tipped pen and drew a circle on the map. Inside the circle, he marked bases used frequently by Task Force aircraft. They were Lai Kai, Tay Ninh, Tay Ninh East, An Loc, and Loc Ninh. Zane drew smaller circles around Bu Dop and Song Be.

"Gents, you are looking at our area of operations for one hell of a fight. Right now Loc Ninh is cold meat. They didn't stand a chance. Next, the NVA will go after An Loc because it is the next major town along QL-13 toward Saigon. The only thing in the NVA's way is the ARVN 5th Division and some ARVN Rangers. With them are some American advisers. They're having to direct this fight because the ARVN have never seen anything like this. Hell, I've never seen anything like this," Zane said with an intensity never before seen by the others.

Zane continued, "Bet your ass that General Hamlet will use Lai Kai, Tay Ninh as major staging areas. That means we're going to be hauling a lot of aviation fuel, artillery ammo, rockets for Cobras and small arms ammunition. Think a minute how much they're going to need to fight this fight. We have to get it to them."

"Terry, have cots setup in the main meeting room. Pilots will be there if not on a mission. Get the guys together and moved from their quarters."

"Earnest, be sure to brief every AC before he leaves that when they're in this circle, they will fly NOE. There are no exceptions. There is heavy ass AAA out there."

"Top, get with the mess sergeant and have chow around the clock. We still have to defend this place. Mess personnel will deliver hot soup, sandwiches, and coffee to people on perimeter duty. Let the maintenance NCOs know they are on duty around the clock. Work out a shift schedule as best you can. Safety is first. I don't want some sleepy inspector overlooking something."

As Zane conducted his briefing, Captain Caldwell saw a young PFC from Ops enter the room. He appeared nervous. Caldwell went to him and the soldier whispered to him and left. Caldwell returned to the desk.

Interrupting Zane, Caldwell said, "Sir, I hate to bother you but you need to know this."

"What?" Zane asked impatiently.

"There's a Major General at the big maintenance hanger. He's pissed and screaming for you," Caldwell related.

"Damn," Zane cried. "Just what I needed. Terry you take over. I will be right back," Zane said, rushing from his office.

Zane brought his jeep to a quick halt, rushed to an irate Major General Hollingsworth, and reported.

"This is the worst shit I have ever seen in my fucking life. Jesus H. Christ Zane, how the hell can you fix Hooks in the dark? I demand to know why in the hell you don't have lights in this hanger," Hollingsworth bellowed.

"General, I don't have lights because you won't let me have any. That dumb ass PA & E committee you set up won't approve any capital improvements over 50 damned dollars. They've turned down three request because of your silly ass ruling," Zane answered.

Hollingsworth clamped his jaws tight and glared at Zane saying, "You better have Hooks when I need them damn it. If you don't I will have your ass."

General Hollingsworth went to his waiting C & C Huey and immediately departed.

Zane knew Major General Hollingsworth by reputation. During World War II, he developed a leadership style like that of General Patton. He was a no nonsense, get the job done commander, and his tongue held expletives to sear one's ears.

Currently, he was Commander of Third Regional Assistance Command (TRAC). He was responsible for providing advisors to ARVN units in Military Region Three (MRIII) which included Saigon and surrounding provinces. Furthermore, MR III included Loc Ninh and An Loc. The advisors fighting with the ARVN were his people. NVA General Giap made a big mistake attacking an area that Hollingsworth had to defend.

Within six hours after Hollingsworth's departure, work teams from Saigon were installing lights throughout Zane's aircraft hangers. They would burn night and day for the next three months.

After meeting Hollingsworth, Zane returned to his headquarters building. Cots for aircrews lined his meeting room's walls. Hook crews began moving into the new "Ready" room for short notice missions. Zane found Caldwell manning radios in Ops. Zane got his attention and gestured Caldwell join him.

"Earnest, I forgot something. Make sure that each AC knows to make a weapons check before entering the AO I outlined. When they need those M-60s, I want to be sure they work. In addition, I'm counting on you to cover my butt. You are the Operations Officer. When you see something that needs doing, do it. Do not wait for my approval. We do not have time for that," Zane explained.

Caldwell said, "Along those lines, sir. I have made the road between An Loc and Loc Ninh a no fly zone for the Hooks. I plan to do the same for QL-13 south of An Loc. If the NVA flank An Loc, anything flying down that highway will be an easy target."

"Good thinking, Ernest. That's the kind of thing I mean. Both sides of that road are clear and parallel the tree line on both sides. That road is a death trap," Zane agreed.

Zane left Ops and went to his office. He called supply.

"Sarge, I need a 40-mm grenade launcher and a case of ammo. How long before you can get the items?" Zane asked.

"Sir, I'm Specialist Morray, the supply clerk. The Supply Sergeant is on a supply run."

Zane asked. "Well Morray, how about it?"

"They're on their way sir," Morray answered.

Zane loaded the launcher and ammunition on his C & C ship. He returned to Ops and spoke with Caldwell. He advised him that he was going to An Loc to do a reconnaissance.

As Zane and Robertson approached An Loc from the south, they saw two Hueys orbiting. In addition, an Air Force Forward Air Controller (FAC) would dive and fire white phosphorus rockets at potential targets. Various Air Force and Navy jets attacked the marked targets with a variety of bomb loads.

The most used combination appeared to be a mixture of cluster bombs and napalm. Cluster bombs were particularly deadly against personnel targets. When a fighter pilot dropped his load, two large bombs left the plane. However, these burst hurling smaller cylinders (bomblets) throughout the target area. These would explode spraying deadly metal fragments, which cut unprotected personnel to pieces. Napalm unleashed a boiling cauldron of flame with a jelly like consistency. It stuck to whatever it touched, burning it. Armored vehicles became ovens toasting those inside.

Moving in and out among the other aircraft, Spectre AC-130 gunships devastated ground targets. The Spectre ships had a particularly deadly effect. The original aircraft was a four-engine transport. Through major modifications, a variety of weapons converted it to an attack airplane. Armed with 20-mm Vulcan cannons, it could deliver 6,000 rounds a minute onto a target. In addition, it came equipped with 40-mm, automatic Bofors. During World War II, Bofors were an air defense weapon. Later, designed with four barrels, it proved exceptionally effective as a firebase defensive weapon in Viet Nam. The Air Force added the Bofors to its Spectre ships. Later, they added 105-mm, artillery howitzers as part of its armaments.

NVA by the thousands succumbed to the Spectre's deadly systems. They were ideal targets for the Spectre. Anytime they gathered to make an attack, the Spectre cut them to pieces.

Zane told Robertson, "L-T, we better hold out here. There is too much air traffic over the place. We will confuse the situation."

Robertson began a right turn and went into a holding pattern. Everyone aboard watched for tracers but did not see any. It appeared that the AAA threat was in the Loc Ninh and An Loc region.

Zane contacted his Ops.

"United Three, this is United Six, over," Zane transmitted.

"United Six, this is three, over" Caldwell answered.

"Three, this is six. Advise that the only remaining landing site that I see available for Hooks is a soccer field on An Loc's south side. In addition, do not plan to use the Quon Loi airfield at An Loc for refueling. Make sure our people know to refuel elsewhere, over," Zane instructed.

"Six, this is three, roger, over," Ops acknowledged.

"Three this is six, out," Zane ended his transmission.

Zane's C & C contained a communications console that gave him access to practically every radio frequency used in Viet Nam. He turned on its radios and began monitoring other frequencies. He quickly recognized General Hollingsworth's voice. He was transmitting to advisors trapped in Loc Ninh. He used the call sign Danger Five Seven.

"Hold on for me. We'll have you out. You're doing a tremendous job," Hollingsworth said in a calm voice as if they were having a casual telephone conversation.

However, when Hollingsworth changed his frequency to one the trapped could not hear, he howled, "Get some more nape on those goddamned tanks. Where in the hell are the sons of a bitching B-52s? Get them here now damn it."

Zane could hear an advisor on the ground at Loc Ninh. When he transmitted, sounds of exploding artillery and small arms fire filled in as background noise. During another transmission, he heard a child crying. Finally, the adviser with the call sign Zippo called for fire on his own position. Despite the horrendous supporting fires, NVA took the southern defenders at Loc Ninh. They were the final holdouts.

"L-T, let's see if we can get fuel at Lai Kai," Zane said.

"Roger that sir," Robertson said as he turned to a heading for Lai Kai.

Minh Than awakened to find Jean asleep. She took her two children and left quietly. She knew Jean needed rest. In the communal area, she poured tea for Anh her elder son. Now, almost six, he held his own cup with both hands and sipped the hot brew.

Removing some rice from a pot, she crushed it in a saucer. Her youngest boy, Jean Diem Danjou, just became able to eat solids. Crushed rice, lightly flavored with condensed milk and sugar, was his favorite. She held him with his head nestled in her left elbow. With her right, he removed small morsels of the mix with a spoon. Touching it lightly to his lips caused him to smack his tiny lips and kick his feet. He quickly took it and wriggled for more.

"Jean says I spoil him," she thought. "Too much sugar is not good for him. Look at his chubby cheeks he says and then laughs."

Ngoc's wife picked Anh up and spun him around to hear him laugh. She hugged Anh and came to sit with Minh Thanh.

"Your babies are good children," Linh said. "They remind me of my son when he was a baby. Enjoy them while you can. They grow old way too fast."

Minh Thanh felt sympathy in her heart for Linh. She had one remaining son. The others died fighting for the VC. She lost three and each loss seemed to carve away a part of her heart. Her eyes no longer sparkled as in the past.

Looking at her Minh Thanh asked. "Does the fighting continue?"

"Yes," Linh answered. "If you go up the rails, it is very loud. It never seems to stop. It has been a week and it continues. Surely it will end soon."

"Jean says it is very different this time," Minh Thanh said. "Most of the fighters are from the north. They are NVA and few VC are with them. Our village no longer stands. It is mostly rubble. When they leave, we will rebuild it."

The two ladies heard a noise and looked up to see Jean. He stretched and yawned. He came to Linh and Minh Thanh and sat with them. Anh struggled from Linh's arms and ran to Jean.

"How is daddy's little man?" Jean asked, lifting Anh high above his head.

"I am daddy's man. I am daddy's man," Anh cried out with laughter.

Jean lowered Anh to embrace him. The boy grasped Jean around his neck and squeezed.

"When can we ride the tractor, daddy?" Anh asked, pouting his lower lip.

"Soon, I hope," Jean answered.

"Are you hungry?" Minh Thanh asked Jean.

"Not right now. I have to check the watch. If you have something in about 30 minutes I will eat," Jean answered.

Leaning over, Jean caressed Minh Thanh's check with his lips and said, "I must go. I will return soon."

Jean arrived at the stairs leading to the storage bin. Quietly, he began climbing. Next, he came to a steel ladder built into a tower that extended nine feet into the storage bin. When he reached its cover, he raised it slowly to avoid noise. He gripped the cover and allowed it to hang along the tower's side. The leather hinges he installed helped reduce noise.

Jean saw Nanh peering through a small opening with a removable cover. He stood in Macadamia nuts to his calves. Hearing Jean arrive Nanh turned his head to look at him. He excitedly beckoned to Jean to join him. Walking in the stored nuts was difficult. They rolled from underfoot, causing a person to lose balance. Slowly, Jean made his way to Nanh side. Nanh moved away from the opening and indicated that Jean look.

Parked by the main house were five vehicles. Each had a mesh covering to destroy its outline.

Two were Soviet PT-76 Armored Personnel Carriers (APC) with large cables running from their lowered ramps and into the main house. The others were 57-mm cannons mounted on tracked bodies. Each had a radar antenna to track aircraft. They were formidable AAA weapons.

Near the main road to Loc Ninh, Jean saw five destroyed APCs. Their rears faced each other as if in a star-like, defensive formation. They sat beneath rubber trees from an old plantation. Their charred, melted bodies indicated destruction by intense heat.

"The people in those vehicles fought to their deaths," Jean thought. "The ARVN will fight if their leaders will.

In the distance toward Loc Ninh, Jean heard almost continuous explosions and small arm's fire. From their position, it was impossible to see the fighting but Jean knew from experience that it had to be vicious.

Returning his attention to the main house, Jean watched NVA soldiers entering and leaving. Judging by the number of antennas, Jean knew it was a major headquarters. Looking closer, he saw many holes in the walls and ceilings

"With its excellent camouflage, from the air it must look like a destroyed building," Jean thought. "I hate to lose our home but I must inform the American advisers of this."

Turning to Nanh, Jean whispered, "Get some sleep. I will complete your watch. Tonight, you will take a message to an American adviser. The message that I give you will tell him that the plantation house is a NVA headquarters. Try An Loc first. If the NVA control it, continue south until you find an American advisor. Do not return here tonight. It is too far and dangerous. Wait until the next night to return."

Inside the plantation house, Commanding General Nguyen Van Anh looked through a family album brought to him by one of his infantry commanders. One of his soldiers found it during their initial search of the house. They arrived at the plantation less than an hour after their main attack. They found it deserted.

Later, when the fall of Loc Ninh seemed assured, word went to Anh that he could move his headquarters. Anh made the plantation his forward command post. The other command post in Cambodia was still operational and reported to Hanoi information received from the forward position.

Another found item, a family bible, confirmed Anh's suspicions. Comparing the photo album with the bible gave him a complete history of Minh Thanh since she married. One particular entry showed a son to be his namesake, Anh Vinh Danjou. There was another, still a baby, named for his father's brother, Diem.

"Minh Thanh is as beautiful as ever," he thought. "The pictures of her with her sons shows her radiance. What a lovely woman she is."

Someone knocked on his door and Anh said, "Come."

His Aide opened the door wide enough to see inside and said, "Sir, General Bien to see you."

"Send him in right away," Anh directed.

General Bien commanded the 9th Division and had the responsibility of taking An Loc. Anh's superiors, General Giap in particular, considered him Anh's most talented commander.

Anh arose as he entered. Bien bowed and Anh returned Bien's sign of respect.

Looking around Jean's former study, Bien said, "The plantation owners rob the people to live in such opulence. We will put an end to this."

"Yes," Anh answered. "How can I help you general?"

"Commander," Bien replied, "It is essential that I receive reinforcements. My regimental strength is quite low from casualties. Every time we gather for an attack, the American gunships decimate my forces. Worst of all is the B-52s; we have no defense against them. I have lost too many tanks. The helicopter gunships attack whenever they appear in the open. Their rockets do extensive damage. If I am to take An Loc, I need armor and infantry replacements soon."

Anh dared not refuse Bien. Taking An Loc was the purpose of everyone's attacks. To deprive the 9th Division would be ludicrous.

Anh promptly responded, "You shall have them tonight. Leave your requirements with my operations officer and he will see that you receive what you need."

"Thank you," Bien replied and asked. "I have information that an ARVN regimental commander surrendered his unit at the DMZ. Is this information correct?"

"Yes, it is. He is Lieutenant Colonel Pham Van Dinh and he surrendered his entire regiment. Later, he made broadcasts trying to convince other ARVN forces to join him," Anh explained.

"I am curious to know the difference between there and here. The ARVN are giving strong resistance to our advance. Some of them are deserting but not many. POWs tell us that American advisers are commanding many units. I did not expect this," Bien commented.

"Do not concern yourself," Anh said. "We have more than enough forces to accomplish our mission. Your men are fighting with enthusiasm I am told."

"The report is correct," Bien said, as he turned to leave. "I must visit my forward regiments. They are reporting that helicopters are still delivering supplies to An Loc. I must stop that."

Anh accompanied General Bien to his forward operations center located in the next room. At one time, it was the living area for the building. Anh's Operations Officer took Bien's reinforcement request and Anh signed it.

"Transmit this immediately," Anh said. "Add to it that I expect them in position with the 9th Division tonight."

After General Bien departed, Anh remained in Ops to review the tactical situation of each unit. They were not advancing as anticipated.

Anh knew that their mission would fail. The Americans had an unlimited supply of air power. If the French had such power at Dien Bien Phu, the Viet Minh's attack would have failed. As an artilleryman, he understood the use of firepower.

"Why couldn't they wait six months or a year. With the Americans gone, they could win but not now," Anh thought.

Colonel Biap, Anh's Intelligence Officer, joined him at the map board. He leaned close to Anh.

Whispering, Biap said, "Come with me general. I need you to see something."

Anh followed Biap to the cooking area. When they arrived at its doorway, Biap stopped.

Again he whispered, "Sir, look at the butcher's block."

Anh saw a cook with half of a freshly killed hog. It lay atop the tall, wooden block. Using a large knife, he cut pieces from the carcass.

"What?" Anh said, keeping his voice low.

"Sir, look at the block's base," Biap answered.

Anh saw blood from the carcass. While considerable amounts flowed down the block's sides, it spread on all sides except one. Occasionally, a bubble appeared in the blood and burst. Blood was flowing through the floor on one side of the block's base. Since the house was on a cement slab, the blood should accumulate as it did on the other sides.

Anh leaned slightly toward Biap and asked. "Have you told anyone?"

"No sir, I came directly to you. How do you want to handle this?" Biap asked.

Major Zane kept on the radios as Captain Leroy Billingsly flew their Hook toward An Loc's soccer field. Billingsly, a relatively new Hook pilot, found their flight route to An Loc "hairy." This was their sixth trip of the day.

When Zane briefed the crew that morning, he explained that their approach into An Loc had to be fast. As soon as they came within 15 miles of the besieged town, they were to descend to treetop level. Once they cleared trees south of town, they would make a low, fast approach. Zane explained that he would make the first run.

Loaded with ammunition, food, and other desperately needed supplies, Zane descended to tree top level beside the main road into An Loc. He put the ship's four tires and underbelly into trees that seemed to claw at the Hook. He kept the old A model redlined at 145 mph as they skimmed the forest's surface.

Once clear of the trees, Zane decreased altitude to slightly above the ground. He explained that An Loc's soccer field would soon appear. When it did, he began a slow deceleration. When within 100 yards, Zane lifted the ship's nose slightly and applied power with the Hook's thrust lever. Once the slowing started, the FE began lowering the Hook's ramp.

Earlier, when loading the Hook, the FE piled crates high on the ramp. When loaded, he raised the ramp causing the supplies to tumble into a pile at the ramp's base and extending up it.

When touching down, Zane gave no hint of a hover. The crew began throwing supplies from every possible place. The gunners threw crates through their left and right ports.

The FE dumped much of their load by simply lowering the ram to full down position. The supplies stacked on it tumbled to the ground. Those remaining, the FE pushed down the ramp.

The FE's effort was the most difficult. While unloading, he had to fight ARVN to keep them from boarding. They had one obsession. They wanted out of An Loc. When the ARVN deserters became more than he could handle, the gunners came to his aid. One held an M-16 set for full automatic firing. When an ARVN tried to board, he fired a burst in front of his feet before he made it to the ramp.

When the FE gave an all clear, Zane departed to the east or west. Sometimes he would make a wide arc at low level while accelerating. His next goal was to get to the trees as soon as possible. Zane always made sure that Cobra gunships providing escort knew his intentions. Without the Cobras, they would receive much more AAA than they did.

Later that day, the refuel and rearm point at Quan Loi came under NVA control. It was three kilometers northeast of An Loc. It was becoming apparent to Zane that their use of the soccer field would soon end.

As soon as Billingsly cleared the trees, they saw a Vietnamese Air Force (VNAF) Chinook sitting in the soccer field.

Zane said, "Put her down well to the right of the VNAF Hook. Two Hooks close together makes too good of a target."

While the crew was unloading, Zane watched the VNAF Hook to his left. A group of ARVN soldiers were running toward it when it began coming apart. Pieces flew in all directions, as its intermeshed blades went out of sync. A fire immediately developed and exploding fuel sent a mixture of black smoke and red flames skyward.

The soldiers, who had been running toward it, were getting up after diving for cover. Two mortar rounds exploded in their midst.

Zane calmly said, "I have the controls. Barry bring up the ramp now."

As Zane applied power, he did a hard right turn to an easterly heading. Billingsly swore he could see individual blades of grass passing beneath the Hook's nose as they rapidly accelerated.

Transmitting to the gunships, Zane said, "United Six, turning niner zero to one eight zero."

From the vicinity of Quan Loi, Zane saw tracers streaming at his Hook. From the corner of his left eye, he saw the area begin to explode as Cobras from F/79th ARA poured rockets into the position.

Once over the trees at top speed, Zane said, "Leroy, remind me to buy the Blue Max pilots anything they want at the club. In addition, we can forget the soccer field as a LZ from now on."

The night of 14 April 1972 Zane flew Lanny Briscoe on another high altitude mission. It was getting harder and harder to make an aircraft available for Briscoe's clandestine operation.

NVA forces surrounded An Loc. When the NVA took the high ground around Quan Loi, they were able to bring artillery and rocket fire onto any portion of An Loc. The city was receiving the most intense artillery bombardments of the Viet Nam war. Someone figured an artillery, rocket, or mortar shell struck every eight seconds.

In an effort to reinforce An Loc units, lift elements of the 229th Aviation Battalion were making assaults into LZs south of An Loc. Their Hueys were delivering eight ARVN troops per ship. The NVA had major AAA weapons in use at An Loc. Trying to approach the city by helicopter was a deadly act. The Huey pilots flew under Cobra cover from F/9th Cav and F79th ARA.

Zane's Hooks had to supply fuel and rockets to rearm and refuel points to keep the Cobras and Hueys flying and firing. It was a massive task to move the essentials to where they were most effective. The toll of doing so was showing on the Hook crews.

"I've got it," Briscoe said. "You can take us down now."

After landing, Zane asked Briscoe to accompany him to his quarters. As they entered, Briscoe exclaimed, "Damn major, you live good."

Briscoe looked through a doorway to the bedroom and bath and whistled. He turned to Zane with an astonished look.

"That's a damned king sized bed in there. Where did you get that?" Briscoe asked.

"Lanny, it was here when I arrived. Most everything you see is as it was when we occupied this area," Zane replied.

A wet bar divided the living area. Its top had alternating, colored, translucent tiles lighted from beneath. On the opposite side was a sink with running water and a stocked bar. A full sized refrigerator occupied one corner. The living room area had a large sofa with a coffee table and easy chairs placed conveniently throughout. The floor was inlaid tile. Two large air conditioners, one in the bedroom and another in the living room, chilled the air.

"You think this is something," Zane said. "Just out back there is a swimming pool and a band stand. The guys here before the Cav knew how to live."

Zane added, "Lanny, I didn't bring you here for a tour. How about letting me know what the NVA plans are?"

"All I can tell you is what they report and orders they receive," Briscoe answered.

"Hell, that' great. Let's hear it while I fix us a drink," Zane commented.

Opening his plastic binder, Briscoe said, "The commander of this NVA attack says that they took Loc Ninh sooner than expected. They have to slow their advance in order to rebuild their supplies. They're using ammunition and fuel faster than they can get it. Furthermore, the air strikes are hurting them. Their commander, General Nguyen Van Anh is requesting reinforcements to replace those used from his reserve. He's having to send tanks and troops to the 9th Division because of their heavy losses."

Someone knocked on Zane's door and yelled, "Hey, Dale. You big mother. Are you in there?"

Zane handed Briscoe his drink as he went to the door. He removed the metal rod serving as a lock and opened the door.

"Hi Daryl, he's here. Come on in," Zane said.

As Scott entered, Briscoe stood up as Zane said, "I believe you two know each other."

"We sure do. Good to see you again Briscoe," Scott said as he shook Briscoe's hand.

"Same here. What's happening in the SIGINT business?" Briscoe asked.

Zane handed a drink to Scott as he said, "The SIGINT business is why I asked Daryl to come tonight Lanny. I cannot continue flying these missions. My ships are too committed. However, Daryl has a solution for both of us."

Scott sat on the sofa next to Briscoe. He took a swallow of bourbon.

Looking at Briscoe, he said, "The withdrawal of RRU assets is being stopped. Not only is it being stopped, some units are returning to active status. I will be able to support your missions Lanny."

"Damn, that's good news. I've been trying to convince NSA about this for a long time. When did you hear about this?" Briscoe asked.

"Two weeks ago," Scott answered.

Looking stunned, Briscoe exclaimed, "Those sorry assholes. They told me yesterday that there was no chance. Someone really has their wires crossed. I sure hope it's the nerd I talked to."

"This is solid Briscoe," Scott stressed. "I already have the aircraft in place at Nah Trang."

Zane sat in an easy chair directly in front of Briscoe and said, "Lanny, I still want access to this information. It could save lives of my people. I realize that most of this stuff is senior officer talk. However, it could contain information that I could use planning our missions."

"You have it," Briscoe replied, "Daryl can show you anything I get."

"It's not that easy Lanny. Later, someone could nail Daryl for showing me this stuff. I want a clearance," Zane stated firmly.

"Dale," Briscoe began, "There's no way I can prove a 'need to know' status for you. I will make sure you get the information. It will be my rear on the line but what the hell, I'm not a virgin."

Zane set his glass on the coffee table and looked directly at Briscoe as he said, "I have one more request. A confidential source says that the 362nd is going to move an artillery unit in the near future. This move is to support an attack south of An Loc. It's not the move that bothers me Lanny. It's heat-seeking missiles that have my highest respect. My source says that the NVA have them. They have fired them at Air Force aircraft. The Air Force denies this. If you see anything remotely mentioned about these things, please expedite that info directly to me."

"Heat seeking missiles, they've been firing those over North Viet Nam for a long time," Briscoe replied.

"No Lanny, I'm talking shoulder fired, SA 7 Strellas," Zane made clear.

"Hell, the Soviets are not going to give those to North Viet Nam," Briscoe scoffed.

In frustration, Zane retrieved his glass and went toward the bar, as he said, "Lanny, damn it. They've given them their best surface to air systems. At An Loc, they have radar controlled .37-mm and .57-mm AAA weapons. Why wouldn't they give them the SA-7?"

Zane scooped some ice into his glass. He looked at the others while holding his glass up.

"Anyone else?" He asked.

With no takers, Zane poured his bourbon. He swirled it around in his glass watching it cling to the ice cubes. He returned to his seat.

Falling into his easy chair, Zane said, "Lanny think about this a moment. The one defining feature of this entire suck-hole war is the helicopter. Put SA-7s in here and there's a whole new ball game. This war, as we know it, will be no more."

Briscoe saw the logic in what Zane said. In fact, he began to wonder why the Soviets did not send SA-7s earlier. They were the poor man's defense against U.S. technology.

"Dale, you're right," Briscoe said as he got up from his seat. "Get me to MACV and I will start tonight. Shit, why didn't I think of this?"

Zane looked up from his chair at Briscoe and said, "Because you don't fly these things."

Nanh, Jean's messenger, never heard the shot that knocked him to the ground. Looking up, he could see ARVN soldiers staring down at him. Their faces would fade into a fuzzy blur and then into focus, as he continued to lose blood from his leg wound. From their conversation, Nanh could tell that his appearance confused them. They were used to fighting uniformed NVA regulars. Nanh was the perfect picture of a VC guerilla.

Slowly Nanh moved his hand toward his loincloth. As he reached inside, one of the ARVN put a bayonet to his throat and held it there while others searched him. He felt someone remove the tightly wrapped message and cry out in elation. Nanh heard him jabber something about being a great hero to his commander. He lapsed into unconsciousness.

Unexplainable bliss held Nanh and he didn't dare move should it leave. He ignored the shaking of his head and refused to open his eyes. A ghastly stench filled his nostrils causing him to gag and cough. He opened his eyes to see a Caucasian's face close to his. He closed them again only to cause the stench to return.

Nanh heard someone say, "Give me another ammonia caplet. I'll get him awake."

The stench became so strong that he began to retch and rolled onto his side. Opening his eyes again, he stared at a pair of boots. He felt hands in his armpits lifting him. The same face returned and he realized it belonged to an American.

Fully awake, he tried to talk but his mouth would not keep pace with his thoughts. He spewed forth unintelligible babble.

"Easy young man. You've lost a lot of blood. Just listen. You are in the 5th Division Headquarters in An Loc. We need to ask you some questions," the person explained.

Fully conscious, Nanh had difficulty understanding the American. Minh Thanh tried to teach them but he found it difficult to learn. Yet, he could speak some words.

Nanh formed each word in his mind, as he asked, "You American?"

"Yes, I am the senior adviser to the 5th Division Commander," the American said.

As Nanh clutched at his loincloth, the American held Jean's note up and asked. "Are you looking for this?"

Nanh tried to answer, but the face faded. The stench returned and he awakened. The person's face before him appeared familiar but medications fogged his mind.

Speaking perfect Vietnamese, the person said, "Nanh, it's me, Vinh. Minh Thanh's brother."

Slowly memories began to erase effects of his wound and medications, "Vinh, I need to see an American adviser. Please," Nanh pleaded.

"An American adviser has Jean's message," Vinh answered. "Are Jean and the others in the tunnels?"

Nanh turned his head away and would not answer. Despite repeated questioning and explanations, he would not betray Jean's instructions.

"Sir, Jean is a former French Legionnaire. He married my sister and they live at Peace Retreat Plantation. They're likely hiding beneath it in tunnels that Jean built for protection. Do not use B-52s or Tac Air on the place. You will kill them. Let me take a Ranger team. We'll destroy the headquarters and try to save those beneath it," Nanh heard Vinh telling someone, before he collapsed into his morphine induced world.

Major Vinh, and his 12-man team, had no difficulty moving through NVA positions surrounding An Loc. Dressed in NVA uniforms, they appeared to the enemy as one of their sapper squads. Once through ARVN positions, they moved openly without any hint at deception. Vinh's time serving with the Viet Minh paid immense dividends. Twice sentries stopped them momentarily but let them pass. Their security measures were practically non-existent. At one stop, Vinh did notice an apparent morale problem. There was talk of NVA commanders chaining armored vehicle drivers to their tanks or APCs. They were losing so many armored vehicles to ARVN using LAWs that they did not want to lead an attack.

Before dawn, they arrived at LTL-17. This was a secondary road that intersected with QL-13, the main road between An Loc and Loc Ninh. By moving through the old rubber plantations, they could arrive at Peace Retreat much quicker than by road. Vinh led the way and soon they were out of the rubber trees and into Jean's orchards. Even in darkness, they could see the storage bin's outline. Vinh stopped his group for a quick rescue plan review.

"I will climb the storage bin and rappel inside. That is their only observation point. Someone will be on guard but I should know the person. I must identify myself before they fire," Vinh explained to the others.

Vinh explained farther, "When I transmit for you to begin, the snipers take out every posted guard. Immediately place the satchel charges on the AAA weapons and take them out. Use one satchel charge near the unloading chute of the storage bin. Move to defensive positions while snipers provide covering fire. I will use the explosions as a diversion to move back to the storage bin and exit. There will be women and children so we won't be able to move fast."

"Regroup on the north side of the main house. We must clear the area before dawn. An Arc Light (B-52 carpet-bombing) mission on the house takes place at 07:00 hours. We must make our way to the 5th Division camp at Bu Dop. We cannot return to An Loc or travel south. We will move around An Loc to the north and then east to Bu Dop. Expect NVA troops the entire route. If we have to, treat the civilians as POWs. If separated, try for Bu Dop. If you have questions, ask them now."

Vinh did not expect questions. He had the finest Airborne Rangers in his regiment with him. Each was a former TIA tribesman from his mountain tribe north of Kontum.

Wearing night vision goggles, Vinh climbed the storage bin tower. His most difficult task was next. He had to open the chute without alerting the person on guard. With great care, he lifted its cover a millimeter at a time. Twenty minutes later, it rested against the bin's top and Vinh looked into the bin's darkness as if it were day. Sitting at the viewing port, he saw the expected guard. He could not recognize him from the rear.

Vinh decided not to rappel. It would require unnecessary noise. Instead, he clutched his hands to his chest and fell directly upon the unsuspecting guard. Both boots struck the young man's neck and shoulder area. Surrounding nuts silenced and softened the impact. Rolling him onto his back, he immediately recognized the guard. He was Hiep, a youth from Loc Ninh.

Checking for a pulse, Vinh determined that he was only unconscious and not dead. Vinh feared he might have broken his neck. Not able to leave him, Vinh began trying to revive him. Fifteen minutes passed.

"This is taking too long," Vinh thought.

Cupping his left hand over Hiep's mouth, Vinh felt for a nerve in the unconscious youth's face with his right. He straightened his left elbow to increase pressure on Hiep's face and pressed his right thumb into a nerve on his face. The result was an immediate tensing of Hiep's body as a searing pain coursed through his head. He immediately opened his eyes. Unable to see his assailant, he began to struggle.

Vinh placed his mouth near Hiep's right ear and whispered, "Be still. It's me, Vinh."

Hiep continued his struggling until Vinh identified himself four times. Keeping his hand over Hiep's mouth, Vinh explained his mission and why. He released his pressure as Hiep relaxed.

Whispering, Vinh said, "Let's get to the others. We do not have much time."

Still wearing his night vision goggles, Vinh went into the room filled with munitions. Since he could see clearly, he did not need a candle. As he approached the main passageway, he stopped and removed the vision-enhancing device. If he entered the lighted passageway with them on, he would lose his vision. Light from candles would become like powerful searchlights.

As he placed the device into his backpack, he saw the outline of two persons on the doorway's cover. Through a small, vertical opening, he saw their NVA uniforms. Vinh raised his hand to alert Hiep. Through hand signals, Vinh indicated that he would attack the one in front. Hiep would take the second. They could not do both simultaneously because the passage was too narrow.

Vinh removed his survival knife t from its scabbard on his belt. Upon his signal, the two dove through the curtain. Vinh placed his left hand over the man's mouth while placing his left leg behind his knees. In one fluid motion, he pulled him down and leapt upon his chest. At the same time, he raised his knife to his left ear and started a knife stroke that would sever arteries, veins, and the NVA soldier's windpipe. His victim stared, wide-eyed with fright, into Vinh's eyes.

Before his blade cut flesh, recognition struck Vinh causing him to stop. His body screamed kill but his mind said no. In a millisecond, he saw green rice fields and Muong Valley. He peeked into the next room and saw a gun while his brother pulled on his leg. Outside a tunnel at night, he and Anh looked at stars and talked of his future.

One word left Vinh's lips, "Anh?"

Colonel Biep died beside his commander. Jean taught Hiep well. With his throat cut, Biep could not cry out in pain but only gurgle. Without blood to his brain, he lapsed into unconsciousness and died.

Hiep arose totally confused. He watched Vinh rolling on the floor with a NVA general. They held each other close amid sobbing and floods of tears. Looking up, he saw Jean approaching with an AK-47 at the ready. He was coming to kill. Hiep knew the look but did not know how to respond. Even when Jean stood over them, he gave Hiep questioning looks but could only stare in disbelief.

When the pair gained a semblance of composure, they saw Jean. Anh saw Jean's look and knew it for what it was. He understood his passion because he saw before him his mortal enemy. He knew that Jean's total desire was to end his life. Perhaps it would solve his dilemma. Although Vinh wore an NVA uniform, he represented what his life's work had been, to remove those stifling his nation's unification.

Others in the underground complex began to gather. Among them, Anh saw Minh Thanh. He felt that he would recognize here anywhere but he did see her in photos and had an advantage. His namesake clung to her dress as she held her other child in her arms.

Realizing that Jean did not yet know who he was, he said, "Minh Thanh. It's me, Anh."

As she ran toward him, Jean took the child from her arms. Stopping a few inches from him, Minh Thanh raised her hand and slowly moved it through his gray hair. Large tears formed at the corners of her eyes and coursed down her face.

Her chin trembled as she looked into Anh's eyes and said, "My beloved brother. We have lost a life together. We must not lose anymore."

Turning her head sideways, Minh Thanh placed it upon his chest. Her arms reached around him, holding him tight as she sobbed. She did not speak or look at him. She simply stayed close and wept.

Vinh explained the situation to Jean. He told about his waiting team members and explained about the Arc Light. He gave his assurance that Jean's tunnel would not protect them.

Pointing at Anh, he asked. "How can we leave with their Southern Front Commander."

Without pause, Jean continued, "We cannot trust him. He will betray us at his first opportunity."

Hearing this, Minh Thanh pulled away from Anh and looking into his eyes, asked. "Would you?"

Without hesitation, he replied, "Never little sister."

Raising his gaze to Jean, Anh said, "We gained entrance to your tunnel with great difficulty. We had to destroy the butcher's block. Others will soon find it and come here. You must act swiftly to escape."

"Come with us Anh," Minh Thanh cried.

Anh cupped Minh Thanh's face in his hands and kissed her eyelids. He pulled her to him.

"I cannot but I will not betray you. Make your escape. The others will think that you over powered me. You must go now," Anh said from a part of his innermost soul.

Even Jean knew that he spoke the truth. He had Hiep gather the others while he and the young men armed themselves. With the group gathered in the weapon's storage area, Vinh gave his final instructions.

"When we hear the explosions, climb into the storage bin. There will be an opening to the outside. Go through it and around the house to your left. We will take refuge in the large ditch past where the old Land Rover sat on blocks. Keep your heads down and open you mouths so the explosions do not rupture your eardrums. After the air strike, we will follow the ditch and cross beneath the bridge on QL-13. Our destination is the 5th Division Camp at Bu Dop."

Vinh transmitted the attack signal with his radio. They heard rifle fire and then a short silence. Next, loud explosions shook their tunnel. Dirt fell from between the sandbags as red dirt covered them. Some of the children began crying. Their mothers tried to calm them.

"Follow me," Vinh said as he went up the stairs to the ladder.

After only two rungs, he was looking into the outdoors. The storage bin's side had a gaping hole. Without stopping, he continued outside to help the others. He saw that the APCs and AAA weapons were twisted and burning. He grabbed others' hands and pulled them through. He pushed each person towards the left side of the main house.

Vinh pulled Anh through and close behind was Jean. Anh didn't move when pushed.

Putting his arms around Vinh, Anh said, "Goodbye little brother. Explain to Minh Thanh."

Anh turned and ran toward the Cambodian border. Jean raised his rifle to fire but didn't.

Vinh saw his snipers racing toward them and said, "Let's get out of here."

Vinh and Jean jumped into the ditch together. The snipers landed on top of them. Vinh could see a dim glow in the east. He climbed the ditch's side and looked over its top toward the house. Behind him, he heard Minh Thanh screaming Anh's name.

One moment the plantation house was there and the next it disappeared amid massive explosions and flying debris. The blast threw Vinh against the ditches' opposite side with a hard impact. He knew enough to open his mouth as he slid to its bottom where he lay still. He tried to breathe but his chest seemed overcome with a massive pressure. Pieces of dirt, rubber trees, and other materials fell from the sky into the ditch. Vinh watched the others covering their heads. Minh Thanh lay in a fetal position with both sons clutched to her. Jean lay atop them fending off falling debris.

Vinh, running down the ditch pulling people to their feet, yelled, "Let's go. We have to make the bridge before full daylight."

Two days later the group arrived at Bu Dop. They never would have made it without Jean, Vinh, and his Rangers. Their route went through NVA controlled territory the entire trip. They bypassed motor parks with tanks and APCs. The number of mobile, radar controlled AAA sites was overwhelming. Vinh, thinking that Bu Dop was a haven, was in error. NVA forces surrounded the place. Refugees were quickly filling the area in an effort to stay away from the fighting.

Across a river, and to the southeast, was Song Be. Many refugees said that it was an American rearm and refueling point for operations against NVA at An Loc. Vinh had to return to his unit. However, he wanted to move Minh Thanh and Jean to safety. He figured the Cathedral in Saigon's Cholon District was the best choice. He met with Jean to try and arrange a move.

"It is a short distance from here to Song Be," Vinh stated. "Once we cross the river, we will practically be at Song Be."

"You are correct," Jean agreed. "However, the children have no strength. They need food. I will go with you to Song Be. Surely, you can get a few cases of rations. We will bring the food here so they can regain strength before making the journey."

"Jean," Vinh began, "I will not return here. I must return to my regiment. They cannot get out of An Loc. The way I see things, the battle of An Loc is becoming a siege. It will last for months. My men need me."

Jean thought for a moment and said, "Hell, I bet you can get a helicopter to return you to An Loc. You are a regimental commander. Go to Ops here and request one. When it comes, we will put the others on board."

"You know what they will send. They will send an OH-6. It won't hold as many people as we have," Vinh said becoming frustrated.

Continuing, Vinh said, "I will request a Huey. All they can say is no."

The pair made their way to 5th Division Operations. Vinh explained his situation to the Operations Officer.

He smiled and said, "Major, the NVA will soon overrun our base. I have requested relocation to Song Be. There will be Chinooks arriving tomorrow afternoon. Wait for them."

At Long Thanh North, Major Zane discussed an upcoming artillery move to support troops at An Loc. With him were Captain Caldwell, Operations Officer, and Captain Greenletter, Executive Officer.

Caldwell pointed to an area three kilometers southeast of An Loc and explained, "Sir, this high ground is next to Windy Hill and Hill 169. It is an excellent place to control artillery fire against the NVA. General Minh ordered that the 1st Airborne Brigade move from their positions along QL-13 to this area to support the 5th ARVN Division in An Loc. 229th Hueys moved them on a combat assault today. They landed without any NVA opposition. However, the NVA saw their landing and attacked later. The Airborne forces took some causalities but are still a viable fighting force. Our advisers with them called in Tac Air and kicked some butt driving off the NVA forces with heavy casualties."

Zane asked. "Why Tac Air? Didn't they have artillery support?"

"No sir they didn't but tomorrow they will," Caldwell answered.

"Explain," Zane directed.

"In the morning, lift companies from the 229th will insert the rest of the brigade. We will lift a battery of six 105s, of the 3rd Artillery Battalion, from their position beside QL-13 to the original landing zone near Windy Hill. I've arranged for Cobra cover throughout the flight. Our pickup time for the howitzers is 06:30 hours. We will rendezvous with the Cobra's at RP (release point) 135 at this location," Caldwell explained as he pointed to the RP southeast of An Loc.

"Earnest, here's how I want to run this lift," Zane said. "Get in touch with the advisors with the 1st Airborne Brigade. Tell them that we will not move as single ships. The best way to reduce AAA exposure time is to move in flights of three. This way they only get two chances to blow us away. With single ship moves, they get six. Make sure they know to have the howitzers rigged with two groups of three 30 meters apart. I will fly the lead Hook. We will sling out the first three. Five minutes later, the second group of three will take out the other three howitzers."

"Each group will fly a different route to the LZ. We will not use a RP. Their AAA people will spot that in a heartbeat. Have the gunships join up along the way. We will take the howitzer in as flights of three. Exits from the LZ will be different for each group. We will fly NOE throughout the mission. I want those howitzers tearing tops out of coconut palms," Zane said with emphasis by pounding three times on the map with his fist.

"Uh, sir, won't the howitzers snag a tree's top?" Greenletter asked.

Disappointment flooded Zane's face and voice, as he answered, "Terry, think a little. What tree top is going to snag a multi-ton howitzer traveling 145 miles per hour?"

Greenletter blushed and replied, "You're right sir. I didn't think. Lord help any poor monkey in those trees."

Zane could not help but burst into laughter as he said, "You've got it."

Caldwell interrupted to say, "We have another mission after that sir. We will need every ship we have flyable."

"What?" Zane asked.

"We're to make fuel and 2.75-inch rocket runs to Song Be. After we drop those loads, we're to fly north to Bu Dop, which is on the Cambodian border. We're to relocate 5th Division Forces to Song Be. C-123s won't land there because it is too dangerous. They'll board the C-123s at Song Be," Caldwell explained.

Zane examined Bu Dop's map location and said, "That place is going to be crawling with AAA. When the NVA see us pulling those people out, they're going to put every anti-aircraft weapon to work. Make damned sure we have Cobras and Tac Air Support for that one Earnest."

"Yes sir," Greenletter said, as he reached for a field phone.

"Terry, walk with me," Zane directed.

Outside, the tarmac reflected heat in shimmering waves. Row upon row of Chinooks appeared to float in a lake with tall walls for guards. Zane and Greenletter walked between the rows while Zane talked.

"Terry, I am worried sick about this SA-7 missile business. Correct me if I'm wrong but I believe the SA-7 works like our Stinger missile. The operator must get the aircraft in his sight and get a lock. After that, he must maintain a ten second lock on the ship before he can launch. Is that about it?" Zane asked.

"Yes sir, that's my understanding," Greenletter answered.

Zane stopped and glanced from Chinook to Chinook as he commented, "Terry, those ships cost almost $15,000,000 each. Some dummy with an IQ the same as his waist size can bring one down with a heat-seeking missile. Did you ever do any duck hunting Terry?"

"Yes sir, quite a bit," Greenletter responded.

"Well then you know how hard it is to hit a duck flying overhead when you are in the woods. A duck can fly at about 60 miles per hour. The only time you can see it is when it passes through overhead clearings. It is gone before you can lead it and pull the trigger. Like the duck, we can use NOE to beat these missiles but we need something else. How many flare guns do we have on each hook?" Zane asked.

"There's one in the ship's over water survival raft," Greenletter answered.

"Get with Top and Snuffy. We need six per ship. Make sure to load up with flares. Put 2 flare pistols in the cockpit so that the AC and FP have one loaded and in easy reach. In addition, put one by each gunner and two in the rear for the FE. If anyone sees a missile coming, they are to fire a flare and then announce its location. For example, missile at six o'clock low."

"These flares float down with a parachute and burn magnesium. They make a heat signature much hotter than our engines. Until someone comes up with a defensive system, we'll have to use the flares," Zane instructed.

"Sir," Greenletter asked. "What makes you think they're going to use heat seeking missiles?"

Zane answered, "Remember that Major Vinh that visited us? He mentioned before he left about seeing some metal crates with special markings in Cambodia after we made that napalm run. From his description, I think the crates have SA-7s in them. We can't take any chances. Get us those flares Terry."

On 15 April 1972, Zane's flight of six Hooks left Long Thanh North to move six artillery pieces to a position approximately three kilometers southeast of An Loc. Within sight of their pickup point, Zane had the flight form two groups of three in a "V" formation. Zane, in the lead Hook, saw three ARVN artillerymen standing atop three 105s rigged for sling loads. The first three Hooks arrived over their loads, hooked up, and departed as one aircraft. The total pickup time was less than five seconds. As they left the pickup zone, the other three Hooks were inbound.

Zane, flying AC in the lead ship, said, "L-T, you did an excellent job on that pickup."

Lieutenant Billingsly answered, "Thank you sir."

"Now, let's run some of our primate cousins out of their homes. Put her on the deck L-T," Zane directed.

As Billingsly started a descent toward the trees, Zane received a radio transmission. With so much noise, Zane increased his volume and listened for another transmission.

"Good morning United Six. This is your friendly escort service for today," someone said.

Zane began searching the sky until he saw a Cobra gunship to his flight's left and right. Their markings showed them to be from F Troop, First of The Ninth Cavalry.

Zane replied, "Morning gents. We thank you for your support. Watch out for flying timber."

"Roger United Six," a gunship pilot replied, his voice filled with doubt as to what Zane meant.

Keeping his gaze straight ahead, Zane told Billingsly, "Son, I will get a nose bleed at this altitude. Let's get close to mother earth."

Billingsly, having flown with Zane before, reacted and began to lose altitude while maintaining his airspeed. Zane glanced occasionally in his rear view mirror, which allowed him to see through the cargo area and out the ship's rear. When he could see trees, he knew when Billingsly approached the altitude he wanted.

"Just a touch lower L-T," Zane instructed, keeping watch to the rear.

Within seconds, Zane could see treetop parts going skyward behind his ship. The 105-mm howitzer, hanging beneath, cut a trough through the trees.

"Perfect L-T. Hold that," Zane instructed.

"Whoo-weee, United Six, you are chopping some timber," the gunship leader transmitted.

Zane kept checking the other two ships in his flight. They were in perfect position so that they did not fly over the same route as Zane. Furthermore, they were cutting treetops as he explained to them earlier.

Zane transmitted to his flight, "United Ultra One, this is United Six. Looking good LZ 2 clicks ten o'clock. You know what to do."

To Zane's left front, he saw three ARVN artillerymen waving their arms. They were where they wanted their weapons placed.

"They're exactly where they should be," Zane thought. "That's where I would put my howitzers."

"United Six, breaking left," Zane transmitted.

"Ultra 2 roger, Ultra 3, roger," his other ship Aircraft Commanders replied, indicating they understood and would comply.

"Maintain speed L-T," Zane said.

Billingsly, anticipating his approach path, began a left turn while maintaining his airspeed. He ended his turn flying directly toward the middle artilleryman waving his arms. At the last moment, he decreased his forward speed and leveled his hook.

"Drop it," the FE said.

Billingsly activated a switch releasing the howitzer and immediately began his takeoff from the LZ. He began a right turn, which was the shortest distance to nearby trees. He transmitted his intentions to the others. His total time, stopping, and dropping the load, was three seconds.

As they entered the treetops Zane said, "I've got it."

"Ultra Flight United Six, good show. Next mission," Zane radioed.

"Ultra 2 roger, Ultra 3, roger," the others answered.

"L-T have you completed a PE (Periodic Inspection) in maintenance yet?" Zane asked.

"Yes sir, last week," Billingsly answered.

"Fine, you handle the missions the rest of the day. I will play Peter Pilot. If you lead as good as you fly, you will be an AC tomorrow," Zane explained.

"Thanks sir. I'll do my best," Billingsly replied quite surprised.

"Where's our cover?" Zane asked.

Billingsly began searched the sky for the Cobras. After locating them, he reported their position to Zane.

"What's the call sign and frequency for Tac Air?" Zane asked.

Billingsly began leafing through charts and notes on a metal sheet holder strapped to his left leg. In a few minutes, he reported them to Zane.

Zane immediately asked. "What's our pickup time and when do we contact the FAC (forward air controller)?"

Again, Billingsly scramble through his notes. After about five minutes, he located the information and told Zane.

"What's the problem L-T?" Zane continued to ask.

"Sir, you caught me by surprise. The thought of being AC never entered my mind for today. I have the info but just have to get it organized," Billingsly explained.

"L-T, what would you do if I took a round between my eyes? Would you be surprised then also?" Zane asked.

Billingsly began organizing his notes on his kneeboard. He put the most often used items within easy reach. The rest he marked as to their content and placed them beneath the higher priority information sheets.

When completed, he said, “Sir, you made your point big time. I came to rely on the AC too much. I could become AC at any moment.”

“You still are L-T,” Zane advised.

Chapter Forty Seven

April - May 1972

Therefore the skilful leader subdues the enemy's troops without any fighting;
he captures their cities without laying siege to them;
he overthrows their kingdom without lengthy operations in the field.
Sun Tzu (6th–5th century BC), Chinese general. *The Art of War,* ch. 3, axiom 6

It was not winter's chill that made Haughton House cold for Vanessa. It was the loss of the one person who made it warm and inviting, Frederick. Vanessa knew this before she left Saigon for the only home she ever had.

When she saw Buff Winslow and Befford Redding at her door, she knew. Redding was Frederick's executive assistant at Air America's headquarters in Saigon. He ran things when Frederick flew missions, which was too frequent. Winslow and Frederick became friends, during their years working together at Tan Son Nhut. In addition, he was a neighbor and friend.

"I'm sorry Vanessa," Redding said. "We've not located his ship at any base in South Viet Nam, Cambodia or Laos. His last reported sighting was at Long Thanh North.

She didn't expect more information than Redding told her. It would be fruitless to ask. Redding would simply lie and there was no need for that. She could not fault Redding because Frederick delivered many such messages himself during their time with Air America. Finally, her time came and she was home without him.

Her tears lasted two months as they seared her love for Frederick forever into her heart. The first time she was alone the major hurt came. It was the knowledge that she could never hear his voice, touch him, and love him that caused unbearable pain. She only thought she prepared herself as she followed him around the world. She consoled others thinking that she could deal with it. Her perception made a fool of her. It was a false perception that lulled her mind. There was no way to prepare for what she felt.

She wore a wool sweater beneath her riding jacket to ward off England's damp cold. She descended the stairs and left the main house for the stables. She looked forward to seeing their newest colt Quasar. He carried Daytran's genes and had great promise as an Arabian. Her heart ached as she thought of Daytran and the wonderful string of champions that he provided.

"What a wonderful steed he was," she thought. "When I rode him it was as if we were one soul moving together over the hedges and barriers. Oh, how I loved that gallant horse."

Walking to the stables, she thought, "There are those who would laugh at my portraying Daytran as gallant. Gallant was a human attribute and not one to be applied to a horse. He was always courteously attentive, especially to women. I consider that gallant."

Opening the door to the main stalls, she saw their veterinarian's assistant standing near their new fold's stall. She knew that Phillip Dellar would be with Quasar.

"Good afternoon Lady Earling," Dellar's assistant greeted her.

"Good afternoon, Garland. It is so nice to see you. How is Quasar?" Vanessa asked.

"Oh, he is such a beauty mam. He is in perfect health," Garland answered.

Garland opened the stall's gate for Vanessa to enter. As expected, Phillip Dellar was caressing the lovely Arabian.

"Hello Phillip. How is Quasar today?" Vanessa asked.

Dellar looked at Vanessa with a beaming smile and answered, "It must be the luck of the Irish. Your sires never fail to deliver beautiful, intelligent Arabian's mam."

"Maybe so," she replied. "However, I think most of the credit belongs to Daytran."

"Oh yes mam. What a grand horse he was too," Dellar agreed. "When Gulag sired Tular, I thought I had seen the ultimate Arabian. However, Tular has sired this beautiful creature. You can start letting Quasar run free. He doesn't need the mare anymore. Do you intend to keep Tular at stud?"

"Yes I am. He will continue for one more year," Vanessa replied.

"That's superb mam. I'm plagued with calls for his services. Your decision will make many breeders happy," Dellar responded with obvious joy.

"If the breeders would refer a new trainer, that would make me happy," Vanessa answered. I do not intend for Tular to compete this coming year unless I get someone soon," Vanessa stated.

Vanessa hoped that Dellar might have a recommendation. When he did not suggest anyone, she felt considerable disappointment. She was most anxious to begin riding in competitions again.

"Please excuse me. I need to visit with Tular," Vanessa said, as she opened the stall to leave.

She walked her usual route. As soon as she opened the back door and stepped outside, she heard Tular call to her. As he raced toward the fence between them, she could swear that he was Gulag or Daytran. His tail held high, he lifted his feet with the grace born of a thoroughbred. When she reached inside her sweater, Tular neighed with pleasure. He knew, like the others before him, where she kept their treats.

As she approached the fence, he pawed the ground and raised his massive head. His powerful neck rippled with strength born of the vast desert where his forefathers ran.

"Hello Tular, you are a showoff. All you want is the sweets that I bring," she said while putting one foot on the bottom rail.

Placing her left hand on the top rail, she pulled to raise herself. With both feet firmly placed, she removed two sugar cubes from her sweater with her right hand. Tular pranced with delight. Vanessa extended her right arm, with her fist clinched, toward Tular. He reared with his deep brown eyes wide.

Vanessa opened her hand and Tular walked forward and gently nibbled the offered sugar cubes with his big lips. If a horse could smile, Tular did. As Tular enjoyed his treats, Vanessa stroked his big neck and whispered praise to him.

As she lowered herself to the ground, she saw a black sedan approaching the main house. With Tular protesting, she quickly walked to the corner of the building where they repaired equipment. From her position, she could see the curved drive in front of Haughton House.

The auto was a taxi. She could not see the person exiting the rear seat. He left the vehicle on the side away from her. She could see he wore a plaid cap buttoned down in front. He paid the driver.

Vanessa watched with curiosity as the taxi driver departed. They were not expecting visitors. Now, in full view, she saw that the man braced himself with a cane. At his feet was a leather traveling case. He looked directly toward her.

"Oh, it cannot be," she thought as she took one step forward.

He lifted his bag with his left hand and braced his right leg with the cane. He began walking in her direction. She could see his smile.

She took two more steps as disbelief and joy coursed through her. As he continued in her direction, doubt left her and she began to run.

"Oh my God, it's Devon," her mind screamed, as her heart beat faster.

He dropped his leather case and increased his pace toward her with a noticeable limp. Now, they were close. He stopped and waited.

Stopping directly in front of him, she felt her legs trembling. She fell forward as he opened his arms.

"Pardon me mam," he whispered in her ear. "I understand you will be needing a trainer."

Holding Devon close, she could hear his heart beating as she pressed her cheek against his chest. She felt the scars across his back with her hands.

Pulling away, she stomped her right foot and said, "What kind of man is it who brings his bag as if the job is his for the taking? Devon Elder you are a conceited lout and a worthless trainer at that."

Grabbing Devon's left hand, she pulled him along cursing the entire way. She stopped where Tular stood at the fence.

"That sir is a horse. His son is inside. And, if it is work you are a looking for, there is plenty of it awaiting. That is if you are not too crippled for the job," she cried, as tears steamed down her shanty Irish cheeks.

Meanwhile, in South Viet Nam, Giap's invasion continued. The siege at An Loc grew more intense as NVA continued a desperate effort to take An Loc. American advisers, trapped in the town's center, continued coordinating air strikes against them.

Major General Hollingsworth remained overhead directing strikes against targets the advisers could not see. Not a moment passed that he did not have B-52s, Spectre gunships, or tactical aircraft ravaging the exposed attackers. When he wasn't attacking the NVA, he bolstered the trapped adviser's morale with reports of their slaughter.

"Sir, Song Be will be on our right in a few minutes. We should be able to see red dust soon," Billingsly told Zane. "It's a major refuel and rearm point. Our birds have been hauling to it since this An Loc business started."

"Ultra 2, Ultra 3, trail," Billingsly transmitted.

"Two roger, three roger," the other Hook pilots answered, as they modified their aircraft's position.

Hook number two moved directly behind Zane's craft. Hook number three moved behind two to form a trail formation.

"Sir," Billingsly said, "I did that because of the dust in the LZ. Bu Dop is a mess of red dust. It's about the same at Song Be. I think it's safer to go in this way. Since jungle encircles it, we can use different routes in and out of the place. The AC on 2 and 3 now have that choice."

"Roger that L-T," Zane replied.

"Kid's using his head," Zane thought.

"That's it on the left. Make your approach straight in from here. The others will have time for our dust to clear," Billingsly instructed.

Zane made his approach fast and directly to the ground with no hover. A red cloud spread around them completely blocking their view. Only by looking through the chin bubble could Zane determine where the ground was. As soon as they were on approach, the FE lowered the ramp halfway. Upon touchdown, he lowered it to the ground.

Crowds ran from the surrounding jungle. Some were military while others were civilian refugees. They appeared consumed with fear.

"Sir, what do I do back here? There's women, kids, and soldiers mixed," their FE asked pleadingly.

Zane looked into the rearview mirror. The cargo compartment was full and more piling inside every second.

"Close the ramp Braddock," Zane ordered.

"Ramp coming up sir," Braddock answered.

As with cargo missions, people on the ramp were pressed forward. The group became a crushed together mass of people fleeing for their lives.

"How many you think we got Braddock," Zane asked.

"At least 100 sir," the FE reported.

"No sweat," Zane thought. "I remember a guy on first tour that hauled out one 180. They're women and kids mostly. They are small and not heavy."

Zane gave Billingsly a questioning look. Billingsly returned his look and hesitated for a second.

"Shit sir, take her out," Billingsly directed.

Zane added power quickly in order to move out of the dust cloud that he knew would come. The Hook trembled slightly and began its ascent. As the dust began to form, he lowered the ship's nose slightly to obtain some forward motion. With the dust cloud behind, he added just enough power to clear the tree tops directly in front.

Once above the trees, Zane lowered the nose again to increase forward airspeed and remain low. Billingsly watched as tree limbs crashed against the Hook's chin bubble.

"Tracers at nine o'clock," Braddock yelled over the intercom.

"I'm on it," the left door gunner cried.

Zane could hear the gunner's M-60 firing over the intercom while the gunner spoke.

Suddenly, a Cobra gunship passed Zane's side and began a climb to the left. Zane heard explosions over someone's intercom because they had their talk button pressed.

"Holy shit. They kicked their ass," Braddock yelled as a second Cobra passed on Zane's side.

Looking in the rearview mirror, Zane saw a smoking hole in the trees behind them. The first Cobra that passed on his left was already firing rockets into the same spot.

Zane began a hard turn to his right to a course for Song Be. Now flying in the opposite direction of their takeoff, they had a clear view of support ships attacking the AAA site that fired at them. Billingsly appeared frozen in place. His eyes seemed riveted on the gunship action.

"Get your ass back in this Hook L-T," Zane yelled over the intercom.

Billingsly turned his head away from the firing and looked forward. He blinked a few times and seemed to regain his composure. Zane could see Billingsly's hands trembling.

Slowly, with deliberation, Zane said, "L-T, you have the aircraft."

As soon as Billingsly had the controls, his trembling stopped. He had the aircraft completely under control. He continued a NOE course toward Song Be.

"Thanks loads to F Troop," Zane transmitted.

"Anything to help the guys who bring us goodies to deliver to the VC," a Cobra pilot answered.

"Braddock, do you see the Cobras?" Zane asked the FE.

"Yes sir, There's two of them to our left and right rear. They are slightly higher than we are, sir," Braddock said.

The Cobra flight leader advised Zane that they needed to rearm and refuel. Zane advised them that it was necessary to refuel the Hook. He advised them that they would wait for them.

"No sweat United. There's a couple already waiting for your return," the Cobra lead advised.

"L-T, when we refuel, I need to take a whiz. How about you?" Zane asked.

"You go first sir," Billingsly replied.

Zane made a mental note to talk to Billingsly later. He suspected that was his first time in a firefight.

Dust and debris was worse at Song Be than at Bu Dop. Crating material, paper, and other extraneous material was lying amid thick, red dirt. Zane was glad they did not have a sling load on their approach. Trying to hover would be a mess.

Parked at the refueling point, the FE and a gunner began refueling on each side of the aircraft. With the turbines still running, Zane removed his shoulder harness and left the cockpit to urinate. Remaining in the cargo compartment were a group of civilians and an ARVN major. They looked familiar and then he remembered the Land Rover. Zane removed his helmet and the group broke into smiles.

Zane took the Frenchman's outstretched hand. Quick behind him was Major Vinh who had come to Long Thanh and requested he fly out his relatives. As fate had it, he did fly them.

Because of the engine noise, they had to yell to be heard as Vinh said, "We did not realize it was you Major Zane. We ran for the first ship we saw. Bu Dop is not a safe place."

Zane laughed aloud and replied, "Now, you tell me."

Zane asked. "Where are you trying to go?"

Major Vinh answered, "I must return to An Loc. I am sure I can get a Huey from here. The others are going to Saigon. They need to get to Tan Son Nhut."

Zane thought a moment and said, "If they can wait about two hours, I will return here to refuel on my way to Long Thanh North. I will take them to Tan Son Nhut. It is on my way."

Vinh's face became one big smile as he ran to the others. He was waving his arms and relating Zane's offer.

He returned and said, "Sir, they are very happy. I told them to watch for your ship's tail number. When they see you return to refuel, they will board. Is that okay?"

Zane slapped Vinh on his shoulder and answered, "You bet it is. Now, take the ladies away. I need to answer Nature's call."

"Oh, go right ahead," Major Vinh stated, "They don't mind."

"I do," Zane answered and pushed Vinh toward the ship's rear.

Standing on the ramp, Zane wondered, "Why can I do this here and not at a drug test? This is the second time I've been through this."

He waved at Minh Thanh, Jean, and the others as they moved from Song Be's landing area. Finished, he returned to the cockpit while Billingsly went to the ramp.

During the rest of the day, Zane's unit continued their relocation mission. Each time a Hook landed, military personnel and civilian refugees clamored aboard. There were continued incidents of anti-aircraft fire. F Troop OH-6s scouted clear routes for the Hooks to follow from the hot LZ. One OH-6, from F Troop/9th Cavalry, went down from AAA fire, killing its pilot while he sought safe passage for the Hooks.

One of the 362nd Hooks took AAA rounds through its rotor blades while leaving Bu Dop. Since Bu Dop could be overrun at any time, the AC elected to continue to Song Be. At Song Be, an examination of the damage revealed that the ship was not safe to fly. An emergency request for replacement blades went to Long Thanh North. After arrival, anyone available for work helped replace the damaged blades. The ship was able to depart before sunset but arrived at Long Thanh North after dark. This was the first time that a 362nd Hook sustained damage from ground fire. Zane thanked God that no one received a scratch, including the passengers.

As dark neared, Bu Dop was empty of people trying to evacuate. Zane decided it was time to leave.

"L-T, let's make a refueling stop at Song Be and head to Long Thanh North and a beer," Zane told Billingsly.

"I'm for that sir. Damn, it has been one hell of a day," Billingsly responded.

After refueling, Zane loaded his passengers. Zane learned from Jean that their plantation no longer existed. It was rubble. Zane saw the hurt in Jean's eyes as he related the loss of a dream, a life's hope. Yet, he rejoiced that his family lived and they would find a future in France, if not in Viet Nam.

At Tan Son Nhut, Zane waved to the group as they crossed the tarmac toward the terminal. The sadness of the moment became bewildering and almost overpowering. This was something not learned in a philosophy class or political science. At the time, Zane wished he had the hippie staff from every university here to taste the real thing.

"Major," the FE said over the intercom. "A flag of some type fell out of that French guy's back pocket. Actually, it is not a whole flag but part of one. What do you want me to do with it?"

"Run him down and give it to him," Zane said.

Zane saw his FE get to Jean before entering the terminal. The two talked and the FE passed the flag to Jean. Jean turned and looked toward Zane's Chinook. He came to attention and rendered a long salute. Turning away, he entered the terminal.

"Major, that guy from France really appreciated that torn flag. He cried when I gave it to him. Have any idea why sir?" Zane's FE asked.

Zane answered, "I don't have the slightest idea. Let's go home."

After returning to Long Than North, Zane gathered mission data in Ops. That day alone, the estimated number of people relocated from Bu Dop exceeded 100,000.

The siege at An Loc continued unabated. The trapped 5th Division continued its battle with T-54 tanks, massive artillery bombardments, and continuing infantry onslaughts. Through April and into May, it continued. NVA died by the tens of thousands as aerial firepower slaughtered them.

Zane's Hooks continued their missions despite repeated reports of SA-7 missile firings. The only reason Zane could figure that they never saw one was their NOE flight tactics. The United Ducks of the 362nd remained unscathed until May.

Zane was flying with Captain Billingsly. Billingsly, promoted to captain, received his AC orders as promised. They flew resupply missions through the An Loc area during the morning. An emergency recall message arrived for Zane. It was necessary that he return to Long Thanh North immediately.

The next mission was to pick up a load of U.S. Infantry at Ben Hoa and fly them to Vung Tau's R and R site on the coast. They were through with the war and on their way for some rest and relaxation before going home. Since Ben Hoa was near Long Thanh North, Zane advised United Ops to have a pilot ready to take Zane's seat in order to continue flying missions.

At Long Thanh North, Zane climbed from the cockpit as his replacement, Lieutenant Robertson, waited to take the right seat.

As Zane passed Robertson in the cargo area, he said, "Go get them tiger."

Robertson gave Zane a thumb up and a smile. Zane exited down the ramp and went directly into Operations.

"What's the big emergency?" Zane asked, as he entered Ops.

Captain Caldwell answered, "Sir, Captain Mullins has the details. I'm not sure."

Leaving Ops, Zane entered his orderly room. Captain Mullins was waiting for him.

"What gives Chris?" Zane asked.

"Sir, we received another group from the 101st today. They're still sending us people as they close down their units. One of the men in their group arrived with no records, identification, or anything else. He appears to be on drugs of some kind. You're the only one who can commit him for a psychological evaluation," Mullins explained.

"Where is he?" Zane asked.

"He's sitting in your office, sir. We couldn't let him out of our sight for a second" Mullins responded.

"Fine, I will see what we have," Zane said, as he went toward his office.

As Zane entered, he saw a young man seated in a straight back, wooden chair facing the wall. He wore a fatigue shirt, trousers, and sandals. He continued mumbling to himself while playing with his fingers. He did nothing to show that he even knew Zane entered the room.

"Hello, young man," Zane said. "What kind of problems are you having?"

Turning to look in Zane's direction, his fatigue shirt had no buttons and lay open. Zane looked for ID tags but he had none. He did not have a nametag on his shirt. He presented a broad grin and began mumbling again.

Moving across the room, Zane got another chair and set it beside the young soldier. Zane sat and tried to gain his attention but he did not respond.

"What unit are you from?" Zane asked.

Again, he smiled broadly and replied, "The devil's."

The soldier raised his right index finger in front of his face, rotated it and said, "See where the devil circumcised me. I sleep with the devil and live on the devil's time."

Zane asked. "How do you live on the devil's time?"

"Oh, that's easy," he answered. "The devil grabs the hour and minute hand's of my grandfather clock and holds them."

After an hour's questioning, Zane concluded that he could not shake the man's story. Zane decided to send him to the flight surgeon for evaluation. Zane went to see Mullins.

"Chris, fill out the forms. Let's get this man medical care," Zane directed.

After an hour, Zane received a call from their flight surgeon, Captain Lester Wilhelm. Mullins told Zane that Captain Wilhelm was on the line.

"Zane here," he said.

"Hi sir. This is Les. In my opinion, this soldier will be a vegetable the rest of his life. He's been taking some powerful drugs. There is no way to tell here who he is. It will take a finger print check. I'm recommending a Medevac to Brooke Army Medical Center in CONUS," Wilhelm explained.

"Thanks Les. I appreciate the help. Brooke is the best place for him," Zane commented.

While talking to Captain Wilhelm, Mullins burst through Zane's office door and blurted, "Billingsly's ship is down outside our perimeter. It's on fire."

Momentarily caught by surprise, Mullins' words did not make sense. Zane cupped his hand over the handset's mouthpiece.

"What?" Zane asked.

Before Mullins could repeat his words, what he said registered. Zane dropped his telephone and ran through operations and out onto the ramp. Across the airfield, and outside the base perimeter, black smoke boiled skyward with flames at its base.

Zane's C & C Huey was only a few feet from where he stood. He ran and began untying its main rotor blade. Seeing this, Mullins sounded the alarm for the C & C" standby crew. Two door gunners got to the ship before Zane had it airborne solo. The pilot who was on standby, Lieutenant Robertson, was aboard the burning Hook. He took Zane's seat and Ops had not replaced him with another standby pilot.

Cleared across the field, Zane never went higher than 50 feet with the Huey. After touchdown near the roaring wreckage, he locked the ship's controls and left the ship operating. He ordered the gunners to remain to provide cover if someone should attack. In addition, he didn't want the gunners to step on an abandoned mine.

From the size covered by the wreckage, Zane concluded that the craft came apart in flight at a relatively high altitude. Immediately, he knew that it was a SA-7 missile hit.

As he pushed through heavy, head-high brush, he felt heat from burning remains and thought, "No one made it through this."

Next, he started finding bodies. Checking ID tags, he did not know any of the soldiers found. Suddenly, brush disappeared and he was in a clearing. At its center were the remains of the Hook. After one look at the cockpit area, he slowly turned and walked away. He returned to the clearing's edge and stopped. He began a visual examination of the crash site. Scattered across the area, he saw bodies. Their uniforms were intact and none showed burns.

Greenletter and Mullins arrived. Zane pointed them toward the main wreckage area. As they walked away, nausea struck, causing Zane to bend over and rest his hands on his knees. He did not understand this reaction for he had seen much worse on his second tour.

Taking deep breathes, he still couldn't shake his symptoms. His skin grew wet and clammy. He lost his sense of time. Finally, he stood erect. In the distance, he saw a man in U.S. fatigues approaching. He carried a long wooden staff like what he saw Charlton Heston carry in the movie, "Moses." This struck Zane as particularly odd. The person kept walking toward him. Behind him, others appeared.

They were spread laterally and carried M-16s. He recognized them as U.S. Infantry. Their leader, now close, was a Lieutenant Colonel. Zane could not read his nametag.

As he came closer, Zane saw the name Hendrix over his left shirt pocket. Now, directly in front of Zane, he stopped.

"I'm here to help. What do you want me to do?" He asked.

Zane stared and said nothing.

Again, he asked. "What do you want me to do?"

Finally, Zane answered, "We need to gather the bodies."

Hendrix nodded and continued past Zane to the wreckage. He had his men begin helping Greenletter and Mullins.

Zane went to his C & C Huey and flew to Ops. He parked the ship and saw Caldwell approaching.

After shutdown, Zane told Caldwell to assign a crew to his Huey. Zane had difficulty talking, as his chest became tight.

"Earnest, make the Huey available to Lieutenant Colonel Hendrix for any purpose he sees fit," Zane said, as he went into the building.

Zane went directly to his office and did not speak to anyone. He locked his door and went to his desk. He slumped into his chair and stared at the ceiling. Finally, he could not withstand his pain. Crossing his arms on his desk, he lay his head upon them and began to sob.

With his pain diminished, Zane contacted Lanny Briscoe at MACV. After a considerable period on hold, Briscoe came on the line.

Zane said, "An SA-7 took out one of my Hooks. Get you ass here now."

Not waiting for Briscoe to speak, Zane put the telephone handset in its cradle. Leaving his office, Zane went to Scott's headquarters. Scott, anticipating Zane's reaction, had a security pass waiting for him. As he made his way to Scott's office, Zane's pain began turning into fury. As his best friend's office door closed behind, he unleashed it.

"I want to see every decryption by Briscoe for the last month," Zane demanded.

"Dale, you know I cannot do that," Scott answered.

"Perhaps you are deaf. Get me the damned messages," Zane stated with a determination not wasted on Scott.

"Just a minute," Scott said as he left his office.

Shortly, he returned with a thick folder and gave it to Zane. He immediately opened it and began reading the decrypted NVA transmissions.

After repeated readings and thorough study of each message, Zane found nothing relating to SA-7 missiles. He slammed the folder closed and began cursing.

Scott sat beside Zane and said, "It's a bitch I know. There's nothing that I can do or say to stop what you are feeling right now. The best thing to do is wait for the accident board's findings."

Zane contacted Briscoe and apologized for his behavior. Briscoe understood and offered his help if Zane needed it.

On 12 May, two days after the crash, Zane officiated at a memorial service for his five lost aviators. On board the ship, 42 infantrymen perished. Zane stood behind a rostrum overlooking a table draped in white. Beyond the table, the 362nd stood in formation. Behind Zane, General Hamlet and Colonel McDougall sat to pay their respects. Overhead, the American flag snapped in a crisp breeze. There were no other sounds.

Zane's throat locked. Only with a Herculean effort could he announce each name. Upon announcement, the closest friend of the person carried a snow-white helmet to the table. The helmet's black visor was in the down position. The individual carrying his comrade's helmet stood at attention while Zane read a eulogy for each crewman. They were not only crewmen but comrades-in-arms. In his entire life, Zane could not remember such emotional pain. Once he thought Lieutenant Ludlow's loss was pain. It paled in comparison.

Department of the Army sent an accident investigating team from Fort Rucker, Alabama. They arrived within 48 hours of the crash. The Rucker team examined every facet of Zane's unit. In particular, they focused on maintenance procedures. One of the team members, who knew Zane well, talked to him about the accident. It was a clear violation of investigation procedures but he felt Zane should know. He came to Zane's quarters late one night.

"Come in Randy," Zane said.

Randy was Major Randolph Ewing. Ewing was a member of Zane's flight class. Now, he was a safety specialist with Rucker's Center for Aviation Safety.

Ewing entered and asked. "You understand why I haven't seen you since we've been here I hope?"

"Sure Randy but why now?" Zane asked.

Zane got Ewing a beer and they sat on his couch in front of Zane's coffee table. Ewing made some idle talk and then answered Zane's question.

"I'm sure you've been wondering why we haven't questioned you about this crash. First, you need to know that a missile did not bring down your Hook," Ewing revealed.

Stunned by this revelation, Zane asked. "What the hell did?"

"Please understand that there has not yet been an official determination. We have an idea based upon what we found and related events. Do you know Buff Winslow?" Ewing asked.

"Sure," Zane answered.

"While we were gathering aircraft parts, we could not find the forward green blade. We couldn't even find parts of it. The whole thing simply was not there. We asked Winslow to examine the crash site. He took one look and told us to look about three kilometers forward of the crash site. We found the green blade intact exactly where Winslow indicated. Our report finds no maintenance or pilot errors. Your guys are some of the best maintenance people we have ever seen. We figure that it was a materiel failure," Ewing explained.

Zane, deeply interested, asked. "What failed and why?"

"Something in the forward rotor head and we don't know why. We do know that Boeing Vertol has a field rebuild team on their way to the 362nd. They are going to replace rotor heads and blades on every Hook that you have at their expense. They are going to install C model blades on your A models," Ewing explained farther.

"Jesus, C model blades are a hell of a lot bigger than A models," Zane exclaimed. "Has this ever been done?"

"Not to our knowledge. They are sending their engineers and test pilots to rebuild your ships. As of today, they are grounded," Ewing related.

"Damn Randy, we have a board full of missions to fly tomorrow. Who's going to provide fuel and ammo for the An Loc invasion?" Zane asked.

"I'm told there are six Hooks processed for turn-in. MACV is assigning them to the Command and Airplane Company until Boeing gets yours up. There must be a reduction in the number of refueling and rearm points. On station time for every helicopter will diminish significantly, which means they will have to fly longer. Refueling will take place farther than usual from the An Loc area," Ewing explained.

In frustration, Zane and his fellow soldiers could only stand and watch. Boeing personnel arrived with everything they needed to rebuild the 362nd Hooks. After rebuild, their test pilots would taxi the aircraft for a specified time. If all went well, they began hovering the ship. This also had to meet some specification of which Zane was not aware.

As each ship progressed through rebuild, it ultimately had to pass a test flight. Boeing's test pilots put the ships through every conceivable test. They executed every possible maneuver repeatedly before releasing it to Zane's maintenance personnel. They did their test flights.

The new ships looked peculiar with its new oversized blades. However, their load capacity increased from 10,000 pounds to 18,000 pounds because of the rebuild. The hybrid ships flew smoother and faster than their predecessor A models.

As soon as possible, 362nd ships joined the An Loc battle still in progress after two months. The feared SA-7 missiles were in full use by NVA forces. Fortunately, United's Hook crews were ready. However, other ships succumbed to the heat seekers.

Despite the missiles, U.S. air power continued to devastate NVA forces. It was a common occurrence to find NVA gunners chained to their weapons. According to NVA POWs, food and munitions were in short supply. Medical care became practically non-existent. NVA armor no longer played a role in the battle. Their charred hulks littered the battle area. At one point during the battle, Soviet T-54 tanks fired directly into the 5th Division's command post. When ARVN infantrymen learned they could stop tanks with their shoulder fired LAWs, their morale soared. They would remain and fight.

Sadly, ARVN helicopter use became shameful. At Lai Kai, ARVN Medevac ships remained on the ground. Their pilots would not fly to evacuate their wounded. American Medevac crews flew their missions. Fear still overcame many ARVN when medevac ships arrived. There were reports of ARVN soldiers, carrying wounded comrades, dropping their stretchers, and running to medevac ships. They tried to board and leave their wounded lying on the ground. Some helicopter crews used cattle prods to drive away deserting soldiers.

In late June, Zane attended a meeting at MACV headquarters. He knew that his unit was to stand down but did not know when. The purpose of the meeting was to determine procedures for the transfer of 362nd aircraft to the VNAF. Zane vehemently opposed the first proposal.

The first proposal was how to train Hook maintenance crews. MACV's plan was to transfer Vietnamese recruits directly to Zane's unit. They would eat, sleep, and work beside their U.S. counterparts. Zane explained that it took almost a year to train a reliable Chinook FE. To attempt this with Vietnamese, with no language or proven mechanical abilities, was pure folly. The cultural and social barriers were enormous. A simple thing like feeding them created vast problems. With only two months to accomplish the task, Zane convinced MACV that their plan was totally unfeasible. Their second plan fared better.

It was necessary that the VNAF have pilots trained to perform in a combat environment. Some students would already have Huey skills while others were fighter pilots who never flew a helicopter. Zane agreed to train Vietnamese pilots who had Huey skills. The selected pilots would not live at Long Thanh North but would commute to training.

The first Vietnamese pilots were well educated and proficient in English. They were fighter pilots who attended helicopter flight courses in the U. S. They drove from Saigon as if going to work at a daily job. They would arrive in Mercedes and BMWs when reporting for flights. Paired with selected Aircraft Commanders, they flew well and learned fast. Zane interviewed and worked with every trainee. He found one discouraging factor.

The trainees lacked aggressiveness. They did not have a desire to engage with and defeat the enemy. One particular individual told Zane that he would simply go to the U.S. rather than fight the NVA.

By late June, NVA attacks diminished. The siege ended with the North Vietnamese units slaughtered by air power and those ARVN who fought. Tens of thousands of NVA died during the Spring Invasion of 1972. This battle saw the most intense fighting of the Viet Nam conflict. Time was near for the 362nd to end its participation.

Orders arrived for the transfer of 24 Chinooks to the VNAF. Before the transfer, the aircraft had to go through an extensive preparation process. Critical parts required replacement with like new components. Each ship received a complete overhaul from front to rear. Maintenance personnel removed interior panels and flooring to steam clean every nook and cranny of each Chinook. Instructions required the transfer of all parts in inventory.

When time neared for transfer, Boeing's technical representative met with Zane. He relayed a message from his counterpart with the VNAF. Their message was simple. To avoid undue delays at transfer time, place a flight jacket and two cases of beer in each cargo compartment. If the 362nd met this request, the VNAF officer in charge would sign for the ships without an inspection. If we didn't, they could not say how long it might take to make the transfer.

Zane initial response was, "No. Hell no. I will not submit to blackmail."

However, when he saw the faces of his men beaming at the anticipation of going home, he relented. If he did not agree, meant they would have to stay and repair every nick that VNAF inspectors designated. He would not keep them a day longer than necessary.

In early August of 1972, 24 Chinook helicopters departed Long Than North for Tan Son Nhut. A 100 percent availability rate existed the only time in the

362nd with this flight. With the Chinooks gone, any reason for their unit's existence left with them. Mullins and Greenletter prepared historical records and unit heraldry items for shipment to the U.S. They could not locate one item required for return, the unit flag. One person knows where that flag is.

At the airport lounge in Seattle – Tacoma Airport, Major Zane, Captain Greenletter and First Sergeant Kubble had drinks in their hands. They lifted their glasses in a finale salute to the brave men of the 362nd Fly United Team.

The End

Epilogue

North Viet Nam's fabled leader, General Giap, began a major invasion of South Viet Nam during the spring of 1972. This three pronged attack took place at three different places and times. He attacked when America's forces were at a low of 65,000 and decreasing daily. (See Appendix)

First, he had North Vietnamese Army (NVA) forces strike in the demilitarized zone (DMZ) area on 30 March 1972. Three NVA divisions attacked with heavy artillery bombardments followed by tanks and infantry attacks. They attacked across the DMZ toward Quang Tri and Hue. Three days later three more NVA divisions attacked from Cambodia into Binh Long Province. Their objective was to capture the provincial capital An Loc. On 14 April 1972, his forces made another across border attack in the Central Highlands toward Kontum and Pleiku. All three attacks consisted of NVA conventional forces on a large scale. Total troop strengths were 120,000 and tank/armored vehicles totaled 1,200.

Some historians classify the Battle of An Loc as the most intense battle of America's involvement in the Viet Nam War. North Viet Nam's intent was to establish a Communist capital in An Loc. South Viet Nam's capital, Saigon, was a mere 60 miles away along QL-13. This attack had political as well as military significance. With a provisional Communist capital in An Loc, the NVA would have a Communist political entity in South Viet Nam.

For the first time, General Giap used his elite divisions fighting as conventional forces. Preparation took four years to assemble armored units to fight alongside infantry. In addition, he employed massive artillery fire and antiaircraft units fighting in concert.

NVA infantry advanced openly with armored personnel carriers and tanks to subdue An Loc. They expected a victory similar to that at Dien Bien Phu. After a three-month siege, Giap withdrew his forces after suffering horrendous losses at An Loc.

General Giap failed on all three fronts. He grossly underestimated America's ability to deliver massive firepower. The French fell to Giap at Dien Bien Phu because the fortress had to fight in isolation. The French did not have the resources to combat Giap's forces. However, the United States had the means to deliver extremely effective firepower on every front.

General Giap lost his command for incompetence. For public consumption, the North Viet Nam leadership assigned General Giap to a bureaucratic post. His days commanding NVA forces ended after the An Loc Battle.

After the Spring Invasion of 1972, North Viet Nam sought a cease fire agreement in Paris, France. Before the invasion, they walked out on the talks assuredly knowing about Giap's attack plans.

An interesting side note to the battle of An Loc is the internment of an Air Force pilot to the Tomb of the Unknowns in Arlington National Cemetery. An Air Force A-37 aircraft went down on 11 May 1972 at the An Loc battle. It was not possible to identify the pilot's remains. For 26 years the Air Force pilot remained unidentified, and since 1984, he rested in the Tomb of the Unknowns at Arlington National Cemetery.

Claims arose that the remains in the Tomb of the Unknowns were those of First Lieutenant Michael Blassie. In May 1998, officials authorized removal of the remains for DNA tests. These tests confirmed his identity June 30, 1998. Lieutenant Blassie received full military honors at his subsequent burial at Jefferson Barracks Memorial Cemetery in St. Louis, Missouri.

Appendix

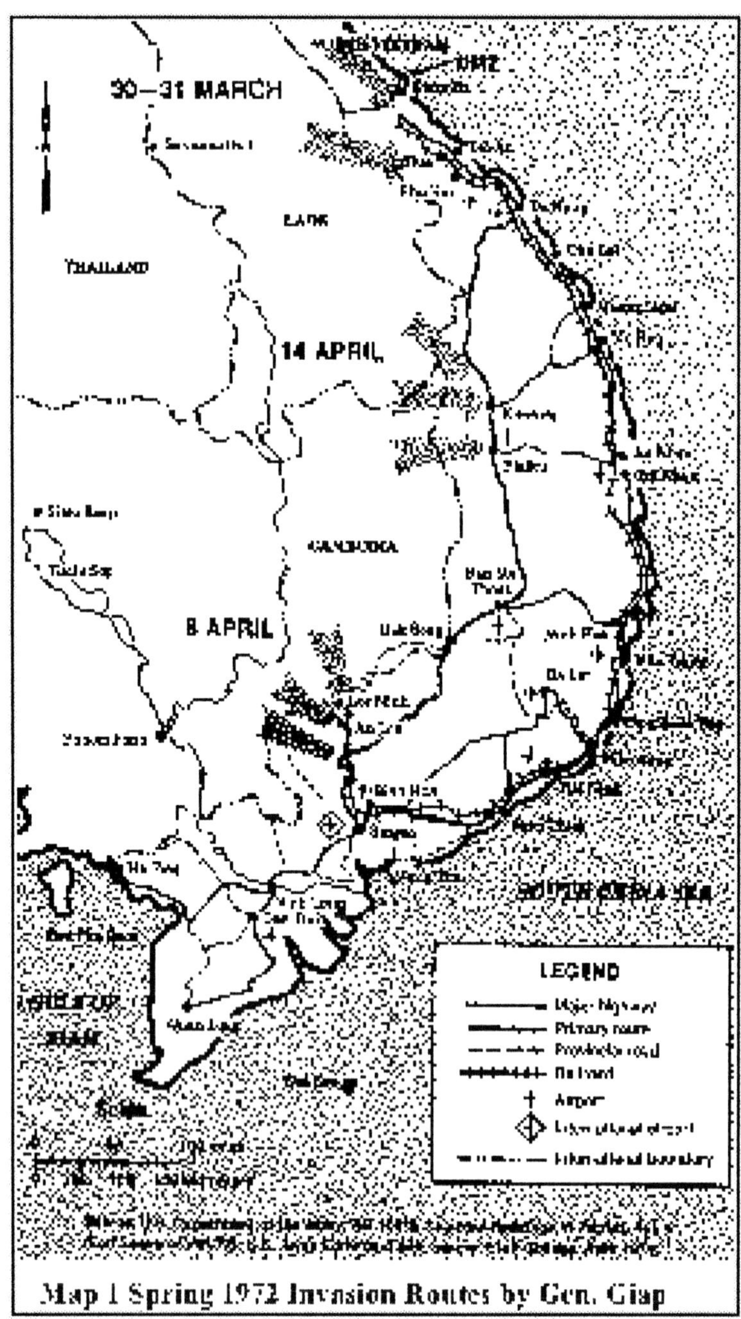

Map 1 Spring 1972 Invasion Routes by Gen. Giap

Appendix (Continued)

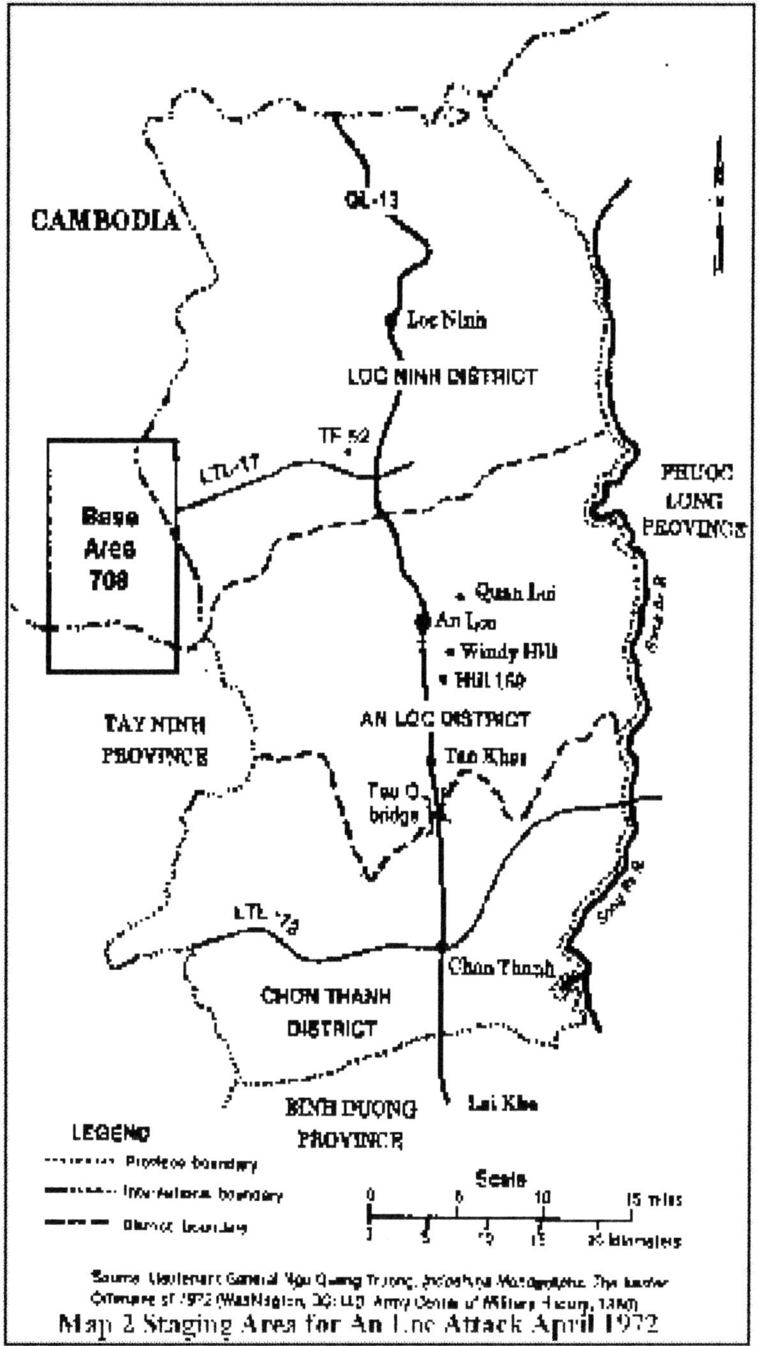

Map 2 Staging Area for An Loc Attack April 1972

Appendix (Continued)

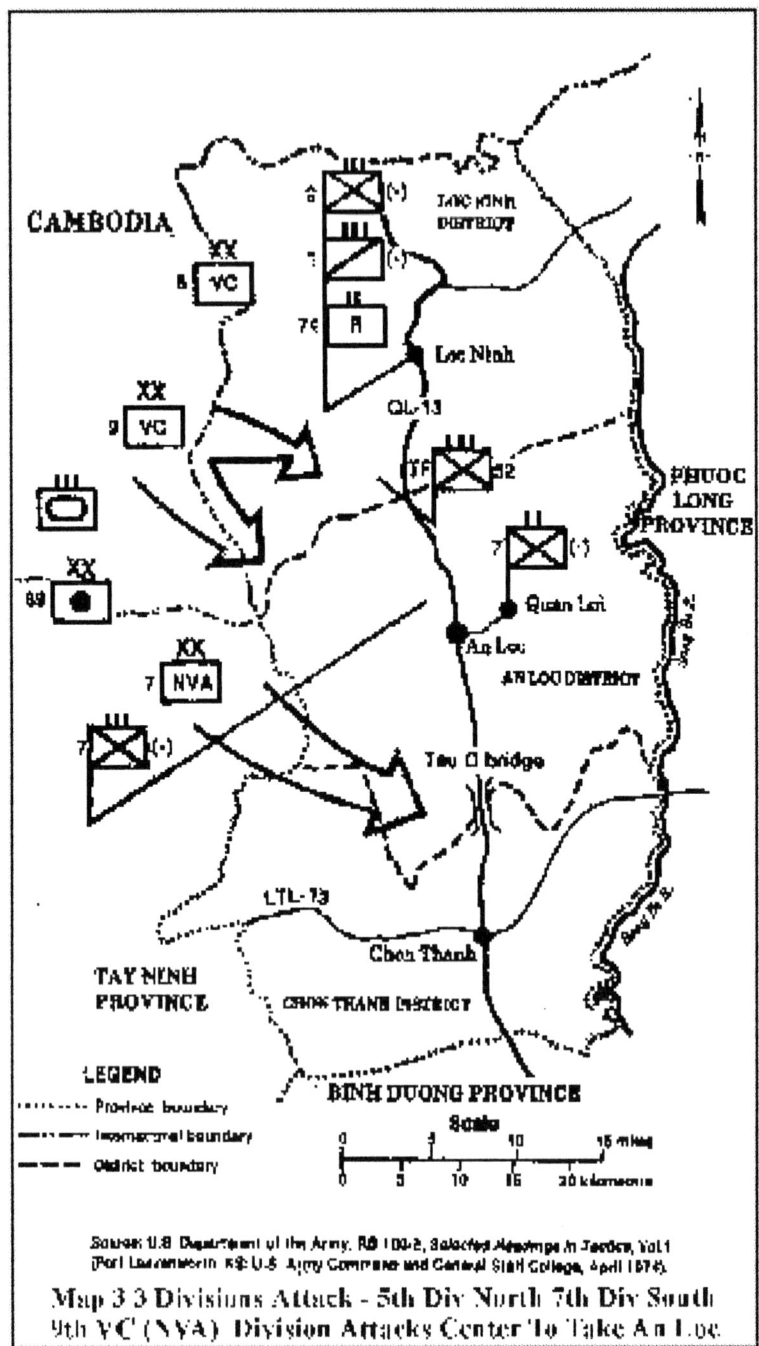

Map 3 3 Divisions Attack - 5th Div North 7th Div South 9th VC (NVA) Division Attacks Center To Take An Loc

Appendix (Continued)

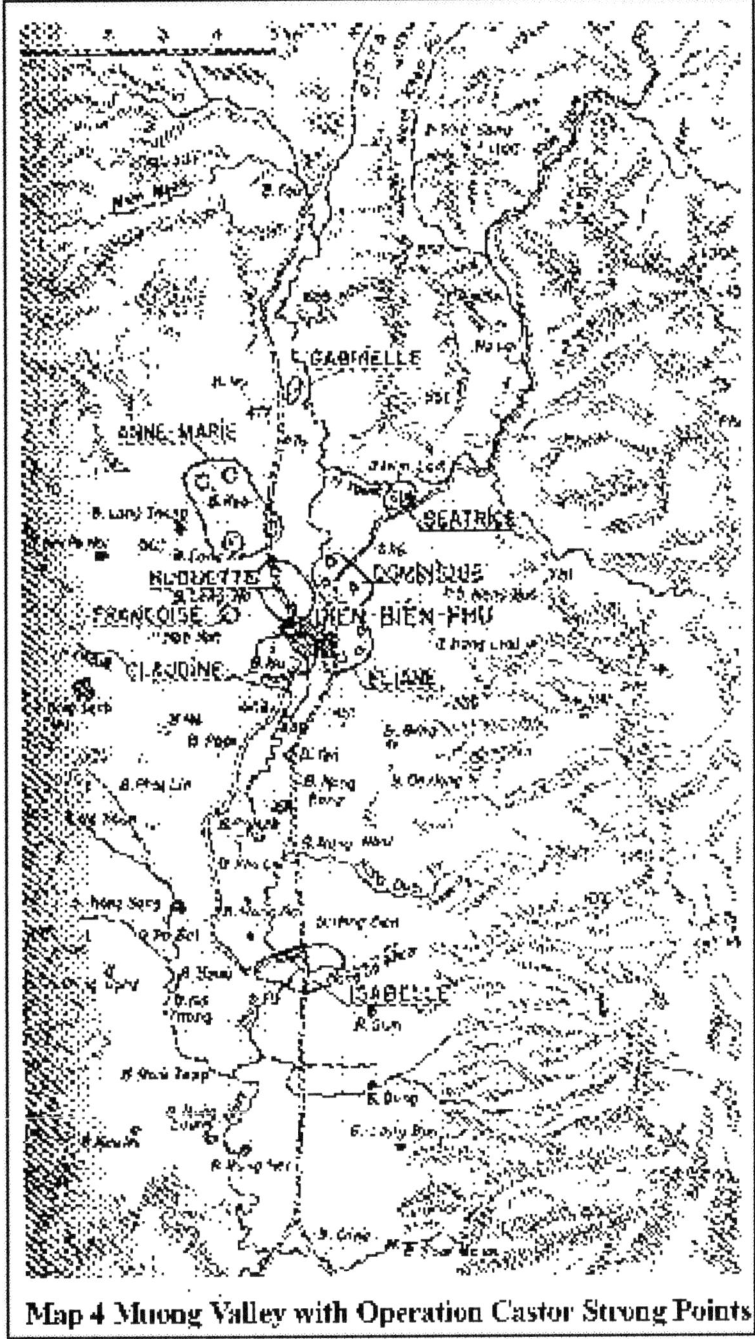

Map 4 Muong Valley with Operation Castor Strong Points

Printed in the United States
16582LVS00002B/125

9 780759 655935